Crafty Cat Crimes

Crafty Cat Crimes

100 Tiny Cat Tale Mysteries

Edited by

STEFAN DZIEMIANOWICZ, ROBERT WEINBERG, & MARTIN H. GREENBERG

BARNES & NOBLE BOOKS

NEW YORK

Contents

Introduction

THE MURDER WAS ALL BECAUSE OF A CAT.
The murderer was a dissipated man and a drunk. He had grown to hate his cat. The animal reminded him of feelings of caring and kindness that had died in him. The cat bore peculiar markings, which the man interpreted as symbols of the gallows to which he would inevitably be led. One day, in a fit of anger over a supposed slight, he lashed out at the cat. When his compassionate wife tried to intervene and protect the animal, the man turned his rage on her—with ghastly results. He did not shed a tear over his unpremeditated murder. Instead, he set about thinking of ways to cover up his crime.

He dismantled a portion of the cellar wall and secreted his wife's corpse inside. He then remortared the bricks, scrupulously matching the look and technique of his handiwork to the appearance of the rest of the room. It seemed the perfect concealment of the perfect crime. So certain was the murderer he would not be caught that when the police arrived to investigate several days later, he willingly showed them through the house and boasted of the building's solid construction. He emphasized his point by smugly tapping on the wall behind which his wife's body lay. From the wall a single damning noise was heard by all—

"Meow!"

When the police tore down the wall, they uncovered the grisly crime, along with the cat—which the man had inadvertently interred with his wife!

The murderer was tried and convicted, and justice was served.

All because of a cat.

Readers will recognize the foregoing as the plot of Edgar Allan Poe's 1843 crime classic, "The Black Cat." Poe understood the affinity between cats and crimes. In the century-and-a-half since his story was first published, hundreds of writers have incorporated felines in the plots of their tales of mystery. You don't have to be an *ailurophile*—a cat lover—to appreciate why they figure so prominently in crime fiction, and why authors such as Rita Mae Brown, Carole Nelson Douglas, Shirley Rousseau Murphy, and others have produced bestsellers in which humans and their cat sidekicks share detective duties. Unlike many other members of the animal kingdom, cats embody many of the personality traits we associate with both the crime-solving and criminal sides of the law. Consider the following:

Cats are independent. Like the traditional detective, they remain aloof from the world in which they move and are particular about whom they trust. And, like the craftiest criminals, they are secretive and detached.

Cats are stealthy. They move quietly and easily insinuate themselves into situations. It's no wonder that the sneakiest thieves are called "cat burglars."

Cats are meticulous. They are attentive to the details of their surroundings and particular about the order of their environments. Cats perform rituals and routines that seem puzzlingly opaque to humans but which make perfect sense to the animals themselves.

Cats are predatory. Can there be any better metaphor for a criminal stalking a victim—or a detective pursuing his quarry—than a cat playing with a mouse?

A whole mythology has grown up around cats that links them—for better or for worse—to the sinister side of human experience. We typically think of cats as nocturnal creatures, who are out and about when only the meanest walk the mean streets. Black cats are especially notorious for bringing bad luck to the guilty and innocent alike.

It is said that all cats have nine lives—an enviable trait for good guys and bad guys engaged in a dangerous profession. And what criminal wouldn't want to always land on his feet?

The stories in *Crafty Cat Crimes* draw from this reservoir of feline folklore and cat ratiocination. Here you will find cats of all stripes playing a variety of roles—from domesticated detective to feline felon—in mystery tales as short and carefully calculated as a cat's pounce. Though we tend to think of cats as finicky and inflexible by nature, here they prove surprisingly adept in tales that expose them to unpredictable dangers and perplexing puzzles that call for intelligence and resourcefulness that would be the envy of their two-legged counterparts.

The cats in this book get their claws into virtually every crime you can imagine. There are burglars foiled by felines in Kathryn Ptacek's "Cat Burglar" and Ron Goulart's "My Career as a Cat Burglar." And there are actual cat burglars—of the four-footed persuasion—who save the day by snatching a timely clue and bringing it to the attention of their owners in Sidney Williams's "Miss Daisy and the Rosary Pea" and Joe Murphy's "Shiny." Catnapping is the order of business in Kimberly Brown's "Just a Little Catnap," which softens the seriousness of its crime with the unusual rehabilitation of its softhearted crook. Rags, the feckless hero of Will Murray's "The Catawampus Caper," helps put the "pet" back into petty larceny. A cat gets its dander up and a sneeze foils an allergic crook in Leslie What's "The Happy Homewrecker." A curious cat prevents war criminals from succeeding at espionage in Connie Wilkins's "Cat Among the Pigeons." There's even a tale of cat consciousness, Max Allan

Collins's "Cat's-Eye Witness," the psychological ramifications of which Poe himself would have appreciated.

It stands to reason that cats can solve murder mysteries as well as any other crime, and *Crafty Cat Crimes* offers a harvest of homicide stories like Steve Lockley's "All for One and One for All," where cats help the innocent and falsely accused escape prosecution by just a whisker. In Michael A. Black's "Six-Toed Ollie," feline fealty leads a loyal pet to properly pin a murder rap on its owner's killer.

Naturally, if cats are capable of solving crimes, they can also commit them. A small subset of stories feature kitties with justifiable criminal tendencies, proving that human perfidy is never a match for cat cunning. Kris Neri presents a cat with an ingeniously crafted retirement plan in "Roscoe's Little Secret," and Beverly T. Haaf describes an unusual partners-in-crime relationship in her allusively titled "Copycat Killer." Read John Sullivan's "How Things Get Done in the French Quarter," and you just might begin to wonder why cats let amateur humans even think of leading lives of crime.

To understand the mystique that cats have for writers of crime fiction, one need only look at the respect the feline kind have enjoyed throughout history. Janet Pack, in "Guardian of Souls," reminds us that cats have long been venerated in some cultures as protectors of their human owners. Couple this duty with the wisdom of the ages and the result is a formidable fighter for truth and justice. It could make you believe, as we see in Pat MacEwen's "A Game of Cats and Queens," that a cat could have had a hand—or paw—in preserving the crown of Elizabethan England. Or, as Darrell Schweitzer gleefully suggests in "The Adventure of the Hanoverian Vampires," that Sherlock Holmes's pet puss may have saved the feline stock of Queen Victoria's time from a fate worse than death, in the Transylvanian vein.

Their distinguished historical pedigree gives cats a lofty eminence that sets them above other members of the animal kingdom. Cats seem to be the first to know that they are exalted creatures, and writers who take the cat's-eye view in their stories translate this haughty attitude into a savvy sense as to how crimes are committed and solved. Delilah, the proud Persian in Gary Lovisi's "Mrs. Milligan's Cat" considers revenge against her human antagonists as their just reward and as her personal entitlement. In William F. Nolan's "What a Cat Has to Do," it is "an ordinary, run-of-the-mill house cat" with "an average feline brain" who is equipped to stop a series of crimes against cats and their owners—proof that for all the efforts humans make to stop crimes, when the cat's away vice holds sway.

Selections have been made to cater to all tastes in cat crime fancies. There are cat cozies for those who like their mysteries homey and housebroken. There are comic cat capers that consider the funny side of human and animal relationships. And readers who prefer their mysteries hardboiled will find a wide variety of stories featuring cats and gats.

Prepare yourself for a collection where a twist in the tale is natural—and every crime is purr-fect.

—Stefan Dziemianowicz
New York City, 2000

The Adventure of the Hanoverian Vampires

DARRELL SCHWEITZER

I FOUND IT. IT WAS MINE, a pretty, shiny thing, which I found amusing to swat about on the ground for several minutes, watching the evening sunlight gleam off the polished surface. Then, of course, I lost interest and left it where it lay. But it was still mine. So when one of the "street arabs"— verminous *boys*—snatched it up, I yowled in protest and gave the villain a fine raking on the calf.

He yowled right back and kicked me away. I landed nimbly and hissed, ready for another round of combat.

"What have you got there, Billy?" came another voice.

"I dunno, Mr. 'olmes."

"I'll give you a shilling for it."

The transaction was done, though the shiny object was still mine.

But now I was content, for the trouser leg I rubbed against belonged to the most perceptive of all human beings, the Great Detective himself, and the result of that encounter is the only Sherlock Holmes adventure ever narrated by a cat.

It is not possible for me to give you my name, for the true names of cats are never revealed outside of our secretive tribe, and not even Sherlock Holmes may deduce them; whether the street arabs or Dr. Watson called me Fluffy or Mouser or something far less complimentary is, frankly, beneath notice. Suffice it to say that Holmes and I had a certain understanding by which we recognized and respected one another. You won't read of any of this in the chronicles penned by the doltish Watson, an altogether inferior lump of clay, *who once owned a bulldog pup*, probably without ever appreciating the crucial distinction that one *owns* a dog but *entertains* a cat. A dog is a useful object, even as, I suppose, Watson was at times useful.

But he tried to shoo me away, hissing, "Scat!" and other ridiculous imprecations, before Holmes drew his attention to the object in hand.

"It is the clue we have been seeking," said he. "Come Watson, we have much to do this night. It would be well if you brought your revolver."

Moments later all three of us were clattering along the rapidly darkening streets of London in a hansom. At first the driver, like the boorish Watson, objected to my presence, but Holmes gave the driver an extra coin. Watson, dog-like, acquiesced. Holmes would have found it useless to explain to him that cats partake of the most ancient mysteries of the dark, and so have a proper place in any night of intrigue and adventure.

It was indeed such a night.

As we wove through the narrow, filthy streets of the East End, past increasingly disreputable denizens, Holmes held up the shiny thing—which I now conceded I had *loaned* to Mr. Holmes.

"Deduce, Watson."

I assume this was a game for Holmes, like swatting a ball of string.

"It is a very thin locket," said Watson, "for I see that a spring-lock opens it—"

"Look out Watson!" cried Holmes, for Watson had unthinkingly sprung open the locket, allowing a scrap of paper to flutter out into the air. Deftly, Holmes snatched the paper out of the air.

"What is it, Holmes?"

"Momentarily, Watson. First, the locket."

"It is gold-plated."

"Not silver, Watson. Perhaps you will see the significance of that."

Obviously not. Watson continued. "On one side is a female portrait—not an attractive one, I dare say—"

"I shall entirely trust your judgement in that department, Watson. Pray, continue."

"She wears a royal crown. The inscription is in German, and reads: VICTORIA KAISERIN GROSS BRITANNIEN—Good God, Holmes!"

"Yes, Watson, it is an emblem of the current Hanoverian pretender, whose plottings against our king and country never cease, even after the failure—so ably chronicled by another writer—of the desperate scheme to place St. Paul's Cathedral on rollers and wheel it into the Thames, at the coronation of James the Fourth."

"God save His Majesty, King James the Sixth, and all the House of Stuart!"

"A sentiment I echo, Watson, but we must hurry on and save the patriotism for our leisure. As you see, we are running out of time."

I placed my paws on the high dashboard of the hansom for a better view. We were near the London docks. A fog had settled in among the poorly lit streets. The air was thick with strange smells. Many of the passersby were foreigners of the most unsavory sort.

"Recall, Watson," said Holmes, "that the notorious Dr. Moriarty, before he turned to crime, wrote, in addition to a curious monograph about an asteroid, a treatise on the possibility of an infinity of alternative worlds existing side by side, which may perhaps be *realized* by the use of certain potent objects—he actually used the word 'numinous'—which suggest all manner of fantastic combinations, such as, for example, one in which bonnie Prince Charlie was *defeated* at Culloden and England today is ruled by this same unhandsome *Victoria* of the House of Hanover—"

"Good God, Holmes!"

"You could as well imagine a world in which you, Watson, are Grand Panjandrum of Nabobistan, complete with harem. You would enjoy that, would you not?"

"I wouldn't be with you, Holmes," he said with some regret.

For an instant I almost admired Watson, though I knew his was mere doglike loyalty.

"But to conclude," said Holmes, "it was Moriarty's theory, which I believe he has passed on to his Hanoverian confederates and which will perhaps be put to the test tonight, that with the use of such an object, *which has been manufactured in one of the alternative worlds and conjured into ours,* all manner of what the ignorant would call supernatural happenings or creatures may be imposed—"

At that moment the hansom came to a halt. We three debarked. The cab hurried off. I ran ahead of the two humans, into the gloom. The hideous smell of the river and of river rats was ahead of me.

Holmes and Watson hurried to keep pace with me, their great, clumsy feet thundering on the pavement. Dr. Watson gasped between breaths.

"This theory, Holmes, seems perfectly insane—"

"Watson, at such times it pays to be a little mad!"

"And you, the rationalist!"

Holmes made no reply to Watson's taunt, for we had come to our destination, a deserted wharf amid tumbledown warehouses. The fog was so thick it seemed a solid thing. Even I shivered.

Holmes struck a match for light. He held the paper from inside the locket up so Watson could read it.

"It is a shipping document," said Watson. "In receipt of five boxes of earth . . . What would anybody want with those, Holmes?"

"Observe the crest, Watson."

"An odd one. With a bat—"

"It is the arms of a certain *voivode* of Transylvania, a Count Dracula, about whom many terrible things are whispered. Now all the pieces of the puzzle come together. This Dracula, in the employ of the Hanoverians, under the direction of Moriarty—"

"I don't understand, Holmes."

Impatiently, Holmes got out the locket and showed Watson the reverse.

"It's the same crest, Holmes, to be sure, but—"

I let out a screech of challenge, and at this point Holmes had no time to deal with Watson's thick-headedness. A low, flat barge drifted out of the fog toward the wharf, heavily laden with long, rectangular boxes.

"Quick, Watson! Under no circumstances must that vessel be allowed to touch land!"

The two of them ran to the end of the wharf, and with a long leap all three of us landed squarely in the middle of the approaching barge. Watson's thick head proved to be of some service at this point, I must admit, because even as we landed one of those disreputable foreigners arose from behind one of the boxes and clubbed Watson with a shout cudgel, which would have broken his skull had it not been so thick, but instead sent him tumbling back against his assailant who was thus set off balance.

Sherlock Holmes, strikingly agile for a human, had all the advantage he needed. He swiftly dealt the single *live* crewman on the barge, leaving him unconscious at his feet.

But even he could not quite grasp the *true* danger. *I* was the one who first appreciated the significance of the horrible carrion smell which wafted from the boxes, now all the more intense as the lids of those boxes creaked and rose up, *opened from within.*

In the struggle, Holmes had dropped the gold locket. It gleamed even in the poor light.

The *thing* which streaked out of one of the earthen boxes far more swiftly than the other occupant could emerge went straight for the locket, swatted it to one side, then to the other, then turned to confront me.

"Mine!" I communicated, in the secret language of cats, which no human may ever understand.

When I call it a cat, I use the term loosely, for though it had the form of a huge, black-furred tom, it was a *dead* thing with burning red eyes and glistening fangs. We struggled even as Holmes and his opponents did, both seeking to regain the shiny locket and chain, while we rolled right to the edge of the boat's deck, mere inches above the noxious water.

That was when the inspiration came to me, though I paid a terrible price.

I let go of what was *mine.* Instantly my enemy grabbed hold of the chain with both forepaws and became entangled, and it took but a single swipe for me to knock him over the side into the water. The carrion-thing let out a hideous yowl, then *exploded* into steam upon contact with the water and was gone.

As was my pretty treasure.

The rest is less interesting. Holmes, seeing a variety of carrion *humans* emerging from the wooden boxes, heaved first the boat's anchor, then the semiconscious Watson and the inert crewman over the side and leapt into the water himself. He stood up, awash to his shoulders. I might have been in a difficult situation had he not allowed me to ride atop his head all the way to shore, while he dragged Watson and the nautical thug.

Once on land, we watched the hideous spectacle of the carrion-things stumbling about, seemingly unable to figure any way out of their present predicament.

"The vampire is rendered helpless by the running water of the good Thames," Holmes explained, "so enfeebled they cannot even raise the anchor. Daylight will force them back into their boxes, where they are easily destroyed."

"What I don't understand," said Watson, the following morning, back at Baker Street, "is how the locket got where we found it in the first place."

While they spoke, I lapped a well-deserved saucer of milk, despite Watson's disapproval.

"I think Count Dracula—who was not among the vampires destroyed, and has yet escaped us—was betrayed by his cat."

Holmes got out *the locket* and dangled it by its chain.

Watson stuttered. Even I looked up in amazement.

Holmes laughed. "When the sun rose and the tide went out, I hired one of the Irregulars to splash around in the shallow water until he found it."

The thought of a "street arab" immersing himself in the nasty element to recover my prize made me think that even boys have their uses.

"Dracula's feline," said Holmes, "must have passed from ship to shore many times, perhaps carried by a human agent, to serve as a scout. On one of those missions, it stole the crucial locket, then, losing interest, abandoned it. The object is the perfect cat-toy, don't you think?"

He dangled the beautiful thing on its chain. I watched, fascinated. But I continued with my milk. The locket was *mine*, after all, and I could play with it later.

A.k.a. Pookums

MARTHA BAYLESS

COULD SEE FROM THE MOMENT she opened the ornately carved front door that Mrs. Sachs wasn't your usual lovelorn and suspicious wife.

"Mr. Bernetti," she said. "Please come in." I started to ask her to call me Nate, but then I thought better of it. The Chanel suit, the pearls—she looked like Jackie O. in her Kennedy period, and she obviously wasn't going to get friendly with commoners, even if she had hired one of them to tail her husband.

We sat down at a mahogany dining table, which was large enough to serve twelve. She had a pitcher of lemonade and two glasses all ready, with little marble coasters to set them on. A folder of papers was neatly arranged at the side— in fact, everything in the room was immaculate. No kids, I guessed. A rich woman of a certain age with a lot of time on her hands. Time enough to be suspicious of her husband.

"So when we spoke yesterday you said you thought your husband was stealing money from you? What makes you think so?" I took a polite sip of lemonade. My glass dripped a bead of condensation onto the mahogany, and she dabbed at it with a linen napkin. Meticulous.

"Mr. Bernetti," she said, laying the napkin to the side, "I don't ask much from my husband. He's a busy man. He sells luxury cars—oh, it's not what you think, he's not one of those sleazy car salesmen. These are customized luxury cars. The buyers require a lot of attention, and Albert is very good at that. He gives attention to everyone but me."

A cat came wandering into the room, and suddenly Mrs. Sachs shifted her focus from me and what I could do for her. I've only had a couple of cats, but even I could see that this was one magnificent animal. He was huge, with much of his size being luxurious long fur and a tail like a feather boa. He was that dark tiger-stripe color, with a single off-center white blotch on his nose.

"Pookums!" said Mrs. Sachs. She pushed her chair back from the table and patted the lap of her Chanel skirt. The cat jumped up and circled around in her lap, its tail brushing the top of the lemonade glass on the table. She began to stroke him with one finger under the chin, and she and the cat gazed into each other's eyes.

I got the feeling I knew where Mrs. Sachs's attention had gone when her husband started his funny business, whatever it was. Even her meticulousness was forgotten. Cat hairs drifted down onto the mahogany table, but she only had eyes for Pookums.

"Pookums is certainly a beautiful cat," I said politely.

She straightened. "Actually, his name is Little Albert," she said. "My husband thought I needed something to keep me busy."

I took a notebook from the inner pocket of my jacket and flipped it open. I realized I had nothing to write down. "Little Albert," I wrote, "a.k.a. Pookums."

"So your husband devotes most of his time to his business?" I asked.

Pookums—or Little Albert—settled onto her lap, and a large purr started up. "He spends two weeks out of every month going around the state delivering cars and courting customers."

I made notes. "That's a lot of time to spend on your own."

She nodded. "I have Pookums, anyway. I know *he* loves me. Except for the summer." A troubled look crossed her face.

"Something happens in the summer?"

"Sometimes he disappears. For days at a time. I let him out at night— Pookums is an adventurer—and he always comes back in the morning, except during the summer. He disappears for days! It was a whole week once! He just scares me silly! What if sometime he doesn't come back? Don't do that to me, honeybunch!" she said, and gave the cat a long stroke. The purring intensified, and a large paw began spreading and contracting, kneading the air over her knee.

"Couldn't you just keep him in at night?"

She tilted her head at me. "Keep Pookums in!" she exclaimed. "But Pookums would complain! Wouldn't you, my sweetie?" She fixed her eyes on the cat again, and her expression softened. He certainly was a beauty. I wondered how he kept all that fur so neat, being out in the underbrush all night. But, like Mrs. Sachs, I was straying from the real order of business.

I glanced at my notes again. "Okay," I said. "So your husband's out selling cars a lot, where you can't keep tabs on him. Anything else funny going on? Where does the missing money come in?"

She pulled papers out of the folder. "Here. He's been a salesman for years, and obviously a profitable one—that's not what I'm worried about. I thought I knew where all the bank accounts were. I thought I knew how much he was bringing in. But look at this! A separate bank account at a different bank! Mr. Bernetti, I calculate he's been running fifty thousand a year through this account—money that I never see. Where's it all going, Mr. Bernetti? What's that man doing with that fifty thousand?"

I took the papers and studied them for a moment. She had done her homework, all right. A lot of money was going through these accounts.

"I'll make copies of these," I said. "But how did you get hold of them?"

She gave Pookums another rub. The purring sounded like an Evinrude motor. "Albert said I needed a little something to keep me busy. So I got a little secretarial job at the bank."

She smiled at me, a sweet, innocent, calculating smile.

The first thing to do was to tail Albert, to see what he was up to when he wasn't selling and delivering expensive cars. But this was his two-week period out of town, and the first problem was that I couldn't locate him. He operated out of an agency, but the secretary said he only reported in once a week.

"But I need to get hold of him right now," I said, lying smoothly in my best phone voice. "I need a new Caddy to surprise my wife for her birthday." Never mind that I didn't have a wife, and that if I did she'd have to be the kind who liked Honda hatchbacks.

"You can leave a message on his voice mail," said the secretary. "He checks it several times a day."

"But you don't know where he is right now? I'm in Norwalk; is he nearby?"

"I'm sorry," she said. "Shall I transfer you to his voice mail?"

I needed to think out my strategy, so I declined. First, best to look over those papers. I had just settled into my easy chair with my reading glasses when the phone rang. It was Mrs. Sachs, and she had lost her patrician composure.

"You've got to help me!" she said, her voice climbing in pitch. "He's gone!"

"Albert is gone?" I said. "How do you know?"

"Not Albert! Pookums! It usually doesn't happen till July! But he never came back this morning! What if he's gone for good? I can't stand this! Albert's doing something funny with the money, and now Pookums deserts me again! Call the police! They won't listen to me!"

I calmed her down enough to last until I got over to her house. I charge a pretty high hourly rate, but that didn't deter her. She wanted action: phone calls, missing pet signs, visits to the pound. If she was paying, that was all fine by me.

We looked at Pookums's photo album to choose a picture for the lost pet poster. There was Pookums, so small he could curl into the palm of a hand, a tiny wisp of fur with that nose a splotch of white. Pookums in boxes. Pookums in grocery bags. Pookums asprawl on the dining room table. Pookums asprawl on Mrs. Sachs's lap. Pookums in mid-leap, going after a bit of cellophane on a string. Pookums looking adoringly at Mrs. Sachs. Mrs. Sachs looking adoringly at Pookums.

It was clear to me why Pookums going missing was a heck of a lot more upsetting to Mrs. Sachs than her husband siphoning money away. Money was money, but Pookums was love.

We chose some photos and divided up the list of vets' offices and animal shelters to visit. I went to the copy shop at the nearest strip mall and made up several dozen posters, and on my way home I stopped in at a couple of vets' offices and put up signs. Nobody had seen Pookums. It was a little early, but you never know when you might strike it lucky.

I live several towns over, but I thought I'd put one up at my local vet's too. It was a good thirty miles away, but you do hear funny things about cats wandering hundreds of miles from home.

"Hi, Mr. Bernetti," said the receptionist. "Are you paying us a visit? Got another cat?"

"Nope," I said, "just putting up a poster for a friend. You haven't seen this cat, have you?"

She looked at the picture. "What a beauty," she said. "And that white patch on the left side of his nose—you can bet I'd remember that one. If I see him, do I call you?"

"It's Mrs. Sachs's cat," I said, and showed her the number.

"Oh, I know Mrs. Sachs," she said. "Young woman with two Pomeranians?"

I laughed. "Pomeranians wouldn't last a day with the Mrs. Sachs I know," I said. "Pookums would squash them by just sitting on them."

Pookums had been missing for eight days, and I hadn't gotten a single lead—not on him or Albert. Mrs. Sachs was getting impatient, and I could understand why. But how could a cat—or for that matter, fifty thousand dollars—vanish into thin air?

I parked the car around the corner from the Sachses' house and locked it up. True, Albert was still supposed to be out of town, but if he arrived back unexpectedly, I didn't want him to see my car parked in his driveway—the surest route to being conspicuous. It was a warm day, and families were out all along the street: hosing off their cars, shooting hoops, running in sprinklers. It sure was nice to see good old-fashioned families where nobody was disappearing or running around. Being a private investigator, it was easy to forget that kind of family existed.

I had to pause on the sidewalk at the end of the street; a white minivan was just pulling into the driveway. It parked and two kids and two parents spilled out, evidently just back from a vocation; they started hauling in suitcases, duffel bags, and inner tubes. A small girl hefted a strangely shaped container from the van. "There you go," she said to the container. "I know it's not the cabin, Trixie, but at least you don't have to sit in the cat-carrier any longer." She opened a grill on the front and out sprang a cat.

He was a large cat with long striped fur. He stretched himself out on the lawn and then turned to look at me. Off-center on his nose was a large white blotch.

He stared at me another second and then bounded out of the yard.

I turned the corner and walked down the street to Mrs. Sachs's house. It was several minutes before she answered the bell, and when she did a very familiar large striped cat was in her arms.

"Oh, Mr. Bernetti!" cried Mrs. Sachs, nearly weeping with joy. "Pookums is home!"

※   ※   ※

The McLaughlins were gathered in Mrs. Sachs's living room: both parents, the boy, Martin, and the girl, Tina, all perched uncomfortably on the edges of Mrs. Sachs's formal crushed-velvet sofas and chairs. Mrs. Sachs had *not* offered lemonade, which showed how rattled she was.

"His name is Pookums," said Mrs. Sachs.

"His name is *Trixie*," insisted Mrs. McLaughlin.

The cat—whoever he was—was sprawled on the Persian carpet, stomach turned upward, one paw in the air—the picture of repose.

"Hang on here," I said. "Mrs. McLaughlin, how long have you had Trixie?"

"Four years," said Mrs. McLaughlin, pushing a strand of light brown hair out of her face. She looked like a determined woman, and the children had their teeth gritted. "He was a stray," she added.

"He's *our* cat," Tina chimed in. "We feed him. He comes in every night at eight, and we give him a special dinner of Kitty Nibbles with gravy."

"Nonsense," said Mrs. Sachs, sitting straight as a ramrod in the most imposing chair in the room. "*I've* had that cat four years. His name is Pookums, and I feed him Nibbles Deluxe with meat sauce."

"What time?" I asked.

"Seven o'clock," she said.

"And then—"

"And then I let him out for the night at seven-thirty."

I turned to the McLaughlins. They all had expressions that brooked no nonsense, even the little girl.

"What happens after Trixie comes in and eats his dinner at eight?"

"He stays in all night," said Mrs. Mclaughlin.

"He sleeps on my bed!" put in Tina.

"And we let him out in the morning."

"And what time is that?" I continued.

"Seven-thirty," said Mrs. Laughlin smugly.

"And Mrs. Sachs," I said, "what time does Pookums usually come home?"

But Mrs. Sachs was staring at Pookums with a face filled with dismay.

And suddenly I had an idea.

When I next visited Mrs. Sachs, she had a new folder of papers to display: the divorce papers. She had initiated proceedings as soon as I'd found Mr. Sachs over in Norwalk. And the other Mrs. Sachs.

"Well," said Mrs. Sachs—soon to revert to her maiden name, Fay Oliver. "I always knew his attention had to be going somewhere. And I knew it wasn't going to me."

Of course, bigamy's still against the law, and since Mrs. Sachs—Miss

Oliver—appeared to have been the first wife, she'd get the lion's share of the wealth.

"Good thing I got those bank records," she said, and a brief but determined smile crossed her face.

Pookums wandered in, and Mrs. Sachs pushed back from the table and patted her lap. He made a lazy jump into it and then turned around a couple of times before settling down.

"So you and Pookums have reconciled?" I said.

She showed me the tag on Pookums's collar: one side had POOKUMS and her address, and the other had TRIXIE and the McLaughlins' address. "I figure he had my interests at heart," she said. She stroked that long fur and Pookums began to emit a deep rumble of a purr. "If he hadn't been two-timing me, you might not have caught on to Albert. So I'll share him with another family." A paw reached out and began to knead the air.

She gave him another long rub. "Some people you can't forgive," she said, "and some you can."

Ali's Cat

DIANE ARRELLE

ALI WAS WATCHING THE KITTENS sun themselves when she heard the sirens. She glanced away from her neighbor's five little felines as two police cars pulled into the driveway next door. She put down her book, got up off the lounge chair, and walked over to the hedge that separated her yard from Mrs. Henderson's.

She got there just in time to see the ambulance pull up. "What's wrong with Mrs. Henderson?" she called to the E.M.T.s who were rushing into the old stucco house.

Not knowing what else to do, Ali stood and watched, feeling embarrassed for gawking and at the same time concerned for her neighbor, a nice, quiet woman who always greeted her with a smile.

After a short time the E.M.T.s wheeled Mrs. Henderson out on a stretcher. The older woman was paper white, attached to an IV and wearing an oxygen mask. As they loaded her into the ambulance, she turned her head toward Ali and feebly signaled her to come over. Ali pushed through the hedge. "What can I do for you, Mrs. Henderson?" she asked leaning down. "How can I help you?"

Pushing away the mask with a palsied hand, the woman whispered in a weak voice, "Take care of the kitties."

"Of course I will," Ali promised as the E.M.T.s put the oxygen mask back on the older woman and finished loading her into the ambulance. Ali stood there as they slammed the doors, jumped in the front, and drove away with sirens blaring and lights flashing.

The police officers came out a few minutes later, but Ali was still standing there deep in thought. She was thinking about the dozing kittens and wondering how to take care of them. She'd never had a pet, never wanted one, and now she was responsible for five cats. She turned to see the three officers watching her.

"Hi," she said, wishing she had on more than a bikini top and bike shorts. "I . . . um . . . I was just sunning next door, I rent the place from Mrs. Henderson and I . . . um . . . just promised her I'd take care of her kittens."

One of the officers started writing in a small notebook. "Go on," he said.

"Hey, why are you writing stuff down?" Ali asked, suddenly remembering her curiosity. "What's going on. Why did they take Mrs. Henderson to the hospital and why are you guys still here at her house. Aren't you supposed to follow the ambulance and notify next of kin, or something?"

The officer stopped writing and stared at her. Ali, a middle-school teacher, was used to stares, stares of all kinds, from early teenaged lust, to stares of disbelief over grades, to stares of anger over assignments. She stared right back at the officer blink for blink.

The officer gave in first. "Mrs. Henderson's house was robbed this morning while she was out back watering the flowers. Front door was unlocked, perpetrator just walked in and helped him- or herself to the late Mr. Henderson's coin collection."

"That collection was in a locked glass case," she said with surprise. "How'd they get it?"

"Familiar with the stolen property?" the officer asked and started writing in his notebook again.

"Will you stop that!" Ali snapped and noticed that the officer—she glanced at his name tag—Russell Gray was sort of good-looking in that sandyhaired, hazel-eyed kind of way. Angry at herself, she quickly sneaked a peak at his fingers on his left hand and noted that he didn't have a ring or a ring mark.

The other two officers had left them and were searching the front and side yards. "Just doing my job, Ma'am," he said with a straight face.

Ali fought a giggle, but it was hard.

He must have seen the smile behind her eyes because he suddenly seemed to relax a little. "Look, Mrs. Henderson came in, saw the case opened, the display trays missing, called 911, and had a heart attack. Did you see anything or anyone suspicious?"

Ali began to answer but he interrupted, "I'm going to write this down. Just wanted to let you know." Ali nodded and noted that he had said it with a very disarming smile.

Ali thought for a moment, "I was out back reading and watching the kittens, so the only people I saw this morning were Mrs. Henderson and Kevin, who does our yardwork. He's a nice boy, I taught him about six years ago. He should have gone to college, he was just so smart, but he took over his father's lawn service after his father and uncle had a falling-out."

Officer Russell Gray stopped writing and grinned. "Are you sure that's all you can remember? Perhaps Kevin's girlfriend in seventh grade?"

Ali flushed, she could feel her cheeks burning and she nervously brushed back at some wayward strands of her long, curly auburn hair. She silently cursed her pale red-headed complexion.

"Relax, Ms. Bennett. By the way, is Ali your full first name."

Feeling her cheeks growing even redder, Ali started to ask, "How'd you know my na—. Oh, now I know why you're so familiar. You're the officer that spoke to the students last winter. My first name is just plain old Ali. My mother saw the movie *Love Story* about a dozen times while she was pregnant."

"Nice name," he said. "When and where did you see Kevin this morning?"

"I saw him out front mowing the lawn, you can always tell it's him by the mask he wears over his mouth and nose for his asthma. That and the Phillies cap he always wears. Such a shame that a young man with grass and tree allergies has to go into the lawn and tree business."

"And did you see him in the backyard?" Officer Gray prompted.

"About fifteen minutes before you showed," Ali said. "He was using that long tree-branch saw to take down some branches from that big oak."

"Did you notice anyone else? It would have to be someone who knows the value of the collection. They didn't touch anything else in the house."

Ali watched him finish writing, wondering what else she could say. She'd just bought a half-dozen doughnuts but thought it too much a cliché to invite a police officer over for coffee and doughnuts. And anyway, with that narrow waist and flat stomach, she didn't think Officer Russell Gray the sugar and cholesterol type. Maybe he knew something about cats and could help her out, she thought.

"... sometime if that's all right?"

Ali looked at him, startled. She'd been so busy trying to figure out how to not let the moment end, she'd been ignoring him. "I'm sorry, I was ... I was just wondering about the kittens. I promised Mrs. Henderson that I'd take care of them. I guess I got distracted. What did you say?"

"I said if you remember anything else important, don't hesitate to call," he said. "Oh yeah, and if you'd like to think about it over dinner, I'll call and check with you tomorrow."

"Yeah," Ali said. "That sounds like a good idea. Why don't you come over tomorrow night and maybe we could even look for clues."

He frowned. "Don't get any ideas about solving the robbery. Civilian interference only causes problems, destroys evidence, and could be dangerous. Please, leave crime-solving to professionals."

Ali frowned back. "I was only kidding about the clues." Then she smiled and added, "But I was serious about dinner here."

"Sorry," he said. "Sometimes I take myself too seriously, but I'd hate to have to worry about you. Sure, dinner sounds just fine."

Ali blushed then asked, "Can I get into Mrs. Henderson's house? I need to feed the kittens and get their beds and whatever."

He led the way into the house and Ali could feel him watching her as she tried to figure out what she needed. As she stared at a bag of gravel, he finally said, "It's kitty litter for their commode. See that large pan filled with it. Cats are very clean animals and will take care of all their hygienic needs."

Ali stared at him wide-eyed. "I won't need to put out newspaper and walk them in the middle of the night?"

"Poor Mrs. Henderson," he sighed. "She'd really have an attack if she knew she'd asked a novice to care for the kittens. Come on, I'll set everything up for you in your house."

After all the excitement was over Ali was once again back on her lounge chair. She was amazed that she had actually invited Russell to dinner. She was thinking of neither poor Mrs. Henderson nor the kittens, until the kittens tried to go home.

Ali jumped up and rushed next door. "Come on, kitties," she called. "Come with me. I've got your dinner and potty and beds."

The five kittens, two tortoise-shell tabbies, a gray and white spotted kitten, a red-striped tabby and an orange-cream-colored kitten, turned their eyes toward Ali then looked back to the door and meowed. Ali kept trying to lead them but they didn't budge. Finally in desperation, she scooped up the orange-sherbet cat and carried it home. To her surprise the others followed, but in their own fashion, stopping here and there along the way to sniff a bug or chase the blowing grass.

Ali quickly poured food into a large bowl and the kittens came running the rest of the way, their tails sticking straight up in the air like antennae. Ali laughed, amazed that she'd actually picked up the little animal and even more amazed that she liked the feel of the warm body and silky fur. After they ate, she led the kittens onto her screened porch where she'd set up their beds and litter box. She sat and watched them explore under the wicker chairs and bat at the hanging leaves of her plants. The phone broke the spell and Ali bid the kittens good night and went inside.

The next morning Ali woke late. She jumped out of bed as soon as she remembered the kittens. They needed breakfast! Rushing out to the porch, Ali called, "Chow time, kitties, come and get it." To her horror, only one kitten, the gray and white one with the spots, was sitting on the wicker sofa. The others were nowhere to be seen.

"Oh no," she groaned noticing that the lightweight screen door was ajar. "Oh no! Kitties! Come back, kitties. I've got your breakfast!"

What am I going to tell Mrs. Henderson. I promised to care for her cats and now they're missing! "What should I do, Spots?" she asked the kitten, not even realizing that she'd named it. "Should I call the police?" Then she laughed despite her panic. Call the police for a bunch of wayward cats?

Ali stepped onto the front steps and called, "Here, kitties. Come home and get your breakfast." To her utter surprise, she saw them lift up their heads from different areas of her backyard. "Come on," she called, relief making her weak.

The kittens ran to her, three little tabbies, two gray and one red. Ali opened the door, counting as they strode in, hoping she'd made a mistake; the orange-cream kitten was missing. She fed the others then went out and searched. She remembered how good the kitten had felt in her arms, how soft, how warm, how comforting, and was upset to find she was blinking back tears. "Oh Kitty!" she called but there was no answering head peaking out, no welcoming meow, only silence except for Kevin, in his cap, mask and, strangely enough, long jeans and a long-sleeved shirt.

"Hi," she called halfheartedly. "Awfully warm day out."

Kevin waved back, the lawnmower making small talk impossible.

After a futile search, Ali sat on her lounge chair watching out for her missing charge. But the kitten remained MIA all morning. It was after she had fed the kittens a light lunch and was eating a sandwich herself while sitting near the huge old oak that she heard it.

"Meow! Meow!"

It was a pitiful cry, a kitten's form of yelping.

"Meow!"

Ali looked up at the big old oak and saw a vista of leaves overhead. She looked all around the trunk and the nearby bushes. Nothing. She heard the cry. It sounded like it was coming from above and to the left. She strained to look up into the tree and made out a huge limb above her. No cat. But she heard the cry again. This time from the right side of the tree. Looking at the ivy-covered trunk she could see another huge branch almost even with the one on the left, but it was empty. She heard the cry again, this time from the left. Sighing, she moved to the left and heard the cry move to the right. *I'm going to wait this one out,* she decided and sat down. Sure enough the meows moved until they were directly overhead. She looked up and there was her orange-sherbet kitten. It looked down at her, then ran back to the middle of the tree and onto the other branch.

Ali reached up, but the branch was too high. She jumped but it was still too high. She looked at the poison-ivy-covered trunk and wondered how the kitten had gotten up there.

She sighed again and went to the garage and took out the late Mr. Henderson's ladder. She put it up against the branch. Then, praying that the ladder would hold without any support except at the top, she climbed up and onto the branch. The kitten sat just out of reach. "Hey, why don't you come over here and we'll get down," Ali coaxed.

The kitten didn't move. "Meow," it cried and clawed the trunk above its head.

Ali shook her head. "Come on Kitty. My dinner guest won't have any dinner if we don't get down soon."

The kitten stared at her and scratched the trunk. "Meow!" it said in a commanding tone.

Ali shook her head. "Look cat, that's poison ivy and although I've never reacted to it, now is not the time to test out a rash."

"Meow!"

Ali got up and, holding on to a branch above, carefully walked toward the middle. As she neared the thick, hairy vines, she noticed a hole in the tree, about a foot long and five inches wide. "Why the tree has a hollow spot," she mumbled, and then said louder to the kitten, "That's very nice, Kitty, but we really need to get out of here."

The kitten clawed at the hole and Ali saw there was something sticking out of it, something like the clear plastic coin-holder cases that were missing from Mrs. Henderson's house. Ali started to back away from the center and toward the spot where the ladder stood. "Wow, are you a smart kitty. Just wait until we get down and call Russell."

"Sorry, I can't let you do that, Ms. Bennett."

Ali looked down and saw Kevin taking away the ladder. "Now, Kevin, why are you doing this? Why don't I come down and we can talk."

"Oh, Ms. Bennett, I don't think I'll let you or that nasty cat down."

Ali saw the kitten now resembled a Halloween cat, fur up and back arched. It was even making little hissing sounds. "Kevin what is going on?" she asked, although from the sore-looking red rash on his hands she was sure she already knew.

"Come on, Ms. Bennett, I think you understand everything. I'm going to ask you for my coins and then leave with this ladder so you and your kitty can just stay away from a phone until my dad and I get away from here."

"Really Kevin, you didn't think this through at all. I have the coins and you are stuck down there."

"That's not a problem," a deep male voice said from behind her. Ali turned fast, almost losing her balance. Another ladder had been put up on the other side and a strange man was reaching into the hole. The kitten rushed forward and took a swipe at his hand with claws fully extended.

"Damn," he yelped and fell backward. Ali watched as man and ladder hit the ground with a loud thud. "Damned cat," he snarled as he cautiously stood up. "Almost broke my neck."

Ali noticed with a sinking feeling that he had the coins. "Come on," he said, "let's get the hell out of here."

Just then, the kitten leapt from the branch and landed on Kevin's head, knocking off the baseball cap and brushing the mask from his face. He grabbed at the cat, but the damage had been done. Ali saw that the young man wasn't a young man at all, but a bald middle-aged man with claw scratches on one cheek. Obviously, Kevin had been framed by this man who she was sure was the uncle who left the family business. And, she thought, he and his accomplice were trying to pin the blame on Kevin and his father.

Ali sighed when she realized that she was treed, just like the kitten had been, only now the kitten was down there and she was up here. "Guess there's nothing to do but wait," she muttered and sat down on the huge limb. To her pleasant surprise, the kitten immediately climbed up the trunk, came over and curled up on her lap. "Why, you sound like Kevin's lawn mower," she mused, deciding that it hadn't been Kevin mowing the lawn yesterday but his uncle. He'd grabbed the coins and, using his ladder, climbed the tree from the back. The kitten had obviously surprised him, knocking him into the poison ivy and scratching his face.

By the time Officer Russell Gray arrived for their dinner, Ali was more than ready to get down. "Hey Officer!" she called. "Would you mind giving me a hand here? My cat Ivy and I have quite a lot to tell you. We know who stole the coins and if you'll just help us down we'll be glad to help you solve the case."

Ali saw the look in his sparkling hazel eyes, and for a moment worried that he was going to leave them up there all night. But instead, after calling in her information, which he had forced from her with threats of abandonment, he used the ladder to join Ali and her cat for a glorious sunset.

All for One and One for All

STEVE LOCKLEY

THERE IS NOTHING WORSE THAN the sound of a telephone ringing at 3 A.M. The best you can hope for is that it will be a wrong number or a drunken friend, just about anything else means bad news. The glowing digits on my alarm read three-o-five when mine rang.

"Hnnng?" I said although my intention had been to say something more intelligible.

"Al?" said a faintly familiar voice.

"Yeah, who is this?"

"It's Danny. Look Al I think you ought to come down here soon as. Phil's in trouble."

Danny. Good old Danny, always choosing the worst time to call. And Phil, the other one of our Three Musketeers. The last three to be chosen for basketball. One-time losers who had drifted together and stayed together. "What kind of trouble?"

"His mother's dead," he said. "They think he did it."

"Okay, okay, give me twenty minutes. Tell him not to worry. I'm on my way."

This was crazy, it had to be. Phil couldn't hurt a damn flea even if he tried. He didn't have an aggressive bone in his body and more than once that had got him into trouble. The Three Musketeers. All for one and one for all. Phil was smart; Phil was a drinker; but he sure wasn't a killer. Still having a lawyer and a police officer for friends must have made him feel a little easier.

Danny was waiting outside the police station when I arrived. "You took your time," he said.

"Didn't want to get a ticket on my way over did I?"

"Why not? Would have given the boys a good laugh."

The boys. That meant uniform. Danny's people. On the phone he had said 'They.' That meant plain clothes. "So what's the score?"

"We got a call from one of Phil's mother's neighbours. She was dead before the paramedics got there. She had been strangled."

"Why pick Phil up?"

"The neighbour said that he had been around earlier and that they had some kind of row. Loud by all accounts. When they picked him up he was covered with scratches, probably courtesy of that damn Persian of hers."

"We've all got some of them," I said raising my hand to show off the long-standing white scars that stretched from my knuckles to my wrist. "Good job she never had the thing when we were kids. We would probably have given it a taste of its own medicine."

"Never bothered me," said Danny revealing scar-free hands.

"Hmm, cat lovers," I said, feigning to spit in the road.

Danny raised a smile and thumbed towards the door. "He's waiting for you."

"Who's running the show?"

"Baker," said Danny as we started up the steps. "And he's convinced that Phil's his man."

Baker was from the school of hard knocks and had been around longer than most of the criminals in the area. Anyone who had been a first offender in the last five years had probably had their ears clipped by Baker when they were in short pants and Baker had been a beat officer, but promotion had been his undoing. Now he seemed more interested in convictions than in justice.

"Why *Mister* Anderson," said Baker as I was let through. "And why do we have the pleasure?"

"I'm here to see Phil Bradley."

"Oh and I suppose he's your client."

"That's right, so perhaps you'll show me where he is."

"Of course Mister Anderson right this way. But there's just one thing."

"And what's that?"

"Your client hasn't made his phone call yet, so how did you know he was here?"

"Telepathy," I said.

"That's a new one," he said. "I always thought that there were three main forms of communication in this town. Telephone, telegram or tell Danny."

I held back a smile. It never does to let the enemy feel they've got one over on you.

"My client?" I said.

"I'll bring him through for you," he said. "We weren't exactly expecting you."

"You are so kind," I said.

"You're wasting your time though," he said. "He was placed at the scene of the crime and it looks like his mother's cat tried to fight him off. If the cat could speak she would be our star witness."

"How did you know it was a she?" I asked.

"Saw her, lovely thing. Wouldn't mind taking her home myself if there's no-one left to look after her."

"I don't think Phil would object to that."

"I doubt if he's going to have a lot of choice where he's going."

"Whatever happened to innocent until proven guilty?"

"Those cat scratches are enough to convince me."

"Right, you said. What time did the victim die?"

"Sometime between eleven and twelve last night."

"Phil was with me until a little after ten," I said, desperately trying to remember the name of the bar we finished up in.

"Out of town?"

"No," I said knowing that I had not cut any ice. Phil could have made it back to his mother's apartment by eleven thirty at the latest. "Witnesses?"

"We have reports from a neighbour that he was at the apartment yesterday afternoon, that they had a blazing row and that he returned last night."

I couldn't believe this; it just didn't ring true. Not Phil.

"Penny starting to drop?" he said with a smug grin on his face. "You'd better speak to your client."

Phil was looking tired when they brought him through to the interview room. "Al, thank God," he said. "They think I killed her. I couldn't, you know that don't you."

"Course I do, Phil. We've just got to prove it to these clowns. Just tell me what happened."

"I went round to see her this afternoon, or yesterday afternoon I suppose. She asked me to call, said she had something important to tell me."

"And did she?"

"Oh yes," he said with a look that approached disgust in his eyes. "She told me she was going to get married again."

"Oh," I said. I had never expected her to marry again despite the fact that Phil's father had died more than five years ago. That was why she had bought the cat. "Who to?"

"A guy called Walter Doyle, lives in the apartment upstairs. He wants her to move in with him but she won't budge unless they get married."

"Sounds fair enough," I said. "Your mom's of a different generation. And maybe she's decided that it's time that she needs a little company."

"Maybe," he said. "But that doesn't stop it hurting."

"No. Maybe not," I said. "You met him?"

He shook his head. "No, I got a little angry, said a few things I shouldn't have and left."

"Did you go back last night?"

"I was with you last night."

"Later."

He nodded, choking back tears that looked as if they were desperate to get out. "I wanted to say I was sorry, tell her it was okay. If she wanted to marry this guy it was okay with me."

"How did she take it?"

"She didn't."

"You didn't have another row did you?" I asked fearing the worst despite my unyielding belief in my friend.

"No, she didn't answer the door. I figured that she was either still mad at me and didn't want to talk, or she was asleep. Looks like I could have been wrong on both counts." He rubbed the knuckles of both hands into his eyes, grinding them there in some sort of mediaeval penance.

I placed one hand on his arm. "It's okay, Phil. Don't worry about it, I'll be back later."

The custody officer led him away, back to a cell, leaving me alone for a moment with my notes. I had known Phil a long time and knew that he could not have done it, but there was nothing on my yellow sheets of paper that would convince anyone else in the world of the same. Except perhaps Danny.

"All done?" asked Baker, sticking his head around the door.

"For now," I said desperately trying to think of something to put him down with, but like Phil I was too tired.

"You said that you went to Mrs Bradley's apartment yourself."

"That's right. Nice place even though she seemed to have a lot of stuff for a place that size."

"Yeah well she used to live in a house, pretty big as I remember."

"Not always easy to throw memories away," Baker said, seeming to mellow slightly. "She was a nice lady."

"Did you know her?" I asked surprised that he might and yet I should have been surprised if he had not.

"Way back when I used to be on the beat, she always used to stop and say hello, ask if I'd had to clip any of you round the ear. I always said I hadn't, even if I had. No need to worry her if everything had been taken care of."

"She was a nice lady," I said.

"One of the best," he said. "That's why I want to get that son of hers put away for this."

"Whether he did it or not."

"Oh he did it all right. No doubt about it."

The softness of the old beat cop had disappeared once more and the gruff detective had returned.

"Where did you find the body?"

"Bedroom," he said. "She'd been strangled with some kind of red cord, maybe even a thin rope. The forensic boys are examining fibers now."

"And the cat," I said. "Where was she when you found her?"

"Kitchen. Her basket was there."

"Figures," I said then searched my pad for a name. "Do you know a guy called Walter Doyle?"

"Doyle? Doyle?" he repeated, obviously trawling his memory. "There was a guy called Wally Doyle, used to hang around Sammy's Pool Hall. Nasty piece of work. Used to beat up on his wife until she felt that he'd broken enough bones and she walked out on him. Did a stretch for aggravated burglary."

"He wouldn't happen to be your witness would he?" I said, feeling for once that maybe things were going to swing our way.

"Don't know," he said. "I didn't take the statement. I was planning to call back later today to speak to the neighbour."

"Would you mind checking?"

Baker left the room for a minute or two then returned with a buff file. "Yeah, the guy's name is Walter Doyle though I can't be sure that it's the same guy I remember."

"Of course not," I said knowing that he was already pretty certain that it was. There could not be that many people with a name like that in the neighborhood.

"Why did you ask about him?" he said.

"When Phil went round to see his mother in the afternoon it was because she wanted to tell him something. She wanted to tell him that she was going to marry this Doyle guy."

"So?"

"So maybe Doyle has a vested interest in making you think that Phil is guilty."

"Come off it. The guy only told us that he has been to the apartment and that they had argued. They did argue didn't they?"

"Sure, Phil's not denying it."

"And it was about his mom getting married again."

"Not just that," I said. "This isn't about replacing his dad if that's what you think."

"What is it about then?"

"Well for one thing, the cat."

"The cat?"

He was starting to annoy me with the way he kept repeating everything I said and turning it into a question. If he just shut up maybe I would get it all out and save him a lot of bother.

"Mrs Bradley bought the cat after Phil's father died. Said she needed the company while Phil was out at work. One day Phil was in a hurry to get to work and tripped over the cat and they both fell down the stairs. Phil had a mild concussion but the cat managed to break its hip. When Mrs Bradley came rushing out of her bedroom to see what the commotion was, she went to the cat first. Phil had to wait."

"Some people feel like that about their cats."

"Of course they do. But even after the cat gets better it can't walk properly. Mrs Bradley blames Phil for this, they row and he moves out, not before time. Mrs B then sells her house to buy a ground floor apartment because the cat can't manage the stairs any more."

"Sounds fair. The lady obviously loved her cat."

"Sure. All Phil did was to remind how she had put the cat first before, and asked if this Doyle guy was going to be quite as accommodating."

"But the scratches?"

"That cat can tell a cat lover from a cat hater, there's no in betweens with cats. She was fine with you because you're a cat lover, but if you're a cat hater and sit down in an armchair she'll tear your hands." I held up my own to show my own trophies. "Phil got his latest set during his afternoon visit."

"He could just as easily have got them while he strangled his mother."

"No he couldn't," I said. "Because the cat can't get up onto the bed. If she wanted to fend off an attacker she would not have made it above knee height."

Baker checked his watch and instinctively I looked at my own. Six ten. "I think I'll pay a call on our concerned citizen," he said. "Make sure we catch him before he goes to work. Coming?"

"Wouldn't miss it for the world," I said.

We called into Mrs Bradley's apartment on the way because Baker said he wanted to feed the cat, but I'm sure that he also wanted to be sure that it really had the injury I said it had. While he crouched on the floor petting it, he spotted something trapped in the cat's claw. The damn cat even let him free it. If I had tried I am sure that my hand would have been shredded.

"Looks like we have ourselves another piece of the jigsaw," he said holding a thread to the light. Together we made our way up the main flight of stairs to the next apartment.

"Hello Wally," he said when the disheveled man appeared at the door, pinching a faded red dressing gown closed in front of him.

"Having trouble sleeping?"

"Only when people keep knocking at my door in the middle of the night," said Doyle.

"I thought that was when you were at your most observant?" said Baker.

"I don't know what you are talking about."

"Not clever enough for murder are we Wally?"

"Murder? What do you mean? That son of hers did it."

"I'm sure that's what you'd like us to believe," he said. "But I'd be surprised if he has a pair of blue pyjamas the same as yours or a red dressing gown with the cord missing."

Baker turned to me and held a hand out for the first time since I had known him. "Looks like I was wrong and you were right," he said. "I'll have your friend out within the hour."

MARILYN MATTIE BRAHEN

HE HAD ONLY FALLEN ASLEEP in the warm sun at the Oxford railroad station for a scant few minutes, but in that time, the manuscript, carefully packaged in brown paper and tightly bound with good string, had been stolen, along with a small brown hamper containing his lunch.

The food and wine were small loss compared to his printer's copy of *Alice's Adventures Under Ground*. He had labored on the book for over a year, since he originally recited it as a series of sketches to the Liddell children as he rowed them along the Thames on an expedition upriver. He had promised Alice, ten years old and dear to his heart, that he would write the tales of the fictional Alice and, now having completed that promise, he was traveling to arrange its publication.

But the manuscript was gone, and he felt a frantic sinking in his heart and took several long breaths, trying to calm himself. *Go about this logically*, he told himself. *You are, after all, a lecturer in mathematics*. The bench he had earlier seated himself on, before nodding off, was partially secluded by a tree and some bushes, a short distance from the station house. He studied the platform. The same two young ladies and their parents still milled about, keeping a close watch on their ample luggage and on a boy around Alice's age, who alternately stared at them sulkily or peered impatiently up the railroad tracks, trying to spot the train. It obliged him, appearing in the distance.

Beyond the waiting family, Charles noticed two new gentlemen who hadn't been there prior to his own arrival. One carried a large portmanteau, which seemed filled to its seams with whatever it held. Still, Charles had no cause to confront them. He wondered what purpose he had now to even board the coming train without the manuscript, and watched despondently as it pulled into the station.

A porter emerged first, then the carriage guard collecting the passengers' tickets. He escorted the family of five into the first carriage, nearly filling it, then waved the two strange gentlemen over to the second. The porter began loading the family's luggage into the baggage compartment.

Charles approached the station master, struggling to help the porter lift an oversized trunk. "Excuse me, gentlemen." They looked up, poised to hoist the obviously heavy piece. "I seem to have misplaced a brown-paper parcel and a lunch hamper while dozing. The parcel is extremely important." He hesitated. How could he accuse the late-arriving gentlemen of theft? Asking to search their belongings would be tantamount to that, wouldn't it? It was quite possible that someone else, unnoticed by the others, had come to the platform, taken his parcel and hamper, then left.

Yet he had to recover the manuscript or hope, at least, that the thief considered it worthless and discarded it. It might be found by someone kind enough to return it, Charles's name and address clearly printed on the wrapper, in case of such loss.

The station master answered him reluctantly. "Did you search thoroughly for them, sir?" The porter ignored him, saying, *"Now!"* Both men heaved upward, swinging the trunk into the baggage area. The porter jumped up, pushed it further in, jumped down, pulled the sliding door closed and secured it.

"They were on the bench right beside me. The parcel contains a manuscript I've written. I was carrying it to my publisher, Macmillan, in London."

"Well, I don't like to say it, sir," the station master began, only to be interrupted by a loud feminine scream, followed by a high-pitched stream of hysterical complaints. "What now?" He rose stiffly.

One of the gentlemen emerged from the train, opening the compartment door and calling to the guard. "There's an animal running loose in our carriage, sir. A large striped tomcat, from the looks of it."

"Now, what the devil . . . " the train man groused, and boarded the carriage. A commotion sounded within, and the cat, orange with large black stripes, bounded from it and onto the platform, its teeth firmly clamped on the string of a wrapped parcel. It dragged it along as it skittered away toward the bench, tree and bushes and disappeared beneath the shrubbery.

"My manuscript!" Charles raced after it, parting the leafy branches to forage in the undergrowth and triumphantly reclaim *Alice's Adventures Under Ground.*

The station master caught up with him, winded with exertion. "Would that be the missing parcel, sir?"

"It is, and I'm delighted to have it back!"

"Can't say I understand how it got aboard the train, much less the cat."

"The important thing is that it's been returned."

"Do you think the cat dragged it off the bench, sir, and then snuck on board with it?"

"I . . . I couldn't really say now, could I? But if you find a small brown hamper under some foliage." He drew apart more shrubbery, which revealed only leaves and dirt. "It might support that theory. I doubt that the cat could have dragged *both* the parcel and hamper onto the train without being seen."

"Unlikely," the station master agreed. "In that case, sir, do you think a thief has boarded at my station?"

Charles hesitated. "I couldn't say that either, sir. I slept through the theft and can't vouch for whether teeth, claws or fingers were employed."

"Then you don't want an investigation?"

He shook his head. "I'd rather not. The hamper wasn't valuable. This was." He held up the manuscript.

"Charles Lutwidge Dodgson, Christ Church?" the station master read. "Well, sir, we'll return the hamper to you, if it's found. In the meanwhile, I'll warn the carriage guard to keep an eye out for persons with a pilfering nature on the train. Will you be boarding, sir?"

"Yes, now that my reason for traveling has been restored."

He handed the guard his ticket and took the remaining seat in the first carriage, introducing himself to the family sharing the compartment. As the train finally pulled out, Charles relaxed by the window, holding the parcel alertly and protectively against himself, and entertaining the young boy and his sisters with a story or two while their parents listened, amused.

At the next station, the two men he had seen on the platform at Oxford disembarked. Shortly afterward, in the compartment they had vacated, new passengers found an empty lunch hamper. They gave it to the carriage guard at the following station stop; he returned it to its rightful owner.

Charles, both manuscript and hamper in hand, dashed madly to the station eatery to purchase some refreshments and ran quickly back to reboard the train before it started up again. On the platform, the station master of that stop, an elderly man with immense white whiskers and a curious habit of wrinkling his nose, held a large, opened pocket watch in his hand, haranguing the carriage guard: "You're four minutes late, sir! Whatever delayed you?"

Charles reentered his compartment swiftly and took his seat, gazing quietly out the window. It was then that he noticed another enormous orange-and-black-striped tomcat, sitting on that platform and preening itself. He pointed it out to the boy beside him. "There was another striped puss, nearly identical to this one, at the Oxford station."

"Was there? I hadn't seen it, sir."

The tom looked up, turned its head, and stared back at the mystified author.

The train wheels began to creak, and the cat continued to gaze at him, turning its head the other way as Charles, at the window, passed by it.

In the few seconds before the cat disappeared from Charles's view, it grinned at him.

After a moment of surprise, Charles grinned back.

"No matter," he told the boy. "Cats like that have a tendency to appear unexpectedly. You might very well see it again someday soon."

The train headed toward its final destination as the sun began setting, streaking colors across the sky.

Allergic Reaction

LARRY SEGRIFF

GOD, I HATE CATS. KIND OF a funny view for a cat burglar, I guess, but it was a cat that got me into this mess. All my life they've fouled me up, and now this.

It started off as a regular job. A three-story Victorian-style house, with an immense snow-covered lawn and a three-car garage. I'd never been inside the place, of course, but it just smelled of money. I watched it for a long while before I felt ready to do the job.

It was a family that lived there, an older couple and a girl that I figured was back from college. She was young enough, and had that attitude about her, like there were no such things as jobs in life. Plus, it was Christmastime, and she was never home. She had to be back from college, or someplace like that, more concerned about her friends than her family.

Why is it that the more a kid's got, the more ungrateful she is?

Midnight brings out the philosopher in most people, and I'm no exception. Even cold, cloudy nights like this one. Not much else to do, I guess, except think and freeze.

I saw the college girl get home around ten and thought that was decent of her, tomorrow being Christmas and all. She had a kitten with her when she went into the house, and I shuddered at the sight. I was allergic to cats, which was why I decided to go ahead and do the job that night. I didn't want the place to get filled up with cat hair.

I went in at 2:15. That's always been my favorite time for working. Late enough so that everyone's sound asleep; early enough that the older folks probably won't be up going to the bathroom; and, just in case I slip up, the cops are busy rousting drunks.

Besides, I just like that time of night.

I went in a window. In all the time I'd been watching the house, I hadn't seen any activity at all on the third floor, so that's where I slipped in. The climb was a bitch, but I'd done this enough to know to be careful, and one good thing about a new cat in the house: I was pretty sure there wasn't a dog.

The window went up quietly, and I was glad to see there wasn't any alarm system. Those things are a joke, really, but they do take a few minutes to deal with, and I didn't like to waste time.

There were six rooms on the top floor, and none of them looked to be used for anything. At a guess, I would have said they'd belonged to the kids when they were growing up, except that I hadn't seen anyone besides the college girl. Maybe the house had been in the family for generations. I didn't know.

There wasn't anything worth taking up there, which was all I cared about.

The second floor was more rewarding. I cleaned out the old couple while they slept. Got some cash and a lot of jewelry, and they never roused up at all. They never do. Sometimes I'd leave a little rose on their pillow, but not in December.

Their room was at one end of the house. Hers was at the other. In between were two guest rooms, a sewing room, and a large bath. I took nothing from any of those.

As soon as I opened her door I knew I'd found the cat. I could smell it, and my nose started to itch. Psychosomatic, I knew—even if the place had been lousy with cats it was too early for any symptoms to show up—but there it was.

Her bed was beneath the window, the curtains open to the cloudy night. The room was cool, and she was bundled up beneath a thick blanket. I could see the kitten curled up beside her head, and I cautioned myself to greater silence. I didn't know how much about cats, other than that I didn't like them, and I didn't know how it would react to strange noises.

I found her purse by the door, but there wasn't much in it, just a few lousy dollars and a college I.D. card. The state university, which surprised me. I'd have guessed Ivy League, but maybe that wasn't important to her. Then I checked her dresser and got a couple of small jewelry boxes. I didn't open them for fear they were musical.

That was it. The job was over. I'd learned long ago not to be greedy, and it was time to get out. I was turning to leave, quite happy with my haul, when it happened.

I sneezed.

I got most of it muffled, but not enough. Spinning back towards the bed, I saw two eyes glaring at me. Not hers. The cat's.

I freaked. When I was a kid, I once saw a cat that had cornered a rat and was playing with it. The rat was as big as the cat, maybe bigger, but that didn't seem to matter. The cat was quicker, and while watching their little game there was no doubt in my mind who was in control. They played for about ten minutes, the cat batting the rat every so often, avoiding the lunging bites easily and flipping these lightninglike paw shots in return. Finally the cat got tired of it and started to turn away. I figured the rat was so mad it would jump on it from behind, but it was smarter than I was; it bolted for a trash can.

It never made it.

I heard its claws click once on the bricks, and then the cat had spun back towards it, pinned it, and disemboweled it, all in the time it took me to blink. It didn't even eat the rat; just batted it a few more times until it finally died, and then it walked away. As near as I could tell, all it had gained from the encounter was a drop or two of blood on its paws.

I never forgot that scene. It was only a month or two later that I developed my allergy. And now this little kitten was looking at me in the same way the other cat had eyed that rat.

I knew I had to get out of there. The college girl was still asleep, which was a lucky break, but one that couldn't last long. My eyes were burning, my nose was running, and I could hear my breath whistling in my lungs. Besides, I wanted away from that cat.

I got out of there, heading back up to the third floor. I knew better than to use the front door. People who wouldn't think to put an alarm on a third-floor window often put one on the door. No sense giving Fate another chance to screw me over.

I got to the window and threw a leg over the sill. Turning to go out butt-first, I saw that that damned cat had followed me. God, but things were not going right for me. At least there wasn't any sign of the college girl.

Catching the sill with my hands, I started lowering myself down slowly. The old couple's window was directly beneath this one, and the decorative molding around it was a perfect place to put my feet. After that, I could easily reach over and grab the same downspout I'd shinnied up on my way in.

That was my plan, anyway.

Going down was trickier than going up because I couldn't see my feet. Normally I tried to find a better route out, but this time I was too anxious. I hadn't wanted to take the time to look for alarms, not when I could start sneezing and wheezing and wake up the whole house.

I was hanging by my fingers, trying to remember just how far beneath me the top of that window was, when I felt something sharp prick my skin. The cat had found my fingers and was playing with them.

I thought of that alley, and had a sudden vision of those sharp claws slicing open my hands, and instinctively I let go.

I was closer to the window beneath me than I'd thought and my feet struck it before I was ready. My knees knocked against the siding of the house, and the next thing I knew I was falling.

Two stories straight down, and I landed on my back. I remember looking up as I fell and seeing that kitten framed in the window, watching me.

I survived, but I broke my back. The doctors say that I'll probably be paralyzed for the rest of my life. The family decided not to press charges, figuring that I'll suffer enough as it is, and they're probably right. The college girl, a sociology major, is taking it a step further. She wants to show that there are no hard feelings or something. And she wants me to have some company in the dark times ahead.

She's sending me a pet, a kitten, to sit on my chest and keep me warm. I can hardly wait.

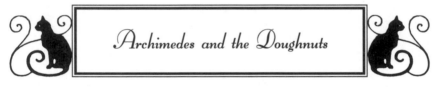

Archimedes and the Doughnuts

GENE DEWEESE AND BARBARA PAUL

'M NOT SURE WHEN IT STARTED, but I know when it ended. It was shortly after noon on Sunday, the ninth of June, just six months ago. That's when Clara Murphy came pounding on my door, surprising me in more ways than one.

At the time I was sitting at the kitchen table staring morosely at an assemblage of grease, cholesterol, calories, and triglycerides that would keep me up all night if it didn't kill me first. I'd been conned into buying it by two small monsters from outer space that my son Warren keeps insisting are my grandchildren. Monster Number 1 had started chanting "Pizza! Pizza! Pizza!" and of course Monster Number 2 had quickly joined in, as he always does. So we'd stopped by a pizza parlor with the fine old Italian name of Willoughby's, and then back home I was faced with the disagreeable prospect of actually eating the stuff.

Clara's pounding on the door stopped me just in time; need I say I was glad to see her? Truth to tell, I was always glad to see Clara Murphy. We'd known each other all our adult lives. Her Harry had been dead for ten years, my Emma for twelve; but there'd been a time when the four of us were inseparable. We had a lot of good years behind us, Clara and I. But we were older now, less active; I hadn't seen her for, oh, three months at least, since last March when she'd brought her cat Archimedes into my clinic for his annual shots.

This time, though, the sight of her shocked me. She'd looked fine when she'd brought Archimedes in, but now she looked as if twenty years had gone by, not three months. I'd never seen her so pale, not even when she'd had the heart attack a few weeks after Harry died. And she looked tired, tired, right down to the bone, as if she barely had the strength to stand up.

But I didn't get to say anything; I didn't even have a chance to say hello before she was grabbing at my sleeve and using what breath she had to urge me to come with her. "It's Archimedes," she gasped, as if it was all she could do to get the words out. "I have him in the car, I came home from church and found him, he's never been like this before, never, and I don't know—"

"Easy, Clara, I'll take a look at him—try to relax." From past experience I knew Clara's idea of a feline emergency could be nothing more than a temporary loss of appetite; the only true emergency she'd come to me with had been a BB lodged in the back leg of a cat named Desdemona. I told the monsters to finish their pizza and went to get my bag; Clara trailed after me, trembling and unsteady. "You didn't drive over here in that condition, did you?" I asked her.

"Jerry drove me." The words were faint.

I nodded and said nothing; Jerry was the one serious point of contention that had ever arisen between us. I held out a hand to steady her as we went down the steps toward her car; I was more worried about her than I was about Archimedes. Despite a sweet tooth that almost matched Clara's—Archimedes was one of the few cats I'd ever seen who would actually eat plain sugar—he'd never been more than a pound overweight and was usually in excellent health. But I knew there was no way I was going to get Clara to answer questions about her own health until I looked after the cat. Clara loved that animal, just the way she'd loved the half-dozen other cats she'd had since she first came into my clinic with Darius (he was a Persian) over thirty years ago.

A lanky young man unfolded himself from behind the wheel of Clara's Mercedes. "Hello, Milton. Sorry to bother you on a Sunday, but . . . " He gave me a look that meant *You know Aunt Clara.*

I didn't answer the look. "Jerry."

"He's in the back." Jerry opened the car door.

The moment the door was open I could see this was something more serious than a BB in the leg. Archimedes, a fifteen-pound tiger stripe, was moving restlessly over the back seat, whining painfully. His breathing was almost as rapid as a human's pulse. And he had thrown up, partly on the seat, partly on the floor.

"He just now lost his breakfast," Jerry said. "Aunt Clara, I told you it was nothing to worry about. Archimedes isn't as young as he used to be and he simply can't digest everything he eats anymore. Isn't that right, Milton?"

I took the stethoscope from my bag and checked the cat's heart. Like his breathing, it was rapid and weak. "We'd better get him to the clinic," I told Clara. "I'll need more than I have in this bag."

"What is it, Milton?" she asked, even more alarmed.

"Has he been outside?"

"No, of course not. Ever since Desdemona—"

"Could he have slipped out? That's happened before."

"Not this time, Milton—I'm sure of it. He was asleep on the dining-room window sill when Jerry picked me up to go to church. You remember, Jerry."

Jerry cleared his throat. "I don't think I saw him, Aunt Clara."

"Well, *I* saw him," Clara insisted. "And he was asleep when we left. He didn't slip out." The effort of talking left her exhausted.

I asked, "Is there anything in the house, then, that he could've gotten into? What about ant pellets? You still put them out in summer, don't you?"

"Yes, but not where Archimedes could get them. I put them under the stove and the refrigerator—he couldn't possibly reach them."

"Well, we'll figure this out later," I said. "We'd better tend to Archimedes first. You two go on ahead to the clinic—I'll follow in my car in just a minute."

I could barely hear the sound of the Mercedes starting up as I hurried back up the steps and into the house. I picked up the phone and tapped out my son's home number. "Warren?"

"Hey, Dad, what's up?"

"You're going to have to come take the monsters home. I have to get over to the clinic—something's wrong with Clara Murphy's cat."

"Aw, too bad. Is it serious?"

"Yes, I'm afraid it is."

"Then you might want to let Jerry know. Clara—"

"Jerry drove her here. Look, Warren, you can pick the monsters up at Mrs. Tanner's next door. I can't wait around 'til you get here."

"Monica will come get them. I have to go to work."

"On Sunday?"

"Bert's sick and Jack's off to Willow Bend today, and I don't have anyone else to send in. But don't you worry about the kids, Pop—you go take care of the sick kitty."

"Don't call me Pop." I hung up the phone, shooed the monsters next door to Mrs. Tanner's, and backed the car out of the garage.

Archimedes' symptoms had me worried. I'd seen this sort of thing before, in farm cats that had ingested something that had had rat poison mixed into it. On the whole cats have too much sense to eat something that will kill them, but they can be fooled; pesticides are getting more sophisticated all the time. That's why I'd asked Clara about the ant pellets, even though it was implausible that

Archimedes would have eaten one. Why would he ignore them for four or five years and then suddenly decide to sample one?

Clara had stopped letting her cats out of the house ever since the day poor Desdemona came dragging herself home, her right rear leg virtually useless. That damned BB in her leg had been a gift from a particularly loathsome ten-year-old who was—and unfortunately still is—Clara's nephew. Yep, it was Jerry who'd shot Desdemona, the same Jerry who was now so solicitously driving the ailing Archimedes to my clinic. I had to wonder if Jerry had slipped the cat something; he was just mean-spirited enough to do a thing like that. But Clara said Archimedes had been all right when Jerry picked her up for church.

All those years ago, Jerry had never admitted to shooting Desdemona. When I told Clara that not only had Jerry done it, but he'd shot her deliberately—she flatly refused to believe me. Said I was just guessing. But I'd seen too many other cats with the same kind of wound that summer. There'd been at least half a dozen during the two months that ten-year-old Jerry and his BB gun had stayed with Clara and Harry—that's half a dozen that I *saw*. How many other cats were wounded or even dead that I knew nothing about? Once Jerry returned to his own home, the incidence of cat-shootings dropped to zero. When I'd tried to point this out to Clara, she'd called me spiteful and unreasonable, saying I'd never liked the boy and always thought the worst.

Well, that last part was true; I didn't like him. And I was pretty much alone in that opinion. Even Warren thought Jerry was an okay guy, and he's usually pretty good at seeing through people's façades. But the first time I'd ever seen Jerry, he'd been holding a wounded bird in his hand—broken wing, I think. The boy was in Clara's front yard and didn't see me walking up the driveway. I was about to offer to take a good look at the bird when he put it on the ground and crushed it with his foot. Ground its head right in. Jerry liked hurting things—small things, that is, things that couldn't hurt back. Of course he'd shot the cats. And probably had a lot of fun doing it.

But Clara steadfastly refused to see that side of her nephew. I could understand why; Emma and I had had Warren, but Clara and Harry had remained childless. Jerry's parents died the year before Harry did, and it was logical that the two surviving members of the family should draw together. I'd taken to checking in on Clara now and then after Harry died; but now that Jerry was grown, she was turning to him more and more. That's why I hadn't seen her for three months; in a way, I'd been abrogating responsibility to Jerry. The thought of that didn't make me any too pleased with myself.

They were waiting at my clinic when I got there, Clara in the Mercedes with Archimedes and Jerry pacing nervously outside. I lifted the cat carefully out of the back seat. His breathing was more shallow than ever.

"Are you going to give him something to settle him down?" Jerry asked.

Inside, the first thing I did was to flush out the cat's stomach, although Archimedes had done a pretty good job of that himself in the car before I got to him. Then I gave a shot of dimarcaprol, to help neutralize any poison still in his system. Then all we could do was wait.

Slumped in a chair under the bright lights I need for my job, Clara looked worse than ever. Her face was gray and pinched; her shoulders drooped forward. She looked old, old. Haggard, even. Clara, pretty Clara, looked *haggard*. I offered her a chocolate bar I found in my desk, but for once Clara had left her sweet tooth at home. She just shook her head, *no*. Jerry kept up his pacing until I was ready to yell at him.

After about an hour Archimedes weakly lifted his head and started sniffing in the direction of the candy bar I'd left out. The cat had almost died of poisoning, and now he was ready to celebrate with a little Hershey's chocolate! Tell me about resiliency. I checked him over; his heartbeat was stronger and his breathing was slow and easy.

"He's going to be all right," I said.

Clara gave a little cry of relief, and even Jerry looked as if a load had been lifted from his shoulders. I told Clara I wanted to keep Archimedes at the clinic for a few days, just to keep an eye on him.

Jerry looked at his watch. "Aunt Clara, now that the emergency is over, well, I have a date, and ... "

"Of course, dear, you run along," Clara said. "Take the car. Oh—you don't mind driving me home, Milton, do you?"

"Be glad to. Just let me get Archimedes settled in." I was putting fresh water in his cage and this time didn't even hear the Mercedes start up and drive away. I wondered if Jerry would clean up the mess in the back seat.

On the drive to Clara's house I again brought up the subject of where Archimedes had gotten the poison. "It had to come from *somewhere*," I pointed out. "And if we can't find the source, Archimedes could get into it again."

"I know," she said tiredly. "I've been trying to think, but there's nothing in the house that could have made him sick. I'm sure of that."

"All right. Then you have to consider the possibility that the poison was given to him deliberately."

"What?" She sounded shocked.

"It's the only other explanation. Archimedes would never have eaten that much poison unless it was mixed in with something else, something he liked. A few licks out of curiosity, maybe, or to clean the stuff off himself if he'd gotten it on his fur—but not as much as I found in him, Clara. I suppose you've already washed his food dish from this morning?"

"Yes." She turned her head away. "You know what you're saying, don't you?" she asked in a small voice. "You're accusing Jerry of poisoning

Archimedes." I said nothing, letting the thought fester. Finally Clara burst out, "This time you go too far! I know you've never liked Jerry, but to accuse him of putting poison in Archimedes' food . . . you're getting obsessive about him, Milton!"

That was a nice cold bucket of water in the face. Obsessive? Me? I tried to think about it objectively . . . but that was impossible, of course. So I said, "Okay, if it's not Jerry, then the source of the poison has to be somewhere in your house. I'd better come in and look for it. We have to find out."

"We'll both look," Clara said.

I glanced over at her tired face. "I'll look. You're going to lie down before you fall down."

Clara's house was on a small rise at the peak of a long curving driveway. It was a magnificent old house, built by her grandfather around the turn of the century and full of the little niceties so sadly lacking in much of modern housing. It was far too big for one person but Clara wouldn't dream of leaving, even though it was costing her a fortune in upkeep. But Clara's family had always had money; if she wanted to spend her inheritance maintaining an Edwardian-style mansion, that was her business. Personally, I thought it was money well spent; it really was a magnificent old house.

We went in the front door, which Clara had neglected to lock when she'd rushed out with Archimedes. "Go lie down," I said to her. "There's no need for both of us to look."

She shook her head. "I want to see this through. Where do we start?"

"The kitchen. Then the bathrooms, then the basement."

Clara led the way into the gargantuan kitchen, but stopped short just inside the door—and laughed. "Oh, that *naughty* cat."

It took a second, but then I saw what she was looking at. On the floor by the kitchen counter was a cardboard box, one of the flimsy white ones you get from the bakery. It was upside down, and the cardboard had been clawed apart until you could see what remained of the chocolate-covered doughnuts inside; Archimedes had had himself quite a feast.

"It's my own fault," Clara said ruefully. "Normally when Jerry drops off the doughnuts I put them in the refrigerator where Archimedes can't get them—you know how he loves sugary things. But this morning I just couldn't seem to get moving. I've been so tired lately, I simply put them down without thinking—"

"Jerry brings you doughnuts every day?"

"Not *every* day, Milton," she said with a faint smile. "A couple of times a week, though. Isn't that thoughtful? I do so love doughnuts, especially the chocolate ones." She bent over to pick up the box.

"Don't touch that," I said sharply, and felt like kicking myself for being such a damned fool. I should have guessed. I went over to the phone on the wall by the

refrigerator and tapped out a number. To the woman who answered I said, "Give me the Sheriff. It's urgent."

"Milton?" Clara said. "What are you doing?"

When the familiar voice came on the line I said, "Warren, listen up. There's a box of doughnuts on the floor of Clara Murphy's kitchen that you've got to get tested for poison." I looked at Clara's shocked face. "Tell them to test for arsenic first."

Warren was quick. "The cat. That's what was wrong with him?"

"That's what was wrong with him. He got into a box of doughnuts meant for Clara, and it was Jerry who brought them here. He's been bringing Clara doughnuts a couple of times a week for . . . how long, Clara?" She was too stunned to answer. "For a long time, I'd guess," I said to Warren. "I've got to get her to the hospital."

"I'll pick up Jerry," he said. "You take care of Clara, Dad—leave the rest to me."

So I bullied that poor sick woman into the car and off to the hospital, where she got the care and attention she needed. And that's when it all ended, six months ago. The lab tests found arsenic in the chocolate frosting of the doughnut, as I'd suspected. I'd gone with Warren to Jerry's apartment, where Warren found the package the arsenic had come from. I hadn't seen one like it for nearly thirty years, since they found safer ways of getting rid of rats. But there were probably other packages like it still around, out in abandoned farm buildings around the county. Still available, and still lethal. In Jerry's kitchen were several containers of the ready-to-use kind of chocolate frosting you can buy at the supermarket.

We found something else as well. Jerry wasn't much of a reader; he had only one two-shelf bookcase in the place, crammed with paperbacks—adventure stories, spy novels, porn of varying degrees of softness. An adolescent boys' book collection. The one exception was the single hardback book he'd bought, a biography of Napoleon.

Warren and I stood staring at the book shelf. "Did you ever hear Jerry talk about Napoleon?" Warren asked me.

"Never," I said emphatically.

"Me neither." He pulled the book off the shelf and riffled through the pages. A newspaper clipping fluttered to the floor; Warren picked it up. "It's a review of this book," he said, reading quickly. "Well, well, what do you know. The author says that Napoleon died of arsenic poisoning and that no one knew at the time because it'd all been done so gradually."

"Huh. So that's where he got the idea." He'd probably enjoyed watching his aunt deteriorate, the sadistic little wretch.

Warren shook his head sadly. "You were right about Jerry, Pop. He's twisted, all right."

"Don't call me Pop," I said.

Jerry never did confess, of course, any more than he'd confessed to the BBs. But this time even Clara knew the truth; she had to accept the evidence of the lab reports, as did the jury when Jerry was tried for attempted murder. Clara is still anemic and I check on her almost every day. Other than that, she's pretty well recovered from her ordeal—only it took her six months instead of the six days it had taken Archimedes.

But I knew Clara was getting better when she announced one day that she was worried about me, living alone as I do, and that she was going to start checking in on me now and then to make sure everything was all right. I didn't say no to that. We'll watch out for each other—and for Archimedes, of course, who gets a doughnut for breakfast now and then; he's earned it. We still have a few good years ahead of us, Clara and I, thanks to his sugar-thieving ways.

Assault of the Yow-Ling Jewels

VIKI S. ROLLINS

PHILLIPE DE MAURIER, *chef de train* of the Orient Express, checked his watch: 10:21. He glanced out the windows at the passing countryside, Germany's ancient forests and distant mountains cloaked in the misty darkness. An hour more would see them in München, as per the schedule. He frowned, sipped his cognac, and turned his attention back to the efforts of the cleaning staff working in the dining car. It had become Phillipe's habit as the train's commander-in-chief to perform a routine inspection after dinner—drink in one hand, pocket watch in the other—to converse with staff members and guests to verify that all was well before retiring to his compartment to complete the day's records.

Which was why he stood here now, scrutinizing every movement of his staff. A few of his wealthier guests from runs in the past weeks had reported missing items from their compartments. The apparent thefts were few, but significant in value. Careful examination of the passenger list had eliminated the possibility of an outsider, considering the times and dates of the burglaries. The thefts had occurred over a period of several runs and between the hours of

11:00 P.M. and 5:00 A.M. and no single passenger had been on each of those runs. Only his staff remained a constant in this equation.

Phillipe took another sip from his cognac as he turned the mystery over in his head. His broad, imposing frame combined with gentle, grandfatherly features normally radiated confident assurance. Tonight, he slumped against a table near the rear of the restaurant car, his eyes red and weary from too many sleepless nights. Most troubling was how to deal with the guests themselves. The desire to protect conflicted with the need to maintain calm. Discretion, too, was the code of the Orient Express. Approaching each guest individually and inquiring after personal effects proved arduous, but necessary for the moment. Fortunately, the passenger list on this particular run from Varna to Paris was especially light, startling Phillipe from his reverie all the more when he heard the door to the restaurant car open behind him.

The *chef de train* turned and found himself face-to-fuzzy-face with a pair of yellow, almond-shaped eyes.

"*Waow!*"

"*Mon Dieu,*" Phillipe exclaimed, stepping back from the disarming sight of an impeccably dressed English gentleman with a slender feline perched regally on his right shoulder. Owen Gould, British Consul General for trade in the East, smiled and bowed his head.

"My apologies, m'sieur. Pho is rather demanding, I fear." Mr. Gould rubbed his shoulder-riding companion behind its chocolate-colored ear. The cat responded with soft mewls of pleasure.

"M'sieur Gould. A pleasure, regardless," Phillipe smiled, recovering his poise. He cocked his head toward the animal. "*Et votre ami, aussi.* It is, indeed, a fine creature. I had heard descriptions, but they do not do your beast justice."

The cat lifted one dark, delicate paw to its mouth and began preening, as if conceding the compliment. The fur on its body was light brown, while its tail, face, ears, and all four legs were a deep, rich chocolate color. No longer a kitten, but not quite a full-grown adult, its body was slender and a bit gangly. Mr. Gould chuckled.

"Ah, m'sieur, you will not find these animals elsewhere to my knowledge. Pho and his mate were a farewell gift from the King of Siam. This type of cat was bred for use as a temple guardian and considered quite holy. Kept only by the noblest families in Siam, so I am told. I must admit I am normally not fond of cats, but this particular breed insinuates itself upon your affections."

The cat ceased grooming and yowled. Silence ensued as the restaurant staff turned to stare at the two men and the disgruntled feline.

"Which is why I am here, m'sieur," Mr. Gould continued. "My cats are hungry. Could I impose upon your kitchen staff to part with some scraps from this evening's repast?"

"Nonsense, my good sir. Scraps will not do. All guests on L'Express d'Orient receive only the finest cuisine. André!" Phillipe called to a tall, muscular gentleman with graying sideburns who was instructing a boy on the proper method of table presentation. After a quick exchange in French, André strode toward the kitchen, while the rest of the staff resumed their duties.

"André will instruct the *chef de cuisine* to prepare a roast partridge for your pets. In the meantime, could I interest you in a drink?" Phillipe asked, raising his own toward Mr. Gould.

"Thank you, no. I should probably return to my berth. If you could have someone . . ."

"Of course, M'sieur Gould. Compartment three, *n'est-ce pas?*"

Mr. Gould nodded, expressed his gratitude, and turned to go, his cat still balanced perfectly on his shoulder, when Phillipe laid a hand on the Englishman's arm. The *chef de train* hesitated, then spoke in a low, conspiratorial voice.

"One thing more. If you are concerned with the safety of any of your valuables, I can provide you with a lockbox for the duration of the trip."

Pho, sensing his master's tension at the statement, growled deep in his throat. Mr. Gould stroked the cat's head reassuringly. "Is there a reason I should be concerned, M'sieur de Maurier?"

The two men faced each other, the question compounding the silence that followed. Phillipe could not resist the stare of the animal, its eyes narrowed to glittering, golden slits. Demon eyes, he thought, that steal away your soul. The cat's tail whipped hypnotically back and forth across Mr. Gould's shoulders. The *chef de train* forced himself to look away, back into the beckoning darkness just outside the railcar's windows. Phillipe's head ached, and fatigue wracked his body. Why not confide in M'sieur Gould? He seemed an intelligent, worldly man not easily frightened by the darker aspects of human nature. Look at what he carried on his shoulder.

"But no physical harm came to the victims?" Mr. Gould asked after the captain's disclosure.

"None thus far. Only the loss of materials: heirlooms, precious gems, rare artifacts. The thief is not greedy insofar as quantity; but in quality, his taste is exceptional. I suspect . . ."

"M'sieurs. I apologize for interrupting, but the cook says the partridge will take some time to prepare," André said, coming up behind Phillipe. "I will have Georges, the porter, deliver it to your compartment once it is complete."

"Thank you very much, André." Mr. Gould offered his hand to Phillipe, who set his drink on a nearby table and shook the Englishman's hand. "And you as well, M'sieur de Maurier. And I appreciate your offer regarding the other matter. I have only two rare jewels in my possession on this trip, but I doubt that they would do very well in a lockbox."

Owen Gould turned and exited the restaurant car, the cat on his shoulder glaring back at the two Frenchmen as its master walked away. Phillipe noted that the pounding in his head decreased as the distance grew between himself and that insidious feline beast.

"Quite a unique creature, no?" André commented toward the retreating figures.

"You will not find those animals elsewhere," Phillipe said, rubbing his eyes wearily. "Or so I am told."

Quietly, the slender, uniformed figure slid a key into the door of compartment three. He knew from experience that most passengers at this hour slept soundly, lulled by the rhythm of the train. Even the conductor snored loudly from his little cubbyhole at the end of the corridor. The intruder held his breath as he heard the tumblers roll and click open inside the keyhole. He waited for a moment, listening for sounds of movement inside the darkened compartment. Hearing nothing, he slowly opened the door only as far as required to allow his body access. He closed the door behind him and stood motionless, allowing his eyes to adjust to the darkness.

A shadowy movement to his left surprised him, and he stifled a gasp. He reached for the door latch when he heard a low, threatening growl beside him. A second snarl in front of him prompted him to tear open the door in an attempt to escape, his fear of discovery overcome by the fear of such menacing noises. A high-pitched screech behind him caused the intruder to scream, when a small, furry object struck his shoulder. The impact propelled the uniformed figure into the lighted hall, where he cried out and clutched at the shrieking, clawing creature that had attached itself to his head. Another unearthly yowl and the intruder felt a second set of teeth and claws on his leg.

Awakened by the growing commotion, the conductor bolted from his small chamber into the corridor, as passengers cautiously opened their doors and peeked into the hallway. All were surprised to discover a young porter fighting vainly to extract two exotic-looking cats—fur bristled and yellow eyes aglow—clinging and biting at the boy's face and legs.

Shouts from outside his compartment jolted Phillipe from a deep slumber. He stumbled from the berth and searched in the darkness for a match to light a lamp. He could feel the steady rumble of the train's movement beneath his feet, easing his initial fear of derailment. Upon lighting the lamp, he fumbled in his coat pocket for his watch. Dazed, he realized he had fallen asleep fully dressed, when his fingers chanced upon the fob chain. Tracing the delicate links to the watch, Phillipe pulled the timepiece into the light, and checked the hour: 2:10. It would be another five hours until sunrise.

"M'sieur de Maurier!" A voice called from outside his compartment. Phillipe recognized it as the voice of one of the train's conductors. "M'sieur de Maurier! There is a problem in compartment three! Come quickly!"

Compartment three? M'sieur Gould! Phillipe grabbed his cap from the berth, slid open his compartment door, and ran as quickly as the movement of the cars and the portals separating them would allow toward Owen Gould's compartment.

The *chef de train* fought his way through the crowd that had gathered in the narrow hall outside compartment three, drawn by the unearthly shrieking and howling from inside the small room. Breaking through the human barricade, Phillipe started at the sight before him.

Owen Gould's two cats, tails puffed to bottlebrush stiffness, stalked and yowled on one bunk, across from which a boy in a porter's uniform huddled on another. Mr. Gould, still dressed in his nightclothes and standing between the two bunks, spoke in low, soothing tones in an attempt to calm his pets.

"M'sieur Gould! What happened?" Phillipe asked after the cats' yowling had dissipated.

"Pho and Mia have lived up to their reputations as guardians, my dear sir," the Englishman replied. His smile was wide and triumphant. "My cats have caught an intruder."

"*Aidez-moi, s'il vous plait,*" came the plea from the huddled boy. "They are monsters!"

"Georges?" Phillipe stepped toward the bunk, as the boy raised his face from the pillows. Scratches across the porter's cheeks were starting to clot, but smeared blood made his wounds appear more serious. Georges, one of the youngest members of the staff, wept openly as he saw his captain before him.

"I am so sorry, M'sieur de Maurier. I meant no harm. He told me to get the jewels, or he would beat me and release me from my duties."

"Who told you to get the jewels, Georges?"

"What jewels?" Mr. Gould interjected.

Everyone waited as the boy quieted and caught his breath. Georges wiped at the tears running down his cheeks and winced as the salty moistness mingled with his open wounds. "André, m'sieur. He made all the boys steal for him. We were to go through the guests' baggage and tell him what we found. Oh please, m'sieur. Mercy! I never wanted to, but he was my superior."

"And after your reports?" Phillipe pressed.

"He would tell us what to take. He told us we were never to take any more than what he said, and then bring it only to him. He told us that these people were so rich that they would never miss a few small things. And he promised me that if I took M'sieur Gould's rare jewels, he would not ask me to steal again."

The boy's voice trailed off, ending in a miserable whimper as he warily eyed the pacing cats across from him. The animals had quieted, but still lashed their tails and glared at their quarry.

Phillipe turned to the conductor, who had struggled through the crowd behind him. "Find André and bring him to me now. Then have one of your more trusted men search the restaurant car and company sleeping quarters for any suspicious-looking articles. Lockboxes, trunks, unusual containers, and the like. I'll deal with the boy myself."

The *chef de train* helped the boy from the bunk but kept a firm grip on the porter's arm to keep him from fleeing. Upon seeing their victims rise, the cats arched their backs and lashed out with claws extended. Georges pulled against the older man's grip to distance himself from his tormenters.

"Tell us why you entered M'sieur Gould's compartment, Georges," Phillipe prompted.

The boy's eyes darted from the cats to their master to his captain. "Please, m'sieur. Keep them away," he whispered in a harsh voice.

"Tell us, or M'sieur Gould and I shall leave you to the beasts."

The boy cried out, "For his jewels, m'sieur. That is all."

"But I have no jewels," Mr. Gould said, shaking his head at the trembling boy. "Where on earth would you get such an idea?"

"André overheard you telling M'sieur de Maurier that you did not want to keep your rare jewels in a lockbox."

"My word," the Englishman laughed. "I was referring to my two cats, Mia and Pho. Other than trade reports and traveling documents, they are the only items of great value that I am carrying on this trip."

"They seem to have been of great value to L'Express d'Orient as well, M'sieur Gould," Phillipe added. "This mystery had been plaguing me for some time; but without any evidence, I was unsure of where to start. I will question the other porters to ascertain further information regarding André's part in these thefts."

"M'sieur de Maurier?"

The conductor entered the tiny compartment. "We were unable to find André, M'sieur de Maurier. And we will be entering Ulm in about ten minutes. He may have jumped the train or possibly hid himself in one of the other cars. I have the maintenance men searching now."

"Have one of your men secure the other porters," Phillipe said. "We will keep them locked in an empty compartment until we reach Paris so that I may question them further. When we reach Ulm, I will leave a report with the station authorities to keep watch for André. If he has jumped, his chances of survival are few. Someone will find him."

The conductor nodded and left the room, shooing any lingering on-lookers back to their berths. Still gripping Georges by the arm, Phillipe bowed to Mr. Gould.

"My apologies for any inconvenience, M'sieur Gould. I will notify the company of your ordeal, and take full responsibility for any recompense that you and your pets may require."

With his free hand, the *chef de train* reached tentatively toward the cats as he added, "They do have a certain appeal, do they not, m'sieur?"

Both felines, calmed by the dissipation of the crowds and chaos, nuzzled the captain's outstretched hand and purred loudly. Temperamental, but appealing, Phillipe thought, and smiled softly at the tenderness both cats now displayed.

"I warned you," Mr. Gould said. "They insinuate themselves upon your affections."

All three humans jumped as the cats leapt to the floor and yowled at Phillipe.

"Waow!"

"And now," laughed Mr. Gould, "they insist on a bowl of cream for their troubles."

Aunt Edna's Cats

DEL STONE JR.

AS I STAND IN MY KITCHEN, hands on hips, gazing across the 1,200-square-foot empire of my townhouse, I see things bumped out of place, the dust rings showing like chalk outlines, proof I've murdered my life with sameness.

I can't believe I'm living like this—everything disorganized and messy and, as I said, out of place. I swore I'd never live like this. I swore my life would be a monument to neatness and order and safety. What's going on?

It's Aunt Edna's cats.

Aunt Edna's cats have brought me a present. *Gaaah!* It's a lizard, one of those slippery green monsters. And it's still alive! *Gaaah!* Get it out of the house! I'll be chasing it for weeks!

I would strangle Aunt Edna. If I could find her.

* * *

I never liked cats. I was a dog man. My sisters were dog men. My parents, and their parents too, were dog men. We were all dog men, except my Aunt Edna, who had two or five or forty cats, who knows?

She was the nutty aunt, the one with all the cats.

But it wasn't the cats that made Aunt Edna nutty. Something else was wrong, and that's what I liked about her. While I had the job and the pension and the seven-percent mortgage, she rode motorcycles and ate Spam from a can and never saved a nickel for retirement. "Life is its own reward," she announced on her sixty-seventh birthday, and then she left town driving her ancient Ford pickup to search for D. B. Cooper's loot.

Who?

D. B. Cooper. Oh, you know. Back in 1971, D. B. Cooper skyjacked a Northwest Orient jetliner and parachuted to freedom over the Cascade Mountains with a ransom of two hundred thousand dollars. I thought they'd found his money, but not according to Aunt Edna. It was still out there, and she planned to find it—or have a darned good time trying.

Nutty Aunt Edna. That's what I liked about her. She was a free spirit. What I can't understand is what she liked about me. I'm her exact opposite. Maybe she felt sorry for me. Who can say? But it's obvious she liked something about me.

Because now I have two cats. *Her* two cats. It was a calculated move, I'm beginning to see. Aunt Edna brought them along, did her visiting, then left them to go finish what a skyjacker had begun twenty-eight years ago.

It was something I would never have done, not in a million years, and maybe Aunt Edna shouldn't have done it either.

Because she never came back.

Aunt Edna's cats have brought me somebody's mail. A TV cable bill. A solicitation for the American Cancer Society. And an airplane ticket to Bali.

Bali. I wonder what Bali is like? I wonder if I might go there someday? Probably not. Too expensive, and too dangerous.

Rotten cats. How did they get this stuff? Pick the lock on the mailbox? Just my luck. A kitty larceny.

I live in a townhouse, all alone, and I'm at the office most of the day. So it makes perfect sense that I have Aunt Edna's cats.

I don't talk about them much. I intentionally don't talk about them. Pet stories rank right up there with summer-vacation slides. And I know people wouldn't believe me if I said these are two of the most *amazing* felines God ever let slip into an earthly state, even if they do bring chaos and disorder to my life.

I won't let Aunt Edna's cats hear me say that, or even think that. They shouldn't believe for a moment that I am amazed.

Oh, no. What have Aunt Edna's cats brought me now?

It's a set of keys, lying on the kitchen floor like a stringer of koi, gleaming silver and gold in the fluorescent light. The keys are attached to a key ring that bears the Chevrolet logo. It says "Corvette."

Ah, a Corvette. Something low and sleek and dangerous. I wonder what it would be like to own such a car? Would I prowl the streets, an easy foot on the throttle, playing the role of mysterious stranger? Would women admire me? Would men shrink in fear?

Would I become low and sleek and dangerous?

I glance out the window at my Escort. You're insane, I scold myself. A Corvette costs more than all the money in your IRA. And the depreciation! Dear God. You'd have to be crazy!

Aunt Edna's cats are watching me. They remind me of her. I can hear her voice: "Life is its own reward!"

Which is true only if you're nutty.

The female cat's name is Magpie. I call her Maggie. She's an orange tabby Manx, and her most famous accomplishment is this: When I had her spayed, she had the tiniest ovaries of any cat the vet had ever seen.

The male is anthracite black. His name is Pavlov—Pav for short. He was put on this earth to teach me patience, and lately I only threaten to kill him two or three times a day. The trend is downward.

He waits for me at the door when I come home at night. Nutty cat. But why does that surprise me?

Aunt Edna's cats bring me something every day.

Today's offering is a compass, contained within a dented brass casing. The needle is long and fluted, a kind of art deco design, and the directions are indicated in florid black cursives highlighted in faded vermilion. The needle swings in wobbly arcs.

It's old and maybe it's valuable, looking like an artifact from the '20s or '30s. The days of Charles Lindbergh and Amelia Earhart and the *China Clipper*. Which direction shall I go? I ask myself. North to the pole with Admiral Byrd? South to the steamy Amazon? West to the Orient, or east to mysterious Africa?

Where do Aunt Edna's cats find this stuff?

Why do they bring it to me?

*   *   *

Every moving thing is a game to Aunt Edna's cats, be it a catnip-laced flannel mouse dangling from an elastic string, or a human foot sliding beneath the bed-covers. I discovered this fact early one morning as I awakened to the feel of Pav performing a biopsy on my big toe, his claws hooked knuckle-deep in my flesh and his ears laid back against his skull, his brain shrunken by play lust to the size of a BB shot and rattling around in that too-small cap of bone like a pachinko machine down to its last marble. I came howling out of bed like a Shinto priest in a funeral dirge and danced the way I have danced only three times in my life, all of those occasions prompted by excessive alcohol consumption.

Pav, of course, scrammed for safer playgrounds, having delivered my morning jolt so that I needn't bother with the coffee.

Thank you, Aunt Edna. I am now tuned to your frequency.

Another gift from Aunt Edna's cats.

Goodness. It's a bird. A tiny little bird.

It's still alive.

When I pick it up, it doesn't struggle. There is no blood, and everything seems to be intact—wings, legs, feathers. Not a scratch. Poor little thing.

It's terrified. Surrounded by all these huge, strange, scary things, it's immobilized with fright. I can see its heart pounding in those shining wide eyes.

Oh dear. I can see *myself* in those shining wide eyes.

Outside, I hold it in my open palm. It lies there a moment, its fear at war with its secret hope. Then it springs from my hand and flits to the nearest tree. It flies to another. Finally, I can feel its relief as it takes to the wind and soars and soars, practically shouting with its flight, "I'm alive! I'm free!"

That was me in those eyes.

The bird is a very un-catlike thing. What's going on here? What are Aunt Edna's cats doing?

This is the worm story.

I warn you, it's scary and it's gross. The experience severely damaged my psyche. I am now a good candidate for one of those baboon-heart transplant operations.

Maggie had worms, which I now know she got from fleas. (At the time, I was blissfully ignorant. I assure you, that is no longer true.)

I was warned about tailless kitties. "They aren't sanitary," I was told. So if I happened to be around when Maggie used the litter box, I'd give her a quick check, just to make sure she'd finished her business.

One morning, as I was leaving for work, I saw her climbing out of the litter box. I picked her up, turned her hind end toward me, and lifted her bobtail with my thumb.

Oh.

There really is no polite way to put this. Shall we just say that as I peeked at her bottom, something emerged from her bottom and peeked at me.

I could feel my face hardening into a waxy mask of terror. I set her down, and calmly walked to the door, and opened it, and shut it behind me, and locked it.

Then I ran like hell for the Escort.

What was that! I gasped, once I was inside and locked all the doors and had the air conditioner running. *Something from outer space? Something from the pits of hell?*

"It was something passed on to Maggie from a flea," the vet would chortle later. "It's called a tapeworm."

Dear God. I do not handle the unknown well. The unknown is chaos, and chaos is kith and kin to kitties, and I really wonder what Aunt Edna was thinking when she left these guys with me, because she knows I'm afraid.

At any rate, the fleas had to go, which meant Bob the carpet guy had to come clean the carpet before Charlie from the pest-control place could spray for fleas while the cats were being dipped and dewormed and inoculated.

So $175 later, I found a flea dying on the kitchen table.

Amazing. All my terror amounted to no more than this tiny thing, no bigger than a hangnail.

Be still, my baboon heart.

Aunt Edna's cats have done it again.

It's in the usual place, in the kitchen in front of the refrigerator, where I'd be sure to see it.

A twenty-dollar bill. Now, that's something useful.

Except it's so ratty-looking! Gnarled and eaten at the edges, Andrew Jackson a mere ghost within the green. It must have gone through the laundry— and a couple of times at that.

Where did Aunt Edna's cats find a twenty-dollar bill?

Is it mine? Did I leave it in a pair of pants and run it through the washer?

Or did they find it outside, hidden in the hedges or buried in the deep grass next to the wall?

Or here's a thought: Maybe Aunt Edna really did find D. B. Cooper's money. Maybe she's keeping a low profile to dodge the F.B.I. and the I.R.S., yet she wants me to know, so she sent this bill with Pavlov or Maggie as a message to run away from my world and join her in one last, great adventure.

Oh, sure. Right. That's a knee-slapper.

But you know, Aunt Edna really *did* like me.

She left me her cats.

Assuming I go straight home from work, a moment arrives between the time I open the front door and the time I go to sleep, when the day replays before me. Lightning does not strike, nor does the earth move, but I enjoy my quiet celebrations of things well done, and perhaps a silent regret for that which was not.

And always, no matter how wonderful or rotten I've been, I can lie on the couch and close my eyes and within moments feel the pressure of small paws on my chest, the spreading glow of a kitten lying down, the vibrating compression of a purr monster warming up.

It is the feel of disorder and chaos, but it is also love at its very best, for no reason other than its own, simple transcendence. Which is really, really nutty.

But it reminds me of what I must do.

Don't worry, Aunt Edna. Your message has come through, loud and clear. I am amazed.

The Bed and Breakfast Burglar

JILL GIENCKE

I DIDN'T LIKE THE LOOK of the guy the minute I saw him. Cats are pretty good judges of character, you know. We can spot a rat a mile off and this one, well, he smelled like a rat, too. Cheap cologne.

Mother and I were off on another of her "rest cure" weekends. This time, it was at a little bed and breakfast on the shore of a shining lake. Mother has expensive tastes and, luckily for both of us, the money to indulge them.

We were in the parlor—or the sitting room or whatever old-fashioned name you care to use—on a large, squashy sofa next to a fireplace. It was a cool spring evening and the fire completed the cozy ambience. I sat in Mother's lap with my paws curled under, and she stroked me with those long, soft strokes I love so much. We never stay at places that don't permit Mother to take me everywhere, of course. Sitting room, dining room, front porch. So, here I was, literally in the lap of luxury and quite enjoying it, while Mother held court with the other guests.

There was the doctor and his wife, off on a romantic weekend. The honeymooners, ditto. A middle-aged woman with a sulky teenage daughter. And this man, alone.

He was tall and thin and seemed to be made up of a series of rectangles. Face, body, arms, legs—all long, narrow boxes. I, myself, am a series of triangles. Soft gray triangles. Ears, nose, face, head, body. That's me. Mother insists on calling me—now, no cringing—Cordelia, but I'd just as soon be called Three.

Anyway, as always happens on these weekends, Mother ended up capturing an audience and proceeded to regale them with stories. Stories of the past—past adventures, past loves, past fancy-dress parties. Usually, people are very polite, nodding their heads even as their eyes glaze. Mother's like that. She commands attention. I've never been sure if it's the tower of snow-white hair or the startling blue eyes or the length of real pearls she constantly fiddles with that draws people to her.

But I knew what drew the rectangle man. The smell of money. Oh, he was careful to act quite nonchalant, drinking his coffee and listening to each story as if he were genuinely taking it in. He'd interject a question now and again, which Mother just loved because, by answering, she could put on her "Expert" hat, and that is so good for her ego.

"Belize?" he said now, his voice husky. One long finger gently rubbed the side of his long nose and he sniffed, then extracted a handkerchief from a pocket. "Then you must have been to Tikal? Tell us what you thought of the ruins there." He blew his nose with gusto.

I'd just shut my eyes. Not to sleep, mind you. Just to rest them. But I opened one now and looked at this man perched on a tufted chair not three feet away. I didn't have to listen to Mother's story. I'd heard it all before and seen the snapshots, besides, so I used the time to wonder what he was thinking. Certainly he wasn't really interested in an elderly woman's impression of Mayan ruins. Even if he were an archaeologist, the uneducated opinion of a tourist would be more frustrating than fascinating.

Watching his red-rimmed eyes, I saw them dart over the pearls, tangled, as always, between Mother's bejewelled fingers. If he weren't careful, he'd drool, I thought, and decided it was time to break up the little party.

I stood, stretched and yawned rudely at the assemblage. Then, I turned around on Mother's lap to face her and put both paws up onto her shoulders. She loves this. It just melts her. And I love it, too, because then she carries me around as if I were a baby wanting burping and I like the view from up high.

"Oh, there, look! Baby's ready for bed," she cooed now, scritching that spot behind my ear. I purred loudly and squirmed a little.

"Well, it is getting late. Time we were all in bed," the doctor announced as his wife rose a bit too hurriedly. He began to reach for the after-dinner drinks bill sitting discreetly on the edge of the table, but Mother shook her head.

"Oh, no, Doctor. Let me get this tonight. You've all been my guests." She beamed around the group and everyone, even the sulky teenager, smiled back.

Mother turned to the rectangle man. "Do you have a pen I could borrow?" she asked, and he quickly produced one from the breast pocket of his suit coat. Mother signed the bill, then took a moment to admire the pen.

"It was my father's," the man said proudly. "Sterling silver, chased with gold."

"Well, it's quite wonderful, Mr. . . . . er," Mother trailed off. She's very bad with names.

"Caine. Adam Caine." He bobbed his head. "At your service."

Really, it was too much. Mother ate it up, giggling like a girl and handing the pen back with a flourish. The scene would have gotten even more stagey if, just at that moment, Mr. Caine hadn't emitted a sneeze loud enough to shake the glazing from the windows.

"Oh, Mr. Caine." Mother was the voice of concern. "You've caught cold."

Mr. Caine looked daggers at my back. I could feel prickles along my spine, honestly.

"No," he said. "I have an allergy." He paused. "To cats."

Mother's hands tightened around me and I gave a little yip of dismay.

"Oh, dear. I'll just get Cordelia off to bed then and out of your way. So sorry."

We all tromped upstairs and Mother was asleep just the instant her coiffure hit the satin pillow cover. Behind her knees, I sat awake for hours, listening to the sounds of the unfamiliar house and wondering about Adam Caine.

The next morning at breakfast, Caine was careful to seat himself at the opposite end of the table. He caught my steely gaze once or twice and then quickly looked away. Not many humans can endure my steely gaze without flinching. I've worked on it for years and it now possesses a dazzling intensity.

The discussion at the table centered around the afternoon's excursion on the lake in a fancy pontoon boat. Mother was quite gung ho.

"Of course, I'll have to leave darling Cordelia behind in my room," she told the others as I licked bacon grease from her fingers. "She's not much for water, you know."

Truer words. . . .

So, at one o'clock, off she trotted, a big straw hat shielding her from the sun. I sat on the windowsill and watched her climb gingerly aboard the bobbing boat, assisted by the good doctor. The honeymooners were absent, I noticed, as was—I squirmed closer, gave my tail a flashing whip—as was Adam Caine.

The motor roared to life and off they putt-putted. In the quiet of the old house, I began to feel sleepy, and the jump from windowsill to counterpane was a snap. I curled up on Mother's pillow and drifted off.

When the bedroom door creaked open a while later, I knew it meant trouble. The creak came slowly and stealthily. Mother doesn't do anything stealthily.

I sat up, stretching without lifting my bottom from the bed, and waited. It really came as no surprise to see Adam Caine slip into the room. Moving with purpose to Mother's dresser, he didn't see me there on the bed, so when I leapt from bed to dresser, landing lightly and with great style directly beside his elbow, he gave a satisfying start of alarm.

"Get away," he told me. "Scat!"

Already his hands were opening Mother's jewelry box and selecting small, easily concealed items.

I pranced between him and the box. I'm a trim thing—eight pounds at my last vet visit—so I couldn't use brute force against this burglar stealing my beloved Mother's beloved jewels. I had to be a bit craftier.

"Yeow!" I greeted him in a friendly tone, lifting my back to invite a caress. "R-reow!"

Instead, I got a rude shove.

Mother's jewels were fast disappearing into the pockets of his blue blazer. Really, I thought, he should have gone along on the boat ride, he looked so nautical in the blue blazer and white pants.

White pants. White pants.

I jumped to the floor and continued to sweet-talk the thief. Twining around his ankles in figure eights, I rubbed up against him as hard as I could, depositing much gray fur on the cuffs of those white pants.

Adam Caine lifted one foot, then the other, struggling a bit feebly to disengage me. He was too preoccupied with his job to be effective. I gave a playful swat to his ankle, claws extended only slightly. I didn't even leave a mark! He let out a muffled oath, bending over to swat right back at me. I skipped out of the way, naturally, and noticed what he had not.

When he'd bent over, something had slipped from the breast pocket of his blazer. It didn't weigh much, and the carpet was so thick it hadn't made much of a sound. Silver, chased with gold, it was the pen of which he was so proud.

Ever so casually, I stepped in front of the pen, blocking his view of it. Then, turning quickly, I gave it a bat. My aim was true and the pen slid noiselessly across three feet of carpet and under the bed.

Adam Caine sniffed loudly once or twice and, at great personal risk, I returned to the dresser top to rub against his arms and brush his cheek with my tail. His eyes were already watering and his nose was beginning to flush red. Anyone seeing him now after having seen him last night would have no doubt as to what was wrong.

The sounds of the pontoon boat returning to the dock came through the open window. *Mother, hurry!* I wanted to yell, but, moving to the windowsill and looking out, all I could manage was, "Meow! Meow, meow!"

Everyone on the dock looked up.

"Oh, hello, Cordelia!" Mother waggled her fingers at me.

Adam Caine was out of time. He turned on one narrow heel and ran from the room, leaving the door ajar.

It seemed to take Mother even longer than usual to climb the flight of stairs to her room, where I waited with growing impatience.

Mother went straight to the dresser to remove the jewelry she wore, in preparation for her afternoon nap. It only took her one glance to see what had happened. Her hand lifted to her chest and she gasped. "My jewels!"

Then, in best movie star fashion, she hurried to her open doorway and stood shouting, "I've been robbed! I've been robbed!"

What happened next went a long way toward restoring my faith in human nature. Along the corridor other doors opened and concerned fellow guests came rushing out. Luckily, Mother pretty well blocked the doorway, so none of them came in to disturb the scene.

"Call the police!" the doctor ordered and the sulky teenager dashed off to do it, sweet as you please!

The proprietor, Mr. Kenyon, showed up just then to check on the commotion. He was clearly stunned to think he had harbored a thief in our midst.

"Nothing like this has ever happened before," he said, as if that made a difference.

The sulky teenager's mom stepped forward.

"I'm Police Officer Danis," she told us, producing a shiny silver badge. "I'm on vacation, but I can contain the scene until the local authorities get here."

"R-reow!" I said. Now we'd get some action! Every moment counted. Adam Caine could already be in his car, driving away. He certainly wasn't in the hall with the others.

Officer Danis stepped past Mother and came toward the dresser, her eyes taking in the scene. The other guests stood just outside, their necks craning to see what the two women were doing.

"I came in and it was just like this." Mother pointed at the nearly empty jewelry box.

"Seems whoever did this left in a big hurry," Officer Danis remarked.

"R-reow!" I said again. I was sitting near the bottom of the bed, waiting for my chance. I needed their full attention.

"Oh, Cordelia," Mother cried. "You saw the whole thing, didn't you? Oh!" She bent to scoop me up, but I sidestepped gracefully. There'd be time for cuddling later.

"Yeow!" I hollered again.

Officer Danis turned to smile at me. "If only you could talk," she said.

With the police officer and Mother and all those folks in the doorway as witnesses, I jumped to the floor and wriggled under the bed.

"What on earth—" Mother began, breaking off as I smacked the pen out from its hiding place. It bumped against her shoe.

Leaning down, Officer Danis said, "I think we've all seen this before."

"That pen! It's Adam Caine's pen!" Mother was aghast.

"Where is he?" Mr. Kenyon growled. He and the doctor formed a posse of two and marched off to Caine's room.

If only Adam Caine hadn't stopped to blow his nose and take an antihistamine, he might have had time to vanish. Instead, the proprietor and the doctor found him in his room, hastily packing a bag.

When the police arrived, everyone tried to talk at once, but Mother's voice rose above them all.

"You can tell he's the guilty man," she said, pointing a finger straight at Adam Caine's bleary eyes. "We found his pen in my room."

"And he's sneezing again," the sulky teenager contributed helpfully, "from his cat allergy."

From my place on the floor at Adam Caine's feet I gave a sharp, commanding, "G-g-reow!"

The doctor looked down, as they all did, and noticed what I had hoped he would.

"And just look there! Caine's pants legs. They're covered in gray fur. There's more proof!"

Defeated, Caine sniffed and gave me an angry glare.

I don't want to say I looked smug, but I was quite pleased with myself.

Caine was taken off to the waiting police car in stony silence. When he'd gone, Mother scooped me into her arms and rubbed her chin on the top of my head.

"My Cordelia is so smart! She caught the burglar all by herself!"

And so I had—just in time for dinner.

Beware of Cat

KURTIS ROTH

ALL RIGHT, KID. I WANT YOU to ignore all these people. Forget the lab techs. Forget the photographer. I want you to look at this scene and tell me what you see."

"I see a cat."

"Forget the cat already."

"Well, he's all bloody."

"He's not all bloody. He's cleanin' hisself up pretty good."

"And he looks mean."

"You'd look mean, too, if your owner just got dragged off to the hospital with a massive head wound and your house was invaded by the boys in blue."

"Hey, Joe?"

"What?"

"Why do they call us that? The boys in blue? We're plainclothes."

"We're still cops, kid. Goes with the territory. Now tell me what else you see."

"All right. I see a cat—"

"Forget the cat."

"—who tried to kill his owner."

"Excuse me?"

"Yeah. I mean, I can't say for sure he did it on purpose. Maybe he did. He looks mean enough."

"Kid—it's a cat."

"Hey, you asked me to tell you what I see, I'm telling you."

"All right. Then tell me how you got there."

"Well, first there's the fact that we're here because the neighbors heard the cat screaming up a storm—yowling, whatever—and called it in. And there were shouts, too. A man's voice. And then there's this spot where we found Mr., uh, Mr.—"

"Devoe, kid. Mr. William A. Devoe of four-twenty-three West Hundred-and-Twenty-Fifth Street. For crying out loud. Where's your memory?"

"Sorry."

"Don't be sorry. Just get it right. Put it in your notebook, for crying out loud."

"Okay, look, I'm writing it down. You happy?"

"Very."

"So anyway, Devoe was here at the bottom of the stairs."

"You figure the stairs played a role."

"Yeah. The stairs, and the cat. Guy's coming down the stairs, it's dark—"

"How do you know it's dark?"

"What do you mean, how do I know? It was dark when we showed up."

"No, I mean how the hell did you remember it this long?"

"Hey, cut me some slack, would you? I'm trying to detect here."

"All right. Keep going."

"So the guy—Mr. Devoe—he's coming down the stairs in the dark and the cat gets underfoot, and he takes a tumble and smashes his head. Cat stands triumphantly over his kill—who isn't quite dead, but you get the point—and that's where we found them when we got here. End of story. What? What's that look for?"

"I'll tell you what's it for. Show me where Devoe hit his head."

"Huh?"

"Guy got his head smashed in, show me what he smashed it on."

"Well, jeeze, he smashed it on the floor, didn't he? That's where all the blood is."

"Uh-huh. Tell me, kid, did you even bother glancing at him before they carted him out of here?"

"Sort of. You got to admit, they whizzed him away pretty quick."

"How quick? You didn't get two seconds to look at him? Because that's all it took for me to see that the wound was on the top of his head, near the back. Guy's coming down the stairs, trips over a cat, he falls forward. How do you figure he hit the upper back portion of his head? The cat's an outside linebacker now? Flipped the man end over end? Spun him around while he was at it? Quick, call the Giants. Call the Jets. God knows they could use the help."

"Jeeze, Joe. Settle down."

"Settle down, he says."

"What if he fell from the top of the stairs? He could have flipped, landed head first."

"Kid, I'm no pathologist, but I'm thinking he could have fallen down three times as many steps as you see here, and he still couldn't have landed with enough force to inflict that wound. He didn't hit his head on the floor. So I want you to show me where he *did* hit it. Go ahead. Look around."

"I am looking around, and I don't see anywhere else it might have happened."

"All right. What *do* you see?"

"I see the cat, that's what. And he's looking at me. Hungrily."

"Oh, yeah. You know, now that I think about it maybe you're right. Maybe he killed Devoe because the poor jerk was late with his Fancy Feast."

"You joke, but I'm telling you—that cat's a killer. I've seen the look before. I had this girlfriend once, had a cat just like this one. Stark white. Same icy blue eyes and everything. Eyes of a killer. Thing tried to shred me every time I came over. That's why we broke up, you know. That damn cat."

"Yeah, kid, I'm sure it was the cat."

"It was."

"You ever hear of a psychological principle called displacement?"

"Cut the crap, would you? What do you want from me anyway?"

"I want you to show me where the man hit his head. There's good clues all over the place if you'd just open those beady little eyes of yours. What's with the Clint squint, anyway? You nearsighted?"

"I don't squint."

"Sure you do. Go ahead, make my day. It's written all over you."

"Jeeze."

"No, see that's where you mess it up. Clint would never say 'jeeze.' Anyway—unsquint and look around. Start with the kitty cat. You want to talk about bloody paws, you can tell me what goes with them."

"What goes with them?"

"Yeah. Bloody paws equals. . . ."

"Bloody pawprints?"

"You're a genius, kid. Now look around."

"Hey, wow—bloody pawprints."

"Uh-huh."

"Looks like they go around the corner into the kitchen. Right up to the back door. And—oh, jeeze."

"Yeah. Jeeze. Look at that. Blood all over the back door."

"Wow, Joe. You're really good. So, what, you figure the cat tripped Devoe in here, he smashed his head, stumbled into the other room—"

"Kid."

"—fell over and—"

"Kid."

"What?"

"The cat did not kill his owner."

"But . . . the blood. . . ."

"Yes. Exactly. The blood. That's a splash pattern, not an impact point."

"So? Maybe he tripped over the cat and hit his head on the doorknob."

"Enough with the tripping already. Do you see any blood on the doorknob?"

"Yes. A little. A smear."

"Right. And how would you say that little smear corresponds to Mr. Devoe's massive head wound?"

"Well. . . . "

"Right. It doesn't. But what *does* it tell you? Put it together with the fact that there are spatters on and around the door. Go ahead, think it through. I can see it's going to take you a minute."

"Um."

"Tick. Tock. Tick—"

"Devoe was trying to get out? Because the cat was attacking him?"

"You're getting warm. Now think about Devoe's condition."

"Okay."

"And put that together with the cat's bloody paws."

"Oh."

"Uh-huh."

"I think I see what you mean. The cat's paws—or, more precisely, his claws—don't match up too well to the infliction of an impact head wound."

"They don't match up at all. Not unless the cat inflicted it some other way, then did a little Gene Kelly singing-in-the-rain victory dance in it afterward."

"But jeeze, Joe. The cat—he looks so mean. Look at him. He followed us in here and he's *still* giving us the evil eye."

"He's giving you the eye, kid. Me, he likes. Come here, kitty cat. Look—he's cleaner now, but you can still see the stains. That's the hassle of having this great white fur, huh, buddy? A little bit of blood on the back paws, a lot on the front. And the blood in back is just around the toes. Like he wasn't using 'em so much as weapons, but more to hang on to the guy."

"Wait a second. He was hanging on to Devoe?"

"No. Come on now. I'm only going to give you one more try."

"Okay. He was hanging on to someone else."

"Right."

"But who else would be—oh."

"Uh-huh. Go ahead, open the door."

"Is the lab finished with it? Pictures and prints?"

"Yeah."

"Okay. Woah. Somebody really did a number on the outside of this thing."

"Uh-huh. Forced it with some kind of crowbar. This was the assailant's point of entry."

"And his point of exit?"

"Uh-huh."

"So, okay, let me see if I got this. Someone breaks in here at the back door, Devoe's coming down the stairs to see what the noise is all about, and he gets clobbered, probably with the crowbar. The intruder thinks he's got free reign of the place now, but then there's the cat. The attack cat."

"Right."

"Cat jumps, starts shredding away, guy probably can't even figure out what's happening, and he sure as heck can't smack at it with the tire-iron or whatever, not without smacking himself. All he knows is he wants out and he wants out *now*. So he makes a run for the back door, fumbles with the knob—and this is where he gets the serious shredding."

"Right. But eventually he escapes."

"And the cat goes back to the other room to stand protectively over his owner until we arrive."

"And he gives you the evil eye, kid, because he's had a bad day, and because you clearly aren't a cat person."

"That's not fair. I am so a cat person."

"Really. That why you took one look at kitty cat here— who probably deserves a medal of commendation—and were ready to send him to the electric chair?"

"We don't have the death penalty anymore, Joe."

"Okay, so send him upstate. Same difference."

"Look, I get along with cats just fine."

"No, you don't. And I think you'd better cop to it so I can write off your poor performance as a bias against felines, instead of calling it crappy detective work."

"Jeeze, Joe. You wouldn't really do that, would you?"

"Try me."

"Hey, Joe? Joe—wait a second."

"What?"

"Where you going?"

"To find this guy some Fancy Feast before he rips your throat out."

"Oh. Jeeze."

"Rookie."

The Biggest Crime

JOHN BEYER AND KATHRYN BURDETTE

NED THE BARTENDER WAS NERVOUS.

Most of the people in Gilmore's were nervous. The barmaid, Karen, was standing by the empty tables at the front of the bar, clutching her tray to her chest, her easygoing voice silent for the past half hour. Two untouched fourth bourbons sat in front of the rumpled salesmen from across the street. Even Jerry, the beat cop who had just delivered the bad news, shifted about uncomfortably in the front doorway as he looked into the small, narrow establishment, past the four wobbly tables, past the bar, and at the back of the room.

Down there were the only ones who weren't nervous: the three strangers, who had come in half an hour ago, and Bukka, the bar's resident cat. The strangers were shooting pool and Bukka was reclining on the dark, polished countertop that almost ran the length of one entire wall. His eyes were shut, but occasionally he'd open them and stare irritably at the strangers. Of course, they didn't notice him; in fact, they didn't seem to be aware that a cop had entered the room. When Jerry stopped talking, the only sounds in the bar were the clacking of the pool balls and the rich voice of Muddy Waters emanating from the jukebox against the far wall.

Ned, a stocky, thirtyish guy with shoulder-length red hair and a goatee, had not averted his gaze from the strangers since they had come jostling into his establishment through the back door. And ever since Jerry had announced that he was looking for a robber, Ned had been standing with one arm draped across the till and the other hand cupping his chin, scratching his beard. He didn't feel all that bad about what Jerry said had happened—leave it to Stefan, the owner of the club down the street, to make a night deposit at the poorly-lit bank around the corner. What Ned hated was the upheaval that had been caused by the strangers' presence. Ned was high-strung and soft-spoken and did not like the unexpected. Especially if it resulted in a confrontation.

The first thing the three strangers had done to cause trouble was force Bukka off his roost. They had come in from the alley laughing demonstratively and shoving each other into the cigarette machine by the back door, chucked their cigarettes into the men's room toilet, and upon emerging from the narrow back hallway into the main room, had driven out two college boys about to attempt a pool game. Few people ever came into Gilmore's to play pool—the table had sort of come with the establishment. Ned had left it there as an occasional money trap. It barely fit in the room and had to sit parallel to the bar, with its short sides facing the front door and back wall respectively. There was hardly enough room for a person to walk past any side of it, never mind try to maneuver for a shot. Forget playing at all if Gilmore's was crowded, which happened if more than ten people showed up. And it was nearly impossible to make any shot from the side nearest the back wall, because you had to try to fit between the table and the juke-box, an ancient, dented machine that looked like it should have Sulu or Chekov doing interstellar calculations on it. Consequently, the tall, thin stranger had to reach around it to get at the cuesticks and found himself at eye-level with a gray cat that was as much a large, beat-up relic as the machine it sat on.

The blond stranger with the baseball cap stepped up behind his friend. "Git off!" he shouted at the cat. "Git!" The short, dark-haired stranger with the walrus mustache came around the other side of the pool table and chucked some quarters at the cat. Bukka's ears went back; he flattened himself out as the money pinged against the wall and the jukebox. Then the tall man, obviously the ringleader of the group, swiped his pool cue at Bukka's head.

"Hey, leave him alone, man!" shouted Ned. The cat jumped to the floor and ran behind the strangers, down the back hallway, out his kitty door and into the alley.

"Damn animals. You got an infestation here," the short stranger told Ned. The leader then slapped a huge wad of bills on the pool table; the blond stranger scooped them up and tossed them at Ned. "Coronas. Keep 'em coming."

Ned had considered chasing them out or calling the cops. But in his experience, it was often best to let trouble walk away all by itself. Let them try to get a decent game going around that table. See if they don't get fed up in five minutes.

But twenty minutes later, they were absorbed in a game of Cutthroat and showed no interest in leaving anytime soon. At least Ned felt better when Bukka came skittering back down the hallway batting a piece of crumpled paper and carrying two maraschino cherry stems in his mouth. Ned was so happy to see him that the cat's obvious foray into the trash went unpunished. But it only calmed him for a few minutes, because Jerry came in the door shortly after that with the news that one of the strangers was probably a criminal.

Now Jerry made his way down the narrow pathway between the tables and the bar. The strangers still pretended not to notice him, even as he quietly took the pool cue from the leader and repeated his question.

"Where were you at 8:55 this evening, Porter?"

The leader acknowledged Jerry's presence for the first time. "I was here," he said in a smoker's hack. "Wasn't I here, barkeep?"

Ned's glare darkened, and he shook his head no. He hugged the till a little tighter with his left arm.

Porter returned the glare. The bartender was startled by his eyes: they were a clear, bright blue, the only color on his drab person. Ned pretended to glance at something on the wall behind him, but Porter's eyes stared at him in the giant mirror back there, the only part of him visible between the shelves of liquor bottles. The bottles themselves reflected his whole face in miniature, freakishly distorted.

"You sure?" asked Porter's bizarre reflection in a bottle of Absolut. "I don't see any clocks on the wall. You look at your watch when we came in here?"

Ned turned around. He felt his heart pounding, and tension shot right up the back of his neck. "It was about half an hour ago, Jerry," he said sternly.

"Forty-five minutes," Porter said, folding his arms as if his patience were being tried by an unreasonable bureaucracy.

Jerry's voice was calm. "At 8:55, a man was making a deposit at the First National on Third and Decatur. Someone attacked him and took his money. I'm pretty sure it was you."

"He was attacked from behind. How would you know who robbed him?"

"How'd you know he was attacked from behind?" Ned asked.

Porter leveled his eyes at Ned. "Nobody sneaks up from the front. Don't you watch *Homicide?*" He sounded amused. Ever since Jerry had come in, he had seemed to be stifling a laugh.

Jerry said, "But he says he got a good look when the robber was running away."

Porter took his eyes off Ned, who felt partly relieved and partly disgusted at his relief. "A good look at what?" he asked. "His face? Was the guy running backward?"

The blond stranger laughed. He and the short one had not stopped playing pool and repeatedly bumped into Jerry as they lined up their shots. "Oh, excuse me," the short one kept saying.

Jerry ignored them. "What's your story, Porter?"

"Been with my friends all afternoon. Right, guys?" He took another cue from above the jukebox. "So we couldn'ta done it, since only one guy attacked your friend."

"Where's my next Corona, barkeep?" the short one called without looking up from his shot. The empties had been placed on the jukebox.

"Back here," Ned told him.

The little man looked up. His blond friend gave a short, contemptuous laugh, which might or might not be directed at Ned.

"We gave you our money, buddy boy," the short man said. His eyes were weaker than his leader's, but he didn't need an omnipotent stare—clearly, from the veins appearing on his forehead, he had a temper that was shorter than he was.

Ned remained steady. Jerry's presence didn't hurt. "Didn't take it yet, Ringo," he said. Sometimes you didn't have to let trouble walk away.

But Jerry stepped up to the bar. "Ah, Ned . . . please don't start something."

"Me?! Jesus! How can I start something that started half an hour ago?"

"Have they done anything wrong?"

"They scared Bukka!"

Jerry glanced at the abandoned jukebox. "I admit that's a crime, but I mean legally?"

Ned looked at the floor.

"So I can't do anything," Jerry said.

"Oh, come on! You got your evidence right here!" Ned cried, holding up a few of the twenties littering the countertop.

"Why wouldn't their fingerprints be on their own money?"

"What if Stefan's are on it?"

"They've all handled it too much by now, and so have you. We wouldn't get anything conclusive. Think about how many people touch a dollar bill the whole time it's in circulation."

Ned gave a terse sigh. Jerry had been a patrolman for twelve years and was used to punks; Ned wondered if that had made him too cynical about difficult cases.

"There's just no proof, Ned. You admit the guy came in with his pals."

"Yeah, like probably right after he did it!"

"Probably," Jerry said. "But all Stefan saw was a guy in black and it was dark out. That isn't going to stick."

"Okay, what about video cameras?"

"Muggers account for that."

"So they can just do whatever they want to whoever, and nobody's gonna stop 'em because it's just too hard?"

"Look, Ned, I know he did it. You know it. Karen knows it, your customers over there know it, and even Bukka probably knows it. Guys like these are punks, and all they ever do is break the law. That's all they're good for. That's all they're good *at*, which is why they get away with it a lot." He glanced over his shoulder. "One of these days, they'll commit some crime without even thinking about it, or maybe without even knowing it, and that's when they'll get caught. But what happened to Stefan was not one of those crimes. So until then, we have to let them continue being worthless—"

Porter's raspy voice interrupted them. "What's with this Delta blues crap?" he shouted, and unplugged the jukebox. Bo Diddley's jangly guitar chords were silenced, right in the middle of "Who Do You Love."

Jerry turned around. "Hey!"

"What?" Porter said, holding up his hands in mock surrender. "I'm turning off the music!"

"You're messing with property!"

"No, sir, I'm just trying to help you converse with our friend the bartender." He looked at Ned again. *Just wait till the cop leaves, friend.*

Ned averted his eyes, which came to rest on Bukka. The cat was now sitting up straight in his chair, staring at the silent jukebox, his trashcan bounty of stems and paper forgotten on the seat in front of him.

Ned had brought everyone's attention to the cat. The blond stranger leaned in and hissed melodramatically at him; the short stranger pretended he was going to throw the cueball at him; Porter held his stick out like a sword. *"En garde,* cat!" he cried, thrusting. Bukka crouched low and swiped at the cue with his paw.

"Knock it off, Porter," Jerry said.

"What? I'm just playing with the kitty!"

"Yeah, well, we take people downtown for harassing animals."

The blond stranger backed away from the cat, almost right into Porter's jabbing stick. "Really?"

"He's jerking you, Phil," Porter said.

Bukka jumped to the floor and landed right next to Jerry's feet, rather nimbly considering his bulk. Ned leaned over the counter and saw that Bukka was offering Jerry a gift that he carried in his mouth—the wad of paper he had been batting around earlier.

Jerry reached down and stroked Bukka's head with the back of his gloved hand. "For me? You shouldn't have, Bukka." He took the paper and uncrumpled it.

"Be grateful, Jerry," Ned told him. "Usually it's rats."

Jerry studied the paper and was silent for a few seconds. "No, seriously, I'm flattered," he said, still addressing Bukka, who walked around and between Jerry's ankles until the dark blue trouser bottoms were covered in gray fur. "It's not every day somebody gives me a deposit slip."

Suddenly the three strangers tensed. The short one froze in midstroke, Phil backed himself right into the corner of the pool table, and Porter's cuestick slipped from his fingers as if they were buttered. He had to lurch forward and fumble with it to keep from dropping it altogether.

Ned felt a rush of warmth inside; his neck muscles loosened. His eyes met Jerry's, which were bright with exhilaration the way they probably had been when he caught perps as a younger cop.

"Whose deposit slip might that be, Jerry?" Ned asked him.

"Lemme see," Porter said, lunging toward Jerry.

Jerry stepped out of the way, holding the paper up as if he were playing keep-away with a small boy. "I can't imagine," he said with exaggerated curiosity. "This isn't yours, is it, Ned?"

"Jeez, I don't know. What's it say? Hey, you should find out if *my* finger-prints are on it."

"Oh, we don't need *yours*, Ned, just Porter's and Stefan's."

"All right, just give it here," Porter said.

"Why? Is it yours?"

There was a thudding sound in the hallway; Ned turned around just in time to see Phil and the short man run out the back door, their cuesticks on the floor by the table. When he turned back, Jerry had Porter up against the bar, his left hand holding Porter's head down on the counter, his right hand somewhere behind Porter's back. Ned heard the click of handcuffs.

"It's not mine!" Porter said, his voice slurring as he tried to talk with his chin and nose pressed against the counter. He looked up at Ned; the malice in his eyes was gone, but when Bukka jumped up on the bar next to Porter's head and started hissing, it returned.

Ned gingerly put a soothing hand on Bukka's bristling back. The cat ignored him altogether and growled at Porter while Jerry's voice droned the Miranda rights.

When he was done, Jerry asked Ned, "Where'd Bukka get the slip? The dumpster in the back alley?"

"You think we'll find a deposit bag in there, too?" Ned asked.

Jerry pulled a black pocketknife out of Porter's jacket, held it up for Ned to see, and set it on the counter. He leaned in close to Porter. "And I bet that's what you used to cut the deposit bag open."

Porter said, "Will you get that goddamn cat away from me?"

The cat ran to the far end of the counter as Jerry led Porter out the front door, and he continued growling even after they had gone. Ned tried talking Bukka down, but Bukka only started meowing at the door in his gravelly voice.

Karen put down her tray and came around behind the bar to pour two new bourbons for the salesmen; she placed a handful of tuna-flavored kitty treats on the opposite end of the counter. Bukka only stared expectantly back at Ned.

Then Ned realized that Jerry was right. Punks like Porter committed crimes all the time. And he had committed his biggest crime of all without even realizing it. Ned came around the front of the counter, went around the pool table, and plugged in the jukebox.

"—do ya love?" Bo Diddley sang, his chords ringing off the walls and ceiling. Bukka ate the treats, leaped from the bar to the pool table to the jukebox, and resumed his routine. Ned placed the cherry stems in front of Bukka, nuzzled the cat's head with his goatee, and went back behind the bar to resume his own routine.

The Boys

KATHRYN PTACEK

SARAH KNEW SOMETHING was wrong the minute she woke. The cats weren't snuggled against her. She peeked at the clock radio. 7:30. She'd overslept, and for a moment she struggled with panic. She was late for work.

Wait. It was Saturday. Still, she'd overslept. And that in itself was curious because the Boys, as she called them, never let her sleep late. If she tried to hunker down under the covers for a few minutes longer, she was invariably disturbed by Lovejoy pawing at her. If Lovejoy couldn't budge her, then in trotted Archie who would proceed to walk up and down on top of Sarah. And when all else had failed Lord Peter would start chewing on Sarah's hair.

That always rousted her. Funny, though, Lord Peter never chewed on Brian's hair. Brian. She looked over at the other side of the bed. He was up already. That was odd. Normally she rose long before he did, and would have her morning walk, shower, and breakfast out of the way by the time her husband dragged downstairs.

For years she'd tried to get him up at the same time as she did, but nothing worked, and after a while she'd given it up. She was doomed to a life of solitary breakfast-eating.

Except for the Boys who always kept her company while she munched on an English muffin. They stuck close to her all the time. Actually, the cats had been Brian's idea; as a child Sarah had never had a pet—her mother had run off when Sarah was young, and after that her father had traveled a lot, and Sarah had been passed from relative to relative.

When she and Brian married, he'd insisted they get cats. From the first, though, it was apparent the cats—all rescued from the local animal shelter—preferred Sarah to Brian.

Brian had smiled when the tiny fuzzballs jumped into Sarah's lap, but as time wore on, Sarah noticed his smile grew strained. The cats went to Sarah and meowed for food; they arranged themselves in front of her to get their daily grooming; and in the morning they woke her up, not him. Brian had tried to keep the cats out of the bedroom, but that hadn't lasted long. Lovejoy would sit on the other side of the door and try to dig his way in, or he would throw himself against the door, trying to make it budge. Finally, Brian relented and kept the door open.

Brian. "Hon?"

Lovejoy answered with a squeak.

Sarah threw back the covers, pulled her jeans and a T-shirt on as she padded out into the hallway. She paused at the top of the stairs and listened.

Nothing. Not a sound from below—except the hum of the refrigerator. Brian always had the tv or radio going. He said he hated a silent house; he'd grown up in a house with lots of kids and noise, something neither she nor the cats could appreciate. This was her father's house—she and Brian had just moved in, a few months after the death of her father—and she could never remember a time when there was much noise. Only the ticking of the grandfather clock when it still worked.

The three cats trailed after her as she headed downstairs. She checked the living room—not that Brian ever sat there. When they were first married he'd insisted on buying her expensive furniture, far fancier than anything she'd ever grown up with, then proceeded to throw covers over it—"to keep it good for company," he had insisted, and then later "to keep the cats off." The company, though, had never materialized for one reason or another—mostly because Brian didn't like her friends.

She walked through the dining room, then stopped in the kitchen, the only sounds the faint drip of a faucet and meows and squeaks and rumbling purrs of the Boys as they threaded around her ankles. She glanced out the window at the driveway—Brian's car was gone. Funny. He never went anywhere on Saturday mornings. Maybe he'd gone into town.

She shrugged. Who knew what he was doing? She had to feed the cats, but first she'd start her own breakfast. As she dropped the English muffin into the toaster, though, she was unable to shake the feeling of unease she'd had since waking. As she waited for the muffin to pop up, she wandered around the first floor.

The door to the closet under the stairs stood ajar, and she started to close it. She yanked the chain to turn on the light. Brian's good camel hair coat was gone, and so were the suitcases.

Two steps at a time, she raced to the bedroom and flung open the drawers of his dresser. Empty. In the closet her clothes hung neatly on the right side, his side was bare.

Heart pounding, she ran into the bathroom. Razor, toiletries, prescription bottles—all gone. Weakly she sat on the edge of the tub, her arms resting on her legs. Something inside her seemed to tighten; she could barely breathe. She forced herself to relax . . . and face the truth.

Brian had left her.

Just as her mother had left her and her father.

No! She wanted to cry, but the tears wouldn't come. She wasn't sad, wasn't . . . anything. Just numb.

Meow! Lord Peter butted her leg, sat down on her foot, and stared up at her with his harlequin face. He purred, the low rumble filling the small room.

"You won't leave me, will you," she whispered, and it wasn't quite a question.

He opened his mouth in the silent meow and continued staring, as if trying to hypnotize her to do his bidding—which would be to feed him and his pals.

Sarah laughed, somewhat shakily, and stood up. The tightness in her chest remained. She gazed at herself in the mirror; she didn't look all that bad. Not bad enough to drive her husband away, she told herself.

"Just a minute, Lord Peter." She washed her face, brushed her teeth, ran a comb through her short dark hair. Better. Still not enough to drive someone away.

Or maybe she was deluding herself.

"C'mon."

Downstairs she found her English muffin popped up and now cool. She shrugged. However, the Boys had to eat. As she dumped dry food into the three ceramic bowls, some of the kibble bounced onto the floor. Archie made short work of the errant food, then tackled the bits in his bowl. She opened the kitchen door and stepped out onto the porch. Birds splashed in the birdbath, somewhere in the distance she heard a lawnmower . . . the sun was shining and it was a perfect summer's day. It was all so normal.

Except that it wasn't.

Something soft brushed her foot and she realized that Archie had ventured out onto the porch. "No, you don't." She scooted him back inside and closed the door before the others tried escaping. The Boys were indoor cats, something she had insisted on when they'd brought the little guys home. For their own safety, she'd insisted, although now she realized she was simply afraid it would be one more thing to run off and leave her.

"Sarah, you're so pathetic," she told herself with disgust. The cats meowed, not in agreement, but for her attention. They wanted more food. "You just ate!" But they didn't care, and kept up their chorus.

She sighed and nibbled at the cold muffin. She couldn't be bothered even to spread jam on it. She wandered into the living room and stared out the windows, willing Brian's car to come up the road and turn into the driveway. Minutes passed, and all she saw was Mr. Peterson's old Buick creep by. He saw her and waved; she remained motionless.

She checked the bookshelves—there were gaps from volumes Brian had taken with him. She didn't know what was missing, at least right now. Several paintings were gone, as well as some collectibles.

"How could Brian have done all this without my knowing?" she said aloud.

Lord Peter meowed once as he sprawled in a patch of sunlight and washed a back leg. Archie and Lovejoy curled up together, purring. "I didn't have any hint. Nothing! How long was he planning this? How could he sneak out of the house with all this stuff without my hearing?"

Maybe she didn't want to hear. Maybe she really had been aware that something was going on, but maybe she just refused to believe it.

No.

She had been sound asleep. Possibly, she told herself for reassurance, he had been sneaking stuff out ahead of time. She wouldn't notice if a shirt here and there went missing. He'd probably finished packing up that morning while she slept, then gone downstairs and taken the paintings, and then left.

Left the house. Left her. Without a note.

She moaned and put a hand to her chest where it felt so tight. "What am I going to do, Lord Peter?" She looked down at the cat, his green eyes closed. He opened them when he heard his name. He always looked like he was about to say something to her, Sarah thought. He opened his mouth, but no sound came out. "What am I going to do?"

The long hours of the day stretched out in front of her. All today and then tomorrow, and Monday she would go back to work, and then what? What would she say when someone asked how Brian was? What would she say if they suggested drinks after work? What would she say? What would she do?

Do. She had to do *something*. Clean. That's it. She'd always been the type to start cleaning house the minute she got upset or anxious or whatever. She didn't like housework; in fact, she hated it, but it kept her mind occupied. And she needed that right now.

"I'm going to scrub this place from top to bottom," she announced to her feline audience. "Or from bottom to top, as the case may be."

She found her sneakers and slipped them on, grabbed a broom, dustpan, the heavy-duty flashlight, and a plastic garbage bag, and opened the basement door. She turned on the light, then pulled the door shut. Cobwebs festooned everything, and she thought she heard a rustle in one corner.

"Yuck!" This should keep her occupied all day . . . perhaps even through Sunday night. Where to start, though?

The not-quite-finished basement was split into three rooms. The first was the largest, with the second just beyond it, and then at the end of the house sat the littlest room, the only one with a door. Barrels and crates stood in the shadows, while old furniture leaned against the walls. She hadn't been down here really except to peek quickly at it when they first moved in.

The door squeaked open, and for a wild heart-fluttering moment, she thought it was Brian. The even pad-pad-pad of little feet told her a cat was joining her. Lovejoy. He was the one always opening doors not fully shut. Sometimes even when the doors seem locked, Lovejoy got them open.

He stopped on the last step and surveyed the basement, as if to say, *What a mess.*

"You're right," Sarah said. "It is a mess. This is going to keep me busy for hours! For days!" Archie and Lord Peter soon joined their pal and watched her as she knocked cobwebs out of corners and started sweeping the cement floor. Clouds of dust billowed upward, and within minutes all of them were sneezing. She opened a window, and fresh air poured through the screen.

She'd have to get rid of the worst dust, then bring down a vacuum—no, she'd rent one of those special heavy-duty ones—and then maybe she'd even mop the floor.

Now that the floor was cleaner, the Boys deigned to investigate. Lord Peter scaled an old steamer trunk, while Archie peered into a clothing barrel. Lovejoy prowled further afield.

Sarah wondered what was in the trunk. Lord Peter jumped down as she cautiously looked into the trunk. Women's clothes. She picked up a dress and shook it out. She recognized the style as something quite fashionable thirty-some years ago, and realized these must be her mother's clothes. Who had put them away? Her father? Surely not. He hadn't spoken of her mother after she left; sometimes it was like the woman hadn't even existed. All Sarah had of the woman were a few photos she'd found. What could have pulled her away from her husband and little daughter?

Beneath other dresses Sarah found a purse, some silk scarves, and a cedar box that rattled as she picked it up. In that she found a jumble of rings, earrings, bracelets, and necklaces. Her mother's jewelry. Odd. Her father always claimed her mother took everything with her. And yet here was proof that her mom had left something behind. Sarah poked through the stuff and drew out a ring with a marquise diamond.

Archie had jumped into the trunk and made a nest at one end. "Look at this." She held the ring out to him; he sniffed the diamond, then yawned. Absolutely no interest. "This looks like an engagement ring."

Lovejoy started scratching somewhere, and Sarah waved a vague hand at him. "Knock it off, Love."

At the bottom of the box lay a plain gold band. Sarah turned it over and over in her fingers, then slipped it onto her right hand. It fit perfectly. A woman's ring. Odd, though, that her mother had left these behind. Usually women took their jewelry with them, even their wedding and engagement rings. She selected an oval garnet and pearl brooch. This appeared quite old, like something that might have belonged to a grandparent. Toward the bottom of the trunk Sarah found a pile of baby clothes, handcrafted. Sarah inspected an outfit and knew it had been for her—and that her mother had sewn it. What kind of mother would so lovingly make something for her baby, then abandon her?

Lovejoy's scratching became more persistent now, and Sarah looked up. He stood at the door to the third room, and he was determined to get in. "Here, let me." She turned the knob, but nothing happened. Then she saw the old key that had fallen onto the floor. She picked it up, blew the dust off it, inserted it into the lock, and turned. The door swung open, its hinges creaking loudly.

Lovejoy padded into the room. Lord Peter followed. This room was quite small and contained only two things: another trunk, pushed up against the far wall, and a plain wooden chair facing that. The dust wasn't as heavy here as elsewhere in the basement—almost as if the room had been cleaned from time to time.

Lovejoy jumped onto the trunk, while Lord Peter settled onto the chair, staring at his pal.

And even before she had taken a step into the room, Sarah knew what was in the trunk. "No," she said, and the sound was more moan than word. "No."

It couldn't be . . . she didn't want it to be . . . but . . . she had to know. For sure.

Gently she nudged Lovejoy aside. She lifted the lid and stared into the trunk's dark depths. She gave a little cry, then dropped the trunk lid.

So, night after night, her father had come down here, and he had sat in this chair and watched the trunk, the trunk where he had put her mother's body. Night after night. And then he had gone on the road, leaving his house, leaving his child, leaving his wife alone here in the dark.

Sarah started to cry then, and the cats, alarmed, weaved around her feet, brushing against her. She picked up Lovejoy and buried her face in his fur and wept.

Her mother hadn't deserted her then. Her mother had loved her. The tightness that had been in her chest all day loosened somewhat, and she rubbed at her eyes.

But what was she going to do? Call the police? Her father was dead now. Call the relatives? They didn't care. Or leave her mother in her final resting place?

She had to go upstairs, at least for a while. "C'mon, guys." She picked up the flashlight, and waited for the cats to come up the stairs. She whirled around as she heard a key in a lock.

Brian stepped into the kitchen. Lord Peter made a sound, deep in his throat, and it wasn't a purr.

"Brian." Sarah could scarcely breathe now.

He smiled shakily. "I couldn't leave. Not without saying good-bye. Not without talking to you." He strode across to her and took her in his arms.

"Don't ever leave me, okay?" she said. He nodded, his face pressed into her hair. She wanted him to stay with her, no matter what.

He saw the open cellar door. "You were downstairs?"

"Yes. Cleaning." She smiled. "I've found something, too. It's incredible. You have to see it." Sarah took her husband by the hand, clasped the heavy flashlight in the other hand, and led him downstairs.

Lovejoy watched from the top of the stairs, then trotted back into the kitchen. He stood up on his hind legs and pushed at the door. It swung shut with a resounding clap. Then he went to his food dish to sit with Lord Peter and Archie and wait for their mistress to come back upstairs.

A Breath of Subtle Air

TRACY KNIGHT

IT WAS DEEP NIGHT, SILENT save for the rumors of lonely, love-starved insects and frogs. A lilting humid breeze, praising the sovereignty of mid-summer, danced past us. The towering trees—and we—were lit silver by the moonlight.

"I can't believe I'm doing this," I said, unscrewing the storm window from its frame. "It's one in the morning. Twenty minutes ago we were fulfilling our lifelong roles as pariahs at our ten-year class reunion, drinking beer off by ourselves at the lake with . . . or, rather, *near* twenty of our classmates. Now I'm assisting you in a burglary. Apparently adulthood hasn't brought me any wisdom or will."

"It's not a burglary, Mike," Steve Bentley said. "It's a job I was hired to do." He looked like a rabid mountain man: long blond hair cascading down his back, an untrimmed beard, and a burn-hole-speckled Merle Haggard tour T-shirt.

"And it worked out perfect that we were both going to be back in town for the reunion," Steve continued. "Who else could I ask to help me but you?"

He had a point. From kindergarten on, Steve Bentley and I had been inseparable classmates and friends, two nobodies in a world full of somebodies, though for different reasons. He was the eccentric hyperactive who was as hard to follow as to keep up with; I was the poor, adopted, abused kid who could only participate less in society if I were a comatose slug.

"Who hired you?" I asked.

"Dunno," Steve answered. "Anonymous client, cash in advance. It's the best job I've had since I got my P.I. license—"

"This job—breaking and entering, theft—doesn't exactly fall within the private investigator's code of ethics, does it?" I'd always challenged his schemes, but never expected to sway him. "What's the point?"

"To uncover personal information about our hometown's one and only Cat Lady, Bernice Jefferson: birth records, marriage licenses, photos, whatever."

"Uh, Steve. Ever think of checking public records in the county court-house?"

He stopped, but only for a second, then shook his head. "Naaa. Red tape."

"Then it *is* burglary. Not P.I. work."

Steve shrugged. I could almost see the wheels of rationalization spinning in his head. "Not really. I'm just going to take the materials I find, make copies, and then mail the originals back to her. When the client calls me, I'll report what I found. The Cat Lady won't lose anything."

"Bernice, huh? That's her name?"

"Yeah," Steve said. "What, did you think her legal name was Cat Lady?"

Every town has one. Detached from the company of their fellow humans, their histories and lives remain for the most part unknown, informed only by local legend. They live within a perimeter of untold feline companions, and are universally referred to as cat ladies. Though I hadn't ever known her name, Bernice Jefferson was Lamoine's cat lady. From the time of my adoption by the Livingstone family at seventeen months, through my teenage years when I went to live with Steve Bentley's family, until I reached eighteen and left Lamoine for good, Bernice Jefferson had intrigued me. She remained in my memory as a dark and obscure silhouette glanced fleetingly through the curtains of her front window, her profile always surrounded by an army of cats.

"We're gonna get caught," I said, yanking the storm window from its frame and laying it on the ground.

"Just ride the wave, Mike. Ride the wave. This is exciting. You know she isn't going to wake up. She's hard of hearing, I know that for sure."

Steve Bentley had never been cursed with the burden of common sense. He remained a person who went straight from idle notion to action, without an intervening stop at the weigh station where we ask ourselves, "Gosh, what are the likely consequences of this?" He was a walking, talking platoon of impulses.

We were two halves of a polarized whole. Where he was impulsive, I was so reflective of every nuance of life that it might take me days to make a decision about what shirt to wear. It was probably because of my life as an adopted child that I learned to adjust so well, to "ride the wave," as Steve would say. There wasn't any choice. Who could have known that my adoptive father would beat me daily as soon as I entered school and ceased to be the cute little kid, the family pet. I learned to surf around the complications of human relationships, since as I grew I felt like I'd injured every life I'd touched along the way. Go figure.

Like the Cat Lady, I lived apart from others, alone, scraping my way through existence. My newest job as a rest-stop security guard fit me well.

Steve Bentley was life's fireball; I was its driftwood.

Through the window of the Cat Lady's house I could make out numerous pairs of eyes—yellow, gold, and green—glowing intensely from the moonlight, capturing every flyspeck of illumination and reflecting it back into the world. Twenty of them? Fifty? Impossible to say.

Steve pushed open the window. "C'mon," he whispered.

He crawled inside and I followed.

The first thing I heard when we entered the darkened house was the piercing, singsong speech of the Cat Lady, who apparently was lying down in her bedroom, wide awake in the middle of the night.

"Oh, no," she said. "No way. Can't be happening. Nope. One mustn't become attached to animals because they don't last long enough. Or to people. They last too long. Nope. Opposite for me. Opposite." And on like that.

The second thing I heard was the pattering of uncountable sets of feet. A tiny, muted stampede. Cats poured into the dimly lit room, a worming yet graceful display that made me recall how someone once wrote that cats are embodied patterns of subtle air. How true.

The Cat Lady continued talking to herself. "No way. Not tonight. Oh my God. Can it be?"

Stepping carefully through the feline sea so as not to land on a tail or paw, I trailed Steve through the living room, to the stairway and up to the second floor. When he reached the top of the stairs he took a left and entered the first room off the landing. He reached in and flicked on the light.

The room was a mess, with stacks of magazines and books standing nearly eight feet tall. A corner desk was covered with a scattering of papers, pens, and paper clips.

In the middle of the room sat a large black trunk.

"Fate beckons us," Steve said with a smile, then walked to the trunk and opened it. It was haphazardly stuffed full of documents and envelopes and faded photographs.

"Look at this," I said, pulling out a thick manila envelope with the words "Personal Records" scrawled across its front in black permanent marker.

"Perfecto," Steve said, patting me on the back. "We're done. Keep a hold of it."

Emboldened by our success, Steve strode out of the room and turned on the upstairs hallway light.

Twenty cats sat there on the landing, staring at us. All ages, all colors and shapes and sizes.

I looked directly into the eyes of one cat, and couldn't look away. It was an aged, mangy calico cat, overweight, its proud colors paling. It was missing its left front leg.

"Good Lord!" I said, getting on my hands and knees and crawling to the calico. "I *know* this cat. I'd completely forgotten."

"What do you mean?"

"You're not going to believe this, but I brought this cat here when I was, geez, about five or six. Left it on the front porch."

"Why?" Steve was rocking back and forth, anxious to leave.

"My parents . . . well, my *adoptive* parents, they gave it to me for Christmas. The next summer my dad ran over it with the mower. Cut off its leg. He said he was going to kill it, put it out of its misery. But I took it and ran away. I couldn't think of any place to take it. I ended up walking around for hours, crying with the kitten in my arms, until I finally left it on the porch here, I don't remember why. I can't believe it's still alive."

"Okay, okay," Steve said. "I'm happy you had a sentimental reunion with your three-legged cat. Now let's blow this joint."

I kissed the calico on the head, then set it down.

From the bottom of the stairs came the voice. "Is it Death come for me? Or life? No way, no way. Can't be happening."

Steve took two steps backward, shoving me in the process. "She's got a shotgun! Hide!"

The Cat Lady started up the stairs.

I whirled around and lunged into a room.

The door immediately slammed shut behind me and I was enveloped in complete darkness. I pressed one ear against the door, but I couldn't hear Steve. Or the Cat Lady. Or anything.

What to do? My natural inclination was to wait it out. To ride the wave. I'd lived through worse than this.

Then she muttered, "No way. No way. People don't last too long. Cats last forever. Can this happen? Happen tonight? No way."

I reached up and felt the surface of the door. Finding the lock, I quietly turned it. I had to assume that Steve had made a getaway. Now, it was just me and the Cat Lady sharing the house: me huddled and sweating in a dark black room, her lurking with a shotgun while she delivered her delusional soliloquy.

I pressed my head against the floor and peered beneath the door.

There were two feet wearing tattered house slippers. Just standing there. Surrounded by several sets of little cat feet.

I held my breath.

Then the feet turned away and Bernice Jefferson padded down the stairs, followed by her kindred family of meowing felines.

I breathed deeply and stood up in the dark room, wondering what my next move should be. Assuming she was returning to her bedroom, I figured I could wait a few minutes and then slip out a window, any window, any upstairs window if need be.

Beginning to pace the floor, I promptly hit my shin against something. I hopped around the room rubbing my leg until I realized that even if the Cat Lady couldn't hear, she would likely be able to feel the vibrations from my pain-fueled tango. I limped to the wall and ran my fingers along it until I brushed the light switch, then flipped it up.

The bare bulb hanging from the ceiling illuminated the strangest, most unexpected scene.

What it was I'd bumped my shin against was a large easel, upon which rested an enlarged photocopy of a picture.

Of me.

My forehead tensed as I stepped forward for a closer look. It was a picture taken when I was in the sixth grade and part of the local Boy Scout troop. We'd just finished our weekend camp-out at the lake when the local news photographer came out to snap our picture. My scarf was crooked, my hair was tousled, and on my forehead were the last vestiges of a bruise. Still I smiled.

The photocopy had been colored with crayon. My eyes had been rendered a bold plum color; my hair was golden as sunlight; the skin on my face was a warm orange hue.

"What is this?" I said aloud, now noticing that the crayoned photocopy was only the beginning.

The room was filled with photos of me from childhood onward. They were thumb-tacked to the walls, taped to the windows, strewn randomly across the floor.

Sudden resounding thumps on the door startled me. I simultaneously jumped a foot into the air and spun around to face the sound.

There was a final thump and the door flew open.

Bernice Jefferson—the Cat Lady—stood at the doorway, having kicked through the lock. Seeing the shotgun in her hands, I was terrified. But not so terrified that I didn't recognize that, for the first time in my life, I was looking directly into the face of the reclusive, mysterious Cat Lady of Lamoine.

She wore a ragged bathrobe covered with a bleached-out flower pattern. Her white hair was pulled straight back and tied into a long ponytail. Her face was tattooed with deep creases of weariness, heartbreak, perhaps even fear. Her mouth was toothless.

"You?" she said, waggling the shotgun. "Tonight? No way!"

I held up my hands. "I'll leave," I said. "We didn't mean any harm, Mrs. Jefferson. Honest."

She let go of the shotgun with one hand and pointed to her ear. "Can't hear," she said.

I pressed my hands together, like I was praying, hoping she'd see the helplessness in my eyes. "Please," I said.

Her eyebrows angled downward as if she were confused.

Then I saw him. Steve was creeping up the steps behind her, sneaking up on the Cat Lady.

Eyes locked to mine, Bernice Jefferson tipped her head to one side and almost smiled.

Steve was within two feet of her when I shouted, "Don't, Steve! Stop!"

Grinning, Steve took the last two steps to her, reached around with a calmness I'd never seen in him before, and wrapped his fingers around the barrel.

She turned toward him and released the gun.

Articulating his words excessively, Steve said to her, "It's . . . okay. Remember? You don't need a gun. You go back downstairs. We'll be down in a minute."

Amazingly, she complied, trudging down the stairs and out of sight, followed by twenty or so feline attendants.

Steve pointed to the personal records envelope I'd left lying on the floor. "Open it."

So bewildered I was dizzy, I complied as automatically as the Cat Lady had.

I shook the contents into my hand and began flipping through the pages. There was a laminated newspaper article detailing the unexpected death of her husband, city councilman Max Jefferson, in 1972. There were discharge summaries from her many stays at the state psychiatric hospital in Springfield, diagnosing her as schizophrenic and pointing to her husband's death as the stressor that triggered the psychotic episodes. Her hospitalizations had ceased in the summer of 1978.

And there were the adoption records.

Steve touched me on the arm. "Happy ten-year reunion," he said. "I bet you never thought I'd have the patience to do the legwork and research to find your real mom, did you? I figured it out, all by myself. I got together her records and put them at the top of the trunk. I did good, didn't I? Of course I had to make a production out of it. Make it interesting."

I couldn't say anything.

Steve continued, "It's amazing, ain't it, that a little gossip-infected town kept a secret like this all these years. Kinda nice of 'em."

"Amazing," I echoed.

"One thing, though," Steve said.

"What?"

"When I came over here yesterday to talk this over and tell her we were coming, she claimed she didn't remember you. At least not as her son."

"But what about all the pictures up here? She's been keeping track of me all my life."

He shrugged. "Let's go downstairs and find out."

And so we did.

Bernice Jefferson sat on the couch, arms folded in her lap, and I sat down in a chair facing her, Steve standing behind me.

"I know now," I said, smiling tentatively. "You're my mother."

She ignored me, saying, "You brought the kitten to me when you were a little boy. I saw you through the window. I remember. From then on, I took care of it and any other cats that came along."

"Why?"

"To make you proud. To show you I could care for things in the biggest way, that I mattered. Thank you for giving me the cat. That started it all. You were a wise little boy to help me. I never went back to the hospital after that. Thank you."

"For what?"

"Giving me something to be alive for. It was hard. . . ." she began, then fell silent.

I reached over and held her hand. It was cold. "You did make me proud," I said. "The cats are all so lucky they found you. I'm lucky I found you, too." Then I touched her chin and lifted it until she was looking me in the eyes. "You're my mother."

She wiped away a tear. "No. No. I'm nobody's mother. I'm the Cat Lady."

I raised an index finger and started to say more, then dropped it. Bernice Jefferson had found her place on the planet, one that meant something to her, that gave her meaning. Bernice and her cats had been blessed with lives more substantial and coherent than mine. Who was I to complicate things? Particularly since I was the one who had given birth to her career as a cat lady.

Here was evidence: a house full of lives I *hadn't* injured. In my own way, maybe I'd made them whole a long, long time ago.

"And you're a perfect cat lady." I stood up, leaned over, and kissed her gently on the cheek. "It was nice to meet you."

"Wait one minute," she said, then called, "Elizabeth!"

The obese, aged calico cat skittered to her with three-legged elegance. Bernice lifted the cat, then handed it to me.

"She's yours again," she said. "Take care of her. She'll keep your life together. It works."

I cradled the old cat. It purred. "Thanks." Turning to Steve, I said, "I think that's our cue. Let's go."

"Sure, buddy," he said, patting me on the back.

We left her house and as we were walking down the deserted streets of Lamoine, Steve said to me, "Did I do good?"

The midnight breeze caressed the three of us.

"You did fine. Now let's be quiet. Let's just walk."

That moment, I shared something with Elizabeth, the ancient cat who'd been mine briefly, a lifetime ago. I sensed the slightest bit of grace in my body.

Perhaps like the cats, there are times we human beings can move as subtle air.

Perhaps driftwood sometimes finds the shore.

Burning Bright

CAROLE McINTYRE

WHOOO, DAWGIES!" VINCE looked over George's shoulder at the stopwatch clamped in his hand. They both turned to stare at the colt easing up near the clubhouse turn. His head was as common as dirt, and his legs were none too straight. Churning down the stretch to the wire, he'd looked like an eggbeater. They'd shared a few six-packs trying to name him, and filled in the third choice on the registration form as a joke. When the papers came back a month later, there it was: they were going to race a horse named Stringbean.

There had been nothing glamorous about the colt until now, when the sweep hand on the watch stood frozen four seconds from the top.

"And that's with shoes on!" Vince sighed in wonder. That was another thing. The colt wouldn't be in racing plates until the day before the race, and that should make him faster. 1:56. George thought. A 1:56 mile. Whoo, daw-gies, indeed.

Rajah weighed fifteen pounds on a good day, and fourteen when he was feeling peckish. There were no resident mice in Rajah's barn, and immigrants were promptly dispatched. No one could figure out how Rajah got up to speed to catch a mouse, rumor had it that he sat on them. Mostly he looked down from the hay storage over the horses' stalls, forepaws curled under his massive chest, tailtip twitching faintly. When he descended to pad up the shed row, humans would actually step aside for his passage.

Rajah did not play. Efforts luring him to chase a piece of baling twine were met with a cold stare, and anyone foolish enough to try to pick him up learned just how many sharp-pointed things a cat owned. His only concessions to humans were to use a muck basket as a litter box and to accept his favorite brand of cat food. He had been known to confuse off-brands with the muck basket, and the humans had humbly learned the lesson.

Rajah was not only a mobile mousetrap, he was a good-luck charm, and lately he had taken to favoring Stringbean's stall. Telltale tufts of golden fur gave George the good news. He smuggled in an extra supply of Rajah's favorite food and put a can in each corner of the stall. Cheap insurance at the price. They were emptied without comment.

When the vet came to make rounds, Rajah was sunning himself, lolling on one of the jogcart seats. He pretty well covered the seat, with his legs and tail hanging over the edges.

"You guys ought to put that cat on a diet." Dr. Mack was unequivocal. Lean animals were healthy animals.

"Diet? How do you put a barn cat on a diet? He'd move to another barn," George said.

"No, he wouldn't. It'd be too much trouble to clean up all the mice in a new barn. He did this one when he was a lot smaller. Look at him. His jowls have jowls." Dr. Mack was tucking bottles and syringes into his pockets, and flipped a stethoscope around his neck.

"Well... How 'bout we wait a coupla weeks? We've got a big race coming up."

"I promise you, he's not going to win it. He couldn't trot from here to the manure bin. Here, I need some hot water."

George took the stainless steel bucket with the tube for worming. "He doesn't have to. He's, uh, shown an interest in Stringbean."

"So?" The vet picked up the jug of wormer.

"Rajah's horses win races. Remember when Silk Pennant had that winning streak? He was camped by her stall. She didn't lose until he left her for Sassy Frass. Sassy moved up from claiming then. If he likes the Bean, it's fine by me. I'm glad to see him there."

"Are you helping him along any in his thinking?"

"A little cat food here and there. Nothing major. Hey, Doc, a buck a day! I spend that much on supplements for the horse."

"That horse weighs half a ton. At the rate that cat's going. . . ." He handed George the twitch and stuck two thermometers in his pocket.

"Doc, Doc, that cat's never gonna weigh half a ton. A *tiger* doesn't weigh half a ton! Besides, he only thinks he's a tiger."

The object of these comments stretched luxuriantly and fell off the seat. He was barely able to twist to land on his feet. He stalked off into the cool barn.

Starting at the first stalls inside the door and working his way down the barn, it would be a good hour before the vet got to Stringbean. George hurried down to Stringbean's stall and retrieved the empty cat food cans.

Henry's conformation was every bit as bad as Stringbean's, but he couldn't trot nearly as fast. In fact, he seldom raised a good walk, and worked best within arm's length of supervision. He had a few honesty problems, and answered, with a smirk, to "Weasel." Right now, he was holding the head of Super Saga, who had slit her haunch on a vagrant nail, then chewed on it until they'd put a cradle on her neck to prevent her turning to her side. Then, as her rump still itched, she'd rubbed it on the wall.

Dr. Mack sighed as he looked at it. Her otherwise gleaming hide was marred by this oozing sore. She was still working, but not at the top of her form. He sedated her, cleaned up the mess, dusted it with sulfa powder, injected some antibiotics, and beckoned to the trainer.

"She's going to keep after this as long as it itches, and we need to get it cleared up. Can you give her a week's stall rest?"

"Yeah, I guess so. She's not going to race much like that."

"Okay. Here's what we're gonna do. We'll keep her under just a little, so it doesn't matter to her. She'll leave it alone and give it a chance to heal. Once it starts coming along, it won't itch so much. Keep an eye on her. If she starts to wake up, give her five cc's of this. You want her just a little foggy."

Weasel's eyes widened a little when he saw the label on the vial the vet handed to his boss. Roofies! He'd heard legends of roofies! If he could just figure out how to get some, he'd get lucky on Saturday night. And he was Soupy's groom, so, logically, he'd be the one to dose her.

* * *

By the time the vet worked his way to Stringbean's stall, the farrier was also there, and was rasping off the edges around the last aluminum racing plate he'd tacked on. Tomorrow was the Big Day.

"What d'ya think, Doc?" George was getting obsessive about everything that might possibly help this colt.

"Looks right to me." Rajah, reclining above, shifted position just as Dr. Mack stepped into the doorway of the stall. Strands of hay landed on his neck and edged down his collar.

"Why don't you go work for a living, cat?" he asked, pulling his shirttail and flapping it to work out the tickling hay wisps.

"Now, Doc, that cat's doing just fine. You leave him be. Rajah's welcome to sit up there until doomsday, as far as I'm concerned. At any rate, he can sit there until tomorrow."

"That day you clocked the Bean—anyone else see it?"

"Cripes, Doc, everyone saw it. The word's out. I figure we'll win tomorrow, but the odds'll be lousy."

"I have to be out of town tomorrow. Put this on his nose," said the vet, eyeing the crooked but clean legs, and the Roman profile. Once he got past that, though, the colt had a deep chest and a serious set of haunches.

"Jeeze, Doc, that's the first time you've ever been givin' money to me!" George stared at the wrinkled ten-dollar bill in his hand.

"Don't tell anybody." Dr. Mack winked at him and went on to the next horse.

"He's never been raced here before. Just got in last night. They stuck him on my string." The grooms were having a few late-night beers, lounging on tack boxes. "I figure he'll show 'em all, first thing tomorrow." Weasel hated to have an extra horse, but since Soupy was laid up, it was his turn in the barrel.

"Nah. The Bean's in the first. He clocked a 1:56 the other day. Ol' George has him turned." Sammy's brother was a driver, and he'd been the one to open up Stringbean on the clock.

"Yeah, well . . . this is supposed to be a pretty good horse."

" 'Pretty good' isn't gonna beat the Bean. He'd have to have a rocket in his crupper."

They laughed and chugged some more beer, but Weasel got to thinking. If he couldn't put a rocket on Working Man, maybe he could slow the Bean. Nothing permanent, just an off day. He lay back on the tack trunk and stared up at the rafters for inspiration. He didn't even know he'd dozed off, but the rain on the tin woke him up. He liked the sound of rain on the roof, he thought. Rain on the . . . he sat up and looked around. Everyone else had gone to bed.

Soupy was drowsing in her stall, and Weasel smiled at her as he passed on his way to the fridge. Yep. Some roofies ought to take care of the Bean. Say, ten cc's.

Stringbean's serious haunches were facing the door as he slept with his head in a corner. Weasel wanted to wake him up before he stepped in, because a startled horse might kick first and ask questions later.

"S-s-s-t! Hey, Bean! Look here!"

Rajah, reposing above the door, woke...stretched...and fell sprawling onto Weasel's head, driving him to his knees and plunging the syringe deep into his thigh. Rajah strolled off to get a drink of water, and when George came to feed the next morning, Weasel was still lying there.

He wasn't making sense, and everyone saw the syringe, so they shipped him off to the hospital.

The odds had, indeed, been awful, and the next time George saw Dr. Mack, he handed him a twenty to go with the ten. "I told you he was ready, Doc! Didn't I tell you? And the cat's still there! Man, he shaved another eight-tenths off, and he cooled out like gangbusters! And Rajah still likes him! We can't lose!"

Rajah's four paws and flicking tailtip stuck out over the edge of the loft floor. His actual body was situated a little farther back. It had been nice of the human to break his fall, but no more than he deserved. Still, there was no reason to take chances.

The Canary and the Cat

BRIAN PLANTE

THE CANARY WAS PASQUALE Alphonse "The Whip" Messere, Pat to his friends, but he would only keep that name a few days more. Once the canary was finished singing before the Grand Jury, he would be given a new whitebread American name and disappear forever into the Witness Protection Program.

The cat's name was Tigre, a five-year-old, orange-striped tabby, and it would get to keep the name after its master finished ratting out his former employer.

The canary and the cat were holed up in an FBI safe house somewhere in

Queens until the Grand Jury hearing. To kill time, Pat played cards with the FBI agents who were assigned round the clock to watch over him, and cooked pasta e fagiole in the cramped little Fifties-style kitchen. Pat also played games with Tigre to keep the animal amused. It was a boring time for everyone involved.

Tigre's all-time favorite toy was a laser pointer. Pat aimed the pen-like instrument to shine a bright red spot of light on the walls, and chasing it drove the cat bonkers. Unlike the FBI men, who grew weary of too many hands of poker, Tigre never seemed to tire of the laser pointer. Pat would wiggle the light high, out of the cat's reach, and the feline would respond by swatting, jumping, and rearing up on its hind legs to try and catch the dancing spot of light. Pat could even get the cat to do a somersault if he maneuvered the light just right. Even the FBI men were impressed for a while.

"Funny how you can make him jump like a puppet on a string," said Agent Moody. "Just like how the District Attorney can make *you* jump."

Pat kept his mouth shut. He wasn't used to other people showing him such disrespect. Certainly not some underpaid punk cop. Under other circumstances, Pat might arrange to have a little accident happen to a person who was so rude. Perhaps a broken arm or a smashed nose. Maybe worse.

Of course the FBI men hated him. Pat was the kind of hoodlum they were dedicated to ridding society of, and here they were now, assigned to protect his miserable life. How it must gall them, Pat thought, that he would get away with his life of crime scot-free, just for testifying against some other, bigger hoods. And to top it off, he'd be set up with a new identity and a cushy home in some Norman Rockwell community in the Midwest. He'd start a brand-new, exciting life, comfortable and happy, while the poor G-men would just keep chasing the next two-bit hoodlum. Dumb working stiffs, the G-men were, but for the next few days Pat needed them to stay alive.

Pat's old employer, Don Conigliaro, was the mob's regional boss for half of New Jersey, and in his position as a soldier, Pat had participated in murders, kidnapping, blackmail, bribery, illegal gambling, and drug running, all on behalf of the Don. For nearly all of his adult life, Pat had been loyal to Don Conigliaro, performing his dirty deeds without question. But where had it gotten him? When a distant cousin got the post Pat was being groomed for, his loyalty wavered. When Pat was busted in a sting operation and offered immunity in exchange for his testimony, it crumbled away completely. Pat had agreed to spill his guts about all of the Don's nefarious activities before the Grand Jury. He was just a small-fry, and the Feds were after bigger fish.

Needless to say, Don Conigliaro wanted him dead, now that he was playing ball with the Feds.

It was late the night before Pat was scheduled to begin his testimony before the Grand Jury, and the pasta e fagiole had been cooked and eaten, and many hands of cards had been played. Pat sat in a well-worn La-Z-Boy recliner, teasing Tigre with the laser pointer for a good half-hour, wearing the both of them out. The FBI agents were nodding off to sleep, bored, and Pat finally clicked the device off and put it on the coffee table. Tigre quietly jumped up into his lap.

"Just you and me, huh?" Pat said to Tigre. "It'll all be over soon."

In response, Tigre began purring and kneading Pat's spaghetti gut. Pat stroked the cat behind the ears, and after a while, they both settled down.

Shortly, the canary and the cat both shut their eyes and dozed.

Sometime later in the night, Pat was awakened by the cat. Tigre was tapping frantically at his chest, slapping him gently on the collarbone with its paws.

"Go to sleep," Pat mumbled to the cat, without opening his eyes.

The cat continued for a few more seconds, whapping Pat's chest with its paws. Pat reached up feebly to push the cat away, but the feline began hopping up and down excitedly on his lap. He tried to push the cat down and away, but Tigre became more and more agitated.

Pat opened his eyes when Tigre performed a somersault in his lap.

Looking down, Pat immediately saw the red laser spot centered on his chest, moving from side to side. The cat took a swipe at it and patted him square on his sternum, but the spot instantly jerked a few inches over to the left side of his chest. The cat was going wild.

"Guys?" Pat said to the FBI agents. "Are you doing this?"

Pat looked away from his chest to the couch where the two agents were just rousing from their slumber. It wasn't them. He turned his head and saw the laser pointer, right where he had left it on the coffee table before he had fallen asleep.

"Guys, there's something going on here," Pat said, with a note of urgency.

Tigre faithfully tracked the red spot wherever it lighted, swatting at Pat's shoulder, then neck, chin, cheeks, and finally his forehead. It was such fun.

"Down, Tigre," Pat said forcefully, and luckily the cat obeyed.

The single bullet followed the pencil-thin beam of light to its end, making only the tiniest tinkle as it passed through the window and found its mark.

Tigre did another somersault.

The Case of the
Incompetent Police Dog

SUE ANN BOWLING

THE POLICE DOG CLEARLY HAD no idea of what she was doing, and her handlers were no better. Normally I would have enjoyed the sight, but just now I was worried. I lifted an already snowy paw to my tongue—not that it needed cleaning, but there is nothing like washing for settling the mind and focusing one's concentration.

The dog, a big black and silver shepherd, wore an arrangement of straps that would not have held me for a moment. It held her quite nicely when she first saw me and made an abortive lunge in my direction, though. I tried to tell her that the burglars had loaded their loot into my provider's car in the garage and driven away, but she seemed to have no knowledge of Cat, and I have never lowered myself to learn Dog beyond the most obvious phrases.

As to the humans—I had tried several times to lead them back into the house, where they should have been. The best said "Hello, kitty" and patted my head; the worst actually tried to kick me. They did not even seem to realize that my provider herself had not driven her car away, but persisted in talking about her as if she were away on the vacation trip she had planned. My presence alone should have told them differently—my provider would never have left without making arrangements for my comfort.

I am a properly reared cat, and there are rules one follows. One does not show undue affection to one's provider. One does not respond to the requests of humans, much less their commands, on any regular basis. One does not, in short, behave as a dog. Neither does one do anything to make a dog appear anything other than the blundering fool it was made to be. But in my situation—

I spread my toes, the better to wash between them, and studied the humans and the dog from the corner of my eye. The dog, I was forced to admit, was actually not doing badly. The humans kept leading her in a circle around the house, and she kept trying to lead them up the driveway to the garage, where the burglar had entered. The humans apparently were convinced that the burglar, weighted down with the computer and the television, would have left a trail leading away from the house. Television and computer—I would miss them both, as they were the best places in the house for a nap. That, however, was a secondary problem. Who was going to feed me tonight?

I ducked my head and took a thoughtful lick or two at my white bib. One does not show undue affection toward one's provider. Still, a reliable provider is not easily come by, and I had mine quite well trained. Freeing her, I decided, was not so much a matter of affection as of assuring my next meal. It was also beyond my abilities—unless I could use the dog. And that would make the dog look good.

The humans were dragging her off to the back of the house again. She gave me a look as she passed, and while I may not be fluent in Dog, her lifted lip and the flick of her tongue were unmistakable. She looked fast, too, and I am . . . not fat, exactly, but not in my best racing form, either. The humans had left the door behind me open, but were the doors inside open, too?

I turned and entered the house, trotting through the living room and up the stairs. How right I had been to investigate! The door to the guest bedroom was closed—probably closed by those thick-skulled humans. I am reasonably adept at doors, but I would not have wanted to try this one with a maddened shepherd close on my tail! With the police dog still outside, however . . . I stretched to my full height, pawing at the round doorknob.

Round doorknobs—how I hate them! Levers are best, of course, and even the patterned glass knobs give some purchase to one's paws. Round metal is maddeningly difficult, especially since I could hear the humans talking of giving up with the dog. Much as I hated the idea, I needed the dog—they would never follow me. Then I felt the catch give, and the door swung open. I meowed as loudly as I could—a promise of help on the way—turned, and trotted briskly down the stairs.

The straps had been removed from around the dog's shoulders, leaving her sitting alone. One of the humans stood on the long strap hanging from her neck, but that would not slow her down for long. I ambled around the side of the yard, breathing deeply. The shepherd glanced at me, then turned her head away at a sharp word from one of the humans. I continued my walk, spiraling in slightly, until the dog was almost between me and the open door. Once there, I dropped into a stalk, my heart pounding as I let myself realize the danger of my plan.

I did not pause to rake the shepherd's nose with my claws. I swiped on the run, and felt the satisfying pull on my nails. By the time she jumped to her feet and yanked the strap from under the human's feet, I was streaking through the open door to the house.

She was no more than two body lengths behind me when I reached the stairs, and gaining with every leap. The humans were shouting—behind her, I thought—but I had no time for them. A spin to the right—a few inches gained as the shepherd slipped and scrambled on the old wood floor—and a great leap to the top of the wardrobe almost as soon as I entered the guest room door. The shepherd tried to follow, leaping and snapping at my tail. I moved back as far as I could from the edges, listening to the pounding of the human feet on the stairs.

I could feel the vibration of the wardrobe beneath my feet, but between the hysterical dog and their own shouting the humans seemed not to hear it. I peeked down, cautiously, to be sure that the humans had the dog's collar. Then I gave my most strident meow and leaned down, pawing at the edge of the wardrobe door. Most of the humans just looked at me, but they were quiet for a moment. The one who had petted me went stiff. "Listen!" he commanded, as he finally heard the thumping from the wardrobe.

It took them a few minutes to find the key. I tried to help by staring at the spot where the burglar had tossed it under a bureau, but with the dog still in the room I felt it wiser not to attempt to hook it out myself. I am not certain whether the dog noted the direction of my gaze or smelled out the key, but she found it for them, and they unlocked the wardrobe. My provider was stiff from being tied up and gagged, but her usual sensible self. She insisted that the dog be removed at once, to my considerable relief. It even occurred to the humans that since she had not driven her car away, the burglar might have. By the time she had convinced them that she did not need to be taken to the hospital, others had found car, burglar, and loot—still together.

I dined that night on king crab and poached salmon—far tastier than my usual fare. My provider, at least, knew whom to thank for her freedom. The television with its warmth had not yet been returned, but I fell asleep on my provider's lap wondering if there were not an opening for a police cat.

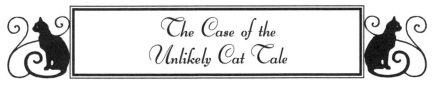

The Case of the Unlikely Cat Tale

LLOYD BIGGLE JR.

CLEANTHA, DOWAGER DUCHESS OF Rutley, fumbled for her handkerchief and blew her nose in a most unladylike manner. Lady Sara and I waited politely. In Lady Sara's study, as elsewhere, members of the peerage were accorded certain privileges, and the dowager Duchess of Rutley was an old friend of her father, the deceased Earl of Ranisford. Because Lady Sara was England's finest private detective, her study was a haven for persons in trouble.

It was not the first time tears had been shed there, but it certainly was the first time anyone had wept over a cat and a canary.

The Duchess dabbed at her eyes and managed to regain her composure. She was a rotund little woman, stylishly—and expensively—dressed but with the kind of wrinkled ugliness that only a cat could love. 1904 was an exciting year both in England and abroad. To the Duchess, however, both national and international events were trivialities compared with the loss of her pets. She had been so disgusted with the local police that she complained directly to Scotland Yard.

"It is such a nebulous place," she said. "Men coming, men going, no one in charge. I kept insisting on seeing someone higher up, and finally Chief-Inspector Mewer consented to see me."

"And what did the Chief-Inspector say?" Lady Sara asked.

"He said Scotland Yard had the wrong kind of organization for locating missing cats. He thought you had far more experience with that type of crime and I should see you about it—which if I'd been thinking clearly, I would have done in the first place."

"I will thank Chief-Inspector Mewer for the compliment the next time I see him," Lady Sara said darkly. "Let me summarize your problem. Your cat, Biffy, and your pet canary, Archie, are missing. Since they were great friends, and the canary was fond of riding on the cat's back, you think they must have gone somewhere together. You reject the possibility that a door was carelessly left open, allowing them to escape, because your servants are trained not to leave doors open and because both animals were contented and wouldn't have left your home if they'd had the opportunity. The police promised that constables patroling the neighborhood would keep their eyes open for a canary riding on a cat, but none has been seen. Now, five days after the animals were first missed, you want me to find them. Is that a fair summary?"

The Duchess nodded, blubbering into her handkerchief again.

"Very well," Lady Sara said. "I'll do what I can for you."

The Duchess floated out on protestations of gratitude, and Lady Sara returned to her desk. I resumed my chair and sat waiting for instructions. When none were forthcoming, I suggested, "I might procure a piece of liver or a fish and wander about attracting stray cats. Perhaps one would have a bird riding on it. Without the bird, how could anyone possibly distinguish between Biffy and any other stray street cat?"

One might have expected the pet cat of a duchess to be a Persian, or Siamese, or Manx, or some similar choice breed. But the Duchess of Rutley was a bird fancier, and when she saw a common street cat stalking birds in her garden, she sent a platoon of servants to catch it and ordered it placed in captivity until the gardener was available to wring its neck. In that interval, the cat so managed to ingratiate itself with the household that the Duchess adopted it instead, and the cat, named Biffy, responded so well to its sudden prosperity that it even became friendly with the Duchess's pet birds—especially with Archie, called a canary by the Duchess but actually a goldfinch Her Grace had purchased at a street stall in Holborn. Archie was so fond of riding on the cat's back that the pair had achieved a certain local fame among the Duchess's friends.

Now both were missing.

Lady Sara said, "There are two homes for stray cats that I know of. One is the Gordon Home for Lost Cats, in Hammersmith. The other is the Camden Town Home. The latter's cart ranges all over London picking up stray or unwanted cats. It is said to receive six or seven thousand cats a year, but for all anyone knows, this represents only a fraction of the stray cats in this city. If the Duchess had lost a dog, we would know it probably had been stolen, and we could take steps to recover it. But who steals an ordinary street cat?"

"We could visit the Gordon Home and the Camden Town Home and inspect the cats in residence," I said, "but my question still stands. Unless one happened to have a bird riding on it, how would we recognize Biffy? If Biffy had some highly individual characteristic, such as a tattoo of a dog on its chest, or a strange passion for eating pickled artichokes, we might have a chance of identifying it. Otherwise, I doubt if the Duchess herself could pick it out of the Camden Town Home's annual six thousand cats."

Lady Sara made no comment, and I lapsed into gloomy silence. Neither of us enjoyed failure, but this looked like a case no one was going to solve.

Finally Lady Sara said, "We must at least visit the Duchess's home and talk with the servants. Tell John to get the carriage ready."

When we arrived at the Duchess's town house in Holland Park, a small-sized country manor with high brick walls and a large garden, we found the place in an uproar. Biffy had just been sighted in the Duchess's own garden. We went immediately to the garden, which was cluttered from one end to the other with plantings of trees, bushes, and flowers that the Duchess deemed attractive to birds. It could hardly have been better designed for a cat to hide in.

I joined the search. One of the footmen thought he knew where the cat was, so we craftily approached from opposite directions and cornered it against the tall garden wall.

As I reached for it, it went up the brick wall in a flash, and over. I wouldn't have thought it possible. I grabbed a ladder a gardener had left leaning against a tree and went over the wall after it. The footman followed me. The garden on the other side of the wall was much tidier, and there were fewer places for a cat to hide. We quickly located Biffy, surrounded it again, and cornered it.

Whereupon it ran off in three directions. There were three cats, and in the brief glimpse I had of them, I saw nothing that would enable me or anyone else to distinguish between them.

At that moment two gardeners collared both the footman and myself and demanded to know what we were doing in their garden. By the time we had explained ourselves and listened to their complaint that the Duchess should keep her cat at home, a sentiment we heartily agreed with, all three cats had vanished. We borrowed a ladder from the gardeners, got back over the wall, and reported total failure.

The Duchess was crushed. I looked about for Lady Sara; she was nowhere in evidence.

I found her in the house talking with Libby Brown, a pert young lady who was an assistant cook. In other households she would have been called a slavey, but in that of a duchess she carried a higher rating. She had just returned from her afternoon off. She couldn't have been more than fourteen, and she was neatly, even stylishly dressed, another unusual distinction for a slavey.

She was adamant that Biffy and Archie had not escaped through the kitchen. "They weren't allowed," she said. "Her Grace wouldn't permit animals where food was prepared and eaten. No one wanted that bird flying around and leaving droppings in it. They had to keep out of the kitchen and dining room."

"A wise rule," Lady Sara said. "Then you think they must have escaped by the front door?"

Libby dropped her voice. "The cat was all right, see, no one minded the cat. But the housekeeper and the downstairs maids complained all the time about having to clean up after that bird. I'm not surprised that it somehow managed to get away."

"Do you think the front door may have been left open accidently on purpose?"

Libby laughed heartily. "That's it—accidently on purpose—but I don't know nothing about it. I'm not allowed in the front of the house."

Lady Sara thanked her and gave her a shilling for being such a good witness.

We returned to the carriage, and Lady Sara sat meditating for so long that Old John dismounted and came around to see what the trouble was. "Just thinking," she told him. She said to me, "We have one of the villains and half our case. The other half is going to be a problem."

"One of the villains?" I exclaimed. "How can you know?"

"Libby Brown," she said. "Didn't you notice how she was dressed?"

"I thought she was stylishly dressed, for a slavey, and showed very good taste in her hat and frock."

"Indeed she did. How do you suppose she managed it on the shilling or two a week the Duchess pays her? She spent at least two pounds on that out-fit."

"The accomplished little liar!" I exclaimed. "Let's go back and make her tell who paid her."

"We might not succeed, and we would get the girl marked for life. If the Duchess so much as suspected she was involved, she would dismiss her without a character and turn her over to the police. Two pounds would be an over-whelming temptation to a kitchen slavey. Obviously someone thought the cat and canary were worth money."

"No doubt they are. The Duchess would willingly pay to have them back. But in that case, why hasn't anyone asked for ransom?"

"Exactly. Why has no one offered to return them for a reward? For you can be certain that money is involved." She thought again. Then she turned to John, who was still waiting for orders. "Have you seen a Happy Family lately?"

"Not for years, my lady," John said.

"Did you ever see one?" Lady Sara asked me.

"I've seen families that certainly appeared to be happy. I suppose one would have to know them intimately before—"

"No," she said. "This is a special kind of exhibit that had a mild popular-ity fifty years ago. At that time there were several Happy Families working in and about London. When I was a child, there were one or two left. My father took me to see one. It wasn't doing well, and shortly after that it faded from sight. I haven't seen or heard of one in years. I'm wondering if someone is try-ing to reestablish one. That is our next step. We must find out."

Lady Sara's agents were scattered throughout the metropolitan area on every level of society, but they were most numerous among people with the best op-portunity to observe: street-crossing sweepers, costermongers, omnibus con-ductors, various kinds of street people. It took time to notify even a portion of these that Lady Sara needed information. Along with Lady Sara's two footmen Charles Tupper and Rick Allward, both accomplished investigators, I started at once, and by evening Lady Sara's interest in a Happy Family was widely circu-lated.

Early the next morning, she had a response: "Tower Hill."

We went together, waiting until afternoon because Lady Sara thought the exhibitor might not operate mornings. We found a large cart with, at one side, a stage like that of a Punch and Judy show except that it was actually a cage. The name "Happy Family" had faded into history. This exhibit was called "Barnley's Animal Theatre," and the animals appeared in a series of acts to the accompaniment of a cheerful patter supplied by the exhibit's owner.

A monkey served as a sort of master of ceremonies. Various unlikely com-binations of animals were released into the cage where they went through simple routines: a hawk with sparrows; a cat and a dog; a ferret with rats; an owl with pigeons; a dog with rabbits; a cat with mice. All of these combinations of deadly enemies were so unlikely that I—and other members of the small audience—stared in disbelief. The animals behaved like seasoned theatrical performers and the best of friends.

"How does he do it?" I asked Lady Sara.

"With very patient and skillful training," she said. "Of course he has to love animals. In the old Happy Family exhibit, an unlikely combination of animals appeared together in a large cage, and the entertainment consisted of merely seeing such an unusual spectacle. This is an attempt to make the exhibit more attractive."

The animals really did very little, but one was astonished to see deadly enemies placidly occupying the same cage.

Finally came the pièce de résistance: "Damon and Pythias," announced the owner. "Two friends whose friendship will become legendary."

A large, unusually fat street cat was released into the cage. It had a goldfinch riding on its back. It crossed the cage and ate a tidbit that it obviously knew would be there. The goldfinch hopped down and consumed some scattered seed. Then the goldfinch hopped back onto the cat's back and rode back across the cage to another tidbit and more seed. Another crossing, and they made their exit. Against all odds, Lady Sara had found the missing cat and bird.

Reclaiming them was not so simple. The owner obviously considered Damon and Pythias his prize exhibit. He knew nothing about any theft. He had bought the pair legally.

"What did you pay?" Lady Sara asked.

He sullenly admitted to investing five pounds in the pair.

"The person you bought them from used two pounds to bribe one of the Duchess of Rutley's servants, leaving him a profit of three pounds on the transaction. Isn't five pounds a steep price for a street cat and an ordinary goldfinch?"

"Not with them already trained," Barnley said.

"They trained themselves," Lady Sara said. "That's why they were so easy to work with. I'll give you a choice. Give the animals up immediately and tell me who sold them to you, or the police will close your exhibit and charge you with receiving stolen goods."

The argument was prolonged, but we finally departed with a small cage containing Biffy and Archie. Lady Sara promised to return the cage later.

The Duchess was delighted, and, as far as we could tell, both Biffy and Archie were pleased to be home again. I never heard what the servants thought.

Lady Sara managed a private interview with Libby Brown, telling her in no uncertain terms what the two pounds might have cost her. She also had an interview with the man who bribed her, frightening him with the specter of a long prison term. More than that she would not do because she didn't want to get the girl in trouble.

The Duchess complained directly to the Prime Minister, a remote relative of hers, about the inefficiency of Scotland Yard. In almost a week it had failed to solve a crime that Lady Sara unraveled in one day. The Prime Minister called the Home Secretary on the carpet; the Home Secretary reprimanded Chief-Inspector Mewer, who visited Lady Sara in a state of resentful bewilderment and demanded to be told how she managed to find the escaped animals so quickly. But Lady Sara had had enough of Biffy and Archie, and she refused to discuss the case further, not even with a Chief-Inspector.

There the matter ended; except that, sometime later, we learned of a wholly unexpected result. Biffy had given birth to a litter of kittens.

Chief-Inspector Mewer was still trying to find out how Lady Sara solved the case, and he announced, "If that cat ever publishes her memoirs, I'm going to buy a copy."

Cat Among the Pigeons

CONNIE WILKINS

MOLE'S GRAY FUR WAS ALL BUT invisible where he crouched under the sideboard, but the firelight turned his eyes to glowing amber. The angry words hurtling back and forth above didn't worry him as much as the shiny, stamping boots that had nearly succeeded in kicking him.

"What bloody idiocy, keeping a cat at a signal station! The other two missing birds must have ended this way as well!" Captain Winslet shook the bloody mass of feathers in Moira's face.

"He always brings me his catches—if there had been others I would have known—" She struggled to keep her voice from shaking. The Captain's face was flushed with rage, and his harsh voice was quite unlike his seductive tones last night, in the garden, with the moonlight shining on his fair hair. Not that she had taken his blandishments seriously; she was scarcely that young and foolish; but it had been nice to pretend that love might come again, to try to forget for a while all that she had lost....

"That creature ought to be destroyed!"

Moira backed away in a panic. She hadn't been so weak-kneed! But Mole was all she had left. She had come to the coast to get out of London and get a grip on her life after . . . after the bombings had taken away everything else she loved. But she mustn't think of that. She must focus on what she could do here, keeping house for her second cousin Edwin now that there were so many comings and goings and always several mouths to feed. She had a duty here as essential as anything she could do as a Wren or in the Volunteer Service. But she couldn't give up Mole! Maybe a farmer would take him for a while—he was such a good mouser—still, this hardly seemed the time to mention his hunting prowess.

A large brown hand reached across the Captain's shoulder and plucked the dead pigeon from his grasp. "The moggy never killed that bird," Edwin said in his slow, deep voice. "The pigeons home directly into the loft, and even that furry shadow could not slip in there without wings. Not to mention that someone is always on watch."

Captain Winslet made a visible effort to curb his speech. Edwin, though he wore no uniform, outranked him. "But Major, he was caught with it in his mouth!"

Edwin turned the bird over gently in his one good hand; the other arm hung useless, a casualty of the Great War that had turned out not to be the one to end all war after all.

"He scavenged it, then. Chaser was too sharp a bird to come to ground within reach of a cat. And look here—" he probed among the feathers on the stiff breast. "A hole . . . and a bullet." With a flick of his forefinger a small pellet arced through the air to fall with a metallic clang to the floor. Then he peered closely at the bird's beak. "Shot somewhere out over the downs, from the look of this bit of chalky soil."

"Shot?" the Captain asked with a frown. "Don't the local farm lads know better?"

"One would hope so," Edwin said. "And any marksman with that much skill should be off with the invasion."

Moira was pleased to see a different sort of flush on the Captain's face. There was considerable conjecture in the village as to why he was here instead of across the Channel in Normandy. His recently announced "liaison" post was quite unnecessary; a radioman and two privates were here already, and Edwin himself opened every message capsule and read its contents before they were wired to London.

"But where is the capsule?" Winslet asked.

"Cut off. With a sharp knife. And the cat never dragged the bird all the way from the downs. He never strays that far from Moira. There's more to this than lads' pranks."

Edwin turned toward his office and the transmitter there. Moira saw with a pang that his thumb absently stroked a motionless wing. She knew, though he never spoke of it, that he loved each of his birds no less than she loved her cat, and felt their loss as keenly as she would Mole's.

The Captain's anger rose again once Edwin had left. Moira edged between his rigid body and the sideboard. "We can search for the capsule, at least," she said breathlessly. "Maybe Mole will show me where he found poor Chaser." She turned, bent swiftly to gather the gray cat into her apron, and went out into the cool June evening.

Mole, of course, would do no such thing. He had found the bird behind a hedgerow under heaped-up leaves and sticks, but right now he was more concerned with where his prize had been taken. If Shiny Boots had still been in possession he would have stalked him (taking care to stay out of range of kicks) in hopes of a chance at a quick grab. But it was the man with the gentle voice and strong hand who had taken it away. That man was Master here, Mole knew, though it didn't much concern him, and the birds belonged to him. More to the point, even a sleek gray shadow of a cat could not slip in where the Master wished to keep him out. Still. . . .

He struggled out of Moira's grasp and squeezed back inside before the door had quite shut.

"Mole!" Moira looked around the hall, but there was no trace of gray fur and not much place to hide, once she had eliminated the umbrella stand. All the connecting doors were closed. Mole must have gone up the stairs. If only he had the sense to stay out of Captain Winslet's way!

The Captain himself came through a door just at that moment and said to her curtly, "Have my shirts been ironed? Bring one up directly. I have that damned bird's blood on this one, and on my coat as well. What possessed that bloody beast to bring it here instead of polishing it off elsewhere?" He pounded up the stairs without waiting for an answer.

Moira sighed. War or no war, Winslet must have his pre-dinner bath and change of clothes, and never mind that it would take the old boiler hours to provide more hot water for washing up the dishes. At least it got him out of the way for a while.

Mole crouched on the upper landing behind a carved oak chest. He watched the Captain stomp past to his room, and noted that the slammed door didn't latch but rebounded to leave an inch or so gap.

Mole's mood wasn't quite as foul as the Captain's but he was still peeved at the loss of his prey, and even more peeved at the kicks the man had aimed at him. Worst of all had been the angry shouting that had made Moira tremble. Something ought to be done.

After a few minutes he sauntered to the door and peered in. The room was empty. The Captain had taken the best guest chamber, the only one with a private bath, and was taking advantage of the luxury.

Mole stepped farther in, looking about for anything of interest. Shoes were his preferred target for demonstrating his displeasure; he proceeded toward the shiny boots beside the bed and considered the possibilities. A swipe of sharp claws across a gleaming surface was a good beginning; he did it a few more times to both boots. When one fell over he poked his head inside, but it was clear that soiling the interior might soil his own fur as well. He contented himself with liberally spraying both exteriors.

When the other boot toppled he heard something roll across the floor, and pounced on it, then batted it so that he could pounce again. The little metal tube made a wonderful toy. He forgot his ill humor altogether until Moira entered with an armload of folded white shirts and nearly tripped on the rolling capsule.

"Mole!" she cried in dismay as she surveyed the damage he had done. "What am I going to...." Then she saw the metal capsule more clearly. She froze for an instant before picking it up. She backed into the hallway, turned, and ran down the stairs, and Mole was so startled at the lack of scolding that he bounded after her.

"Edwin! See what Mole found in Captain Winslet's room!"

Edwin twisted open the capsule with practiced fingers and drew out a tiny roll of paper. Moira watched anxiously as he read it.

"This was sent just before dawn today, from paratroopers behind enemy lines." He started for the stairs, calling over his shoulder, "Get Jones and Renton. And make sure they're armed!"

Moira reflected later that Winslet might have tried to bluff it out if he hadn't still been in his bath when accosted. Any sort of dignity was out of the question. When a search of his room turned up two more missing capsules any sort of defense was out of the question as well.

She didn't ask the identity of the dark-coated men who drove up an hour later and whisked the Captain away, declining her offer of dinner or at least tea, but she suspected that they would manage to pry from him the other names in a treacherous chain of command.

Edwin was quiet over supper, which had grown quite cold. Moira eyed him anxiously. "I'm sorry Mole had to maul poor Chaser's ... remains." Mole himself was twining in and out around her ankles, puzzled but pleased to have been allowed into the dining room.

"Don't fret yourself. If not him, some fox or ferret would have had a meal, and then where would we be?"

"At dinner with the pompous Captain," she answered, and then was afraid she'd been too pert until he laughed for the first time since she'd come here.

"Quite right. A narrow escape. Your gray friend has done a good turn for us, as well as for King and country."

Mole, who always knew when he was spoken of, moved under the table to chance a tentative rub against the Master's leg. A strong hand came down and scooped him up. "So, Mole," said the deep, gentle voice, "if a grateful nation doesn't build you some sort of cat palace, do you think you and Moira could settle for a permanent home here?"

Mole's only answer was to snuffle at the shirt that had still, since Edwin hadn't bothered to change for dinner, an aura of bird about it.

"I'm sure we could," said Moira, "if only I can manage to keep him from among the pigeons."

Mole's amber stare across the table looked a good deal like a challenge, but Edwin just gripped him firmly and said, "We'll manage."

 Cat and Mouse

K. D. WENTWORTH

I ORIGINALLY MOVED IN WITH old Herm Sidley because he can't abide cats. I divined this by the fastidious set of his shoulders that first fateful morning and the way he edged around me in his driveway. The day was already steamy and promised to make the pavement sizzle by noon. Traffic was whizzing its foul-smelling way down the street. Mockingbirds were singing just out of reach and I had unfortunately found it necessary to abandon my most recent residential situation due to the management's acquisition of a slavering Rottweiler puppy.

Head high, I strolled down Sidley's modest driveway, then struck my most elegant pose, tail wrapped around my gray and white body while I stared up with narrowed green eyes. The man actually shuddered as he stepped around me and opened the door of his drab blue car.

That did it. I knew I had sniffed out my next mission. No way could I let this pathetic creature pass through life without experiencing the utter euphoria of cat companionship.

After checking out the neighborhood female feline population and finding it bountiful, I hung out on the porch. Then, when Sidley came home that evening,

I bolted through the front door as soon as he opened it, a useful talent acquired at a very early age. Sidley, being much closer to the rabbit side of the Force, was of course too taken aback to catch me and toss me out, as a more assertive human would have done. I've been a resident of his vapid little bungalow ever since.

Sidley works somewhere downtown in a big office building with a multitude of two-legged bores. I always smell them, as well as paper and ink and coffee, on his clothes when he stumbles home each night. Occasionally, there's the faintest hint of some female's musk, but let us be frank, he's a very timid tom and probably wouldn't know what to do with a female even if she knocked him to the ground and licked his face until the moon rose.

At any rate, Sidley came home the other night, just about yowling-on-the-fence time, unusual for him. He's strictly a sunset sort of guy, likes to stare at that stupid talking box of his all evening until he can't keep his eyes open, then totter off to bed. (I always get him up once in the middle of the night just to give him a bit of exercise. Otherwise, he would get fat and lazy and what would the neighbors think?)

He had this dazed look on his thin face, much worse than usual, and didn't even close the front door behind him. He dumped his briefcase just beyond the threshold, then sat at the kitchen table and held his head in his hands. It was November and the wind sang through the house, chilly and invigorating.

"Hudson," he said (having named me after his ex-father-in-law, not a warm relationship I've been given to understand), "I don't know what I'm going to do! I didn't take that money, but the evidence is overwhelming. I'll never make the management believe me!"

I put my forepaw on his leg and unsheathed my claws for a second, just long enough to prick through the cloth into the skin beneath. It was long past dinner time, after all. First things first. He winced, but made no move toward the can opener. I sat back and gave my whiskers a thorough wash. This was serious. I mean, a cat could starve to death. Steps had to be taken.

I leaped up onto the table and sniffed his grandmother's antique delftware blue salt shaker. He hates that.

He just shook his head and turned away. "So much money, Hudson! Three hundred ninety-two transfers over the last six months—using *my* authorization codes! I'm headed for the big house for sure." He pressed his trembling hands over his eyes.

I wrapped my tail around my feet, my best thinking position, and considered. When Sidley starts using terms like "big house," I know he's been watching the idiot box too much again.

An idea tingled in the back of my mind and I scratched vigorously at it with a hind foot. Trouble at the office, obviously, could not be solved by sitting at home and wailing. And dinner, it seemed, was not to be forthcoming. Perhaps there would be dinner at the office, I mused, as well as resolution to Sidley's dilemma. Sidley always took food with him in the morning and never brought any back home. He was too skinny to have eaten it all. A veritable mountain of it must have accumulated there.

I leaped down from the table and went to work, rubbing against his navy blue suit pants, back and forth, leaving a lovely trail of gray and white hairs. Usually this elicits bitter muttering about "dry cleaning." Not tonight though.

Humans can be so utterly dense. This situation obviously called for more aggressive action. I began to yowl. Sidley raised his head and shuddered. I batted his pants leg with bared claws and yowled louder, approaching that subtle key which makes the windows vibrate.

"Oh," he said finally, "dinner." He fumbled in the pantry for a yellow and white can, then opened it and dumped the slimy contents in my bowl. "Enjoy it, Hudson. It may be your last. They don't allow cats in prison."

It was nasty stuff, unadulterated chicken, and not exactly the best parts of the departed bird either, if you catch my drift. Obviously, there had been another sale down at that wretched Piggly-Wiggly. I hissed at my bowl and resumed yowling. Whatever Sidley had stashed at the office must be better than this.

Sidley paced the tiny kitchen, muttering about "encumbered moneys" and "restricted accounts." His pale blue eyes bulged and he resembled a rabbit more than ever before. I followed him at every turn, caterwauling helpfully at his heels. We had to get out of this house, back to the scene of the apparent crime. Hiding here would do no good at all.

In desperation, he opened another can and dumped the contents in my bowl on top of the inferior chicken. I sniffed delicately—salmon. My ears twitched. This was much harder, but I managed to turn up my nose again and go back to yowling unabated at his heels. *Think of females on a fine summer's night when the wind ruffles your fur,* I told myself to drive the luscious scent of salmon from my mind. *Think of fat indolent mice lying in the sun, waiting. Think of . . . catnip!*

Finally, just before my willpower gave out, he snatched up his car keys. "For pity's sake, Hudson! I can't even hear myself think!"

I followed him to the door. He tried to shut it in my face but I slipped out between his legs in a long-practiced move. He mumbled all the way to the car, so jangled that he dropped his keys after he opened the door and didn't even notice when I slipped over the seat into the shadowy depths of the back.

The ride to his office was longer than I expected, at least three times the length of a ride to the vet's (may she be pierced by a thousand needles in unspeakable places and immersed in nasty cold water all the rest of her days!). I was surprised. Sidley did this morning and night? Maybe he'd be better off without his job after all—except for the part about me starving.

When he parked, the building before us was as tall as a dozen houses stacked on top of each other and had windows of black glass. I could see my noble profile reflected in them. *How bizarre*, I thought as I kept up with Sidley. *Were there so many birds in the vicinity that they were afraid the people inside would just stare outside all day?*

The doors opened without being touched and stayed ajar long enough for me to trot through. Sidley was still muttering and shaking his head. We passed a uniformed man at a desk who waved without really looking up from his newspaper. Sidley stopped at the far end of the lobby, punched a button, then waited, arms crossed, until the *walls* opened. I followed, tail high with curiosity. *Why didn't we have such cool doors at home?* I wondered.

He glanced down. "Hudson? For cripes' sake, what are you doing here?"

Yes, I thought, gazing up at him inscrutably. *Rather clever of me, wasn't it?*

He scooped me into his arms, a sign of great distress, since he never touches me unless it's absolutely unavoidable. "Well, it's after hours," he said. "Probably no one's here but Security and the cleaning crew."

I twisted, then sank my claws into his forearm to hint at my displeasure. I was doing just fine on my own, thank you very much. No need for us to get all touchy-feely.

He flinched, but held on as the doors opened again. The hall before us was quiet and deserted, the gray carpet deep as unmowed grass. Sidley lowered his head and walked quickly past a set of glass-topped doors. I sniffed a vase of flowers on a table at the far end—plastic. How vile.

He opened the door with his keycard, still juggling my weight, and edged into a vast room filled with desks and computers and piddly half-walls that wouldn't keep a kitten out. Somewhere, a machine was humming faintly. I squirmed free of his arms and jumped to the floor. Vague hints of food drifted in the air—crackers (stale), cookies (Oreos), pizza (darn near petrified), and—

My ears pricked. A ham and cheese sandwich! Close by too. My stomach rumbled and I trotted off into the maze of desks and walls.

"Hudson!" Sidley cried and dashed after me.

I avoided him with a graceful twist, rounded several more corners and then leaped up onto a desk holding the aforementioned sandwich. A brown-haired female seated before the desk gave a convulsive shout and rolled backwards in her chair.

"Ms. Smythe-Jones!" Sidley slid to a halt. "I—"

The ham was quite fresh, sugar-cured, with just a touch of mayo. I breathed in its exquisite bouquet, then nibbled a corner that overlapped the bread.

The woman glanced up at Sidley, then reached across and tapped a small curving gray thing with her forefinger. The computer screen changed from a field of white with black squiggles to yellow and green fish swimming back and forth in a deep-blue sea. Two hectic spots of red bloomed in her cheeks. "Mr. Sidley," she said. "What on earth brings you back to work at this ungodly hour?"

Unable to resist, I abandoned the ham to swipe at the fish, but they were protected by glass and I didn't even get my paw wet.

"I—" Sidley's Adam's apple bobbed. "I had some accounts to clean up before—" He grimaced. "And you?"

"My cursor keeps jumping all over the place," she said with a smile.

Look out, Sidley! I thought. *She's showing her teeth. She's getting ready to bite!*

"So I requisitioned a new mouse from Stores to replace it," she went on, then shoved the gray thing aside. "I wanted to get it installed before my big report is due tomorrow."

My ears twitched. Mouse? I stepped over the sandwich and sniffed the hard plastic shell. It smelled faintly of ham, but that was the only thing the least bit appetizing about it. On the other hand, it did possess a marvelous long, winding tail.

"I—could do that for you," he said. "If you like."

She stiffened. "Don't be ridiculous. Are you implying I need a *man* to do even something as simple as that!"

"N-no, of course n-not," he stammered. "I didn't mean—"

I batted this so-called "mouse" with my paw. It didn't jump, but I heard a definite click. Interesting.

On the computer screen, the silly flat fish changed into a field of tiny static pictures.

"You're not supposed to be here anyway!" She bolted up out of her chair and stood in front of the screen. "Didn't I hear gossip floating around the office this morning about you and 'embezzlement'?" She advanced on Sidley, her face thrust forward, just like one cat backing another off a fence. "So, just exactly what is it you're here to 'clean up'? Maybe I should say 'clean out,' perhaps some funds you overlooked before?"

I batted the mouse again. This time I saw the left side move downward and I realized suddenly it was a *toy*. Old Sidley was clueless about toys, so it'd been a long time since I'd seen one, but I still remembered from my kitten days. How utterly cool! I pounced, batted it twice in quick succession, lashing my tail with pleasure. Up on the screen, the tiny pictures winked out. The white field with its boring black squiggles returned. I laid back my ears and growled deep in my throat with disapproval.

"Hudson!" Sidley looked horrified. "Leave that mouse alone!"

The woman snatched at the so-called "mouse," but I raked the back of her hand with bared claws and drew blood. She squealed and put the wounded hand to her lips.

I hunkered down with the thing between my forepaws. It was my toy, mine! I wasn't about to relinquish it without a fight—unless maybe she wanted to trade me that sadly neglected ham and cheese sandwich.

Sidley made an abortive move toward me, then froze in mid-grab and stared at the screen, mouth hanging open in that unappealing goldfish way he has. "Wha—?"

"Get that verminous beast out of here!" The woman looked mad enough to spit, almost feline. "Or I'll call Security!"

Sidley turned to her. "Those are *my* authorization codes, Ms. Smythe-Jones! What are they doing in *your* files?"

She tried to grab the mouse again, but I arched my back and hissed. She backed away, cradling her injured hand. Blood dripped to the tiled floor at her feet. "Don't be ridiculous." Her voice sounded squeaky. "What would I be doing with your codes? We're not even in the same department!"

"No," he said. His back straightened, and for once, he didn't sound like my timorous Sidley. "We're not." He reached across and picked up the phone, punched a bunch of the white buttons. "I think Security should come up and check this out." He turned back to me. "And, Hudson, don't let her at that blasted mouse or we'll lose the evidence!"

Sidley wanted the mouse too then. I gave it a tentative lick, but it wasn't a bit nice, not nearly as tasty as even the much despised Piggly-Wiggly store brand special. *Well,* I thought, *there's no accounting for taste.*

Security came of course, and then, not too long afterward, the police. Fortunately, Sidley made them leave their stupid yammering dog out in the hallway. There was too much noise, flashbulbs going off in my face, the female sobbing as they dragged her away. I sneaked another bite or two of the ham sandwich, before someone bagged it up, but all in all, as a dinner party, it was pretty much a bust. If this was what Sidley did with his days, I thought, no wonder he preferred staring at that boring TV.

When it came time to head for home, Sidley picked me up, but I seized the mouse in my mouth and its tail was somehow stuck in the computer. We were brought up short after two steps. "Let go, Hudson," Sidley said gently. "It's all right now. They have her files and everything is going to be okay."

It's my mouse! I thought crossly. *Mine!* I rumbled deep in my chest and whipped my tail to show my displeasure.

Several police officers standing nearby laughed.

"Come on, Hudson!" Sidley said, considerably less gently. "You were magnificent, but we have to go!"

I wriggled out of his arms and leaped back to the desk. I flattened my ears and dared him to try and take the mouse away. It wasn't much, as mice went, but I had caught it all by myself.

"Hudson!"

"Oh, let him have it," one of the officers said. "After all, he's earned it!" He reached around behind the computer and detached the mouse's tail. "Here you go, big guy."

Sidley picked me up again, mouse and all, and we trooped back down the hall with the skinny tail dragging along behind.

So, that's about all, except that Sidley never buys me the nasty Piggly-Wiggly special of the week these days. Instead, he stocks Bast's Tidbits, cat food of the gods, and it's actually not too bad. I like the steak tartare flavor the best.

The mouse still lives with us, if something that has no legs or fur can be said to "live." The little black ball in its stomach came out during a romp a few days after our visit to the office, so Sidley bought a replacement. This new ball is much superior because it's stuffed with catnip and has a tiny bell inside, just the thing for a mad scamper about the house.

I do allow Sidley to scratch behind my ears occasionally now, mostly on alternate Tuesdays in months that end with an "R." After all, we wouldn't want this affair to go to his head.

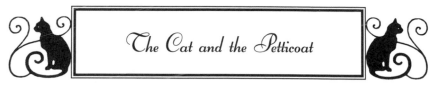

The Cat and the Petticoat

REBECCA LICKISS

THE WEEKLY SADDLEBACK STAGE was late. This being more usual than not, Burkett was unconcerned. He'd become a patient man since the war. He watched the dry, sandy desert valley below his scrub-covered promontory, while loosely holding the reins and leaning over the saddle horn.

"Think maybe they ain't coming? Maybe got tired of being robbed?"

Burkett looked back in time to see Elmore spit a stream of pungent tobacco juice, barely missing the rump of Burkett's horse. "Naw. They're just late. Like always."

It took another hour of waiting in the hot sun, sweating in their dun-colored dusters, before Burkett spotted the plume of dust thrown up by the stagecoach. He pulled his neckerchief up over his nose. "Let's go."

They planned to meet the stage just after it came out of the dry wash. They'd been stopping the stage at various places along the route, so as not to rile any one lawman too much. And they paid bribes to any that took particular exception to their activities. Burkett figured another six months and he could retire, not rich, but comfortably enough not to have to break his back plowing the unforgiving soil, or picking and shoveling through cruel solid rock.

Stopping the stage was the easy part. It was a cheap outfit, no one riding shotgun, mostly used by passengers unable to afford the Wells Fargo-guarded runs. The only gold would be on the passengers as jewelry, or that smuggled out by mine workers highgrading in the big mines, slipping a nugget or two in their pockets or lunch buckets. Those nuggets would be hidden in packages in the freight. Burkett had no qualms about stealing from thieves, and thieves couldn't scream to the law for help.

The coachman, well practiced at this, threw down the luggage and freight at Elmore's command. Burkett ordered the passengers out, and herded them and the coachman away while Elmore ransacked the bags, trunks, and crates, putting anything interesting or valuable in his sack.

Burkett sized up the passengers. They consisted of an older gray-haired man with a gold watch and chain prominently displayed across his ample blue vest, and that irritating petite brunette woman.

As always, she clutched desperately to a large black and white cat, who seemed undisturbed at these proceedings. The woman's eyes puddled with tears, and her lip wobbled in a silent sob. Her dress was familiar. She wore the same one every time. It was old, lace and linen, fraying at the hem, with straining seams. It looked like the cast-off from someone's better days. In spite of that she'd almost be pretty, if it weren't for the red, teary eyes and fearful expression. Burkett didn't need to check to know she had no jewelry, little money, and no other valuables.

He swore silently to himself. She wasn't on every weekly run, but every time she rode the stage the haul almost wasn't worth the trouble. She had to be hiding the ill-gotten gold somewhere, but he'd be damned if he knew where. He holstered one of his Colts.

"Take off all your jewelry. Turn out your pockets. Take off your coats and vests. Put all your jewelry, money, and any other valuables you might have in this sack." Burkett pulled a sack from his pocket, and extended it to the coachman.

The coachman, as always, had prepared for this, and had nothing to contribute. The older man put in his watch, his wallet, two gold rings, and a silver cigarette case.

He was about to pass the sack to the woman, when Burkett said, "We'll take the silk handkerchief, too. And that pin you tried to hide by fastening it to the inside of your coat."

The woman took the sack when it was passed to her, jostling the cat, though the cat never opened his eyes. She extended it fearfully to Burkett without adding anything.

"That cat ain't real," Elmore said coming up behind Burkett. "I swear I ain't ever seen it move. It's a puppet. She's hiding something in it."

The woman half turned away from them, putting a hand protectively over the cat's head, her eyes widening in terror. The cat had no reaction. "Checkers is real. He's a sweet kitty. Don't you dare harm a hair on his head."

"He ain't moved," Elmore said. "I want to look at that cat." He nudged Burkett, and took a half-step toward the woman.

Burkett sighed and nodded. It was possible the cat was only a smuggling puppet. Elmore wouldn't rest till he'd figured out how she was hiding the gold.

She screeched as Elmore pulled the cat from her arms. The cat proved his vital state by raking his claws down Elmore's chest, shredding Elmore's shirt.

Elmore dropped the cat. The cat stepped away from Elmore, sat with a disdaining back to Elmore, and began washing itself. The woman started to get the cat, and Elmore grabbed her by the arm. "Where're you hiding it? You got that gold tucked away somewhere, I know it." His free hand groped across her breasts, squeezing and prodding.

The woman screamed. The cat turned to look back at Elmore.

Drawing his holstered Colt with his left hand, keeping it pointed at the coachman and older man, Burkett flipped the Colt in his right hand around, and struck Elmore on the back of the head with the grip. Elmore crumpled to the ground.

"Sorry, Ma'am. He's been getting a mite frustrated, but that's no call to rough you up. You all right?" Burkett holstered his right Colt, and scooped up the cat.

The petite brunette nodded, gulped down a sob, and took the cat as Burkett extended him to her. She cooed soothingly in the cat's ear, stroking his fine thick fur with a shaking hand. He yawned, and snuggled in to resume his nap.

Burkett motioned to the coachman and passengers with his Colt. "You can be going on your way now. We thank you much."

He watched them walk back to the stagecoach. The men hurried, and started throwing the baggage back on top. The woman walked slowly and deliberately, head held high. She seemed to almost glide, the bustle on the back of her dress never twitched, as those of most of the women of his acquaintance would have.

Elmore roused as the stagecoach left. "You idiot." He pushed himself up to glare at Burkett. "She ain't no lady. She's just some whore, smuggling gold that should rightfully be ours. If you'd have just let me get it."

"No." Burkett picked up their small sacks of plunder, and put them in the saddlebags. "We may be thieves, but we don't hurt people, if we can avoid it."

"Gentleman Bandit." Elmore spat another stream of tobacco juice. "If they catch you, they'll still hang you. Whether you acted like a gentleman or not. Idiot."

"Let's get out of here."

They robbed the stage again the next week. The woman wasn't on that run, and the haul was better. Elmore took a portion of it into the town not far from their hideout, and got himself killed in a barroom fight. Burkett took that as a sign that it was time to retire. With the money both he and Elmore had saved up, Burkett decided to travel somewhere no one knew him, and see if he could set himself up somehow.

He sold the horses, shaved his beard, trimmed his hair, bought some nice clothes, and left for good. He traveled through Nevada, California, Arizona, New Mexico, and Colorado, looking for a place where he could stay, but anywhere gold mines flourished he could see wanted posters with bad renderings of his neckerchief-covered face. Kansas wasn't far enough east, so he took the train to Iowa, and got off at Cherokee. It looked small enough to be friendly.

Burkett strolled down the street carrying his two large bags, heading for a hotel recommended by the train's porter. The setting sun at his back helped warm him against the crisp autumn evening. The air smelled damp to his desert-acclimated nose, and was richly scented with the perfumes of the cultivated flowers, the thick green grass, and the dark black dirt. Still, he thought he could grow accustomed to it.

Around him shops were closing for the night. Various storekeps wished him good evening as he passed. He nodded and returned their salutations, until he saw ahead of him, closing a shop, a petite brunette woman, carrying a black and white cat.

The cat blinked at him lazily, and meowed.

He'd paused momentarily, but caught himself before he could stare outright. Burkett walked on, boldly. He nodded and said, "Good evening."

The cat smiled at him, he would have sworn to it. The woman whispered as he drew close, "Well, well. If it isn't the Gentleman Bandit."

"I beg your pardon, Ma'am. You must have mistaken me for someone else."

Burkett made as if to walk on, but she said, "I'd know those eyes anywhere. So would Checkers. And I saw you stop in surprise when you saw us."

"I—" Burkett scrambled for something to say. "I was merely admiring your cat."

The cat twitched his black and white nose, yawned knowingly, and snuggled in for a nap.

Smiling, she said demurely, "You needn't worry over me. I wouldn't turn you in. You might turn around and do the same to me. The owners would dearly love to know who, how, where, and how much gold disappeared from their mines."

Unable to resist, Burkett asked, "How were you smuggling the gold past us?"

"I retired when you did," she said, ignoring his question. "I was afraid the next bandits wouldn't be so gentlemanly, and the mine's supervisors were beginning to take note of my visits to my 'brother.' My cut was enough to set Checkers and me up here. Almost respectable." She stroked the cat, who acknowledged the attention by opening his eyes momentarily.

"Almost?" Burkett glanced at the sign on her shop. It said merely "Emma's," giving no hint of what business was conducted inside.

"An unmarried businesswoman is never completely respectable. And, of course, I had to use what knowledge and skills I acquired. So, I make, mend, and clean women's foundation garments." She started walking the way he'd been heading, very slowly.

Burkett stepped up beside her, trying to sort her words into something that made sense. He knew houses had foundations, but what sort of foundations would women have?

"A corsetiere." She giggled at his confusion, a lilting crescendo, and stroked her cat. "I make women's corsets, bustles, and hoops."

"Oh. I see," he lied. They strolled on through the growing twilight.

"I thought Checkers was a good distraction. He has always been so calm and lazy. I expected you thought I was palming or sleight-of-handing the nuggets around him. That's why I carried him all the time, and I couldn't bear to be parted from him."

"Elmore did," Burkett said. "I didn't."

"No?"

"No Ma'am. I knew you were smarter than that."

She stopped and looked at him seriously. "I thank you."

"Ma'am, before I leave for the hotel, would you please tell me where you were hiding the gold."

Giggling again, she buried her face momentarily in the thick fur of her cat. "You haven't figured that out yet?" She turned the cat to her, nose to nose. "Should we tell him, Checkers?" She cuddled the cat closely again, then looked up to smile coquettishly at him. "I sewed them into the stuffing of my bustle."

"I wouldn't have looked there." Burkett shook his head ruefully.

"No. I knew you wouldn't. Not the Gentleman Bandit."

They walked in silence for a moment. Burkett moved his gaze around the storefronts nervously. He cleared his throat and said, "I had thought about settling here. I was wondering . . . Ma'am, would you join me for dinner, and perhaps tell me about this town?"

"Carry Checkers?" She extended the cat to him.

Burkett and Checkers contemplated each other momentarily. Burkett shifted his bags, so they were both in his left hand, and held the cat in the crook of his right arm.

Checkers looked from Burkett to the woman, yawned, and settled in for a nap. The woman smiled up at Burkett and said, "Well, Checkers likes you, so I suppose it'd be all right to join you for dinner."

Cat Bay on Cat Cay

BILL PRONZINI

October 21

Dear Blanche,

Well, here we are at Cat Bay on Cat Cay. Finally! Three different planes, the last one a twelve-seater, and then a forty-five-minute trip by ferry launch, and then Arthur had to rent a car and drive us all the way around this primitive little island to get to Tweed's Resort. Talk about remote. I was afraid it couldn't possibly be worth all that trouble. But it is, Blanche. This isn't just another Caribbean island—it's a vacation paradise!

Cat Bay on Cat Cay. Isn't that wonderfully alliterative? And wonderfully descriptive too. Did I show you the brochure before we left? I can't remember if I did or not. Anyway, the island is one of the outer Leewards, twenty miles long and fifteen miles wide, and from the air it really does look like a sleeping cat. There's a long, narrow, curving peninsula at the south end shaped exactly like a tail, and at the north end there's a rounded projection that resembles a head and two wedge-shaped promontories, one on either side of the head, that are perfectly symmetrical. The natives call the promontories East Ear and West Ear. Isn't that cute? They're the highest points on the cay—about one hundred fifty feet above a rocky shore-line. The rest of the island is at sea level.

Cat Bay curves in from East Ear, a mile-long sweep of brilliantly clear water and the most dazzling white coral sand beach. The photos in the brochure don't do justice to it. Wait until you see the ones I took. Tweed's Resort is at the south end, and it's just the most marvelous mix of provincial and retro-modern. Large bungalows with terraces practically hanging over the beach, and a huge main house where meals and drinks are served that you'd swear was lifted right out of one of those thirties tropical movies, like the one with Dorothy Lamour about the hurricane. I mean, there are ceiling fans instead of air-conditioning! And the grounds are fabulous. Most of Cat Cay is flat and treeless, with a lot of unattractive scrub growth, but at Tweed's there are palms and flamboyant trees and frangipani and... oh, every kind of exotic plant you can imagine. And old stone fences and rusty cannons from the days of the Spanish Main pirates, when Captain Kidd, Blackbeard, and Anne Bonny and Calico Jack Rackam (whoever *they* were) came all the way out here to pillage and plunder. The whole place simply *drips* atmosphere.

The owner, Jeremiah Tweed, is a delightful old graybeard, the last member of an African slave family that first settled here two or three hundred years ago. He speaks a charming native patois and tells the most breathtaking stories. His wife, Vera, does most of the cooking and is an absolute wizard—the meal we had last night was to die for. Crayfish, curried conch, and a barbecued meat they claim is beef but Arthur and I are convinced is *goat*. Not that I really want to know, Blanche, because it's delicious no matter what kind of animal it came from.

And here's the big surprise, not mentioned at all in the brochure: the place is positively teeming with cats! Dozens and dozens, nearly every variety of mixed-breed shorthair and longhair, and most as friendly as can be. Mr. Tweed says he and his wife are lifelong cat fanciers and maybe they are, or maybe they feed them and let them roam free as a promotional ploy because of Cat Bay on Cat Cay, but in any case I certainly approve. You know how I love cats. Of course, Arthur started grumbling as soon as he saw how many there are. He never has been able to warm up to felines, at least not the non-feral, four-footed kind.

We practically have the resort to ourselves, since the season is still a few weeks off. That would suit me just fine if it wasn't for the Tweeds' only other guest. Her name is Gloria Bartell and she's a widow from Chicago. *Claims* to be a widow, at any rate. She can't be more than thirty-five, one of those slinky blondes with ball-bearing hips and a Lauren Bacall voice. As soon as I laid eyes on her I said to myself, uh-oh, here's a woman on the make. Arthur doesn't think so, naturally. He says she's just a lonely widow with no designs on anything except crayfish and rum punches. But he doesn't fool me. I caught him ogling her in her skimpy bikini this morning, when we came out to the beach. She was lying under one of the little palm-frond lean-tos they have scattered around for shade, and without even asking me he sat down under the one closest to her. And then started a conversation that all but excluded me. Believe you me, I told him what I thought of *that* behavior when we were alone afterward.

Anyhow, Blanche, I'm not going to let myself worry about the widow or anything else. I'm here to have fun. Cuddle with Arthur, swim, go sailing, lie in the sun as much as I can stand to so I'll come home with a glorious tan that will make you green with envy, even if it is on a pudgy forty-three-year-old body. I'm not going to worry about my weight, either, not with all those scrumptious Caribbean specialties of Mrs. Tweed's and Mr. Tweed's special rum punches.

I'll write again in a day or two, whenever the mood strikes. Meanwhile, take care and be sure to let me know if and when that handsome tennis pro at the club says yes next time you ask him for a private lesson. If I wasn't a hopelessly old-fashioned, one-man woman, I'd be terribly jealous of you.

Love and kisses,
Janice

October 23
Dear Blanche,

Greetings again from beautiful Cat Bay on Cat Cay.

We went snorkeling yesterday, all the way out to the coral reef that protects the bay from sharks (the kind that live in the ocean, anyhow). The water is only about six feet deep the whole way, and so clear it's like looking down through layers of glass; you can see starfish and anemones and all sorts of other sea creatures. I worked on my tan most of the afternoon, until clouds piled up and it rained for a while. This morning I went for a lovely catamaran ride around to West Ear. Arthur didn't go along. He said he just wanted to lie on the beach and read and I couldn't talk him out of it.

Do I sound less enthusiastic than I did two days ago, Blanche? If I do, it's because I am. I'm not having near as good a time as I thought I would. You know I planned this trip as more than just a vacation, as a second honeymoon for Arthur and me. But it isn't working out that way. We don't seem to be communicating—not in *any* way, if you know what I mean. Our bungalow has two double beds and we haven't shared the same one for even a minute since we arrived.

I blame Arthur, of course. And that Bartell woman I told you about in my last letter. She hardly has a civil word for me, but she flirts shamelessly with him. He preens when she does it, too—not that I have to tell you about that annoying habit of his when he's around an attractive female.

Last night he went for a walk after dinner, without asking me to join him, and a little while later I happened to step out onto the terrace and there they were, Arthur and the widow, walking along the beach side by side, talking and laughing. One of the Tweeds' cats came bounding out of the bushes just then and ran toward them. Just being playful, the way cats are. And Arthur picked up a piece of driftwood and threw it at the poor little thing. I think he hit it, too, because I heard it cry before it ran off. Then they both laughed as if they'd shared a wonderful joke. I mean, have you ever heard of anything so cruel and heartless?

Then today, after I returned from the catamaran trip, there they were together again, in the garden at the main house, drinking rum punches with their heads about six inches apart. A few minutes ago, when we got back to our bungalow, I confronted Arthur point-blank and of course he laughed it off. All perfectly innocent, my dear—*he* says. Well, we'll see.

So that's why I'm not my usual cheery self today. I know you understand, Blanche, and I wish you were here so we could talk about it. You're the only person I can really talk to—my one true friend.

More later. Until then,

Love and kisses,
Janice

October 24

Dear Blanche,

Last night after dinner Arthur left on another of his walks. I tried to join him, but he wouldn't hear of it. Well, I waited fifteen minutes and then I went down to Gloria Bartell's bungalow. The lights were on inside, but when I crept onto the terrace and peeked through the jalousies, she wasn't there. I went straight to the beach. It was a beautiful moonlit night—one of those magnificent frosty white Caribbean moons that make everything seem as bright as day—and I could see all the way to East Ear. There was no sign of either of them. And no sign of them at the main house or anywhere else on the grounds.

It was more than two hours before Arthur came back. I asked him where he'd been, and he said walking on the beach, enjoying the moonlight and the peace and quiet.

Oh, Blanche, it looks like he's at it again. I don't want to believe it after he swore to me the last time that he'd never again be unfaithful. I keep hoping I'm wrong, imagining things. But under the circumstances, what else *can* I believe?

Your troubled friend,
Janice

October 25

Dear Blanche,

I wasn't wrong. It's all true.

Arthur *is* having a clandestine affair with that Bartell witch. And he doesn't even care that I know it!

He disappeared this afternoon for four and a half hours. And so did she. And when he came back . . . well, one look at him and his clothes and it was painfully obvious to anyone with half a brain what he'd been doing for most of the time he was gone. I came right out and accused him of it, naturally. He didn't even bother to deny it. All he said was, "What I do is my business, Janice. I'm tired of answering to you. In fact I'm tired of *you* and of pretending I'm not just because you control the damn purse strings."

I cried my eyes out afterward. Then I swallowed the last of my pride and went to him and begged and pleaded—and he laughed at me. Exactly the way he laughed after he hit that poor little cat with the piece of driftwood. As if I were nothing to him anymore—if I ever was in the first place—except a cruel joke.

Oh, Blanche, what am I going to do?

Desperately,
Janice

October 27

Dear Blanche,

I just tried to call you. But the telephone system on Cat Cay is so hopelessly antiquated I couldn't get through. At least the Tweeds have a fax machine, one of their few concessions to modern technology. Otherwise I wouldn't be able to let you know this quickly what's happened.

Blanche, I have some ghastly news.

Arthur is dead!

It happened last night, around ten-thirty. He hardly said a word to me all day, and after supper he left me alone again and went to meet *her*, and he didn't come back. I thought . . . well, I thought he'd given up on our marriage completely and didn't care about keeping up appearances and had spent the night in her bungalow. I didn't go to check because I couldn't bear to know for sure. I just lay awake the entire night, waiting for him and crying hopelessly.

When dawn came I couldn't stand it any longer. I *had* to confront him and get it over with. So I got dressed and went to the witch's bungalow. Well, she was there alone and she claimed Arthur hadn't spent the night with her, that she hadn't seen him since nine-thirty last night. Oh, they'd been together then, she admitted that, but only for a walk over to the bottom of East Ear. He wanted to climb up onto the promontory to take in the view, she said, but she didn't because there are signs warning you the footing is treacherous and not to make the climb after dark. So she left him there and walked back alone.

I was frightened that something had happened to him and she acted as if she was too. We both ran to the main house and told Mr. Tweed, and he and two of his employees hurried out to the East Ear and that was where they found Arthur. Not up on the Ear but among the jagged rocks at its base. He fell more than a hundred feet, Mr. Tweed said. He must have been a horrible sight, too, because I wasn't allowed to go and look at the body.

Everything since has just been a blur. The local police constable, a nice little man named Kitts, drove out from the village and asked a lot of questions. Then he and his men left to transport Arthur's remains to the village hospital. He'll be back later to "attend to formalities," as he put it.

When he does I'm going to tell him about the witch coming on to Arthur, trying to seduce him. But not that she actually succeeded, because I don't *know* that she did and because there's no reason to open up that can of worms unless it's absolutely necessary. Why say anything at all, you're wondering? Well, everybody seems to think Arthur's death was an accident, but was it, Blanche? I mean, for all I know the witch went up onto East Ear with him after all and they had some kind of argument and she *pushed* him over the edge. And if that's the way it happened, then I want her to get what's coming to her too.

More about that later. I'd better fax this right now, before the constable returns and while I still have my wits about me.

In deepest despair,
Janice

October 28

Dear Blanche,

Thank you so much, my dear friend, for the heartwarming words of solace and sympathy. You've always been there for me in my hour of need, and never more selflessly than now. I can't tell you how much it means to me.

No, you mustn't even think of flying all the way out here. By the time you arrived I'd be on my way home. Constable Kitts says I can leave tomorrow and I've already arranged to take the most direct route possible. I'm sure I can hold up well enough until I get there, and once I see you I'll let myself go and we'll have a good long cry together.

I'm sorry I wasn't able to fax this reply to you yesterday, but your fax arrived just after the constable's return. And after that, the rest of the day simply melted away for me and I was exhausted by nightfall. Constable Kitts and his "formalities," which translated into more questions and all sorts of papers to sign. Mr. and Mrs. Tweed fussing around, trying to console me. Even the witch tried to offer her sympathy, but of course I wouldn't let her anywhere near me. The sheer gall of the woman!

But evidently she's not a murderess. At least the constable doesn't think so. For one thing, she did leave Arthur when she said she did and walk back from East Ear alone. She stopped at the main house for a nightcap, and the Tweeds both remember that it was just ten when she got there. And Arthur's watch was broken in the fall and the hands were frozen at 10:34. So the official verdict is that his death was a tragic accident, which I suppose, when one takes the long view, will be much easier on me. Constable Kitts thinks one of two things must have happened. Either Arthur lost his footing on the rough ground, or he tripped over one of the Tweeds' cats— a more likely occurrence than you might think because many of them go wandering up there at night to hunt birds and rodents. Wouldn't it be ironic if he *did* trip over one of the cats, considering how he felt about them and his inexcusable cruelty on the beach the other day?

The witch has left Cat Bay and temporarily moved into a hotel in the village. Constable Kitts is letting her leave the island tomorrow too, and good riddance, even if she didn't get what was coming to her. I'm still here at the resort, though in a different bungalow than the one I shared with Arthur. The Tweeds have been marvelous, bringing me food and drinks and hovering around to see if there's anything else I need. A cynic might say they're worried that I'll sue them for negligence or something and that's why they're being so solicitous. But I'm not a cynic, Blanche, you know that. I'm just a poor, unlucky woman who seems fated to lead a tragically unfulfilled life.

No, no, don't worry, I'm not *that* depressed. I'll survive this setback and press on. Always have, always will.

One thing that is keeping me from becoming too self-pitying is that I have a part-time roommate in my new bungalow—the cutest little calico with one orange paw and the longest whiskers you've ever seen. She follows me around and coaxes me at every opportunity into picking her up and cuddling her. It's as if she understands and sympathizes with me and is determined to give me comfort. Isn't it a shame that all people aren't as sweet-natured as most cats? Men particularly.

Husbands definitely.

I didn't tell Constable Kitts about Roy and George, of course. It's really nobody's business but mine—and yours, dear Blanche—that Arthur was my third husband and the third to die in a terrible accident. Coincidences do happen, after all, and everyone knows that tragedies come in threes. It's not my fault I keep falling in love with men who turn out to be faithless fortune hunters *and* prone to fatal accidents.

I mean, you and I both know I'm not only a poor and unlucky woman, but a helpless one. Don't we, Blanche?

Love and kisses,
Janice

Cat Burglar

JILL MORGAN

RAIN RATTLED THE WINDOWS of the stately old house, boiling at loose-fitting panes and leaking into cracks along the weathered seams. There had been wetter winters in Lee County, Texas, but none as cold as this one. The house had been in Aletha Huber's family since the days of her Texas Ranger ancestors, and seemed to be showing every day of its two hundred and forty-eight years during this storm. Worn with time, like Aletha herself, the Rangers' house had a grace and dignity few modern homes could touch.

"Mother," said Aletha's son, Charlie, "I'm leaving now. I'll be at Susan's apartment if you need anything. Will you be all right by yourself till I get back?"

"Of course I will. You go on and have a good time on your date with Susan. Tell her 'Hi' for me."

"I'll do that," said Charlie.

He looks so handsome, like his father, Aletha thought. Jackson Huber had been more regimented in his ways. Charlie was cut from a different cloth. *No, Aletha* thought, *he may have his father's eyes and height, and even the same color of his hair, but Charlie is much more of a free spirit than Jackson ever was.*

"I like Susan," Aletha said as Charlie opened the door to leave. "She seems good for you."

"You mean that I've been a rascal and Susan is taming my ways?" Charlie said with a hint of a smile, just enough to charm his mother.

"I mean that I like her, and that's all I meant."

He came and kissed her on the cheek. "You're always my best girl."

"Go on, now. Don't keep that beautiful young woman waiting."

Charlie had been a real comfort to Aletha in the last two years. Having her son still at home made her widowhood less lonesome. She missed Jackson deeply, a hurt that would not heal. Charlie gave Aletha someone to take care of and fuss over. He wasn't a child anymore, but when that light came into his eyes as he teased, he might have been seven years old and charming her into allowing him an extra cookie before dinner. She found it hard to deny her son anything at all.

"The storm's bringing in a real downpour," Charlie said from the open doorway.

Aletha feared storms. When Jackson had been alive she'd felt safe, but since his death she'd let her terror of storms gain control over her. Having Charlie around had helped. In many ways, she depended upon him.

"I set the security alarm," Charlie said, pulling the front door closed. "Don't worry."

"I wasn't worried. And you don't need to hurry back. I'll be fine."

Charlie left. The steady blue light of the security system glowed from the wall panel above the front entry. Aletha was comforted by the blue eye's constant watchfulness, as if Jackson were still here and looking after her.

The house *was* isolated. She didn't mind the distance from neighbors. She enjoyed her privacy and the luxury of space this old settlement of the Rangers' had given her family . . . but on nights like this the old place did seem a little too deserted. A crash like an avalanche of steel girders dropped from overhead slammed against the roof, walls, and ground of the house; the noise invaded everything.

"Oh, I wish you'd stop," Aletha said to the storm, her fingers holding tightly to the stair rail.

And then it went dark.

For one instant Aletha half expected an answering reply from the storm, as if the lights had disappeared in response to her asking the thunder to stop. She waited a few seconds, hoping the comforting hum of power would surge back to life. It didn't.

"Bully," she said, with as much dignity as she could manage.

It would be best to simply go to bed. She worked her way up to the second-floor landing, feeling blindly for each step with the soft toe of her slipper. With hands held in front of her, she scuffed along the hallway, found the door to her room, and slipped inside. She fumbled in the drawer of her bedside table; she found a candle, matches, and flashlight. Only when the candle was burning did she notice that the thunder had stopped.

She climbed into bed and waited for power to return. She reserved the flashlight for emergency purposes, if needed. Time slowed to unrecognizable minutes until it seemed that what must have been an hour had passed in this dark quiet.

That's when Aletha heard the noise downstairs. It sounded like a heavy *thump*.

The mother cat was soaking wet, her calico coat slicked with mud from the rain-saturated garden. In her mouth was a tiny white kitten, five-and-a-half weeks old. The kitten mewed softly; a cold, soggy lump of white fur, blue eyes, and an open pink mouth full of tiny pointed teeth.

The calico didn't belong to anyone. She didn't have a name. No one fed her. No one gave her shelter. She was a stray. Her claws were sharp, and if backed into a corner she had teeth that could inflict a serious bite. She was not tame, not a pet, but gentle with her kittens.

The shelter from the storm was dark and quiet, and far away from barking dogs. The calico had carried the second of her three kittens up a rose trellis and through an open window, dropping silently onto a carpeted floor. The room was a warm cave. The white male kitten stopped his fretful cries. His body relaxed in the luxury of heat and dryness. Quickly, the calico padded to the alcove beneath the stairs where she'd left a black and white female kitten a few minutes earlier. She put the white kitten down in this same spot. In the time since the calico had been gone, the black and white kitten's coat had dried and felt warm to the touch when the mother cleaned its face.

The calico stared into the darkness, watchful and wary in this new place. She made no sound, other than the soft purring noise that helped to calm her mewing kittens. Silence was their best defense from danger. Mothering instincts warred within her. Should she go back for the third kitten or stay to protect these two? If they were fed and warm, they would be quiet while she went back outside. The other kitten would be cold and hungry. She wanted to go back for it right now, but the danger was too great that these other two would cry for her if she left them alone. There were two of them. She chose their welfare over the single kitten still outside in the cold. The kittens curled into the warmth of her body. They pressed their heads against her and fed on her milk. The calico's body rested, but her eyes stared in the direction of the open window, where she had left the little one outside.

When their stomachs were full and their eyes closed in exhausted sleep, the calico stood to leave the two kittens. She was very hungry, but would not hunt for food until she had brought the last of her kittens in from the cold. Only then would she be free to hunt for her own food. Only when all her young were warm, fed, and sleeping.

Moving silently, she retraced her steps down the long corridor toward the room with the open window. She was halfway there when she heard a loud noise that stopped her in her tracks. It was a heavy *thump*.

The second of the two men dropped from the window ledge into the room but slipped, turning his ankle, and fell hard on the carpeted floor. His body hit with a solid *thud*.

"Idiot," hissed the man already in the room. He was dressed in dark clothing and wore a black ski mask.

"Sorry," said the second man. He wore a ski mask too, dark pants, and a bulky black sweatshirt.

"Who's there?" a woman's voice called from the top of the stairs.

The men froze in place.

"Is someone in the house?" the woman asked.

"What do we do now?" whispered the man who had fallen.

"Quiet," said the other one.

Still as still, the two men waited. Above them, on the second-floor landing, boards creaked with the weight of someone slowly descending the stairs.

"She's coming down," said the second man. "She'll see us."

"No, she won't," whispered the leader. "Power's out. She won't see anything."

"She'll notice the open window," said the injured man.

"Close it," said the leader. "Hurry!"

The man pulled the window shut. The two men then ran hugging the wall, and into a room off the hallway. The limping man stumbled over a chair in the dark. The overturned chair made another loud *thump*.

"Careful!" said the leader.

The footsteps on the stairs had stopped at the sound of the second thud, but the footsteps began again, moving slowly but steadily toward them.

"What should we do?" the injured man asked.

It was too late to risk any answer. The woman was right in the hallway directly outside the room where the thieves hid in the dark. In another instant she would be in the room with them.

In the hallway, Aletha Huber shone her flashlight along the length of the corridor. Her hands trembled. She told herself it was foolish to be alarmed by a sound in the night. She was reacting like a frightened child instead of a sixty-eight-year-old woman. She wouldn't tell Charlie about this. Thinking about Charlie made Aletha wish he were here now.

She took one more step, moving toward Jackson's den on the left of the hall. Something small and close to the ground bolted past her in the dark. Startled, Aletha dropped the flashlight.

She gasped. "Oh, my goodness."

A reckoning of trapped fury unleashed itself on the closed window at the end of the hall. It sounded fierce, snarling, and clawing at the glass. Aletha bent and scrabbled along the floor for the fallen flashlight, which had gone out when it hit. She found it and thumbed the switch.

Beamed light shone a straight path down the corridor. Aletha saw nothing out of place at first. A swift movement caught her eye and she turned the flashlight in that direction. Glaring back at her were two amber-colored eyes.

"Why, how did you get in here?" Aletha asked, absurdly relieved that a cat was her prowler. Relief flooded her senses. The question of how the cat had come into the house troubled her. The small blue eye of the security system in Aletha's bedroom had shown a steady beam, which meant the silent alarm had not been triggered. Jackson's valuable collection of rare coins, and jewelry he had given her during their marriage, was kept in a safe in the den. The den was where she'd first thought she'd heard the noise....

She stared at the closed door of the den. "There won't be anything at all," she told herself for courage. Three steps to the door. Her hand reached for the knob. "The *thump* was only a tree branch hitting the wall." She pushed open the door and stepped inside the den.

"H-hello?" Aletha said.

No one answered.

Feeling more confident, she walked further into the room and shone her flashlight ahead of her. Her heart beat wildly. "Pure nerves," she told herself firmly, "nothing else." *Silly to have been so worried. Silly to make a fuss just because Charlie was gone and a storm caused a power loss.*

"Just as I expected, no one here," Aletha said. It was only the cat she'd heard. She'd have to disconnect the security system long enough to put the stray back outside.

She was still facing into the room when power suddenly returned and the overhead light came on in the den. "Oh, thank goodness," Aletha said, immensely relieved, and turned to leave.

Two men stood to the left of the doorway. They would have been visible if she had simply looked in their direction and pointed the flashlight at them.

They were dressed in dark, loose-fitting clothes, and had knitted ski masks pulled over their faces.

Aletha had one clear and burning thought. *Thank God Charlie's not home.*

The burglars bound the woman to an office chair with duct tape. It was the same duct tape they had brought along to attach a small mirror to the inside frame of the window where they had entered the house, preventing the alarm system from recognizing that the window was actually open.

The men filled bags with Jackson Huber's rare coins and Aletha's jewelry, sparing not a word for the woman in the chair. Aletha found that to her surprise, she wasn't very frightened. It made her furious that they were stealing Jackson's entire collection of coins. Those coins were meant for Charlie. Anger flamed in her, thinking how sad Charlie would be to lose this inheritance from his father.

Necklaces and earrings that Jackson had given to Aletha on their wedding anniversaries and many Christmases were roughly dumped from velvet-lined trays into the bags. The jewelry was more precious to Aletha for sentimental reasons than for what it might be worth. Each piece had been a gift of love. She watched them from the chair, bound and unable to move, but determined to see them come to justice.

The cat stood in the open doorway, watching them too. Only Aletha seemed to notice. The men were too busy. *The poor thing is still trying to find a way out*, she thought, feeling pity for the stray. *It must feel a prisoner in here, just like me.* The cat glanced at Aletha, then moved stealthily across the open doorway and disappeared into the hall. *Good luck*, Aletha thought. *Good luck to both of us.*

The men weren't satisfied with only the coins and jewelry. One of them took Jackson's antique dueling pistols. At last, their greed seemed satisfied and they prepared to leave. They turned to her, and the chilling thought crossed Aletha's mind—*Will they kill me? I am a witness.*

"What do we do with her?" asked the shorter of the two men.

The other one didn't answer. He pulled open the window and left the same way he had entered. The other man followed his lead.

Aletha sat alone, still bound in the chair. Now that the thieves were gone, tears stung her eyes. *At least they didn't kill me*, she comforted herself, *but the dueling pistols and my jewelry, and the coins meant for Charlie!* It was cold with the hall window open. She shivered and closed her eyes, waiting for Charlie to come home.

A man's shout interrupted Aletha's misery. A second shout followed the first, then sounds of a struggle. *Charlie!* she thought, terrified that her son had come back from his date and intercepted the thieves.

"Police!" a man's voice called from the hallway. "Mrs. Huber?"

Aletha lifted the chair legs off the floor and thumped down as heavily as she could manage. The police found her still strapped to the chair in Jackson's den. The duct tape was a nuisance coming off. Once free of it, she went into the hall. The first thing she noticed when she stepped into the hall was the little blue security light just over the front door. Its beam was no longer a steady blue. The beam was broken flashes, meaning the silent alarm had been triggered.

The cat must have set it off, thought Aletha, realizing that the calico must have left by the same open window that the thieves had used. The cat must have jumped to the ledge and knocked away the mirror. When the mirror fell, the security beam had recognized an open window and set off the silent alarm. That's how the burglars had been caught.

"We apprehended two intruders on your property," said the police officer. "Are you willing to look at them and tell us if you can identify either of them?"

Aletha nodded. The first suspect was clearly the man who had asked his partner, *What do we do with her?* Aletha recognized his voice. She believed she was ready to identify the second man as well, merely by the clothes and ski mask, but wasn't prepared for her reaction when the officer pulled the ski mask away. Standing in handcuffs was her son, Charlie.

"Mother," Charlie said softly.

"Do you know this man?" asked the officer holding Charlie in custody.

Aletha thought carefully before answering. Those were her son's eyes, her son's face, but the man before her was a stranger. "No," she said, "I guess I don't know this man at all."

The police took Charlie and his partner away, charging them both with assault, breaking and entering, and grand theft. In the morning, Aletha would send her lawyer to inform the police that Charlie was indeed her son. She didn't want to see Charlie herself.

Long into the night, Aletha thought about what she should do. Charlie had not committed any crime by breaking into his own home, and she wouldn't press charges against him for grand theft. The other man was another matter. She would drop all charges against her son except assault. She couldn't drop that because the police had found her strapped to the chair. The law required them to charge him with domestic violence. Charlie would have to stand trial.

Sleep did not come. Instead, Aletha spent the hours considering what she should do. Charlie would have to move out of the house. She couldn't let him live with her anymore. The coins and jewelry would have been his one day, if only he'd waited. She supposed he must have needed to sell them to pay gambling debts. Gambling had been Charlie's weakness for years.

Taking up pen and paper, Aletha wrote a codicil to her will. Charlie would remain her heir, he was after all her son, but he would not inherit anything until after his fortieth birthday, even if she should die before that time. He must wait, and hopefully mature enough not to squander his inheritance on gambling.

Thin cries caught at Aletha's senses, distracting her from thoughts of

Charlie. She followed the sounds to the bottom of the staircase, and there, hidden in the recessed alcove of the stairwell were two kittens.

"I guess I know how you got here," she said. "Your mother found a cozy place for you." The calico hadn't returned for them. Aletha suspected she never would. The kittens appeared old enough to be weaned. She first picked up one and then the other. They stopped mewing when held close against her, and began to purr. "I'll look after you," she said. "I owe your mother that much."

She carried them upstairs, and in the quiet that came after the storm, all of them drew warmth and comfort from each other. They settled into the soft folds of Aletha's winter quilt and closed their eyes to sleep.

In the early morning, the calico carried her one remaining kitten to a different place of shelter. There she curled around it, warming it from the cold, and finally rested.

Cat Burglar

KATHRYN PTACEK

BLANCHE AWAKENED IN THE darkness and wondered what it was that brought her out of her sleep; then she heard the faint scraping noise at the window and knew.

She shivered, and clutched at the covers with her wrinkled hands, and waited. There was nothing more she could do; she was confined to the bed, unable to get up by herself. Trapped.

Wait! she thought. The phone extension that her daughter Julia had insisted on installing in the room—the small phone sat on the bedside table. She reached out, trying to find the phone in the clutter. It sat out of arm's reach. She remembered then: Julia had dropped by earlier and called her husband to tell him she was on her way home, and she had left the instrument there, forgetting to put it back in its usual place. Blanche tried to find the cord so she could pull the phone toward her, but the cord was draped on the other side of the table. She couldn't move the table closer, either; it was too heavy, too solid.

Now, if she could just push herself up. She managed to struggle up onto her elbows and was leaning over, when she knew she couldn't do it. It was beyond her capability, and she sank back onto the bed.

Maybe her kids were right, she thought sadly; maybe it was time she went to the nursing home. She was eighty-two now; but others her age lived by themselves. She really could take care of herself. She only needed the nurse's aide to come in the morning and help her from the bed and get ready. Once that was done, she was on her own, and she did well enough, even if she did it very slowly nowadays.

One of the cats on the bed—she thought it was Snowflake because in the moonlight the cat's coat was white, but then it might have been Fred who was silvery gray—lifted its head and stared at the window.

The scraping grew louder, then she heard the soft sound of something touching wood. The window was being lifted. Snowflake—or Fred—yawned, ears pricked forward, alert. Tammy, the scrawny tabby, crawled out from under the covers and crouched by the woman's pillow, her tail flicking back and forth, the tip of it brushing the woman's chin. One of the other cats ambled in from another room and settled in the doorway, waiting. The cat was big so she knew it was Bear, and beyond Bear she could see the white of Snowflake.

Blanche waited.

She saw the window was now halfway up. A foot emerged, then a pants leg, followed by the lower half of someone's torso. Within seconds the burglar stood inside her room.

Blanche held her breath, afraid to make a sound. What if he heard, what if he attacked her? She tried to smother the rising alarm. She could yell. But who would hear? Her neighbors in the houses on either side worked hard all day and slept heavily at night; besides their houses sat far from hers. An old woman's thin scream could go unnoticed in the night sounds of the city. Too, her bedroom faced the back of the lot; no one could see anything from the street.

No one would come to rescue her. She was on her own. But what if he raped her, killed her? What if, and she could feel the tears welling in her eyes, what if he did something to the cats? She would have called them to her if she could, but fear had robbed her of her voice. Besides, how could she protect them when she couldn't protect herself?

The other cats had wandered in now, lured by the unfamiliar sounds, and they watched the intruder as he glanced around. He held a small flashlight, more like a penlight, which he had switched on, and he hissed, an inward breath, when he saw the cats arrayed in the doorway. The thin light traveled across a chair, a dresser, and then finally the bed, traveling up the foot, past Sylvester who had perched himself alongside Fred on the neatly folded quilt there, past Mittens, the Siamese, who crouched by the woman's hip, past Tammy who growled a low sound, to the old woman's face.

She stared at the dark figure behind the light.

"Well, this changes my plans slightly," he said. "I didn't expect to find you here. I thought you'd left."

"Not yet," she said, finally managing to speak. "My daughter wants me out, but I've been stubborn."

"Old people can be that way." There was a hint of amusement in his voice.

"I know." She took a deep breath. "What do you intend to do?"

"I'm here to rob you." He gave a short laugh and flicked off the flashlight.

Her eyes needed a few minutes to adjust to the sudden blackness, although with the light of the moon streaming through the window she could still see fairly well. Age had taken away many things, but not her sight. The large limb of the oak just outside her bedroom cast a long shadow. She wondered if he had climbed up the tree, or had he been more practical and used a ladder? She decided he must have used a ladder.

"I didn't know you had all these cats," he remarked as he picked his way across the room to her antique oak bureau. He ran his gloved hands across the surface and found the jewelry box her grandson had given to her for her birthday, before he went off to southeast Asia and stepped on a land mine and came home in a box.

"Don't destroy anything, please!" she called out, and wished she could have kept the quaver from her voice. She bit down on her lip. Tammy huddled closer and the old woman stroked the cat, feeling the silky texture of the stray's fur beneath her fingers.

The burglar looked in her direction, then back at the jewelry box. "Relax, lady. That's not my kind of thing. I'm here for the goods. I don't get off on destruction." He lifted the top and, now with flashlight on, he examined the contents, lifting earrings and necklaces and bracelets to inspect or put back in the satin-lined tray for the moment. She saw now that he had a small bag, like one used for gym clothes, a bag he would put all her belongings in.

Or rather, she corrected, the belongings that were worth something.

She couldn't tell much about him. He was slender, dressed in black, and she didn't know if he was black or white. For years Julia had insisted that Blanche lived in a "bad part of town," and Blanche had been puzzled by that, until Julia had explained there were more black families moving in and things were getting worse and real estate prices, she claimed, would be going down with this "undesirable element." And Blanche had said she was ashamed to know that her daughter was a bigot, and that she thought she had raised her better than that.

The burglar sounded young, too, but she realized at her age that *anyone* sounded young, even those folks in their sixties and seventies, and she supposed, compared to her, they were young.

He spoke well, she noticed, and he wasn't particularly rude. Perhaps that was a bonus.

Perhaps he wouldn't do anything awful.

On the other hand, she watched the nightly news, read the newspapers; she knew what was happening in this city and others across the country. Violence wore the face of the neighbor next door, who one day could smile at you and who the next day might slaughter his family with the gun he kept in the hall closet, the gun meant for intruders.

Her burglar didn't seem in a hurry, and that puzzled her.

"Aren't you afraid I'll call the police?" she asked after a moment.

"I cut the phone line before I came in," he said matter-of-factly.

"Oh." She wondered what would happen if Julia tried to call. Would she get a busy signal, or a message saying the line was out of order? But it didn't matter, really; Julia never called at night, not after she'd left for home.

Once or twice Blanche had timidly asked her daughter to stay the night with her, and Julia had simply stared at her with the cool gray eyes of her father and said she had her own life to conduct. Blanche knew that, and she appreciated what Julia did for her, however reluctantly at times, but sometimes . . . sometimes Blanche would have liked having someone stay with her at night, just to be another presence in the house, a presence beyond the cats, that is.

It had been well over two decades since Randall had died. In all that time she'd lived alone, just her and a progression of cats. Sometimes her daughter came to visit, bringing her children; sometimes her son flew in for the weekend, and then he would be gone for another six months or more.

She was lonely. Very lonely.

She was glad, though, that she had the cats. They were there to talk to during the long hours of the day, there to love her, there with her during the lonely hours of night.

Tammy licked the back of her hand.

"What's your name?"

He was sorting the jewelry now, rejecting the inexpensive brooch that had been a present from a grandchild, and selecting the sapphire and diamond one given to her by Randall on their fifteenth anniversary. He laughed. "That's a good one, lady. Think I'm going to tell something like that?" He shook his head.

"My name is Blanche."

"Yeah?" He didn't look up. He had scooped up the family bracelet she'd put together over the years, the one that held the gemstones for each of the grandchildren's birthdays. "That's an old-fashioned name."

Snowflake jumped up onto the bureau and paraded back and forth in front of the thief, trying to get his attention. She's such a flirt, Blanche thought. Absently the thief patted the cat as he sifted through the rest of the jewelry.

"Yes, well, I was born a long time ago."

"You don't sound all that old, not ancient, I mean."

"I'm eighty-two, almost eighty-three. My birthday is next month."

"Oh yeah? Mine too. The fifteenth."

"Eighteenth."

Fred had joined Snowflake, obviously wanting to know what was going on, and they watched from their perches as the burglar pulled open the drawers of the bureau now, going through the contents, and she was embarrassed when he reached her underwear drawer. Almost immediately he found the box of silver coins hidden under her panties.

He made a *tsk*ing noise. "Didn't anyone ever tell you not to put something like this with your underwear, lady? It's the first place guys like me look."

"Blanche," she said.

"What?"

"My name is Blanche."

"Uh, right, Blanche. Didn't anyone tell you that, huh?"

"My son-in-law told me to put them there. He said no one would ever look at an old woman's underwear."

The thief brought his head around and stared at her, and she thought she could see his features, and then realized it was the markings of a ski mask. "That wasn't a very nice thing for him to say. What's with this son-in-law anyway? And why aren't you living with your daughter and him instead of by yourself and a bunch of cats?"

"They don't want me with them." No one had ever said that to her, but it was plain enough; no one had to say the words aloud.

"Yeah? What's wrong with them? You're their family. They should want to take care of you. You get around okay, don't you?"

"Yes. I just need help getting in and out of bed. That's why I can't get out now," she said, sounding almost apologetic.

"You got all your marbles, right?"

"Certainly!"

He shook his head again as he put the box of silver coins into the bag. "Then what's their problem? If you'd been with them, this wouldn't be happening now."

"I know," she said, and she couldn't keep the sadness from her voice. Sylvester moved closer to her feet, and Tammy licked the back of her hand again, the narrow tongue rasping so much it tickled.

He was examining the rest of the room now. "Got a safe in here or downstairs?"

"No. Randall—my late husband—always planned on putting one in, but he never did." There had been many things Randall had planned on doing; we have all the time in the world, he would always say, plenty of time. But of course, there hadn't been. "Why are you doing this?"

He looked at her. "Stealing?"

"Yes."

"I need the money."

"Don't you have a job?"

"Yeah, and I work my butt off. But I need more money than I can earn at that."

"Why? You aren't on drugs, are you?"

He laughed, harshly. "No, hardly. I got an angry ex-wife who's out to make my life hell. She wants more and more, and the courts don't much seem to like me. So I steal. I take what I get and pawn it, and it's a bit more to help ends meet."

"But that's not right—not fair to you. You should find a judge who's sympathetic, who's—"

"This isn't TV, la—Blanche. The real world doesn't work that way."

"Sometimes it does."

He laughed and headed toward the open door of the bedroom. Bear growled at him and arched his back.

"This cat bite?"

"Not usually. But maybe he thinks you're a threat."

The thief brushed by Bear and the other cats, and Bear snarled and lashed out at the man's leg.

"Dammit! He got me with his claws!"

The thief kicked out with his foot and Bear jumped onto the bed, narrowly missing getting booted.

The thief turned his light on the flesh below his pulled-up pants leg. Blanche could see several rivulets of blood.

"Goddammit." He rubbed away the blood with his gloved fingers, but new droplets sprung up in the gouges. "I hope that cat's got all his shots."

"They all do." She was stroking Bear's thick ruff; the big cat squatted on the bed and as he watched the thief, his tail snapped back and forth. Blanche could hear the low growl in his throat.

"I'm going downstairs," the thief said.

She heard him reach the first floor and listened as he searched there. He didn't make a lot of noise, so she guessed he really wasn't trashing her house. He would find her antique silver service in the dinning-room hutch, and some money in her pocketbook although she never carried much more than twenty dollars at a time; there were one or two pieces of cut crystal, and some odds and ends, but most of the good stuff was in her bedroom. There was nothing in the other bedroom, although she supposed he would check on that when he came back.

He did, and when he came back into her room a few minutes later, he was limping a little.

"I'm sorry my cat hurt you," she said, and she was. She thought she might have grown to really like this young man—if he hadn't been here to rob her.

"Yeah. Me, too. Guess I'll put some iodine on it when I get home."

"Be sure to wash it out thoroughly with warm water and soap first. Cats' claws can be dirty. From the litter boxes, you know."

"Yeah."

He stood over the bed now. Bear's growling increased, and she rubbed his head, trying to get the cat to relax.

"I'm sorry, la—Blanche. I'm sorry that you turned out to be such a nice lady. I don't usually meet many people in this line of work. Usually they're out of the house, or they sleep through my burglary."

"I hope you go to court and get those payments lessened, so you won't have to do this any more. I would hate to see you get hurt." And she meant it.

"Yeah. Maybe I will. And give your daughter and son-in-law a real chewing-out for me, okay? They should be taking better care of you, you know?"

Briefly his fingers touched the top of her head, and then he was crossing the room. He slung the strap of the bag across his shoulder, and tucked the pen-light into a pocket. He climbed back through the window and was about to start down the ladder when Bear with a bloodcurdling yowl launched himself from the bed.

"No, Bear!"

The cat, who weighed close to twenty-five pounds, hit the thief solidly in the chest. The man's fingers slipped from the ladder, and his arms flailed as he lost his balance. Desperate, he tried to grab the ladder. It was the wrong thing to clutch. Ladder and man fell away from the house. Bear yowled again and leaped to the branch of the tree outside.

There was a thud, and an agonized cry, then nothing.

"Hello?" Blanche called, horrified by the turn of events. "Hello?"

Maybe he's been knocked unconscious, she told herself, but as the minutes passed, she began to think it was more than that.

Bear paced along the branch. Blanche could see his silhouette on the branch's shadow, and after a while, the cat leaped lightly onto the window sill, and sat there with his tail hanging down over the sill and washed his paw as he stared down at the motionless man below.

And alone, Blanche wept.

The Cat Who Knew Too Much

DOROTHY CANNELL

ALFRED MORRISON WAS SEATED in his favorite chair by the fireplace, making cheerful plans to murder his wife, when her booming voice destroyed the moment.

"Don't just sit there like a sack of flour, you great lummox, do something!"

"Yes, Edith!" Alfred planted his feet more firmly on the fine Persian carpet and opened one eye, a typical response on his part to the daily domestic crises that had enlivened six months of marriage to a woman who looked like Winston Churchill in drag.

"Is it too much to ask, Alfie," raucous sobs filled the room, "for you to take that vacant stare off your stupid mug? Just for once, look at me when I talk to you." Edith's bulldog face swam into view as Alfred strove for an expression of male sympathy suitable to whatever the current tragedy entailed, be it a broken vase or the death of someone near and dear to Edith. No, couldn't be the latter. Alfred bit down on a mirthless smile. His better half had no family, nor any friends that she wouldn't happily have traded in for a flashy rhinestone brooch. The only creature in the world for whom she would gladly have laid down her life weighed nine and a half pounds and looked like the Victorian muff Alfred's grandmother had used as a hot water bottle cover.

"Ah-ha!" A congratulatory slap on the knee. "You don't have to spell it out for me, Edith. This is about Charlotte Rose, isn't it? What's the little sugar bun done? Gone and got herself run over? There, there, old girl! It's a crying shame, all right, but none of us gets to live forever."

And that's what I've got to keep telling myself if I'm not to end up losing my marbles, Alfred reflected wistfully as he stood up and patted his wife's weight-lifter shoulder. Three failed attempts in as many months on the life of the woman he had married in hope of a speedy inheritance would get any man down. But it wouldn't do to cave in and meekly accept the status quo. One of the nastier things he had discovered about his wife on the honeymoon was that her heart condition wasn't as bad as she had led him to believe. And as he had always told himself, the devil helps those who help themselves.

"Charlotte Rose isn't dead, you stupid gawp!" Edith dropped down onto the sofa with a mighty thud. "Do you bloody well think I'd be fit to put two words together if the angels had come for my little darling? She's upstairs in her canopy basket. Oh, Alfie," a series of heaving sobs, "she's got something wrong with her meow."

"What?" Alfred was shocked into joining his spouse on the sofa. Before he could inch away from her he was swallowed up in a bear hug. Edith had her grotesque moments of being cuddly. And there was nothing to do but lie still with his nose impaled in her Styrofoam bosom and pray that he would be allowed up for air before he turned as blue as his lady wife's hair.

"I noticed at lunchtime that she didn't sound herself. And what terrified me was she didn't touch her shrimp mousse or the fricassee of chicken livers. So while you were having your afternoon snooze I drove the sweet precious down to the vet's. I was sure dear Dr. Stanley would tell me Charlotte Rose had a nasty sore throat and he'd prescribe medicine, along with lots of fluids, bed rest, and perhaps a drive in the country for a blow of fresh air. But—" Edith's tears plopped down on Alfred's neck as she kneaded his face into that well-sprung bosom. "We're not talking about a sore throat!"

"We're not?" Alfred mumbled as his mind leaped hopefully to proper illnesses—here he managed a squashed smile—like the Black Death.

"Charlotte Rose's trouble isn't physical. Dr. Stanley broke the news as gently as he could that she's developed a speech impediment. A stammer. Or was it a stutter? I can't remember which one he said." Edith clapped a meaty hand to her forehead, sending Alfred flying backwards so that he lay three quarters off the sofa in the manner of a magician's assistant about to be levitated to the ceiling. "It was all such a shock I blacked out and the nurse had to come in and help Dr. Stanley get me up on the examining table. A coldhearted woman. She told me to take a look at my bill and if that didn't bring me round nothing would."

"So the cat needs a course of elocution lessons, is that it?" Alfred rolled onto the floor, hobbled around on his knees until his head stopped spinning, and got to his feet. "You'll be out a few quid, but that shouldn't bother you, Edith. You've never counted the cost where dear little Charlotte Rose is concerned."

"You great dolt!" A pillow whizzed past Alfred's head, giving him a closer shave than he routinely got with his electric razor. "My angel baby's problem is psychological. We're talking about a mental illness. She's having . . . oh, I don't know how I can bear to say it . . . a nervous breakdown. Could a devoted mother ever receive a worse piece of news? Any fool knows the feline mind is a perilously fragile thing, not nearly as easily cured as taking out the poor little moppet's tonsils. Dr. Stanley asked me"—heartrending sob—"if Charlotte Rose had recently suffered any sort of trauma."

"And what did you tell him, dear?" Suddenly the room tilted like the deck of the *Titanic*. Knees trembling, Alfred sat down across from his wife.

"Well." Edith's eyes shifted sideways. "I did explain that we recently changed milkmen, and Charlotte Rose doesn't readily adapt to new tradespeople. She's started taking her tea black with a squeeze of lemon. But Dr. Stanley didn't think that the new milkman would have caused her to break down so completely. He said Charlotte Rose must have been exposed to a catastrophic event, or in all likelihood more than one, to have been robbed of normal speech."

"Watching too much telly, that's my guess. Horribly violent, most of the stuff they put on nowadays." Alfred's voice came out in a croak and he had to close his eyes to stop the room from spinning. Unfortunately, hiding out behind his lids proved no escape. His mind zoomed in on his three attempts to murder Edith. Scenes flip-flopping off kilter, as if being captured for posterity by a video camera in the hands of a rank amateur. The colors livid. The sounds blurred.

There was the April day when he and Edith huffed and puffed their way to the top of St. Michael's medieval tower in Riddlington, Suffolk. Realizing they were the only idiots to have made the climb, Alfred had seized the moment to give Edith a shove that had sent her slithering headfirst down the toe-hold stone steps. She had survived that experience with a bump on the head and no memory of ever having been in the tower.

The result was much the same after her dip in the sea at Brighton. Bloody hell! Edith had been begging to be bumped off that day. Flexing her brawny arms, she had insisted on taking a rowing boat out into rain-shrouded waves in an area known, so a local had warned them, for its savage undertow. It had been a piece of cake for Alfred to fake enthusiasm. The moment they were out of sight of the beach he begged to be allowed to take an oar, and never in his fifty-seven years had he enjoyed anything more than giving his wife a bash on the back of the head and seeing her topple overboard. But talk about rotten luck! Edith had refused to sink and before Alfred could regain control of the boat a busybody Coast Guard had showed up and callously ruined what should have been the surprise funeral of the year. Edith had spent a couple of days in bed with a bad cold but no memory of why she had ended up overboard.

Poor Alfred. For several weeks he had nursed his sense of grievance against the guardian angel who would seem to be working overtime on Edith's behalf. A lesser man would have given up. But not Alfred. A fortnight ago he had suggested a day's shopping in London. When he and the wife were waiting to board their train home in the crush of rush hour at Liverpool Street underground station, he had maneuvered Edith to the edge of the platform and shoved her onto the line as the train rocketed into sight with hurricane velocity. This time there could be no escape! Alfred finally knew the meaning of connubial bliss when . . . the brutal reality hit him like a ton of manure. The third time was not the charm. Edith had been dragged back to safety by a Boy Scout heaven bent on doing his good deed for the day. And what did the bloody woman have to show for this near-death experience? A sprained shoulder and . . . again no memory of events after entering the tube station.

"That's right, Alfie. Sit there like a lump on a log, why don't you!" Edith's voice rivaled the roar of the train that was supposed to have made him a free and very rich man. "Here I am at my wit's end, wondering if my Charlotte Rose will ever again be a fully functioning pussycat, and what do I get from you? Not so much as a crumb of comfort. Sometimes I wonder what possessed me to marry you. Oh, I know you came on like I was the queen of Sheba, but I should have seen you for what you are. Unfeeling, that's the word. I don't suppose you'd turn a hair if my little darling should end up taking her own life before we can find out the root of her problem."

"There, there, my love!" Alfred sat down next to his wife on the sofa and patted her shoulder. The panic that had gripped him was receding. It was rubbish to worry that in mulling over the last few months Edith's eyes would be opened and she would reach the chilling conclusion that her series of mishaps had traumatized Charlotte Rose. The cat had not been present to witness any of the events, and to give his buggering wife her due, Edith had not made a major production out of recovering from her accidents. A couple of days in bed with the aspirin bottle within reach had been the extent of each convalescent period.

"I say the vet's got you worked up over nothing," Alfred spoke with increasing cheer. "My guess is Charlotte Rose will be like a cat with two tails come morning."

"That's easy for you to say." Edith gulped down a sob. "I don't think you ever really took to my baby."

Alfred almost said that the boot was on the other foot. The first time he had set eyes on the pampered Persian she had recoiled from him as if he were a viper let out of a shoebox. And after the marriage Charlotte Rose had treated him with a studied indifference that at times got under Alfred's skin.

"You're talking a lot of bosh, Edith," he said stoutly. "I'm almost as fond of the little tyke as you are. I'm just trying to put a good face on a bad situation for your sake, my love."

"Oh, Alfie!" Edith nuzzled up to him on the sofa. "I don't deserve you. I'm such a cow most of the time. I don't mean anything by it. Having pots of money can be rough on a woman, particularly"—sniff—"when she's got a face like the back of a bus. You get so's you don't trust men, even the salt-of-the-earth ones like you."

Alfred submitted to a smacking kiss without puckering his lips. "Now, Edith, you know I never wanted your money. I told you that from the word go. It was me as told you not to change your will, but you insisted!" His voice cracked convincingly. "As if any amount of money could make up for being without the love of my life. We're a family, Edith. That's what we are, you, me, and Charlotte Rose."

"Bless you!" Edith swallowed him up in a rib-cracking embrace. "You've buoyed me up so's I can face what has to be done, whatever the cost in anguish to yours truly."

At that moment Alfred experienced a flicker of admiration for the woman he had married. The old bag was dotty enough about Charlotte Rose to end the cat's misery by having her put to sleep. A pity life wasn't as simple in other ways, but there it was.

"You'll come with me, won't you, Alfie?" Edith was saying.

"To the vet's?" Alfred had his moments of squeamishness.

"Dr. Ventura isn't a vet in the usual sense of the word. He's the senior cat psychiatrist at the Royal Feline Infirmary in York. According to Dr. Stanley, the man is a giant in his field and could be Charlotte Rose's one hope of recovering from her nervous breakdown, before she slips into permanent psychosis." Edith's voice trembled like an avalanche about to let loose. "Not to scare you to death, Alfie, Dr. Stanley said there's no time to be lost and we should rush our little angel up to the institute this evening."

"But we haven't had dinner." Alfred could not keep the irritation out of his voice."

"I know, love." Edith got off the sofa like an elephant in a trance. "But it's best for you and me, not just Charlotte Rose, if we don't put this off a moment longer than needed. Dr. Stanley warned me that part of a patient's recovery program includes family therapy sessions that can be emotionally draining for everyone concerned."

"I'm not sure I like the sound of anything to do with this business." Alfred fought down the uneasiness that was worming its way up from his stomach, but he couldn't keep his hands from trembling. Edith didn't notice. She went upstairs to fetch Charlotte Rose and swaddle her in a powder blue blanket with the cat's initials monogrammed in the corner. "You drive, Alfie," she instructed in a voice that even though gentler than usual made his head spin. "What with all I'm feeling right now, I wouldn't be safe behind the wheel."

The Morrisons lived in Rotherham, so motoring to York was hardly a taxing trip under normal circumstances; but from the moment Alfred pulled away from the house, he knew he was going to have trouble keeping his mind on the dark ribbon of road. He'd been in such good spirits before Edith came in with her news about Charlotte Rose. He'd decided he hadn't been thinking on a grand enough scale in his earlier attempts to make himself a widower, and that had given him an idea. He would suggest to Edith that they go on a holiday to America to see the Grand Canyon. He'd read that every year some overly eager tourist took a fatal tumble while viewing that scenic wonder.

But now, even as he cautiously negotiated his way around a car going twenty miles an hour, Alfred felt as if he were the one falling through space down into the blackest of pits. Out the corner of his eye he could see Charlotte Rose nestled on Edith's lap. Her pose suggested she was dozing but he knew that at least one of her eyes was cracked open. He could feel her counting the hairs on his head. Worse, he could feel her picking apart his thoughts the way she might have plucked the feathers from a sparrow had Edith ever allowed her to set her paws outdoors.

Bugger the little varmint! Alfred almost wrenched the steering wheel out of its socket. Charlotte Rose had him sized up from day one.

"Watch the road, Alfie!" Edith's bellow brought the lorry ahead of him into wavering focus. "Now look what you've done, you great clot! You've jolted our Charlotte Rose out of what was like as not the best sleep she's had all day."

"Me . . . me . . . ow . . . ow."

Bloody hell, sweat broke out on Alfred's forehead. The cat had developed a stutter! Could anything be more horrible than the humanness of the condition, particularly when coupled with that icy blue feline stare?

"I'm sorry I shouted at you, love." Edith rubbed his knee. "It's on account of me being that worried is all."

Worried! That was a tame word for what Alfred was feeling. Charlotte Rose knew all about his attempts on Edith's life. The cat hadn't needed to be present to witness the events. On some telepathic level she had been there on the stone steps at St. Michael's tower, in the rowing boat at Brighton and at Liverpool Street tube station. She, the oversized powder puff, had been Edith's guardian angel. And now she was headed for a cat psychiatrist's couch where, under the tender care of Dr. Ventura, she would become the means of everything coming to light.

"You're not a bad old stick, Alfie," Edith rumbled affectionately. "How about we stay over a few days in York when Charlotte Rose is on the mend? Have ourselves a second honeymoon. We could go and have a gawk at the cathedral. Really do the tourist bit. You'd like to see the railway museum, wouldn't you? And to show you love me, Alfie, we could go window-shopping in the Shambles."

"Whatever you say, dear," Alfred was doing better at watching the road. His mind had suddenly become crystal clear. He could picture himself along with Edith and Charlotte Rose being ushered by a sober-faced nurse into a stark white admitting room. There waiting for them would be the world's foremost cat psychiatrist. He would be foreign, Alfred decided, with a receding hairline and a sallow complexion.

"I am not Freud." Alfie could see Dr. Ventura bowing a greeting over steepled fingers and hear the thin piping voice inside his head.

"No, of course you're not a fraud," Edith would bellow, already having trouble with the doctor's accent. "Dr. Stanley says you're a genius. And I know you can make my Charlotte Rose all well again."

"I am not Freud." Dr. Ventura's face vanished for a moment when Alfred turned on the windshield wipers, but returned seconds later with even more fanatical clarity. "What I am is a man with the mind of a cat. I understand how my patients think. I talk their language. Slowly, layer by layer, I will peel away the face that Charlotte Rose shows to the outside world and discover what torment lurks within her soul."

Rain was coming down fast now, but Alfred turned the wipers down to low in a vain attempt at blurring Dr. Ventura's face.

"Watch the road, Alfie!" Edith's voice tore through his head and Alfred drew a shaky breath. The phantom doctor was gone, but there was no escaping the real man waiting for them at the Royal Feline Infirmary. He would require full cooperation on the part of Charlotte Rose's parents in pursuit of her recovery. Edith would explain that Alfred was the little angel's stepfather. Dr. Ventura would ask how long Alfred and Edith had been married, how Charlotte Rose had reacted to the event, and if the last few months had been relatively uneventful. Edith would mention she'd had rather a run of bad luck in the way of accidents recently. Dr. Ventura would probe more deeply and express himself very interested that Edith's memory of the events was so clouded. He would mention the words *traumatic amnesia* and gently suggest that while Edith might have blotted out whatever was particularly troubling about the accidents, Charlotte Rose had been able to pick up her mistress's subliminal distress calls and had reached a point of emotional overload. Her sense of powerlessness had manifested itself in her present vocal problems.

"Alfie, are you asleep at the wheel?"

"No, dear."

"I've been thinking, Alfie," Edith kissed the top of Charlotte Rose's head, "that if Dr. Ventura is everything he's cracked up to be and does right by our precious here, I'll change my will and leave everything I've got to his infirmary. You said right from the beginning you'd never take a penny of my money."

But you weren't supposed to take me at my word, you stupid cow. Alfred could have bashed his head against the windshield.

"That day, soon after we were married and I went down to see the solicitor, he talked me into seeing I was wrong to go against your wish. And the will I made out left the lot to various charities, but this will be better. And such a nice tribute to our Charlotte Rose."

What a bloody bad joke. He could end up at the Old Bailey charged with attempted murder. And that might be preferable to what Edith would do to him if he was left to her mercy. Alfred turned his neck an inch to look at his wife, but it was Charlotte Rose's eyes that met his and he could have sworn the rotten little beast was laughing at him.

"A penny for your thoughts, Alfie?" Edith said as York Minster rose up before them in the not too far distance.

"Just watching the road." Alfred Morrison spoke with remarkable cheerfulness. His nimble brain had come up with the perfect way out. He was humming a tune as he drove along thinking up ways to kill himself.

A Cat with a Gat

TINA L. JENS

IT WAS A COLD AND DRIZZLY NIGHT when the white, powered-and-puffed French poodle pranced into my office. It was no place for a class dame—dog or not. Her pedicured nails would scuff on the cracked linoleum. That fancy tail-bouffant would muss if she sat on my rusty metal chair. But she was a dame in trouble.

Trouble had brought her to the seedy side of town, to my office, to bat her baby-blues, wiggle that powder-puff tail, and beg me to help her . . . but be discreet about it.

Yammer's the name. Mickey Yammer. The best private gato in town. I don't usually take dogs for clients—I'm not a speciesist, or anything—it's just dogs yap too much. Plus, they tend to chase you down the alley when you deliver the second overdue notice on the bill. But, my litterbox was full, my pantry was empty, and I had a hankering for some Tender Vittles with extra tuna—the expensive kind. So, I took the case. My other lives would live to regret it.

The dame barked, danced and shivered, and did all the things a pedigreed poodle does when it's nervous—except piddle—I was glad of that 'cause I wasn't about to let her borrow my litterbox.

"Mr. Yammer, I need your help. I need you to clear my family name."

She did that poodle-shiver again, making the rhinestones on her designer collar flash in the neon light that shone in from the bar sign hanging outside my office window.

"My name is Fifi," she said.

It always is, I thought to myself.

"Fifi Lamour. I have some money of my own. I can pay you."

I flicked my tail and licked a dust mote off my front paw before I purred at her, "Tell me the details, toots. We'll worry about how many pounds of Purina chow it'll cost you, later."

She crossed her fluffy paws in front of her, then finally settled down and got to the meat of the story. "You know that horrid painting of seven dogs playing poker?"

"Seen it hanging in a milkhall or two. . . . Seems like there was some cheating going on."

"That's the problem!" Fifi yipped. Then she yapped, "The two dogs in the front of the picture appear to be cheating, but they're not! The golden Terrier on the left has three aces in his hand, and the English Bulldog to the right appears to be passing him a fourth ace—but it's a set up! The Terrier, my great-uncle, swore on his deathbed that he was innocent. But thanks to that picture by that fiendish Cassius Marcellus Coolidge, everyone thinks my uncle was guilty! Coolidge even gave the painting an incendiary title, *A Friend in Need*." She ducked her head and covered her eyes with one little, white poodle-paw.

I hissed. There's nothing I hate worse than a dame faking distress and trying to play me for a sap. She must have realized the drama act wasn't working, 'cause she raised her head, shook her ears back and went on with her tale.

"I think Coolidge was in on it with that brutish Bulldog. They set my uncle up. After the picture appeared on that cigar box no one would believe my uncle. He lost his job. He lost his papers. And he died—in the doghouse."

I licked my paw again, spreading the toes wide so I could polish my razor-sharp nails. "If the mutt's kicked the bucket, why do you care? All dogs go to Heaven anyway, and Heaven's pretty good at sorting this sort of mixup out. Why spend all that dough to clear a dead dog's name?"

"It's not just his name that's sullied!" Fifi yapped. "It's the entire bloodline. They've yanked our pedigrees and dropped our name from the roster of the New York Garden Kennel Club. The family is ruined! And I've pups on the way! Please help us, Mr. Yammer. Please!"

I took the case. All right, I'm a sap. I'm a broken down, tiger-striped, alley cat with half a tail, clipped ears, and a gimp when I walk, thanks to an unhappy love affair with the front tire of a city bus. I'm eighteen pounds of muscle and creaky joints. Haven't got much, but what I've got's mine, and I got it the honest way. Some of my friends uptown are in the rackets—criminal, civil, and tennis—they haven't been shy about stepping on my game foot if it suited their scam, either. Dog or not, I had sympathy for the Terrier, and his whimpering niece—if he'd really been set up and the family was taking the fall—I'd give him the benefit of the doubt, at least 'til I had a chance to stick my whiskers into it.

I didn't tell the dame this, but I had a handle on the case already. There was a milkhall around the corner that claimed to have the original painting on display. I figured that was a good place to start.

I donned my battered gray fedora, grabbed my gat, checked that it was loaded, then fastened my string holster around my haunches. I don't usually carry heat, but it was a rough neighborhood, and a rougher drinking den. And sometimes, a dog'll take a look at my docked tail and gimpy leg and peg me for a pushover. But this is one cat that's never been declawed. If they take me alone, they leave the worse for wear, but if they attack in a pack . . . well that's when a gat's a cat's best friend.

The bar was called Curly Tails, strictly a cat-and-dog joint, no humans allowed. Word at the water bowl is Cassius Coolidge had set up shop in the alley, and painted his series of poker pictures while peeking in an open window. Some critters whisper that he called the cops himself, so he could get that fourth-in-the-series painting of the fuzz busting up the game.

The bartender on duty was an old flame; a little calico with a skittish tail and a hot libido. She was a little run-down, a little saggy around the jowls, but she could keep a tomcat warm on a cold winter's night, and not howl at you the next morning. I leapt up on the barstool and shook my whiskers at her.

"Mickey Yammer—Mr. Scruffy himself—what brings your whiskers to this side of town?"

"Got a caper going, doll, and a powerful thirst. Hit me with some moo-juice, make it a double. Pour one for yourself, while you're at it."

"Sweet talker," she purred, before pouncing off to pour the drinks.

I sat back and studied the picture behind the bar. It was a massive canvas; at least twelve tail-lengths on every side—that's full-length cattails, to you—with the famous CM Coolidge signature scribbled in the corner.

There were seven mutts clipping cards, betting high on hands that didn't deserve it. I've never bothered much about canine kinds, but near as I could tell, that was a Collie on the far left, leaning back, looking smug about his hand—probably why he had so few chips in front of him—he had a lousy poker face. Behind the table was a St. Bernard and a Bloodhound with several bottles of booze between them. Wasn't clear who was doing the drinking; both breeds were known to over-imbibe. On the right side was a chocolate-speckled Doberman with pert ears and a pipe, next to something—looked like a bad cross between a Labrador and a Beagle. In front: the two canines in questions; a feisty white Bulldog with a spiked collar, who seemed to be passing the ace of hearts under the table; and Fifi's uncle, a golden Terrier, with a front paw full of three aces, and a back paw that sure seemed to be reaching for the sweet-heart card.

The big dogs were all behind the table—the two mutts in front were half the size of the rest of the pack. It takes gumption, or stupidity, to try to rig a card game when you're the smallest dog. 'Course, size don't matter to a bulldog. Species got its name from fighting bulls; dog'd leap up, latch onto the bull's lip, and hang on 'til the bull flipped him off or the lip ripped away.

In the picture, the Terrier's back paw placement was borderline. The foot seemed to be reaching for that card—but then again, it was resting pretty much along the edge of the wooden chair, right where a leg would need to be to sup-port him in the awkward human-sitting position.

A final fact remained that didn't look good for the little guys—they'd cleaned house, but good. They both had stacks of chips the size of Rin Tin Tin's royalty check in front of them. The other dogs had crumbs.

Mutts will give away everything with their tail. The two little guys may have been winning simply because they didn't have a big bushy brush to tip the other guys off. The Terrier's tail was loosely curled, relaxed, and happy, as he should be with a paw full of aces. The Bulldog's tail was ramrod straight, pointing down and dirty. But his guilt wasn't in question. The ace under the table proved that. The question was, did the Terrier take it? Did he ask for the card, or was the Bulldog offering it up, out of the goodness of his little black heart?

I wandered out of my reverie and found a saucer of moojuice in front of me. I lapped it up and tried to think. The job wasn't made any easier by a cou-ple of canines that were growling and barking, and generally bringing down the class of the joint in a nearby booth. They were all wearing felt hats with spiked rims, a studded collar, and oversized milk-bone shaped dog tags. Had to be a new gang in the hood. I hadn't seen them around before. But then, I didn't get down to this neighborhood much anymore.

I called the old flame over. She took her time, but I didn't blame her. Cat's don't like to come when they're called. "Hey sweetheart, know anything about that painting?" I pointed a paw at the picture.

One of the milk-bone boys started barking, but I put it down to bad man-ners. It never occurred that he might have been barking at me.

"Not a thing," she hissed. "And I can sure think of more interesting things to talk about than a painting full of pooches. Call me when you've got some-thing interesting to say."

I watched her prance off, knowing what she wanted, and knowing that wasn't what I was after . . . tonight.

I'd gleaned everything I could from the picture on the wall. I needed to talk to someone who'd been there. There weren't many four-footers left from the days that picture was made, cat and dog life spans being what they are. But the bar owner was one of those rare long-lifers. He was an old Russian Blue, with green eyes and a coat with a silvery steel sheen. Wagging tongues said he was twenty-five. Vets say that's impossible, but I've seen it happen, now and again.

One of the ugly pugs had muscled his way to the bar, squeezing me, and the poor schmuck on the other side, nearly out of our chairs. I thought about ripping his milk-bone off to teach him a lesson in manners, but I figured he was just trying to get another round of whatever dogs drink these days.

I licked my dish clean then swished a paw at my calico cutie. "Is Curly around?"

The dog growled, and the cat wasn't much friendlier. She rewarded me with a defiant twitch of her tail. When she deigned to answer me she said, "He was asleep on the radiator in the backroom 'bout an hour ago. No reason to think he's quit."

I arched my back at her, making vague promises about being social that I didn't intend to keep, then jumped down off the chair and went in search of the ancient Blue.

Curly was still curled up on the radiator, the knob long ago being set to where the metal was just toasty warm, and not too hot on the paws.

I gave a rumbly-purr to see if I could wake him without scaring him out of one of his nine lives. It took a few minutes, but he snuffled and huffed, stretched and yawned—I listened to the symphony of his cracking joints—then he slowly sat up and looked around the room in a daze.

I gave him a moment. It's hell getting old, but it beats the alternatives.

"Well bless me whiskers and kittens, if it isn't Mickey Yammer! What brings you to this neck of the catnip patch?"

We batted the breeze back and forth for a while, before I got down to business at the scratching post. "Got a job about that picture out front," I said finally.

"Oh, it's not for sale."

"Nah, I mean, did the dogs do it? Did the two little pipsqueaks dupe the dopey mutts? Or was the Terrier set up to take a fall?"

Curly's fur bristled. Arching his back he spat, "Don't go digging in that litterbox. Stinky stuff buried there. Always liked that little Terrier. Wasn't like him to cheat, but he was down on his luck, trouble at home, and that Bulldog was a fast talker—called himself Lucky—mebbe for him, not for his friends. The Terrier did some hard time down at the city pound. Pretty payment for a single ace, and him with three in his hand!"

I nodded.

"The dogs are all dead. Went to Harry the Doberman's funeral just last year."

Curly was confused. The Doberman had been dead for more than a decade. But I didn't interrupt.

"That human's still alive. Talk about double-dealing. Never paid those dogs royalties, and ruined more than one life in the pack. Couldn't face the fame, or the shame of having their gambling predilections exposed," he hissed. "Now he's sniffing around the next generation—wanting them to put their paw prints on legal papers. Says he's got a buyer for some of the original paintings that never sold. Don't know how that could be. Sold six or eight of them, back then, mebbe more. I finally run him off." He scratched the air with a feeble claw. "Stay away from that two-legged swindler, Mickey, if you want to keep what's left of your tail."

It was good advice, but I didn't take it.

Instead, I went back out front, decided it was too late to do any more work anyway, had another bowl or four, and flirted with the flame. The pugs were still there, and they seemed to growl every time they looked at me, but I put that down to the docked tail and my personal paranoia of pooches. I staggered out of the bar under the influence of too much cream around midnight.

I didn't realize the mutts had followed me until I turned down the alley and headed for home. The streetlight behind me backlit them, and suddenly their shadows were looming over me on the brick wall. I turned around to meet my challengers. They were shorter in the flesh, but no less menacing. Great, I was tipsy as a kitten in clover, and about to be roughed up by a pack of pugs.

It wasn't much of a fight, what with there being four of them, and only half of me. They'd been tipped off about the gat—they went for that first thing. I watched an ugly pug bounding down the alley with my gat in his mouth, the string holster dangling behind. Every muscle in my body wanted to chase after that string. But a pug had me pinned from behind, while the other two went to work. I arched my back, extended my claws, and hissed, but it didn't do any good. The mutt behind me hung on, and I just looked like one of those cheap vampires in the movies.

The ugly pug mug in front of me sneered, "Things ain't what they seem, Cat. You're stickin' your whiskers where they don't belong. And they're liable to get clipped."

I was working on a clever comeback, but they'd already rushed past that part of the script. I took a couple of sucker punches to the gut, a roundhouse to the kidneys, and a cuff to the muzzle. Then a black hole opened up in front of me and I jumped into it. Unfortunately, I didn't land on my feet.

Several hours had passed when I came to. A drummer was pounding a Latin number in my head, and a sour taste was leaking out of my mouth. I'd landed on my back. A barrel-load of pain shot through my side as I rolled over and climbed to my feet. With the help of a friendly brick wall I made it. I picked up my fedora and found a milkbone-shaped dog tag lying underneath it—must have fallen off one of the mutts in the scuffle. I tucked it in my hatband, figured it might come in handy somehow. Then I gathered the shreds of my strength together and stumbled to the mouth of the alleyway, where I found my gun. "Great," I thought to myself, "the cat's got his hat and his gat. Now it's time for bed."

I dragged myself out of bed at the crack of noon, and tried to ignore my bruises as I tossed down a bowl of cream and a double-helping of catnip to perk me up. A warm ray of sunshine was poking its nose through my kitchen curtains, and I wanted to go drown in it, but I had work to do.

I headed over to the public library first. You hardly ever get roughed up in the stacks. I figured I could lick my wounds and learn a little something, too.

I started with the phone book, to find out where this Coolidge character lived. It was a good play, but no dice. The book listed a Calvin Marcus Coleridge and a Renford Coolman, but no Coolidge at all. . . . So maybe the Coolidge pedigree line wasn't big on phones.

I checked the Who's Who in the City, but no luck. Then, I tried the Who's Who in the Art World, and hit gravy. Just under an entry about Calvin Marcus Coleridge—especialty cloth art, was CM Coolidge. He had a whopping three-line writeup. Trouble was, one of those lines said he'd died back in '34.

A dead man wasn't stirring the pot, so where did that leave me?

Hopefully with an ace up my sleeve, in the form of a silver bone. On a hunch I fished the dog tag out of my hat and looked it over. The bruiser's name had been, well . . . Bruiser. There was an address on the tag—though I couldn't imagine wanting that mutt back if he chanced to get lost. The address looked familiar.

I flipped the phone book back open to the "C's" and sure enough, the address, and the mutt, belonged to a CMC, just not Coolidge. The address was an exact match for Calvin Marcus Coleridge.

I hiked my tail and skedaddled.

The house was a modest little bungalow, run down at the corners and sagging in the middle. The roof looked like it leaked when it rained, and I wasn't certain the frame porch would support my weight. The place looked quiet, but the pugs had my fur up. I didn't see, hear, or smell any of them around, but I wasn't about to go charging into the rat-trap. I cased the place first, prowling through unmown grass high enough to tickle my ears.

A salsa band was playing on the radio inside. It was the only indication the joint was occupied. Something felt wrong about the place. I jumped onto a low-hanging tree branch that brushed the side of the house, and peeked into the window. My peepers got filled up real quick.

I could see a beer-bellied man who was pushing fifty, and still wore his black beret in the house—in case his artist credentials were in doubt. Had to be Coleridge. Neither art nor time had been kind to him. And he wasn't in a kind mood. He was standing on a threadbare carpet yelling at a run-down couch. I wondered what the couch had done to him to rate that kind of treatment.

He started pacing, and I realized he didn't have a problem with the furniture. On that couch, crouching in fear, was Fifi. I was so surprised I fell out of the tree. I scraped my claws along the side of the house as I fell. I landed on my feet, of course. But by then the damage had been done.

I heard Coleridge shout, "What was that?" as he ran through the house. I clawed my way up to the window sill and knocked frantically on the dirty glass. Fifi looked terrified, but managed to shiver her way over and raise the window with her nose.

"Hi, doll," I said, with more bravado than I felt.

"Yammer! He'll kill you if he finds you here! Hide!"

I heard the sound of heavy boots returning, so I scampered into the bedroom and dived under the bed. The footsteps followed.

I saw the edge of the bedspread being lifted. I darted back out, past the human, and into the next room. What I saw hanging on the wall stopped my flight cold.

It was another painting in that series of card-playing mutts. This was a later version though. Much later. Unfinished, with the paint still wet, kind of later.

It made sense of the whole crazy puzzle. Same mutts, same poses, same ace-passing trick under the table. But instead of a couple of gray walls and a grandfather clock hemming all that in, this had a more interesting background. Behind a bar a pooch was polishing a beer stein while a poodle delivered a bottle of whiskey to the table. The waitress was the spitting image of Fifi, right down to the pink bows pinned behind her ears. I sat on my haunches and let my tongue loll as my brain scratched through the implications.

That quip about her pedigree being taken away made sense now. It'd rung wrong when Fifi had said it, but I hadn't realized why. If she had an uncle who was a Terrier, her pedigree would have been taken away long before he was caught cheating at cards. She was looking to clear her name, but not because of the Terrier's card-sharking. She was trying to hide the fact that her powdered-and-puffed white roots covered a blue-collar barmaid. But why pose for the picture in the first place . . . unless she hadn't been pregnant when the picture was started.

One look at the pooch convinced me I was right.

"Mickey, you have to understand!" She yipped and shivered. "I'd been sold across country, separated from my family. Then my humans abandoned me by the side of the road. They kept my papers—I couldn't prove my pedigree. So I took the barmaid job. But I got fired after I spilled a tray of drinks when that horrid little Bulldog goosed me. Then Coleridge came sniffing around. Offering money if I'd pose for his dirty little painting for him."

I snarled, "So you made a deal with him. And now you want to weasel out."

"But, I didn't know I was pregnant then! What kind of life can I offer my pups if this gets out? They'll be just another pack of mutts tipping over trash cans in the alley, their reputations ruined before they even get their eyes open."

She yapped and shook her head, making the tags on her rhinestone collar jingle. "Besides, isn't what he's doing worse? He's painting new pictures, passing them off as originals. I figured if you could discredit the original artist, prove the first painting was a fake, they'd never release the rest of the paintings. I know I lied to you—but I did it for my pups!"

She was all teary-eyed. If you know anything about dames or dogs, you know poodle-tears are the worst kind. I started to sneer, but the human was standing behind her, and he did enough sneering for both of us.

"Your pups can go to the pet shop, or the pound, for all I care! No one's interested in my designer dresses, but the cigar company wants to revive this dreck! Anniversary editions of the worst art ever put on canvas!" Coleridge waved angrily at the painting. Apparently he wasn't a fan of the original CMC's work.

"Found one of these horrible things hanging on the wall of the house when I moved in. I was hauling it out to the garbage when one of the cigar company executives drove by. Made me an offer on the spot for the whole series. So I passed myself off as the artist, started painting new pictures—the company was willing to buy the whole series. Nobody knew for sure how many there were. So I talked some dogs into posing. Stupid mutts never knew the difference, they thought I was the old man reviving the series."

That made sense. The mutts and Curly would have been taken in by the act. Four-footers don't pay much attention to stray humans. We keep tabs on the ones we keep, but who can keep track of all the humans running loose on the street?

And technically, it wasn't even forgery. He was signing his own name: CM C—a squiggle then an—idge. It was close enough to pass, but left just enough room to weasel out if somebody tumbled to the scam.

Coolidge was still yelling at Fifi. "They're offering good money—obscene amounts of money—it'll set me up with my own shop on the expensive side of town! You think I'm going to let you mess that up! I'll show you what meddling mutts get!"

He pulled his boot back to give the pregnant poodle a swift kick. I leapt forward and shoved her out of the way.

I saw her slide across the hardwood floor just before the boot connected with my head, and I went diving into that black pool again.

I opened my eyes—but it stayed black. I closed them, then tried again, thinking maybe I'd gotten the procedure wrong the first time. No, it was still black.

I didn't buy it was nighttime; I couldn't have been out that long. I heard a whimpering off to my left.

"Fifi?"

"Oh, Mickey!" She sounded relieved.

I didn't see how my waking up made things much better.

She whimpered, "I thought you were dead! That horrid man tossed you in the closet, then shoved me in afterward, and locked the door. He's out there now, ruining my life!"

I didn't point out that my life wasn't any grander from the encounter, either. Instead I asked, "What's going down?"

"The sale! The truck pulled up a few minutes ago. They're loading up all the paintings. They've chosen the 'poodle shot' as the premiere print, but they're going to run the whole series on the cigar boxes. I'm ruined!" she wailed.

"Hold on to your powderpuff," I said. "Maybe not."

My eyes had gotten used to the dark, and I was up on my back legs, trying to pick the lock with one claw. I twisted my paw 'til I heard a faint click. I put a paw on either side of the knob, and gave my body a sharp wrench to the left. It woke up the old bruises, but it released the latch. We were free.

"Quick, Fifi. Out the back and into the truck! Wait 'til they go into the house."

We scampered outside, hid in the bushes, then made a run for it. A quick jump later and we were in the truck, scrambling to hide behind some of the canvases before the workmen could come back.

We were just in time. They shoved one more canvas inside then slammed the door. I heard them say something about Midtown. I gave a Cheshire grin. The ride would take more than an hour—plenty of time to apply paws and piddle to the stack of paintings.

Cat's-Eye Witness

MAX ALLAN COLLINS

PIERCE HARTWELL REMOVED the pillow from his wife's face, relieved to see her expression was not one of agony but peace. She had not suffered. She had, as Pierce expected her death certificate would verify, passed away in her sleep.

The lanky, darkly handsome, pencil-mustached Pierce, wearing the wine-colored silk robe he'd received from Esther on their tenth anniversary not long ago, took one step back, pillow still held delicately in two hands as if he had brought it to his wife's bedside to present her with comfort, not oblivion. He stood poised there, as if waiting for Esther to wake up, knowing—hoping—she would not. The once beautiful, now withered features of the eighty-year-old woman had a calm cast, the simple white nightgown almost suggesting a hospital garment.

"Good-bye, darling," he whispered to the dead woman, feeling something almost like sadness. He was breathing hard, as hard as when of late he'd made love to the woman, an act that had increasingly taken his full effort and intense concentration.

When he had married Esther Balmfry ten years ago, she had been an attractive matron, slender and elegant on the cruise-ship dance floor. Pierce, at that time forty-five and wearying of his gigolo existence, had considered Esther a prime candidate for settling down. Prior to this, he had flitted from one fading flower to another, providing love in return for financial favors; but he had never married. Never considered it.

But—on that cruise ship a decade ago—Pierce had noticed several others of his ilk plucking the faded flowers from his field, men younger, newer at the game, fresher. Pierce had begun dyeing his hair, and wearing a stomach-flattening brace (he could never, even mentally, bring himself to say "girdle"), and had sensed that perhaps it was time to settle down. Pick one rich old girl who he could put up with for a few years before that "tragic" day when his beloved went where all rich old widows eventually go.

And Esther was childless, had no close relatives—except for Pierce, of course. Her loving husband.

These ten years with Esther had been increasingly difficult. The remnants of her beauty waned, though her health remained steadfastly sound. Her last physical—a few weeks ago—had elicited a virtual rave review from her doctor, who said she had the body of a woman twenty years younger.

That was easy for the doctor to say: the doctor hadn't had to sleep with her.

"My mother lived to see one hundred," Esther had announced over muffins and tea last week in the breakfast nook, her creped neck waving good morning to him. "And father lived to be ninety-eight."

"Really," Pierce had said, spreading strawberry jam on his muffin.

"Looks like you're going to be stuck with me for a while, darling," she'd said, patting his hand.

He'd always been given a generous allowance, but Pierce knew that Esther's fortune was a considerable one, and the life he could lead with access to that kind of cash would go a long way toward making up for the indignities of the last ten years. At fifty-five he had living left to do. If he waited around for Esther to pass away of natural causes, he'd be a geezer himself.

Or, if her health did finally go, but gradually, that fortune could be decimated by medical bills.

Pierce didn't dislike Esther, though he certainly didn't love her. He didn't feel much of anything for her, really: she was just a means to an end. And now her end could be his means to a new, unencumbered life.

And then there was that goddamned cat: that had been another factor, another catalyst to spark this unpleasant but necessary deed.

Clarence (named for her late husband), the mangy brown beast, had turned up at the door last year and Esther had welcomed it in, grooming it, taking it to the vet to be "fixed," lavishing attention upon the thing as if it were a child. Pierce and the cat kept their distance—once the cat learned that Pierce would kick it or toss something its way any time its mistress wasn't about—but just the presence of the animal meant distress to Pierce, who was after all allergic to cats.

His first act, as the master of the house, the sole human inhabitant of the near mansion (they had no live-in household staff), would be to toss that animal back out into the winter night, into the cold world from which it had emerged.

Just thinking about the beast—as Pierce stood at the bedside, taking his wife's pulse, making sure she was in fact deceased—made his eyes burn, his nose twitch.

No ... that was no psychosomatic response: *that wretched animal was somewhere nearby!*

Pierce turned sharply and there it was: sitting like some Egyptian statue of a feline, the brown, blue-eyed beast stared at him, eyes in unblinking accusation.

"Did you witness it, then?" Pierce said to the animal. "Did you see what I did to your mistress?"

It cocked its head at him.

Sniffling, Pierce said, "I liked her. . . . Imagine what I'll do to you."

And he hurled the pillow at the creature.

But Clarence leapt nimbly from harm's way, onto the plush carpet, padding silently but quickly out of the bedroom, a blur of brown.

Pierce ran after the animal, chasing it down the curving stairs, past paintings by American masters, into a vast dark living room where the cat's tiny claws had damaged precious Duncan Phyfe antiques. The thing scampered behind a davenport and Pierce threw on the lights, pulled out the heavy piece of furniture . . . but the cat was gone.

For hours he stalked the house, with a rolled-up newspaper in hand, looking behind furniture, searching this nook and that cranny of the expansive six-bedroom spread, checking in closets and in the basement and the most absurdly unlikely of places . . . even under the bed where his late wife slept her dreamless sleep.

No sign of Clarence.

By dawn Pierce had given up the chase, figuring the cat had found some way out of the house. Exhausted, he sat in the breakfast nook with a cup of coffee, drinking the bitter brew, wondering if it was too early to phone 911 about the unsettling discovery of his deceased wife next to him in bed. He raised the cup to his lips and the cat jumped up onto the table and stared at him with its deep blue unblinking accusatory eyes.

I saw what you did, the cat seemed to say.

Spilling his coffee, Pierce reached for its throat, but the beast deftly, mockingly, dove to the floor and scampered across the well-waxed tiles and into the living room.

Racing after it, Pierce spent another hour searching high and low before he finally gave up—and realized the house was in a terrible disarray from his search. It took better than an hour to straighten the furniture, smooth various throw rugs and otherwise make the place look as normal as possible.

At eight o'clock Pierce called 911, working up considerable alarm as he said, "Come quickly! I can't rouse my wife! She won't wake up!"

The paramedics came, and Pierce—not even taking time to dress—accompanied them in the ambulance, but Esther was of course D.O.A. at the emergency room. Rigor mortis had begun to set in. He put on his best distraught act, working up some tears, moaning to the attending physician about his inadequacy as a husband.

"If only I'd been awake!" Pierce said. "To think I was asleep beside her, even as she lay dying!"

This melodrama seemed to convince the doctor, who calmed Pierce, saying, "There's no need to blame yourself for this, Mr. Hartwell. There's every indication that your wife slipped away peacefully in her sleep."

"I . . . I guess I'll have to find solace in that, won't I?"

By eleven A.M., Pierce was back home, driven there by one of the ambulance attendants. He was whistling as he went up the curving stairway, almost racing to the bedroom where he had murdered his wife. He went to the closet to select appropriately somber apparel for the day—there were arrangements to make, starting with the funeral home—and when he reached for his charcoal suitcoat, the cat leapt from the shelf above, as if jumping right at him.

But it wasn't: Clarence scampered up onto the bed and resumed its Egyptian-style posture and again affixed its blankly reproachful blue-eyed gaze at him. Pierce moved slowly toward the animal, which twitched its nose; as if at this bidding, Pierce's own nose twitched, and began to run, his eyes starting to burn. He leapt at the cat with clawed hands, but the animal adroitly avoided its master's grasp and again fled the bedroom.

This time Pierce did not follow. He sat on the edge of the bed, at its foot, and caught his breath. Slowly the symptoms of his allergy eased, and he rose and finished dressing.

The cat's next appearance came when Pierce was seated in his study, at the desk, calling the Ferndale Funeral Home. He was halfway through the conversation with the undertaker when the cat nimbly jumped up onto the desk, just out of his reach, and stared at him as he completed his phone conversation. Gradually the allergy symptoms returned, his eyes watering, burning, puffing up.

The undertaker, hearing Pierce's sniffling, said, "I know this must be a difficult time for you, Mr. Hartwell."

"Thank you, Mr. Ballard. It has been difficult."

And as Pierce hung up the phone, the cat sprang from the desk and scurried out of the room.

Pierce didn't bother following it.

The police came that afternoon, two of them, plainclothes detectives, a craggy, thickset lieutenant named March with eyebrows as wild as cat's whiskers, and a younger detective named Anderson, ruggedly handsome but also quietly sullen.

Pierce knew Lt. March a bit, as the onetime Chicago homicide cop who had married a wealthy widow several years before, the couple a staple of country club dances, where the detective was viewed as a "character" among the city's captains of industry and inheritors of wealth.

They sat in the study, with Pierce behind the desk, the two men across from him, as if this were a business appointment. Pierce hadn't offered to take their topcoats and neither man took his off as they sat and talked—a good sign. This wouldn't take long.

"Pierce," Lt. March said, with a familiarity that wasn't quite earned, and with a thickness of speech that reflected a stroke the detective had suffered a year before, "I hope you know that you have our deepest sympathy."

By "our," Pierce wasn't sure whether March was referring to Mrs. March or his fellow detective, the younger man whose unblinking gaze seemed to contain at least a hint of suspicion.

"I appreciate that . . . Bill."

March smiled; one side of his face seemed mildly affected by that stroke, and his speech had a measured manner, as if every single word had to be cooked in his mind before he served it up. "There is the formality of a statement. We can do that here, if you'd like. Save you a trip to the Public Safety Building."

"Certainly."

Anderson withdrew a small tape recorder from his topcoat pocket, clicked it on and set it, upright, on the edge of the desk. The recorder emitted a faint whirring.

"When did you discover that Esther had passed away?" March asked.

"When I woke up," Pierce said, and his nose began to twitch.

"What time was that, would you say?"

"Well, just minutes, probably moments, before I called 911. I didn't look at the clock." His eyes were running now; that cat—that cat was somewhere in this room! "Don't you record those calls?"

"Yes."

"So you can verify the time that way."

"Yes we can."

Pierce felt a rustling at his feet; glancing down, he saw the damned thing, sitting under the desk, at his feet, staring up at him with those spooky, un-blinking blue eyes.

Sniffling, he reached for a tissue from a box on the desktop. Blew his nose, dried his eyes, and said, "Sorry, gentlemen."

"We know this is difficult for you," March said.

"Terribly difficult," Pierce said, and withdrew another tissue.

The statement was brief—what was there to tell?—but once the tape recorder had been clicked off, Anderson said, "We'd like you to authorize an au-topsy, Mr. Hartwell."

"Why is that necessary?"

"I think you know."

There was something nasty about Anderson's tone, and Pierce said, huffily, "What are you implying, sir?"

March frowned at his partner, then, smiling at Pierce, sat forward. "Pierce, I'd like to be candid, if I might."

"Certainly."

"When a wealthy elderly woman—who has recently married a relatively younger man—dies under circumstances that are even remotely questionable, it's incumbent upon the police to investigate."

What did he mean, "relatively younger"?

"An autopsy," March continued, "should establish your wife's death by natural causes, and we can all go on with our lives."

"Bill," Pierce said, invoking the lieutenant's first name, "considering the fact that many people in our fair community have accused *you* of marrying for money, you're hardly anyone to—"

"Mrs. March isn't dead," Anderson interrupted.

"Gentlemen," March said, holding out two palms. "Please. This is an unfortunate situation . . . a tragic situation. Let's not get into name-calling or personalities."

Eyes burning, Pierce said, "Of course I'll authorize an autopsy, distasteful though a debasement of my dear late wife's remains are to me. Just tell me what you need me to do."

When Pierce had seen the detectives out, he returned to his study, hoping the cat would still be in the well of the desk. Pierce's intention was to trap the cat, perhaps cage it up in a wastebasket, and hurl the creature into the cold late afternoon air, where it could either fend for itself or freeze itself to death—preferably the latter.

But there was no sign of the cat. He looked everywhere, irritated but relatively calm, not allowing himself the indignity of turning the house topsy-turvy again, which would only require him to set it aright. Clearly the cat had finally sensed the obvious: that Pierce meant Clarence harm.

Sooner or later it would come out, to its water and food dishes.

So Pierce set out fresh water and food for the animal—the cat food liberally laced with rat poison—and, whistling, dressed for dinner.

Since they had no cook (Esther had enjoyed preparing breakfasts and lunches herself), the couple's habit was to dine out. In a town the size of Ferndale, only a handful of suitable restaurants presented themselves—the country club and the hotel, chiefly. Pierce chose the latter, not wanting to chance running into March and his wife at the former.

He was famished and hoped the staff at the hotel restaurant—who went out of their way to express their sympathy, to stop by and comment about how much they would miss the sweet, kind Esther—did not consider him callous, to eat so heavily and drink so heartily. He hoped they would consider him to be drowning his sorrows, as opposed to what he was really doing, which was celebrating.

At home, mildly tipsy and extremely drowsy, his stomach warm and full, Pierce lumbered up the curving stairs. When he found himself in the bedroom—the bedroom he and Esther had shared—a chill passed through the room, and him. Winter wind rattled frost-decorated windows. Telling himself he wanted to get away from the draft, he stumbled down the hall into one of the guest bedrooms.

Clothed in the Armani suit he'd worn to dinner, taking time only to step out of his Italian loafers, he flopped onto the bed, on his back. Had his conscience sent him into this bedroom? Did he feel guilty about what he'd done to Esther? These thoughts were worthy only of his laughter, with which he filled the room, laughing until his tiredness took over and sent him almost immediately into a deep sleep.

He awoke, not with a start, but gradually, groggily, with the growing sensation of pressure on his chest. He reached for the nightstand lamp, clicked it on, and stared into the blue unblinking eyes of the brown animal sitting on top of him.

Staring at him.

Staring into him.

The accusatory stare of the witness to the murder he'd committed. . . .

Screaming, Pierce sat up, flinging the cat off him. The beast rolled and came up running, scurrying out, claws clicking on the varnished wood of the hallway.

And Pierce was after the animal, chasing it down the winding stairs, darkness relieved only by moonlight filtering in through frosted windows. This time there would be no frantic search of the house. This time he would prevail.

As the cat headed into the living room, Pierce dove, and in a careening tackle that took over an end table and sent a lamp clattering, crashing, to the floor, Pierce scooped the animal in his arms and held it tight. Clarence fought, but its claws were facing outward as Pierce hugged it around the belly.

The nearest door was the front one, and, lugging the squirming beast, Pierce made his way there, holding tight around the cat's belly with one arm and with the other reaching to open the door, swinging it open, flinging the beast into the deadly cold night.

Slamming the door behind it.

No sounds came from beyond the closed door: that cat didn't want back inside, no matter how cold it was. For the longest time, Pierce sat on the floor with his back to the door, folding his arms tightly, laughing, laughing, laughing, until tears were rolling down his cheeks, never aware exactly when the glee gave way to weeping.

At some point he found his way back to the bedroom, where, exhausted, he quickly fell to sleep. He had nightmares but on waking didn't remember them—they just clung to his mind the way the taste of sleep coated his mouth. But he was able to brush his teeth and deal with the latter; the taste of the unremembered dreams stuck with him.

Nonetheless, the morning passed uneventfully, without any particular stress. Noting that the poisoned cat food had not been touched, he emptied the bowl into the sink and down the garbage disposal. He washed his hands thoroughly before preparing himself an English muffin and coffee. He showered, shaved, and was feeling fairly refreshed, wearing the same silk robe he'd killed his wife in, when the phone rang.

"Could you come down here, to the Public Safety Building?" Lt. March asked.

"Am I needed?"

"We have the results of your wife's autopsy, and we'd like to discuss them with you . . . if it's not inconvenient."

At one o'clock, wearing a Pierre Cardin sports jacket and no tie, Pierce Hartwell walked to March's office on the first floor of the modern Ferndale Public Safety Building. The door to the modest office was open and March was seated behind his desk, with Anderson in a chair by a cement block wall.

And on top of the desk, seated off to the left like an oversize paperweight, was the cat.

Clarence.

Sitting and staring with its terrible blue eyes—right at Pierce.

"Have a seat," March said.

Swallowing, Pierce pulled up a chair, opposite March and as far away as possible from the brown beast. The goddamn thing looked none the worse for wear: no sign that it had spent a terrible frostbitten night, perfectly groomed, even purring, as it stared accusingly at Pierce.

March said, "Mr. Hartwell, there is a disturbing aspect that's turned up in the autopsy."

"What . . . what are you talking about?"

The cat seemed to stare right through him. The cat. The witness. Could they somehow know this cat had witnessed the murder? The goddamn thing couldn't have told them. He was a cat!

March was saying, "Your wife's eyes . . ."

The cat's eyes. . . .

". . . had severe hemorrhaging."

Pierce began sniffling. "Uh . . . uh, what do you mean?"

Anderson, sitting back, arms folded, said, "Clotting. The whites of your wife's eyes were so clotted with burst vessels they were damn near completely red."

From the nearby desktop, Clarence, the cat, stared at Pierce, whose eyes had begun to burn. *I saw what you did,* he seemed to say.

"A person suffering suffocation tries so hard to breathe," March said, "the blood vessels burst in the eyes."

Eyes.

Cat's eyes. . . .

His own eyes, burning, burning. . . .

"We've been doing a background search on you, Mr. Hartwell," Anderson said. "You met your wife on a cruise ship, isn't that correct?"

"*How could you know?*" Pierce blurted.

"Very simple," Anderson said.

Pierce lurched forward in his chair. "You found it outside in the cold, didn't you? What did you do, go into my house and find that poisoned food? Did you have a warrant? Perhaps I should call my attorney."

The two detectives glanced at each other; but the cat was looking right at Pierce—and the animal seemed to shake its head, no. . . .

"He couldn't have told you anything," Pierce said, and laughed as he nodded toward Clarence. "A goddamn cat can't talk."

Anderson started to say something, but March waved a hand and the younger detective fell silent.

"Go on, Mr. Hartwell," March said.

"You're very clever, Lieutenant. How did you do it? How could you know that that cat witnessed what I did?"

"*What* did you do, Mr. Hartwell?"

"You know damn good and well." Water was running from his eyes—not tears, just that burning goddamn allergy kicking in. "You just said so yourself. I smothered her—with a pillow. But she didn't suffer. I would never have done that. Never."

Nodding slowly, March got on the phone and called for a uniformed cop. Pierce just sat there, avoiding the gaze of the purring cat on the detective's desk. The damn thing seemed to be smiling, a Cheshire cat, now.

"If you'll go with this gentleman," March said, standing, gesturing past the animal to the police officer who was now standing in the doorway, "he'll escort you to a room where you can make your full statement. We'll be with you momentarily."

Pierce could only nod. He needed help to get to his feet and the police officer gave it to him.

"How did you know?" Pierce asked from the doorway, eyes watering, nose running. "How in God's name could you know about the cat?"

The two detectives said nothing.

Then Pierce was gone, and Anderson said, "That's one for the books. We could never have made our case on those clotted eyes alone. His gigolo background woulda helped, but . . ."

"Maybe he had a conscience."

"That guy?" Anderson snorted and waved at the air. "No way in hell."

Shrugging, March got on the phone and arranged for a technician to meet them at the interrogation room.

Then, hanging up, March shook his head and asked Anderson, "What do you suppose he was going on about?"

"What do you mean?"

"You know—that business about a cat?"

The two men widened their eyes, shrugged at each other, and left the empty office to take the confession.

The Cat's Jewels

T. M. BRADSHAW

THE WEDNESDAY AFTERNOONS SPENT at the library, surfing the Net, sometimes generated leads for Sheila to follow, but she much preferred actually following them to sitting in front of a screen. This Wednesday, she was just about to sign off when she saw an odd little news item.

> *CULTISTS WANT EYES RETURNED*
>
> *The Knighted Issue of Tum-Tum's Enlightened Neophytes (KITTEN), a new-age group with a philosophy that combines astrology, alien research, and Egyptian-style cat worship, has demanded that the Rehnquist Museum return two jewels, a sapphire and an emerald, to their rightful positions as the eyes in the golden statue of a cat, believed to have been owned by Cleopatra. The statue is in the Rehnquist's Egyptian collection. A spokesman for the Rehnquist said that when the museum acquired the statue at auction in nineteen forty-six, the eye cavities were empty. KITTEN maintains that that was the year the gems disappeared and referred to old rumors that Jacob Rehnquist removed them from the statue as gifts for his mistress, actress Astrid Cygnet. The group believes the gems are currently hidden somewhere in the museum.*
>
> *Felix Kopff, Grand High Priest of KITTEN, said that if the eyes are not in place at the stroke of midnight for the start of the new millennium, Tum-Tum will be unable to see into the future and the world will end. Recently, there have been several small fires at the museum. Mr. Kopff denies allegations connecting KITTEN with the fires, although he has previously been quoted as saying his organization "will spare no effort to smoke out the stones."*

Well, here was an interesting little piece. Just the sort of thing she could use to generate articles on art, terrorism, archaeology, and quasi-religious cults. Yes, just exactly the right sort of thing. The place to start of course would be the Rehnquist. Sheila checked her watch—1:30. If she were really lucky, she might even get an appointment for this afternoon. She pulled her cell phone and the phone book out of her backpack. Her boyfriend, Tom, always teased her about toting a Manhattan phone book around, but she said that not having to pay for information calls was like getting paid to exercise.

"Mr. Avery, I appreciate you seeing me on such short notice." While appearing to have difficulty deciding which seat to choose, Sheila surveyed the room with a reporter's eye. It was tastefully decorated, about what one would expect an office in a nineteenth-century-home-turned-museum to look like—lots of maroon leather, mirror-polished wood, heavy drapes, and brass lamps with pleated shades.

"Not at all, Ms. Fremont. That is my job here, press liaison." He gestured to one of a pair of wing chairs pulled up to a mahogany table. "Please, sit down. I thought that perhaps we could have tea while we talk. Which paper did you say you were from?"

"Well, actually I didn't. I'm not from a paper. I freelance."

"Oh, I see. And what sort of article are you researching now?" He poured tea from a china pot that was a replica of the museum building. "Sugar? Lemon? Cream?"

"Lemon and sugar, please. I was browsing around, looking for an idea when I stumbled on this KITTEN story and as I've always been fascinated by Egyptian art...."

"The KITTEN story! There is no KITTEN story." Edward Avery was obviously very agitated; the museum teapot in his hand was shaking as if in an earthquake. "Who are you really? You call out of the blue, you have no press card, no credentials, no way for me to know that you are who you say you are! Why should I talk to you?"

"Mr. Avery, I didn't mean to upset you. If you want I'll leave and come back another time. I'd be happy to bring some clips, references, whatever would make you more comfortable. The only thing I have with me now that I could show you is my driver's license, if that would help. Or would you like me to just leave?" Sheila hoped the offer to leave would calm him down enough to talk.

Avery set down the teapot and collapsed back into his chair like a starched tea towel dropped into hot water. "I'm really very sorry, Ms. Fremont. Those KITTEN people have been a trial around here for weeks, calling, accusing, and threatening. And of course, it's my job to straighten it out without involving Mr. Rehnquist. Forgive me, please. Of course there's a story. It's not every day that the lunatic fringe threatens to set fire to an important museum. Would you pour? I'm not quite up to it."

"I'd be happy to, Mr. Avery." Sheila thought that, since Avery was being so apologetic, she'd better cover as much ground as she could. "Would you mind if I record our conversation? Taking notes distracts from one's attention, don't you think?"

A platinum tabby entered the room and wove a figure eight around their ankles. Her hind legs were black to the knee, but only in the back, giving the appearance of gartered black stockings. She was soft and fluffy and a little small for an adult cat.

"Oh, what a beautiful cat. Is she yours, Mr. Avery?"

He sneezed in response "No, Ms. Fremont. I don't like cats and am allergic to them, but Mr. Rehnquist allows Katie the run of the place. One of these days she'll probably knock over a Ming vase. Shoo, go on, shoo, get out of here." But of course, cats do not shoo easily. Katie jumped up on Edward Avery's desk and settled down with her front legs tucked under her body. With her eyes closed down to little slits, she purred through the entire interview. But Sheila noticed that Katie's ears twitched now and again.

Sheila and Tom stopped just short of the steps of the Rehnquist.

"I don't understand what the big deal is, Tom. Lots of people go to museums."

"Sure. But they don't go to snoop around behind doors that say 'No Admittance.' Can't you work from the interview tape? Why do we have to do this?"

"Tom, we are not snooping, we're absorbing atmosphere. That's just as important as the facts—more important, if the only 'facts' you uncover are what you knew in the first place. Avery didn't tell me anything that hasn't already been printed. Come on. I wanted you to see this place inside anyway. It's fantastic to think of it as someone's house. How long has it been since we went to a museum?" Sheila took Tom's hand and led him up the steps. They stopped just inside and looked around. The black and white floor tiles were marble and two identical sweeps of stairs curved opposite each other in giant mirror-image S-curves. They did not connect with a landing at the top; if there was a connection between the east and west wings somewhere else upstairs, it was not visible.

"I wonder where these go," said Sheila, walking toward the flight on the left. Tom squeezed her hand. "Upstairs. They go upstairs, where we don't belong. Shall we go look at the cat? That is why we're here, isn't it?"

"Okay, okay. We'll go absorb a little atmosphere."

The hushed museum silence was intensified in the long, narrow Egyptian room. Tum-Tum occupied the place of honor at the far end, the focal point of the room. It was quite large, almost tiger size. Its blind stare somehow seemed to focus on a glass case of papyruses. There was a vague scent of incense in the room.

"Tom, I'll be right back. Wait for me here, all right?"

"Oh no, Sheila. I can't let you go trespassing around here alone. I'm coming with you."

"To the ladies' room? I'll be right back, Tom. Have a look at the mummy."

Sheila walked briskly out of the Egyptian room and into the main entrance hall. As she stood surveying the room for a sign of her destination, she felt a soft rub against her ankles. "Well hello, Katie. Do you remember me or do you rub up against all the guests?" The cat *riaow*ed in response and ran toward the stairs. "Bye, girl. See you later." Sheila spotted the door to the ladies' room and strode toward it. Katie ran back and wove between Sheila's feet, almost tripping her. "Hey, cut that out. You don't want me to fall and crack my head on the marble, do you?" A guard approached, looking apologetic. "Do you want me to remove the cat, Miss? Katie can be quite a nuisance." Katie hissed at him from behind Sheila's ankles. "No, thank you. Katie and I are old friends. But could you tell me where the ladies' room is?"

"Just behind you."

"Thanks." Sheila smiled at him and then she and Katie went through the door together, with Katie swishing her tail at the guard in a gesture of superiority.

When they came out, the guard had left. Sheila started walking toward the Egyptain room, but Katie *riaow*ed, ran toward the curving staircase on the right and back again.

"Katie, Lassie was a dog and I don't believe I'm talking to a cat." Katie ran back and forth again, *riaow*ing insistently. Sheila looked around furtively and headed toward the stairs.

"Okay, Katie. You lead and I'll follow. Boy, is Tom going to be mad." The long flight led to a corridor of doors, all shut. Katie sat in front of the third one on the left. Sheila tried the door—it opened into a lovely sitting room, full of overstuffed pink floral upholstered furniture. A fire roared in an ornate rose marble fireplace. Over the mantle hung a large portrait of a stunning brunette woman with a black swan on her lap. The woman's right arm curved around the swan's neck, stroking it in a protective embrace, while her left arm lay draped over the swan's body, hand extended, palm up, offering what appeared to be two eggs, one blue and one green. "Oh wow, Katie . . . the jewels. This must be a picture of. . . . "

"My beloved Astrid. Who are you, young woman, and how did you get in here?"

Sheila wheeled around. A very elegant, very old man stood near the window. He looked angry. "Mr. Rehnquist? Jacob Rehnquist? I'm Sheila Fremont. I interviewed Mr. Avery earlier today and well, this is going to sound silly, but your cat, Katie, brought me here."

"The only part that sounds silly is suggesting that Katie is my cat. We share this house, but she is most definitely her own cat." He sat down in a chair near the fire and Katie jumped up onto his lap. She purred while he scratched under her chin. "Isn't that right, girl?"

"Mr. Rehnquist, this portrait of Ms. Cygnet is beautiful. But the eggs, aren't those the missing jewels that KITTEN is demanding?"

Katie stood up in Jacob Rehnquist's lap and turned around a few times before settling back down. Sheila wasn't sure but it seemed that a few tail flicks were aimed at her in an admonitory way.

Rehnquist sighed. "Oh those ridiculous KITTEN people again. Didn't Avery explain all that? There aren't any jewels, there never were. When I first saw Tum-Tum, in the Thirties, her eyes were there; when she came up for sale, they were gone. Things do disappear during wars, you know."

"But, Mr. Rehnquist, what are these in the painting?"

"Ms. Fremont, is the sophistication of your generation limited to technology? I thought your music videos were supposed to be layered with meaning. You seem to be an intelligent young woman. I don't imagine you believe the *bird* actually sat for the artist, do you? It's something of an allegorical painting, Astrid giving me something I missed. The painting was a gift from her on my thirty-fifth birthday, in 1946, the same year I bought that damned eyeless cat." Katie jumped down from Rehnquist's lap. He brushed the cat hair from his trouser legs. "I'm very tired, Mrs. Fremont. I believe Katie can show you out." He leaned back in the chair and closed his eyes.

Sheila resisted an urge to slide down the walnut banister more from fear of landing on the marble floor than of preserving her dignity. Walking with and talking to a cat wasn't very dignified. "So, Katie, thanks for introducing me to Mr. Rehnquist, but I don't really know anything new." An alarm sounded. "What's that?" Sheila raced down the stairs.

Guards were rushing around, grabbing fire extinguishers and talking on walkie-talkies. The exit lights were flashing. Sheila spotted Tom as he ran into the main lobby from the west wing. "Tom, over here, Tom. What's going on?"

Katie was *riao*wing and running back and forth between them and the foot of the other flight of stairs.

"Why ask me? I figured you triggered the alarm snooping around. Where have you been?"

"Upstairs. Katie took me to see the jewels. Here, let's go in here." She pushed him, and with Katie they disappeared into the ladies' room.

"Oh, great. Will they prosecute me as a trespasser or a pervert?" Tom sank down onto a sofa. "Hey, this is nice. There isn't a lounge in the men's room."

Sheila sat down beside him. "A holdover from the age of fainting. You never know when a woman will need to sit down. It's pretty convenient, actually." She looked over at Katie, who was sitting in the chair opposite the sofa and chewing on a spider plant on the end table. "Well, what do you suggest we do now."

"I think we should get out of here. The building may be on fire."

"Tom, I was talking to Katie."

Katie jumped from her chair to Tom's lap and began kneading his chest and purring.

"She likes you, Tom. Isn't she a sweet girl?"

"She's just trying to keep me here, Sheila. Actually she reminds me a lot of you."

After about half an hour, although the museum seemed very quiet to Sheila and Tom, Katie's ears twitched and she jumped down from Tom's lap and rubbed against the door.

"Guess it's time to go. Katie's ready," Sheila whispered.

"Go where? You're planning on going somewhere other than out the front door?" Tom looked skeptical.

"If the museum is closed, going out the front door will definitely set off an alarm. We're better off following Katie." Sheila opened the door a little and peered out. The entrance hall seemed to be empty. "Come on. Let's go."

Katie headed straight for the left staircase and trotted up, pausing every ten steps or so to glance back and check that they were still following. At the top of the flight there was another corridor of doors. She paced back and forth in front of the third one.

Sheila reached for the doorknob and Tom reached for her hand to stop her. "You know what they say—curiosity killed the writer who was with the cat. Let's go. We can still get out of here without any trouble."

Sheila opened the door and they all tumbled in. It was a mirror image of the room with the swan portrait—except it was all blue with an onyx fireplace. The portrait above the mantle must have been Jacob Rehnquist in his late twenties or early thirties. In it he was standing with an elbow resting on a bookshelf, his fist against his cheekbone. In his other hand he held a copy of *Gulliver's Travels*. There was a muffled sound, like a soft sneeze. Katie leapt up and paced on one of the shelves *riaowing* insistently. Two more sneezes seemed to come from the corridor. As Sheila walked toward the bookcase, Katie jumped down. Sheila scanned the titles on the shelf and picked up a book. Behind *Gulliver's Travels* was a key.

"What do you think this is for, Tom?" Sheila said, turning around. Edward Avery was standing behind Tom, holding a gun to his head. Avery aimed a kick at Katie and missed as she ran out the door.

"Your boyfriend probably hasn't got a clue, Ms. Fremont, but I do. There's a locked chest in the Egyptian room that old Jake is very touchy about. Since the best place to hide something is in plain sight, I believe that's where I'm going to find the jewels. Just put the key on the desk and lie down on the floor, please."

"What good will that do? The jewels and the statue belong to Mr. Rehnquist. If he chooses not to display them. . . ."

Avery laughed. "Don't be so naïve. I'm not a member of KITTEN. I had hoped that their ranting would get Jake to take me into his confidence, so when he dies I could just pocket the jewels, but this works just as well. With all that's been going on, who could blame me for shooting a couples of trespassers. The key, please."

"No, Edward, the gun please. The key is mine." Jacob Rehnquist stood behind Avery, holding a gun to *his* head. "And I've already called Security, so there's no point in anyone getting shot."

Tom stepped away and took the gun from Avery's hand.

"And Edward, don't waste any time in your cell dreaming of what might have been. I never had the jewels."

"But the rose-room portrait . . . and the locked chest?" Avery looked thunderstruck.

"Ms. Fremont can explain the portrait, and the chest is filled with pictures and letters from my years with Astrid. Oh good, here's Security now. Here you are, gentlemen, our arsonist and would-be murderer and jewel thief. When the police arrive, they'll find us in the rose room, having a brandy."

Katie *riaow*ed.

"And some catnip. Ms. Fremont, have you ever considered writing a biography? I think Astrid would have liked that."

The Catawampus Caper

WILL MURRAY

BILL BRUNT PULLED UP TO THE faded lavender Victorian on the corner of Lost Squantum Street and Muskonontip Road. The Squantum Street entrance bore a shingle that read: MISS GINA, PSYCHIC READER. Brunt carried the wrapped package to the more discreet Muskonontip side door.

The doorbell read: G. SCONDERELLA. He rang it.

A moment later, a tall, striking redhead popped open the door. Her brown eyes warmed at the sight of Brunt. He lifted the package, and they leaped with childish glee.

"Happy birthday," Brunt said, poker-faced.

"You remembered! Come on in."

Brunt followed Gina Sconderella into a modest kitchen decorated in stark black and white floor and wall tiles.

"You're staying for the surprise party, of course," she said, plopping the box onto the kitchen table.

"If it's a surprise, how do you know about it?" Brunt asked.

"Because I'm a professional psychic, you silly private dick."

"At least you didn't say dickhead," Brunt muttered. "And I can't. Have to stake out a place."

Her eyebrows quirked. "Oh. Can you use my help? Business is slow."

"I'll call you," Brunt said quickly. "Now open it. I want to see the look in your eyes when you. . . ."

Gina placed her hands against the package. She closed her eyes. Her Italian features bunched in concentration.

"It's black and white, whatever it is."

Brunt looked surprised. "That's a pretty good guess."

She shot him a withering look. "I'm also seeing fur. . . ."

Brunt looked even more surprised.

"You bought me a fur!" Gina squealed, reading his expression. Eagerly tearing away wrapping, she exposed a plain cardboard box. Punch holes decorated all sides. Her face fell.

"If you bought me a pet turtle, I will throttle you."

"It's not a turtle," Brunt promised.

Flipping the box flaps, Gina Sconderella peered within.

The box was filled with white Styrofoam packing peanuts. Nestled at the bottom slept a tiny tuxedo cat decorated with a red ribbon. One white-mittened paw covered its eyes protectively.

"A *kitten*?"

Brunt grinned blandly. "Her name is Spooky. I knew you'd fall in love at first sight."

"I already *have* a cat."

"Rags? He's old. You never know when he's going to take that great catnap in the sky. Spooky's perfect for you, what with your business and all. Black cats provide atmosphere."

"Are you up to something?"

"Am I ever?" Brunt countered.

Gina lifted up the cat. Spooky cuddled in her hands as docile as a baby chick. The cat's eyes opened. They were a yellow-green color. "She does have cute eyes. . . ." she ventured.

Brunt started for the door. "I'll just let you two get to know each other better," he said hastily. "Gotta run."

"Don't you want to say hello to Rags?"

"Naw. Tell the big gray wampus cat I'll catch him later."

Brunt drove around the corner, shook open a copy of the morning *Globe* and began reading patiently.

A police prowl car drifted up, and the driver's-side window rolled down.

"You up to anything I should know about, Brunt?" a dark-featured cop asked.

"Just trying to reclaim some property from a certain party, Walter."

"You keep hanging around that fortune-teller and people are going to think you've gone soft."

"They think that already," Brunt said. "I'll survive."

The prowl car slithered away. Dusk fell.

After about forty minutes, Brunt heard a ferocious frenzy of hissing and spitting, followed by the hard smack of a rolled newspaper against flesh and fur.

Out of the open second-floor window leaped a gray and white ball of energy that looked like a genetic collision between a Maine coon cat and a Russian forest cat, with touches of Siamese and Persian thrown into the mix.

Rags the cat raced around the porch roof to a spindly pear tree that grew too close to the house. Leaping into the tree, he came crashing down, ears pinned back in feline frustration.

"Right on time," muttered Brunt, keying the ignition.

Rags was galloping across the street when Brunt pulled up and popped open the passenger-side door.

"Rags! Here. In here, boy."

Rags hesitated. His ears went forward and backward. His pale golden eyes fell on Brunt's familiar face. He let forth a meow of recognition. He took his shot, leaping onto the front seat.

Pulling the door shut, Brunt sped off.

After giving the cat's ears a scruff, Brunt said, "Did that mean old Gina bring a strange cat into your house? Poor boy. Well, you can come back to live with me for a while."

Rags lay down on the front seat, with his chin and white paws hanging over the edge. He was the picture of dejection.

"Maybe if you're good, I might buy you a catnip mouse."

Rags failed to stir from his dejection.

"But before we head home, I have a little job for you."

Brunt drove five miles into a residential neighborhood where the brick homes were spaced well apart.

"It's like this," he told the inconsolable Rags. "Someone stole a very expensive painting from the Museum of Fine Arts. A Bama. I have a good idea who might have commissioned the theft, based on rumor and innuendo."

Rags did not look up, even after Brunt pulled into a shady little street whose ranks of ancient New England oaks formed a natural arcade.

"There's a handsome reward for the painting's recovery," Brunt continued. "There are also stiff laws against breaking into a person's home to search for stolen property, especially when said person is Samuel Simms, the quasi-millionaire."

Brunt extracted a tiny stainless steel device from a briefcase, attached it to a flea collar, and affixed said collar to Rags's fluffy ruff. Rags allowed his head to be lifted up for this purpose. It dropped back down again.

"These laws are designed to discourage those of us of the higher animal kingdom. You, being a cat, and not subject to higher kingdom laws, are not so constrained."

He flipped a switch, and a laptop monitor showed a dim picture of the rubber floorboard mat. Brunt waved a hand before Rags's blunt nose and a fleshy blur showed on the screen.

Satisfied, Brunt got out of the car. Taking Rags from the other side, Brunt slung him over his shoulder. Rags clung, purring, like a toddler wearing a fuzzy gray snowsuit. His bushy tail switched back and forth.

Brunt carried the contented cat to a fieldstone fence fanged with embedded rock shards. He gave Rags a boost to the top.

Balancing precariously, the huge cat tried to find comfortable spots to set down his oversized marshmallow paws. He found only three. Letting out a plaintive mew, Rags placed his free paw on Brunt's wide shoulder as a first step in crossing back to more familiar territory. Brunt pushed him away.

"Look, just take a stroll through the guy's yard. I happen to know he's a cat lover. Nothing will happen to you. Daddy promises."

Rags hesitated. Brunt gave him a firm push. A ball of gray fluff, Rags tumbled from sight.

Rushing back to his Taurus, Brunt set the monitor on his lap and watched a cat's-eye view of Rags's prowl through a twilight of rosebeds and lilac bushes.

Rags meandered for a time. Eventually he found his way to the front door. There, he intercepted a security beam. The front entry became a blaze of halogen lights. Rags took a seated position, apparently to await developments.

The door opened and a puckered-faced man looked out. He spied Rags. His puckery features softened.

His *"Whose little kitty are you?"* came distinctly through the monitor.

"Take the bait, buddy," Brunt muttered.

Rags gave a plaintive sound.

Moments later, he was lapping up milk in a spacious gourmet kitchen. Milk droplets spattered the screen. Frowning, Brunt took a handkerchief to the monitor to no avail.

"Watch the milk, you swivel-eared tree ape," he muttered. "That camera set me back a cool four grand."

After that, Rags went on a tour of the house. He encountered two cats, both Siamese. They took one look at his hulking form and muttonchopped mask of a face, and sought solace in the basement.

As Rags went from room to room sniffing curiously, rubbing scent onto assorted doorjambs, Brunt rotated the camera lens, searching the walls. Paintings abounded. Most were Western landscapes. One depicted a yellow-slicker-clad cowboy brandishing a Winchester in the pouring rain.

"Bingo," he said. "The purloined Bama."

Brunt picked up the car phone and dialed a number.

"Hello?"

"Gina. Brunt. Listen: Rags is in trouble."

"What!"

"You gotta help him. He wandered into someone's house and I can't get him out. Meet me at Hickory Circle."

"On my way."

Gina's red Jeep Cherokee pulled up twenty minutes later. She popped out of the vehicle, saying, "What happened to my poor Ragsdale?"

"My Rags*well*, you mean."

"What did you pull on me?"

"Nothing you haven't pulled on me in the past. I'll explain later. See that house? He's in there. I can't go knock on the door, but you can."

Gina looked at him with naked suspicion. "Why can I, and you can't?"

"It's business."

"Is this the place you're staking out?"

"No comment."

She eyed him seriously for a long minute. "Does this by any chance have something to do with the painting that was stolen last month?"

"Absolutely not," Brunt assured her. "That kind of action is way out of my league. I'd be a fool to go chasing that thing, what with everyone from the FBI to the local constabulary after it. Besides, it's probably in Europe by now."

Gina got back into her Jeep and pulled up to the gated entry. She hit the buzzer twice, insistently.

A metallic voice came back. *"Yes?"*

"I think you have my cat. Big, butch, and wears a permanent milk mustache. I want him back. *Now.*"

"He wandered onto my property," Sam Simms said defensively.

"Well, boot his fuzzy *tokhes* out of there."

"Why don't you just come in and get him?"

The gate opened electronically, and Gina drove up the gravel drive. She gave Brunt a loose-fingered wave. One finger looked suspiciously straight.

Brunt waited. It was a long wait. Splashed milk had dried on the surveillance lens, making the picture an opaque blur. He turned off the monitor to conserve the expensive batteries.

When she came out again, Gina roared past Brunt's vehicle at high speed. Rags, standing up in the passenger seat, looked out with a mixture of feline pleasure and wide-eyed surprise at his sudden change of fortune.

Brunt decided to let them go. He drove to the police station house and asked the desk sergeant, "Is Walter around?"

"Out."

"Know when he's due back?"

"Is this an emergency?"

"No, I guess not." Brunt slid his business card over and asked, "Have him call me, will you?"

"You want fries with that?"

Brunt left. He drove home, and turned on the TV. The theft of the Bama painting led the evening news. The newscaster quoted police sources as saying they were pursuing several promising leads.

Nervous impatience got the best of him. Brunt went out again, and after a little aimless wandering during which Walter's prowl car did not turn up, returned to Sam Simms's palatial home.

Walter's cruiser was parked in the driveway. So was Gina Sconderella's Jeep.

"I don't like the looks of this," Brunt started to say.

A moment later, a slump-shouldered Sam Simms was led out in handcuffs. A flat crate about the size of a painting was gingerly placed in the trunk. And off on the lawn, Gina Sconderella was doing a celebratory jig.

Brunt rushed up. "Walter! Been trying to catch you all night."

"I'm busy, Brunt. We just recovered the missing painting."

"Who tipped you?"

"Your psychic friend."

Brunt made helpess fists of rage. He composed himself before he approached Gina.

"Nice night," he allowed.

Gina gave her long auburn hair a careless toss. She smiled. "The best. I just earned myself a cool ten grand."

"That so," Brunt said evenly. "How ever did you do that?"

"When I went in to fetch Rags, he gave us a little chase. Right into a room where I saw no less than the missing painting hanging on a wall. In plain sight."

"Imagine that. . . ."

"Rags has always been good luck for me. Tell you what, why don't you keep Spooky? She's your type."

"I don't like female cats," Brunt growled. "Some days, I don't like females in general."

"You seem to be in a bad humor tonight. Come over to my place. I think there's still some birthday cake left. White with chocolate frosting. Your favorite."

Brunt blinked. "How'd you know that?"

"Same way I know a lot of things. I'm psychic. And very, very lucky." She started past him.

Brunt grabbed her slender arm.

"Okay, enough games. You know I was casing Simms's place."

"Do I?"

"This is *my* case. *My* commission."

"The police say it'll be a week or two before *I* can collect the reward."

Brunt's blocky face began resembling a climbing thermometer. "We'll go halfsies," he said sullenly.

"Why should I share with you?"

"I got Rags into the joint. You just got lucky."

"If you had bought me a winning lottery ticket for my birthday—which by the way would have been an excellent idea—would you expect me to split it with you?"

Brunt gnashed his teeth.

Gina smiled coolly. "Serves you right for that dirty trick you pulled on me last time we teamed up."

Gina started back to her Jeep. They were pushing Sam Simms into the back of a prowl car. He spotted her, and his look was venomous.

Gina halted. She seemed to struggle with a conflicting impulse, then doubled back.

"I have a proposition for you," she told Brunt.

"What's that?"

"I'll give you half of the reward if you'll take all of the credit."

"How's that again?"

"Sam Simms. He just threw me a look you don't have to be psychic to read. I think he's planning on having me kneecapped, or something."

"People of that caliber don't do that," Brunt said thinly. "They find even more insidious methods."

"That's what I'm afraid of," Gina said.

"What do you want me to do?"

"Go over there and boast. Tell him all about it. How you caught on to him in the first place. Rags. The camera in the flea collar."

"How do you know about that?" Brunt demanded.

"Don't take me for a dunce, okay? Rags didn't buy that collar at the five-and-dime."

Brunt walked over to the prowl car and engaged Walter in conversation.

"Worked like a charm. Although I have to give ol' Rags most of the credit."

"Say what?"

"Rags. I boosted him over the fence wearing a camera collar. I spotted the painting. The rest was up to Gina."

"She didn't mention anything like that."

"You know what a glory-chaser she is. But I prevailed on her to do the right thing. Gina was just hired talent."

From the back of the cruiser, Sam Simms threw Brunt a dirty look.

Gina suddenly appeared beside them. "That's right," she said in a too-loud voice. "It was Bill's caper. I'm just a pawn in a larger game. I owed him a favor. Now we're even. And believe me, I've learned my lesson. I'll never get tangled up in one of your sneaky little schemes again."

Sam Simms spat out the window.

Then a TV-news van pulled up and Brunt was telling his story to a local reporter while Gina fumed in the background, looking like a bride who had been left at the altar.

After the cruiser had departed, Brunt found Gina kicking a clump of milk-weeds apart.

"Let me know when to pick up my third," he said.

"No problem," she said darkly. She climbed into her Jeep. Her voice brightened slightly. "Oh, by the way, how much does this cost?"

Out of the window dangled the flea collar with the mini surveillance camera.

"A lot."

"Sell it back to you for a reasonable price. Say, your share, plus a modest recovery fee?"

"You wouldn't dare...." Brunt growled.

Gina bestowed upon him a feline smile. "I would and will. Happy birthday to me. Happy birthday to me."

And, singing, she drove off, leaving Bill Brunt chewing figurative nails and spitting out literal pejoratives.

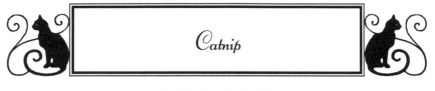

Catnip

RON GOULART

EVEN BEFORE HE FOUND OUT ABOUT the murder, he wasn't in an especially good mood.

Almost as soon as Mack Bullmer drove onto the Paragon Pictures lot late on that gray autumn morning in 1937, people started waylaying him and dumping problems and complaints on him. The head of Publicity was afraid that the business about one of their top male stars and the high school girl was going to leak to the press after all. The cowboy who was starring in Paragon's most successful horse opera series had gotten into another hit and run accident and wanted it hushed up right away. The Latin bombshell whose jungle epic was being released in just two weeks had run off to Tijuana with the guy who mowed the lawn of her new Beverly Hills mansion.

By the time Mack reached the entrance to Sound Stage 6, his hangover was worse and he was near certain he was going to have another one of those ocular migraines that had been hitting him lately.

Then Vincent Delborgo hailed him. "You've got to do something about that damn mouse," he said, giving the studio troubleshooter an angry look and setting down the two animal carrying cases he'd been lugging.

"Which mouse?"

"The one I've been complaining to you about, Mack," said the animal trainer. "Pharaoh is an important cat. MGM is after him and I may just switch over to—"

"Hi, Pharaoh." Crouching, which made his headache worse, Mack poked a forefinger through the wire and nudged the chubby black cat inside.

It snarled, whapping at his finger with a clawed forepaw.

"That's Leroy, Pharaoh's stand-in," pointed out the trainer. "Pharaoh's in the other case. The way you can tell them apart is that Leroy's a mean son of a bitch."

"Yeah, that's exactly how I just differentiated." Mack stood up, licking at his injured finger. "What mouse?"

"That second-rate hambone you've got working in *The Case of the Curious Cat.* He carries a catnip mouse around in his coat pocket."

"At last count, Vince, we had sixteen—make that seventeen—second-rate hambones employed in this B-epic. Be more specific."

"Arthur something. Arthur Remmington I think. He's the guy playing a bit part as a plainclothes cop."

"And?"

"He keeps sneaking that catnip mouse out of his pocket between scenes and dangling it under Pharaoh's nose," explained the annoyed Delborgo. "That gets the little guy all agitated and goofy, and I have one hell of a time cueing him from off camera. You know."

"I'll find him when we start shooting in there this afternoon and take care of it, Vince," he promised.

"MGM is very anxious to get Pharaoh over there. They're thinking of replacing that hambone dog, Asta, in the Thin Man pictures with a smart cat, aren't they fella?" He squatted, patted one of the cages, and picked them both up.

Inside his cage, Leroy made some negative, sputtering noises.

"You going in there now?" asked Mack, nodding at the sound-stage door.

"Going to leave the fellas in their dressing room. I like them to get acclimated for a couple hours before Pharaoh and Leroy have to do their stuff," explained Delborgo. "Then I'm heading over to the commissary for a cup of coffee and a bowl of chicken soup."

"Okay, fine," said Mack, keeping the annoyance out of his voice as he opened the big metal door and stood aside.

Delborgo carried his cats on into the vast shadowy building. "Don't forget about that damned catnip mouse."

" 'Remember the mouse' shall be my slogan." He followed them inside.

Sylvia Diamond didn't kiss him.

Mack had quietly, avoiding the animal trainer, made his way to the slim, brunette actress's dressing room at the edge of the *Curious Cat* set. Nobody was supposed to be shooting in this particular sound stage until this afternoon. That made it an ideal place for a married troubleshooter and a married actress to meet.

Sylvia was pale and fully dressed. "Today of all days," she said, her voice more nasal than usual. "What bum luck."

"Hmm?" he inquired as he crossed the threshold into the dressing room.

"I mean, I'm on my way up," continued the pretty actress. "This turkey is my last cheap movie. Next month I go to work in *Here Comes Cleopatra*, a big-budget A-film with VanGelder directing. It's my big break."

"I know all that," he said, impatient, reaching for her. "But what's it got to do—"

"Dummy, Ella Blanton's coming over here this afternoon to interview me." She backed out of range.

"Ella Blanton from the Hearst newspapers?"

"How many Ella Blantons are there, dimwit?"

"At last count it was twenty-seven in captivity and a rumored dozen more roaming loose. But what exactly are . . . oops."

She'd pulled aside the screen at the rear of the room.

And Mack got a view of a man sitting in the dressing-table chair. He was slumped, arms dangling. A pair of scissors had been plunged into his chest, and the front of his shirt and the front of his coat were bloody. He was completely dead.

"How'd a corpse get here?" he inquired.

"Well, how do you think? I stuck my scissors into the blackmailing jerk."

He eased nearer the dead man, eyes narrowing. "Hey, it's Arthur Remmington," he said. "Well, at least that solves the catnip problem."

"Whatever are you blathering about, Mack?"

Mack turned, eyed her. "Why'd you kill Remmington?"

"I just told you. Don't you pay attention to anything I say? The guy was blackmailing me."

"About what?"

Sylvia took a deep breath, brushing at her dark hair. "I haven't been completely truthful with you, darling," she began, a girlish quality entering her voice. "Or with the studio, actually. You see, I didn't actually attend a convent on the outskirts of San Diego, nor did I appear in summer stock in New England before signing with Paragon. Actually, truth to tell—"

"You worked in a bordello in Tijuana," he supplied. "I already knew all about that."

She inhaled, did a mild take. "Well, sweetheart, so did the late Arthur Remmington. And he had pictures to prove it."

"He should've come to me. We've got a budget for buying incriminating stuff that might—"

"He wanted more than money, Mack."

Nodding, he looked again toward the dead blackmailer. "Where are the pictures?"

"A set of them's there on my dressing table, next to the powder puff. The negatives. . . ." She shrugged.

Approaching the body, Mack searched it. He found no more photos, nothing else pertaining to the actress. He came across the catnip mouse in a side pocket of the dead actor's coat and left it there. "Okay, I'll have to get rid of the body," he told her. "Dump it in one of the canyons above Hollywood, try to make this look like an underworld kill. Although they don't usually use nail scissors when they take some poor gink for a ride."

"How're you going to get him out of here? We're supposed to start shooting in—"

"Trust me." Mack moved to her door, opened it a few inches, and listened.

He heard one of the cats, no doubt Leroy, yowling over in their dressing room some hundred yards away. Mack stepped out of the room and looked around. No sign of Delborgo or anyone else.

He returned inside. "There's no shooting over on the next set—that's the one for *Dime-A-Dance Dame*," he told Sylvia. "I'll stash Remmington in the folding bed in the hotel room layout. Tonight I'll collect him, with the help of one of my assistants, and get him out of here in a panel truck. It'll be a cinch and nobody'll ever tie his death in with you."

"Can't you do it alone? It makes me nervous that somebody else is going to know about this, Mack."

"There's nobody working for me that I can't trust, kid," he assured her.

After rubbing his hands together once, he moved toward the body.

Mack started seeing spots of colored light about five minutes after Ella Blanton had come waddling onto *The Case of the Curious Cat* set, escorted by the redheaded girl who worked in Publicity.

The lights, little flashes of zigzagging color, were the symptoms of what the studio physician had diagnosed as an ocular migraine attack. They usually lasted no more than a few minutes and weren't supposed to be serious. Caused by stress probably.

Serious or not, they annoyed the hell out of Mack.

So he was standing there watching them shoot a scene with Sylvia and Paul Vaughn, who played the two-fisted attorney in this series, and he was seeing everything through what seemed like a collection of abstract neon signs.

Just as Vaughn lit his cigarette and leaned back in his desk chair, somebody yelled, "Cut!"

Only it wasn't the director. He'd been over near the coffee wagon flirting with the script girl.

The man who'd shouted was a big, husky fellow in khaki shirt and trousers. "Damn," muttered Mack, "it's William Francis Storm."

Storm was the author of the books that these B-films were based on. He was unhappy with the way Paragon Pictures had been handling his characters.

So unhappy that Mack had issued orders not to allow him on the lot. Today somebody had apparently screwed up.

Mack smiled at Ella Blanton, who seemed to have yellow and green lines all across her pudgy face. She was taking a notebook out of her fat black purse.

"Nothing serious, Ella," he assured her and started making his way over to where the disgruntled author was standing.

"My lawyer character is a tough guy," Storm was telling the assistant director and a couple of stagehands. "He's not a sissy. He wouldn't light a cigarette like a sissy."

"I heard that, you lowbrow oaf." Tossing his cigarette aside, the actor got up from the desk and came striding over to the edge of the set. "You're the one who's a sissy. I'm damn tired of your—"

"Easy, guys," Mack advised, stepping between them. "Let's settle this in a friendly way right now. And then we can talk about it some more *after* Ella Blanton leaves."

"Who in bloody blue blazes is Ella Blanton?" Storm tried to get around Mack and take a swing at the actor.

"See, you don't even know anything about the movie industry." Vaughn tried to get around Mack and take a swing at the author.

"Gentlemen, if you please." The director had joined them. He hit at the side of his jodhpurs with his riding crop. "This, let me remind you, is Paragon and not Paramount. We don't have the kind of budgets that De Mille does and I want to get this scene done in one more take." He held up a suntanned forefinger. "*One.*"

"We may have a problem." The animal trainer was coming toward them. "Pharaoh is missing."

The director paused to scowl at Delborgo. "We don't need your cat until the next scene. If you haven't located him by then, we'll use his stand-in."

"Leroy is missing, too."

"How'd you allow that to happen?"

"I had them out of their cages so they could use the catbox before their scene," explained Delborgo. "When I heard the fracas over this way I left them for a minute. I came back to find them both gone."

The director waved his riding crop in the direction of the attorney's-office set. "We'll hunt for them after we shoot this."

Stepping close to Storm, Mack said quietly, "If you don't shut up from here on, William Francis, I'll have a couple of guards give you the heave-ho. Understood?"

Storm scowled and moved away into the shadows.

Mack returned to Ella Blanton's side. "Just a little clowning around that got out of hand."

The movie gossip was making shorthand notes. "That *was* William Francis Storm, wasn't it?"

"Was it? I'm not certain, Ella." He realized he was over his attack of flashing lights. Maybe that was a good omen and things would go okay from now on.

"Roll 'em," someone said.

The interrupted scene began again.

As Vaughn struck a match to light his cigarette, considerable yowling and sputtering commenced.

"Cut!" This time is was the director who said it.

"That disturbance is coming from over there." Ella Blanton pointed a beringed finger to the left.

Toward the dim-lit *Dime-A-Dance Dame* set.

"Might be," said Mack, taking hold of her arm. "But it doesn't sound like anything serious."

She broke free and started for the noise, notebook still in her hand.

The crew, the director, and most of the actors were heading that way, too.

Sylvia gave Mack a very worried look and was then escorted over to the next set by her co-star.

Mack headed there, too, catching up with the columnist.

The howling and snarling was coming from the three-walled hotel room set. It sounded like a cat fight.

"Inside the folding bed," said an electrician.

The angry director nudged Delborgo. "It's your cats who've disrupted my shooting."

"No, both Pharaoh and Leroy are well behaved and never—"

"Go break this up."

Shrugging, the trainer entered the hotel room and reached for the shut folding bed. He grunted as he tugged it open.

Pharaoh and Leroy, a large, furry black tangle, came tumbling out. And next the bloody body of the dead actor.

"Hey, it's Arthur Remmington," exclaimed Delborgo, jumping back as the corpse sprawled out on the threadbare rug.

Ella Blanton opened her notebook to a fresh page. "Those cats found a murder victim," she said, impressed. "Wasn't that intelligent of them?"

"It wasn't intelligence," Mack told her. "It was catnip."

Catnip

JANE YOLEN AND HEIDI E. Y. STEMPLE

WHEN WE GOT TO THE ALLEY, he was stone dead. And cold. Except for the place where the cat was snugged up to him. That was the one warm spot on the stiff. It was full of these long orange hairs.

The cat was a beauty, well fed, well groomed, and stoned out of its gourd. At first we thought it was dead, too. But it was just limp with ecstasy. No collar or tags, though, so we didn't know if he belonged to the stiff. But as Gillam pointed out, the only place there was cat hair was in the snugged-in place, right by his suit-jacket pocket. So we guessed probably not. Cat hairs aren't particular; they'll cling to anything, like a girl I once knew.

There was another peculiar thing—the dead guy's pocket was full of catnip. Which, of course, explained why Amber Dextrose (Gillam named her) was so content to lie next to him and act like a happy dishrag. I knew a girl like that, too.

The uniforms who secured the crime scene tried everything to shoo the cat away. One guy even tried to swat at her with his boot, but received only a slight hiss for his troubles. Shrugging, they left the cat where she lay, curled up with the stiff.

If I didn't know Gillam like I do—and you certainly do get to know a guy who's been your partner for the better part of ten years—I would have thought what he did next really odd. Lucky for us, the crime lab guys know Gillam, too. They agreed to leave the body bag partially unzipped and, on his say-so, toted the whole package—cat and all—off to the meat wagon. Gillam is know for his sick sense of humor and his unlikely relationship with the chief medical examiner, Doc Strangelove, who is as humorless as she is beautiful, two qualities Gillam has never been accused of. They do have one thing in common however. They're both big into books. Especially poetry.

Gillam is forever trying to get a rise out of Strangelove. (OK, her real name is Stanlow, but that's what I call her.) He even went so far as zipping himself into a body bag one April Fools' Day a couple of years back. She never even cracked a smile.

We arrived at the morgue about half an hour after the stiff and his companion. The sterile steel and glass greeted us with the silence of the dead. Disinfectants can't really cover the smells, but they try hard.

Doc Strangelove was seated at a steel desk taking notes beside the John Doe from the alley. A paperback book called *Poems of e. e. cummings* sat on a steel table next to her instruments. Doc was gloved, masked, and capped, but still recognizable by her arrow-straight posture. She acknowledged our presence only by a quick shifting of her amazing gold eyes.

We waited in silence, the four of us, Gillam and me in the doorway, Doc at her desk, and the stiff on the table, until Doc put down her silver pen and pushed her chair back, sending it rolling.

It was then I noticed the cat. Amber Dextrose was curled up contentedly on Doc's lap. In one movement, the cat and Doc looked up at Gillam and me. Four huge round gold eyes staring at us.

"What's the word, Doc?"

"He's definitely dead."

Not a smile from her, but this was the closest to a joke I'd ever heard her make.

"Cause of death?" I asked. Although it came out more like "carse of derth?" Pretty women do that to me.

Both Doc and the cat blinked. A long, slow deliberate blink. "Massive cranial damage, right lobe." And then, as if to clear it up to the non-medical staff, i.e. me, she said, "Bullet hole to the head." She turned and smiled at Gillam and in that low tone she uses for him alone, added, "I wonder how Mr. Death likes his blue-eyed boy now!"

Gillam chuckled, some secret had passed between them, some poetry I guessed. So as to seem in on it, I nodded, which, of course, was unnecessary. Besides, the mystery wasn't how this guy died. The mystery was why and who did it.

Luckily, by the time Gillam and I got to our desks, part of the who had already been cleared up. Fingerprints revealed the stiff to be one Robert E. Lee. Not *the* Robert E. Lee obviously, but Robert Everest Lee, a diplomat. His mother was the infamous Climbing Granny Lee who at ninety-six had attempted Mount Rainier. Funny thing, memory. There when you don't need it and on walkabout when you do! I have all these little bits of trivia running around in my head, and not one line of poetry.

Records revealed that Mr. Lee had just returned from a diplomatic trip to the Netherlands. That's Holland to working guys like me. Attached to the paperwork was a note that said a complete passenger list was on its way. I sure hoped the airline was one that was known to be on time!

I looked up to tell Gillam the new info but was interrupted by the buzzing of my telephone intercom.

It was Sgt. Johnson. "Fax, front desk."

Never one to mince words, Johnson.

I went out through the big glass doors and picked up my fax. A minute later, I was looking at the names of passengers on Flight 277 from Amsterdam. I made a note of the airline. If I ever got any actual vacation days and some extra cash at the same time, I'd fly their friendly skies. Must have been some tailwind on those fax lines.

Gillam read the list over my shoulder and pointed. He's always quicker than me on paper. I'm quicker than Gillam on the shooting range. Which makes us about even. Though with the way police work goes these days, he saves me a lot oftener than I save him.

"Number seventy-three. Recognize the name?"

Indeed I did. "Jasper Cornwell" was one of the aliases of a guy we lock up every now and then for racketeering. But nothing ever sticks. He's connected up to his eyeballs. We just can't ever figure out who he's connected to.

Gillam and I brainstormed on the way to the stiff's place. Maybe Cornwell, aka Cromwell, a.k.a. Callahan, a.k.a. Callan was in with the diplomatic corps, too. That could explain why every time we got him into court, the charges were nol-prossed. The Feds were already breathing down our backs on this one, what with a big name showing up dead. And, like most detectives, we guarded our turf with the fierceness of a lioness protecting her cubs. If we didn't solve the case fast, it would be yanked from under us.

As it turned out, there was no need to waste time at Lee's penthouse condo. We weren't the first ones there. We weren't even the second ones there. When we arrived, the Feds were already dusting the place. We took a quick look at the sparsely furnished chrome and glass bachelor's pad and knew instantly that it had been tossed professionally even before the Feds had arrived.

We bowed out quickly.

"Let them have the condo," I said to Gillam. "We need a better angle."

"Acute or obtuse?" he asked.

"Whatever."

Back in the morgue, we found Doc in an uncommon state of disarray. She was trying to steer Amber Dextrose away from a gunmetal gray locker. The cat was letting out an altogether unpleasant mix of growl and meow. Each time her claws dragged at the locker, I could feel the sound reverberate in my molars.

Doc must have sensed our presence, because she straightened and smoothed her hair and lab coat before turning to us.

"The cat seems to want to get at Mr. Lee's effects," Doc explained. "The catnip from his pocket was sent to the lab already. But the odor must still be on his jacket."

"Pretty strong sense of smell for a cat," commented Gillam.

"More like a dog," I added.

"Open up the locker and let's see what she does," Gillam said.

I probably should have objected since the closet contained evidence that might get contaminated, but before I could object, Doc had the door open and the cat went right inside. She curled up and began purring.

"At least she's stopped that infernal howling," Doc said.

"Allen Ginsberg would be pleased," Gillam responded.

He and Doc traded glances.

"Who the hell is Allen Ginsberg?" I asked. "Another diplomat?"

Doc shot me a pitying look. "American poet. Beat Generation. Wrote a poem called 'Howl' that knocked everyone's socks off."

"Oh—that Allen Ginsberg," I said, as if I had known all along.

While Gillam went over the final autopsy reports with Doc, I stood around smarting over that "Howl" stuff.

"Can I use your phone?" I asked. Without waiting for Doc's permission, I called Johnson at the front desk.

"Listen," I said, "do me a favor. Call it a whim or an educated guess." Actually Gillam was the educated one of the two of us, but I had hunches that were as good as a bachelor's degree. "Make a quick call to the airline. Ask for a complete baggage report on that tulip plane, especially any live cargo." I had a feeling that the cat was no innocent bystander. She knew something. We just didn't know what.

"Consider it done," he told me. I like Johnson. Nice, uncomplicated, didn't read much.

Johnson had the airline paperwork waiting for us when we got back to the station. Long shot or not, Mr. Alias Cornwell had checked one bag in Holland and one live-animal cargo cage. With cat.

Sometimes things do work like in the movies.

The rest of the morning we drank coffee, ate bagels, and traded cat jokes while we made a barrage of phone calls.

Most turned into dead ends. But then—that's a policeman's life. There ain't any poetry in it. Just hard work.

There was one very promising lead, though. We were told by someone who handled such things—a Ms. Marshal, with a very pleasing voice—that there was an overcoat, a paperback novel, and a pager left at the baggage carousel for that flight. The airline would messenger all three to us if we needed them for a murder investigation, as long—said Ms. Marshal, practically purring into the phone—as they received a receipt for anyone who might want to claim them later.

I answered that I might want to claim *her* later. She giggled something that might have been a "yes," and hung up. It was the best offer I'd had in weeks.

"So," I said to Gillam, "we have a cat, catnip, an old pro, and a stiff. I know there's a connection somewhere, but I just don't see how they fit."

Gillam was staring up at the ceiling. There's a crack there that makes the Grand Canyon look like a paper cut. Suddenly he turned and said, "My God, Montresor, they have walled the cat in the tomb."

I shook my head. I mean—he's often like that. Making literary quotes out of nowhere. But I just let him go on. Between the two of us, we manage to do good police work anyway. Though sometimes even I wonder.

"No tomb," I said.

"But a cat carrier," he answered, biting his lip.

The rest of the day was filled with more phone calls—making them and dodging them. We figured we had precious few hours left till the Feds officially nabbed our case. Nabbed the cat too.

To tell the truth, I think that cat was now Gillam's primary concern since three of his calls were from Doc asking him to bring various feline supplies to the morgue. This, of course, became fodder for the joke mill around the station.

Meanwhile I was busy on the phone again, trying to coax information out of the rental car clerk who'd been on duty within eyeshot of the baggage carousel when Johnson's voice beckoned from the intercom.

"Delivery, front desk."

I signed the invoice for the airlines while Gillam opened our package. The lovely Ms. Marshal—I'd have to call and thank her for such promptness—had sent us the overcoat, digital pager, and paperback.

While I rifled through the coat, Gillam picked up the book.

When the coat yielded no new clues, I checked out the pager. A recurring number appeared. What the hell. More calls.

"Hello?" A nervous voice answered.

I introduced myself, explaining quickly why I was calling.

A huge sigh and a waterfall of tears answered me.

When the woman on the other end calmed enough to speak, she explained—punctuated by hiccups—that our now cold old guy, Lee, was her boyfriend and he had called her from the airport. She had been in the shower so he left a message that the "strangest thing had happened."

According to the girlfriend, Lee had collected his bag and then stopped to take off his coat because it was a lot warmer than he'd expected. When he picked the bag up again, he saw the tag end of a document sticking out. That's when he discovered that someone had slipped papers into his bag as well as a small package of what he assumed was drugs.

I said the last word out loud.

"Drugs?" Gillam looked up, surprised.

"Good he didn't try to smoke the stuff," I said. "Or he'd have had a catnip buzz!"

Ignoring my aside, the girlfriend continued. "Bobby wanted me to know he would be late because he was going first to the authorities. He said I should go on to the party without him." She sighed. "I paged him repeatedly, but he never called back. And he never got to the party. I was furious with him. But when the paper arrived this morning and I saw that he had been killed, I was so frightened, I didn't know what to do."

I thanked her for the information and told her we would be at her apartment within the hour to retrieve the answering-machine tape.

I hung up just as Gillam turned a page of the book and a neatly folded pack of papers fell out.

We looked at the papers on the floor.

We looked at the book.

Then we looked at each other.

Since the morgue was on the way to the girlfriend's apartment, Gillam convinced me to stop at the store and pick up some cat food, litter, and a squeaky toy mouse.

But we arrived moments too late. Ahead of us the shadowy figure of a man in an impeccably tailored suit was just entering the autopsy room.

"The Feds," Gillam whispered.

I agreed. No one I know but Feds wear clothes that nice. So, we did what any twelve-year-old boys would do when the bully takes over the playground: we skulked in the doorway, cursing quietly.

But then the Fed turned and I noticed he had a gun. We should have known a lone man wasn't a Fed, no matter how well he dressed. They're like Noah's ark animals, always arriving by twos. I kicked Gillam in the shin and drew my own weapon.

Even as we started forward, the cat leapt from a locker where she had been sleeping and headed straight for the feet of the suited man. In a meowing frenzy she wound between his legs. He stepped over her, then lifted her up with a foot, but gently. It was clear they were old friends.

Doc looked up, saw the gun, stifled a scream, then looked past him to Gillam and me.

The cat scrambled up the man's front like Granny Lee on Everest and tried to lick his chin.

Gillam shouted, "Freeze!" and the guy turned.

At which point, Doc hit him with a hardcover book and down he went. His head bounced on the steel corner of the autopsy table and he was out.

That's when the Feds flooded into the room.

The Feds, of course, got the collar.

Gillam and I didn't even bother going to court. We had to read the newspaper for all the details.

Cornwell—officially James Connor—had been stealing confidential documents from European governments which he would deposit in some unsuspecting business traveler's luggage along with a bag of catnip. When his cat was let out of the air freight bag, she was trained to follow the luggage with the catnip in it. Unfortunately for Connor—and worse for Lee—the patsy had discovered the stash which he put in his coat pocket. But in the muddle, he'd left the coat, with the pager, book, and documents behind.

The cat had dutifully followed him, with her master close behind. Connor had pushed Lee into a handy alley, then killed him for the bag and still came up empty-handed, because the stuff he wanted was in Lee's coat left back at baggage claim. Somebody had heard the shot, called the cops, and a pair of uniforms got there before Connor could search further. That's why he went after Lee's effects in the morgue.

But, no one can say the Feds got the bad guy. The honor of identifying and taking Connor down belongs entirely to Amber Dextrose. With a healthy assist from Doc.

The press got a mysterious leak about the particulars of the arrest. No one can ever trace that leak to me, but the headlines read: "Catnip Catburglar Catnabbed by Cat."

And if that ain't poetry, I don't know what is.

The Chocolate Cat

KRISTIN SCHWENGEL

IT WAS THE SNEEZES THAT wakened Paulina—great painful sounds echoing up the stairwell to her flat. It took a moment for her sleep-fogged brain to realize what they meant. Someone was in the shop!

Leaping out of bed, she grabbed her robe and pulled it on, tying the belt as she fumbled with the bolt on her door and tore down the stairs to the entrance hall. A great clatter erupted to her left as she reached the landing. The door to the kitchen was open a crack, though she was sure she had closed it before she went up to bed.

A white cloud enveloped Paulina when she opened the door wider, and she started coughing. Waving her hand to sweep the powdered sugar away so she could breathe, she entered the room, pausing only to flick on the overhead fluorescents.

A soft brushing wisped against her bare legs and feet, and she glanced down.

"Claudette, was it just you?" The tremor in her voice belied the gentle scold. "But how did you get in here? The shop and kitchen are off-limits, you know that."

The cat meowed, the sound neither a purr of comfort nor a questioning chirp, but holding a note of urgency.

The air having cleared, Paulina inspected the damages. The sugar had settled over everything, giving the kitchen a dusty, long-abandoned appearance. An eerie shiver passed down Paulina's spine as she walked forward, leaving ghostly dark footprints on the floor.

The indoor snow had come from one of the ten-pound bags of powdered sugar, which had fallen and burst on the floor in front of the steel shelving units that ran along the wall, fitting right into the corner next to the back door. A few bowls had fallen as well and shattered—the noise that had led her in here. But the sugar and bowls were too heavy for Claudette to move, even if she had managed to get on the shelves.

Looking at the back wall, Paulina sucked in her breath and felt her heart rate go back up several notches. Claudette was not to blame for the incident. She had not noticed it before, shadowed as it was in the corner, but the back door stood just a few inches ajar.

Her pulse skyrocketing, Paulina backed out of the kitchen, followed by Claudette. She closed the door with extreme care, then moved across the hall to the shop door, which was still locked. Without thought her hand went to her pocket for the key, and she stood fumbling for a few moments before she remembered that she was still in her pyjamas. With a nervous laugh she reached to the top of the doorjamb for the spare key and let herself into the shop.

All was still in order here, and Paulina breathed a sigh of relief. Not wanting to go back upstairs with an unknown intruder still nearby, she reached for the phone while Claudette, more at ease, explored this forbidden area.

"Ms. Thomas?" Paulina nodded at Officer Carlson, and he continued. "The area around the building is clear. We did see some tracks in the sugar, but there was no trail. The shoe pattern was kind of unusual, with several strong swirls across the bottom. The size could have been either a man with small feet or a woman with large feet. There's really no way to know for sure. The sugar drifted a few feet through the back door, but beyond that. . . ." He shrugged. "That door was the point of entry, forced with a knife blade or a screwdriver. Lucky thing the shop is dead-bolted, as well as the inner door to your flat upstairs."

Paulina shuddered at the thought of what could have happened. "Yes, you're right. Definitely a good thing."

"Was the breaking of the bowls the first thing you heard?"

"Actually, a very strange sneeze woke me up. I'd never heard a sneeze like it—probably a reaction to the powdered sugar in the air. But at least the place was already dusted for prints," Paulina joked, although her voice cracked. The officer gave her a sympathetic smile, then returned to his questions.

"What was so unusual about the sneeze?"

"It sounded as though it hurt. It was violent, and quite loud. It had to be, in order for me to hear it upstairs." Paulina paused, trying to remember those hazy moments when she had been awakened. "Not just one sneeze, either, but a whole series of them, each more intense than the last."

"No one you know has a sneeze like that?"

"No, I don't think so. My father had hay fever and would sometimes have a series of sneezes, but his were softer. These were new to me."

"Your ex-husband, perhaps?"

"Robert? Certainly not. I lived with him for enough years to know what his sneeze sounded like. Besides, he'd have no reason to do something like this. Our divorce was amicable enough, as divorces go. He just remarried, too, a cute little thing who moved into town last year. He's happy now—and one of my best customers. Says no one makes praline like I do."

"How about his new bride?"

"Why on earth would Jeannie have it in for me? We've met a couple of times . . . there's no bitterness on either side that I can see."

"Any business competition?"

"No. Mine is the only chocolate shop in town since Josh Richards went back to computer programming." The officer raised his eyebrows, and Paulina blushed. "It can't be Josh. He's become a regular, too. He wanted to find out what made my stuff so special, he said. To learn my secret." She smiled, her eyes half closed in a dreamy memory. "I think it's more than chocolate that brings him back."

"Well, if you remember anything more, just give me a call. We're going to take samples of the chocolate and caramel, the unfinished batches, to test just in case. Don't use any of it until we're through. We'll get back to you by tomorrow afternoon if we find anything."

"I'm closed on Mondays anyway, so that's nothing major. I've got enough left from the weekend to get through 'til Wednesday. By then I'll have fresh made."

"One of the officers will drive past during the rest of the night, but you should be all right if you lock all inner doors. Once they're scared off, they don't usually come back."

"I'll pull the steel table in front of the back door, too, since the lock is useless now," Paulina said. "I'll sleep better for that, I think."

On Monday night, Paulina was able to go to bed feeling much safer, but more confused. The back kitchen door had been replaced by one of steel construction with a solid dead bolt. The only prints the police found, however, had been her own. The most perplexing thing was the test results. Her chocolate was fine, but her caramel, made in the same environment and with shared ingredients, showed high levels of a bacterium. The levels would be sufficient to cause a bad case of food poisoning in sensitive individuals.

Less than a month earlier, Paulina had been tested for renewal of her license. The health inspection had included the same tests—and she had passed. Someone had poisoned her caramel, and it was nearly untraceable. But if anyone had gotten sick, she could have been shut down. For the second night in a row, Paulina did not sleep well.

Still uneasy, Paulina broke her own hard-and-fast rule and allowed Claudette free run of the shop and upstairs when she opened up to a rainy, gray Tuesday. Even the bustle of her regular customers failed to soothe her, for now she suspected everyone. A number of them had heard about the break-in, but Paulina interpreted their well-meant sympathy as guilt.

Miss Allston came in, picking out a different sweet for each of the children she would be giving music lessons to that day, and Paulina noticed that she bought nothing with caramel. Could it be her? No longer young, was Miss Allston jealous of Paulina's financial success? Of her flirtation with Josh? Paulina's eyes narrowed on the other woman, all but ignoring her attempts to chat.

When Robert stopped by for his week's supply of praline, Paulina couldn't help examining him for any sign of guilt. He bought no caramel, but then he never did. A sudden shock struck her. Jeannie, his new wife, taught biology at the high school. Paulina remembered cultivating bacteria in her own high school science classes. It was easy to do. If not Robert, maybe it *was* Jeannie who had poisoned her caramel, knowing that Robert never ate it himself. Paulina could hardly wait for Officer Carlson to stop by in the afternoon so she could suggest that he had been right to think of Robert and Jeannie.

The shop emptied at around noon, and Paulina began to balance her accounts. Soon after, the bell over the door jangled and she looked up from the books with a smile. The cheery greeting stuck in her throat when she saw who it was, and her mind raced back to the last time she had seen him, when he had complimented her caramel, among other things. Paulina blushed and shook her head to clear her thoughts.

"Hello, Josh," she finally managed. "I'm all out of praline for today, but I've got plenty of butter toffee. Or your favorite, caramel chews?" Glancing down, she saw that he had not managed to avoid the mud puddle on the sidewalk and was leaving muck on the hardwood floor. She grabbed a towel and came out from behind the counter to wipe up the mess.

"I really didn't come in for candy this morning, Paulina," he said. "Mostly I wanted to stop by and see how you were doing. I hear you had a scare Sunday night." His eyes flickered over her and around the shop. As he took another few steps, the marks on the floor changed from blobs into clearer tracks, and Paulina's eyes widened when she saw the pattern from the soles of his loafers.

At that moment, the door chimed again and Officer Carlson walked in. Paulina caught his eye and angled her head toward the clear prints as she wiped up the larger splotches. He looked down and nodded, then gestured for her to finish the conversation and stepped back, just within hearing range.

"Yes, well, I was fortunate. I lost a few ceramic bowls and had to replace the back door, but no one made it into the shop. It could have been much worse." She stood up, the worst of the mud cleared away, and returned to the counter.

Josh nodded. "Maybe you should think of investing in a guard dog. I've got a German shepherd. They're cheaper than one of those security systems."

Paulina suppressed a shudder at the thought of her beloved Claudette with such a large dog. "Perhaps. Are you sure I can't tempt you with some pecan caramels?"

"I don't think my dentist likes me to eat so much candy." Josh shrugged, then grinned at her. "Let me look around. You take care of the officer."

Officer Carlson came over and leaned against the counter, reading the sudden panic in Paulina's eyes. "I can't believe it," she murmured to him. "I don't want to believe it. I thought he liked computers." The officer looked at her in expectation. "The shoe prints match, and he won't take any caramels, even though he loves them." Her voice trailed off, her lips tightening on her fears, and she stared at the pen in her hands.

Paulina felt the pressure of Claudette's head against her legs, and she reached to scratch the cat behind the ears. "So you decided to come back in here, huh?" she asked her pet, glancing down.

Claudette's ears were flat against her head and her back was arched. She lashed her tail back and forth, staring at Josh. Startled, Paulina looked up and met the policeman's eyes. He nodded in understanding, his eyes flicking over to where Josh stood.

"Josh, could you step over here a moment?" Paulina asked, her voice barely trembling.

He turned to face them and saw Claudette next to the counter. "No wonder I feel like this," he said, his eyes red and puffy and his breath coming in short, sharp gasps. "I'm allergic to cats." Then he sneezed, and Paulina's heart sank in recognition. She nodded at the officer, who led Josh outside.

"Well, Claudette, I guess it's back to you and me," she sighed, running her fingertips over the cat's head. Claudette purred and rubbed against Paulina's ankles in contentment.

The Church Cat

MARTHA JOHNSON

CERTAIN THINGS ARE EXPECTED of a church cat. Dignity, decorum. Perhaps even a sense of aloofness. Needless to say, I have these qualities in abundance.

I half-dozed on the step outside the sanctuary, enjoying the weak April sunshine. All was in order in my world . . . the small trail of people leaving donations in the kitchen for tomorrow's bake sale; Ella Hargrove, the estimable church secretary, clattering the typewriter keys as she prepared the worship bulletin; Pastor Jeffries in his study, deep in contemplation of Sunday's sermon.

Everything was as it should be. Except . . . the tips of my whiskers twitched. Something was out of kilter. Despite the surface calm, something was wrong.

I lifted my head, alert for any sound. Was that a whisper of movement in the sanctuary?

No. My eyes narrowed, my whiskers twitched. A dog, that's what it was. And no ordinary dog, either. It was Amanda Fulbright's over-bred, over-pampered miniature poodle. Bells on his blue collar jingling, he headed for the daffodils along the church wall and lifted his leg.

I soared off the step in a move reminiscent of a stealth fighter. I had personally supervised the planting of those daffodils last fall. I'd even put in extra duty keeping the moles away from the bulbs.

I landed a scant foot away from Percival, trapping him neatly between myself and the sanctuary wall. He darted a swift glance left and right. Seeing no way out, he responded like the cowardly creature he was—he yelped for his mistress before I'd so much as laid a claw on him.

I hissed. The yelps turned into frenzied yaps, piercing my tender ears and sending the black fur standing on end along my spine.

"Absalom!" Pastor Jeffries rushed out the office wing door, followed by his secretary. "What are you doing?"

Ms. Fulbright surged through the opening behind them. She snatched up Percival, ending his yelps as she snuggled him against her fluffy pink sweater. She dropped a pair of flower shears, narrowly missing my tail.

"Poor Percy," she crooned. "Did the bad cat hurt you? Did he hurt Mama's boy?"

If I had, she wouldn't have needed to search for the marks. I sat down, curled my tail around myself, and gave the silly beast a scornful look.

Two pairs of round eyes met mine; two curly white heads tilted. His mistress looked ridiculously like Percival. The last surviving member of the family which had donated the land for Grace Church a century ago, she was a reminder of a long-gone era. She occupied herself with rounds of bridge, arranging the flowers for Sunday service, and occasionally donating some useless item to the church.

"That cat is a menace." Convinced her precious Percival wasn't harmed, Amanda turned her ire on Pastor Jeffries. "We don't need a cat around here, I've said so time and again. He'll give one of the children cat-scratch fever, that's what he'll do."

Pastor Jeffries looked harassed. "I'm sure Absalom has never scratched anyone, let alone a child. He was just protecting the flower bed."

"Protecting it against what, I'd like to know!"

The pastor seemed reluctant to mention the obvious extent of Percival's visit to the daffodils. I began washing my white bib, waiting for Amanda to bring up her latest donation. She used the remnants of the family fortune like a whip to bend others to her will.

Ella bent to stroke my head, wafting the faint scent of chocolate my way. "Absalom's a good cat, aren't you?"

I'd object to the condescending tone, but she'd found the precise spot behind my ears where I like to be rubbed.

Amanda gave her a withering look, then focused on Pastor Jeffries. "I assume you'll be using the new chalice for communion Sunday."

Furrows crossed the pastor's usually placid brow. "Of course we appreciate your generous donation, I'm not sure such a valuable object . . . "

"It was my father's wish." Her tone left no doubt the late judge's wish would be obeyed. "I'll expect to see it then." Clutching Percival to her breast, she marched to the elderly Chrysler that took up two spaces at the curb.

"We can't get away from it," Ella said when she'd gone. "We'll be polishing that antique silver from now until the last trump sounds."

Pastor's frown deepened, and I wound around his legs. "I'm sure our Lord didn't use antique silver for the Last Supper. And the value of the thing . . . have you finished the paperwork on it yet?"

She whisked toward the door. "Working on it now."

Pastor and I exchanged a glance. We both knew she wasn't. Ella ignored the new computer that was supposed to make her life easier and her work faster. Consequently she was always behind and always working late.

"Well, try to finish soon." He called after her. "I just don't like . . ."

The door closed behind her, cutting him off. He leaned over to tickle my white bib. "I just don't like any of it, Absalom. Not any of it."

I wasn't sure whether he meant the edict to use the expensive chalice or his futile efforts not to be dominated by the women in his life. Either way, I purred agreement.

"Pastor Jeffries! Pastor Jeffries!"

I skittered away from running feet in the hallway between the sanctuary and the office, leaping to the nearest windowsill for a convenient view.

The deacon in charge of setting up for communion dodged through the bake sale traffic and slid to a halt at the study door.

"The chalice . . . the new chalice. I opened the cabinet to get it out, but it wasn't there. It's gone!"

So. I blinked slowly. That sliver of warning the day before had been accurate. Something was indeed wrong at Grace Church.

* * *

"The police must be called at once." Amanda planted both fists on the pastor's desk and glared at him. "I don't know why you haven't done it already."

Pastor wilted, and I retreated a bit farther under the bookcase. Percival was sniffing at my tail, but this was clearly not the time to teach him manners.

"Perhaps it's just misplaced."

"Misplaced! It was locked in the vestry cupboard. Only church staff and deacons have keys. It's been stolen."

He winced at the strident words. "But the police . . . you can't be thinking one of us would have taken it."

"Everyone in the church knew how valuable that gift was." Amanda drew herself up. "There's no doubt in my mind. The police must be called."

"Not yet." Pastor stood, facing her. "We don't want a scandal. Let me have twenty-four hours to find it before we report it."

She sniffed. "Very well. But it won't take twenty-four hours to find if it's misplaced. I'll give you two. Then I'll make a police report, like it or not."

She scooped up Percival and departed, her air that of an avenging angel.

I leaped to the desk as Ella appeared in the doorway.

"What are we going to do?"

Pastor stroked me absently. "Find that dratted chalice, I suppose. I don't want to try and explain to the insurance company why such a valuable item was sitting in a cabinet to which half the church has keys."

Ella paled. "You won't have to. I haven't completed the paperwork yet. Officially, the chalice still belongs to Amanda."

The mutual recriminations began to bore me after a few minutes. I leaped down from the desk. My church, my responsibility. I'd find the culprit myself.

Where to begin? Our previous minister had been addicted to television police dramas; Pastor Jeffries was more of a Sherlock Holmes fan. Surely between the two of them I'd learned enough to conduct an investigation.

Motive, first. Humans seemed to have a natural acquisitive sense for any object they thought valuable. As far as I was concerned, if I couldn't eat it, play with it, or sleep on it, it had no value. However, I've learned not to judge other creatures by my standards.

So any human who'd entered the church yesterday might have wished to acquire the object. I considered the possibilities. Pastor, Ella, George the sexton. People dropping off goodies for the bake sale.

I trotted through the hallway to the church kitchen, to be promptly shooed away from the array of baked goods. Several of these people had been in the day before, but none had gone out carrying anything. They'd been delivering, not picking up. The only humans I'd seen carrying anything out of the building yesterday had been George the sexton, Ella, and Pastor himself.

I was tempted to eliminate Ella and Pastor on the basis of long friendship and tuna treats, but that would be akin to Holmes taking a bribe. Unthinkable.

George would be in the catacombs beneath the sanctuary, my favorite haunt for the occasional mouse to vary my diet. He'd fixed up a snug little den for himself behind the furnace, and he wasn't likely to come out as long as the bake sale ladies were present. They might want him to move a table, haul a package, or do any of the things for which the church paid him. I flowed down the stairs and through the boiler room door.

"Absalom, my lad." George the sexton waved me in. "On a hunt, are you?"

He dropped a careless caress on my head, and I dodged it with the ease of long practice. With George the sexton, it was equally likely to be a pat or a blow, but he never laid a glove on me.

"They're not hunting for me, are they, laddie?" He frowned toward the ceiling. "You'd let me know if they were coming after me. You and me are pals."

Only in his dreams. However, I thought I'd seen enough. What George the sexton's wife called his "sick spells" were relatively predictable, and he'd been playing least-in-sight for the last two days. It was safe to assume the only thing he'd carried out of the church in his toolbox yesterday had been his bottle.

I trotted back through the cellar, ignoring the faint lure of mouse. No time for that now. I had other business to tend to.

Ella had also been carrying something when she left the premises the day before. I'd wondered at the bulge in her embroidery bag, hoping she wasn't making Pastor yet another stole. Liturgical needlework had become popular with some of the ladies since the advent of a bachelor parson.

Dodging through the half-opened office door, I checked out the room. Beyond, in the study, I could hear Ella's sniffles. She apparently was still mourning her failure to complete the paperwork on the chalice, while Pastor did his feeble best to comfort her. The embroidery bag lay on the floor near her desk.

Hmm. This didn't look good for Ella. The bag lay flat. Whatever had distended its sides the day before was gone now.

I reached for the bag's handle with one black and white paw, flipping it over. It fell open with a gentle *whoosh*.

Sniffing quickly, I quartered the bag, checking every fiber, identifying smells. Wool, linen, the metallic hint of needles. And . . . I stopped, sniffed again, and took a lick. Chocolate.

Understand, I am not a chocolate addict. It is, I believe, not especially healthful for felines, and I prefer to keep my digestion sound and my coat glossy. However, I have, on rare occasions, tasted the food some humans found irresistible.

This was no ordinary chocolate. Oh, no. Two flavors of chocolate, a hint of crème de menthe, the satisfaction of butter . . . I knew what we had here.

Mrs. Lang's double-chocolate mint cake, baked at great effort from the secret recipe she insisted she'd will to the church when she passed on. I'd seen her carrying the concoction into the kitchen for the bake sale the previous day.

Ella had apparently anticipated the sale by a few hours. Etiquette insisted donations for the sale not be touched until the sale officially opened. But Ella had made a raid on the kitchen and absconded with the double-chocolate mint cake.

Not absconded, that wasn't the right word. Knowing Ella, I was sure she'd left an appropriate donation. But she hadn't been willing to wait until the sale opened and risk losing the prize to someone else.

I licked my whiskers, considering. The only other human who'd left the building carrying anything the day before was Pastor, with his briefcase. It was a large one. Large enough to hide a silver chalice? I didn't know, but I didn't like to think it. And furthermore, I didn't know how to prove it, one way or the other.

"We'll just have to search, that's all." The study door opened. "Let's start with the vestry closet. She may simply have overlooked it."

None of us believed for a moment that Amanda had overlooked a silver chalice, but Ella and I trailed dutifully behind Pastor to the vestry. He unlocked the cabinet where the communion ware was kept. Only the old pottery set met our gazes.

"Nothing." Ella opened the doors to the other cabinets, one after the other. Candles, vestments, serving trays, the heavy vases used for altar flowers.

"It has to be here." Pastor gave me a helpless look. "I refuse to believe one of us would do such a thing. It's impossible. And if it's impossible, it didn't happen."

I thought I heard echoes of one of his favorite Sherlockian tales. Perhaps he imagined me his Doctor Watson. I had a differing view of who should play the Great Detective, however.

"Have you phoned for the police yet?" Amanda's strident voice boomed from the walls in the tiny vestry as she entered. "Well?"

"Not yet." Pastor shot a nervous look at her. He was probably trying to think how to bring up the delicate subject of the insurance, or lack thereof. "Let's just talk this through, first."

"Nothing to talk about."

Percival wore the same insufferable expression as his mistress. I leaped to the counter, then up to the shelf which held the flower vases, so that I could look down at him. Dogs find my head for heights infuriating. Carefully out of reach, I let my tail dangle.

Percival yipped once, and Amanda glared at me. "Get that cat down from there."

The edge in her voice intrigued me. I rose, weaving my way among the metal flower containers.

"Pastor, that cat is going to break something."

"Absalom never breaks things," Pastor declared. "He can walk along the shelf as easily as you or I would walk across the floor."

I froze, my eyes zeroing in on one of the vases. I sniffed, delicately. And I knew.

I hated to make a liar of Pastor, but it was for a good cause. I hit the bronze vase with one paw.

It didn't move. I'd forgotten how heavy the things were. Still, a good head butt should do it.

"Absalom!" Pastor shouted as the vase hit the floor with a resounding clang. I flowed down after it, intent.

Some of the floral foam with which the vase was packed dislodged at its rough treatment. Percival, snarling, attacked it. I diverted him with a back-handed swipe on the nose that sent him yelping for cover.

I hooked one paw into the vase, pulling out the object that someone had wedged securely between the vase and the floral foam. The silver chalice slid out. Caught on its rim, entangled in a bit of the foam, was a long, fuzzy pink thread.

"So she never intended to give us the chalice at all." Ella poured another cup of coffee and sat down opposite Pastor.

He shook his head. "Apparently she discovered it was much more valuable than her father thought. She couldn't bear to part with it, but she also couldn't go against the judge's wishes."

"So she handed it over and then stole it back."

"I suppose she didn't want to risk walking out with it yesterday, so she hid it where she didn't think anyone would look." He reached out to stroke me. "Anyone but Absalom."

"I still think you should have turned her over to the police and taken the chalice back. After all, the judge intended us to have it." Ella's face flattened with displeasure.

Pastor shook his head. "I suspect she's learned her lesson. She's agreed to sell the chalice and turn the money over to the homeless shelter. That's a better use for it." He stroked me again. "I'm satisfied."

I purred. I was satisfied, too. Not that I cared about the disposition of the chalice, but because I'd restored my world to its proper order. And scratching Percival's nose had been pure pleasure.

I stretched. I'd been right all along about Percival and his mistress. But then, I usually am.

Close, but No Cigar

BARBARA PAUL

HERE, KITTY! COME HERE, YOU stupid cat. I'm not going to hurt you! Why does he think I'm going to hurt him?"

"Stop screeching at him, Richard—you're frightening him."

Feeling insulted, Richard gave Justine his best villainous glare. "I do not," he said, "screech."

The cat opened his mouth and gave a loud hiss.

The third member of the group spoke up. "Just keep quiet, Richard," Lyle said softly. "Your voice is aggravating him."

Richard rolled his eyes. "Et tu, Lyle?"

"Oh, look!" Justine exclaimed in alarm. "Come down, kitty! You'll hurt yourself!"

The yellow tom had leaped up to the balustrade and was crouching there uncertainly, looking for a way to escape from these three noisy and insistent humans.

Lyle approached the cat cautiously. "C'mon, kitty, no one's going to hurt you. Come here."

The cat glowered at Lyle's approaching hand, and after a moment's hesitation launched himself away from the theater box. His three pursuers watched in awe as he sailed through the air, landed on the stage, and scampered away into the wings.

"My god, did you see that?" Richard asked, dumbfounded. "Just like John Wilkes Booth!"

"And from the very same spot, too," Lyle added, equally impressed.

"But John Wilkes Booth broke his leg when he landed," Justine said anxiously.

"Nothing got broken this time. You saw him run away," Richard pointed out. "Cats aren't like people—he's all right."

"What the hell are you doing up there?" They looked down to see Mona Armstrong standing on the stage and glaring up at them. "Nobody's supposed to go into that box!"

"We were trying to catch a cat," Justine explained. "And, Mona, he jumped! All the way from here to about where you're standing. Did you see him? Is he all right?"

"Oh, is that what that yellow blur was?" Mona asked. "Don't worry. Anything that can run that fast can't be injured. How did a cat get in here anyway?"

No one knew. The three actors left the private box where Abraham Lincoln had met his untimely end and went down to join Mona. Ford's Theater was to see the debut of a new play called *Inchmeal*; the buzz had it that the dark comedy was a winner and would prove a career boost to everyone appearing in it. The hiring of Mona Armstrong to direct upped the odds even more; Mona was on a streak, having directed four successful productions in a row.

When all fifteen actors had arrived for the day's rehearsal, Mona told them what she wanted. "We're going to walk through the blocking for the first scene of the second act. Something's not quite right and I want to fix it now. When you—" she broke off to look at a young man chewing on a hamburger. "Sammy, you know the rule. No food onstage."

The young actor stopped in midchew. He swallowed and said, "Oh, right. I forgot." Sammy dropped the rest of his hamburger into its paper bag and trotted offstage. He set his lunch on a folding chair and never saw the yellow paw that darted out to snag the paper bag the minute his back was turned.

The director finished giving the cast its instructions. As the actors moved to their places, Lyle stopped Richard. "When we get to the newspaper bit," Lyle said to him, "if you pick it up with your left hand instead of your right, you won't look so awkward to the audience."

Richard gaped at him.

Mona had heard. "You don't look awkward, Richard," she said hastily. "Just keep on doing it the way you've been doing it."

Lyle shrugged and moved away.

Mona put them through their paces. When she was satisfied that they'd got their stage movements right, she called a break and motioned Lyle aside. "I want you to stop it, Lyle," she said. "No more of this 'friendly' advice to Richard."

"Oh, hey," Lyle replied, all sympathetic concern. "I didn't mean to step on your authority."

"Cut the crap," she snapped. "We both know what you're doing, and I'll not have you undermining Richard's confidence with all these little helpful suggestions that have him thinking he's doing everything wrong. Ever since Day One you've been 'helping' him. I've watched you giving him little exercises to get rid of what you call the abrasive quality in his voice and—"

"His voice is abrasive," Lyle interrupted.

"To you it is. He got the role *you* wanted. That's what this is all about, isn't it?"

Lyle nervously twisted the ring he was wearing on his left hand, round and around. It was a Thespian Society ring, the preferred article of jewelry of an organization whose main order of business seemed to be thinking up things to complain about to Equity, the actors' union. Lyle saw Mona staring at his ring-twisting and put both hands in his pockets. He also saw that further protest would be useless and opted to play it straight. "Richard's wrong for the role, Mona. He has no presence, no stage weight—"

"Whereas you do? Forget it, Lyle. Richard's playing the lead and that's that."

"I know the role. Every word. I could step in for him on a moment's notice."

Mona took a deep breath. "I should hope so, since you're understudying him. Look, I'm sorry you're feeling frustrated, but you're right for the role you're playing. And I meant it about your making no more suggestions to Richard. None at all. If you keep it up, I'll have to replace you."

He smiled icily. "Threats, Mona?"

She nodded. "Threats, Lyle. Now behave yourself. Concentrate on your own role."

Mona left him standing there and headed toward the ladies' before resuming rehearsal. On her way she passed Justine and a woman named Ginger sitting on the floor; Justine was cuddling a big yellow cat in her lap. "Is that the cat you were chasing?"

"This is the guy," Justine said happily. Mona nodded and moved on.

The cat licked his lips, belched politely, and snuggled down for a nap.

Ginger stroked the cat's head. "Wonder where he came from? He must be a stray."

Justine shook her head. "He's too sociable for a stray. He has to be somebody's pet."

The cat purred.

"I doubt it," said Ginger. "People are pretty good about getting their cats altered these days. But this one—well, he's still all boy."

Justine perked up. "Then he doesn't belong to anybody?"

The other woman laughed. "You want to keep him."

"I think I'll call him Abe."

Ginger looked surprised; she'd heard about the cat's flying leap to the stage floor. "Not John Wilkes Booth?"

Justine made a face. "I'm not going to name a nice innocent cat after an assassin. His name is Abe."

Mona returned and called everyone back onstage. She should have told Justine and Ginger to get rid of the cat; but she was a sucker for felines herself so she let him stay. Lyle, she noticed, was keeping to himself, brooding and playing with his ring. Richard, as usual, was champing at the bit. "Okay, everybody," she called out, "act two, scene one. Full out, this time. Remember your new blocking."

"Somebody stole my hamburger," Sammy complained.

It was Abe who found the body.

The next day, the minute Justine let him out of his new carrier, the cat crouched low to the floor and began to growl.

"What's the matter with him?" Ginger asked.

"I don't know." Justine bent down and tried to stroke Abe's back, but he slunk away from her touch.

Sammy wandered up. "What's with Abe? Why's he gone into attack mode?"

"That's what we're trying to figure out," Ginger replied. "Oh—where's he going?"

The three actors followed as the cat assumed a stalking posture and crept slowly to the head of a stairwell leading to the substage area. There he stopped, growling low in his throat.

Ginger was the first to look. "Oh, my god—it's Richard!"

The other two joined her. "Shee-ut!" said Sammy.

The play's leading man lay in a heap on the first landing of the stairwell. His head was bloody, and there was blood on the brass handrail where he'd hit. Richard's feet were tangled in the coil of lighting cable that had evidently tripped him.

"Sammy—go get Mona," Ginger said. She put her arm around Justine, who was trembling violently. "He must have been there all night."

Abe's growl turned into a high whine. They waited.

Sammy came back with Mona, who took one look and went down the cement steps two at a time. Although Richard was clearly dead, she felt for a pulse. She looked up at the others and shook her head. Justine began to cry.

"Shee-ut," Sammy said again.

Mona was fingering the lighting cable. "Who the hell left a coil of cable at the top of the steps? Anybody with half a brain could see that's a safety hazard! Some stagehand is going to get fired," she muttered, "union or no union."

"Shouldn't we call someone?" Ginger asked.

"Yeah." Mona came back up the steps. "I'm going to do that now."

"Poor Richard," Justine said between sobs.

It took the D.C. police twenty minutes to get there, with an ambulance not far behind. The medical examiner's guess was that Richard had been dead at least fifteen hours, probably a little longer. The police took statements.

The director and cast of the new play *Inchmeal* said their rehearsal had broken up shortly before six the day before. They'd drifted out singly and in pairs over a ten- or fifteen-minute period. Spread out like that, no one had given any thought to not having seen Richard leave. Mona told the police that Richard's official residence was in New York and that he'd lived alone in Washington; he'd been using the apartment of a friend who was spending the next few months in

London. She didn't know about next of kin, so she gave the police the name of Richard's agent.

While the police were questioning the cast, Mona spent the better part of an hour on the phone with various Ford's Theater officials. The PR office wanted a statement. Even though she hadn't completely absorbed the shock of Richard's death, Mona knew she had to think ahead.

Lyle was going to get to play the lead in *Inchmeal* after all. Sammy had been understudying Lyle, so he'd take over Lyle's old part. The only problem was that Sammy was a bit young for that role. But he was a good actor, and it would be easier to find a replacement for Sammy's old role than for Lyle's. So Lyle would move into Richard's role, Sammy would move into Lyle's, and Mona would make some unemployed actor deliriously happy by calling him in to take over Sammy's small role. She had a long list to choose from, actors who'd auditioned but who had not been cast. Then tomorrow they'd start rehearsal earlier than their usual hour to make up for lost time. Mona felt callous treating Richard's accident as an obstacle to be worked around, but it had to be done.

The police were finally finished; they started leaving, taking Richard's body with them. Members of the cast were standing around helplessly, not wanting to linger but not wanting to go, either; Mona was going to have to say something to them. After she'd seen the last police officer out, she started back toward the stage. But her eyes were drawn to the stairwell as if by a magnet. Abe was down there where Richard had been, playing with something that made a light metallic sound as it rolled over the cement landing.

The others were waiting for her on the stage, the fourteen who were left of a fifteen-member cast. They'd fallen into the informal half-circle they adopted when listening to their director. Mona took her usual place, facing them, back to the empty auditorium. She cleared her throat.

The damned cat was playing with something right where Richard had died.

"Wait here," she told her numb-looking actors.

She ran back to the stairwell. Abe was still on the landing, but now lying on his side and looking bored. Mona approached him cautiously; when she stroked his throat for him, he let her pick up his toy. It was a Thespian Society ring.

Mona clenched her fist around the ring, trying desperately to think what to do. She took her time getting back to the stage. Lyle was staring gloomily at his feet, a scowl on his face. Stumbling over her words and having trouble finishing her sentences, Mona told the actors there was no point in trying to rehearse today. Go home, she said, do something to take your mind off Richard. You need time to catch your breath.

And I need time to think.

* * *

Mona had spent a sleepless night, trying to decide what was the best thing to do. She ought to call the police and give them the ring. But if they arrested Lyle, *Inchmeal* would close before it even opened; where was she going to find a leading man at this stage of the game? Sammy wasn't experienced enough to carry a lead. Oh, maybe someone was available; but finding him could take weeks and they didn't have weeks.

But she couldn't let Lyle get away with murder. No way. She thought about calling a lawyer. She thought about calling the chairman of the board of Ford's Theater. She thought about calling her mother.

And what if she was jumping to conclusions? There could be some perfectly innocent reason Lyle's ring was on the landing where Richard's body had lain. *Yeah, sure.* But shouldn't he be given a chance to explain? She thought about confronting him privately, hearing what he had to—

Whoa. A private meeting with a man who could be a killer? Good god, what was she thinking of! No, that kind of thing happened only in dumb movies. She would *not* talk to him alone.

So what was the opposite of a solo confrontation? A group confrontation. A group like the cast of the play. Safety in numbers. The more she thought about that, the more she liked it. She, Mona Armstrong, would call everyone together, explain what had happened, and finger the killer. Straight out of Agatha Christie. Only this time the suspected killer would be given full opportunity to offer his explanation. If he had one.

So the next morning she told the actors to find a place to sit; they had something to talk about. Mona herself was seated behind a card table that held a copy of the script and her usual notes, but for once she ignored them. As the actors found seats, Abe wandered in from the wings, sat down in exact stage center, and cocked his head at her. Mona noted that Lyle was to her left, sitting between Ginger and Justine. He was slumped in his chair, both hands jammed into his pockets.

"I have reason to believe," she started out, "that Richard was murdered." She was expecting an outcry at her announcement, but she didn't get one; they all sat staring at her blankly. "You know ... *murdered?*"

Finally Sammy responded. "You mean, like, on purpose?"

Mona sighed. "Well, yes, Sammy, if it's murder it would have to be on purpose. I'm telling you Richard didn't just trip and fall. Somebody pushed him down those stairs. Then whoever did it must have put that cable around his feet to make it look like an accident."

"No!" Justine gasped.

Mona got the general outcry she'd been waiting for. She waited for the hubbub to die down, but it never really did.

Finally Ginger shouted, "Why, Mona? What makes you think so?"

They fell quiet to hear her answer. "Before I tell you that," Mona said, "I have to ask a question myself." She turned to Lyle. "Lyle, just how badly did you want to play the lead in *Inchmeal?*"

He sat up straight, his eyes wide. "What?"

"You'd been doing everything you could think of to demoralize Richard and make him appear incompetent, in the hopes that I'd kick him out and give you the lead. What else did you do to him that we don't know about?"

Lyle swallowed and said slowly, "Mona, that sounds very much as if you're accusing me of murder!"

"Did you push him down those stairs?"

"No! Goddammit, Mona! Where the hell do you get off, asking me a thing like that!"

Mona took out the ring and held it up so everyone could see. "A Thespian Society ring. It was on the stairwell landing where we found Richard's body."

Every eye in the place turned toward Lyle.

His look of astonishment grew even greater. He shook his head incredulously and pulled his left hand out of his pocket. He was wearing his Thespian Society ring.

The hubbub broke out all over again. Mona buried her head in her hands. Her one chance to play Miss Marple and she blew it.

Salvage what you can. "Okay, I was wrong," Mona said, waving the others to silence. "I'm sorry, Lyle. I'll apologize more adequately later. But right now, who else here belongs to the Thespian Society?"

"Not me," said Sammy. "Dues are too high." The others were shaking their heads.

"Lyle, you must know," Mona insisted.

"I have no idea," he said. "It's a national organization, big membership. And we come from all over."

Ginger turned to him. "Don't you have a membership directory?"

Lyle's face lit up. "Yeah! Mine's back in L.A., but we shouldn't have any trouble getting hold of one!"

"Good!" Mona exclaimed happily, feeling like a detective again. "And whichever member of this cast is listed in that directory—"

"Never mind," Justine said in a high, choked voice. "It's my ring."

There was a startled silence. Then:

"*Yours!*"

"Justine?"

"Shee-ut."

No one knew what to say. They were all staring at Justine in disbelief. Abe jumped up on her lap and started butting her with his head.

"*You* killed Richard?" Mona finally asked.

"It was an accident," Justine said unhappily, absently stroking the cat. "Just what it looked like. And I didn't put the cable around his feet, he really did trip, and I couldn't do anything, I just had to stand there and watch . . ."

Mona sighed. "Start at the beginning."

"Well, he was teasing Abe," Justine said. "And he was being really mean about it, real nasty. Richard kept poking at him with a ruler, and poor little Abe thought he was being attacked and was hissing and swiping at Richard with his claws. I told Richard to stop it, but he said they were just playing and he went on poking and poking. Anyone could see the cat was traumatized."

She stopped to wipe the tears off her face with the palm of her hand. Ginger handed her a Kleenex.

"Anyway, Richard was *enjoying* it—tormenting an animal! I'd never seen that side of him before and it scared me. I kept telling him to stop, but he wouldn't listen to me. Finally I got myself in between Abe and him, and I pushed him, like this." She demonstrated, thrusting both hands forward, palms out. Abe growled at the sudden movement and jumped down from her lap.

"And that's when he fell down the stairs," Mona said.

"No," Justine replied, "that's when he pushed me back. So I pushed him again and he pushed me again and we were pushing and shoving and not look-ing where our feet were going and Richard got all tangled up in that lighting cable . . . and, and down he went." She took a long breath, let it out. "It was an accident."

"And the ring came off your finger during the tussle?"

"I wore it on a chain around my neck." Justine reddened at the high-school-ishness of it. "Richard must have hooked a finger in it. I found the chain caught in my bra when I got home."

"So what did you do when Richard fell? Did you go for help?"

"For a dead man? I did the same thing you did, Mona. I went down and felt for a pulse. I even put my ear against his chest to listen for a heartbeat. He was *dead*. I was scared. I'd been kind of fighting with him, and I was afraid of being accused of . . . you know. Murder." She shivered. "It was just a stupid ac-cident. Abe had taken off, and it took me some time to find him. Then I, er, I went home."

The actors were all exchanging startled looks. Ginger said, "You should have told someone. Right then."

"I know," Justine wailed. "I can see that now. But I was so upset with Richard and when I saw what happened to him . . . aw, my brain just turned it-self off."

Lyle patted her clumsily on the shoulder. The entire cast proceeded to an-alyze Justine's emotional state at the time of crisis and draw conclusions as to whether her own trauma excused her subsequent behavior or not. "Are you going to tell the cops?" someone asked Mona.

"Oh, why?" Ginger interposed. "They'll just let her go after they hear her story. Why put her through all that?"

Lyle said, "I agree. But I feel I must point out you were all ready to turn me in when you thought I did it."

"That's when we were still thinking murder," Ginger told him. "Big difference between murder and accident."

"Besides, Richard started it," Sammy said judiciously. "If he hadn't been tormenting Abe, Justine would never have given him that first push."

Yes, that's true. Heads were nodding sagely in agreement.

"Mona?" Justine's voice was tiny. "What are you going to do?"

Pin-drop time.

They all seemed to be holding their breath. Mona let the silence build and then said, speaking slowly: "Richard's death is on the police books as an accident. We now know for certain that that's exactly what it was. I see no reason to cause the police more paperwork."

A cheer broke out among the actors. Justine rushed over and hugged Mona, knocking over the card table. Abe scooted off the stage to get away from all the dancing feet.

Mona watched the actors with a smile, shaking her head. Fourteen of the original cast—fourteen extroverted, gregarious, talkative people. How long could they keep a secret like this?

Long enough for the play to open.

"Do you suppose we could get in a rehearsal sometime today?" Mona shouted over the clamor.

Good-naturedly, they made the effort to settle down. Playscripts were located, the rehearsal furniture rearranged, places taken.

Mona gathered up her spilled notes and folded the card table. As she was carrying them offstage, she glanced toward the auditorium and caught a glimpse of Abe, who was comfortably ensconced in one of the seats in the first row.

She could have sworn the damned cat was laughing at her.

Club Macavity

DAVID BISCHOFF

AS I THINK MY CAT WOULD AGREE, it was not a case solved by the book—but then, in a way, it was.

I got the call from the captain late in the morning. I would have let the phone machine take a message, except that the cats had been fighting on the table the week before and they knocked the thing off the table and busted it. The phone was on its eleventh ring when I picked it up.

"Yeah?"

"Need a favor, Carol."

Captain Ed Reynolds was the obnoxious kind of guy who didn't go through niceties or formalities, just barged right into your ear. I hate that obnoxious kind of guy.

"Long walk, short pier, Captain."

"You owe me, gal."

Crap. I did.

And as the kind of pseudo-dick with a pseudo-code of honor, I kind of kept my word.

Sigh. "Okay, okay. Look. My brain is still in bed. See you late afternoon?"

"I'll get you a cup of Full City Coffee."

"Cap. . . . ."

"Grande. Now get your butt over here. Pretty please!"

"So. What's going on?"

He told me and it woke me up.

He hung up and I sat down and rubbed my eyes. Just as well. No coffee in the trailer and it was only a short hop across the river. I'd probably get a donut out of the visit, too. Besides, the Eugene City Police Department had put me on a consulting payroll and it was doing lots for my lifestyle, if not for that pseudo-code I've got tucked away somewhere.

Carol Marshall, ex-L.A. Police Detective. Sherlocka Holmes, formerly tan, with shades and an attitude. That's me.

So I pulled on some jeans and tucked in a flannel shirt and ran a brush through my long tangled hair. I looked outside. I needn't have bothered. January-in-Eugene, Oregon, rain was coming down. No motorcycle today. Today was Volkswagon weather.

I threw on my trenchcoat which not only makes me look way cool, but keeps out the drippy damp. I was about to take off when Macavity kicked up a fuss.

"You've got plenty to eat," I told my ginger tabby.

She made that cat noise again and stroked my leg. Cabin fever? I didn't know, but it gave me an idea.

"You know, come to think of it . . . you really should go along on this thing."

"What the——" said the captain.

Macavity was peeping out of my coat. She meowed and I let her out. She hopped up onto the desk and started walking across some papers.

"That's my cat," I said, grabbing my cup of coffee so it wouldn't get knocked over.

"No kidding!" said Captain Reynolds. "What's she doing here?"

"She's standing on your papers."

He glared at me. "You know what I mean! What did you bring your damned cat here for!"

I shrugged. "She's a crime-solving cat. I'm thinking about writing a series of cat mysteries. So I figured—let's try one out. Let's see if cats really got what it takes. I got cats . . . And now, I've got a mystery." I took a sip of coffee. Ah. Yeah, it was just right. By now Eugene's finest knew how their consultants liked their coffee. "Anyway, it's totally appropriate that I take Macavity on this one. You'll see."

"You want to put her on it now and get her off my desk? I guess I really don't care if you take your cat. You always seem to get the job done, you've got unorthodox methodologies, and, strictly speaking, you're not a cop anymore." He shook his head. "Sometimes, though, Carol, I think you do these things just to annoy us."

"Why should I do that? I love cops!"

He gave me a hard, "yeah, right" look.

We knew each other well enough by now for Captain Ed Reynolds to have done some digging into my past. And that past was simple. Topflight woman police lieutenant-detective in the L.A.P.D. confronts macho, corrupt system and crashes, bad. Pieces move to Eugene, Oregon, and cool heels, write, hike, motorbike—mend.

Cops are pretty much cops anywhere, and they were crawling around Eugene, but often enough they were too dumb to figure out lots of cases. Their record for solving things was piss poor. So when someone moves into the neighborhood with real detective skill. . . .

All in all, I'd rather write books, but so far I'd only sold a few confessionals. After a while of playing hard-to-get, I started getting easier. All in all, it was a heck of a lot better than butting heads with hard-nosed career jerks in L.A. who were either on the take or on the make. But cops are still cops, and attitudes were still attitudes, and I guess there was still a lot of the bad side of both in Eugene, and in yours truly.

"So what's up?" I asked, after getting some smooth, milky paradise down.

"A theft. Victim's a cousin of a City Council member, and frankly, from the looks of it, I don't think our people are going to be able to recover the property."

Macavity knocked over the portrait of the captain's wife and family and then complained loudly of the clatter it made.

The captain righted it and gave me an aggrieved look.

"Priceless!" said the man, rolling his eyes beneath their bushy brows. "Absolutely priceless!"

"I'm sure. But what would you say it would get at auction on Christies or better yet—eBay." I said. Captain Reynolds had already explained my connection to the Eugene Police Department and my role in this investigation.

The man pursed his lips. "Now? Well, I'd have to say . . . oh, fifty, sixty thousand dollars, minimum."

That sounded a little steep for me, but the stocky man before me, with his extravagant gestures, looked like he was capable of extravagant exaggerations. I let it go and had a look around the place, just to get the feel of it better.

It was a bookstore, of the antiquarian variety. I'd heard of it, but hadn't had a chance to visit yet. It was nice, with lots of old books and tasteful displays of ancient matted prints. There were books under glass at the front counter, and it smelled of old leather and paper—my kind of smell.

The stolen item, it turned out, was a rare first edition of the poem collection *Old Possum's Book of Practical Cats*, in tip-top condition and signed by T. S. Eliot himself, along with drawings and notes, and even a shred of a piece of unpublished verse. There were a few other books of note swiped—a first of Mark Twain's *Huckleberry Finn*, goofs and all; a first of John Steinbeck's *Of Mice and Men*, signed by the man himself, but far and away, T. S.'s book was the top prize in the burglar's haul.

After all, it had been the inspiration for Andrew Lloyd Webber's hit show, *Cats*.

The owner of the book was an antiquarian book dealer named Mark Harness. He was a roly-poly fellow, with ruddy cheeks and a cultured accent that was odd and New Englandish for Western Oregon, but he had my approval from the git-go, immediately adoring Macavity and allowing her free reign of the shop. He'd been especially appreciative of the name, as Macavity was the name of one of the cats in the poetry collection. Macavity was already striding about, sniffing old editions of Edgar Rice Burroughs and pulp magazines in plastic wrap, in the way of kitty investigations.

The captain said, "Of course, we've dusted for fingerprints and the usual things, but we've come up with nothing."

Mark Harness shook his shaggy, disheveled locks. He looked a little like the card-magician Ricky Jay, minus the cynicism and puffiness. "I've got a modern alarm system. I don't know how they got through it."

"The book was on display?"

"Yes. But I thought it was safer here than at my home!"

"Sounds like a professional job to me," I said. "I'll have to look at what we've got here."

I got to look at the door, whose lock had been picked. I got to look at the alarm system, which wasn't quite as modern as the guy claimed, but which no amateur would be able to deal with either. Finally, Mark Harness led me into the back room where the book had been set up for inspection by visitors.

"Nice," I said, as the captain and I followed our host through some beaded curtains.

"Thank you," said our host. "We call it our Cozy Room."

The room was filled with stained-walnut bookshelves, jammed neatly with old books. There were a number of fancily upholstered chairs and a single beautiful fainting couch next to a tasseled lamp. It was like stepping into another dimension, and I guess I was damned enchanted. Macavity had already found the couch; he was curled up on it, resting from the day's exertions, and snoring lightly. My kind of detective!

"Cozy Room! Yes!" I said.

"We keep a lot of old collectors' editions of mystery novels—many English mysteries. You know what I mean?"

"Agatha Christie," I said. "Ngaio Marsh. Oh and about two hundred thousand since."

"You're familiar with cozies then?"

"Like a junkie's familiar with his needles."

A huge smile split the guy's face. It was a genuine smile, disarming and rich. No mere affectation here—I felt a connection.

"Well then. These are just a collection of mysteries that you might be interested in. And we afford our browsers a comfortable place to sample the wares. Or just enjoy the atmosphere."

For sure Macavity was enjoying the atmosphere. She yawned, stretched, looked out at us through inscrutable eyes—and then started looking for the missing books in her cat dreams.

"Right over here is where my book was," said Harness.

It was kind of a pedestal arrangement, covered with a plastic case. The top had been sawed off. Some sort of portable electric saw probably.

"There were alarms in the case, too?" I asked.

"Yes. The circuits were somehow nullified so there was no alarm.

"But there's a latch here I see," I noted.

"Yes, but as you can also see there's a combination lock."

"And who has the combination?"

"Well, I have four people on payroll and I trust them all, so they all have the combinations of safes and locks here."

"I see. I wonder if you'd call the ones who aren't here and tell them to come in. I need to speak to them."

"You think it's an inside job?" asked the captain. He was smoking a cigarette. We were outside the store in the outdoor mall.

"Well, the book's been on display for months, so lots of people must have known about it. I can't tell. I want to talk to the help.

"I'd gotten a look at the alarm system the burglar had gotten through."

"Any thoughts?"

"You're pushing too hard, Captain. I need to consult Charlemagne, anyway."

"Jeeze," said the captain, turning his eyes toward heaven, home of Jeeze.

They looked nervous. They smelled nervous.

There were four of them, and we sat in chairs in the main part of the shop, now temporarily closed for this meeting.

One guy's name was Mitch Williams. He was a skinny guy with a pale complexion but great big brown eyes. He stuttered a bit.

Another was Alexis Pulaski. He was part time. He worked as an English teacher and had his own book collection. He just loved old books. He had fading brown hair and a big nose.

The third man, as Graham Greene might say, was Frederick Alexander. He was a graduate student at the University of Oregon, working on his doctorate in American Literature. His dissertation was on Dashiell Hammett, John D. MacDonald, and modern crime fiction.

The fourth fellow was Richard Moss. Richard was the science-fiction expert and some of the old SF books that the store had were his, on consignment.

I asked them the usual questions that the cops had probably asked them, but then I also asked them about books. They all seemed genuine. They all seemed to know their stuff. They all had tentative, reflective, and awkward manners, variations of social skills hampered by hours and hours spent reading, reading, reading.

I was asking them about their roles with the alarm system, when Macavity strode out. He stretched, got a look at the assemblage, and then made for the nearest one, Richard Moss.

"Hey there! What a beautiful cat!" Richard stroked Macavity in just the right way. All the men looked at Macavity with admiring smiles, and the royal personage gave them all their chance to pay homage.

I asked a couple of more questions, and then thanked them.

"Well," said the captain, as we walked out.

"I'd like to borrow the reports of the inspecting officers," I said. Macavity was on my shoulder, looking back wistfully at the shop. "Then I want to think about it."

There were no customers in the store when I entered, five minutes before closing time. The only guy there was Mark Harness. He looked a little startled to see me.

"Hello! I didn't expect—"

"Okay if you put up the CLOSED sign a little early?" I asked.

"Uhm— sure. . . ."

He lumbered over to the door, locked it, then turned the sign to its CLOSED side. His face was blank when he turned around.

"Can we talk? The Cozy Room would be a good place."

"Of course." He looked and sounded subdued. He led me back to the Cozy Room.

I hadn't brought Macavity along, but I'd brought a couple of bottles of Mirror Pond Bitter Ale.

"Do you like beer?" I asked.

"I do."

"How about a church key?"

"I've got a Swiss Army knife."

I smiled. "You look like the sort who'd carry one of those," I said.

Puzzled, he opened the beer bottles and we sat down. He immediately guzzled a good quantity of the beer. He didn't look nervous, but he didn't look calm either.

"Macavity and I have talked about this whole business and we've looked at the police reports. We've come to a conclusion."

"Oh?"

"Yes. Mr. Harness . . . Mark, if I may . . . Macavity smells a rat. Macavity's a very ingenious cat, you see, unlike the clods at the Eugene Police Department. Macavity is very curious as to how a burglar with the technical finesse to get through your security system wouldn't also have the finesse to pick the lock to the case holding that most valuable signed novel."

Harness started to speak, but I held up a hand.

"Mr. Harness . . . Mark. Pardon me. Macavity, being a bookish cat, also knows a little bit about antiquarian books and about that market. She also knows a little bit about insurance. She also knows that antiquarian book lovers just like to own books sometimes. They don't necessarily need to show them."

The guy's beer was almost gone. I pushed mine across the coffee table to him. He looked puzzled, but he took it.

"Frankly, Macavity thinks that what's happened here is that you and your folks did this—and then planted clues to lead suspicion away. Maybe it would have worked, except that Macavity came onto the case. However, I've got to make a confession here. My dear cat lacks usual human ethics. She's a very selfish creature. Besides, like I say, she likes book dealers and books . . . And she understands that keeping this kind of operation going must take money and sacrifice . . . And too often the former gets a little messed up and shortcuts have to be taken to preserve . . ." I smiled, ". . . standards."

The guy sighed. "What does . . . Macavity . . . want?"

"You have to understand, Mark. Macavity is a regal cat. I got her from the Greenhill Humane Society. I keep her in a hovel of a trailer and she has to deal with a bunch of cats way below her station. I think that Macavity would like to have a new home. She was very comfortable here. She loves cozies too, she loves books . . . And frankly she felt that you and your employees paid her the respect she was truly due. As a part of your bookish family, she could not possibly go to the police and tell them her conclusions. In fact, she might even be able to give you a few pointers to cover loose ends you've left. And, of course, as my loyalties swing more toward her than our most pure legal system and its spotless lawkeepers—and since we're both aware that insurance companies are operated by Satan and his minions—well, I wouldn't be able to say a thing, either."

"That's all?" He looked like a man spared a bullet to the head, but baffled.

"Well, I must say that I should like to visit Macavity. And I should like to keep company here and get to know you and your employees . . . And it would be fun to hear about your bookish world and your bookish contacts."

I leaned back in the high-backed chair and savored the leather. Silence hung over us for a minute and the guy drank some more of my beer. He shook his bushy head and smiled.

"You—I mean, Macavity is really serious about this, isn't he?"

"I apologize for the overt blackmail. But Macavity does cut corners sometimes to get what he wants. And after all . . . he is the Mystery Cat."

"You know, I happen to have a very nice cognac in the back. I could do with some now. Would you like to join me? I'm sorry that Macavity can't join us, but I look forward to having a new addition to the crew here. We've been looking for quality cat rulership."

"Yes. A cognac would be nice," I said, and settled back comfortably into my new club chair.

Copycat Killer

BEVERLY T. HAAF

THE ONLY WITNESS WAS THE CAT. It lay watching us from under a bench, its eyes silver in the dim light.

"Look—" I said to the man, and pointed into the midnight sky.

Obediently the man looked where I directed. The hour was late, the street was deserted, and we were strangers, but he anticipated no threat from a woman. He stood with his head angled away from me, his fatty chest and plump stomach relaxed and unprotected.

My blade slipped in and up and out.

He gasped and turned to stare, startled but not alarmed, unaware of the fatal inner hemorrhage already begun. That's the magic of a properly mastered blade; there's so little time for pain.

"Goodness," I said. "You're having a heart attack!"

It's what I always say. It disarms rather than alarms for it provides a sensible explanation for the mysterious sensations. Instead of thrashing and crying out for help, the victim submits meekly to my direction.

The man's legs buckled. He collapsed and rolled to his back. A hissing breath escaped his slack lips. Then silence.

His wallet held two tens and a membership card to a porno club. His watch was unremarkable.

I glanced at the cat. "Nothing of value. Why him?"

The animal flicked its ears in arrogant disdain.

"I've missed something?"

The bonanza was in a money belt. Ten one-hundred-dollar bills.

The cat slipped from under the bench, my fellow creature of the night.

I lifted an eyebrow. "Same time next week?"

It gave me a flat, silver gaze and disappeared into the shadows.

I was raised a thief, the daughter of a pickpocket and one of her brutal companions. Another of her companions taught me skill with the knife. He also became my first victim when he tried to creep into my bed.

My specialty was breaking into houses; my problem was the horror of being apprehended. A five-foot-tall woman with a knife lacks a certain authority when confronted by an irate homeowner. A knife is best when there is an element of surprise. Murdering the members of the household in their beds would have solved my dilemma, but that would have meant death to women and children, too. I'm a thief and worse, but I have no desire to bring death to innocents.

The Bus Stop Killer showed me a new path. He first drew my attention because he also used a knife. His victims were women and I despised him for that. He was also careless, for he had left a thumbprint on the clasp of a victim's discarded purse. Still, I was curious enough to pay a late-hour visit to Quince Street, where he had made his third kill, a woman coming home on the 11:30 bus.

It was that night on Quince Street that I first met the cat. It came up to me as I stood in the shadows. Small and lithe, the creature boldly sniffed my shoes. It then gave me a long, piercing stare, eyes glowing like crescent moons.

Amused, I said, "You have ten sharp weapons, while I have only one. Have yours also tasted blood?"

A man in a trench coat came along the sidewalk. The cat darted out. Uttering throaty sounds, it circled the man. I assumed the animal knew him, and its fawning repelled me. A dog might beg for affection, but cats should be aloof from such needs. I was taken aback when the man cursed and kicked. The cat danced nimbly, avoiding harm.

That's when I saw the possibilities. Before me was an ideal victim. His distraction would provide my blade with the necessary element of surprise, and as a side benefit, the police would deem him Bus Stop Victim Number Four and redouble their search for a male killer.

I was about to slip on my ever-present gloves when a couple approaching the bus stop dissuaded me.

At home, I further pondered the new idea. When I entered an occupied house, I was on the defensive, but as a copycat Bus Stop Killer (excuse the pun, but you will soon see how apt it is) I would be the aggressor, the advantage all mine.

That next night found me in the shadow of a building on the corner of

Maple and Third. The cat reappeared. I had difficulty believing it was the same animal, but its dark gray coat and scimitar-like gaze convinced me.

"Come to join me for the kill?" I whispered.

Two men came to the bus stop and stood waiting. The cat glanced my way, then padded out. It paused as if sizing them up, then it circled the legs of one of them. After another look in my direction it faded into the concealing brush.

The bus arrived. One man boarded, but the one the cat had circled remained, apparently waiting for another bus.

I emerged from around my corner.

"Hi," I said, and moved in close.

That first kill went smoothly, resulting in a fat wallet, a nasty pistol, and a gold neck-chain decorated with a diamond-studded razor blade.

"Good choice. The world is better without him." I spoke to the cat, who sat watching. I joked, of course. Although I didn't understand the animal's behavior, I didn't believe it had deliberately chosen my prey.

The next morning's paper headlined: BUS STOP KILLER STRIKES AGAIN. I clipped it and started a scrapbook. In the library I retrieved back-issue articles about the real killer's crimes. Wicked though he was, he had been my inspiration; he deserved a place in my records.

A week later, I set out again. The true Bus Stop Killer had taken yet another female victim. Now that the deaths totaled five, late-hour bus riders were wary and inclined to travel in pairs. The true killer might have reasons for selecting those who took public transportation, but any male alone after dark was meat for me.

I found a hiding place by a hedge-flanked lane. When the cat joined me, I quelled my surprise. "Come for another lesson?"

A man's approaching footsteps silenced me. I was about to emerge, as if on honest business, when I realized the cat had not budged.

Not him? I questioned silently.

Pure superstition made me pause. It cost me, for it gave the man time to pass by.

Annoyed, I glared at the cat. Although I found its company oddly enjoyable, it had proved a nuisance.

Another man strode into view, keys jingling in hand. He approached a parked car. As if from nowhere, the cat darted out and went through the man's legs, almost magically escaping harm as the man stumbled.

The opportunity was too good to miss.

I hurried out. "Is my little cat bothering you?"

Straightening the man turned to face me.

"Damned cat," he said.

The last words he ever spoke.

The man's jewelry was boon enough, but the real prize was in the briefcase in the car trunk; forty thousand dollars in bills of small denominations.

"Perhaps you're not a nuisance after all," I said to my four-footed friend, experiencing an unexpected sense of camaraderie. Although it was a male, the sex I distrusted and despised, it was after all only a cat.

I went off on a well-deserved vacation and came home wondering what my little friend had made of my absence. A newsstand headline jumped out: COPS SEEK COPYCAT KILLER.

My first thought was that the police had finally recognized my superior skill with the blade. A look at the paper told me I was wrong. The "copycat," who had murdered two women and a man during my absence, had slit his victim's throats, a technique used by neither the true Bus Stop Killer nor by me.

Since I was a copycat myself, it was foolish to feel usurped, yet I did. I went home and soothed myself with the thought that I was the only killer assisted by a real cat.

My TV had been playing in the background; a newscaster's voice abruptly drew my attention. He spoke of a bizarre set of circumstances: the police had now determined that the victim of the previous night's copycat murder was the original Bus Stop Killer. His body had been identified by the fingerprint he had left on a victim's purse clasp.

The camera showed the dead man: a sprawled figure garbed in a trench coat. Something about him looked familiar, but before I could figure out why, the scene switched to the newscaster interviewing a woman who was a witness to the crime.

"I saw a man trip over a gray cat," she said into the microphone. "Another man rushed up. I thought he had come to give aid, then I saw his knife."

The woman rattled on, but my brain had stopped at hearing about the gray cat. It was *my* cat that darted out to distract a potential victim. Questions arose. During my absence, had the cat switched his alliance to the other copycat killer? And why had the victim in the trench coat, the true Bus Stop Killer, looked so familiar?

That's when I remembered the night on Quince Street when I first met the cat; remembered how it had circled the legs of a man dressed in a trench coat.

I tore open my scrapbook and read of the Bus Stop Killer's early crimes, seeing what I had missed before: the woman killed on Quince Street had lived alone, *except for her cat.*

A sense of betrayal gripped me. The cat had never been my friend and willing helper. It had been *using* me.

I stormed out into a night gloomy enough to suit my mood. The cat soon appeared, standing in an eerie, rain-misted glow.

"Deceiver," I accused. "You never cared for me and my work. You were only luring me on, seeking revenge for the murder of your mistress. As soon as my back was turned, you sought someone else to complete your task."

The creature stared for a moment, then disappeared around the corner.

I continued walking, mumbling vile words under my breath. I should have known better than to trust a male of *any* species.

I rounded the corner and continued along a walkway lit by old-fashioned gas lamps. The cat stood watching from beside a thicket of fog-shrouded lilacs. It darted into the thicket, then reappeared. It gave me another look, then dashed inside again.

The lilacs, I realized, offered the kind of shelter that either I or the other copycat killer might like to hide in.

This thought came too late to save me. A man burst from the thicket and seized my arm. His knife flashed. The cat leaped. For an instant it seemed the blade had found its target there, then the animal, unharmed, sunk its claws into the startled killer's hand. I twisted and drove my own blade home.

The dead man's pockets held only a stained ribbon, an earring, and a money clip; trophies, no doubt, from his successful kills. But I felt lucky to be alive and was in no mood to complain.

I met the cat's steadfast silver gaze.

"With your nine lives and my one blade, I think we're going to have a long and beautiful friendship."

Together, we walked home through the rain.

Cricket Longwhiskers

CAROLINE RHODES

WHEN SHE HEARD THE SOUND of Mom's car pulling into the veterinary hospital parking lot, Cricket scooped the hoppy bug that shared her name into her mouth and scampered for the back door. While Mom was trying to get the beepy alarm shut off, Cricket slammed her tiger-striped head into Mom's purple scrub-clad leg.

"Mmmmrrow," Cricket said, her greeting muffled by wiggly legs.

"Hi, cat," Mom said, leaning over to pat her head.

It wasn't nearly enough of a "good morning," and Cricket let her know by running alongside, bumping her legs as they made their way down the hallway back to the office.

Mom stopped abruptly at the office door. "Cat!"

Cricket paused, cocking her head to one side . . . ahhh, that would be the very battable box of gauze left on Mom's desk. "Mmmmmrrruph," Cricket said by way of apology.

Mom gave a heavy sigh, scooped the streamers of gauze into a wad and deposited them in an empty box that had an intriguing look to it. "Don't even think of it," Mom warned, meeting her gaze.

Mom sat and eyed the pile of charts on her desk that still needed notes and callbacks. "Paperwork. They didn't tell me about the paperwork at veterinary school."

Cricket dropped the bug into the middle of the hated paperwork, and opened her mouth to make an appropriately sympathetic noise.

"Eeewwww. Did I need a mangled bug before breakfast?"

Cricket leaned closer, studying Mom's face. Was she kidding? Who *wouldn't* want a bug before breakfast?

Mom pushed her away. "Back, bug breath," she said, helping the cricket to the floor, where it crawled behind more files, promising a tempting mid-morning diversion.

The alarm chirped, and Susan's voice called a greeting. A moment later, she appeared in the office, green scrubs smelling of her own kitties. Cricket flew from the ground to Susan's chest in one agile leap. Susan's arm went around her, and Cricket began her morning greeting, scenting, and marking ritual.

"Good morning, sweet kitty," Susan crooned, running her finger down the white fur on Cricket's nose. "Has anyone called in response to the ad on her?"

"No. I'll run it another week. She's a pretty nice little cat . . . someone's got to want her."

"It's been two months, Katie. Why don't you just take her home? It's unnatural for a veterinarian not to own any animals."

Mom sighed. "She needs a home where someone is actually there from time to time. She doesn't need a house where she's abandoned all day long. She needs . . . supervision," Mom said, her gaze going to the box of tangled gauze. "Besides, if I take her home, I'll bond with her, and then I'll never look for a home for her. And I have more than enough animals here every day."

Cricket patted Susan's cheek with a white paw. "Stop bugging Mom . . . she'll take me home when she's ready. It won't be much longer now . . . I've been working on her," she *mrrowed* confidently.

There was a frantic knock at the back door. Cricket shrank down, ears slightly back.

Mom took a look at Susan, arms full of cat, and headed for the door. Cricket heard the whimper as soon as the door opened, heard the frightened tone of the woman's voice.

"I need the doctor...my dog...he's bleeding."

"I'm the doctor," Mom said calmly. "Let me get him on the table."

Cricket jumped off Susan and went to watch, pausing at the doorway. There was something strangely wrong with the big dog. He didn't smell sick, he smelled...injured...and scared. Cricket crept closer, watching Mom touch the dog gently, while Susan escorted the woman to the waiting area.

Cricket jumped up on the table next to the dog and froze. There were two holes in his skin, and blood...she sniffed. They smelled of metal and human anger...male human anger. And more than just scared, the dog was terrified, and had been that way for a long time.

"Shoo," Mom said, elbowing her off the table. Cricket ran down the hall, and watched from the edge of the office door as Mom went to the cabinet where the bottles of liquid medicine were, grabbed a syringe, and filled it.

Mom carefully injected the dog, then ran her hand over his head while his breathing evened out and he stopped whimpering. Susan returned about the time Mom was putting on the cap with the dangly ties in back.

"Did you ask her who shot him?" Mom asked.

Susan got out the intubation and surgery pack and shook her head. "She didn't know. I sent her home and told her we'd call later."

Mom snorted gently, then started scrubbing up for surgery.

Cricket was so upset that she couldn't even nap, but sat curled in Mom's chair, listening to the clink-clank of instruments, the breathing gases, and regular beep of the heart monitor.

Finally, she heard the dog whuffing against the tube in his throat, followed by the gagging choke as they took the tube out, then the sounds of him being moved into a cage. A minute later, Mom came into the office, scooped her out of the chair, and hugged her tightly. Cricket mewed and relaxed a bit. Even if nobody truly loved her, at least nobody was trying to hurt her! She snuggled closer under Mom's chin, getting her ears scratched in return. It was even possible that someone did care about her.

Mom sat down in her chair, allowing Cricket to remain on her lap while she dialed the phone.

"This is Dr. Weis calling about Sonny. Do you have any idea who shot him?"

Cricket could hear the woman's voice saying she didn't know who would do such a horrible thing. Then the woman started sobbing.

"Sonny's going to be all right, I think. I took out two bullets, and he was pretty lucky that they missed all his organs. He's resting comfortably now, and you should be able to take him home in a couple of days. But I really need you to talk to the police and file an animal cruelty report. Talk to your neighbors, find out if anyone saw anything."

Cricket heard the woman going on about nothing at all. She was scared, but pretty brainless, it seemed. She wasn't willing to get involved with the police over "just a dog." Cricket snorted and began grooming her front foot, striped tail twitching sharply.

When Mom got up to start seeing clients, she scratched Cricket behind the ear for a minute, looking into her eyes, really seeing her, instead of thinking about all the work she had to do. Then she smiled.

Once Mom left, Cricket went and curled up beside the dog's cage and watched over him. No stupid electronic alarm could beat out *her* vital sign monitoring. Even the bug rustling under the office papers couldn't entice her away today.

Later, after all the pets had been treated, and they'd all been sent home with medications, instructions, or vaccination certificates, Mom and Susan stood before Sonny's cage. Mom listened with her stethoscope, then patted the dog and closed the cage door.

"He sounds good, seems like he's pretty comfortable."

"I just gave him his pain meds and antibiotics, and his temperature is still normal," Susan said.

"That's it, then." Mom reached down and patted Cricket's head.

"Look at her . . . she hasn't left his side since he came out of surgery," Susan said, amazed.

Cricket let out a tiny meow, one that wouldn't disturb Sonny.

"Mmmmmm. C'mon, let's get out of here," Mom said, walking over to the burglar alarm. "Ready to run?" she asked, then pushed the buttons that made the chirpy noise start.

Cricket watched them close the door behind them, heard the lock click into place. It would be a long night, and she could both sleep and monitor Sonny's breathing.

She closed her eyes and dozed lightly, dreaming of bugs and food, waking when the dog sighed or whimpered in the night.

Her eyes snapped open three hours later, when she heard the chain-link fence rattle. Her ears went back. She had heard a lot of strange noises here at night, but never this one. There were big, rumbling trucks, car horns, people running and laughing on the sidewalk out front, but never this delicate noise. A footfall, then two, quiet, creeping ones. Nothing like a cat's, of course, but trying to be quiet, which was worse. Whenever humans tried to be quiet, it was usually a bad sign.

She sat up quickly as a shadow crossed the treatment room window. Her pulse sped up. It wasn't Mom, wasn't Susan, and nobody else should have been there at night, sneaking around. She made herself smaller as she heard the metal rattle of someone trying the doorknob. She glanced back at Sonny, who was lying in the back of his cage shivering, eyes wide. Oh-oh. This was very bad. The footsteps faded toward the far end of the building, but Cricket listened sharply.

Shattering glass brought up all the fur on her neck, and a low growl to the back of her throat. The dog whined, reeking of terror. This was very, very bad. As the soft footfalls came closer, Cricket moved further into the shadows behind the teeth cleaning machine knowing that she had to save Sonny.

She held her breath as a thin man appeared in the doorway. Even without the glow from the nightlights, Cricket's keen vision could have made out the expression of dull anger on the man's face. He stank of it as well.

"There you are, damned mutt." The dark, hurtful edge to his voice made Cricket tremble. She had never met up with any humans like this before.

The man reached into his pocket and brought out an object that he pointed toward Sonny. It smelled metallic, like the wound in Sonny's side had earlier, before Mom had operated. She had seen kids play like that before, at her old home. They pointed the object, water came out, and the other kid got all wet. Not only did Sonny need to stay dry for seven days until Mom took the stitches out, she didn't like the smell of that thing, didn't like it pointed at Sonny.

"Say good-bye, Sonny boy," the man said.

Cricket didn't like the way he said "good-bye" either. She bunched the muscles in her hind legs and jumped, flying onto the man's neck. There was an explosion, but it didn't cover up the man's scream. Cricket dug her claws into the bony shoulder and leapt off, streaking down the hall to Mom's office. There were curses, then another explosion, and powdery dust flew around her, plaster chips pelting off her fur as she turned the corner.

In two bounds, she was up on the file cabinet, her heart pounding. She would only have one chance, but she'd done this before. Not on purpose, really, but still. It was cute to see how she looked in the TV set in the other room, and sort of fun when everyone arrived all excited to see her.

When the man was perfectly framed in front of the little camera that took the pictures, she pounced on the white button that made people come quick, then stood up on her hind legs and waved her front paws directly in front of the little white box with the blinking lights on top. A siren immediately filled the room—this was the part she didn't like. But seeing the frightened look on the man's face made up for it. It was nice to see *him* being the one frightened for a change.

He fled, his footsteps echoing through the treatment room where, rather than taking the time to go out through the broken window, he grabbed the doorknob, threw the lock, and yanked the door open. She felt disappointed watching him disappear into the night. Still, they should have everything they needed, and Sonny was still alive, cowering in the back of his cage.

It was a long, long time before the people showed up . . . at least as long as it usually took Mom to go get the kibbles and fill her bowl. She mrrowed her greetings, and they were excited to see her. For a moment, she was nervous, because they were pointing those metal things like the bad man was, but then she relaxed. They were the same men who dressed alike, and had shown up last time. After a moment, the painful noise stopped.

"Police! Put down your weapons and identify yourself."

She mrrowed dutifully, apologizing for not having a weapon to put down.

"Don't tell me it's a false alarm from that damned cat again," one of the men whispered.

"Oh no," she mrrowed. That was only a mistake last time, couldn't they see how different it was this time? She ran toward the front lobby, leading them toward the broken glass, but careful to keep her sensitive paws away from the sharp edges. Finally, one came.

"Forced entry in the front, but it's secure up here now," the man called to his partner in the back. She chirruped her agreement, then ran to the back. The man back there was looking in the surgery, which was altogether wrong. She jumped up on top of the row of cages, ran over to where the metal thing had gone into the wall, then back to the nice man, then back, mrrowing all the time. Finally, he stopped in front of the damaged wall, studying it.

"Looks like there was gunfire back here," the man called to his partner. The other man joined him, and they both looked intently toward the office.

"It's okay," Cricket chirruped, then ran ahead of them. They followed, but left the office before she could show them the picture-maker. They ignored her in the room where the little TV was. They walked back toward the door, and she started to panic.

"Don't leave," she wailed. "You haven't seen it all yet."

Just then, Mom pulled up outside. The men started moving toward the door, but Cricket ran ahead, calling for her to help make them understand.

As soon as they explained everything to Mom, she led them to the TV room, pushed some buttons, and the whirly picture thingy lit up the TV with the man. Just seeing him, Cricket's fur ruffled, and her ears fell back. She knew from the smell that it wasn't him, just like it was never really her in the picture either. Mom and the nice men talked, and then they took the little plastic box away, and pretty soon a man arrived to put wood over the window and sweep up, and another man was there doing something exciting with the doorknob and black powder that made her sneeze. A nice woman dug those metal things out of the wall. Another woman took pictures, and Cricket tried to figure out how the camera worked by looking at it really closely. Mom checked on Sonny, gave him some medicine to make him sleep, then watched everyone work, looking overwhelmed.

By daylight, all the people were gone, and it was just her and Mom, snuggled into the couch, sleeping for a few hours before the pets arrived for their appointments.

When Susan got there, Mom explained things.

"When I called her, she said that she hadn't told anyone that Sonny was going to be all right—nobody except her boyfriend—and when the police showed her the tape she positively identified him. Still doesn't know why he shot the dog, or why he thought it was important enough to come finish the job...."

"Probably just a sicko who figured he wouldn't get caught," Susan said.

Mom reached a hand out and ran it over Cricket's back. Cricket lifted her head, but stayed snuggled on Mom's lap.

"He wouldn't have if it weren't for her. If he'd stayed in the treatment room, where there were no cameras, no motion detectors, he would have been fine. It was only because she lured him down the hall that he got on tape."

Susan smiled. "Isn't that a bit much? I mean ... *luring* him? But you're right ... it is a good thing she ran that direction instead of up front."

"Mmmmm. You should have seen the tape ... she never got in front of the camera ... almost like she knew what it was. And her flailing around was what set off the motion detector. Well, that and she hit the panic button."

"Nothing strange there ... she's done the panic button before."

"I guess you're right. Still, it just seems a little odd...."

"No odder than anything else she does."

Cricket woke up enough to give a yawning meow of protest.

Mom ran a hand over her. "Call the alarm people, schedule them to install motion detectors and a camera in the treatment area and up front. And cancel the ad for the cat."

Alone again, Cricket lowered her head, purring contentedly as Mom rubbed her ears.

"From now on, you'll be coming home with me at night, young lady. You just get in too much trouble here alone. You're lucky your whiskers will be getting any longer."

Cricket squinched her eyes closed, pulling her whiskers forward as Mom scratched under her chin.

"Besides, a big dog can watch the place at night."

Cricket's head popped up. "A *dog*? Mom, how could you entrust this place to a dog?" she yowled.

"I guess there's room enough in the bed for us both," Mom said.

Cricket considered the trade. Getting to sleep by someone who loved her would be ample compensation for her pride. She bumped her forehead into Mom's chin, content at last.

Curse of the Cat People

RON GOULART

DOGS DIDN'T BOTHER HIM AT all, but cats made him sneeze violently.

Throughout his life he'd done his best to avoid them. Nevertheless, at the age of thirty-seven Ned Beecham accepted a job editing a magazine for cat fanciers. He'd been out of work for seven months by that time, he was behind in alimony payments to both his former wives, and Ned figured that he could edit *Catmania* effectively without ever having to go near a cat.

Unfortunately, however, he had to work in close proximity to Peggy Pont Ybarra. Wife of Lionel Ybarra, the publisher of the fifty-three titles that made up the Connecticut-based Ybarra magazine empire, she was twenty-nine years younger than her husband and managing editor of the company's nine pet magazines. These included, in addition to *Catmania—Dogmania, Birdmania, Fishmania,* and *Bunnymania.*

During his job interview with her, Ned had indicated he'd prefer working on *Dogmania.*

"Impossible," the lovely redhead had informed him. "Lionel, my husband, is goofy about dogs and he insists on editing that one himself personally. You know how older men get. Stubborn."

"Well, I love cats, too," he lied when she offered him the position as editor of *Catmania.* "And during the seven years I was with Bockman Brothers in Manhattan, I edited several best-sellers about cats."

He'd been downsized out of Bockman back in January, shortly after the company had been taken over by the German publishing giant, Luftwaffe Books.

Actually the only cat book he'd ever had anything to do with was an unsuccessful kids' title, *The Pussycat Princess*.

Peggy was staring at him intently as he told her the lies that got him the job. Finally she observed, "I know what it is I like about you, Ned."

"Oh, so?"

"Yes, it's the fact that you look quite a bit like Arturo Alcazar." She tilted her head to the left, narrowing her eyes. "Even handsomer, though."

"I don't think I know who—"

"Oh, sure, because you probably aren't a soap opera fan," Peggy said, smiling. "Before I married old Ybarra three years ago I acted on *Rage to Love*."

"The soap opera," he said, nodding.

"I played twin sisters, one of whom was a homicidal maniac. It was a terrific part," she explained. "Arturo was, and still is, for that matter, Dr. Gahagen and he had an affair with both of us."

She leaned back in her chair, smiling. "And, wouldn't you know it, life imitated art."

"Um," he said.

"I hope Lionel doesn't notice your resemblance to Arturo," she told him. "He can be insanely jealous at times and . . . But, hey, it's no use worrying over something he probably won't even tumble to."

Ned inquired, "Did your husband do bodily harm to Arturo?"

She shook her head, made a dismissive gesture with her right hand. "Well, not much," she replied. "Only broke his arm, though I suppose if they hadn't pulled him off he might've fractured poor Arturo's skull. You can do a lot of damage with one of those metal baseball bats and—"

"And this was *after* you were married?"

She sighed again. "For old time's sake I had lunch with Arturo, at that nice little vegetarian Mexican place down on Crosby Street in Soho in New York. Lionel got wind of it and came storming in, swinging his—"

"How'd he happen to find out?"

"Oh, I was really dumb when I was first married," the pretty red-haired woman answered. "Never occurred to me that the old coot would have all the phones in the mansion bugged."

"Arturo recovered, didn't he?"

"Eventually, yes. And they wrote the broken arm into *Rage to Love*. Made for a nice sequence," she said. "Well, when can you start, Ned?"

"Monday?"

"That'll be neat," she said, smiling at him. "I'll take you out now and introduce you to Mercedes Opper."

"Who is?"

"Oh, she's assistant editor for *Catmania*." Peggy stood up behind her metal desk, smoothing her short black skirt. "I suppose I'd best warn you that Mercedes may be a little rude and nasty to you at the outset."

"Because of my resemblance to Arturo?"

"No, because she was expecting to take over the editor spot on the magazine," she said. "But she's only twenty-two and Lionel and I decided she's not old enough for the top spot yet. But don't worry about it. I'm pretty sure she'll eventually like you as much as I do."

She did. And that, eventually, caused Ned considerable trouble.

Mecedes Opper was a moderately attractive young woman in her early twenties. Although she was a mite too plump for his tastes, Ned, nonetheless, set about to charm her. If he was going to succeed with the job of editing *Catmania*, Ned was definitely going to need the assistance of someone who could safely go near cats.

By the end of his second week in the Westport offices of the Ybarra publishing empire, he and Mercedes had fallen into the habit of having lunch together at least twice a week. Since his assistant editor was a dedicated vegetarian and there were few vegetarian restaurants in Fairfield County, this meant they usually ate at a place in Norwalk called Reggie McVeggie's.

"Okay, we've got the August issue safely to the printer," he said one afternoon as they shared one of the small tables. "Now there's some stuff I'd like you to handle for me pertaining to the September issue of *Catmania*. Visit the Northport Animal Hospital and do that feature on their cat adoption center. Hit the Manhattan Cat Show this Saturday afternoon and take Larry with you for photos. And, when you can fit it in, drop in on that nitwit matron in Westchester who's turned one wing of her mansion into a shelter for feral cats. Then—"

"You don't like cats, do you, Ned?"

"What gives you that notion?"

"Well, thus far, you haven't gone anywhere near a live cat. Or a stuffed one, for that matter, because you had me cover that Long Island taxidermist who—"

"I adore cats," he assured her.

"I like cats, too. So much so that I put up with working for the two Ybarras," she told him. "But you never—"

"Okay, I'll confide something to you," he said, leaning forward and lowering his voice. "But, please, Mercedes, don't mention this to anyone else ever." He lowered his voice further. "I'm allergic to cats."

Snapping her fingers, she said, "Dr. Cohen."

"Beg pardon?"

"That's why you had that sneezing fit last week when Dr. Cohen, the fellow who wrote *Some of My Best Friends Are Cats*, was in the office to be interviewed. Sure, he must have had cat dander all over his clothes."

"Probably, yeah," he admitted. "But keep this a secret, huh?"

"Sure, what are pals for?"

"I sort of need this job. Thanks."

She studied him for a silent moment. "I only hope the curse doesn't strike you."

"What curse?"

"Eventually it hits most of the men who work on any of Peggy Pont Ybarra's magazines," she explained, starting to eat her tofu burrito. "They, each in his turn, get hit on by Peggy. Romantic interludes follow and then Lionel Ybarra finds out and resorts to violence." She paused, chewing. "In your case we could call it the Curse of the Cat People. You know, like the old movie that—"

"That was about a ghost," he said. "How many of these guys have there been?"

Mercedes considered his inquiry. "Quite a few," she responded finally. "And what worries me is that Lionel is getting more and more violent. I mean, he's accelerated from breaking bones to resorting to firearms. Thus far a generous severance package has kept any of Peggy's beaus from suing or calling the law."

"My relationship with Mrs. Ybarra is strictly professional."

"Thus far maybe, Ned. But I can tell she's got her eyes on you and she's not calling you into her office five or six times every blessed day just to discuss *Catmania*."

Ned didn't think it wise to mention that he'd already had dinner with Peggy Pont Ybarra three times since he'd started working for her. Always on evenings when her husband was out of town. "Trust me," he said. "I don't fool around like that."

"Or, hey, darling, here's an idea," said Peggy, naked, from the doorway of the motel bathroom.

Ned shifted his position on the wide, rumpled bed so that he wasn't looking at her. "About what?"

"This dilemma we found ourselves in." She retreated for a few seconds, returned with a midsize towel wrapped around her.

"You're talking about the October issue?"

Peggy seated herself on the edge of the bed. "I'm talking about this torrid romance of ours, dummy, that's been going on for almost a month now."

"A couple of hours in Ye Olde Nutmeg Inne once a week doesn't actually constitute a—"

"Don't pretend to be obtuse, Neddy." Reaching under the quilt, she dealt him a punch to the lower back.

"From what you've told me about your husband, Peg, anything remotely torrid would annoy the—"

"That's it exactly." Peggy moved onto the bed, pressing against the headboard and hugging her bare knees. "We don't want you to end up with a broken leg or a load of buckshot in your tush."

"I thought Lionel broke that actor's *arm*." He sat up, easing about a foot further away from the lovely managing editor. "What's this about a leg?"

"Different actor," she explained.

"Did he *also* get shot?"

"No, that was my agent. We were having a purely innocent business meeting in his hotel room in Atlantic City when Lionel, roaring like a lion with a sore paw, burst in and started shooting," she said, sighing. "Fortunately those suites are soundproof."

"We have a terrific relationship, Peggy," he assured her, moving further away just as she was reaching out to take hold of his hand. "But, maybe, all things considered, it would be—"

"No, listen," she cut in. "I haven't even gotten to the really neat idea I just thought of in the john."

"I don't think maybe this—"

"All we have to do is kill him." She assumed an I've-just-discovered-the-lost-city-of-the-Incas expression.

"We do what, Peg?"

"You know, like in that movie with Fred McMurty," she continued. "We arrange an accident that nobody—"

"That's Fred MacMurray," he corrected, getting entirely out of bed and starting to hunt for his discarded boxer shorts. "And in *Double Indemnity* he ended up dying."

"I've never watched the ending when they show it on American Movie Classics," she admitted. "Too depressing. But my point is—"

"Check it out at Blockbuster, along with any version of *The Postman Always Rings Twice*," he advised while tugging on his trousers. "People who plot the—"

"We're not going to make the kind of mistakes they did," Peggy said confidently.

"No, nope, not at all."

Smiling faintly, she watched him buttoning his shirt. "But just consider the rewards, Neddy," she said. "There's me, of course. And, once poor old Lionel has shuffled off this mortal coil, I inherit all fifty-three of the damned magazines plus all his assets. The total, as of this afternoon, is $360,000,000."

Ned sat down beside her. "And you get it *all*?"

She smiled more broadly, taking his hand. "Every blessed penny, darling," she said.

The following day, a shade past noon, he was having what seemed, initially, a perfectly natural conversation about his salad with Mercedes.

"You're not eating your fiddle ferns," she mentioned, resting both plump elbows on the checkered tablecloth.

Looking down at his plate, he inquired, "Which ones are they?"

"Those curled up green things there."

"Oh, I thought maybe they were these squiggly black things. I'm not eating them either."

"I bet you eat all your salad when you're with *her*," Mercedes accused, anger slipping into her voice. "Although lately you don't even bother with dinner and just go directly to Ye Olde Nutmeg Inne."

"You don't pronounce the final e's on those." He sat up straighter in his chair. "And how come you know about that place?"

"I know a lot about the sleazy side of your life and your tacky relationship with Peggy Pont Ybarra," she said evenly. "The woman, you know, that you swore you weren't having an affair with."

He reached across the table, took hold of her chubby hand. "Hey, it's simply a way of assuring my job security," he told her. "There's really nothing at all serious going—"

"When I invite you over to my place, you always have an excuse," she said, pulling her hand free of his grasp. "But when Peggy snaps her fingers, you hop into the sack and—"

"C'mon, you can't be jealous."

Mercedes, after taking two more quick bites of her tempeh steak, stood up. Very quietly she informed him, "I'll continue to work with you on *Catmania* in the office to the best of my ability, Ned. I'll also strive to prevent you from having any direct contact with a cat. But our social relationship is over." She spun on her heel, and went hurrying out of Reggie McVeggie's.

"Jealous," he said to himself. "I guess I was *too* charming."

He started noticing the cats a couple days later.

Ned was living in a rented cottage in the town of Brimstone. He had no immediate neighbors on the narrow woodland road and stretching uphill behind the place were about twenty acres of woods. Deer lived in there, raccoons, squirrels, all sorts of birds, including some immense wild turkeys.

But in all his months there, he'd never been aware that any stray cats were residing in the woods.

On a chill Tuesday, when he had a night free from Peggy, he was depositing a bundle of newspapers in the blue recycling bin, when he heard a low snarling off in the growing dusk.

Narrowing his eyes, he looked into the thick brush beyond his porch. Something was rustling among the spiky leaves. He reached back, and turned on the overhead porch light.

All at once he saw at least a half-dozen pairs of cat's eyes glowing out there in the darkness.

"Shoo, scram, you bastards!" he shouted, starting down the steps.

A fat calico cat came scooting out of the brush and went running for the cover of the surrounding trees. The rest of the cats scattered, rattling away through the scrub.

"Go away. No cats allowed."

He started sneezing, deciding not to chase them up into the woods.

Going back into the house, he paused, sniffing at the night air. There was a vaguely familiar smell in the air. "Cat food," he realized, frowning and looking around.

There was no sign of anything like that on his back porch. Shaking his head, he went back into the cottage.

He didn't return home the next night until close to midnight, and he didn't spot any cats lurking around. But about two A.M. he was awakened by the yowling of a cat out in the woods. He turned on the porch light and stared out into the darkness, just in time to see the fat calico go bouncing away into the woodland beyond.

The following day he went to a Westport pet shop and bought two kinds of cat repellent. He sprayed both liberally all around his cottage before going to meet Peggy for dinner.

Ned still wasn't sure he wanted to go ahead with her plan to arrange an accident for Lionel Ybarra. But the possibility of having access to over three hundred million dollars was an enormous incentive.

Before he left the motel that evening, he'd agreed to help her work out a foolproof plan.

And that Saturday afternoon, when Lionel was supposed to be attending a dog show in Philadelphia, Ned and Peggy met at his cottage to come up with a scheme.

"You're not very romantic," Peggy was saying.

"Put your clothes back on," Ned said. "It's distracting. We have to figure out how to—"

"We can do that after we—"

"We'll take care of this first." He was sitting at the small butcher-block table in his kitchen with a legal tablet open in front of him.

"Okay, you're the practical one." She wandered away for a moment and returned wearing his yellow terry cloth robe.

"All right," he said, "Lionel has a violent temper. How many other people would you say are aware of this?"

"Every damn person who knows the old fool," she answered. "What are you getting at, Neddy?"

"Maybe this accident he's going to have can grow out of some situation where we can make it look like he lost his temper and did something stupid."

"That sounds good, yes." She came closer, leaned and put her arms around him from behind. "What sort of situation exactly?"

"That's what we have to think up. Maybe he—"

The phone on the kitchen wall began ringing.

"Ignore it," she advised.

"I don't like to do that." Working free of her embrace, he ran over and grabbed the receiver. "Yeah?"

"I'm really sorry, Ned. I shouldn't have done it," said Mercedes forlornly.

"Done what?"

"Told Lionel Ybarra that I'd found out you and his wife were going to be shacked up at your cottage this afternoon."

"Holy Christ, why did you—"

"I guess I *am* jealous, Ned," his assistant editor admitted. "I told him about it last night at the office and he canceled his plans to go to the dog show. I was going to let him burst in on you two, but then I got to thinking about the semiautomatic pistol and—"

"What semiautomatic—"

"The one Hilda in accounting says he bought last week and charged to the company," said Mercedes, sounding very unhappy. "I think you better put your clothes on and get out of there until this blows over, Ned. I'm really sorry, but—"

"We'll have lunch sometime and talk about it." He hung up. "Get dressed, Peg."

"Now what?"

"Your husband is heading over here to shoot us."

She shook her head. "He never shoots me, darling," she said. "Only the men who—"

The kitchen window exploded and a scatter of slugs came chattering into the room. All of them hit Peggy and she fell to the floor, the yellow terry cloth all bloody now.

Ted sprinted to the back door, yanked it open and ran from his cottage.

A late afternoon fog was closing in, the woodlands were blurring all around him as he made his way, striving to move both swiftly and silently, uphill and away.

Judging from Ybarra's yells, Peggy's husband had gone into the cottage first to look for him.

Ned was heading toward a hiding place where he was certain, or nearly so, that he'd be safe. No sign yet of Ybarra's pursuit.

Up ahead, the ruins of the old farmhouse that he'd discovered while exploring the woods some months ago materialized out of the fog.

Much of the slanting roof and two of the walls were gone. Most of the living room and dining room remained. And inside the living room was the big stone fireplace he'd investigated on his earlier visit.

He was taking off his shoes, tying the laces together, when he heard the first sounds of Ybarra. From far below, muffled by the thickening fog, came the sounds of his stomping his way uphill.

Ned, hanging the shoes around his neck, stepped into the living room of the long-abandoned house.

The wooden floor was thick with dead leaves, which were dotted and spattered with bird droppings. On tiptoe, he made his way over to the huge fireplace. The old room gave off a damp, decaying smell and the leaves underfoot were soggy.

As far as he could tell, looking down as he made his way carefully to the fireplace, his passing left little or no trace on the slushy blanket of decaying leaves.

He ducked his head and stepped into the fireplace. As he'd remembered, there was a ledge inside. It ran around the fireplace, roughly a foot above the top of the opening. Wide enough, he was sure, for him to stand on.

All he had to do was boost himself up there. He'd stay on the ledge until Ybarra had gotten tired of hunting for him. Then he would, very carefully and cautiously, climb down, return to his cottage, and phone the police.

It would be too late to do much for Peggy. He was pretty certain she was dead.

Ned took hold of the ledge and, somewhat awkwardly, got himself up onto it.

Just as he pressed his back against the rough interior wall of the chimney, he heard several shots from close outside.

"I thought I had you that time, Ned!" bellowed Ybarra outside. "My mistake, it wasn't you. But I'll kill you eventually, you bastard. Same way I fixed Peggy!"

Breathing carefully, Ned listened.

In a moment he heard the sound of heavy footsteps on the floor of the farmhouse kitchen.

Then he heard something else.

Meow.

His eyes had become used to the darkness inside the chimney.

Sitting comfortably on the ledge, about six feet from where Ned was perched, was the fat calico cat. The same one he'd chased away from his cottage.

Mewing again, she stretched to her feet and started working her way along the ledge toward him.

Dogs didn't bother him, but cats made him sneeze violently.

The Day Frank Hollings Died

JO-ANN LAMON RECCOPPA

"HE SAW IT ALL," THE WOMAN in the funny-looking outfit tells my owner.

I hate that word—*owner*. It sounds so possessive. Like I'm a lamp or a car. I mean, Katie's a nice lady. A little stupid maybe. She doesn't really own me. It's kind of a trade-off. I look out for her, keep her company. She feeds me and gives me a place to stay. We're companions. Roommates.

But hey, I'm no gigolo.

"Tom's been edgy ever since Frank Hollings died. I think he's traumatized," Katie tells the flaky lady dressed up like a fortune-teller.

Traumatized? Me? Like I'm some kind of, you'll pardon the crude expression, pussy.

"That's his name? Tom?" the flake asks.

Yeah. Tom. What can I say? Katie is as short on imagination as she is on brains. She thinks it's cute. Tom Cat. Real original.

"Well, he kind of looks like a Tom, doesn't he?"

"I suppose," the flake says, noncommittally.

What the hell kind of pet psychic is she supposed to be anyhow? I mean, how psychic is she if she doesn't even know my name? Besides, I do look like a Tom. I'm big, strong, agile, orange and white and gray—and look meaner than a pack of hungry wolves. I can prove I'm tough, too! I've got scars! Loads of them! I've fought every cat in the neighborhood and haven't been bested yet.

"Can you help him?" Katie asks.

I don't need help. It's Katie who needs it. That's why I stick around. If she had to look after herself, that Hollings character would have killed her weeks ago.

"Let's take him into my office and get started," the gypsy-loony says as she grabs the handle on my carrier and takes me into another room.

I hate being cooped up inside this thing. It's cramped. Every step the flake takes feels like turbulence. I get tossed back and forth, slammed against the sides of the carrier. I slide backward, then slip forward and mash my face against the plastic grill door. If you treat a human like this, you get arrested for kidnapping and assault and battery. Treat a cat the same way, they call it humane.

Go figure.

Katie reaches inside and lifts me out. She keeps me in her lap as she sits on the sofa, face to face with the gypsy woman. "Tom, my name is Brandy," the flaky gypsy says. "I want you to think back to the day Frank Hollings died."

Brandy! I wish cats could laugh. The flake has this dark red hair—like wine. Maybe Katie named her too!

"Tom!" nutty Brandy repeats. "What happened on the day Frank Hollings died?"

Frank Hollings. What a bad guy. He walked too fast, for one thing. And talked fast, too. It made me nervous just being in the same room with him. Katie met him through her computer—something called a chat room, though I don't remember chatting, just typing.

Anyway, this guy Hollings shows up one night looking way too polished. He has that gel crap slicking back his hair, his clothes are pressed and they look brand new. He must have splashed on a whole bottle of cologne. It made me sneeze my brains out. And even with all that fake fragrance, he couldn't cover it up. You could smell the bad on him the minute he walked though the door.

He brought Katie flowers. Nobody ever brought Katie flowers before.

I knew this guy meant trouble.

"I've never done anything like this before," Katie tells him, smiling. She's dressed to the nines. Her hair is done up. She even put on makeup.

A whole lot less than that phony crap you painted on your kisser, Brandy!

"Oh!" Brandy says suddenly, her clown face looking totally shocked.

Katie looks worried. "What's wrong?"

"Tom thinks I'm wearing too much makeup."

"I see," Katie says, and I know what she's thinking—the gypsy *is* wearing too much makeup. The broad looks like an old prostitute.

"Watch it!" Brandy snaps at me.

Oh, yeah! I almost forget. She's a pet psychic.

"Back to business. Then what happened?"

✳   ✳   ✳

Anyway, Katie runs out to the kitchen to put the damn flowers in a vase and I see Hollings going through a pile of mail she left on the coffee table. He opens an envelope and pulls out a paper and gets this really big grin on his face. "Rich bitch," he whispers, really low, but my hearing's aces. He folds up the letter real fast and stuffs it back inside the envelope when Katie pushes open the kitchen door.

"I'll be back later," Katie says, coming over to the windowsill and giving me a quick scratch behind the ear.

This Hollings character says, "I didn't know you had a kitty," real cheerful and I nearly barf. He tries to pet me too, just like Katie did, but I wasn't gonna let the scuzz-bucket touch me. No way! I extended my claws and took a swipe at his hand. Caught him, too. Three nice, long scratches right along the back of his hand.

Most people say little bastard *when a cat draws blood, but not old Frank Hollings. He just smiles and tells Katie, "I guess he isn't used to me yet."*

That scared me. I sat up half the night waiting for Katie to come home.

"So, you knew Frank Hollings was up to no good the first time you met him?" Brandy says, her eyes narrowing like Hollings tried to scam her instead of Katie.

"Tom *knew* something was wrong?" Katie asks, looking totally confused— which is how she looks most of the time anyway.

"Right from the start!" flaky Brandy tells her, then turns back to me. "Go on, Tom. Tell me what happened next."

Frank Hollings starts coming around the house—a few times that week, a couple more the next. And Katie is walking on air—humming and singing and looking moonstruck like Fi-Fi down the block does when she's in heat. And this Hollings character is as smooth as an alley cat, sniffing around Katie and going through her stuff when she ain't looking.

One day, I catch him ripping a couple of blank checks out of the checkbook Katie keeps on her desk and he slips them inside his jacket, real casual-like. Poor stupid Katie never suspects a thing. A couple of days later, he's rifling through her purse and taking money from her wallet.

Last week, I figured I'd follow Frank Hollings home after he dropped Katie off. So he gets in his crappy old car and heads for town. I couldn't keep up with the car, of course, but I didn't have to. Like I said, you could smell the bad of Frank Hollings a mile away. I just follow my nose, and before long I'm sitting on the fire escape outside his apartment window.

The windows were filthy, but I could see through them all right. His place looks like a garbage dump, with clothes thrown everywhere and newspapers all over the place. Hollings switches on a light, see, and I notice all these pictures hanging up on the wall. I mean, they're everywhere! Big ones. Little ones. All women. And they're not pictures like in a frame either. This guy cut them out of the newspaper and plastered them all over his walls. Nice-looking broads for humans, too. But there was one I didn't like—a lady with her eyes closed.

She looked dead.

✻   ✻   ✻

"So, you knew he killed those women," Brandy says, staring at me like she would stare at a human.

"Are you saying my cat *knew* Frank Hollings was a serial killer?" Katie asks her, and she's got this little smirk on her face like she doesn't believe it.

"Miss Denton, you have one brilliant cat," Brandy tells her, and all of a sudden the flake doesn't seem so flaky after all.

"Tom doesn't even know what a serial killer is," Katie insists, and now she's the one looking at Brandy like she's two sandwiches short of a picnic basket.

"He knows exactly what a serial killer is," Brandy tells her, and looks down at me perched on Katie's lap. "Go on, Tom. Finish the story."

I ran all the way back to my neighborhood. I cut through alleys, darted among cars in the streets, took shortcuts through the woods and the backyards of the houses in the development. I stopped twice—once because the pads on my paws were raw and I needed a breather, and once to check on Fi-Fi, but she wasn't in heat so that didn't slow me down.

I got back inside the house by sneaking through an open basement window—hey, I told you Katie isn't the brightest human I've ever met. I slept on and off all day, stretched out on the sunny ledge of one of the living room windows. Frank Hollings would be coming over later, I knew, and I needed to rest up for the busy night ahead.

When Katie came home from work, I made a beeline for her desk and started slapping at her checkbook, hitting it around a little like it was a game. She thought it was real cute until I knocked it on the floor and it opened. Stupid as she is, she noticed the missing checks right away.

Her face went blank for a minute, which isn't exactly earthshattering news where Katie is concerned, and then it was like a light bulb lit over her head.

Hollings was the only other person to come inside the house for weeks.

"I'll bet I didn't lose the money from my wallet either," she tells me, like she wants a confirmation. What can I say? I never got past the meow stage.

So she waits for him. Sits in the chair, real calm, and stares at the door waiting for this bum to arrive. And when he knocks, she calls out, "Come in." Her voice is cold, controlled anger. Like humans get when they're really, really mad.

Hollings opens the front door and steps inside, and he's got these stinky flowers behind his back to surprise her. She gets up and takes them, then gives them a quick sniff before she tosses them out the open door.

This time it's Hollings's face that goes blank. I mean, this guy looks like he just landed on a strange planet or something.

"I know you're stealing from me, Frank," Katie tells him. "I know about the blank checks and the money you swiped from my purse. Get out before I call the police."

I think her talking about the police is what did it. He starts backing up toward the front door and I think, if he gets away, he's gonna do this to some other dumb broad—only he'll probably kill the next one, like in the pictures on his wall.

* * *

"So what did you do?" Brandy asks, and she seems awfully anxious to find out the truth.

You'd think being a pet psychic, she'd have figured it out. After all, she's supposed to know how our minds work. Like all dumb humans, they go on facts and ignore instincts.

"I keep telling you. Tom had nothing to do with it," Katie tells her. "It was an accident—purely luck that Frank Hollings fell down the front steps and broke his neck. The police said as much. That nice detective told me Frank would probably have killed me if he hadn't tripped."

"Is that how it happened, Tom?" Brandy asks me.

Not exactly. Hollings probably was trying to get away, but maybe, just maybe, he was thinking of closing the door and dousing Katie's lights for good. I was right there in my usual spot, on the sill, and you know, me and Katie have this arrangement. I look out for her, and she feeds me and gives me a place to stay.

So I did what any self-respecting tom would do. I sprayed him. Shot the slime ball right in the eyes—perfect aim! Hollings screams like a scalded cat and grabs his face. He's still backing up for the door, mind you, so he doesn't realize he's outside until the wind hits him on the top step. By that time it's already too late. He's rubbing his eyes and teetering on that step and before you know it, he's flying down the stairs backward.

It's a thing of beauty, seeing a full-grown human male in flight. It's even prettier seeing them land. They have no grace at all, no sense of balance. There is no animal I know of with less co-ordination than the human male. He lands smack on his head and you can hear his neck crack clear inside the house. Now, you'd figure with all that gel crap he put on his hair that his head would have at least slid on impact, but no. It hit like a sack of potatoes. Thud. Crack! Way cool.

"Did the police figure out you sprayed him?" Brandy asks me, and Katie is hugging me close, like she's afraid the cops are gonna cuff me and haul my ass off to jail.

That young guy, Detective Burns, figured it out. He said Hollings's face was wet, that he stunk to high heaven. He comes inside to talk to Katie, who by this time is hysterical because one of the uniformed cops told her Frank Hollings was "The Lady Killer," that serial murderer who was wanted in four states for killing young women and taking their money.

Anyway, this Detective Burns is trying to calm Katie down, and you can see right off the bat that he's kind of sweet on her. And in between dabbing her eyes and blowing her nose, Katie is looking at this guy like he's RoboCop or something.

"So, actually it was *you* who killed Frank Hollings," Brandy says.

"Tom didn't kill anyone," Katie tells her, like she's my attorney. "He's only a cat, for God's sake. He didn't know what he was doing!"

"Oh, he knew all right. And I'll tell you something—he ought to get a medal."

Katie sighs, like she's relieved, and gives me a quick kiss on the head. "And the whole episode didn't traumatize him?"

"Oh, he's fine with it. You're the one who's traumatized," Brandy tells her.

Of course, there's a little more to the story. That detective has been coming around the house for the last few days. He's even got a great cover story. He tells Katie he's just checking up on her to make sure she's okay. But I know for a fact he's staking his claim—the way I'd mark my territory. I told you he was kinda sweet on Katie. Hell, he was making a play for her on the night of the murder. So maybe humans aren't that much different from felines after all.

Oh, yeah. There's something else. I know Detective Burns is a good guy because you can smell a good guy just like you can smell a guy who's bad news. And there's an added bonus here— a little something in it for me, too.

My sense of smell tells me the detective owns a cat.

Her name is Fi-Fi.

Deputy Cat

JERRI M. OAKES

DON'T CARE WHAT HE SAYS, AMOS, if that old she-devil of his can go, I don't see any good reason why you can't."

That's my mom talking. She's the new deputy sheriff of Raleigh County, Kentucky. I'm Amos, her tiger cat. We haven't been on the job very long and mom's had a tough time. Not only did Hank Jones, the sheriff, not want a deputy, but he definitely didn't want mom. It wasn't because she was a woman, but because she was the granddaughter of Riley Pike, the most notorious moonshiner and scoundrel ever to come out of the hills. At least that's what I'd heard the sheriff telling Miss Boone. Miss Boone was the sheriff's old Siamese cat. She was the most beautiful cat I'd ever seen. She was also the meanest. Far as anybody could tell the only creature Miss Boone had ever tolerated was Hank. They say that she once whipped a state police dog for just looking at her. She clawed him up real good. Miss Boone always rode everywhere with the sheriff in his squad car. I'd heard people say behind the sheriff's back that she was the brains of the two.

Mom wasn't really mad about Miss Boone riding with the sheriff, but like I said she's had a tough time. Mom had been on duty the night that Billy Newman had escaped from the jail. Billy had only been in jail for drunk and disorderly, but when he'd escaped he had stolen the mayor's car, a brand new Cadillac. Mom had stepped over to the café for a cup of coffee and wasn't gone a minute, but somehow Billy had gotten out. The mayor had been plenty mad. Now the sheriff was going out looking for Billy, and mom was going to help. I think it was a matter of pride for her since no one had ever escaped from the Raleigh County jail before. The sheriff and mom were going to meet out at Billy's house and look around.

The trees dipped toward the squad car as mom and I bounced our way over the bumpy dirt road that led up to Billy's. The old Appalachian Mountains rose high on either side of us with just the creek, the hollow, and the road in the middle. Frost was on the ground and I could smell squirrels and field mice through the half-open window. I whipped my tail back and forth as I imagined chasing them through the hollow. Autumn in Kentucky was the best. Billy lived in a trailer across the creek about halfway up Rattlesnake Road. I twitched my tail some more when we got there and I saw Miss Boone. She was sitting on Billy's porch with her tail curled around her. She looked so still, just like one of the cat statues at the dollar store. You wouldn't think she was real except for the movement of her blue Siamese eyes. When mom let me out of the car, those eyes looked at me before they half closed and she yawned. I raised my chin as I walked through the frost-stiffened grass to the porch. To tell you the truth, Miss Boone kind of scared me, but I wasn't going to let her see that. Mom was having a bad enough time without me embarrassing her in front of Miss Boone. Mom went inside to where the sheriff was looking around Billy's trailer. I heard the rough tone in the sheriff's voice when he said hello to mom, and it made me mad.

"The sheriff has no call to talk to mom that way," I told Miss Boone. "It's not her fault that Billy escaped."

Miss Boone just blinked her eyes sleepily at me and started washing her face, which made me even madder.

"Mom's a good human. It's your human that's mean."

Miss Boone opened her eyes and looked at me. "You're too young to recognize a good human from a bad one. Sheriff Jones is perfectly fine. You shouldn't call your human 'mom.' It's not dignified. She's not your real mother."

"She's the only mother I remember and that's good enough for me."

"Hummpf," was the only sound Miss Boone made before lapsing into silence.

I could see Miss Boone's gray ears twitching back and forth as we sat there on the porch watching the sun melt the frost on the grass little by little. It always took the sun a long time after sunrise to make its way down between those old mountains. It was the same way at sunset. The valley was covered in shade long before the sun had said its final good-bye to the rest of the state.

I could hear mom and the sheriff talking about where Billy might be hiding out and the sheriff's voice sounded a little friendlier now. Mom was smart and would make a good deputy if she got the chance.

"Humans never seem to ask the right question, have you noticed that?" Miss Boone's voice was a purr in the morning air.

I looked at her. "What do you mean?"

Her whiskers twitched with the sigh she gave. "How do you expect to be of help to your human if you don't know how they think? Right now they are wondering where Billy is instead of wondering how he got out."

I looked at her confused, and she sighed again.

"Deputy Pike is concerned with where Billy is so that she can get him back because she thinks she's responsible. The sheriff wants him back because there has never been a jailbreak in Raleigh County. But how did Billy escape in the first place, and why would he steal the mayor's car? That seems to be asking for trouble."

Just then mom and Hank came out of the house.

"Well I've put it off as long as I can. I'd better go on over and talk to the mayor," Hank said.

Mom gave the sheriff a real long look. "I'm going with you."

Hank looked back at mom for a minute as he chewed on a hunk of tobacco, and then nodded.

The mayor's house was one of the nicest in the county. His family had lived there for a long time and they were real proud of themselves. He and his wife had two snobby daughters, just like them. Everyone knew that the mayor spent a pretty penny every Election Day to keep getting elected. People no one had seen since the last election would make their way out of the deep hollows with entire voting families to collect the money or the pint of whiskey that he would have ready for them. It was that kind of town. They were cutting down on election graft all through the South, but Raleigh County still clung to the old ways. I personally didn't know what people got so upset about. One human was about the same as any other, the kind that ran for office anyway.

I wasn't sure about going into the mayor's house at first. My kind weren't always welcome in people's houses, but Miss Boone set me straight when she met me outside on the porch.

"Don't be a silly cat. My relatives have lived here longer than that Johnny-come-lately mayor. We lived in Squash Hollow with one of the first families.

The mayor's people weren't so high and mighty then," Miss Boone sniffed. "They didn't even have a cat."

I guess the mayor didn't have anything over on Miss Boone when it came to snobbery.

The mayor was a big ruddy-faced man who liked to hear himself talk and he was hearing himself a lot at the moment. He was huffing and puffing at mom and the sheriff about his car, and police incompetence, and firing mom. That didn't seem fair to me. I thought about making my opinion known, but just then out of the corner of my eye I saw a door move. It was a door off to the side of the living room that had been closed when we arrived but now was open a crack. My nose twitched. The longtime instinct to explore the mysterious kicked in and drew me toward the door. I looked for Miss Boone, but she was up in one of the mayor's best chairs taking a nap. I was on my own.

Trying to act casual, I kept low as I stalked the door. When I got closer I noticed that there was barely a crack there now and I had to push my paw through the space and wiggle it before there was enough room for my head. I looked around and then went in.

It was a bedroom. It wasn't very big. It just held the bed in the center of the room and the small kitchenette set up in the corner. I figured from the maid's uniform laid out on the bed that this was where one of the mayor's staff slept; but where was the person who had been behind the door? I prowled around the room. No one under the bed. . . . No one in the closet. . . . There was a closed door with daylight showing underneath and I could smell a faint old smell of horses. An outside door, but it was locked. How could I get out? I jumped up on the stove and checked the window. Ah, enough of a crack if I could just squeeze myself through. I didn't think I was going to make it at first, but the rest of me just slid out after I got my head through.

I hit the ground and looked around. There were footsteps in the soft dirt outside the door and I followed them to an old, rundown stable. The air was musty inside the stable and I had to swallow a sneeze when I heard voices. I could hear a man's voice talking about the sheriff and a woman's voice saying that they were married now so what did it matter. I jumped on top of a stall to see better and then almost fell right off again.

I saw Billy Newman and Sally, the mayor's oldest daughter. The mayor's car was there too. They probably figured they were safe in the old stable since no one ever went in there any more and so far they had been right. I thought about what Miss Boone had said about wondering how Billy had got out, and I started to get mad. Sally must have let Billy out. Raleigh County still kept to the old custom that all of the town buildings could be opened with a master key. A master key that the mayor kept. Sally must have taken it from the mayor without him knowing. Then she had broken Billy out of jail and eloped in the mayor's car. That really got under my fur. Everyone had blamed my mom, including the mayor.

I looked over at the blue Caddy, and at the open window on the driver's side. I jumped down from the stall and moved quickly over to the side of the car. I could hear the newlyweds talking. They were talking about going back over the Virginia state line to where they were married and hiding out for a while until they sent the mayor a letter telling him what had happened. Not if I could help it they weren't. Mom would be fired by then.

I jumped in the window on the first try, and groaned silently. The keys were still in the ignition, but when I looked closer I saw that they were only partly in, like someone had started to take them out and then changed their mind. I raised my head to check on Billy and Sally. They were looking inside a suitcase.

I swiped gently at the keys with my paw trying not to jingle them. Nothing. I swiped again a little harder shuddering at the jingle. A little movement. I peeked at Billy and Sally. They were closing the suitcase. I took a deep breath and swiped again. The keys hit the floorboard with a crash. Without thinking, I grabbed the keys up in my mouth and jumped through the car window. I heard commotion behind me as I sprinted out of the stable and I knew that Sally was coming after me. I picked up speed as I crossed the yard, trying to think what to do. Where should I go? I didn't think I could make it back in through the bedroom window before she caught me, and if she caught me I was finished, and so was mom. I rounded the side of the house to where the squad car was parked and I dived in the window. The door was locked but it wouldn't take but a minute for Sally to get her arm inside and unlock it. I dropped the keys on the seat and started yowling loudly.

Making more noise with every breath, I put my paws up on the steering wheel. I knew there was a horn there somewhere, but I wasn't strong enough. I couldn't push it. I paused in my yowling long enough to hiss at Sally when she got to the window. I put my body between her and the keys. Whatever happened, I couldn't let her get them. I hissed and spat between yowls as she reached in the window. I moved toward the door lock, but that was a mistake. She caught me on the side of the head with her hand and threw me to the car floor. I was momentarily stunned and thought for sure I was finished, but then I heard Sally screech and start cursing. Climbing back up onto the seat, I looked out the window.

Miss Boone was out there and every hair on her arched back was standing on end. Sally was clutching the back of her right ankle where long red claw marks showed clearly between her fingers. Sally seemed hesitant to come back near the window, and I didn't blame her. I could see every one of Miss Boone's teeth when she hissed and both her front and back claws were sticking out. I noticed the front door opening and I started to yowl again. Surely someone had heard all of that ruckus.

I was relieved when mom and the sheriff came running down the steps followed closely by the mayor. Everybody was babbling together wanting to know what was going on, and Hank picked up Miss Boone. I heard Sally complaining that Miss Boone had scratched her and that she was dangerous. I was afraid no one was going to look in the car so I picked up the car keys in my mouth from where they were lying on the seat. I put my head up to the window as mom approached and to my relief she took the keys, looking at me in confusion. Sally was talking, saying that I had stolen her keys and that she wanted them back. However, mom kept hold of them turning them over one by one in her hand, a tiny frown between her brows. I saw her finger one of the keys on the ring. She touched the sheriff's arm, and I heard the words "master key."

Feeling that the time was right, I jumped back out of the car window and wound my way around and through mom's legs over and over before heading off toward the stable. At first I wasn't sure they were going to follow, but the hissing sound Miss Boone made after she jumped down from Hank's arms and joined me convinced them. Miss Boone and everyone else followed me to the stable and all the chaos that had come before couldn't compete with the scene that came then. Mom, Hank, the mayor, and Sally all had a whole lot to say and in the end we left the mayor and his family to work it out. Mom and Hank let Billy off the hook for the drunk and disorderly. It was pretty clear that he would have enough trouble belonging to that family.

Later that day, I lapped up the milk contentedly from my bowl and looked over to where Miss Boone was more delicately, but no less contentedly, licking hers from her bowl. It was starting to get dark now, and mom and Hank were in Hank's kitchen having dinner. Hank had even cooked. I heard mom tell him that if it hadn't been for Miss Boone and me, Billy and Sally would be long gone by now. Hank laughed and said that if the truth be told, Miss Boone was as much the sheriff as he was. Mom hugged me hard and kissed the top of my head, murmuring that I made a good deputy. I drank some more milk and settled down sleepily for a nap. *Deputy Amos,* I thought dreamily before I dozed off. I liked that.

A Drop o' the Pure

PAUL DUNCAN

WHEN I ENTERED THE SADYE house I could see nothing, but I could smell the damp, woodsy aroma of books, magazines and paper accumulated over several lifetimes. My job was to tear apart those lives and scatter them to the four corners of the earth. To dispose of the remains.

The lawyer had arranged for a place for me to stay, just a couple of streets away—she had met me there earlier, handed me the key to this place, and jumped into her car. I could tell by the rust on her car that she had not reached the top of her profession, and that by the off-handed way she treated me, she was unlikely to reach it any time soon.

I should talk—she rang me, said she was a friend of a friend, asked if I knew about books and offered to pay for a two-week trip to Boston, room only mind you, paying me five percent commission on anything I sold. It was hard to work out who was more desperate—her for asking, or me for accepting.

Walking from my guest house on Beacon Street to the Sadye house, I had a tremendous feeling of well-being. I felt safe in the dark, shuffling my feet through the fallen leaves. Although cold, it was the kind of crisp cold that makes you alert to the world, makes you see things more clearly. Perhaps it was just the fact that I was in a new place that made me so happy. Whatever.

I checked the number of each house. It was easy to see the numbers because light came from inside each building, to show that it was still alive. In the back of my mind, I instinctively knew when I had arrived at my destination because the house was dark. It had died, and I was here to perform the autopsy, to dissect the rooms, to drain the river of paper which clogged the corridors.

I had arrived at the Sadye house.

After that first night, when I stumbled around the house purely out of curiosity, I quickly fell into a daily routine. Up at 6:00 A.M., straight down the corridor into the bathroom to shower and shave before all the hot water ran out, dress, breakfast of cornflakes, nuts and orange juice (from the local convenience store) in front of the TV, then to the Sadye house via Starbucks on Newbury for a venti house blend. Once inside the house (leaving my coat and scarf on since there was little heating, and I didn't want to bring in an electric heater with all this paper around), I'd systematically list and value all the books, placing them in appropriate piles around the house. Absolute dreck (bad condition mass-circulation paperbacks, romances) could go to the thrift stores on Mass. Ave., just across the Charles River. Good condition paperbacks and book club editions were for those eccentric people in the Ave. Alex Dumas bookshop on Newbury Street—(hell, they were the closest so I didn't have to lug the boxes too far). The first editions, illustrated books, Americana and magazines were for me—I have a list of people who are looking for this stuff, and the Internet would deal with the rest of it, no problem.

There is an unusual pleasure in creating order where there was once chaos. It's like solving a mystery. Let me give you some idea of what it was like.

When I first entered the house, and took a few steps, I thought I was still shuffling my feet through the leaves—there was so much paper, it had ruptured the rooms and flowed through the house. When I first saw the house in daylight, my heart sank at the enormity of the task. As well as piles of books precariously balanced against walls and each other, scraps of paper, written and typed, filled the spaces in between. I picked one up at random and saw that it was a rejection letter from Stuart Rose of the *Saturday Evening Post*, dated 1961, handwritten, saying that Josiah Sadye's article was "eminently suitable for the old *Post* but, unfortunately, the new powers-that-be have their own ideas of what passes for content," etc. I had never heard of Josiah Sadye, but knew that the beloved *Post* had undergone a complete revamp in September 1961, one which signalled the beginning of the end of its illustrious publishing history. I'm sure there was a book on the subject by a guy named Friedrich.

As interesting as this stuff can sometimes be, I was here to sell the books. I circumnavigated the house, which took some doing. There were four rooms on each of the floors, and four floors. Only one room on the first floor had been lived in—it had a bed, clothes, washbasin, toilet, kitchenette—the rest were used for storing all the books and papers. That meant I had 15 rooms to sort. If I could do two rooms a day, there would be time left over for some sightseeing in Boston. I decided to start with the first room by the front door.

I was deep in thought, trying to figure out whether the Fredric Brown I had in my hand was a priceless first edition or a worthless book club edition (and secretly cursing those publishers who failed to print the magic words "first edition" on their copyright pages), when I heard a flapping sound, followed by a series of *ssh-ssh*es. A cat stood in the doorway, looking at me, questioning my right to be there. It entered the room, smoothly jumped onto the desk in front of me (cats always seem to move in slow motion, don't they?), and lay down on my notes without a care in the world. I was not too pleased, not being the sort of person to enjoy the company of cats or dogs, so I put my hand under the cat to remove it—it hissed, lashed out, tore a chunk out of my mint copy of *The Lenient Beast*, and shot out of the room, leaving a cloud of letters in its wake.

I placed *The Lenient Beast* on the pile for Ave. Alex Dumas.

The house bore bitter fruit. Most books are worthless as a matter of course, but these were tacky with it. Occasionally, I would find a first edition by Faulkner, Hemingway or Mailer, then discover it was a library copy, or the front end papers were ripped out, or a child had scrawled all over the pages, or the remains of some long-digested meal had left its stains, or insects had devoured the binding and edges. I could have made a definitive list of book defects if I had taken the time. I did not have time—I was working late into the night to keep to my schedule as it was. Even his magazines were annoying—articles had been cut out of most of them and pasted into scrapbooks.

On day four, I was in book room eight, on schedule. As usual, I first collected all the loose papers into one corner, and then systematically worked my way around the room, shelf by shelf, bookcase by bookcase. This room was different. It had its own quality. The authors, the condition of the books, the handwriting of the loose papers, spoke to me of somebody who was more cultured, more refined. Here I found Dorothy Parker, Jean Rhys, Gertrude Stein, George Sand. Not only first editions, but review copies, and some personally signed by the author to J. Sadye. Josiah?

I was sorely tempted to investigate when my lawyer friend called up through the staircase.

"Ahoy there! Anyone on board?"

I tried to speak but my mouth had dried up, so I stumbled over to the banister and grunted an acknowledgement.

"Have you seen a cat?" she asked, looking up the centre of the staircase.

"Urr . . . Yes. A couple of days ago. A vicious one."

"That'll be her." She rubbed the back of her neck, then took a puff of her cigarette. "Why don't you come down so we can talk in a civilised manner?"

That'll be a first for you, I thought.

Over a coffee, she told me that she had been looking after the cat at her house but it hadn't come back, so she assumed it had returned here. She produced a bagful of leaky cat food and said I should leave it out for the cat. I was not impressed. She was oblivious to my attitude and asked how much money she should expect to make on the books.

"Enough to keep the cat in cat food for at least a month."

"That much, eh?" She didn't seem bothered. "Ciao," she said, on the way out, without a hint of irony.

I opened a tin, forked the smelly contents into a dish, and left it—with some water—for the mistress of the house, wherever she may be. After washing my hands, I returned to the third floor and began reading the papers in room eight. Immediately, a mystery was solved. These books belonged to Josephine Sadye, older sister of Josiah, who was an educated woman, a respected reviewer of books (clippings from *The New Yorker* and *The Smart Set* proved it), and later a writer of fiction herself (copies of the *Saturday Evening Post, McCall's, Cosmopolitan*) under the name Alice Drood Powell—a name I recognised. It seems she was well-known among the literary crowd—a paperback edition of Dorothy Parker's *Enough Rope* was even inscribed "To Jo—Men dare not make passes, at girls with beer glasses—Mrs Parker." And then, the letters stopped in the mid 1950s.

Did she stop writing? Did she die? What had happened to her? I was determined to find out.

Things were not going well. Every morning I left out food for the cat, and every night I threw it away untouched. One day, as I placed the stinking mixture on the floor, madam cat blithely entered the building, sniffed the food and hissed at me, arching her back. I really thought it was going to attack. I decided to back down. It could starve for all I cared.

As I worked my way towards the top of the house, the books became more interesting, older, more unusual. I found many illustrated books and magazines by Howard Pyle, and especially his student N. C. Wyeth, who surpassed him in my opinion. (This wasn't evident in Wyeth's first book commission, *Boys of St Timothy's* by Arthur Stanwood Pier in 1904, but there was certainly more humanity in his excellent pictures for Mary Johnston's *The Long Roll*, which depicted the pain and suffering of the Civil War rather than the superficial glory of that engagement—both books valued and placed on my pile.) As joyful as these discoveries were—and each find egged me further on to the next shelf and bookcase—each one took me further and further away from Josephine and Josiah Sadye. These books belonged to their childhood. I wanted to find out what happened to them in adult life. I had to go deeper to get to the bottom of this, so I returned to the first floor.

It was difficult to resist reading Josiah's letters, notes and suchlike as I rearranged them into chronological order, but it was done. I then skipped through them to find out who his main correspondents were. He had various agents in New York whose main job seemed to be to pass around manuscripts to the magazines, compile an edited summary of rejection letters for the poor Mr Sadye, and then regretfully inform him they think him unsaleable and advise him to find other representation. However, the earliest letters are fairly verbose and addressed to Bobbie Parler in Canada. 18 Feb 1950, Josiah now living with his sister. (Implication is that she's supporting him.) 2 Aug 54, siblings have major falling-out. (About what?) When 1955 arrives they are not talking, and Josiah has started writing articles. (The subtext here is that he's doing it in competition with his sister, and perhaps to pay his own way.) This is when all the rejections begin. Then comes the letter I'd been waiting to read: 9 Nov 1955, Josiah writes that "Josephine passed away after a protracted illness," and that he was taking over her estate.

It was becoming obvious to me that Josiah was not the best of writers (his letters were often dull and unimaginative) and was not embarrassed at trying anything to earn some money for himself. He proceeded to submit every scrap of paper Josephine wrote to all the women's magazines. Josiah was somewhat unlucky with his timing—perhaps he should have been christened Jonah? What happened is this: with the advent of the teenager, all the major magazines changed their outlook in general and their fiction in particular. Once bristling with soft, petite women of a certain age, they now required something more robust, if they wanted fiction at all. Alice Drood Powell was from a different era, was not "with it" or "happening" or part of the "Beat Generation."

Josiah thought about this and made a practical decision. He would write what the market demanded. They wanted crime. They wanted juvenile delinquents. They wanted women in adult situations. Then the public would get what they wanted. He worked for all the worst publishers: Bee-Line, Kozy, Boudoir, Merit, Night-Lamp. Just skimming through them tells me that they were pure unadulterated rubbish—and that's me being kind. Some nice cover art on a couple though. A Heade cover on one, DeSoto on another. Interestingly, he was caught "borrowing" a couple dozen novels from a famous bestselling author, and caused Night-Lamp to fold after they had to pay for compensation and costs.

The best book he ever wrote was his first, *A Drop o' the Pure*, published in 1956 as Lion 234—their last book. Lion Books had a reputation for publishing some of the hardest-boiled novels of writers like, for example, Jim Thompson, David Karp and David Goodis. *A Drop o' the Pure* was the story of a femme fatale who slowly murdered her rich lover by introducing a poison into his daily dose of liquor. Perversely, the more she kills him, the more she loves him—that's always the way with those sorts of novel. Inevitably, it ends melodramatically with him dying and her getting away with the murder and the money, but continuing to be haunted by her love for him. Believe me, it's very affecting the way he wrote it.

Now, you don't have to be much of a detective to ask the question "Did this story have any connection with his real life?" Since writers generally write about the things they think about (often subconsciously), I think you have your answer right there. So, Josiah killed off his more successful sister and reaped the benefits. (Well, he got a good novel out of it if nothing else.)

My problem was proving it.

✳   ✳   ✳

With all this going on in my head, I'd completely forgotten about Boston. I could have been anywhere in the world and it wouldn't have mattered. I only existed within these pieces of paper. For sustenance I relied on Starbucks, a great old-fashioned deli I found on the corner of Newbury and Fairfield, and a pizza place on Mass. Ave. For supplies of tapes and batteries, I went to the nearby Tower Records (I was dictating all the letters into a tape recorder I'd brought along—it's quicker to annotate on tape than to write it all down). I packed all my books and shipped them home.

On day twelve of fourteen I was feeling the pressure a little. I had concentrated on reading Josiah's letters dated around the period of Josephine's death. Now I wanted to read the later letters, to see what happened to him. I found out that he went a little mad. There are pages and pages of made-up words, as though in code. Sometimes they are turned into nonsense poems. Occasionally there is a kind of coherence—one letter, to a person named Felix, mentions a cat which haunts him. (I knew the feeling.)

Josiah became obsessed with the cat—he thought it was the reincarnation of his sister—and called it by several names: Jo, Josie, and peculiarly Adropo. He'd try to kill it, and sometimes even succeeded. But every time he killed a cat, another would come to take its place, and the whole thing would start again. This is what the writings said, anyway.

There was no confession of a crime, just his guilty conscience, ever-present, in the form of a cat.

In the back of my mind, I knew I was not going to find the proof I was looking for.

I had packed all my luggage and stored it with those very nice people at the guest house on Beacon Street. My last morning in the house, I went to open a can, and found a cat dead on the floor. I poked it with my foot and it stayed where it was, so I figured it really was dead. It wasn't *the* cat—no such luck—but one like it.

The lawyer turned up, another bag of dripping cat food under her arm, and she looked down dispassionately at the cat, drawing in smoke from her cigarette.

"About time, too," she said, blowing out the smoke. "That cat, must have had a cast-iron stomach." Did I mention this woman was stupid as well?

"That isn't the cat."

"Oh shit."

I sat her down and disposed of the cadaver out the back door. I made the coffee and she told me everything. When Josiah died he left the house to the Mugar Memorial Library (part of Boston University, a few blocks away on Commonwealth) for literary meetings, wanting to be remembered as a patron of the arts. But he wanted to provide for his sister as well (i.e., the cat) and said that the sale of the books should cover the expense. The "smart" lawyer, who is getting paid a pittance for this, decides to get an out-of-towner to do the valuation and selling, kill the cat, and use the proceeds to buy a new rusty car or somesuch. She told me how difficult it is to succeed as a lawyer in Boston, what with Boston U and Harvard and the like.

"We're overrun with lawyers here," she explained. "Something like sixty-five thousand lawyers, and more graduating every year." She saw how broken up I was about it. "Okay, okay. I won't kill the cat. But, you could at least give me a few valuable books to sell on the side, to make it worth my while."

I pulled out some paperbacks I had—er—put by—two Lion Books: one by David Goodis, the other by Jim Thompson. She looked somewhat sceptical. I told her she'd get at least $200 apiece on them, perhaps as much as $600 if she put them up for auction with a dealer like Black Deuce or Sphinx. She left on a puff of smoke, beaming, thinking I was a good guy. I wasn't about to disabuse her of that particular notion.

Having rid myself of that dreadful woman, I then dusted off a copy of *Tales* by Mr Edgar Allan Poe. I'd come to collect it and take it home for myself. I opened it flat on the bed, so I didn't get too many finger marks on the pages. A first edition, 1845, it was inscribed by Poe to "Mr. Nathaniel Hawthorne," hoping that the aforementioned thought these tales had the desired "effect." This referred to a favourable review that Poe gave Hawthorne, where Poe described his ideas about the purpose of stories. Obviously Poe was toadying up to Hawthorne, perhaps hoping for a favourable review in return. Although most would consider it a forgery, dated as it is 1854 and Poe having died in 1849, anyone who knows their Poe knows he was a prankster and hoaxer—I was sure this was by his pen.

The cat chose this moment to appear. It meowed and pressed its back up against my legs. Anyone would think it knew what was going on.

"I loathe cats. I'm never going to like you. I'm not even going to give you a name. Give it up." I couldn't believe I was talking to it.

The cat jumped onto the bed and curled itself up on the open Poe. Slowly, it started drawing its claws across the fragile pages, playing with them.

Great! What do I do now?

The black cat just purred.

The Duel

J. A. JANCE

HOWARD WAS NOTHING IF NOT dependable. Living up to his reputation for constant vigilance, he was at his assigned post and standing guard, carefully studying the parade of home-bound cars that tooled down the rainy, winter-darkened street. He examined each pair of fuzzy, rain-softened headlights, waiting for the one, all-important pair which would slice away from the others and turn onto the graveled driveway.

The atmosphere in the room was charged with floating particles of waiting while the graceful old Seth Thomas clock on the mantel ticked hollowly away. Every fifteen minutes it gave sonorous voice to each quarter-hour interval. The only other sounds in the chilly and ominously expectant house came from a single person playing cards. The cards slapped down angrily on the faded finish of the rosewood table where Anna played her ever-present game of solitaire.

The hands of the clock marched slowly, inevitably past the delicate Roman numerals on the mother-of-pearl clock face. It was late and getting later and still Edgar wasn't home. With each passing moment, Anna's playing grew more impassioned and frenetic. The cards hit the table with increasing force and urgency. The periodic shuffles were like threatening claps of thunder preceding an approaching storm.

"Any sign of him?" Anna asked without looking up.

Howard didn't move, and he didn't answer, either. That was to be expected. Howard never had been the talkative kind, nor was he particularly sociable. He seldom remained in the same room with them once Edgar arrived home. As soon as the Lord and Master stepped inside the front door—Lord and Master was the nickname Anna and Howard called Edgar behind his back—as soon as L&M came home, Howard would stalk off upstairs, leaving Anna to fend for herself, to deal with her husband on her own. Howard's position was that Edgar was Anna's problem.

Up to a point, that was true. But now, thank God and Federal Express, the two of them were evenly matched. Edgar no longer had her outgunned, as it were.

Her use of the word *outgunned* made her smile in spite of herself. Pausing briefly from her game of cards, Anna slipped one hand into the deep pocket of her heavy, terrycloth robe and let her fingers close tentatively around the rough grip of the still-almost-new Lady Smith and Wesson she kept concealed there. She touched the gun because it was there for the touching. She touched it for reassurance, and perhaps even for luck. Stroking the cool metal of the short barrel, she wondered if the confrontation would come tonight. If so, it would finally be over and done with, once and for all.

Anna Whalen no longer cared so much what the ultimate outcome would be. She just wanted out of limbo. Whatever the cost, she wanted the awful waiting to end.

And how long had she been waiting? Forever, it seemed, although it was probably only a matter of months since the situation had become really intolerable. Howard, ever observant, was the one who had first pointed Edgar's dalliance out to her. He was also the one who had realized and warned her that Edgar might try poison.

Initially, the idea of Edgar's poisoning her had seemed like a wildly farfetched idea, a preposterous, nightmarish joke. Anna had laughed it off, but later, the more she thought about it and the more she observed Edgar's increasingly suspicious behavior, the more it had made sense. After all, he was the only one in the house who did any cooking, such as it was. Eventually she realized that it would be a simple thing for him to slip some kind of death-inducing substance into her food.

Faced with this possibility, Anna and Howard had wisely hit upon a countermeasure. True friend that he was, Howard had generously agreed to taste whatever food appeared on Anna's plate. Howard tried everything first—everything that is, except green beans and snow peas. Howard despised green vegetables. Unfortunately, the frozen-dinner people were very big on snow peas this year. Friend or not, when servings of suspicious green things turned up on Anna's tray, Howard wouldn't touch them.

If she hadn't been cagey about it, green vegetables might well have been Anna's undoing, her Achilles' heel. Instead, she carefully slipped the offending green things off her plate and surreptitiously stuffed them behind the cushion of her recliner whenever Edgar wasn't watching. Every morning, as soon as the Lord and Master was safely out of the house, she'd return to the chair and dispose of the previous evening's incriminating evidence. So far, so good.

Outside a passing car slowed, but it turned left into the Mossbecks' driveway across the street. Anna still called it Mossbecks' although the Mossbecks hadn't lived there in fifteen years. She had no idea who lived there now—some nameless, childless young couple who both had important, well-paying jobs in the city. Why someone like that needed a house as big as the Mossbecks' Anna couldn't imagine.

But then, to be fair, she and Edgar didn't need such a big house, either. They lived in only four of the downstairs rooms in Grandmother Adams's gnarled old house. Edgar was too tight to heat the rest of it. He claimed they couldn't afford it. He slept on a day bed in what had once been Cook's room off the kitchen. Anna's ornate bedroom suite had been moved downstairs into what had once been her grandmother's parlor. For years, no one but Howard had ventured upstairs, but he had assured Anna that he didn't mind the cold. In fact, he preferred it.

Actually, the escalating warfare between Edgar and Howard was what had finally alerted Anna to her own danger and to the possibility that another woman might be the root cause of all the trouble. Most of it anyhow. For at least six months now, Edgar had been coming home late on Tuesday nights, and only on Tuesdays. Howard, whose nose was particularly sensitive to such things, had detected a hint of very feminine perfume, the same scent every time, lingering on Edgar's clothing on each of those selfsame Tuesday nights. Anna had racked her brain to figure out who this perfume-drenched homewrecker might be.

Anna's forty-year marriage to Edgar had never been an especially happy one, but then neither one of them had been brought up to believe in happy marriages. Marriages lasted, of course, because that was expected. How one functioned inside those lasting marriages was left to the good grace and wit of the individuals involved.

Part of the problem was due to the fact that there had been certain misunderstandings from the very beginning which were traceable to parental meddling and mismanagement on both sides. Edgar had been touted to Anna's family as having "good breeding and good prospects" although the chief touter, mainly his widowed mother, should have been somewhat suspect as a source of reliable information. But then Anna's family wasn't entirely blameless when it came to stretching the truth either.

Edgar had presumably married for money without realizing that Anna's father, Bertram Quincy Adams III, had done an excellent job of concealing his own foolhardy squandering of the family fortunes. By the time Edgar discovered his wife was practically penniless, except for her grandmother's house and a small trust fund, he himself was far too committed to the gentlemanly lifestyle.

Anna Quincy Adams Whalen wasn't rich, but her pedigree opened doors that otherwise would have been closed to her husband on his own. Constitutionally unfit for regular work, Edgar shamelessly used Adams family connections to procure himself a couple of corporate directorships and a private school trusteeship. The small income from those combined with minimal Social Security checks kept the wolf from the door and paid the property taxes, but that was about it. They lived on the right side of town with a fashionable address but behind a closed door which carefully concealed their genteel poverty. To Anna's way of thinking there was nothing genteel about it.

She looked around the chilly room. What had once been a large, elegant dining room had been forced into the mold of dining and living room both. The extra leaves had long since disappeared from the rosewood table. Grandmother Adams's remaining furniture, quality once but now faded and dingy, had been pushed up against the walls to make room for a monster television set and two La-Z-Boy recliners which Anna found ungainly and uncomfortable both, but that was where she and her husband sat, night after night, matching bookends in their matching chairs, eating frozen dinners on TV trays while CNN droned on and on.

It would have been nice, every once in a while, to watch a sitcom or even one of those dreadful made-for-television police-dramas, but Edgar was the keeper of the remote control, and he liked to watch the news. When he was there they watched what he wanted. When he was gone, the television stayed off completely because Anna found the push-button controls far too complicated to understand.

Naturally, Edgar had bought the set without consulting her which may have been one reason why Anna hated it. The first she had known anything about it was when the delivery man rang the doorbell and asked her where she wanted him to set it up. Oh well, she had gotten even. Anna had made an unauthorized purchase of her own. The mail-order Smith and Wesson had come to the house less than five days after she phoned in her order. She had intercepted the VISA card bill for three months in a row, paying it herself out of her own paltry Social Security check until she had gotten the balance down low enough that Edgar hadn't questioned it.

Just then headlights flashed across the rain-splashed window. Tires crunched in the driveway. Edgar was home.

Howard got up at once. "Please don't leave me alone with him tonight," Anna begged, but Howard only shook his head and wouldn't stay. She resented it that he could so callously abandon her and leave her to face Edgar alone, but that was just the way Howard was. Over the years, it seemed as though she would have gotten used to it.

Edgar came into the room, set down his briefcase and grocery bag, and immediately closed the drapes. "How many times do I have to tell you to close the drapes in the winter? You're letting all the heat out."

"I forgot," Anna said, and continued to play her game of solitaire with diligent concentration.

Edgar went over to the television set and picked up the remote control. For a moment he stood staring down at the small electronic device on top of the set.

"Have you let the damn cat sit up on the cable box again? You let it wreck the last one. That's what the guy said, you know, that the insides were all plugged full of cat hair."

"Maybe it keeps his feet warm," Anna offered.

"Don't start with that 'the house is too cold' stuff again," Edgar said irritably. "If the house is too cold, close the damn drapes. Are you hungry?"

She wasn't, but Edgar liked to eat as soon as he got home so he could watch the news for the rest of the night without any unnecessary interruptions. "Yes," Anna said. "I could eat a horse."

"It's chicken," he said, picking up the groceries and carrying them into the kitchen. "Fried chicken, mashed potatoes, and corn."

Good, Anna thought. Howard liked corn. She listened to the familiar sounds from the kitchen—the tiny bleatings of the control on the microwave, ice tinkling into a glass, something, gin probably, being poured over the ice. Suddenly Anna found herself feeling sorry that it was corn instead of snow peas. She had wanted it to be tonight. She had wanted to end the uncertainty and get it over with.

The swinging door to the kitchen banged open. She knew without looking that Edgar was standing behind her, staring down over her shoulder at the cards scattered across the smooth surface of the table.

"Did you win today?" he asked.

"No."

Anna played a complicated, two-deck kind of solitaire which she won only once every year or so. If she had cheated, she probably would have won more often, but she was always scrupulously honest. She didn't like it when Edgar looked over her shoulder, though. Having him watch made her nervous, and she missed plays she could have made.

"Why don't you try a different game?" Edgar asked.

"I like this one," she replied.

The beeper on the microwave went off. Edgar returned to the kitchen. As soon as he left, Anna could see that she had missed putting the six of spades on the descending spades pile for at least three turns. Damn him. She threw down her cards in disgust and went to set the table.

That's what they called it, setting the table, although it was really nothing more than setting up the two TV trays. Edgar always brought the silverware and napkins in with him from the kitchen, but he liked to have the trays set up by the time he got there so he didn't have to stand there with his hands full and wait for her to do her part of the job.

The microwave was going again, and the door to the kitchen was shut. Edgar couldn't hear her.

"Howard," Anna called softly. "Howard. You come back down here. I need you." But for some strange reason, Howard didn't appear.

"Where's Howard?" Anna asked when Edgar brought the food in from the kitchen.

Edgar shrugged. "Beats me," he said. "I haven't seen him since I got home."

Anna waited, but still there was no sign of Howard. She didn't dare make a fuss or call to him again. Edgar was soon eating away, his eyes glued to the television set. Only when there was a station break did he turn to look at her.

"You're not eating your dinner," he said accusingly. "I thought you said you were hungry."

She was hungry, now. The smell of the food, the look of it, had made her hungry, but without Howard there to try it for her, she didn't dare eat any of it, and she was afraid to stuff the chicken, bones and all, down behind the cushion.

This must be it, she was thinking. He must have locked Howard away somewhere, so he can't help me. She slipped her hand into her pocket and screwed up her courage.

"Why are you doing this?"

He looked over at her, surprised. "Doing what? Watching television? I always watch television. You know that."

Her fingers closed around the grip of the pistol, but she didn't take it out of her pocket. Not yet. She didn't want to give everything away at once.

"Why are you trying to poison me?" she asked.

Edgar choked quite convincingly on a piece of chicken. "Me? Trying to poison you? Anna, you've got to be kidding! You've been reading too many books."

"There's another woman, isn't there, Edgar?" she continued. Anna kept her voice low and even. She didn't want him to think she was just being hysterical. "You've been seeing another woman on the side for some time now, and the two of you are trying to get rid of me."

"My God, Anna, that's the wildest thing I've ever heard. Wherever did you come up with such a crazy, cockamamie idea?"

"Tuesdays," she answered. "It's because of Tuesdays. You're late coming home every single Tuesday without fail."

He looked relieved. "Oh, that," he said. "I've been seeing a counselor, trying to sort some things out in my own mind. And it's been helping more than you know. Maybe you should try it, see if it wouldn't help you as well. I could come home early enough to pick you up, and we could go see the counselor together. What would you think of that?"

The story about the counselor sounded vaguely possible, but she wasn't about to fall for it. "I don't believe you," she said, and pulled the gun.

Edgar's eyes filled with shocked disbelief. "My God, Anna! Where did you get that thing? Is it loaded?"

Of course it was loaded. What would be the point of carrying a gun that wasn't? Edgar started to get up, but she shot him square in the chest before he ever made it to his feet. The force of the blow flung him back into the chair which shifted automatically into the reclining position, leaving him with his feet jutting into the air like a helpless, overturned turtle. He lay there for some time, groaning and clutching his chest.

Anna watched him curiously. If he had tried to get up, she would have shot him again, but he didn't. Eventually he stopped groaning. His hands fell limply to his sides. Meanwhile, the news droned on and on, talking about something that was going on in the Middle East again . . . still. Anna didn't pay much attention. She wasn't particularly interested in world affairs.

After a while, though, when they started talking about a nationally known murder case, a trial that had been in process for several months and was just now going to the jury, she got interested in the program. Forgetting her customary caution, she began to eat her dinner. Anna was so interested in what the lady news commentator was saying, she barely noticed the funny almond taste of the corn.

Howard did, though. Much later, thinking Anna and Edgar must have fallen asleep in front of the droning television set, he finally crept back down from upstairs. The big yellow cat sniffed disdainfully at what was left of the corn on Anna's plate, but he had sense enough not to eat it. Howard's nose was far too sensitive for that.

Eight
A Rick Winslow Mystery

KURTIS ROTH

THINK THE WORD I'M LOOKING for is *synergy*. You know, you're going along, living your life right up there on the surface of the world, doing the little things you always do. Everything looks normal. But, whether you realize it or not—and you almost never do—your little day-to-day actions are cranking giant gears into motion underneath the surface. Sometime, somewhere, somehow, the little things you do make big things happen.

As a private investigator, I have occasionally found ways to harness that synergy. But generally speaking, my life is as accidental as anyone's. Maybe more so.

This time I was sitting on a park bench, just reading the paper and enjoying some fresh air when the gears began to groan.

I don't know why I read the paper anymore. All the news is bad news, and the story I was reading on that particular August morning was particularly bad. A front-page item about somebody the *Kansas City Star* had dubbed the "Hourglass Killer." He had been inactive for the last few weeks, as far as anyone could tell. No more mutilations. No more bodies found with the little hourglass figure etched onto their bellies. The Johnson County Sheriff's Office and the Overland Park police had been baffled from the outset. According to the article they weren't any closer to naming a suspect, and I can't say this came as any real surprise, because the *Star* wasn't any closer to printing a new article either.

Anyway, I was just about to set it aside when something rubbed up against my leg.

I looked down, figuring it for a panhandling pigeon or squirrel, but found myself looking instead at the arched back of a yellow cat—a stray I had seen around a couple of times before. It blinked at me through glassy green eyes, then uttered what I suppose was the feline equivalent of *Hey, how's it going?*

"Could be worse," I said, giving it a scratch. It. Him. It had the boy parts. "How about yourself?"

He purred and did a little figure eight against my leg, rubbing his left side, then his right, tail twitching this way and that. That's when I noticed his injury. A narrow ring of skin was missing about halfway down the length of his tail.

I sat back and said, "Well, that's what you get for prowling the mean streets, huh?" I had seen a similar injury before. As a kid, one of my neighbors had a Great Dane, whose tail they hadn't troubled to bob. Left in its natural state, a Dane's tail is very long. It's always whacking into or getting caught under something. The dog in question left hers in the path of a car. She had barely pulled it away in time, and it still got nipped by a tire, and that one instant was enough to tear away not a patch of skin, but a ring, running the full circumference of her tail.

No cat could possibly be as inept as a Great Dane, but out here he wouldn't have to be. Our "park" was the concrete northern bank of Brush Creek, on the Country Club Plaza. On the north side, there's the Plaza proper. The south side is occupied by a row of ancient apartment buildings, one of which I call home. There's parking up and down both sides of the creek. Hundreds of cars for a cat to sit under.

House cats worry about rocking chairs. Street cats worry about Plymouths.

Thing is, he didn't really look like a street cat. He was thin, as if he hadn't eaten properly in some time, but he had a collar and a tag. Red collar. Green metal tag, shaped like a bell. I was hoping it would tell me his name, or maybe his address, but all it had was a phone number.

"I don't guess this is your voice mail," I said.

He gave me a very human look just then, a shrug that seemed to say, *No, that level of connectivity doesn't really appeal to me.*

"You're a rolling stone, is that it?"

Another look.

"Well," I said, "if this isn't your answering service or your beeper, I suppose it must belong to your owner. I could ring him or her and find out what to call you, but you know what? I have a feeling it's the wrong name. I bet they call you Fluffy or Tiger or something."

No comment.

"But that's not you. You're a rolling stone. A travelin' man. You're Travelin' Jack. How's that for a name?"

He did another figure eight against my leg.

"Jack it is then," I said. "And my name's Rick. Rick Winslow. But you can call me whatever you want."

His name for me sounded suspiciously like a purr.

"What say we go get that tail fixed up? I'll give your owner a call while we're at it, see if we can find out where you belong."

I found a stray cat once when I was a kid. It was wintertime, snow falling, and I had taken a short cut through the woods on the way home from school. Halfway through I heard a cat yowling somewhere off out of sight. It sounded pained, and I knew there were rabbit traps all over the place that time of year, so I figured it probably needed rescuing.

I didn't find it until I realized its cries were echoing from a drainpipe that let out into the little creek at the bottom of the woods.

I looked into the pipe and saw a pair of yellow eyes sparkling back at me.

He wasn't hurt. Just cold and alone. I fed him cans of tuna smuggled from my mom's cupboard, and I called him Sparkle, and he was my very own cat right up until I found the courage to bring him home.

I should have known better. My dad—his world was one of pitch blacks and stark whites, with nothing in between. In his mind, Sparkle belonged to someone else. By failing to return the cat, I had effectively stolen it. So he did the only honorable thing there was to do. He put up some flyers in town, located Sparkle's real owners, and handed him over without a word of apology to his son.

I learned two things that day. One: the cat's name wasn't Sparkle, it was Kitty. Two: there are pet owners, and there are pet lovers. These people were owners. They didn't care about Sparkle. They didn't look for him when he was lost, and they sure as heck didn't hand-feed him Chicken of the Sea all winter. But they knew what kind of collar he'd been wearing and what kinds of shots his tags said he'd had, so they got to take him away. End of story.

I never realized it before, but that was probably a big turning point for me. After that, I began to systematically strip my life to the bare necessities. No pets. No toys. No real pals or steady girlfriends. Don't commit to anything or anyone who might not be around tomorrow. Work hard, move forward—life as economy of motion. I eventually followed my dad into the Navy, where life was very Spartan, and then I joined the CIA, where Spartan began to look pretty lush.

Now, self-employed for almost two years, I looked around my apartment and found that things hadn't changed much. There was a chair and a lamp by the living room window. No television. One bed with one pillow, one sheet, and one blanket, buttoned up tight. In the bathroom: toilet paper, soap, razor, deodorant. There were enough pans in the kitchen to get the job done, and that was pretty much it. The place was a dead zone.

Until Travelin' Jack crossed the threshold. He scrambled from room to room, inspecting the facilities while I sorted through a few items from the drug store. When he seemed satisfied, I put him up on the bed where I could see what I was doing. A dab of salve here, a dab there, a little gauze, a strip of medical tape. He accepted my ministrations as if we'd been through it a hundred times before.

Afterward, I teased him with a shoestring for an hour or so, and in that time I came up with a long list of reasons why I really should just keep him for myself.

But he wasn't mine. He belonged to someone else, so I did the only honorable thing there was to do. I picked up the phone and dialed.

You'd think things could go smoothly, just for once.

No such luck.

The number was disconnected.

There are plenty of ways to track down the owner of a disconnected number. First thing I did was head down to the library and check the Crisscross directories. I took it back several years and came up with the same name and address every time. David A. Kirby, in a Ninety-fifth Street apartment, across the state line in Overland Park, Kansas.

I checked another directory, got the name and number of his apartment complex, went home, and called the main office. A young woman answered, cramming too much energy into her official greeting. I told her my name and who I was looking for.

"Oh," she said. "I'm sorry. Mr. Kirby moved out last month."

"I don't suppose you have his new number, or a forwarding address."

She hesitated. "Well, I'm sure we must. We had to get his security deposit back to him somehow. But we have a policy against giving that sort of information out. Especially with someone like Mr. Kirby."

"What's so special about him?"

"You don't know him?"

"We haven't met," I said. "But I think I found his cat. His old phone number—"

She interrupted me with a squeal of delight. "You found Bail?"

"Bail? Is that his name?"

"No," she said, "you're saying it wrong. It's Bay-ull. Bee-ay-ay-ell. Like the devil."

Baal.

If you listen to the Phoenicians, he's an angry sun god. Christians think of him as one of Satan's fallen comrades. I asked what the hell kind of name it was for a cat.

"I think it has something to do with his coloring," she said. "See, he's gold, and he's a target tabby."

"A target tabby?"

"Yeah. Look at his stripes. If you look at them just right, you'll see the circles."

She was right. I studied at him in profile and saw concentric rings, as if someone had pasted targets to his sides. I couldn't believe I'd missed it before.

"Anyway," she went on, "Mr. Kirby said that makes him a dead ringer for Baal."

Gold rings. Sun god. "I guess he agrees with the Phoenicians," I said.

"Huh? All I know is, he's a very weird guy. You should have seen the inside of his apartment. Weird paintings. Candles everywhere. We almost had to evict him once because of the fire hazard."

This knowledge didn't make me any more eager to return Jack—or Baal, or whoever he was—to his rightful owner, but I asked again if I could have the forwarding info. This time she gave it up.

Turned out he lived just a block or two down from my building, surprise, surprise.

I tried his new number. It rang, but no one answered. No machine either. When I called his building's front desk and asked if I could leave a message, the guy on the other end told me to hold. He came back a few seconds later and said, "Kirby. Right. That's the fella took off right after he moved in. Which is a real pisser, because I usually charge two months up front—but not with this guy. He didn't have the cash, and I wanted to fill the room, so I said I'd wait. Figured, why not help a guy out? Now I know. He's long gone, and I'll bet you his back rent he ain't ever coming back. Which wouldn't be a problem, if I could move his stuff or sell it or something, but I can't. Not for a hundred and eighty days. There's laws.

"Just goes to show you," he said. "Try to do a good thing, all you get is a kick in the head."

* * *

The next morning, I was halfway through another article about the Hourglass Killer—still in the headlines; still no further activity—when the vet poked his head into the waiting room and said, "Mr. Winslow? Could you come on back? I've got a few things I'd like to show you."

Too much poise. Way too much for a chubby guy in a Hawaiian-print shirt. He was supposed to be the Happy Fun Vet.

I rolled up my paper and followed him back to an examination room. Jack was sitting there on a high narrow table, peering carefully over the sides. His tail was no longer wrapped. The wound looked as fresh as before.

"What's the prognosis?" I asked.

"Well," he said, "there's nothing to be overly concerned about, not in terms of his ongoing health, not now that we're taking care of him. He'll, uh . . . he'll be fine . . ."

"But?"

He shook his head. "You say this cat was a stray?"

"Until yesterday, yes."

"And you think his tail was run over by a car."

I shrugged. "It was just a guess."

"Right," he said. "Come closer and have a look at this." He took Jack's tail in one gloved hand and pointed with the other. "You see, this is actually a very old wound. Our buddy Jack here has kept it nice and clean, it's only slightly infected, but he's also managed to keep it from healing. If I had to guess, I'd say it's been open for about two months. Maybe as long as six. That's okay, of course. We can manage it now—"

"So what's the problem?"

"Well," he said, "the thing is, I'm pretty sure it wasn't an accident."

I looked at Jack. Jack looked at me. We both looked at the vet.

I said, "You're not saying someone ran him over on purpose. It was something else?"

"I'm afraid so. The wound has tried to heal, so the edges are a bit blurred, but if you look here, and here, you can see that it's not a tear at all. These are incisions, made with a sharp cutting tool. A razor, or a surgical instrument of some kind."

"Someone cut him. Intentionally?"

"Yes. I can't say I've ever seen anything quite like this, but animals are abused by their owners all the time, so whenever we find one indicator of abuse, we look for others."

"Let me guess," I said.

He nodded, nudged Jack over on his side, and held the left foreleg up for inspection. "Here. You have to look very closely. See the scars? I believe they're consistent with the types of cuts made on his tail. There are similar cuts on each of his legs. And then there's his belly," he said. "Did you notice the shaved area when you found him?"

"No," I said. "Looks like I didn't notice much of anything beyond his tail."

"Don't feel bad. It was mostly grown in. But I *did* notice, and I found some contusions in that area, so I shaved it again and came up with something very, very strange. A design of some sort. I could be wrong, but I think it's the number eight."

He turned Jack over on his back. Jack, who was taking this all like a champ, actually looked like he was having fun.

When I saw the design on his belly, I could understand why.

He had escaped a monster.

Maybe it was the number eight. Maybe it wasn't. What I saw was a pair of once-inch isosceles triangles, arranged nose-to-nose. A tiny hourglass. And its sands had run out.

The vet was shaking his head. "What do you think it means? Is that how many lives he's supposed to have left now? Why would anyone do something like this to a cat?"

I unrolled my newspaper, pointed at the headline. Watched the vet turn pale.

"Maybe," I said, "it was a practice run."

Synergy. Sometimes, the little things we do set giant gears into motion.

Once the gears were turning, and I was aware of it, I had some decisions to make. Call the police and pass on what I knew, or go out and find Kirby myself. Give him a little practice run, let him see how it feels.

In the end, I did the only honorable thing there was to do. I made some calls. I swore out a statement. I cheered when they put David Allen Kirby away.

But that was the beginning and the end of it for me. No vigilante rampage. No stalking the courtrooms. I had bigger fish to fry. Salmon, actually. Jack can't get enough. Although his opinion seems to waver, depending on how I fix it. I'm still trying to figure that one out.

Evinrude

DAVID OWENS

ABOUT SEVENTY PERCENT SURE that a noise in the house had awakened me, I moved nothing but my eyes. 1:07 A.M. glowed on the face of the clock radio, which worked out to be just under half an hour of shut-eye. A sharp *whang* down on the first floor launched me.

Rummaging through the clothes dropped next to the bed turned up jeans and a sweatshirt. I pulled those on, not bothering with underwear, before easing open the drawer of the nightstand.

My Smith & Wesson .38 special was there and loaded. With the pistol in my hand, and more or less dressed, I felt nervous but not vulnerable. Pausing a moment to slip my bare feet into elkhide moccasins, I made my way through the darkened bedroom and down the stairs.

Neither the front hall nor the living room contained anything I didn't really want to find. With a tight grip on the revolver's butt, I entered the kitchen.

A dark shape was hunched in the far corner. The shape's tail was twitching.

Evinrude, my big gray cat, is a Russian Blue. His lightning swat sent an object flying out from under him. A roll of thirty-five millimeter Kodachrome film zinged across the floor. *Whang*, it ricocheted off the base of the dishwasher. Evinrude lunged and nailed it on the rebound.

Wresting the film from the cat, I said, "So, the burglar is after my film. Well, buddy, you'll never get away with it."

I should have known better than to leave exposed film from a shoot where Evinrude could find it, but I was getting lax. More than two years had elapsed since his shenanigans had cost me a regular client.

That time a roll of film had disappeared. The result was an expensive reshoot. Spring cleaning, two months later, the film had turned up behind the refrigerator.

Luckily my cat hadn't managed to lose anything this time. The other half-dozen thirty-six-exposure rolls were still up on the counter with the shredded plastic sandwich bag that had been intact when I'd sealed in the film. To free up my right hand, I shoved the .38 into the waistband of my jeans and scooped up all seven rolls of Kodachrome.

Evinrude brushed against my leg and began his deep, loud purr. That purr is the reason he's named after a brand of outboard motor.

The big Blue followed me into the living room and watched as I put the film in the drawer of an end table. Straightening up, I saw movement outside the front window.

In the dim light of a crescent moon, two figures approached an old Plymouth Voyager parked at the curb. The minivan belonged to Jasmine Nichols. She's my across-the-street neighbor and the divorced mother of two young girls.

The pair stopped next to the Voyager's left rear quarter panel. It was too dark to actually tell what they were doing. But it was a safe bet it wasn't anything Jasmine would be real happy about.

My cell phone was on the coffee table, so I snagged it with my left hand as my right pulled the tail of my sweatshirt down over the butt of the Smith & Wesson. Once the gun was concealed, I headed out the front door.

Evinrude darted out with me. I'd closed the door sharply in a failed attempt to head him off and caused one light clap of the knocker. In the night, that was loud enough to send the two across the street scrambling.

They darted between Jasmine's house and the Delgados' next door, making for the backyards. From the middle of the street, I saw them round the back corner of the Delgados' and head left down the street. Five doors down that way was a small apartment building with an adjacent parking lot. I glanced at the minivan.

The gas flap was open. Dropped on the street was a bag of sugar, its contents spilled. Knowing what they'd just done to the neighbor's car, I took off running down the street.

My gut feeling was that they were headed for a car parked inconspicuously in the apartment lot. My guess was that the car would be an older model Corvette, one painted burgundy with patches of gray primer, driven by a teenager with whom Jasmine had recently had a run-in. With an eye out for that particular car, I sprinted into the lot.

Two people were moving through. Crouched low, they were slinking between the cars. I shouted, "Hold it right there!"

Instead of halting, they took off. Arms and legs pumping, the duo tore out of the rear of the parking lot, across the next street and into a small patch of woods. I didn't pursue. I didn't think there was any need.

It looked like I was right about their car being in the lot. All I needed to do was make a quick circuit of the lot, find the 'Vette and call the police on my cell phone. Then just wait beside the car and see who shows up first. A good plan, only there was a hitch—no 'Vette.

I thought, *That battered old 'Vette isn't here. But, they headed straight for this lot. Surprisingly, between the two of them there may have been enough sense to realize that a Corvette with loud exhaust pipes is not exactly a stealth machine. One of these cars must be what they're driving. I still just need to wait. They'll show up. Meanwhile, time to get the police out here.*

The 911 operator took all the information about what happened, where, and who I was. After telling him I would wait in the parking lot entrance, I said, "Be sure you tell the responding officer I'm wearing blue jeans and a green sweatshirt. But, be especially certain the officer knows that I'll have a cell phone in my hand."

The fall night was more than just a little crisp. Regretting not having slipped on a jacket, I realized socks would have been nice too.

Waiting for the police, it finally dawned on me that I should give Jasmine a call. I did that.

Standing there waiting for a cruiser to show up, I heard his incredibly loud purr a moment before Evinrude brushed against my leg. While petting him as he wanted, I saw Jasmine in the street with a flashlight.

A cruiser rounded the corner and stopped beside Jasmine. It paused only briefly, then rolled slowly toward where I was standing. Its spotlight came on and swiveled to shine on me. I squinted and held up the cell phone with its dial toward the squad car. The spot was extinguished. The car stopped and the officer climbed out.

She looked to be in her late twenties, with short red hair and a very fair complexion. "I'm Officer Sullivan. You the one that called 911?" she asked.

"That's right. I'm Collin Ryan," I answered, extending my hand. She took it in a brief but firm grip.

"I saw the gas tank open and a bag of sugar back there. How are you involved?" she asked.

Evinrude began rubbing against her leg. The officer ignored him. He cranked his already loud purr up another notch. She still paid no attention.

"About one A.M. my cat woke me. He was making a racket down in the kitchen, slapping around a roll of film from today's shoot. I'd shot several models in a ladies' spa. A photo shoot, Officer Sullivan."

"I'd pretty much figured that," she said, then pointed at the critter purring and rubbing against her leg. "This the cat that was batting your film around?"

"Right. That's the rascal, Evinrude."

"So, the cat woke you up, then what?"

"From my front window I saw two people beside Jasmine's minivan. Jasmine's the woman that lives across the street from me. So I went out to see what was going on. When I closed the front door, they took off."

"And you gave chase?"

"Well, more or less. I didn't follow along behind them. Instead, I tried to cut them off. I figured the Corvette would be parked in the lot. So that's where I headed."

"Now, wait a minute," she said. "How does a Corvette figure into this?"

"A teenage boy, I believe his name is Preston Williams, drives a shabby older 'Vette with loud pipes. He always roars down our street, trying to impress the Delgado girls.

"The Delgados live next door to Jasmine. They have seventeen-year-old identical twins. Very pretty girls.

"Anyway, a couple of weeks ago the kid came blasting down the street when Jasmine's little girls were playing on the sidewalk. Jasmine shouted for him to slow down. Instead, he shoved his hand up through the open T-top and made a crude gesture. Jasmine called the cops.

"Two days ago there was an unmarked car with radar parked halfway down the block. They nailed the Williams kid for speeding and also wrote him up for the loud pipes. My guess is it was him out here tonight getting revenge."

Evinrude stood on his hind legs, kneaded the officer's leg with his paws, and continued his incredible purr. She looked down at the cat. I said, "He just wants some petting."

The officer pushed the cat away as she said, "I'm not a cat person. Now, where is this Corvette?"

Evinrude ambled off into the parking lot.

"I didn't find it. But, the two guys did head right for this lot. So, they must be driving one of the other cars parked here."

"A possibility but not a certainty," she said.

"You wait. They'll be back after their car," I said.

"If they do have a car here, and they think anyone is watching it, they could wait a month before returning for it.

"Did you get a good look at them? Can you make an identification?" she asked.

"Wish I could. But, they were too far away in the dark."

From the corner of my eye, I saw Evinrude leap up on the hood of a black Toyota. He curled up for a nap. I pointed to the cat and said, "Check Evinrude over there."

"Yeah," she said. "Somebody's cat keeps getting dirty footprints on the hood of my cruiser."

"Officer, they get up on the hood to take a nap. They do it while the hood is still warm."

"Interesting," she said.

The two of us walked over to the Toyota. Evinrude stood. Looking through the windshield, his head moved to follow the beam from the officer's flashlight as she surveyed the front seat. The light stopped on an empty plastic bag from a supermarket. A receipt was visible in the bag. It was a short one, a single item, tax, and total.

"I can't read it from here. But, I'm willing to bet that's a receipt for a bag of sugar," I said.

"Me too," she said. She then used her handheld radio to run the plates on the car. Turned out to be registered to a Valerie Williams.

"Looks like our boy Preston borrowed his mother's car tonight. I'll have it impounded for evidence."

She reached out and began to pet Evinrude. I was standing there with a big grin on my face, when, without taking her eyes off the cat, she asked, "Do you have a permit for that concealed weapon?"

My grin faded. "No, Officer Sullivan, I don't."

"I wouldn't be out here in the dark chasing criminals without *my* gun. Collin, before my sergeant gets here, why don't you stroll on home and get rid of the heavy artillery. Then come on back. And by the way, my name is Arlene."

"Thanks, Arlene."

Still petting Evinrude, she turned, smiled, and said, "Collin, you and junior crimebuster here did all right."

Eyes Wide Open

M. CHRISTIAN

OF ALL THE TIMES OF THE DAY, Margaret disliked mornings the most. It wasn't waking to the warm weight of Tommy on her back, his contented purr a soft vibration that made her feel kittenish: a loved and protected baby, with father close by and happy. It wasn't the first fingers of daylight crawling across her bedroom floor, or the smells of her stepmother's crackling breakfast of pancakes and bacon wafting up from the kitchen below, or even the looming presence of algebra, French, or geography lessons.

The morning was when her father had died. It was too easy to imagine him waking up to see the same lethargic crawl of sunlight across his and her stepmother's bedroom floor, or the smile that always seemed to spread across his gentle face at the thought of a hearty breakfast. Tommy made it so much worse. Not that the big tortoise-shell tabby was a bad cat—far from it; Tommy radiated an affection that Margaret had found unmatched in any other animal, or person, in her life—aside from her father. Tommy and her father had seemed to be part of the same great adoring beast, a happy, furry animal that had always been there for Margaret: a strong, protective arm around her when she cried, a rumbling purr in her lap, a silly joke, a playful chase and cavort after a loose piece of string . . . and so much more.

Tommy stretched; she could feel his strong paws inching along her thick comforter, his back ones pushing down on her full kidneys. Better than an alarm clock—you never had to wind him, her father had said, and, sure enough, a heartbeat later the big gray and white cat let out a purr-rumbling meow of good morning.

Now formally awake, the greeting of her beloved cat ringing in the day, Margaret rolled over slowly. As always, Tommy walked along her turning body till he was sitting, round and heavy, on her tummy.

After her father had died Tommy had been close to death himself. For Margaret, it was as if the gentle giant were dying again. In many ways it had been worse to see Tommy padding around the great Oak Street house, crying mournfully, searching her father's studio, all through the expansive backyard, for any sight of his precious friend. She'd not been home the morning he'd died, having been away at a school overnighter, so she'd been saved seeing his deflated body being brought out the front door. But Tommy . . . she'd been there to hear his sad cries, to hold him—and feel him crane his gray-furred head back and forth, searching for the man who would never be there again.

She'd stayed with Tommy for that hard first week, crying with him over their loss, holding him—and in no small way having him hold her—until they hadn't been able to cry any more, until they'd found what they'd needed to get through the days in each other.

Stroking the fat tom, Margaret giggled as she did every morning while he butted her face and tickled her cheeks with his whiskers. Kneading the comforter with his big feet, his purr sounded like a small avalanche.

With him rubbing her ankles and batting at her shoelaces, she got up and got dressed. Stopping every once in a while to give him a good long stroke, or scratch him—which he adored—at the base of his tail, she made herself presentable for another day of ninth-grade algebra, French, and geography.

Downstairs, her stepmother was going through her own morning ritual. Soon after her father's death, the bacon and pancakes had stopped—but Margaret and in some way Tommy had insisted. It was something from the past, from the good times when he'd still been there to laugh, comment on the morning news, tickle Tommy under his white chin, and look at both of them with bearish love—while the big breakfast had reminded her of his passing, it also reminded her of his presence.

At the bottom of the stairs, the crackle of bacon and the cackle of her stepmother—as always—on the phone, Margaret turned instead to the left. It had taken her a long time to be able to even look at those antique double doors without heavy sadness swelling up inside her. Almost a month after he'd left the studio behind forever she'd been able to go in. The tears had started, of course, but also a greater surge of love—she'd always loved his studio, the warmth of it, the joy in creation that seemed to spill from every paint-covered coffee cup and dog-eared book.

Cautiously, still after all this time, she quietly pushed the doors open— Tommy padding between her feet, rushing inside. Nothing had changed, though Mary, her stepmother, had made firm noises about clearing it out. Whenever she went into the study, Margaret either expected to find it empty—the loving presence of her father swept away, thrown out—or that his death had been some very long, very realistic dream and he'd still be there, brush clamped between his teeth, intent on capturing something with paint and canvas.

A few minutes was all Margaret could really take of the studio—particularly that morning with Tommy meowing so sadly as he walked to all his usual haunts in the huge-windowed room. Originally an eccentric greenhouse, the room had been the deciding factor in buying the house. Margaret remembered it vividly: the real estate agent apologizing for the strange room not being wired for electricity, her father at the same instant saying "Studio" and writing the man a check on the spot. For a man who believed only in daylight, the room had been ideal.

Enlarged on canvas, Tommy stared down at her, as usual. The sweet little cat had been a common subject of her father's work—an experiment in trying to capture his nature, preserve the rumbling love the fat tabby seemed to carry with him wherever he went. Gray and white streaks, wide open eyes—like deep pools of night—mouth always in his all-knowing Cheshire grin.

The real Tommy gave a long, low meow, one that startled Margaret out of staring at her father's last work. The crackling of breakfast seemed suddenly very near, and her stomach gave a loud complaint. "Come on, Tommy," she said, scooping up the fat tom, "time to get on with the day."

Mary, her stepmother, was on the phone—which was no surprise, her happy banter, as always, aggravating Margaret. Mornings were bad—they should have been solemn and sad. It was the last time of day her father had seen.

"Ready for a new day, darling?" Mary chirped over her shoulder as Margaret slid into a chair at the table, never once freeing the phone from where it cradled between her head and shoulder. "It's a brand new day."

Margaret didn't say anything. Instead she sliced her pancakes in half with a neat stroke of her knife. Against her ankle, Tommy was a vibrating warmth.

"We're having visitors this afternoon, sweetheart; some men are coming over to take a look at some of your father's paintings. They made me a very nice offer."

Hatred bubbled up in Margaret. "Don't sell them . . . please," she said, adding the *please* only when she realized she snapped the first part.

"Now, baby; you know as well as I do that your father's paintings were very special to us as well as him. But we have to . . . well, get on with our lives. We have to start to live again."

I don't want to live, Margaret thought to herself. *I want my father back.*

"You'll see, darling; soon you'll understand. It'll be for the best."

An image sat heavy in Margaret's mind: the studio, cleaned and vacant, breakfast becoming something simple—something that wouldn't impinge on Mary's new life, Tommy becoming . . . just a cat, just a fat tortoise-shell tabby. The links would grow weak, then break, and her father would slip away, vanishing into her flawed memory.

"I'm not hungry," she said to herself, as Mary was bubbling over, laughing into the phone to someone named Paul, and couldn't hear. Walking slowly upstairs, she stopped to scoop up Tommy again. Slowly, the tears started—a liquid pressure around her eyes, a heaviness surging up inside her.

At the threshold of her room, Tommy jumped down, giving a playful *murp* before springing up onto her bed. Slowly, robotically, she started to gather her things for school. The memory came hard, the sleep-over and the bad news when she got home that afternoon. Mary with her theatrical tears, wringing her hands, explaining how she'd found him in his studio that morning, how she'd stepped out and come back to find him. Heart failure, they said. Margaret always felt a deeper tug when she thought about that, that her father's heart could have just . . . failed.

The sunlight pouring through her windows was blinding. In its beams, tiny dust mites slowly danced. Tommy looked up at her from the bed, his fur haloed by the hard light, his eyes glowing pink. He had that expression on his face, that deep pool of love in his brilliantly green, narrowly slit eyes—that expression her father had pointed out to her many times, shown her the calm devotion in the tabby.

Looking at him, the ache for her father was too hard, too big for her to contain. The tears started as she stared at Tommy, the memories of her father playing with him; sleeping in his great overstuffed chair, cat and human languishing in their deep dreams.

Her vision blurred with the tears, so she sniffled and wiped her eyes with the ends of her sleeves, the harsh uniform material making her cheeks gently burn. "Have to get on with it," she said, scratching the top of Tommy's head.

Those eyes, though. Those loving, narrow-slit eyes, drew her in and she found herself just staring at the beauty of him, understanding how her father, and now she, had loved the marble-colored tom. She stared for a long time, then longer still, as what she also saw burned, then chilled her.

Later, the hours blurring by—not listening to her friends, not paying attention to her teachers—she had to face it. The anger was quick, lighting through her. She wanted to break, to smash, to release it in blind fury. Instead, though, she walked home—something she rarely did, giving herself time to think.

When she got home, her mind was stilled—calm over a powerful feeling of retribution. When she got home Mary was nowhere to be found, another late night for her, very frequent since her father's death. Tommy greeted her at the door, talking to her in short bursts of rumbling meows, and rubbing against her chilled legs.

Picking up the fat tom, she took a flashlight from a kitchen drawer and walked into the now dark studio.

The painting remained where she'd seen it that morning: Tommy frozen in paint on canvas.

Mary had lied. Certainly. Absolutely—and there was only one reason to lie, just one that Margaret could think of. No, her father hadn't died in the morning, not with brilliant light making Tommy's shining green eyes nothing but narrow slits—no, his last painting had been done near dusk, with the cat's eyes wide and withdrawn into deep, dark pools. Evening, not morning—her stepmother had lied.

Holding Tommy close, listening to him rumble his happiness at being with the girl he adored, she took slow, deep breaths. "Somehow, we'll prove it, Tommy," she whispered to the tom. "Thank you for helping me. Thank you for showing me."

For a moment, the cat stopped purring—a heavy silence in the big, empty room. Then he meowed, sharp and quick, just once—and Margaret knew that the trip would be long and hard, and maybe even dangerous, but they would do it.

They'd do it. For her father, they'd get their proof. Together.

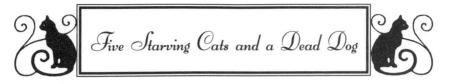

Five Starving Cats and a Dead Dog

KRISTINE KATHRYN RUSCH

WHENEVER A CAR RUMBLES UP the drive, he runs—four feet flying, orange and white tail a flag in the underbrush.

I wish I could run too.

Instead, I grab my husband's .22, and point it at the door, waiting. If I stand right next to the stairs, I can see through the glass panes without anyone seeing me. Usually, it's the man from the electric company out to read the meter. He doesn't seem to notice me. Once it was two Jehovah's Witnesses. I moved closer to the door; they saw the rifle and ran.

No one else comes up here.

I live on a knoll in a company-owned valley, my house hidden among twenty acres of trees that the company can't log. My husband and I bought the house a year ago, on a sun-dappled July afternoon. We had seen the ancient For Sale sign and followed its directions up a mile-long gravel driveway, catching glimpses of a brown building as we drove. We came up the ridge of the knoll and stopped, staring at the house.

Two stories, no basement, three balconies, and dozens of windows. The front door was unlocked, so we let ourselves in. We wandered through the first floor with its cavernous living room, formal dining room, and kitchen large enough to hold twenty comfortably. We didn't have to see the upstairs to know we had found home.

I wish it had stayed that simple. Lord knows, after all the work we did on our business and in our lives, we deserved simple. We had sold our computer company for twice its value and were looking forward to an early retirement in the hills. Neither of us over forty, enjoying our relative youth in relative quiet— or so we thought.

We should have noticed how odd things were from the start. The house's owners didn't want to sell. Their asking price was twice as high as the market would bear. They were waiting for the house to collapse, and the company to buy the land. But we insisted; we hardly negotiated. The house was what we were looking for, and we were determined to have it.

Then there were the cats. The skinny brown one who kept disappearing into the trees, and the starving pregnant Siamese who gave birth to a single orange kitten on the day we moved in. We put out food for them, not willing to let them inside with our four cats, and three more cats appeared, too-thin, starving, grateful for the attention but skittish. They liked me, but it took weeks before they went near Reg. They didn't like our male friends, either, something I'd never seen so uniform in a group of cats before. All five starving cats were purebreds, expensive purebreds: a Scottish Fold, a Tortoise-Shell Siamese, an Abyssinian, a Burmese, and a Manx. People didn't abandon cats like that. Even if they had no affinity for animals, the sheer expense of the cats made them worth keeping.

But the dog unnerved me the most. One afternoon in early September, with the sun setting along the hills, sending ridges of colored light through the trees, I decided to explore the property. I got to the edge of our knoll, where the grass tapered into trees, and found a skull.

Long and slender, canine, a bit too yellow to be sunbleached. It rested on top of a half-dug grave, with more bones littered inside. The skin was gone, but most of the gray matter remained in the cranium. Whatever had dug it up hadn't had time to finish its meal.

I called Reg over. He crouched, gave his inexpert opinion. "Been dead less than a year," he said. Then we stared at each other. People who would abandon purebred cats wouldn't bury a dog, would they? That showed more caring than we thought them capable of.

Reg promised to cover the grave, but dark was setting in, so we left it, forgotten, skull staring sightlessly at the clouds. Maybe if we had taken an extra fifteen minutes, I wouldn't be trapped here. Maybe things would have turned out differently.

We took the purebreds to the vet, got rid of their fleas and ear mites, had the Siamese fixed, renamed them, and brought them back into their old home. Our cats tolerated them with barely hidden displeasure, although few hissing fights occurred. I let them take over our lives, but the one that took over my heart was the orange kitten, whom we named Grubby.

He was a hardy little guy. Born to a starving mother, he barely moved during the first few weeks of his life. As she gained strength, so did he. But he never completely caught up. He remains, even now, two years later, a permanent kitten, stuck between eight and sixteen weeks of age.

But he can run faster than any other cat I have ever seen. And he can hunt. One evening, I sat in my study, reading, when I heard a thrashing on the front porch, followed by squawking, and several pounding noises. I hurried to the front door and peered through the panels at Grubby, who was not yet full-grown. He had trapped a crow three times his size on the porch and was trying to wring its neck. I was about to step out, to prevent my kitten from being pecked to death, when he pounced.

The crow squawked and jabbed at him. Grubby held its head down with one paw while he used his back legs to break its spine. The bird twisted away from him, and Grubby pounced again, this time landing on the bird's neck with an audible snap. The bird stopped moving, and Grub stared at it as if he were a child who had just broken a favorite toy. He tried tossing it in the air a few times, and succeeded only in covering my porch with more feathers.

From that point on, we let him hunt anything he wanted. He brought me field mice, squirrels, shrews, and baby opossums. Once he fended off the raccoon that had been raiding our garbage. Not too bright, our Grubby, but courageous.

That courage fails him now. I don't know why he runs, because he won that last fight. Maybe because it startled him, or maybe because of Reg...

Yet I think it's something simpler than that. For Grubby is still a baby, and he reacts instinctively. I think he realized that human beings can be cruel, and the only one he trusts is me.

The day it happened started poorly. I woke with the acrid smell of smoke in my lungs. Reg was still asleep, his face twenty years younger in repose. Sometimes I stared at him while he slept, seeing the boy I had married in the man he had become. I nudged him awake, and he sat up bleary-eyed, black hair tousled.

"Smell that?" I asked.

"Jesus, smoke," he said.

Our smoke alarm hadn't gone off, but we walked through the house anyway, finding nothing. Then Reg called me from the back balcony. I hurried to him and peered out. On the other side of the ridge, fire licked at the hillside, orange against the October green.

"I'll call," he said, and disappeared. I watched it, eating away at the clearcut, trying to decide what possessions to take, which car would handle the cats.

Five minutes later, he was back. "They said to stay put. They think it's an unofficial slash-burn."

A slash-burn. Something the logging company does after it clearcuts to prime the soil for next year's planting. Oregonians seem to think that fire is the only way to add nutrients to the soil. Grass-growers in the nearby Willamette Valley do the same thing—and pitch-black smoke blowing across the interstate killed forty-three people the summer before.

We watched as the little green fire truck made its way up the logging road that branched off our driveway. It stopped, yellow lights flashing, near the source of the burn, and remained there for nearly fifteen minutes. Then the lights went out. It turned, followed the logging road until it met our driveway and drove up to the house.

Reg slipped on a pair of jeans and was downstairs before they could knock. I took an extra minute to get dressed.

By the time I got downstairs, the fireman was already talking with Reg.

"... slash-burn, like we thought. Don't know why they didn't report it. They been doing it too much lately." The fireman was stocky, in an oversized green plastic-looking uniform. He had clearly come to fight a fire.

"We're safe, then?"

"Oh, yeah," the fireman said. "They got it under control. Something you got to get used to out here. The company owns the valley, they do what they want."

"We were warned about that when we bought the place," Reg said.

We had been warned about a number of things, such as the fact that our twenty acres could be the only stand of trees for miles if the company decided to do some heavy logging in our area.

"Knew the guy who lived here before," the fireman said. "See him every day, and still don't know why he sold it."

My interest was piqued. "Do you work with him?"

"Naw. He works at the grocery down toward town. I stop every night for the wife. We talk some, although we been talking less."

"Did he ever say why he moved?"

The fireman shook his head. "All I know is that he wasn't sure if he wanted to sell the house. Don't know why since he hadn't lived in it for months. That's why he priced it so high. Didn't think nobody would buy it. Then you happened along. Wasn't sure if he was happy or not."

"Was that his dog buried out back?" Reg asked.

The fireman shrugged. "Don't rightly know. We just kinda talk every day, you know. We're not friends or nothing." He tipped his hat. "Best get back to the truck."

"Thank you for coming out here," I said.

"It's our job, ma'am," he said as he made his way through the trees.

Reg closed the door and coughed. "Something we'll have to get used to, huh?"

"Well, this is the first time in almost two months," I said. "Maybe it won't happen that often."

"Hope not," Reg said. "This isn't the way I like to wake up."

He went upstairs and took a shower. I followed soon after. We spent the rest of the day watching the fire slowly burn itself out. By twilight, it had become a glow of embers against the dark.

We were sitting down to a late dinner when we heard a car on the gravel road. It wasn't so unusual then; we just figured it was a friend stopping by for some conversation or wilderness star-gazing.

Reg was halfway to the door when footsteps sounded on the front porch. I had gotten up to put our meal on the counter, out of reach of the cats. The door burst open, and a shotgun stabbed Reg's sternum. The man behind it was short, squat, with brown hair tied in a ponytail. He was wearing a butcher's apron, dress slacks and a white shirt with the sleeves rolled up.

I had never seen him before.

"Didn't think I'd find out about the dog, did ya?"

"I d-d-don't know what you're talking about," Reg said.

I picked up the phone, set the receiver on its side and dialed 911. Not that it would do us any good right away. We were too far out.

"Get that bitch out here where I can see her," the man said.

"Hon?"

I stepped into the foyer, wishing I had gone for the rifle we had in the pantry instead of dialing for help that wouldn't come.

Reg's face was ashen. I stood, hands at my sides, concentrating, trying to see out of the corner of my eye if there was something, anything I could use as a weapon. The hall table beside me was empty, and the coat rack near the door too light to do more than annoy the man, even if I could reach him.

"I didn't think I shoulda sold the house to you," the man said. "But the money, the goddamn money—"

"*You* sold the house?" Reg asked. "*You* owned it?"

Grubby jumped on the table. None too bright, my little cat. The others had run, smelling the fear and anger in the room.

"Why'd you have to snoop? Why didn't you leave it alone?"

"Can't we sit and talk about this like reasonable people?" Reg asked.

Reasonable people. The man holding the gun was not reasonable. He was red-faced and frightening.

"It's the dog," he said, raising his rifle some. I saw my chance. "If you hadn't said nothing about the dog—"

I picked up Grubby and hurled him at the man. The cat flew through the air, spitting and hissing. The rifle went off, Reg moaned and collasped, and Grubby dug his claws into the man's face before bounding out the door.

The man turned to me, blood pouring down his cheeks from scratches that hadn't come close enough to his eyes. "You stupid bitch," he said, leveling the gun at me.

I wasn't about to stand still while he tried to shoot me. I turned, ran through the kitchen, grabbing the knife I had used for dinner off the counter as I passed. I let myself out the back door and into the yard as a gunshot smashed glass around me.

Down on the road, I could hear sirens.

I slipped through the trees, gripping blackberry bushes and trying not to cry out as the thorns bit into my palms. I had left Reg in there with that madman.

Reg.

I made it to the gravel road quicker than I thought. Sliding, sliding on the steep incline, I ran to the sound of the sirens. Two police cars hurried up, with more on the road behind. They had heard it and dispatched someone. Heard everything. Traced the call.

They stopped on the incline, near me.

"He's up there," I said, pointing toward the trees. The cops left their doors open and went up. I couldn't tell anyone that I needed an ambulance. I didn't know how to work the radio, and I was so scared I could barely breathe.

Other cars stopped. More police got out. "Up there," I said. Finally, a woman stayed back with me.

"We need an ambulance," I said. "My husband's still up there."

She called for help. And by the time the ambulance arrived, they had already stopped Reg's bleeding, and were waiting for backup. But they never found the man. He had run into the woods with his gun and disappeared.

The things they never tell you about the forests of the Pacific Northwest. Children disappear in them, only to be found, decades later, skeletal remains under a tree. Adults walk away from a car to take a leak and are never seen again. It's still wilderness here, even if it is wilderness owned by the company.

The search parties combed the woods for three days.

They never found him.

We should move, I know. Find a new place, with new people, get away from all the memories, the bloodstain too deep in the wood-grained floor to remove. But with Reg's medical bills, we can't afford to sell a house we paid too much for in the first place.

Besides, they assure us he's dead.

Reg believes them, even though I find him in his wheelchair staring out the window into the woods more times than not. As if he's looking for something. When we can afford it, I'm going to put in a lift to the second floor. He feels trapped down here, like I feel trapped in the house.

Reg believes the man is gone, forever. "He snapped, babe," Reg says. "He won't be back."

He snapped. As if that's unusual for him. He snapped in the spring and murdered a woman, whether she was a wife or girlfriend no one knew, and buried her in the backyard. Then he shot her dog (I believe all the animals were hers—they never liked men), and buried it on top of her, thinking no one would go past a dog's corpse to see what was buried beneath it. When his friend the fireman relayed his discussion with us, the man snapped—again. How many more times would he snap before he died?

Reg believes he's dead. But I don't. And Grubby doesn't. Sometimes I see that orange and white tail waving through the tall grass, and I realize Grubby's on the hunt. I like to imagine he's following footprints, looking for the man who haunts him in every car that pulls into our drive, in every stranger's glance, in my fear-filled eyes. I like to think that Grubby, our mighty hunter, will catch him someday, trap him on the porch, and use his powerful back legs to snap the man's spine as he once snapped a crow's spine, as a bullet snapped Reg's.

But that won't happen, because that would be justice. And if there were justice in this world, Reg would still be walking, that awful man would be dead, and I would be able to enjoy this house and the woods and the quiet, instead of seeing that gun go off every time I close my eyes. Instead of wondering what would have happened if I hadn't tossed Grubby, if I hadn't interfered. Maybe the police would have arrived in time. Maybe we would all be okay.

Maybe my little orange cat wouldn't scour the woods, searching for prey I hope he never, ever finds.

The Fix

MICHAEL GRISI

HERE'S FOUR THOUSAND. IF YOU guys don't cover the spread, I'll forget about the three thousand you owe me. Are we cool?"

Jake didn't hear a response. He was on the other side of the locker room, out of sight. Voices carried well there, but Jake's hearing wasn't what it used to be. He sat, trying to listen while he petted Mr. Peepers, the stray cat that had become the pseudo-mascot of the Johnson State Jags basketball team. Mr. Peepers had a few battle scars from the fights he had been in over the years. He wasn't exactly a jaguar, or even a junkyard dog for that matter, but he was a mean old locker-room cat.

Jake, the custodian, thought everyone had gone, so he was in the middle of his after-practice cleanup when he heard the voices.

"Not a peep now, Mr. Peepers. We don't want them to know we're here," whispered Jake, "especially if they're planning to fix tomorrow night's game." Things could get a little ugly then, he thought.

"Well, what's your answer?"

"If I get caught, I'll lose my scholarship, get kicked out of school, and probably get thrown in jail. My life will be over."

"What's your alternative? It'll be a little tough playing point guard with a couple of broken legs."

Jake heard a chuckle, then someone reluctantly agreed to the proposition. This might be a golden opportunity, Jake thought. The measly pittance he earned over the last thirty-five years hadn't left him with a pot to piss in. A lousy ten grand was all he managed to save. Not exactly a great retirement fund, but if the boys were going to start fixing games and he was able to cash in, maybe he'd be able to retire before he croaked after all. It was as difficult to control his excitement as it was for Mr. Peepers, who let out a loud meow.

"What was that?"

"It sounded like the janitor's cat."

Jake froze. No time to hide, no place to hide.

The fixer, who looked like a little kid, walked around the corner and saw Jake. A second later, his no-neck, steroid-supplemented sidekick followed.

"Well, well, well, what have we here? A couple of pussies: one with four legs and one with two. What are you doing here, old man?"

"You have to speak up, sonny, I'm a little hard of hearing."

"Were you listening to us?"

"I don't know what you're talking about."

The young punk grabbed Jake by the collar. "Don't fucking play games with me, pops. What did you hear?"

"I didn't hear anything." Jake's palms started perspiring and a bead of sweat trickled down his forehead.

The punk let go, then banged his fist against a locker. "Did you hear that?"

"Yep."

"If I find out you're lying to me, the next time you hear that sound, it's going to be your head bouncing off these lockers like it was a pinball. Do you understand me?"

"I reckon I do." I guess we'd see who the real pussy was if steroid man wasn't around, thought Jake.

"Let's go."

Steroid man hit his left palm with his right fist as a parting message to Jake.

"That was close, Mr. Peepers. You almost got me in big trouble." The cat, oblivious to the harm he nearly caused Jake, rubbed against his leg.

Another head peeked around the corner. It was Billy Todson, a.k.a. Billy the Kid, the senior point guard and leading scorer.

"Hello, Billy."

"Hello, Jake."

"I'm not sure I care for the company you keep."

"I don't care for them much myself."

"Do you want to talk about it?"

"No, and if you know what's good for you, you won't either."

Over the years, Jake had befriended many of the players. He was like a father to many of them, at least that was the way it started out. Now, he was more like a grandfather to them. They usually trusted Jake, but in this case it was just as well if Billy didn't.

Jake had known him for almost four years. He was a nice enough kid. He came from a good family, maybe too good. That was probably why so many of these silver spoon kids got themselves in trouble. Everything came too easily and then they started hanging out with the wrong crowd.

"Are you going to go through with it?"

"What are you talking about?"

"It's OK, Billy, I heard the conversation. I was just wondering how you got yourself into something like this."

"Gambling? It starts innocently enough, betting on other games. It's real easy to get caught up in it and, before you know it, things are out of control. I kept losing, the debts mounted, and now I'm screwed." Billy rubbed a hand across his face. "So what if we don't cover the spread. If we still win the game, no one gets hurt and I get those monkeys off my back. If I only score ten points instead of twenty, who's going to care? It's just this one time. No one will ever know, unless you tell."

"I won't, but this kind of thing is never a one-shot deal. Once they've got you, they've got you."

"No way, they know this is it. One game and I'm done. No more gambling, no more fixing."

Jake got up and patted Billy on the shoulder. "I hope things work out for you, kid. Come on, Mr. Peepers, we've got work to do."

While mopping the rest of the locker room, Jake wondered what he should do. Should he do the right thing and call the coach, or be an opportunist and take advantage of the situation? The kid was right, if the team still wins but doesn't cover the spread, no one gets hurt.

This opportunity would be as good as going down to Atlantic City and knowing what number was going to come up next on the roulette wheel. One-shot deal. No one gets hurt. With an opportunity like that, you bet the house, and that's what Jake decided he would do.

He had his ten thousand in the bank, his life savings. It was really nothing more than chump change to most people, but it was all he had. To double it in one night was a temptation he couldn't resist, but where would he find a bookie that would take that kind of action on such an insignificant game.

He called his brother-in-law, Tony, who was the only one he knew that might be able to place such a bet.

"How much are you looking at?" asked Tony.

"Ten thousand dollars on Lakeview College, plus ten points."

"Ten grand? What are you nuts? You don't have that kind of money."

"Don't worry about where I get my money. All I need to know is if you can place the bet."

"I have to be sure you have the money, Jake. If you lose and they want to collect, it's my ass they're going to come after, not yours. I happen to like all my teeth in my mouth and my bones unbroken, if you catch my drift."

"Don't worry, I've got it."

"I don't get it, Jake, why are you betting against your team? Do you know something?"

There was a silent pause that seemed like an eternity. "What are you talking about?" Jake said, uneasily.

Tony chuckled. "That's what I thought. I'll call you back."

For the next half-hour Jake tapped his fingers on the desk, waiting for the phone to ring. He started getting a pain in his stomach and a lump in his throat that made it difficult to swallow. Maybe this is a mistake, he thought, something could go wrong. Billy can't control the whole game. He was about to talk himself out of such a foolish bet when the phone rang.

"Jake, they'll take the bet, but they'll only give you seven points instead of ten. Do you want to take it?"

"What kind of bullshit is that? If the line is ten, I want ten."

"What you want and what you get are two different things. They smell a rat and I don't blame them. What's going on?"

"I have to think about it. I'll call you back." Jake hung up the phone and sighed. "Shit, now what? What do you think, Mr. Peepers?"

The cat meowed and rubbed against Jake's leg.

"I don't know if that's an opinion or not. Maybe we have another option."

Jake hopped in the car and ten minutes later he was knocking on Billy's dorm room door.

"What are you doing here, Jake?" Billy looked up and down the empty hall.

"I've got to talk to you."

"We've got nothing to talk about."

"Hear me out." This time Jake looked around to make sure no one was listening. "How would you like to make another two thousand on the game tomorrow. All you have to do is make sure you don't cover by seven instead of ten."

"Get out of here."

"Listen to me."

"No, you listen to me. If you don't leave right now, I'm going to call the campus police."

"And when they get here, should I tell them about your friends and to-morrow's game?"

Billy looked down and rubbed his face, which was getting red. Jake backed up a step, not knowing what Billy would do next.

"You're already up to your eyeballs in this," said Jake. "Seven points, ten points, what's the difference? It's like you said, no one gets hurt."

"I can't do it. If it gets too close, who knows what might happen. We could lose the game. That would kill our postseason chances. Then what?"

"You're the point guard. You control the game."

Billy stared at Jake, thinking, wondering, sinking deeper into the abyss. "Please, Jake don't make me do this."

"You're already doing it, that's the point. What difference will a few more points make?"

"Understand me now, if I say yes, that's it. Never again. If you so much as ask, I'll kill you."

"Understood."

"All right. One more thing. Don't you *ever* come back here."

"OK, OK, that's cool." Jake put out his hand to seal the deal, but Billy just stared at it.

"Get out of here."

On the way home, Jake couldn't stop whistling "We're in the Money," but after he put the bet in with Tony, the stomach pains returned. Mr. Peepers looked at Jake quizzically. Jake picked him up and started petting him. "I hope I did the right thing, fella, otherwise it's going to be bread and water for the both of us."

Mr. Peepers meowed contentedly.

Jake laughed. "And you're supposed to be such a tough cat."

The next night, before game time, Jake made sure everything was in place. Plenty of towels were put out, the practice balls were on the racks, and the water cool-ers were filled.

As the players started arriving, Mr. Peepers, as usual, ran around to greet everyone. When he jumped on Billy's lap, Billy swatted him away. Mr. Peepers didn't like the slight, arched his back, and hissed. Billy tossed a strike with one of his size-twelve Nikes, hitting Mr. Peepers and sending him scurrying away.

Jake said, "That wasn't very nice. I'm sure you're a little edgy before the big game, but Mr. Peepers was just wishing you good luck."

Billy flipped Jake the bird and Jake figured it was time to get out of the locker room before he said something that might jeopardize the situation. Jake usually didn't watch the games, but with ten thousand riding on this one, he decided to make an exception. He gave Mr. Peepers a bowl of water and a toy to play with in the locker room, then went out to watch the game.

As the game progressed, Johnson built a lead and was up by fifteen by halftime. It was big trouble for Jake, but he knew there was plenty of playing time and he was still counting on Billy to come through.

With one minute left in the game, Jake's nerves were just about shot. The lead was down to twelve, but Jake was still on the losing side of his bet.

With forty-five seconds to go, Lakeview scored a three-pointer to cut the lead to nine. Jake was biting his nails down to the nubs. If Billy could only keep the Jags off the scoreboard the rest of the way, Lakeview should be able to score three more points.

Jake took a deep breath and crossed his fingers as Billy dribbled the ball up court.

Billy was fouled with thirty-five seconds to go and went to the line to shoot a one and one. The first shot clanged off the front of the rim and the rebound was grabbed by Lakeview.

"Atta boy, Billy," Jake mumbled under his breath.

The Lakeview guard pulled up at the three-point line and launched a shot that caught nothing but net. Lakeview called time-out with twenty ticks on the clock.

"Can we call it a game now?" Jake asked rhetorically. He knew the answer and he knew his fingernails would pay for it.

Mr. Peepers, seemingly from nowhere, hopped onto Jake's lap.

"How did you get out of the locker room?" Jake asked.

It didn't matter. Jake had other things to worry about, ten thousand other things. "Keep your paws crossed, Mr. Peepers, we need the game to end with this six-point spread." The cat nuzzled Jake, looking for affection at a time when there wasn't much being offered.

"Be still, my little feline friend, we have a lot riding on these next few seconds," said Jake as he gently rubbed behind Mr. Peepers's ear. As if understanding the seriousness of the situation, Mr. Peepers turned around and sat on Jake's lap to watch the rest of the game.

Johnson inbounded after the time-out and was quickly fouled. It wasn't Billy shooting this time, so there was no guarantee they would be missed.

Sure enough, the two shots were canned by Dennis Wright. The lead was back to eight and Jake was in some deep shit. There are eighteen seconds left, he thought, plenty of time for another score.

Lakeview moved the ball up court quickly and shot a three-pointer with thirteen seconds to go. The shot banged off the rim, miraculously fell forward and through the hoop with ten seconds left.

Billy inbounded to Dennis, who dribbled the ball up the right side of the court. He beat the press and was about to glide in for an easy game-ending, money-losing layup.

"I can't watch." Jake closed his eyes and crossed his fingers. If it goes in, I'm sunk, he thought. He took a deep breath and kept his eyes closed until the crowd cheered.

Jake opened his eyes and stared at the scoreboard in disbelief. The lead was eight. Dennis had made the shot.

The final seconds ticked off. It was official, an eight point victory and the fact that Jake was now flat broke. His life savings, gone at the blink of an eye or, more precisely, at the sound of the horn.

Jake wanted to jump out of the bleachers and wring Dennis's neck for making the final, meaningless shot. Meaningless to the game's outcome, but not to Jake. How could he blame Dennis? The kid was doing what he was supposed to do: score baskets.

As the crowd filed out, Jake didn't know if he could muster the strength to get up from the bleachers. He had reached the low point of his life. There was nothing to look forward to. It was like the hand of God had just flushed his life down the toilet.

Mr. Peepers jumped off Jake's lap when he began to struggle to his feet. Again, he stared at the scoreboard, letting reality set in. The crowd had exited by the time Jake made it to the locker room door.

"Hey, janitor pussy, how's it going?"

Jake looked over his shoulder and saw the fixer and his no-neck friend. He flipped them the bird and ducked into the locker room. Mr. Peepers managed to follow, just before the door closed.

"Congratulations, fellas, great game," Jake said to the team, barely getting the words out.

Some of them acknowledged Jake, most were indifferent and continued their victory celebration.

Jake continued on, through the locker room, and went out the back door. Again Mr. Peepers followed Jake's footsteps. He walked to the north stairway and he and Mr. Peepers began to climb. He was soon huffing and puffing, out of breath, but continued up in a trancelike state.

Going up the stairs, the only thing he could think about was the money. It was all gone. How could he be so stupid? He went up the rest of the stairs and sat down by the entrance to the roof, no longer aware of Mr. Peepers, who just sat and observed. How did he manage to get himself into these predicaments? No matter, he wouldn't get himself into trouble anymore.

Jake got up, unlocked the door to the roof, and went outside. It was quite cold and snow was falling. He walked to the ledge of the roof and looked up to the heavens. The snow felt quite refreshing as it melted on his face.

He leaned over the ledge and looked to the ground about thirty feet below. It appeared that a few inches of snow had fallen since the game began.

If I do a nice swan dive, maybe I can make one last snow angel. That wouldn't be such a bad way to go.

He would be leaving this life the same way he entered it, with nothing. He had gone full circle and was about to put the final exclamation point on his life, which was a big, fat zero.

He climbed onto the ledge and once again looked to the heavens, allowing a few last snowflakes to melt on his face.

"God, save my worthless soul." He closed his eyes and readied himself for the jump. It'll be over before you know it, he thought.

Then, Mr. Peepers started rubbing against Jake's leg.

"What do you think you're doing, you stupid cat. Do you want to break your fool neck with me?"

Mr. Peepers hopped off the ledge and stared up at Jake.

"Not ready to leave this life yet, are you? It wouldn't be such a big deal for you, you have nine lives, I've only got the one." Jake took a deep breath and pondered a moment. "If I go, who's going to take care of you? Certainly not those jocks downstairs."

Jake sat on the ledge. "Truth is, I'm not ready to go yet either. I'd like to leave having accomplished something. There's little satisfaction in being a big zero all your life. Do you think there's any hope for me?"

Mr. Peepers meowed.

"You really think so? Well, I suppose things could be worse, although at this moment I can't imagine how." Jake petted Mr. Peepers. "I guess it's just you and me, my fine feline friend, and that's not so bad. Friends till the end, ain't that right, fella?"

Mr. Peepers meowed approvingly.

"I thought you'd agree. Come on, we have a locker room to mop."

Jake and Mr. Peepers went back into the school and walked toward the locker room. Echoing through the hall was the sound of Jake whistling the most inappropriate of tunes, "We're in the Money."

Freedom of the Press

BARBARA D'AMATO

I WALKED INTO THE OFFICE OF Representative Peggy Nicklis at 1:55, for a two o'clock appointment. Then I stopped and stared.

She saw my face and started to laugh. When she was done chuckling, she said, "You're Cat Marsala?"

"Yup. Thank you for seeing me, Ms. Nicklis."

"And you expected a much grander office." She was still half laughing.

"Well, I didn't expect—uh—exposed heat pipes, cracked linoleum, a sloping ceiling, two small rooms—I suppose this outer room is for your secretary?—furniture that looks like it was retired from the Library of Congress, and a window the size of the Elvis stamp." In addition there was a slightly off-center bookcase crammed with books, several reasonably adequate bookcases visible in the inner office, some empty cartons, an old desk in the reception room and an old desk in the inner office. Three phones and an answering machine on each desk. Two very large metal wastebaskets. A plush blue cat bed and a litter box in Nicklis's inner office. And a cat. Everything in both offices was tidy; everything was neat and straight and clean, but the place was definitely shabby. Nicklis watched me, smiling.

"It's a matter of seniority. You get better and better offices the longer you're here. Washington is all about how important you are. This is definitely a starter office. Plus, this isn't the only thing," she said. "The nearest bathroom for women is *seven flights* of stairs away from here."

"Jeez!"

"And not just seven flights," she giggled, "but down three, then *up* two, then down two."

"They weren't prepared for you women."

"Well, it also makes you feel sorry for two hundred years of secretaries, dashing for the far-off watercloset."

I had recognized her right away, of course, from a zillion photographs and television interviews. So she seemed like an old friend. She acted like one too, showing me into her office and sitting down next to me in a corner where she had two overstuffed chairs. The cat came over, swept its body across my ankle and told me it wanted to be stroked precisely twice. Cats know exactly what they want. After graciously accepting this homage he allowed Peggy to scratch his ear, then he stared at each of us in turn, collecting admiration.

I asked, "Who is Mr. Cat?"

What I thought she said was:

"His name is Mugum."

"Mugum?" I looked at the tawny, lithe cat. He went to his big, plush cushion and lay down. He lifted one hind leg in the air to inspect it. Apparently decided it was an excellent leg. He put it down and rolled onto his back.

"Mugum is a very unusual name."

"It's spelled 'MGM.' Pronounced Mugum. He's named that because he looks like the MGM lion. MGM is a ginger tom, aren't you, baby?"

"Did you get him after you moved here—"

"Oh, Lord, no! I've had him all his life. He's seven now. We've moved to D.C. together, haven't we, tough guy? MGM goes everywhere with me."

MGM curled up and went to sleep.

Peggy Nicklis was slender, with dark hair cut blunt. An easy-care style. She wore a suit and flat shoes that would be easy to get around in. My mother would have said, "She doesn't do a lot for herself." Peggy also wasn't what United States culture in the waning days of the twentieth century considered especially beautiful.

Peggy Nicklis certainly wasn't the first woman to serve in the House of Representatives, but she was the first from an extremely conservative district just northwest of Chicago. She had received a considerable amount of media attention because she had won without being particularly flashy in her statements or striking-looking in her photographs. The word for Peggy was businesslike, and she had received the trust of the voters, rather than catching their fancy.

Hal Briskman at *Chicago Today* had said to me:

"What we want is a story about how she's settling in, now that she's been in Washington three weeks. Is D.C. intimidating to her? How does she like her office? Are rents breathtakingly expensive? Does she feel like one of the gang yet?"

"That's not very pithy, Hal."

"We don't want pith. Readers are fed up with pith. Don't talk budget deficit with her, Cat. That's not what we want right now. Don't talk health care. Don't talk education priorities. Do a fluff piece."

"Fluff! I don't do fluff."

"Fluff is good for the soul."

"Not this soul. But I *will* do the interview, if you want."

"And do it the way I want. Keep in mind: you play, we pay."

"Oh, very well."

He said he'd pay for the tickets, meals of course, and two nights at a hotel in D.C., which adds up. And pay for the article, of course. Well, that's the business I'm in. I'm freelance, which is always a precarious way to live. And while some of the stories I've done have been big, and my byline is noticed by an occasional reader, I'm not famous.

Being famous would be nice.

Peggy answered my questions straightforwardly. "Well, yes. Rent here truly does take your breath away. For what you'd pay in Chicago for a medium-sized apartment with a Lake Michigan view, here you get one and a half rooms looking out at a fire escape and the brick wall of the building next door ten feet away."

"You're saying we aren't really keeping our legislators happy?"

She smiled. "I wouldn't think of saying that. Anyway, I'm planning to spend most of my time here in the office. I go home mainly to sleep. That way I figure I'll earn more time back in Chicago, too. My folks and my friends are there."

"How about new friends here?"

"I'm meeting a few people. It's slow, though."

"You probably don't have much time to socialize. You have a lot of work and catching up to do."

"Yes. Still, there are parties galore. The White House had the so-called freshmen, the new guys, to dinner. That was exciting. I've been to several special-interest dinners, and a Democratic Party bash in honor of the newcomers. A couple of embassies. My father's family is Polish, so I got asked to their embassy party, of course."

Peggy's secretary came back from late lunch, stuck her head in the door and waved. Peggy introduced her as Annie Boyd.

Peggy said to me, "Could we continue this tomorrow?" To Annie she said, "It was two o'clock Monday and Tuesday, wasn't it?"

In the outer office, Annie nodded her head, yes, it was Monday and Tuesday at two.

The interviewee is always right. I said, "Sure, and thanks." However, it was supposed to be Monday and Tuesday two to three, and this was only two-thirty. Peggy realized that.

"I know we're stopping early. But let me make up for it tomorrow. I'm still backed up with work and I'm barely unpacked."

Well, who could fault a person for that? The last time I moved, it took three months of my life and three years off my life.

Washington was cold but bright Tuesday, and I spent the morning walking. I strolled the Mall, went into the National Air and Space Museum and the National Gallery, and finally walked up Delaware to eat at one of the fast-food places in the underground mall at Union Station. It was truly fast, served coffee in cups as big as soup bowls, and it let me watch the noon news on an overhead TV. There was trouble in the Middle East, fighting in central Europe, and a newsman for United Press International, Lee Chesterton, whom I knew slightly, had driven off the Frederick Douglass Bridge last night and drowned. It was thought alcohol was involved. He was well known here, and it was a big story with a lot of the usual Washington speculation.

After lunch, the Smithsonian beckoned, but a person needs a week to do it justice. No point right now. I strolled through the National Sculpture Garden instead.

A minute or two before the hour, I arrived at Peggy Nicklis's office. Her secretary Annie simply waved me through. No pomp here. Peggy looked tired and the ginger tom was out of sorts too. He hissed at me, then stalked over to the window, jumped up to the ledge and prowled back and forth.

"I heard about Lee Chesterton's accident on the noon news," I told Peggy. "I'd met him a couple of times when he covered a story in Chicago."

"It's a terrible thing to have happened. He was a nice person."

"Yes, terrible. You dated him a couple of times, didn't you?"

She looked up, surprised. "Two or three times. How did you know that?"

"People think reporters just wing it. That must be why they think the job is all glamour and no work." She gave me a lopsided smile. I said, "I always research people I'm going to interview. You were photographed, I think by the Washington *Post*, at a party with him ten days ago or so."

"Yes. It's a shock."

The cat stared at the back of Peggy's neck. He jumped from the windowsill to the desk, and from there to the floor. Peggy got up and shut the door to the outer office. The farther door to the hall was open and she didn't want the cat to get out. The cat stalked past the bed, sheared away, and prowled around the wastebasket as if it were some sort of prey.

I said, "I'm sorry. It must be especially hard for you, so soon after moving in, losing one of the few friends you've met here."

"It is. Although maybe if I'd known him longer it'd be worse." She said this calmly, but there was a lot of sadness in her eyes.

I felt extremely sorry for her. At the same time, I was excited and tense, which made it harder to look relaxed and in charge of a chatty interview. The ginger tom crouched, then sprang forward and ran under the desk. I felt like a cat myself, waiting to spring at a mouse.

"Apparently the investigators believe he'd been drinking," I said. "They're reporting ethanol in the blood."

"He did drink. I asked him not to once, because he always drove his own car. Not like a lot of Washingtonians, you know. They seem to think being chauffeured is proof that you're a real success. Anyway, he didn't like it when I asked him not to drink too much, and I didn't want to upset him, so I just dropped the subject."

Didn't want to turn him off, probably. Unfortunately, Peggy was not a person who would be surrounded by men asking her out.

She said, "Washingtonians drink too much, almost all of them."

I went on. "They think there was somebody else in the car with him. Several cars on the bridge stopped when they saw the Porsche crash through the guardrail. A witness said two people swam away."

"I heard that."

"It looks like they both got out safely. The car floated for a while, and they crawled through an open window. Whoever was with him could swim. But he was a very weak swimmer."

"Unless she—unless whoever it was drowned too."

"Well, no. There was a call from a pay phone reporting the accident. Asking for help. Almost certainly the passenger. I guess she hoped the rescue people might save him."

"I guess."

"I shouldn't have said 'she hoped.' The caller whispered and the news report said the police didn't know if it was a man or woman."

"Yes, I heard that too."

"She has good reason not to want to be identified."

"Yes. The way it is, she could be anybody."

I was profoundly conscious that this could be the scoop of my career. Carefully, I went on.

"Whoever it was, he or she would be guilty of leaving the scene of an accident."

"And that's a crime," Peggy said, placing her hands together, folding the fingers and squeezing.

"Leaving the scene of a fatal accident. I think it's a felony."

She didn't respond. We sat looking at each other for at least half a minute—a *very* long time in polite social discourse. The ginger tom slipped past me, skirted the blue cushion, jumped to the top of a bookcase, and paced back and forth.

Finally, Peggy said:

"Are you going to report that it was me?"

I hesitated too. From feeling excited, I had gone to feeling sick. Some decision had been made viscerally without my brain being involved. It had to do with how I would feel about this six months from now. What I was about to do was foolish. After all, I had my own career to take care of, didn't I? All right. It was my life. I was free to do what I chose. I was going to be foolish.

I said, "No. You've suffered enough."

"What—?"

I pointed to the cat. "He prowls constantly. He's restless. He won't lie down in that bed."

Peggy wrapped her arms around her chest.

I said, "How else would I have known? MGM went everywhere with you. No wonder you're tired. How many pet stores and animal shelters did you have to go to this morning before you found a tom with exactly that coloring?"

Fur Bearing

BRETT HUDGINS

THERE WAS A POEM CALLED *The Rime of the Ancient Mariner* which Gilles Demers knew he would probably never read. He had neither the patience nor the bilingual literacy. However, in the eight years since its publication in 1798, Coleridge's verse composition had achieved such fame that Gilles frequently heard it discussed by travellers.

The chilling example of the Mariner and the albatross had convinced Gilles that he too lived under a curse, though his was bovine rather than avian in nature.

He was six feet tall, muscular—ruggedly handsome, even, if the admiring Métis women could be believed. In short, he was miserable, for there was nothing Gilles wanted more than to be a *voyageur*. Braving the wilderness of his Canadian homeland, shooting frothing white rapids in a *canot du nord* loaded with beaver pelts, singing songs, smoking pipes, passing the days with good friends and hard work.

Except he was too big for the boat.

The ideal *voyageur* was short, thick-set, and possessed of limitless energy. His arms and shoulders were developed out of proportion to the rest of his body. His wide, cheerful face bore testament to brawls and animal maulings.

The last thing he ever did was compromise the efficiency of his canoe with a pressing need for leg-room—the way Gilles would have.

Hence Gilles's curse.

He was stuck living a sort of half-life at Fort William, formerly Fort

Kaministiquia, on the northwest shore of Lake Superior. The fort was the western headquarters of the North West Company, a coalition formed in 1783 by independent traders to compete against the huge Hudson's Bay Company. Each summer all furs obtained from natives and collected at outlying posts were brought to Fort William by *voyageurs* in their North canoes. At the same time brigades of *canots de maître* arrived from Montreal laden with essential supplies and trade goods. The necessary exchanges were made.

Gilles was scorned ceaselessly by his boisterous heroes for the ungainly size of his body, and his dreams.

Yet the devastating truth was that a man could not escape his own body. The one time he'd tried, a blazing summer afternoon, he'd gotten so involved in racing his shadow that he'd hurtled into the wall of the counting-house. Explaining that he thought the building could use a window hadn't saved him from his nickname, his albatross. *Le Taureau.* The Bull.

Gilles had a single refuge against the contempt of his idols. His only solace came from a most unlikely friend, an animal he would ordinarily have ignored: the fort's communal cat. Gilles had named his confidant *Chat du Nord.* North, for short.

Snow-white, sleek and swift as *La Vieille,* the wind that ruled the waters, North displayed an unswerving willingness to spend time with Gilles and listen to his fantasies, as long as the human reciprocated with quality pampering of the sort he had previously reserved for his most prized possession: his paddle. A *voyageur's* paddle, individually decorated to its owner's tastes, was his most distinctive badge of office. Gilles had made one for himself in a burst of wishful thinking and occasionally toted it around when he needed to feel valued.

To his surprised delight, he received the same affirmation of his worth—as well as a great deal of fur on his pants—by petting his cat.

As if sensing his thoughts, North twined around his booted ankles, purring. Thoughts of poems and curses fled before real-life spectacle. Together, man and cat watched a North canoe approach from the mouth of Kaministiquia River. As usual, the *voyageurs* were paddling hard, maintaining their daily average of forty strokes a minute from dawn till dusk. A typical North canoe was eight meters long and over one meter wide. This particular vessel carried a crew of seven men and just over a ton of bundled furs.

Singing raucously, attracting many of the fort's inhabitants to vantage points on the long lakefront wharf, the *voyageurs* put on a burst of speed, paddles striking the water like broad, painted lightning bolts.

The spectators tossed an ebullient chorus of cheers, praise, and questions at the returning travellers, along with more practical anchor lines, as the canoe glided to a halt.

Four Métis women, taken as wives by four of the men the previous summer, rushed to embrace their husbands. Three presented young children to proud fathers for the first time.

Gilles struggled to avoid being trampled by the overly festive crowd and moved to help unload the canoe. The crew's *bourgeois*, a partner in the North West Company and the designated law and order during the rough expedition, tossed Gilles a tumpline and imperiously directed him to get to work.

"I missed you too, Etienne," Gilles muttered, fitting around his forehead the harness which helped him hoist and balance a heavy fur bundle.

"At least the Bull has a strong back, no?" laughed one of the *voyageurs*.

Five red woolen *tuques* bobbed with laughter as paddles slapped the water in appreciation of the jibe.

Still hoping for elusive acceptance, Gilles could not help but answer pleasantly. One caught more flies with honey than with vinegar. "I see you fellows had a good trip."

"Thanks to me!" one man boasted. Even though he was a near duplicate of his comrades in his deer skin leggings, moccasins, and blue capote, Pierre Dumond never failed to distinguish himself with his abrasive, self-important manner. Gilles would never forget this braggart who had given him his nickname. Massive ego aside, however, Pierre was a hell of a trader.

"The richest fur trade I have ever made and we almost missed it. How do you suppose that happened, *bourgeois*?"

Etienne Gauthier shot the *voyageur* a look that invited him to work now, talk later. To the amusement of his partners, Pierre managed to do both, firing back a stream of colorful profanities while affixing his tumpline.

Gilles sighed wistfully at witnessing another special moment in which he could never share. "I wish I could have been there," he said softly to North, who merely lashed his eloquent tail back and forth.

Pierre appeared before him, looking up solemnly. "I, too, wish you were of smaller stature, my friend."

"Really?" Gilles gasped.

"*Oui*. Then I would not have to reach so high to do *this!*" He gave Gilles an open-hand smack to the head and the dock exploded in laughter.

"The Bull must have dull horns for you to abuse his head so, Pierre!"

Almost chocking on the sudden lump in his throat, Gilles let his tumpline slip to the dock, picked up North roughly, and lumbered blindly away.

For perhaps the first time, *Le Taureau* genuinely saw red.

Gilles awoke with a strip of sun across his eyes and North happily kneading his stomach with needle claws.

Of the two, the light hurt more, as if his contracting pupils controlled an inversely proportionate pressure within his hungover head.

He sat up slowly, swaying with the throbbing in his skull. Reaching out to pet his cat, he missed on the first two tries, then rubbed the wrong way and got his hand bitten. This good-natured feline violence helped him pry his eyes open wide enough to recognize, not his lodging-house room, but a stone cell with a single barred window.

Bars. Strip of sun. In his melancholy rage he'd apparently drunk enough to end up in Fort William's jail, known among the *voyageurs* as the *pot au beurre*, the butter tub. As his reputation around the fort was already well-colored by his hero-worship, Gilles supposed it wouldn't be the end of the world if he were accused of emulating one more facet of *voyageur* behavior: sleeping off a drunken revel.

Having abandoned Gilles's stomach when he sat up, North had just finished working his lap to the proper consistency when Gilles upset the whole process by lurching to his feet, dislodging the cat entirely.

Gilles smiled at his hissing friend. "Don't worry, I'm thinking of you. Keeper!" he called. "I think I've got my head together, such as it is. Can I get out of here and feed my cat?"

He blinked in surprise when Fort William's magistrate, Samuel Desjardins, appeared before the cell, accompanied by the *bourgeois* Etienne Gauthier. Where was the ordinary keeper?

"Finally awake, eh Bull?"

"I guess I got a little carried away yesterday," Gilles said sheepishly, *having* to guess because he certainly couldn't remember. "All right if I rejoin the world?" Puzzled by the two men's stern-faced scrutiny, Gilles added, "It won't happen again. I don't even know what I was drinking."

"A *little* carried away . . ." Samuel echoed faintly.

Etienne was much more vocal. "He goes too far, claiming not to remember!"

"Remember what?"

Etienne stepped so close the bars framed his nose. "Do not act the innocent. You bludgeoned Pierre Dumond to death!"

Gilles sat down hard, not noticing what was beneath him. Fortunately, nothing meowed or fought back. "Pierre?"

Etienne threw up his hands and let Samuel step forward. "Last night," he began somberly, "well after midnight, as the revels died down, one of the clerks who had been up cataloging the new pelts was returning to his quarters when he stumbled over the body."

"He looked as if a tree fell on him!" Etienne spat each word like a bullet of outrage. "Several times!"

"We found your paddle, splintered and bloody, where you dropped it a few feet away. You yourself managed to stagger only a few extra meters. We found you slumped against the powder magazine."

"The stone walls were rough and cold," Gilles muttered, vaguely remembering his collapse, though nothing more. He looked up. "My paddle?"

Samuel pointed to a table behind him on which rested the murder instrument.

At the sight of his most prized possession, Gilles could only shake his head in silent denial. But in this matter, silence wasn't, could not be, sufficient. "I would never use my paddle to commit such brutality."

"No?" said Etienne. "Your laughable pretensions are a crime against all *voyageurs!*"

"That's enough, Etienne," Samuel cautioned.

"He murdered one of my men."

A hundred protests clogged Gilles's throat like a logjam. He might have squeaked.

Samuel resumed. "Gilles. Everyone saw Pierre taunting you. Maybe he brought this on himself, but the fact is that even your temper must have a limit. Your jealousy of *voyageurs* is well-known."

"Envy, not jealousy. I. Am. Not. Bitter."

"Regardless. You have the only motive. I'm sorry, but you're in a great deal of trouble." He shook his head sadly. "You may not have lived your dream but you had a good life here, Gilles. You shouldn't have thrown it away." With that pronouncement, it seemed he could no longer look Gilles in the eye. "I'll go see if I can find you something to eat."

"For North. I have no appetite."

Etienne followed the magistrate, casting smugly venomous looks at the prisoner on his way out.

Gilles found he didn't even have the energy to get off the floor. Furthermore, it seemed fitting that all his doubt and worry would settle with him, allowing him to sift through it at his muddled leisure. He was deathly afraid that he might unearth the one crumbly clod of guilt which would confirm that he had indeed murdered Pierre Dumond.

When Samuel and Etienne finally returned, the sunlight had traversed half the floor. The most depressing difference between the light and himself, Gilles reflected, was that the light stood a much better chance of leaving the cell by nightfall.

It had also usurped his position as North's companion. The cat would settle in the beam and bask, wake up in shadow, reposition himself, and repeat the cycle. Gilles wished he were a cat.

"Etienne wants to prosecute you according to trail rules," Samuel said with no preamble. "Where he's the boss. Because Pierre was under his supervision, and because the evidence against you is so positively crushing, fogged memory or not, I've agreed."

"You *will* regret succumbing to the heat of the moment," Etienne promised. He waved his arms theatrically. "Dozens of punishments suggest themselves to me."

Untempered by mercy or understanding, Gilles supposed bitterly. Then again, who was to say he did not deserve such treatment?

"How did you let everything get out of hand, Gilles?" Samuel had regained his sincerity and willingness to make eye contact. He exhibited an almost paternal manner.

"I swear I don't remember. I know that doesn't speak highly of me, but I don't think I've ever been blind, dead, dead drunk before; how could I anticipate murderous tendencies or a mental blackout? I just wanted to deaden my emotional pain, not eradicate its source."

"And your paddle?"

Gilles glanced at the table. "What about it?"

"Should I not aid in the questioning?" Etienne interrupted coolly. "It is my responsibility, and I am less interested in the murder weapon than I am in determining the Bull's fate."

"If the paddle was so important to you, Gilles," said Samuel, "why did you put those scratches in it? They predate the bludgeoning."

"Scratches?"

North meowed loudly, responding to the word, and stalked from his sunbeam to the bars, slipping through lithely. He launched himself to the tabletop, positioned himself on the paddle, and began scratching vigorously. Sinewy forelegs dragged razor claws through tough wood, leaving more furrows of the sort Samuel had questioned.

"Oh," said the magistrate.

Gilles laughed, and felt his mood lighten a fraction. "Yes. Some time ago North settled on my paddle as the perfect tool on which to sharpen his claws. I indulged him. Now, when I take it out, I make sure I display the undamaged face." He blinked. "That is, when I used to take it out . . ."

Samuel sighed. "I suppose it isn't doing any good on that table, nor can you use it from your cell. Etienne, would you get Gilles his paddle?"

"I will not coddle a murderer."

"Then do it as a favor to me."

"I must object—"

"I insist."

"Very well," Etienne mumbled. He walked to the table, his steps almost mincing, and reached for the paddle. As soon as his fingers touched the handle, North exploded into a white blur of fur and claw.

Etienne shrieked and jumped back, cradling bloody hands.

"I should have mentioned," said Gilles innocently, "that North doesn't like to have his scratching interrupted."

"May you find *merde* in your moccasins," Etienne snarled, if not at Gilles, then at the world.

"I apologize, Etienne," said Samuel contritely. "Here, let me have a look."

"I am fine."

"Etienne..." Samuel grabbed his hands for a closer examination. "This is odd. In addition to all the fresh scratches, there are a number that are just beginning to scab over."

"I..."

"As if you've tried before to wrest this paddle from this cat!" shouted Gilles in a rush of understanding. "Perhaps last night in my quarters, before framing me for murder!"

"Nonsense. I got these picking berries."

"You've been hostile to me from the beginning."

"Because you murdered Pierre."

"No, because *you* did!"

"Gentlemen," Samuel interjected.

"I remember when Pierre was bragging on the dock, you gave him a dirty look. What did you resent him for?"

"Nothing! He was part of my crew."

"Etienne..."

"Come now, Samuel. You cannot take *Le Taureau* seriously."

"I take a murder seriously." He swept his penetrating gaze over both men, settling on Etienne. "You may be a big man out in the wilderness with only your crew, but I'm the law in this fort, and I want answers. Neither of you will leave this jail until we clear up this matter."

Gilles regarded the fidgety Etienne serenely and said, "Perfectly acceptable."

"I have done nothing wrong," Etienne said petulantly.

Gilles thought hard about the previous afternoon, willing to relive a painful past for the sake of his future. "Samuel, besides humiliating me, Pierre was bragging about an extremely lucrative fur deal. Maybe Etienne is upset a mere *voyageur* was taking credit for this."

North meowed and hopped from his scratching paddle to rejoin Gilles.

Etienne looked as if he wanted to kick the cat. "He had no business making that deal," he said between gritted teeth.

"Why?" asked Samuel.

"Because I was saving those furs."

"For what purpose?" Samuel bore in relentlessly.

"So I could pass the information on to the Hudson's Bay Company and one of their legitimate agents could return and close the deal. Are you satisfied?" Etienne kicked disconsolately at the floor planks, seeming more ashamed by his confession than by what it revealed.

"You work for the competition?"

Defiantly: "With exceptional skill. You Nor'Westers probably do the same thing among Bay men."

"Maybe," Samuel conceded. "But I doubt we make ourselves conspicuous by committing murder."

"That arrogant Pierre—I was seething! I had to do *something*. The Bull, his paddle, his reputation in general, provided the perfect cover for my revenge."

"Poor Etienne. You should have paid more attention when you were stealing my paddle." Gilles affectionately bumped foreheads with North. "One look at my sad little bed would have shown you how much cats like destroying covers."

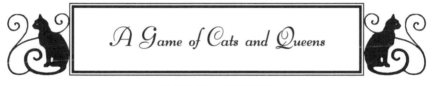

A Game of Cats and Queens

PAT MACEWEN

Hampton Court
December 19, 1571

OFF WITH HER HEAD!" ROBERT CRIED.

The toy sword fell, and with it a round wooden ball with a woman's face and yellow crown. As it dropped to the rush-strewn floor of his father's study, Bryth leaped off Robert's knee to pounce on the bouncing "head" and the Manx cat's heavy rear claws tore through the boy's hose and into his leg.

"God's blood!" Robert shouted. He pressed the doll's straw-stuffed body against his knee, but the doll was yanked out of his hands before he could even draw breath for a second oath.

"What are you *doing?!*" his father demanded.

Despite his plain black doublet, adorned by no more than a tracery of silver thread and a tiny white ruff at the collar, William Cecil cut an imposing figure. Especially now, with his eyes full of thunderbolts. Robert scrambled away from him, falling onto his knees beside the long table that filled half the room. Bryth scrambled too, dropping his prize to evade the man's swift kick.

"Give me that."

Robert picked up the fallen head. His father took it, then fit it back onto the wooden knob of the doll's neck. "Get up," he told the boy.

Painfully, Robert did so. He pulled his crooked spine as straight as possible, trying to make what he could of his narrow shoulders.

William Cecil shoved the doll into his face. "Where, pray tell, did you get this?"

"I ... I ... it was a present."

"Indeed. And who gave it to you?"

Robert hadn't seen the long-nosed man standing behind his father. Now Sir Francis Walsingham took a step forward and reached for the doll. Like the Cecils, father and son, he was dressed in a Puritan's black doublet, trunks, and hose, but over that wore a travel-stained cloak with a collar of fox fur. He turned the doll over, then popped the head off and back on again.

"Answer!" cried the elder Cecil.

Robert shuddered. Somehow he spat out, "Don De Spes."

"The Spanish Ambassador?" Walsingham frowned. "As if we had not troubles enough."

"He ... he said it was my New Year's Day gift," Robert blurted. "He feared he would miss his chance to give it to me."

"Do you know who this doll *represents*?" His father waved at the toy.

"N-no, sir ... my lord said that it was a false queen. That I would serve God and my country well if I learned to dispatch them efficiently."

The two men traded sharp looks. "If Her Grace had seen this," began Walsingham.

"Aye," said his father. "There'd be no explaining it, and my career at Court would be finished."

"But ... why?" Robert startled himself by speaking at all, but he had to know.

To his further surprise, his father softened. Still frowning, but no longer furious, he pointed. "Look, you: Dark hair on the doll, and a sword, not an axe, in the headsman's heads. The 'false queen' you thus beheaded is Anne Boleyn, the mother of our present Queen, Elizabeth."

The same who was killed by command of King Henry the Eighth? Robert felt his own jaw drop. No wonder his father was furious. William Cecil turned, scooped up the toy sword and block, and flung them into the fireplace. Walsingham tossed in the doll as well, then poked at the fire until it consumed the small offering.

"You will accept no more gifts," said his father, "unless I am present. You understand?"

Robert nodded.

"You will speak of this gift to no one."

Again, the boy nodded.

"And you will not swear by Our Savior again! Or His Blood. It is blasphemous and unseemly."

Knees shaking, he nodded a third time.

"Now go find your tutor and ask him why you have the time to play dangerous games with Spanish toys! And take that damned flea-bitten cat with you!"

Pausing to scoop up the unwilling Manx, Robert fled. His unsteady legs did not carry him far, though, before Bryth squirmed free. He ran straight for the chamber they'd just left.

"No! Bryth, stop!"

The cat, of course, ignored him so there was no choice but to catch him again, before he disturbed the two men within. He crept up behind the cat. Bryth had jumped up on a sideboard and was busily trying to paw open the door's latch. With his round jowls and mackerel stripes, his short, dense fur and his nub of a tail, Bryth looked more like a very small tiger-striped bear than a cat from that angle. A bear with exceedingly sharp claws, he thought, mindful of his torn knee.

"Robert has a good mind," said his father, his strong voice muffled by the door's solid oak. "Better by far than his older brother. If only his nurse had not dropped him and injured his spine. . . ."

Robert caught his breath.

"That's why I brought him to Court for the holidays. I have high hopes for him, if he will only apply himself. A man with a good enough mind does not need a strong body."

"The Queen has quite enough servants with strong backs and weak wits," answered Walsingham. "Or we should not be faced with our present problem. How are we to find the missing ring? Especially when we dare not admit that it *is* missing?"

Ring? What ring?

"Why was it ever removed from Her Grace's hand?" his father said. "The ring is never to leave the monarch's hand except to pass to her successor. Thirteen years ago, I myself took it off the dead Queen Mary's finger in London and brought it to Her Grace at Hatfield."

"God's bloody bones," Robert whispered to Bryth. They meant the Coronation Ring, the great onyx ring the Queen wore every day of her life.

"She took ill and swelled up," answered Walsingham. "As she has done now and again ever since her brother died. Her women feared she would lose her fingers if she kept her rings on."

"Why wasn't the ring safely coffered?"

To this there was no answer. Walsingham merely observed, "We must find the ring. If it found its way north . . ."

North lay Carlisle, where the Queen's royal cousin and rival, Mary Stuart, was confined.

"But how are we to gain entry? The quarters we ought to be searching are all well-guarded. De Spes. . . ."

"Fie! A pox on the Spanish Ambassador," answered his father.

"Yes, we must find a way to repay him for his little prank with the boy . . . but the French Ambassador is just as likely a culprit. And then Norfolk's people. . . ."

The fallen Duke? But Norfolk was still in the Tower, and soon to be tried for treason. Was that why Walsingham was here, instead of at his own post in Paris?

Suddenly footsteps neared the door. Robert swooped on the cat. With a whispered, "Hush!" he sped to the nearest garderobe. He ducked inside just as his father emerged and shouted for ale. Heart pounding, Robert clung to both the struggling cat and his father's words. "High hopes," he'd said. "A good mind . . . better than his older brother . . . if only he'd apply himself. . . ."

A fierce determination took hold of him. He'd show his father what he was worth. He'd show them all. He squeezed Bryth, ignoring the cat's growl of protest. "If *we* find the ring, Bryth, just think. We might win a reward from the Queen herself. And my father—he'll be *proud* of me!"

Bryth batted his face, but with sheathed claws, and Robert released him, then sat down to think.

An hour later, Robert picked his way across a slush-filled courtyard outside the east wing of the palace. His hands were quite full, what with Bryth tucked beneath his right arm and his left hand clasping a pocket that squirmed. Despite the icy weather, dozens of servants bustled around him, harried with holiday tasks on top of their normal work. He followed a lad with an armload of firewood into the foyer of the Spanish Ambassador's quarters.

Robert knelt and released the cat, then opened his squirming pocket. Bryth watched intently as Robert drew forth the pocket's wriggling inhabitant. It was a mouse, procured from the rat-catcher's son not half an hour since.

"*Mrowr!*" The cat's nubbin tail twitched but he did not try for the mouse. In fact, he seemed to understand Robert's intention, for he waited, motionless, staring at the panicked mouse.

"Now, Bryth, do your duty. But don't catch him too soon!" Robert flipped the mouse through the open doorway and into the oriel beyond. The rodent bounced but quickly found its feet. Then it froze, as if stunned by the prospect of freedom. Bryth ended that moment by yowling. He leaped like a hare, and the chase was on.

"Get him!" cried Robert, and leaped through the doorway himself. Inside, all turned to chaos in seconds. A woman trimming wicks on a wooden chandelier screamed as the mouse ran across her foot, followed by the cat. She flung candles and trimmer aside and crashed into the lad with the firewood, who promptly dropped it all on the feet of three men who wore clerk's robes and carried slates. The spreading confusion let Robert slip right past two men in soldier's garb. They were too busy watching the woman, who snatched up her skirts and danced away from the scurrying mouse and snarling cat. Overhead, the chandelier veered wildly, swinging ever lower as the rope that suspended it slipped its knot. Amid shouts of anger, the wooden wheel fell upon two of the clerks and the scene became a free-for-all.

Robert smiled as he flitted past the wreckage. He'd never been in this part of the palace, but trusted his instincts. He kept moving inward as others rushed toward the commotion he'd started. He soon found himself in a room with a four-poster bed, tapestries, great wooden chests, a desk, and an armchair. The room had to be De Spes's bedchamber. What better place to hide the Coronation Ring? None but De Spes's most trusted servants were ever allowed in here.

He began with the desk. It had a dozen drawers, one with a cunning false bottom that defied his small fingers, then suddenly yielded. No rings lurked within, though. Just letters, in English and Latin and Spanish. What caught his attention was one that made no sense at all. It was groups of letters that made no words. Frowning, he stuffed that one inside his doublet, then put all the drawers back.

The chests next? Or maybe the armchair. His father had one with a secret compartment built into the seat. And the bed itself, hung with silk curtains and laden with comforters, might conceal anything.

"Ho! A good catch!" cried a man's voice.

Alarmed, Robert jumped, but the owner of that voice was still out of sight. Altogether too close to the door, but he still had a chance.

Robert scrambled beneath the bed, thankful this once for his small size. He pullled his feet in just as a pair of boots and two blue silk shoes walked into his view. Whose? He dared not peek out from under to see, but they were plainly the footgear of important men, not servants. And who should come with them but Bryth? With the no-longer-wiggling mouse in his mouth, the cat paraded back and forth in front of the hidden boy. Purring, he dropped the dead mouse on Robert's foot.

"I wish our Spanish cats were as quick, for we are plagued with just as many mice and rats as your Queen." De Spes's voice, oily, deep, and dark. He must be wearing the boots.

"Aye, but cats will not rid us of two-legged rats, will they?"

Robert blinked, surprised. Surely that energetic tone belonged to the Earl of Leicester, the Queen's favorite. What was Robert Dudley doing, closeted with de Spes?

"You speak of Northumberland?"

"And Westmoreland."

Two of his father's worst enemies! And leaders of the failed northern revolt by the Army of the Five Wounds of Christ.

"You're right, of course," said De Spes. "If Northumberland and Westmoreland had stayed the course, Norfolk would not now be facing the block. He'd be wedded to Mary Stuart. A Catholic succession would be assured whether or not Elizabeth Tudor ever marries. . . ."

Leicester knelt and picked up Bryth. The sight of his ruffled lace cuffs was nearly enough to stop Robert's heart, but the Earl did not bend far enough to look under the bed. Instead, he stood up again. Bryth's purr grew louder. The Earl must be petting him!

"I will do what I can for Norfolk," Dudley said, "for I mislike his chances at trial."

De Spes moved to stand by the bed as well. Was he too petting Bryth? The cat's purring would soon rattle windowpanes.

"You think Her Grace will heed you? Between your affair with the Knollys girl and your earlier involvement in this business. . . ."

Leicester laughed. "The Queen would never truly abandon me. I lie too close to her heart. I assure you, I'll soon be back in Her Grace's full favor. I have just the trick up my sleeve."

"Indeed," answered the Spaniard. "If you can save Norfolk, you must. You will not find King Philip ungrateful."

At that moment, Robert was startled by movement much closer at hand. The dead mouse was not dead after all. It was trying to crawl inside Robert's shoe. He kicked, and the mouse flew out from under the bed as if it had grown wings.

"*Damn* you!" cried Dudley, as Bryth squalled. The Manx leaped straight out of his arms, hit the floor with a stuttering thump and went after the mouse again. Something else thumped on the rush-covered floor, two feet from Robert's elbow. A ring! A heavy ring set with a square stone of gleaming black onyx. The Coronation Ring?

Instantly, everything made sense. The "trick" Dudley had "up his sleeve" was no figure of speech, but the missing ring. Bryth must have knocked it loose when he jumped free of the Earl's arms. Dudley, the Queen's favorite—who would have thought it? But who else had half as much freedom to visit the Queen's privy chambers? And who would now be the Queen's hero, as soon as the Earl "found" the ring and returned it?

Half sick, Robert stared at the ring. But the Earl made no move to retrieve it. Had he even heard the ring fall? Had he felt it? Or Don De Spes? Had the Spanish Ambassador seen nothing?

Bryth squalled again, and ran past the foot of the bed. With his overlong back legs and high hips, the Manx's fast gallop looked more like a rabbit's gait than a cat's. Ungainly as his ka-thumping appeared, though, the cat was a champion mouser.

Bryth proved himself seconds later. A loud squeak announced the true death of the mouse, and the two men applauded him roundly. Without any further thought, Robert snaked one skinny arm out from under the bed and snagged the fallen ring. Pulling it back underneath the bed, he froze again. Had either man seen him? If he were caught, no one would save him, for nobody knew where he was. And what the Earl planned, with De Spes's help, was treason. It might mean the Tower, or even the block for Robert Dudley. What would he stop at to save himself? The man who might well have murdered his own wife in hopes of becoming the Queen's husband?

"Brave puss! Perhaps we should pit him against a fair match," said the Earl. "I would wager on that cat against any rat!"

De Spes laughed. "Instead, let us pit Essex against William Cecil. There's more profit in it."

"But less blood. I swear, Cecil has not a drop in his veins. All he cares for is money, and counting it. You'd think that it was his own, not the Queen's!"

"We will deal with him after we're done with Norfolk," replied De Spes. "And after dinner. I'm famished!"

The two men strolled out, leaving Bryth to his mouse meal.

"God's death!" Robert whispered. His own limbs were shaking so badly that he was hard put to crawl out of his hiding place. Even so, Robert's tight grip on the ring never faltered. He staggered toward Bryth and ignored the cat's protest to scoop him up. "Hush," he said. "I'll make it up to you. First, though, we must find our way out of here, and my father!"

Three days passed, and much that took place in those days Robert did not hear more of till he was grown. Other things, everyone heard of. The Queen expelled Don De Spes, sending him home in disgrace. Francis Walsingham went back to Paris and his role of matchmaker, haggling with Catherine de Medici over the merits of marriage between the Queen of England and her second son, the Duke of Anjou. Robert Dudley was not seen at all, and some whispered that he was again under house arrest. Even his father said little to Robert until the fourth day, when the elder Cecil interrupted his lessons.

"Come with me," he told the boy. "Bring that blasted cat with you."

Through long narrow hallways, Robert followed his father. Bryth did not seem to mind being carried along, and kept his peace until they arrived at a plain wooden door with a single guard.

"Stand up straight," whispered his father.

Robert was led into a small room whose only inhabitant sat facing the hearth in a carved armchair. Red hair spilled luxuriantly over the back of the chair. His breath caught in his throat and he stumbled a bit, nearly dropping Bryth.

"There you are." Though her hair was unbound and she wore little more than a shawl and a dressing gown, there was no mistaking the Queen.

Robert dropped into a deep if awkward bow, losing the cat as he did so, but Bryth did not flee. Instead, the cat leaped into the Queen's lap and nudged at her hand till she scratched his wide head. Then he settled in, purring.

"He's nearly as small as the cat," said the Queen to his father. To Robert, she said, "I shall call you my pygmy. What think you of that?"

"I . . . I. . . ."

"Answer!" his father hissed.

"Oh, never mind." The Queen laughed. "We've been far better served by his tongue-tied bravado than by all the silvery speeches at Court. And since all of this must remain secret, his silence will suit Our needs well indeed."

To the boy, she said, "You have done far more than retrieve Our ring. You have sussed out a plot that endangered us all. But you must never speak of the ring, or of that cyphered letter you found. Understand?"

Robert nodded.

"Good. Then take this in fair exchange for the one you recovered." She pulled off a gold ring encrusted with rubies and handed it to him.

"I . . . but . . . thank you, Your Grace!"

The Queen smiled. To his father, she said, "Take good care of my pygmy, and teach him well. We shall have further need of him when he is grown."

Cecil bowed, all but glowing.

"See you take care of the cat as well. You will find that We do not forget Our loyal servants, no matter how slight their rank!"

Robert grinned, and for once found it easy to stand straight and tall.

Guardian of Souls

JANET PACK

ASSISTANT MEDICAL EXAMINER Darlayne Peters abruptly detoured her morning jog, sudden dread making her mouth taste metallic and her breath become short. Police cruisers and an ambulance bunched in the street near the front door of the small apartment building where her friend Dr. Sam Westenn lived. Their light bars made the old brownstone wall into a spectral kaleidoscope, their growling motors made the A.M.E. shiver with foreboding.

Layne flashed her ID to the cop at the door and entered the brownstone, elbowing through people huddled about the door of the Oriental-history professor's two-bedroom flat. Feeling shocked and trying to delay the inevitable, she ducked beneath the yellow crime scene tape into an improbable standoff.

Dr. Sam's short spare body lay sprawled on its back in the middle of his tiny living room on a throw rug, shadowed by overflowing bookshelves covering almost every inch of wallspace. As usual he wore plastic bandage strips, two on his hands, one on his face, attesting to his accident-prone nature. An empty prescription bottle lay open beside one outstretched hand, along with his silver-rimmed bifocals.

Dr. Sam's female cat, Spirit, defied all comers from the middle of the old man's still chest. The dark tan and chocolate longhair hissed, spat, and clawed with remarkable speed and precision at any who approached. Detectives and police ringed victim and feline, whispering plans to one another regarding the animal's capture. Spirit's dark bottlebrushed tail described wide irritated arcs as a policewoman attempted to distract her while a detective maneuvered a pillowcase behind the cat. Spirit was too alert for that game: she scared off the woman in front with a manic combination of wild eyes, teeth, and threatening claws, then whirled and opened sudden gashes across the back of the detective's hand with a quick left paw.

"Damned cat!" the wounded man moaned, wrapping a tissue over the slashes. "Can't we just knock it out?"

"What happened?" the young A.M.E. shakily asked the detective in charge.

"Oh, Dr. Peters. Dr. Higgins, your superior, just left. He said it looks like medication OD, but he couldn't get any closer than four feet. A neighbor called when she heard the cat screeching." Sergeant Gene Davis, a graying avuncular type in sports coat and tan slacks whom she'd met on a case a couple of weeks ago, answered softly. "You knew him, I guess. Sorry." Noticing her tears he groped for a handkerchief to offer, but found only a tortured, dusty Kleenex. The sergeant handed it to her anyway.

"Thanks." Darlayne swiped her streaming eyes. "This is a shock. Everyone liked Dr. Sam. He taught my Eastern history class at the university. That's how we got to know each other—he stopped me after class one afternoon, said he appreciated my curiosity." She looked at the victim again and shook her head, making her short coppery pony tail bounce. "He wouldn't hurt a gnat. And he's just not the type to OD."

A hiss split the air as another policeman tried to lure the feline away from the body. "You won't get the cat like that," Layne stated, stepping forward. "I know this animal, she's very protective. Dr. Westenn was my friend. Let me try."

"Good luck," sneered a young detective named Rogers. "You'll need it."

The assistant M.E. hunkered down almost to eye level with the feline. "Back off, everyone," she snapped, then her soprano voice became soft. "Hello Spirit, remember me? It's Layne, I was here last week. I'm so very sorry about Dr. Sam. He was a good friend to both of us, and a good man. He'd never hurt anybody." Wide blue eyes stared steadily into her hazel ones. Startling white paws began working up and down, up and down on the victim's gray shirt, leaving smears. "He's gone now, love," she continued. "You did what you needed to do, guided his soul onto the path toward the next life. That's a very good girl, pretty one." Behind her one of the detectives snorted as she slowly, slowly held out her hand to the animal, palm up. "Here, sweetheart. Come on, your job is over. Would you like to go home with me? We can remember Dr. Sam together. I'll never forget him." Her breath caught. "He was very special."

The cat rose from her crouch, uttering a mournful yowl which vibrated from the tip of her tail. Her whole body shook with the keening. When the howl ended she turned, laid a claw-sheathed paw on Dr. Westenn's face, close to the bandage strip on his cheek, then with great dignity stepped from the dead man's chest into the circle of Darlayne's arms. The A.M.E. scooped up the cat, cradling the soft wide head beneath her chin. Detectives and police alike sighed with relief. A few applauded her as the emergency medical team converged on the body.

"I've never seen anything like that," Sergeant Davis said appreciatively, standing near her shoulder as she straightened and pivoted. "You're good with critters, Dr. Peters."

"You just have to know the animal, Detective." She tried to smile at his compliment but couldn't manage one with the cat trembling against her. She felt like trembling, too—why would a man who loved life and was at peace with his world OD? She'd met Dr. Sam for dinner last week, and his mood had seemed normal, quiet but buoyant and gently teasing.

"This cat's pretty unusual," she continued. "As you see, Birman have white feet. According to legend, they were once all dark. Their markings resemble a Siamese and they're very smart. These cats were once temple guards in the Orient, helped the priests there. It's said thieves broke into a particular temple to pillage its treasures, murdering all the priests. One of the cats escaped. That Birman sat on his priest's chest as the man's soul passed into the next world. The cat, who was devoted to its partner, guided him between worlds and mourned. The supreme god saw the animal's dedication as well as its distress, and marked the breed to set it apart from other felines. That cat's feet turned white, and from then on all Birman have had white paws." She paused, hugging Spirit, her voice growing husky. "Dr. Sam thought a great deal of this little lady. They had a relationship similar to the ancient priests and their cats."

Darlayne felt Spirit's front right foot flex against her wrist, claws out just enough to catch her attention. The paw left something sticky on her skin. She looked down. "What's that?"

Davis peered as close as he dared, just beyond the cat's reach. "Might be blood. Probably belongs to the last detective who reached her direction."

"No," the A.M.E. disagreed. "She used her left paw on him. That stuff is on her right."

The sergeant fingered a small plastic evidence bag out of his pocket, opened it, then hesitated. "Will it—the cat—let me get a sample?"

"Better let me. Scrape the stuff off my arm. I'll look for more." Layne disengaged her smudged arm from beneath the Birman while murmuring to the cat. When Davis finished with it, the A.M.E. changed supporting forearms beneath the feline and craned her neck to see beyond Spirit's head and whiskers, running a fingernail down one of the feline's claws.

Brownish-red residue came off. More was matted in the long fur between the pad and the toes. Layne's hopes surged.

"Sergeant, if I hold her like this I think she'll let you clip hair from that paw." The A.M.E. tightened her grip around the small body. The cat felt like tightly-coiled wire beneath her fur, a spring that might release at any moment. Darlayne rubbed her chin between the cat's dark ears as Davis gingerly reached out. "Easy, lady. That's my Spirit girl. Heavens, I'm already calling you the same thing Dr. Sam did!"

"Nice kitty, good kitty," the detective muttered, slowly spanning the short distance between them with small scissors and a clean plastic bag. The cat didn't move, only watched curiously, a faint warning rumbling her chest. The sergeant whooshed out air in a long relieved sigh when the procedure was over. "I hate to overturn the opinion of the Medical Examiner, but this is beginning to look like something bigger than an OD," he said, handing the evidence bags to Rogers. "Take those to the lab now, along with the smudges from the victim's shirt. I want results ASAP. When you get them, call all the hospitals and medical centers in the area. I want reports of anyone having the same blood type who's treated for multiple claw lacerations. And talk to clerks at local pharmacies and convenience stores. If this perp is bleeding badly or hurting he might stop in there, figuring they're safer."

"Yes, sir." The young detective knelt next to the body, cutting away the stained part of Dr. Westenn's shirt with scissors. Spirit hissed and fought Layne for freedom without using her sixteen miniature scythes. The A.M.E. spit fur, but managed somehow to contain the cat. Rogers glanced at the pair once, then finished quickly and disappeared beneath the tape across the door.

"Like I said," Darlayne stated to the sergeant, "Dr. Sam just wasn't the type to commit suicide. He adored life, his books, his friends, and his cat far too much. Especially with a medication meant to help him live longer. He did have a heart condition."

Davis asked, "Did he ever mention owning anything someone might want to steal?"

Layne hesitated, thinking. She scratched Spirit's chin. "He talked about some sort of antique scroll or wall hanging. I never saw it, and I have the feeling only a collector would consider it valuable."

"Why don't you go through the place and try to locate where it hung? You're having better luck today than the rest of us." He smiled at her like a proud relative. "I'd appreciate your help if you could spare the time. Help solve this case, and I may have to make a detective of you."

"Thanks Sergeant, but I've already got a job. I'll do anything for Dr. Sam, though. Hope Dr. Higgins understands. I still have to get home, take a shower, and get Spirit settled."

"No problem there," Davis stated. "I'll let the M.E. know you're working with me on this case, that you'll be a little late."

Darlayne nodded to the detective, then stepped through the rest of the small apartment, trying to see the place as Dr. Sam had. No clean rectangles existed on the few walls lacking bookcases, no nail holes revealed themselves. Only a familiar, faintly minty scent hung about the tiny second bedroom, barely enough to tickle her olfactory sense. Puzzled, she reported her lack of discoveries to Sergeant Davis and left the crime scene. With Spirit cradled in her arms beneath her nylon jogging jacket, ears twitching at every sound, the A.M.E. walked the few blocks to her own apartment.

Uncapping her tube of toothpaste later that night, Layne recalled the faint minty scent in Dr. Sam's second bedroom. Dropping it on the bathroom counter, she sprinted for the phone to call Sergeant Davis.

"Dr. Peters." The policeman sounded tired. "I was about to call you. We have a suspect, thanks to you and the cat."

"Wonderful. And I've got some information for you. Not much, but maybe it will help."

"You first."

"I smelled something familiar when I was in Dr. Sam's smaller bedroom. I didn't mention it because it was so faint. Whoever took the scroll bothered to hide the nail holes where it had been hanging with white toothpaste. Since the walls were white-painted wallboard, only the smell gave it away. If they'd been filled a few hours earlier, even the scent would have dissipated."

"That's impressive, Dr. Peters. Now for the rest." He sucked in a noisy breath. "We sent policemen to local pharmacies and convenience stores asking them to call us if anyone bought antibacterial ointments in association with gauze pads and the like. One guy who works for the local humane association doesn't like us much because we checked him out when he stopped at an emergency room after being clawed by a racoon living in someone's toolshed. Similar pattern to a cat. But the other man turned out to be wanted by Interpol. He's a cat burgular hired by rich collectors to steal distinctive pieces. Apparently he thought Dr. Westenn wasn't home, jimmied the lock, walked in, and grabbed the scroll. He didn't figure on the savagery of the Birman's attack, or Dr. Sam hustling out of the kitchen to see what was going on. The perp knocked the professor out and found that bottle of pills. Got enough of the medicine down his throat to arrest his normal functions, then decided he'd clear out before the cat shredded the rest of his legs. He left through the window after loosening the screen, worked his way up two stories to the roof on the wall facing the next building, aided by one of those special climbing rigs, and escaped. We found some drops of blood on the wall and the concrete ledge, same blood type we took off the cat.

"The thief was on his way to the airport when he decided he couldn't put up with the seeping wounds, and stopped to buy ointment. The clerk had quick eyes, saw some fresh blood on the cuffs of his slacks. He called us soon as the guy left. We got a picture from the security-camera tape, and the clerk gave us a description of his car. We were on his tail when he stopped at the next convenience store to buy Band-Aids. We picked him up just as he turned in his rental car at the airport. A perfect collar.

"By the way, we contacted Dr. Westenn's lawyer. The scroll was ancient Tibetan, has to do with those priests and cats you told me about. It was a real collector's item. Dr. Westenn wanted it to go to the university's museum after his death. They'll put a real pretty bronze plaque next to it with a dedication to him. It's in a security vault now, and will be on its way there under police guard in the morning."

Layne smiled and petted Spirit, some of the darkness left by Dr. Sam's death lifting from her soul. "Congratulations, Sergeant. We're a good team."

"You and that cat make a good team." He hesitated. "If I can't persuade you to become a detective, can I at least make Spirit an honorary one? I'd like to do something for you both. In memory of the good professor."

The Birman purred for the first time since coming home with the A.M.E. "We'd both like that, Sergeant Davis," Darlayne Peters said softly, stroking the beautiful cat who was now her guardian. "And so would Dr. Sam."

Habit

CAROLE MCINTYRE

SISTER FELISA HAD BEEN ADOPTED by the convent because her coat matched their habit: black robes with white wimple and cowl. She had no money, of course, so she easily fulfilled the vow of poverty, and her chastity had been surgically assured. That left only obedience, and the nuns assured each other that two out of three wasn't bad: nobody really expected very much obedience from a cat.

Although she wasn't obedient, she had a natural discretion. She never left the vestry when Father Connor came in to say mass in the convent chapel, but sat just inside the door to the sanctuary, swaying slightly as the nuns sang. If there was incense, she would sneeze, discreetly.

Running the kitchen with the same strict discipline that she'd used to teach French to classes of youngsters, Sister Madeleva relaxed a bit with Felisa, who came willingly to "*Minou, minou, minou,*" having learned that this meant meat scraps: Felisa wasn't really bilingual, but she was very pragmatic. Unfortunately, meat scraps were in short supply during Lent, and Sister Madeleva explained to the disbelieving cat that discipline was good for one's soul.

The kitchen opened onto the gardens, which were Sister Samuel's province. Her efforts supplied vegetables for the table, a practice Sister Madeleva approved for cutting expenses, and produced most of the wondrous flowers that graced the altar of the chapel. Because Easter was so late this year, the lilies would rise from heaps of lilacs, pouring a river of scent down the aisle.

Having made her scrapless way through the kitchen and then toured the gardens, Sister Felisa padded up the stairs to visit Sister Clemenza, who was in bed most of the time now, in the late stages of cardiac failure. Sister Clemenza had celebrated her Golden Jubilee ten years before, and was hoping to die quietly, with a minimum of fuss and expense for her order. She knew her situation. Years of teaching biology had given her a thorough understanding of what it meant when her swollen ankles retained dents from her fingers: she was well into edema, and her kidneys were no longer removing enough fluids.

The cat would curl up by her side, keeping her company as she kept to her bed. Her life, once rigorous, was now mostly dispensations: she no longer wore her habit, no longer kept the hours from matins to compline, no longer fasted and abstained from meat, though it was Lent. Easter wouldn't be the same, she thought, without the little privations to lengthen Lent. And this would doubtless be her last Easter.

"Ah, you'll never get in there!" Joe, Freddy's drinking buddy, had been an altar boy. He knew all the jokes about penguins, and some considerably less amusing.

"Yeah, I will. We're making a big delivery tomorrow. You come with me, and keep that kitchen biddy busy, and I'll get upstairs. We have to go through the kitchen and refectory to get to the chapel, and the stairs are right by the chapel." Freddy delivered flowers all over town, and had been known to get further into private homes than the residents intended. Now he was taking aim at the convent. Their Easter lilies, like everyone else's, came from the greenhouse.

"Twenty bucks says you won't. Besides, if I'm in the kitchen, how will I know you really made it?" Joe liked to gamble, but he wanted to be sure of the terms.

"I'll bring something back. A trophy. What do you want? A rosary?"

"They'd *give* you a rosary, and gladly. They're always givin' 'em away. How about underwear?"

"Underwear? Do nuns wear underwear? I thought they wore hair shirts or something."

"They have to wear underwear. Probably get it from old-lady stores. They can't just shop at Frederick's, you know." Joe and Freddy had a laugh over the notion of a nun with a Frederick's catalog. Joe's knuckles tingled reminiscently: they had known many a sharp ruler in parochial school.

"I'll time the delivery to hit Saturday afternoon. Shouldn't be anyone upstairs then. Piece of cake."

"You haven't known very many nuns, have you?" Joe asked.

"Not a one. None. I say 'hello' when I get there, and 'good-bye' when I leave. What's there to talk about with nuns? I just leave the lilies."

* * *

The warm afternoon air lifted the scent of lilac up the narrow stairs to Sister Clemenza's room across the hall at the top. The urge to see the chapel dressed for Easter was overwhelming. Slowly, with great effort, she sat up straighter in bed—she slept on heaps of pillows because she could no longer breathe lying supine—and worked her legs over the side to tuck her feet into her slippers. She had to move very slowly, and use her arms to assist herself. Felisa bounced off her bed, and began to twine around the old nun's ankles. Sister Clemenza flipped her fingers at the cat. "Shoo. Shoo." She could barely whisper, but it was enough to make the cat move away, as if she knew how terribly unsteady Sister Clemenza was.

The stairs were narrow so the nuns would file singly, avoiding the temptation to talk on the way to prayer, always a problem with novices. The handrails supported the trembling hands that helped to ease the old body step by step, resting frequently, heading obdurately toward the chapel.

Slowly, she limped in, and slumped into the first pew inside. Felisa sat politely in the aisle. The tabernacle on the altar stood empty, door ajar, and the sanctuary lamp was dark, but the Easter lilies rose in trumpeting spires from the frothy lilacs, and the scent was intoxicating. *One last Easter here,* Sister Clemenza considered. *Then I'll go home.* She sat quietly in the golden sunlight that streamed through the windows.

I'd better get upstairs before Sister Madeleva comes with supper, she thought. Painfully, she retraced her steps, climbing back up to her room.

Freddy made it a point to wear cut-offs in summer when he delivered flowers. Sometimes it paid off. And he took especial pleasure in wearing them to the convent, to give the old girls a glimpse of what they'd missed. He'd made so many trips through the kitchen and refectory that he was pretty sure the kitchen biddy didn't know whether he was coming or going, and he'd bounded up the stairs to the second floor two at a time on young, tireless legs. The odor to the first room at the top was open, and he was pawing through the drawers.

"Young man, what are you doing here? You aren't supposed to be here! Shoo!" Sister Clemenza made the same gesture she had made to Felisa when she was afraid the cat would trip her.

Freddy hadn't figured on getting caught, and he had no Plan B. He charged past the old nun, knocking her down, stepping on Felisa's tail, and getting four claws raked down his leg from knee to ankle. Before he could kick at her, he panicked completely, and slid down the stairs with his hands on the rails. On the first floor, nobody would question him, and he carefully sidled through the kitchen with his clawed leg to the wall. He jerked his head to Joe, who politely said good-bye to the busy Sister Madeleva, and they left.

The mixed scent of lilac and lilies still surrounded Sister Clemenza. The last things she thought were how wonderful it was that she'd seen the chapel decked for Easter one last time, and how much brighter this light was than the sunlight pouring through the stained-glass windows of the chapel. When Sister Madeleva came up with the supper tray, she found Felisa curled against the sprawled body, keeping her company still.

"Nightgowns? Whaddaya mean, nightgowns?" Joe was trying to make sense of the report.

"That's what they wear under all that black. Flannel nightgowns. I saw one. A real old one, and that's what she had on. She almost trapped me." Freddy was indignant at his narrow escape.

"What happened to your leg?"

"A cat. I couldn't believe it. I didn't know they could have cats in convents."

"That's gonna scar, you know. It's pretty deep," Joe said.

"Nah." Freddy wore the immortality of youth like a cloak.

"So, what did you get?"

"I told you, she walked in on me. I had to get out of there."

"Twenty bucks."

"Wait a minute. I'll try again. We take hothouse flowers there that they can't grow in the gardens. I'll get in there."

Sister Clemenza's obituary didn't come to Freddy's attention, but others read it, and ordered sprays of flowers for her funeral. On Monday, he was back at the convent, but the instant he entered the kitchen, Felisa began to yowl like a siren. Back arched, tail bushed, she sidled at him until he backed out the door, and then she sprang up to spread herself on the screen he slammed in her face. She dropped to the floor and snarled with bitter menace, her voice bringing nuns from all over the convent to see why the usually placid cat was behaving so.

"What's going on here?" Sister Madeleva came into the kitchen from the chapel, where she'd been sitting by the casket of Sister Clemenza.

"I dunno. The cat just went crazy."

"Nonsense. That's a very good cat. She always behaves herself. What have you done to her?"

"Nothing! I never touched her!" By this time, Freddy had convinced himself that the cat had no reason to dislike him. He made no connection between his foray into the upper reaches of the convent and the funeral which stuffed his van with floral sprays.

Stepping out the kitchen door, Sister Madeleva's sharp eyes noted the red slashes running down the delivery boy's leg. "How did that happen?"

"I . . . caught myself on a wire fence."

"Really? Did you have a tetanus shot? Those are very deep cuts, and they could become infected." She looked at him closely. "If they were cat scratches, for example, they could easily carry a virus which could make you very ill."

The cat was still snarling her displeasure, and Sister Madeleva decided to have Freddy deliver to the door, rather than risk the cat pursuing him to the van. It took many trips: Sister Clemenza had taught quite a few students over the years. Watching him limp from the van to the kitchen porch, Sister Madeleva narrowed her eyes and wondered why Felisa had suddenly taken such sharp exception to this young man who had visited before, and whether those marks on his leg were from a fence or Felisa's claws. They couldn't have happened today, though, or they'd still be bleeding. The opening refrigerator door didn't register with the cat, and even the offer of meat scraps couldn't lure the angry cat from the kitchen door.

There was still another thing, the nun thought. Quite often, people who were dying would hold on until some special day had arrived: Christmas, a birthday, some milestone—a wedding, a graduation. Then, they'd just expire peacefully as though they'd sustained on will alone and flickered out like a candle. The whole convent anticipated Easter. Sister Clemenza, fading though she had been, was no exception. She would have hung on, somehow. If she could have. Why had she been at the door of her room, as though returning? Surely she would have called for help to the bathroom.

"It was that damn cat," Freddy complained as he reluctantly handed over the twenty. "It screeched like a siren. Tried to scratch my eyes out. I barely got out the door. Then that kitchen biddy wouldn't even let me in the building."

"That the same cat that scratched you?" Joe asked.

"I guess so. Looked about the same. How many cats could they have?" Freddy shrugged.

"That nun you saw . . . You know her name?"

Freddy sneered, "We weren't exactly introduced."

"Was it Sister Clemenza?"

"How would I know? Old girl in a nightgown, that's all I know."

" 'Cause if it was, she died."

"So?"

"So . . . you were upstairs in that convent, you scared her or something, and she died. That's murder." Joe was having a sudden attack of conscience on Freddy's behalf, since he, himself, was clearly not at fault.

"Murder? You're crazy. I didn't do nothin'."

"You were someplace you weren't supposed to be, and she's dead. If that's not murder, it's still something. She might still be alive if it weren't for you." It was fun to see Freddy squirm.

"Nobody knows. Nobody can prove anything."

"*I* know. And that cat knows."

"If you know what's good for you, you'll keep your mouth shut. As for the cat, cats have accidents all the time. What's one cat, more or less? For that matter, what's one nun, more or less?"

Freddy's little explorations had always just been adventures before. Of course, nothing serious had resulted before. Slowly, it was dawning on Joe that maybe that old nun had a right to her privacy, and that Freddy had violated it. Joe was thinking about going to the funeral.

As the priest marched around the casket containing the mortal remains of Sister Clemenza, he swung the censer at each corner and at the head and foot. Sister Felisa sneezed quietly from her vantage point at the vestry door. The *Dies irae* was chanted, and the crowd in the chapel emptied out to follow the hearse to the cemetery. Sister Madeleva headed for the kitchen to prepare for the guests who would return after the service there. Joe followed her into the kitchen. "I have to tell you something," he began. "Last Saturday was when Sister Clemenza died, wasn't it?" Haltingly, he told her about the bet, the cat, and his suspicion.

The cat in question had no objection to him; indeed, she sat on his lap as he stumbled through his story. It wasn't that living in a convent had persuaded the cat that all men were strangers, but she certainly had taken exception to that delivery boy. Sister Madeleva stared at Joe, who had been an average student, but no trouble. He was probably telling the truth, but what could she do about it? This was hearsay: Freddy could simply deny it, and how could she prove a connection between his scratched leg and Sister Clemenza's death?

"*Minou, minou!*" brought Felisa off Joe's lap to get her meat. Carefully, she sat up and stretched out her paws to take the scrap from Sister Madeleva's fingers. She never scratched doing this, but used her claws delicately, like a fork. Watching those claws dig into the meat, Sister Madeleva wondered just how carefully the most meticulous cat could clean her claws, and whether there might still be traces of Freddy's skin caught there.

Amazing, Sister Madeleva thought, *how many of this town's people passed through Sister Clemenza's biology classes and went on to study it further.* Sister Felisa, uncomplaining, let her paws be flexed to extend her claws for scraping. Carefully, the technician from the police department cleaned the hollow between the sides of each claw. Felisa even purred at the attention.

"If there's any DNA left, I'll find it. If there's anything human, we'll get a sample from this Freddy. Do you know his last name?"

"No, but the florist would. He works there, delivering flowers."

"We'll get back to you."

"We've got him in custody. He admits to being upstairs, and he admits that the cat scratched him, but he says he didn't do anything to the nun, just that he saw her." The assistant district attorney was trying to figure out just what charges he could make stick. Home invasion, no problem, maybe malicious trespass on the side, but what about Sister Clemenza's death? There were no previous charges on this kid. Making a case that he had been responsible for the death of a nun known to have serious heart problems would be dicey.

Sister Madeleva was thinking much the same thing, coupled with the old nun's name ticking through her mind. Clemenza. Clemenza. Mercy. "Tell me about plea-bargaining. How does it work?" she asked the people's lawyer.

Freddy didn't have much spare time any more. He still worked for the florist, delivering, and most of his off-hours were spent digging and weeding in the convent gardens, under the direction of Sister Samuel. He was learning a lot about horticulture from the ground up, and his attitude toward the nuns, and work in general, was slowly changing. He ate occasional snacks on the back porch of the kitchen, because Sister Felisa still wouldn't let him in, and part of his suspended sentence involved personally keeping up Sister Clemenza's grave. By the time the dirt was really settled, the grass would do credit to a golf green, and the lilac bush was coming along nicely. It should bloom in a couple of years. The black cat with the white face and shirtfront lounged on a garden wall, her tailtip flipping as she watched the young man. He would carry the scars from her claws to his own grave, but his legs were decorously trousered.

The Happy Homewrecker

LESLIE WHAT

SHIRLEY'S JOB OFFERED TRAVEL opportunities, lots of money, and plenty of time off. Although her business card said "Happy Homemaker Housekeeping Services," her true calling was as a burglar. At the moment, a very broke burglar in desperate need of a few new jobs. Her car had broken down outside of Reno and fixing it had used up most of her savings.

She was hoping for a big enough haul this time to take a long-planned vacation to Hawaii.

She pulled her battered sedan off the highway and decided to take up residence in a medium-sized town called Springfield. Within the hour she found a small furnished apartment and paid a month's rent in advance, probably more time than she needed, but those were the landlord's conditions. Now she was really broke. She'd have to clip coupons in order to eat, until payday.

By late afternoon, she got started working. She carried a small suitcase filled with her cleaning supplies, and stashed a handful of pamphlets advertising her services in her pocket. Then she took a stroll around the neighborhood.

Dressed in her powder blue pantsuit with white shoes and a matching handbag, she looked as respectable as a schoolteacher. This community was perfect! Block after block of tidy houses, all left empty during the day. Something about the whole situation told her she was going to love cleaning up here!

The first potential customer looked rushed and exhausted from a hard day at work. A round-faced elementary-aged child tugged at her skirt. From around the corner came the sound of cats howling.

Shirley's eyes began to water. Allergies. "Hello," she said, extending her hand. "I'm Shirley, the Happy Homemaker." The cover of the pamphlet, written in large block letters, read: HOUSECLEANING AT AFFORDABLE RATES!

The woman said in a doubtful voice, "I wish I could hire you, but I just don't have the money." Still, she opened the door enough that Shirley slipped inside. Before the woman could say anything else, Shirley unfolded a pamphlet and pointed to the glowing references from former "satisfied customers." She had written the references herself and knew them by heart.

Her nose itched as if there were wires tickling it from the inside. Must be those stupid cats! Shirley could see that the house needed cleaning. There were toys everywhere and dustballs in the corners.

"I'm new to the area and I'm trying to build up my business," Shirley said. "The first month is half-off—why that's less than the cost of a cup of coffee per day."

The woman looked astonished. "That sounds very reasonable," she said. She introduced herself as Mary Eliot.

Mary's little girl said, "I don't like her, Mommy," and Shirley felt her cheeks redden. What did that little brat know, anyway?

But Mary paid no attention. Absentmindedly, she retrieved a stranded sock from the floor and shoved it in her pocket. "Oh, gosh," Mary said. "I don't know."

It was too easy to make working women feel guilty about their houses! Shirley took a few more steps and looked around and into the living room. She held back a sneeze and felt her ears pop. The furnishings were simple but there was a surprising collection of sterling silver knickknacks—candlesticks and goblets and the like—and on the green velvet couch were two small kittens with white faces and paws and blue eyes. Wiry hairs covered the furniture like pale veins. Shirley sneezed.

"It's dusty in here," Mary said. "I'm sorry. I work until five, then pick up the kids, and come home to make dinner. . . ."

Shirley rubbed her nose. She said, "Doesn't leave you much time. I know how tough it is. I'm a working woman myself." She paused before delivering the next line of her script. "Tell you what. Let me clean your house for free, introduce you to my service. No obligation."

A dreamy look crossed Mary's face. She picked up her child for a brief hug and kiss. "Free?" she said. "Hard to believe."

"Really," Shirley answered. She reached in her handbag and searched for a tissue to wipe her nose. "I just need my foot in the door. Of course, I hope you'll like my work and decide to continue."

"Okay," said Mary. She hadn't needed much convincing. They never did.

Shirley sneezed again.

"Are you catching a cold?" Mary asked.

There was an uncomfortable dryness like a sand dune shifting in her throat. "No," Shirley said, with a cough. "I think I'm allergic to your cats. I'll be all right."

"My mother's allergic to these two," Mary said. "That's where I got them. That's where I got everything, when you come right down to it." She gestured around the room.

One of the kittens jumped up onto the top of the couch and aimed itself at the sofa table and a small silver bell. It pounced and managed to set the bell ringing.

"They're so cute!" Mary said.

"Just adorable," said Shirley.

"They're part Siamese and part Bengal," Mary said. "And playful as can be! My mother fell in love with them the minute she caught sight of them! But she couldn't keep the little sweeties; it's even hard for her to visit us without loading up on allergy pills."

Shirley tried to act interested, but what really interested her was Mary's vast collection of silver. Ornate bud vases and paperweights and tea services! Even the picture frames! And it was all real! She could tell because everything was turning dark as dusk. "Would you like me to polish these things?" she asked. "I'll be glad to start on it next time I'm here."

Mary blushed. "My mother," she said. "She collects all this and gives it to me—says it's her granddaughter's college fund. I just don't have time to keep everything looking nice," she said.

"No problem," Shirley said, suppressing a smile. "That's what I'm here for." Just then, one of the kittens bounced off the wall like a bowling pin. It screeched and ran toward Shirley. Without advance warning, it climbed up her leg, piercing her nylons with its tiny talons. "You little piranha!" Shirley muttered, trying to shake it off. The kitten held tight, taking his time before letting go.

The miserable runts! "I'll bet your daughter just adores them," Shirley said with what she hoped was an appreciative smile. The little girl prattled off something about the kittens turning her new sweater into blue and yellow yarn balls.

"Precious," Shirley said. She had to establish that she was the friendly type. It worked. Mary said, "I can't thank you enough!" and Shirley answered, "No! Let me thank you for giving me a chance to prove myself!" She opened her suitcase and took out a spray bottle and a dust cloth. "I didn't bring the full cart, but I will next time. You'll see! I do twice as good a job at half the price," she said, then got to work.

While the clothes were being washed, Shirley sponge-mopped the bathrooms. She asked to borrow a vacuum cleaner and set to work in the bedroom. Like many people, Mary kept her jewelry box on a chest of drawers. Mostly junk, but a couple of antique silver rings and bracelets that could easily fetch several hundred dollars. Shirley dusted, carefully examining the glass figurines and a coin collection worth at least one hundred dollars. There were silver thimbles in a curio case, but the most intriguing piece was a gorgeous silver picture frame. It was all Shirley could do not to steal it right then! The frame weighed a ton! Solid silver, very ornate, with beautiful engravings of lilies and butterflies. The guy in the photograph was a burly young hunter who held a lion up by its mane.

A tap on her shoulder made Shirley gasp with fright.

Her cheeks blushed hot as she replaced the frame.

"Sorry to startle you," Mary said.

"Just admiring this photo," Shirley stammered. She sneezed. Those horrid kittens had sneaked into the bedroom!

Mary smiled. "My dad," she said. "John Silver. Used to hunt big game. He and my mother met in Africa on safari." She sighed. "Dad's passed on now, but Mom still runs their antique store." She gazed appreciably at the dust-free bureau. "Well, I have to say the house looks great. I'd like to hire you. At least for one month."

Thankfully, that's all the time I need, Shirley thought with a warning look to the cats.

They arranged for Shirley to return later in the week. Before leaving, Shirley said, "Tell all your friends about me!"

And that was exactly what happened. Calls began to pour in. Soon, Shirley had ten clients and the keys to most of their houses. She spent her first few visits cataloguing their belongings so she could guesstimate values and plan to steal the most valuable items. Jewelry and diamonds from the Logans. A collection of fine prints and rare first editions from the Monroes. Collector dolls still in their boxes from the Hamptons. And all the silver she could carry from Mary Eliot.

It was all going according to plan with just one little glitch: she was miserable, with terrible sinus problems and itching. In desperation she visited the doctor, who prescribed some expensive antihistamines, which she didn't have the cash to buy. Those horrid little kittens had made her life miserable, but soon enough there'd be some payback to make it all worthwhile.

Finally, the day arrived when Shirley really planned to clean up. And not a moment too soon. She was flat broke and hadn't eaten a decent meal in two days.

Before leaving her apartment, she emptied all her cleaning solutions down the drain and attached a fresh bag to her vacuum. First she cleaned out Mary's house. Knowing where everything was, it went quickly. She slipped silver rings on her fingers and filled empty bottles with necklaces and silverware. She wrapped the breakables in washcloths, and carefully tucked them into a garbage sack. The coin collection fit nicely in the bottom of a vacuum cleaner bag. The gorgeous silver frame went right into her purse. She was deliriously excited; even those stupid little cats couldn't rain on her parade, though they tried. One used her right leg as a scratching post; she screamed at it, but the kitten only gave her a bored look before slowly sauntering away. She was tempted to drop the silver frame like an anvil on its smug little head, but refrained. No point in denting valuable merchandise. And by the time she was through here, Mary Eliot was going to wish she had watchdogs instead of those horrible kittens! Shirley could barely control her sneezing.

She locked her booty in the trunk and replaced the vacuum bag with a clean one. Then she got to work on the next house. Before long, it was quitting time. There was still plenty of light out, but this was a lot better than banker's hours! Shirley sped away in her car and got onto the highway.

Her eyes were still watering and she felt like there were tap dancers doing the shuffle-ball-change in her throat. She reached inside her purse for a tissue and her fingers traced the cold indentations on the silver frame. Her ears felt like water balloons about to burst. She couldn't wait another minute—she had to stop at the drug store and fill her antihistamine prescription, but before she did that, she'd need to get a little money.

A sign caught her eye. SILVER SHOP. PAWN OR TRADE.

Time to cash in the gilded frame, Shirley thought. She parked and thought herself very clever for removing the photograph. She didn't want to take any chance that the frame could be traced. Another round of sneezing attacked her as she waltzed inside the shop.

It smelled musty and there were ugly animal heads on the walls, and a picture of an old man with a round face standing beside a huge fish above the register. An elderly woman sat behind the counter polishing the silver barrel of a gun. "Gesundheit," she said. "What can I do for you?"

"I lost my job," Shirley said. If she wasn't a thief, she'd have been a terrific actress. "I need to sell some of the family silver." She took the picture frame gently from her purse.

The old woman reached out to inspect it. She got a troubled expression on her face, and then she sneezed. "Excuse me," she said, "but this looks terribly familiar."

Shirley felt more than a little nervous and had the brilliant idea that she better get out of there, but quick.

"Nice frame," the older woman said, suppressing another sneeze. "The kind of thing it's hard to forget." Suddenly, she pointed her gun straight at Shirley.

Shirley looked up at the picture on the wall, and recognized too late where she had seen the round-faced man. It was Mary Eliot's father.

This, then, must be her mother, the one who was allergic to cats. Shirley sneezed, and turned to run out the door. Just as she reached it, she heard the unmistakable click of a ready gun. "Turn around slowly and put your hands behind your back," the old woman said.

Shirley could hardly see, her eyes were watering so.

They exchanged dueling sneezes. "Yup," the old woman said. "Seems we have a lot in common. Allergic to cats and we have the same excellent taste in antiques. I liked that frame enough to give it to my daughter for her last birthday. You might have gotten away with it, if it hadn't been for this!" She coughed as she plucked a silver cat hair from the picture frame.

Shirley blushed beet-red.

"Caught you, you little housebreaker," the old lady said, and dialed 911.

A Harmless, Necessary Cat

NANCY JANE MOORE

THE AFTERNOON SUN POURING through the window made a spotlight on the bed. Sam lay in the dead center of the light, sprawled on his back, his large white stomach soaking up the rays.

Jean Bowers glared at him from the doorway. "There you are, you naughty boy," she said.

Sam opened one eye, looked at her, shifted his position slightly, and then closed it.

"Right in the middle of Anne Wilson's bed, and you know she doesn't like cats."

He yawned widely, rolled over so that his back faced the door, lifted a hind leg and began to lick it. Lazily.

Jean scooped him up. He mewed a protest in the soft, high-pitched tone that always surprised people, coming as it did from a seventeen-pound cat. "I hope she doesn't find out you were in here. She already disapproves of you being in the house. Anyway, you're late for your afternoon appointment with Miss Emily."

Once in Miss Emily's bedroom, Sam became businesslike. He jumped down from Jean's arms, strolled over to the bed, and leaped up on it, landing lightly so as not to jostle the frail woman lying there.

"Hello, Sam," she said, wiggling her fingers just a little to call him closer. He had already begun to purr loudly. He walked up to her fingers, sniffed them, pushed his head against them, and then moved in a little closer so she could rub his head without reaching.

While Sam and Miss Emily engaged in the mutually satisfying ritual of cat petting, Jean unlocked the cabinet in the corner of the room and took out two bottles and two disposable syringes. "How are you feeling this afternoon, Miss Emily?" she asked in her professional nurse's voice as she filled one of the syringes.

"Better than yesterday. I'm sure it's all due to this rascal," Emily Wilson said, scratching Sam's ears. "Look at him, so dignified in his black tuxedo and white spats." Sam nuzzled her hand, and Emily gave him her full attention as Jean stuck the needle into her arm. Her eyes closed briefly—marks up and down her withered arm showed how many injections she'd had in the last few months—but she didn't flinch, just held the cat close.

Jean disposed of the used needle in the biohazard container, and picked up the second one. "How's your pain level—if you're feeling better perhaps you want less morphine today."

"It'd be nice not to feel so doped up," the patient said. "Why not? I feel like living dangerously." She gave a little laugh.

"I'll give you a half dose," Jean said. "If things change, you be sure and buzz me, and I'll give you the rest."

"You just leave this boy here, and I'll be fine."

Jean left her patient in Sam's care, and went downstairs to fix herself a cup of tea. Incorporating "cat therapy" into her work as a home care nurse had been a stroke of genius, though she'd had to fight for it with the agency. Sure they'd read all the studies about how animals could help the quality of life for seriously ill persons, but for a live-in nurse to bring a cat with her! She'd had to find her first patients on her own, but their glowing references had made the difference.

Of course, it wasn't appropriate in all cases. There were always those odd people who really didn't like cats. But for others—and especially those dying from painful cancer like Emily Wilson—the cat was a source of comfort.

Anne Wilson came into the kitchen while Jean's tea was steeping. While she couldn't have been any older than Jean's own thirty-five years, she affected the manners of a much older woman. Probably it helped in her work—she had taken family leave from her managerial job at a large engineering firm to take care of her mother.

"Ms. Bowers," she said. "Your cat has been in my room again. I would appreciate it if you would make a better effort to control him."

"I'm very sorry," Jean said. "I guess I didn't close the door to my room tightly enough, and he got out. I'll try to be more careful."

"Please," said Anne Wilson in a tone that sounded more like an order than a polite request. "I am highly allergic."

Jean looked at her. The woman's eyes did look a little red. Perhaps she did suffer from cat allergies.

"Where is the animal now?"

"With your mother."

"Shouldn't you be there with them? My stepmother"—she emphasized the prefix—"is too weak to make him go away if he starts to bother her."

"I'm sure she'll be fine," Jean said, but the woman's eyes bored into her. She hurriedly tossed out the tea bag, though the tea was only about half-steeped, and went back up to the sickroom, where she found both patient and cat comfortably asleep.

Though Anne Wilson was annoyed by the cat's presence, Miss Emily's only other close relative was firmly in agreement that Sam was a valuable part of her care. Mark Gibson was Emily Wilson's nephew, and though he didn't live in the house, he came by daily, sometimes for several hours, despite his position at one of the city's major law firms. If Anne had come to stay with her dying step-mother out of a sense of duty, Mark made it clear that he spent time with her out of love. He handled her business affairs, and let everyone know he did it free of charge.

"She practically raised me," he told Jean one evening after supper. They were eating ice cream—Anne had left the table, muttering about the evils of dairy fat. "I'd never have been able to afford law school if Aunt Emily hadn't helped me out." He swallowed the last of his ice cream, and then put the bowl on the floor. "Here, kitty, kitty, kitty."

Jean looked up. Sure enough, Sam was in the room. He'd gotten her door open again—thank goodness Anne was gone. He walked over to the ice cream bowl, and started to lick before Jean realized what he was doing. "Mark, please, take that away from him."

"But I put it down for him," the man objected.

Jean had reached the bowl by that time, and picked it up herself. "It's not good for him," she said, apologetically. "The vet keeps lecturing me about mak-ing sure he loses a pound or two."

"You're not fat, are you boy?" Mark said, picking Sam up. "You're just a big guy, that's all." He set the cat on his lap, and Sam promptly jumped off. He sniffed around where the ice cream bowl had been, and finding it gone, gave Jean a dirty look and stalked out of the room.

"Sorry," Jean said. "Sometimes I think cats act like that line in one of Dorothy Parker's poems—'I loved them until they loved me.' "

Mark said, "There must be something I can do to make friends with him."

"Well," Jean said, "He does like catnip. And that won't put any weight on him."

"I'll try it. Maybe you can help me make Aunt Emily see reason, too."

"Why, what's the problem?"

"She insists on continuing to manage her financial affairs. And of course, with her money, they create quite a lot of work. I've tried to get her to sign a power of attorney, let me deal with her stock broker and so forth, but she won't do it. Insists I bring the papers over to her and let her make the decisions. I know it exhausts her."

"Some people have a lot of trouble letting go," Jean said. "But it might be helping her fight the cancer, knowing that she has responsibilities, decisions to make. She's doing better these last few days. I'm sure it's hard on you, being the go-between. . . ."

Mark interrupted. "No, no. I don't mind that. It gives me more time with her. I just hate tiring her out."

Jean found herself thinking about Mark a lot. A handsome man, with the dark hair and blue eyes that always caught her attention. And he flirted in that friendly way she'd always found appealing.

And that always ended up breaking her heart, she reminded herself firmly. Besides, he was younger than she—and all the young women in town chased after him anyway.

Several days later, after she and Sam had given Emily her bedtime medicine—she seemed to be doing fine on less morphine—Jean met Anne just outside the bathroom they shared.

"Ms. Bowers, I'm afraid I'm going to have to talk to the agency about your cat."

"But your mother is doing so much better since he came. She needs less morphine, gets more rest."

"It's all in her head. And I'm reduced to taking antihistamines just to get some sleep." She held a package of twelve-hour capsules in her hand. "I'll call them tomorrow."

Jean tossed and turned, trying to get to sleep. She didn't want to have to leave this post. It would look bad on her record, to be asked to leave because of Sam. And even though she'd get other jobs, she hated the thought of taking him away from Miss Emily. He'd brightened up her days, given her a little joy. Why her daughter—all right, stepdaughter—should be so unwilling to see that, she couldn't imagine. Surely she could get shots for her allergies for the short period of time Emily had left.

Sam didn't sleep well either. Every time Jean turned over, he'd get up and move. It seemed like hours before they both finally drifted off.

Jean woke suddenly. It seemed as if she'd only been asleep a few minutes, but the alarm clock read 3:07. A streak of light shone into her room—the door stood ajar, letting in light from the hall.

She heard a noise—loud scratching sounds and an even louder "meow." Sam must be trapped somewhere, probably the closet. She jumped up, opened the closet door. But it hadn't been completely shut, and no cat ran out.

Putting on her robe, she went out into the hall. The yells and scratches were coming from Emily's room. How had that cat gotten her door open, and Emily's, and then gotten shut in? It made no sense.

Jean opened the door to Emily's room, and Sam shot by her. She saw him race into her own room. *I'll just check on Miss Emily*, she thought, opening the door a little wider. She didn't want to wake the woman.

The room seemed quiet. Too quiet. Emily usually snored a little. In the dim light, Jean could see that her hand hung limply over the side of the bed.

Her professional manner took charge. She turned on the bedside light to get a better look. Emily's wig—she'd hated the hair loss from chemotherapy and insisted on sleeping in it—was completely askew. And her eyes stared at something with blank horror. Jean reached for her carotid artery, to check the pulse, and leaned forward. But she already knew Emily was dead. And not from the cancer.

Jean turned to the phone and dialed 911. As she explained to the dispatcher who she was and what had happened, Sam came cautiously around the door. He jumped up on the bed, and tried to nuzzle Emily's hand. "Mew," he said. His tone sounded sad to Jean.

The police had arrived by the time she'd been able to wake Anne up. And it had taken her a while to locate Mark. She'd only gotten the answering machine when she called his home, so she'd tried his cell phone. From the sounds she heard when he answered, he was partying somewhere.

Now they were all downstairs, waiting for the medical examiner to finish his preliminary exam. Anne was sitting in a corner chair, sniffling. Jean wondered if it was allergies or grief. Mark was pacing around the room. The glass of bourbon in his hand sloshed dangerously as he paced.

Two police officers waited with them. The one in charge—a balding man in his late forties—was drinking a cup of tea. The other, a young woman, leaned against a wall. The forensic team had already left.

The medical examiner came in, carrying something in a large plastic bag. The detective in charge looked at him expectantly. "Suffocated," the examiner said. "I found a lot of cat hair around her face, and. . . ."

"I knew it," Anne said loudly. "That damned cat, sleeping on her face."

"He wouldn't do that," Jean said, shocked.

"That terrible animal," Anne said, but the medical examiner cut her off.

"It wasn't the cat, ma'am. Though it looks like someone tried to hold him over her face—I found some cat hair in his mouth. I'll know more after the lab work, but it looks like the cat struggled to get away. Something ripped a hole in a pillow case; I found a piece of cat claw in it."

He held up the bag. "Whoever killed her used this pillow." He looked around the room.

The chief detective cleared his throat. "So, Ms. Wilson, you said that only you and Ms. Bowers were sleeping in the house tonight."

Anne nodded. She seemed unable to speak.

Jean said, "Mrs. Wilson didn't care for live-in servants. Someone came in daily, to clean and do some cooking."

"Did any of the help have keys to the house?"

Anne shook her head.

"Did anyone else who wasn't here have one?"

Jean felt rather surprised that Mark didn't speak up. She said, "Mr. Gibson has one, of course. No one else that I know of."

"I've been at a party all night," Mark said hastily. "And I must point out that while my aunt thought very highly of Jean,"—he nodded toward her—"she did come here from an agency and we don't really know anything about her. You hear these terrible stories, nurses killing their patients."

Jean was so taken aback by this accusation that she could think of nothing to say.

The medical examiner cleared his throat. "A nurse wouldn't need a pillow," he said. "Had she wanted to kill Mrs. Wilson, she could easily have used the morphine prescribed for her pain. Much harder to detect."

The chief detective said, "We'll check out everyone's bona fides. But unlike you and Ms. Wilson, Ms. Bowers didn't stand to inherit a lot of money when Mrs. Wilson died."

Both Mark and Anne stared at him.

"She was dying anyway," Mark said. "Even if either of us could be so cold-blooded. . . ." He let his voice trail off.

"I loved her," Anne said. "Kill her for money? I loved her." She broke down totally, sobbing. "She helped me so much. Showed me what a strong-willed woman could do in this world." She made great gulping noises. "It hurt me so, to see her in such pain. I couldn't stand it."

The woman detective handed her a tissue. Anne blew her nose loudly, and repeated, "I couldn't stand it."

Jean saw the detective raise her eyebrows at the one in charge. He nodded. Like her they were probably thinking mercy killing. But mercy for whom? Miss Emily hadn't seemed ready to die to her.

And then the medical examiner said, "What's that cat doing?"

Sam, who had been nuzzling Mark's leg for some time, was lying on his back, rolling around, and purring loudly.

Jean said, "He must have found some catnip—that's how he responds. Mark, did you get him some?"

Mark said, "No," loudly. A little too loudly. Sam grabbed around Mark's leg with both forepaws, and nuzzled the sharply-creased cuff on his pants. Mark tried to shake him lose, and something fell from the cuff. Sam pounced on it, and Jean pounced on him. A couple of leaves lay on the floor.

Sam meowed in protest. The medical examiner bent and picked it up. "Is this catnip?" he asked Jean.

She nodded. "Fresh-picked."

"I found leaves just like it on Mrs. Wilson's bed," he said.

"I don't have any, but I did tell Mark he could use it to make friends with Sam."

Everyone in the room turned and looked at Mark. He said, "You don't think I did anything? Why that's preposterous. I would never harm Aunt Emily."

"How'd you get that scratch on your hand?" the woman detective asked.

"I don't know—I did some drinking tonight. Could have happened any-time."

"Looks like a cat scratch to me," said the medical examiner. He started walking toward Mark. Mark moved away, but the examiner turned instead to the cat in Jean's arms. "Let's see if there's anything on your claws, pussycat."

And Mark ran for the front door. He moved fast, but the chief detective moved faster. "I think you'd better come downtown with us, Mr. Gibson."

Jean had expected to have to return for the trial, but once they'd run all the DNA tests, Mark decided to plead guilty. She got a brief letter from the detective:

> Unfortunately, the motive was the most obvious one: money. Gibson had embezzled some money from a client, and was close to getting caught. The loan sharks had told him they wouldn't lend him any against his expectations from his aunt until she died. He was in too deep to wait a few months. The enclosed is for Sam. He made this one easy for us.

The enclosed turned out to be a small version of a detective's gold shield, attached to a cat collar. Sam protested a bit when Jean put the collar on, but when she walked him over to the mirror to admire it, he batted at the reflection of the shield. And purred.

Heidi's Bird Wings

JENNIFER EVANS

YOU HAVE TO FEEL SORRY for talls. For their size they're ex-tremely slow and clumsy, and their almost complete lack of fur breaks my heart if I think about it. Their faces are somewhat expressive, if you learn how to read them, but that can never make up for the lack of a tail. The hands, I'll have to admit, are almost as useful as claws. Talls are very strong and un-doubtedly could kill a cat, yet in general they recognize our superiority, support us and feed us the best food, and never try to mark over our territory marks.

You must pity talls the most, however, for their smell-blindness. I guess that's what happens when your nose is so far from the ground. Still, they're always up to something, making strange sounds, messing around with their endless objects, coming and going, oh, and their wonderful ratlike feet are forever available to stalk and pounce. Fascinating creatures, talls.

The back door was splintered and left ajar, and through it I slipped into the house and wandered into the kitchen.

"Who's this?" said the new male tall sitting at the table.

"That's the neighbor's cat," said the new female.

Well, it's true, I am the neighbor's cat, but I'm so much more than that—Leaping Feline, Warrior with Claws, Thunder Galloping Frenzy. But I'm also the neighbor's cat, and in this delicious-smelling kitchen, I accepted the lesser title meekly.

"Black cats are bad luck," said the female.

"You can't blame what happened on him," said the male. "And besides, he's not totally black. He's got on a tuxedo."

The new neighbor talls intrigued me. The smells in their house enchanted me already: a fishy broth bubbling on the stove, an extremely rank trash can, and not a whiff of dog anymore. Oh joy, I was glad they'd come here, replacing that foul Heidi Busby with her stinks of ammonia, air freshener, cigarettes, and perfume. These might be the perfect tall hosts, if only they'd share some of their bounty.

I like talls, I really do. Of course, you have to be particular about with whom you associate. The teenage males are the worst, and the short talls are troublesome, too, but the rest generally are quite acceptable.

My new ones seemed upset. It was difficult to imagine how they could be upset with so much food available and no one trying to steal it—well, except me, but I'm deserving. I hoped it didn't mean they were leaving the neighborhood already.

The female's feet smelled of talcum powder right now, and the male had stepped in something pleasantly dreadful. They were a real improvement. After Heidi disappeared a long time ago, a series of strangers had visited Heidi's house. And now these two had taken over. The urge to own these people overpowered me, and I rubbed my cheek against his ankle, then hers, so they'd have my mark.

The male bent down and scratched me behind the ear, and the female shoved me away with her heel. I continued to sniff the floor in her vicinity. In my experience, the females bustle to and fro in the kitchen—exactly like this one was doing now—and frequently drop things like a wet noodle, a fleck of onion, even a bit of bacon. When I heard the tall words *big dog*, I stopped sniffing and started listening.

"—a guard dog, Hal, that's what we need," said the female. "A big, mean rottweiler or something."

It is inconceivable that God is a cat, because look at the evidence. Dogs. Dogs are a menace, an insane menace, because of their perverted view that cats are prey. The female was not upset—she was deranged out of her mind. Perhaps the male would bring her to her senses.

"I'm not a dog person, Melanie," said Hal. "A cat would be fine."

Well said, I thought.

"A cat won't protect us from thugs breaking in here," said Melanie. "We never should have bought a drug dealer's house."

"It was a great price, and it was only a drug dealer's *girlfriend's* house."

"Oh right. Then why is she in jail, too?"

"Okay, Heidi's an arch-criminal, a kingpin. A queenpin. How about a security system instead of a rottweiler? Won't pee on your rug."

"I'd rather have a dog. What were they looking for when they broke in? Do you think there are still drugs here?"

"I don't think so," said Hal. "The realtor said the police brought drug-sniffing dogs in here right after the arrests."

Ugh, I thought, remembering.

"Heidi Busby is in jail, Mel. Nothing of ours was stolen or even messed up. The burglars were probably a couple of morons who thought Heidi might have left some goodies behind."

Last night while Melanie and Hal were gone, I'd heard two unfamiliar talls make funny noises at the back of their house and saw them disappear inside. I hadn't thought anything about it, but now I was outraged at the invasion. Outsider talls ought to leave my Melanie and my Hal alone.

"But the realtor said the break-ins would stop after we moved in."

"What can I say? She was wrong. We've only been here three days, Mel, and we've got equity in this place."

"And we've got fourteen dollars in the bank."

"It was a great deal for a great house in a great neighborhood. I love this house. Don't you love this house?"

"Yeah." Glum.

"I'll fix the back door this afternoon," said Hal, "and first thing Monday I'll call about security systems, and then there won't be any more break-ins, okay?"

They went into a long discussion about having no money to pay for a security system. Dull. Boring. Meaningless. I always seem indifferent to what talls say, but this time I really was.

I understood how they felt about defending their territory. My own territory was constantly being invaded by little snips of squirrels and poorly socialized cats from the other block. It's peculiar how talls defend their houses so well, with locks, doors, and security systems, and yet leave the most valuable territory they own, their yards, completely open to invasion by anyone. I guess they don't mind squirrels and sneaky orange toms as much as I do.

I decided to spray every inch of their back door, to lend my weight to theirs.

"Mowr." I said good-bye, meandered out the broken door, and got it done.

That afternoon, loud hammer bangs issued from the back of Mel and Hal's house, and I stayed away. Loud, violent noises shatter my nerves.

The next day was quiet, and I returned to visit several times, but found Melanie and Hal's back door shut, without the slightest crack. While I touched up my spray job, I mentioned out loud a few times that I wouldn't mind being let in, but neither Mel nor Hal came to greet me. Ah, well. They snubbed me, I snubbed them.

In the middle of the next day, Monday, more outsiders arrived. I crept close under a leafy shrub to witness the fight, but instead Hal greeted the two outsiders cordially. Hal and these two went out to the strangers' van and made tall-talk about security systems for a long time, and then the outsiders began trooping back and forth, in and out of the back door. I easily slipped inside with a tall who had his hands full of tall objects. Nobody noticed me, and I kept it that way.

It was high time to inspect the rest of my new house. I usually own two or three houses, depending on which talls are most pleasing to me at the time. I never considered this one truly my own when Heidi Busby occupied it because it stank, but now the smells were rather wonderful and the people were nice. Heidi was generous, though hanging around her was never entirely safe. She smoked and hurried around in hard shoes and stepped on my tender paws several times.

All Heidi's things were gone, and a completely new assortment of tall-objects filled the rooms beyond the kitchen. I passed through the rooms, exploring. The subtly different scents were a delight for a connoisseur—a jar of grease in the bathroom, a closetful of stinking leather shoes, a whiff of dead sea-life inside a shell on the dresser. There were other smells, too, but these were my favorites. Mel and Hal possessed a great many more cardboard boxes than Heidi, half of them empty, and I lurked silently among the boxes, honing my ambushing skills. One of the hiding places inside a cardboard box seemed perfect for a nap. Although you're not supposed to sleep while waiting in ambush, I curled up and dozed off.

When I woke, the house was dead still, Hal and the outsider talls gone, and the back door firmly shut. Learning that I had the place to myself, I did what I'd wanted to do for days. I leaped on Mel and Hal's kitchen counter, walked over to the range top, and sniffed and licked up every delicious spot of fresh grease I found. I leaped to the other counter and tasted the dirty dishes in the sink that appealed to me. When I leaped to the third counter to explore it, I misjudged, lost my footing, and skidded into a white and blue sugar bowl, knocking it off the counter and spraying sugar over the center of the kitchen floor.

The crash triggered my daily frenzy. I dashed off the counter and scrambled in full berserker mode through the dining and living rooms, looking for prey. I scrabbled into the bathroom and lunged at the toilet-paper dispenser. I sank my claws around the neck of the toilet-paper roll and yanked to rip out its entrails. I clawed the fluttering white thing out of its lair again and again. It was no match for me. In moments it wrapped itself around me, but I escaped. We fought in the hall, we fought in the bedroom. I killed it, and killed it without mercy.

Toilet paper is a tantalizing prey yet easy to defeat. Too easy. Unsatisfied, I prowled through the bedroom searching for a more substantial enemy.

Prey, prey, where is prey? I pounced on a coat hanger lying on the floor and overturned the empty trashcan. I was shredding its contents, leaping and wriggling in mid-air to add artistic flair, when some insolent prey thumped me lightly on the rump. I whirled, ears flattened, lips curled, and attacked.

The enemy was a drape, a heavy formidable drape with nubs and lumps irresistible to the claw. I slithered onto my belly and fought the hem of the drape with every ounce of strength in my hindclaws, foreclaws, and teeth. The drape swung and slammed me into the wall. I positioned myself between it and its wall and fought on. It swarmed me from this side and that, and I dug and bit and lashed. The guts of the drape tore open and a rectangular lump spilled out.

Though the lump was an inert prey, I attacked and eviscerated it, too, and it fell apart into wonderful papers that, as I scattered them, reminded me of the wings of birds.

When the frenzy left me, I lay among the scattered papers and imagined that I had killed an entire flock of birds. I'd probably never care to accomplish such a feat, but it was a pleasant dream anyway. As always after a roister, I began to wash my nose. From chaos to order.

As I finished my tail, I heard arrival noises outside, then angry-tall exclamations in the kitchen. Talls often grew angry over the aftermath of an innocent accident or a fine battle, I remembered. I cringed and ran under the bed. They were going to make loud unpleasant noises, I just knew it, and maybe even smack me. I racked my brains, trying to remember a way to escape from the house.

Melanie's shriek came from the hall outside the bathroom. "Look at that! More vandalism! What are they trying to do to us?"

She'd found the dead and defeated toilet paper. The yowl in her voice made me creep far back in the darkness under the bed.

"I—I thought I locked everything. I thought I turned on the system," Hal said. "It was locked. And it was armed. How did the bastards get in?"

His roar and her yowl made me realize that these talls were never going to share food with me, that they were going to grab me by the scruff of my neck and throw me out, if not eviscerate me first. That's what I'd do if I were as mad as these talls sounded. I hunched against the wall and quivered, hoping they wouldn't find me.

In the small part of the doorway that I could see from under the bed, Hal and Mel's feet appeared and froze.

"My God," Melanie said faintly. "It's money." Her tone was completely different, and I began to relax.

"Heidi's money," said Hal.

"Those are hundreds."

"Where did it come from?"

"Look. The drapes are torn. The money was hidden in the drapes."

"If they found it, why did they leave it?" Melanie whispered. "Are they still here?"

Boldly I sauntered out from under the bed and picked my way across the papers, hoping to make it past them and out the kitchen door before their mood changed again.

"The *cat*," said Mel.

"The *cat*," said Hal. They stared at me. I looked up at them, but that's no good for long. It hurts your neck. Besides, I had territory to mark. I gave them each a quick brush, a flirt of the tail, just to show our friendship was intact, and galloped off to the kitchen, and what luck—out the back door.

Later I learned that Mel and Hal had found nine packages of bird wings—I mean money—in the drapes I'd clawed open. They decided to give the money to the police as a way to permanently stop the outsiders from coming around and invading their territory. But Mel and Hal also got some money as a reward, which made them very cheerful, and they've been exceptionally generous at sharing their best food with me every time I visit. They never let me fight their new money, however, or even see it.

I spray the front curb morning and night because furtive outsiders sometimes drive by in cars at odd times. They slow down and stare at my house as though trying to see the occupants, then obviously smell my warning and drive away.

Mel and Hal aren't perfect. They acquired one of those small talls, which grows ever more obnoxious. Even so, their territory is my territory, and I'll help them defend it any day.

Here Today, Dead to Maui

CATHERINE DAIN

AMILLIONAIRE FOUND ME changing planes for Maui! Why is he short and ugly, Lord, when you know I like them tall?" Michael sang as he emerged from the bathroom wearing the hibiscus print shirt he had bought the day before.

"That's gross," Faith said. "Materialistic. Midlife Mick Jagger. And nobody came near you on the airplane. Or in the Hilo airport. Except for the fat woman who put the orchids around your neck."

"Because I was traveling with you and Elizabeth. Everyone was looking at her. If I'd been alone, who knows? Besides, if you're so ascetically inclined, why did you accept the offer of a first-class airplane ticket and a week in a suite at the Lahaina Hilton?" Michael leaned against the central post marking the open french doors to the deck and stretched out his arms. "White sand! Ocean! Clean air!"

"Elizabeth's contract specified two tickets. No point in letting one go to waste when you didn't have anybody else to ask." Faith poured herself a second cup of coffee. She didn't particularly like the Kona blend, but it was all room service had to offer.

"Can't you just enjoy the vacation?" Michael turned back and sighed.

"Elizabeth has one more day of shooting. You're not on vacation until tomorrow."

"To Maui, and to Maui, and to Maui. Life creeps in its petty pace, especially when one is not quite on vacation." He knelt down in front of one of the flowered chintz armchairs so that he was level with Elizabeth. "Say *Maui*."

"Mrowr," she replied, blue eyes focusing intently on his dark ones.

"Maui."

"Mrowr."

"See how smart she is?"

"You didn't feed her this morning. She's actually saying she's annoyed."

Michael straightened up. "When did you become an expert on my cat?"

"I've been part of her environment since you adopted her. She thinks of me as extended family. I felt obliged to return the compliment by paying attention to her behavior. Since I've spent my life—or two careers anyway, the dead one as an actress and the live one as a therapist—studying human behavior, and the cat thinks she's human, it wasn't hard. Trust me. She's hungry."

"So am I." He picked a cheese danish out of the basket on the coffee table. "But she's supposed to be hungry. Otherwise, she might not eat on cue."

"You'd better hurry with that. Elizabeth's call is in half an hour. Eddie will be here any minute with the car."

"They have to set up a shot on the deck of an old whaler. No way are they going to be ready on time." Michael poured himself a cup of coffee and settled in the other chintz armchair.

"Then I think you ought to feed her."

"She only has to be hungry and annoyed for the next couple of hours. She'll be fine."

Faith shrugged. "Suit yourself. But if we're going to be here for a while, could you move to another chair? That one clashes with your shirt."

"All the furniture clashes with my shirt. This is Hawaii—the shirt is supposed to clash. Buy a muumuu and get in the spirit."

"Hawaiian clothes are the best thing that could have happened to the tourist industry. You can't tell you've gained fifteen pounds until you're home and it's too late. If I start to gain, I'll think about the muumuu."

"How can anyone gain on a diet of fish, rice, and fruit? If you're really going to stick to that. Get a muumuu or not. Put orchids in your hair. Drink mai-tais by the pool."

"Maybe when we've finished the shoot." Faith picked a blueberry muffin out of the basket. Blueberries counted as fruit. "I may even search for romance."

"You won't have to search far. Eddie Inouye has made it clear he's available."

"Yes, and he doesn't care who takes him up on the offer. No thanks."

"Well, one of us has to be nice to him if we want him to drive us to the sacred pools of Hana tomorrow. The road through the rain forest is supposed to be challenging, and I don't want Elizabeth's life at risk."

"I'll drive," Faith said. "You can hold Elizabeth and look at the scenery."

"I'll have to think about that," Michael replied. He finished his danish and started on a pecan bun.

"Eddie," they chorused as the phone rang.

Michael stuffed the bun into his mouth and scooped Elizabeth into her carrier. Faith assured Eddie they would be right down.

The elevator took them to the lobby, where Eddie—a short, eager twenty-year-old wearing a shirt that clashed with everything—was waiting.

"*Aloha*," he said, grinning. "Phil said to tell you they're on time. We have to hurry."

"That has to be a lie. Can I go back for the basket of pastries?" Michael asked.

"I told you we should have fed her," Faith snapped.

"No, no," Eddie said. "He means it. Phil promised he'll have her finished before lunch. Okay?"

"Three hours," Michael said to Faith. "We can handle that."

"Elizabeth is on L.A. time, remember. I've never known you to be this callous."

"Oh, for God's sake, Faith. One morning. For two days' deprivation every six months, she gets to eat shrimp, salmon, and chicken the rest of the year!" Michael turned hastily to Eddie. "Only for snacks, of course. Three meals a day she eats Pretty Kitty cat food."

"Don't worry, Eddie isn't going to turn you in," Faith said. "Are you?"

"No way, *wahine*," Eddie answered, still grinning. "Driving is my main livelihood. If I talk, nobody wants to ride with me anymore."

Faith nodded. "Let's go."

Eddie had parked his Honda right in front of the hotel, in the taxi loading zone. Two taxi drivers glared as Faith and Michael got into the back seat.

Eddie whisked the car away from the cluster of tall white hotels, over the causeway, and down the narrow road the short distance to the Lahaina harbor. The day was so beautiful that Faith almost began to enjoy herself.

"What's it like living here?" Michael asked.

"Like this," Eddie answered. "Like every morning when I wake up, it's the first day of vacation."

"It must rain," Faith said. "There's a rain forest on the island."

"Yeah, but it only rains for five minutes at a time. Most of the time. Except for hurricanes, and this isn't the season."

"Stop it, Faith," Michael snapped. "No disasters. I am not anticipating a disaster on Maui."

Faith glared back.

"This is as close as I can get," Eddie said cheerfully. He had maneuvered through the jaywalking tourists to the pier, but there was no place to pull over. Two large silver trucks were taking up three parking spaces apiece. Several horns began to beep the second the Honda's brake lights went on. "I'll find a place to park and meet you on the set. Just yell if you want to make a quick getaway."

"Thanks," Michael said. "I was optimistic enough to schedule a tennis lesson for three and a massage for four."

"No problem." Eddie grinned at him.

The beeps became steady as Faith got out and took Elizabeth's carrier so that Michael could join her. They slipped between the trucks to the wooden walkway.

The whalers were smaller and newer than Faith had expected, but then her idea of a whaler was based on John Huston's *Moby Dick*. She suspected that these had been used since the nineteenth century.

"I don't understand why they're shooting a cat food commercial on a whaler," Faith said.

"Cats love fish," Michael explained, in a tone that let her know any idiot could figure it out. "Pretty Kitty is for cats with a whale of an appetite."

"Yes, but whalers kill whales. When this commercial airs, they're going to lose all the New Agers and Trekkers and Greens who own cats. Maybe half the cat owners in the country." Faith picked her way carefully over heavy cables that snaked from the trucks to a ship halfway down the pier.

"Maybe half the cat owners in L.A., tops. Besides, it's a tax deductible week in Maui for anyone from Pretty Kitty, the ad agency, or the production company who wants to visit the shoot. Although the L.A. ad business is so bad I don't think anyone from the agency came." Michael waved at the deck. "*Aloha*, we're here."

"Oh, good." A young woman in tank top and jeans leaned over the railing. Two days in Maui had given her Southern California tan a bronze glow and turned the peroxide streaks in her stringy brown hair almost white. She waved a clipboard at them. "Phil is setting up for the shot of Elizabeth now. He's lighting her stand-in."

Michael had one foot on the wooden ladder. He stopped so suddenly that Faith hit him with the carrier.

"What stand-in?" he asked.

The woman held a finger to her lips, then beckoned him aboard.

"What stand-in?" Michael asked again, after reaching the deck in two bounds.

Faith clambered up after him, bracing the carrier awkwardly on each rung.

"Mrowr," Elizabeth said.

"Sorry," Faith murmured to the carrier.

"Faith, Jennifer," Michael said as he belatedly reached for the handle.

"Hi, Faith. Hi, Sweetums," Jennifer added to the carrier.

"Mrowr."

Faith nodded assent.

"Where's Eddie?" Jennifer asked.

"Parking the car. What stand-in?" Michael's voice shot up an octave, and Jennifer shushed him again.

"One of the Pretty Kitty executives is here with his wife, daughter, and cat," she whispered. "The daughter really wants to see her cat in a commercial. I hope Elizabeth is in fine form."

"Of course she is! What an outrage!" Michael snapped.

"Okay, okay," Jennifer said, holding up her hand. "I'm just telling you what's going on."

"We have a contract!" Michael lowered his voice.

"I know. But Pretty Kitty hired the ad agency, and the ad agency hired the production company."

"What does that mean?"

"It means that everyone is being very, very nice. Especially Phil. This is his first network job, you know. I think he'd do anything to get more."

"All right." Michael sighed and turned to Faith. "You see why I didn't feed her. One lousy shot and I'd have to get a job."

"Jennifer! Let's go!" a male voice called.

Faith, Michael, and Elizabeth followed Jennifer aft, stepping between cables when possible.

Cameras, lights, and reflectors were all focused on a very fluffy cat the color of an underripe cantaloupe, wearing a cubic zirconium collar. Her amber eyes darted nervously around the crowd. A red-haired, freckled girl about ten years old was sitting cross-legged beside her, smiling at anyone who would smile back.

"That's Marlene," Jennifer whispered to Michael, drawing the name out to three syllables. "As in Dietrich. The girl's name is Boots. Good luck."

She took her clipboard over to the camera.

Michael shook his head, gaze still fastened on Marlene. "She's pretty, but she's not an actress. We're fine." He looked around, spotting a youth with a three-day growth of beard, whose knees were sticking out of his Levi's. The young man was wearing the only Hawaiian shirt that might have come out of a suitcase, not a store. "Phil! I hope we're not late. I didn't realize we were shooting on MTV video time."

"Hey, Michael, how ya doing?" Phil trotted the four steps that separated them and clapped Michael on the back. "Glad to see the star has arrived." He cupped his hands around his mouth. "Okay! Get ready for a take." Then he knelt down beside the girl. "Boots, honey, I'm really grateful for your help. And I'm going to remember what a beautiful cat Marlene is, next time we're casting."

Boots looked at him adoringly. She carefully picked up Marlene, then winced when the nervous cat sank bare claws into her naked shoulders.

Michael lifted Elizabeth from the carrier and placed her down on the crossed pieces of silver tape marking the spot Marlene had vacated. Elizabeth stretched, surveyed the assembled group, winked one blue eye at the cameraman, and settled onto her haunches, pearly tail falling naturally into place.

"Here." Someone thrust a crystal dish heaped with Pretty Kitty into Michael's hand. He put it down on another taped mark to Elizabeth's right.

"Roll the tape!" Phil called.

"Rolling!"

"Slate the camera!"

"Slated. Take one."

"Action!"

"Discover the food," Michael whispered.

Elizabeth turned toward the dish. Her eyes widened dramatically. She approached the dish and sniffed, then looked back toward Michael.

"That's right, baby, time to eat," he whispered.

Elizabeth sniffed again. She shook her head. Straightening up, she made a graceful pirouette and overturned the dish with one kick from her left hind leg.

"Cut!" Phil called.

"Oh my God," Michael moaned.

Faith tugged his arm. "There's something wrong with the food."

"What?"

"Something wrong, damn it, *think*."

"There's something wrong with the food!" Michael yelled.

"What do you mean, son?"

Michael discovered he was standing next to a tall, florid man still decorated with a fading airport lei. Red hair and freckles marked him as Boots's father, even if he wasn't old enough to be Michael's. He was glaring down menacingly.

"I mean sabotage!" Michael gasped. "It can't be Pretty Kitty!"

"Come on, Michael." Phil clapped him on the shoulder again. Michael was starting to feel hemmed in. "We'll try another take. If it'll make you happy, we'll even open a new can."

"Where's Elizabeth?" Faith had squeezed between the men to the overturned dish. Elizabeth was nowhere in sight.

"Elizabeth!" Michael dropped to his knees, to search for her at her own level.

"Hey, guys, anybody seen the cat?" Phil asked.

The murmurs from the crew were all negative.

"Could she have jumped overboard?" The question came from a short, dark-haired woman in a muumuu draped with a fading lei that matched the one Boots's father was wearing.

"Absolutely not!" Michael snapped. Still, he crawled to the edge of the deck and checked the ocean. The gentle blue waves were unbroken. "Elizabeth!"

His stomach churned and he began gasping for breath.

"All right! That's enough!" Faith was standing on Elizabeth's mark. The lights had been turned off, but the reflectors focused enough sunlight to create a glow around her shins. Her arms were upraised, palms out, like an evangelist. Everyone quieted down and stared. She was glad she hadn't worn a muumuu. The way the long sleeves of her white overblouse fell back past her elbows made a more dramatic effect. "I have to ask one question. You!" Her right hand swooped down, index finger pointing to Boots's father. "Are you driving a rental car?"

"Why, yes." His face became even more florid.

"Thank you." Both palms out again, Faith looked at each silent face in front of her. "I know who took Elizabeth. And I know who sprayed the ant poison on the Pretty Kitty." She waited for the gasps to subside. "We will all turn toward the railing, eyes shut, while I count to thirty. During that time, I expect Elizabeth to reappear on her mark. Otherwise, the person responsible will be looking at both civil and criminal charges. Which will not be good for that person's livelihood. Now! Toward the railing. One! Two!"

Faith had reached twenty-seven by the time she heard the soft *Mrowr* and felt Elizabeth rub against her leg.

"Elizabeth!" Michael cried.

"Thank you all," Faith said, bowing, as the crew applauded.

"Let's get ready for the next take!" Phil shouted. "New can of cat food! Clean up the mess from the old one!"

"I'd like to fix the dish," Faith said.

"Down the stairs to the galley." Phil pointed toward the low cabin.

Michael hugged Elizabeth. He even sobbed a little into her fur, which she didn't like at all.

Faith returned a moment later with the crystal dish, piled high. She set it down on the mark.

Michael released Elizabeth in the general area of the other mark. The cat swiftly groomed the spot where Michael's tears had dampened her fur and then settled precisely in the center of the taped cross, tail flaring gracefully.

"Roll the tape!" Phil called. "Let's do it again!"

Take two went without a hitch. Elizabeth approached the food daintily, then attacked it with gusto.

When she was finished, she sat back and cleaned her face, first with her tongue, then with her paw. The camera captured her entire performance.

"Perfect!" Phil said. "Now the high five."

Michael prepared for the signature shot that gave Elizabeth her value. He would kneel, with his right arm raised, and snap his fingers. Elizabeth would leap up and slap his palm with her right paw.

This, too, she did perfectly.

"That's a wrap for the cat," Phil said. "Thanks, Michael. Good job."

"You're welcome." Michael had Elizabeth in his arms as soon as he heard the word *wrap*.

Faith retrieved the carrier from the top of the low cabin, where she had placed it for safekeeping.

"The car's about two blocks away. You want me to get it?" Eddie Inouye materialized next to her.

"I think we can walk back to the hotel," she said. "We want to see a little of Lahaina, and we can do that this afternoon. But tomorrow morning at ten we'd like to leave for some sightseeing, especially the sacred pools of Hana. Do you think you could pick us up then?"

"I'll be there." Eddie grinned at her and took off again.

Michael snapped the carrier shut. Jennifer grabbed his arm before he could pick it up.

"I'm so glad Elizabeth is all right," she said. "Really."

Faith had already started down the ladder by the time Michael caught up. He handed her the carrier, then followed her down.

"All right," he said as they picked their way between cables toward the street. "Which of them was it? Eddie or Jennifer?"

"Both. Eddie sprayed the ant poison, Jennifer grabbed the cat."

"How did you figure it out?"

"Well, I guessed a lot of it. I knew when Eddie said he wouldn't give you away on the cat food that someone else had been talking in his car. It wasn't Marlene's family, because they had a rental. Most members of the crew rode in the trucks with the equipment." She paused until they passed the trucks in question. "And Jennifer pointedly told us that Phil wanted this job to lead to more—not realizing that the best outcome for Phil would be a great commercial, which he wouldn't get if he cast a bad actress in the lead, just to do a favor for the big boss. Favors get more work only at Jennifer's level. Not only that, but from the look on her face when she asked where Eddie was, it occurred to me that he might be a little less available than he was yesterday."

"She enlisted him in the plot?"

"Such as it was. Mostly improvised, I think." They were back on the narrow sidewalk. Faith surveyed the small shops across the street, with their window displays of muumuus. "How about lunch?"

"Tell me the rest first."

"Eddie didn't think we'd suspect ant poison, after you told him that Elizabeth doesn't normally eat Pretty Kitty. He thought you'd suspect simple cat perversity."

Michael raised his eyebrows innocently.

"Mrowr," Elizabeth said.

"I know, dear," Faith said to the carrier. "You're a professional. That's the point."

"But when sabotaging the food didn't work, someone had to grab her, someone who knew her, hence Jennifer."

"Good work," Faith said drily, patting Michael's shoulder.

"How did you know it was ant poison?"

"I didn't. I just thought ants are a problem in tropical climates, so wherever there was food, there had to be ant poison. I checked the galley when I refilled the dish, and I was right."

"I'm awfully glad you're here," Michael said. "I may not always tell you that, but I am grateful for your friendship. I'll buy lunch."

"Here today, dead to Maui," Faith said. "Lunch will do for a start. And did you say you had an appointment for a massage this afternoon?"

"It's yours." Michael sighed.

"Take Elizabeth, run on ahead, and order salmon for three from room service. I'll be there as soon as I've made a quick purchase. Vacation starts now."

"Maui." The word came clearly from the carrier.

"Indeed."

How Things Get Done in the French Quarter

JOHN SULLIVAN

LUCKY'S HUNGER DREW HIM ONWARD, despite the strange smells, the crowds, and the noise. He leapt silently onto the table and hugged the wall behind the boxes. Lucky was jet black and the light in the passageway was dim. The man on the stool hadn't seen him. Lucky licked his chops as the man shoveled a forkful of fish into his mouth. If he could just get a little closer, if the man would set the plate down on the corner of the table again, then he could make a dash for it.

Suddenly there was a warning hiss that froze Lucky in his tracks. An enormous dapple-gray tomcat looked at him from the long wooden bench on the other side of the passage. He had a torn ear and fierce eyes that seemed to pin Lucky to the spot.

"Don't even think about it, kid," said the tom.

"I didn't . . . I didn't mean—"

"I know what you meant. I see your kind all the time, fresh off a barge from somewhere, lost and hungry. Well, you're not in Podunk, Missouri, anymore, kid. This is New Orleans. We got rules here. One of them covers stealing somebody's dinner, but we'll get to that. Get over here."

Lucky edged his way back around the boxes and jumped down to the ground. He thought of making a break for the street, but the tom looked like he could run too. Lucky walked across the hall and stood at the foot of the bench.

"You got a name, kid?"

"There was a girl back home that used to feed me until she moved away. She called me Lucky."

"Pfff. Should have called you Scrawny. I'm Toby. I run the joint. Come with me."

Toby turned with a swirl of his tail and walked down the long bench. The hallway looked like it had been a narrow alley before it was roofed over. It ran from the street to an open courtyard full of laughter and music. A man and woman came in off the street, gave the man with the fish some money, and headed inside.

Halfway down the bench, Toby stopped to let the woman lean over and scratch behind his ears. Lucky hoped she might pet him too, but the couple went on into the courtyard, and Toby strolled down the bench to the end of the hall.

Lucky followed and peered around the corner. Trees dotted the courtyard, and a six-piece band played jazz on a stage at the center. People gathered around the stage to dance or sat at small tables among the trees to listen.

Toby stepped onto a green leather cushion at the end of the bench, turned around twice, and lay down with his chin on his paws.

"This is mine," he said. "Don't let me catch you laying on it. Good view of the courtyard here. I like to keep an eye on things. That's rule one, keep your eyes open. You were so busy watching Joe Joe's fish you didn't even know I was there, did you?"

"No," Lucky admitted. It was still hard to pay attention to Toby with the smell of the fish wafting down the hallway.

"We're half a block off Bourbon Street. Keep your eyes open and sooner or later you'll see everything."

Toby glared down from the cushion. "I've seen voodoo priestesses make the dead get up and dance. I've seen things'll puff up the hair on your tail. Make you arch your back and walk all sideways."

Lucky tried to look brave. "I don't scare easy."

"Yeah? Why's your tail swishing then? Don't get cocky kid. I'm doing you a favor here, so just pay attention."

A cluster of men and women came out of the courtyard, laughing and talking. This time a woman noticed Lucky at the foot of the bench. She bent down and rubbed the top of his head. He purred softly and pressed his head up against her hand.

"What a nice cat you are," she said. "Yes you are." She ruffled his fur once more and then was gone.

A saxophone solo drifted through the warm night air. Lucky's eyes were closed as the woman's heels clicked away down the hall, moving quickly to catch up with her friends. He opened them at last to see Toby staring down at him.

"Try not to be too cute, kid. You'll cost me attention."

"She was nice," Lucky said.

"Yeah, that's rule two. In this town, the classier you are, the farther you'll go. Stealing Joe Joe's fish is cheap. And stay out of those tourist clip joints over on Bourbon. This place has class. No ten-dollar fruit drinks in a souvenir glass, and no fake Cajun food out of a can. We're not easy to find, and we like it that way. The drunk frat boys can go to the Hard Rock that's just like the one back home, and good riddance. People come here to hear real jazz like they used to play it. And they stop and show some respect instead of throwing things at you."

Toby wasn't looking at him anymore, Lucky realized. He followed the tomcat's gaze into the courtyard and saw a man in jeans and a dark jacket moving through the crowd, never settling in one place.

"So I run the place," Toby was saying. "Joe Joe's the bouncer. He's my number-two man. The guys in the band are okay too. The fat guy coming out of the corner office is the owner. Stay clear of him."

Lucky's stomach grumbled. "So what do you do for food around here?" he asked.

Toby glanced into the courtyard again. "Don't worry, kid. We'll eat soon enough. But the Café du Monde's a good bet when you're new in town. Open-air place. They're open all night so it's always warm out back by the kitchen, and there's spilled powdered sugar and half-eaten beignets all over the place."

"Beignets?"

"Kind of like a doughnut."

"Ugh. What am I supposed to do with those?"

Toby took his gaze off the man in the dark jacket for a moment. "You are right off the boat aren't you? You're supposed to let them draw pigeons. You know what to do with pigeons, don't you?"

"Of course I do."

"All right. But that's for future reference. I think we'll be eating a little better tonight. Here, get under the bench, right under me. Be ready to pounce."

Lucky moved under the bench and hunkered down against the wall. He could see legs going past and a man stopped in front of him.

"How you doing, buddy?" the man said. "You keeping an eye on things? There, good kitty." Then he moved on toward the exit.

"Why am I down here?" asked Lucky.

"I'll show you in a minute."

"You just wanted to make sure that guy didn't pet me instead of you."

"You want to eat, don't you? Then do what I tell you. In a minute somebody's going to come through here. When I give the word, you yowl like the devil himself's got your tail and you dart right between his feet. Got it?"

"How's that going to get us fed?"

"Have faith, kid. All right, he's coming. Get ready."

Lucky fell into his hunting stance and rocked his hips back and forth, getting ready to move.

A woman walked past, toward the street, and Lucky heard another set of footsteps coming up behind her.

"Not yet," said Toby. "Ready . . . ready . . . Now!"

A man's legs appeared, dark shoes and jeans. Lucky screamed as loudly as he could and hurled himself from beneath the bench. He had just enough time to see that it was the man Toby had been watching before chaos broke loose. The man cried out in surprise and tried to sidestep him. The woman squealed. Then Lucky was between the man's feet. A shoe caught him in the belly, then the man tumbled forward and went down hard. Lucky darted away and pressed himself against the far wall. Despite himself his fur was standing straight up and his heart was pounding.

The man sprawled on the floor, trying to quickly gather up some things that had fallen out of his jacket. Somehow the woman's handbag had come off her shoulder, and Joe Joe was coming on the run. Lucky's eyes were drawn to the plate of fish, unguarded on the table. So that was the plan.

"Show some class, kid," said Toby, still sitting regally on the green leather cushion, taking it all in.

"That's my purse!" said the woman.

Joe Joe hauled the man to his feet. He tried to break away and run, but Joe Joe shook his head no, and twisted the man's arm behind his back. "Yeah, our friend here's got a lot more wallets than he needs, don't you? Why don't you give this lady her purse back, and I'll take the rest of those. Let's go."

Joe Joe hustled the man around the edge of the courtyard toward the office.

Toby yawned and stretched. "Yeah, I like to run a tight ship. Got to keep an eye out for the riffraff."

He nodded to a spot next to him. "Good work, kid. Come on up. You've earned a place on the bench. Just don't let me catch you on my cushion."

Lucky leapt onto the bench and sat looking out over the courtyard. The band was playing rhythm behind a boogie-woogie piano song, and the customers were dancing.

Before long Joe Joe came back and glanced at the two cats sitting side by side on the bench. "You got yourself a new apprentice, Toby?"

He went to the table and brought back his plate. "Good work buddy. Looks like you could use a meal."

He picked up a slab of fish and dropped it in front of Lucky. Lucky sniffed it and licked the coating. There was a strange, spicy taste to it, but not a bad one. He took a bite.

"Yeah, Toby, one for you too," said Joe Joe as he handed over a second piece. "Thanks guys. Got to go watch the door."

They sat quietly for a while and the fish started to take the edge off Lucky's hunger.

"See kid? I told you. This town rewards style."

"What is this red stuff?" Lucky asked.

"Hot sauce. You're in New Orleans now. Just pay attention to me kid, and you'll do okay. Who knows, someday I may get tired of this easy living and hop a freighter out of here. To South America maybe. Play your cards right, keep your eyes open, and maybe I'll let you take over for me."

Lucky finished his fish and rolled over, contented. The night air was comfortable, the moon shone down on the courtyard, the band was playing a slow number, and all was right with the world. This might work out okay, he thought as he curled up for a nap on the bench.

As Lucky slept, people came and went from the courtyard. Some stopped to stroke his fur or pat his head. He didn't quite awaken, but his dreams were of a warm, safe place full of comfort and affection, and he purred gently as he slept.

I Suppose This Makes Me Sancho

GARY A. BRAUNBECK

NOW I KNOW THAT THERE'S FOLKS around this town who think that I'm just a couple of fries short of a Happy Meal on account of I let Quixote ride around inside my leg sometimes. That's right, I said *inside* my leg, not *on* it—Quixote's my cat, he ain't no dog, and I'm not partial to making off-color jokes about over-friendly hounds, so I'll thank you to get that smutty smirk off your face.

Quixote's nothing special, breed-wise; just a crotchety old tom who kept coming round my back door every night a few summers ago howling for a little food. I'm not the type who usually takes to animals, but that particular summer had been a not-great one for me, what with breaking up with my girlfriend and having to go in for an operation to have the pins replaced in my remaining leg, and I guess I was feeling a bit lonely and blue, and Quixote's coming around every night gave me some company to look forward to—but don't you go feeling sorry for me. I've got plenty of friends here in town and don't never have to be alone if I don't wanna be, but there're times when a soul gets to feeling a little . . . on the outside of things, if you know what I mean. None of which really has anything to do with what happened, but I figured since you asked for all the details, I might as well give you a little personal information, what with this being a—what'd you call it again?—a human interest piece. Stop me if I start to go south while I'm talking. I've never been interviewed by a reporter before.

Now where was I? Oh, yeah; how I came to adopt Quixote.

When it became apparent to me that he was a stray that tended to get in a lot of fights—evidenced by the nightly new scratch or fresh cut—I realized that I just couldn't let him go on by himself much longer. The night following this little epiphany of mine, he shows up at my back door with a serious gash on his side that I knew was gonna shorten his life expectancy something considerable, so I coaxed him into the house with a can of salmon, found an old box to put him in, took him to the twenty-four-hour emergency animal clinic out past Cherry Valley Road, got him all fixed up with stitches and medicine and shots and such (didn't get him declawed, though; didn't like the idea of having him go through the rest of his life unarmed), then brought him back home with me where he immediately set out making himself right at home. He don't take well to strangers most of the time, which comes in handy when I'm sizing up a person: If Quixote don't warm up to them after about, say, a half-hour or thereabouts, they're probably not the type of person likely to win any humanitarian awards.

You're probably wondering why I named him Quixote. Well, part of it's because he saw—and still sees—enemies hidden everywhere. I can't ponder much his opinion of windmills, since there ain't any in these parts, but he's a bit on the paranoid side; the TV he hates on account of all the faces and voices that come out of it (he once actually hissed and jumped at the screen, claws at the ready, when he got a load of that big-ass dumb dog they use on that one Kibbles-and-something-or-other commercial), I'm convinced he thinks the coffee pot is some kind of mad robot out to get him, and I don't even wanna discuss the ongoing battle between him and the vacuum cleaner. The upshot is, Quixote's got himself a suspicious and defensive nature (I can't hold that against him, not when I think about what his life was like on the street before I took him in), and for a while I was afraid things wasn't gonna work out between us, then just this past Veterans Day something happened that made me not only thankful for his suspicious nature, but also made me realize that maybe it's a good thing that not all cats are the warm and fuzzy, friendly types you see like in them cat food commercials.

Okay, here's what happened: Every Veterans Day I participate in the annual parade downtown. I usually ride on the Vietnam vets' float with the other guys who was over there, all of us wearing either our dress uniforms or field outfits (depending on which we can still fit our expanding waistlines into) and on account of I don't drive, Jimmy Henderson down at the VA office always arranges for somebody to come and pick me up a couple hours ahead of time so's him and me can have ourselves a nice lunch with the other vets that the Ladies' Auxiliary fixes up every year, They lay out quite a buffet for us, the ladies do, and they're more than happy to wait on those vets who can't get around easily on their own. It's damn nice of them, and a fella always comes away feeling appreciated.

Okay, so I get myself all ready and have my dress uniform on. I'd gone on a diet a few months before and lost three inches around the waist just so's I could fit into it; I cut, if I do say so myself, a somewhat dashing figure in that uniform, and there was a young lady named Beth at the Ladies' Auxiliary who I suspected was waiting for me to ask her out on a date, so I wanted to look as handsome as possible, an area in which I need all the help I can get.

Because the arthritis in my good leg was flaring up that day, I was rolling around the house in my wheelchair, looking for my Ken-doll prosthetic. I call it that because it always reminded me of the leg on one of them Ken dolls—you know, Barbie's boyfriend. I'm talking the older Ken doll, the one they was making back in the late sixties, early seventies. It was this big, heavy plastic job, with a wider-than-average circumference where I had to fit it around the stump below my right knee. As you can tell by looking at me, I'm a big guy—six-six, two hundred and sixty-five pounds, most of which is still fairly solid muscle. I made 'em crazy at the Veterans Hospital when they was trying to fit a prosthetic on me because my legs were so big. I suppose on the day in question I could've gone for that sleek new alloy job they gave me last year—I mean, sure, it *is* a lot stronger and lighter than my old one, but something about the alloy leg makes me feel like I'm slowly being transformed into Ah-nald the way he got to looking in the last reel of *The Terminator* and it sort of gives me the willies. I prefer my Ken-doll leg. Guess I'm just sentimental about it.

Anyway, I finally find the darned thing buried under a pile of laundry in the back room and I slide down out of the chair and get on my side and roll up my right pants leg and start slipping the leg into place when I notice that it seems to have a bit more *heft* to it than usual. I figure it's just on account of this is one of my aching arthritis days and I'm in kind of a hurry 'cause I'm all excited about seeing Beth at the buffet and asking her to meet me after the parade and all that.

I reach into my pockets and slip my hands through the special flaps I made so I can snap the straps into place without having to actually take my pants off—and if you make any pocket-pool jokes, son, this interview's over—and I almost got it all snug and secure when the phone rings. I figured the answering machine would just pick up after three but it didn't. You see, the answering machine is another enemy of Quixote's; he don't like all the buzzing, all the clicking and whirring, he'll have none of it. Some time ago he had figured out that the red indicator light meant that the monster was awake, so if he just jumped up onto the table and pressed his paw against the button *beside* the indicator light, that put the monster to sleep. Well, the monster'd been put out cold today, so the phone keeps ringing and ringing. I get into my chair, my Ken-doll leg still not entirely attached, and do a Mario Andretti over to the phone stand. I snatch up the receiver and put it to my ear and hear Jimmy Henderson on the other end, already chatting away like I'd answered and we was having ourselves a hearty conversation.

" . . . know that you always get hit up this time of year by door-to-door donation-seekers, but I just wanted to let you know that the Supporters of American Veterans is a fine organization and has my wholehearted endorsement, so I urge you to give them a little something when they drop by—"

"Jimmy, what the hell're you talking about? You know full well that I donate part of my monthly VA check to vets' charity funds—you helped me arrange it when we set up the Direct Deposit with the bank! How come—"

"—representative will be stopping by in a few minutes to see you and ask for your financial support."

Something in his voice wasn't right. At all. Someone who didn't know Jimmy wouldn't have noticed it, would probably have thought he sounded just fine, real smooth and calm, collected-like, but I'd known Jimmy for quite a few years and could tell when he was nervous because he got this little twang in his voice, mostly at the end of certain words—*financial*, for instance, came out sounding like *finansheeal*—not quite that exaggerated, but you get the idea. I first noticed this when him and me started playing poker with a bunch of other guys every other Thursday; if Jimmy had himself a good hand, he got all nervous and excited inside (but looked as composed as you please outwardly) and would almost always give himself away to me on account of that twang. Jimmy loses a lot at poker.

But this time the twang was a bit different. Jimmy wasn't just nervous.

He was scared. Seriously scared.

"Jimmy, is everything all right?"

"Of *course* it is, Daniel."

He *never* calls me Daniel. Everybody calls me Dan or Danny.

"Then why're you letting these folks hit me up for a donation?"

"She's fine, and the kids're great. Said to tell you hi and they're looking forward to seeing you in the parade today."

Now it was getting not only scary, but weird. Jimmy's a bachelor.

I felt my back go rigid in the chair. "What's going on, Jimmy?"

"Sure, I'll be glad to let them know you'll bring your cheesecake recipe. Listen, Daniel, I've got a lot of other guys to call here in the next half-hour or so. An S.A.V. representative'll be over in a few minutes. Give generously—oh, yeah, and make sure you tie that dog of yours up outside, okay? Can't be too safe about tying up the dog."

Then he hung up.

I checked the caller I.D. screen on the phone.

Jimmy had called me from the main office of the VA downtown.

I sat stock-still for several moments, trying to figure out what was wrong and how I was gonna let the police know that there was some kind of an emergency at the VA office.

What tipped me off? Jimmy saying "tying up the dog" right before he hung up. That was a code phrase my unit used over in Vietnam. I'd told Jimmy about it several times. It was a distress call. Translation: We're in deep sewage, send help *now*.

I was picking up the phone to call the police when someone knocked at the door, then turned the knob and just came on in.

Kid must've been in his early twenties but the meanness in his features made him look at least a decade older. He was well-dressed—suit must've put someone back a few hundred—and he was carrying a big donation can with an S.A.V. label on it.

"Mr. Gentry?" he said.

"I don't recall saying you could come in."

He smiled a lizard grin and pushed the door closed, then reached inside his jacket and pulled out the biggest and ugliest semi-automatic pistol I'd ever seen. "I knew the door would be unlocked. Mr. Henderson said you always left it unlocked on Veterans Day so the person giving you a ride to the parade could just come on in in case you were still getting ready. Please hang up the phone."

I did. I've found it's best not to argue with a semi-aut.

"What the hell do you want, son?"

"I'm not your son, and what I want is the second half of the combination of the safe at the VA office."

I glared at him. "You must've done some serious convincing to get Jimmy to tell you that."

"He'll need a couple of stitches and maybe a bone or two reset, but nothing major."

The local VA office has a policy—not widely known—of cashing checks for certain veterans who don't have Direct Deposit, or don't live in a mailbox-safe neighborhood, or simply prefer to avoid banks. There's usually anywhere between two and ten thousand dollars in that safe during the early part of the month. A lot of vets—and this town's got a bunch—have their checks delivered right to the office so they can go straight to the source and not have to bother with a lot of middlemen.

The checks had been late this month—mine still hadn't arrived—so the money was just sitting there in the safe. Jimmy gets nervous about that, so he always has me change the combination every month—the lock is computerized—and every month instructs me to not tell him what the secondary sequence is. For some reason I don't quite understand, the initial series of codes has to stay the same—some kind of manufacturer's safeguard, I guess—but the secondary sequence can be changed as often as you please. I do volunteer work at the office five days a month right after the checks come, so I'm always the one who gets to open the safe. Makes me feel important, and it's kind of neat to watch this big electronic lockbox go through its circuit-dance when it swings open.

Jimmy insists that we do it this way every month so that in case something like this were to ever happen, he could honestly tell any robbers that he doesn't know the rest of the combination. It's all kind of over-complicated and a bit laughable, because you'd think in a mid-sized town like this, nobody'd be stupid enough to try and rob the VA office.

I shook my head at the kid and said, "Well, you at least picked the right day. I imagine Jimmy's the only one down at the office."

"Bingo. Everyone else is either at the luncheon or the parade site."

"How do I know you ain't gonna kill Jimmy and me once you got what you want?"

He jacked back the slide, chambered a round, and pressed the business end of the pistol against my forehead. "You don't."

I took a deep breath, said a quick prayer, and told him what he wanted to know.

Placing his foot against one of the arms, he pushed my wheelchair back about five feet, the gun still aimed directly at my head, then picked up the phone and punched in the number of the office. "Yeah, I got it." He gave them the secondary sequence.

I cleared my throat to get his attention. "Tell 'em that it's gonna take about two minutes for the safe to finish the whole activation sequence before it opens."

"What?"

I sighed. "Once the sequence is punched in, the safe has all these other built-in security programs it has to shut off before it opens. Takes about two minutes. I don't want your buddies thinking Jimmy and me are trying to pull a fast one."

He passed the information along, then hung up the phone and stood there staring at me.

What I knew that he didn't—what no one but me and Jimmy knew, in fact—was that the sequence I'd given to him *would* open the safe, sure, but this particular sequence would also trigger a silent alarm at the police station.

"How many of you are there?" I asked.

He was feeling cocky, I'm sure, having proved his superior intelligence and manhood by holding a wheelchair-bound man at gunpoint. "Me and the two guys at the office, plus the dozen or so folks we've got down at the parade site, you know, going through the crowd and soliciting donations."

"Nice scam. Kind of like what they did in Cleveland a couple of years ago."

"That's how we got the idea."

"Those folks got caught."

"We won't."

"How do you know?"

He yanked the phone cord from the wall, then stormed over and pressed the gun against my head, looking down at the plastic foot of my prosthesis. " 'Cause a one-legged man can't give chase, and since most of your neighbors are gone, it'll take you at least ten or fifteen minutes to get any help. That is, if you can get out of these." He pulled a set of handcuffs from his back pocket, slapped one end around my wrist, then pulled me over next to the radiator and attached the other end to the main gas pipe. "Out of the chair."

It was a little difficult, but I managed to slide down onto the floor and get myself in a half-comfortable sitting position.

The kid knelt down and tugged on my Ken-doll leg; it budged a little, then stopped.

That's when I felt something uncurl just a tad next to my stump, and realized where Quixote was hiding.

"Can you unbutton or unhook this thing?"

"Sure." I reached in with my free hand—my left one, so you can imagine it was quite a reach—and managed to get the harness unsnapped.

"It's loose," I said, hoisting it up so the foot was almost level with the kid's face.

I could feel Quixote's body tense, could feel him give one of those mean, quiet little growls that he always gave before attacking some evil household appliance, and I *definitely* felt the claws dig in as he readied to spring.

The pain must've shown on my face, because the kid said, "Are you all right?"

He actually sounded concerned, so I decided to play the sympathy card for all I could. "It . . . it h-hurts to put this on and take it off . . . I stepped on a damned mine when I was on patrol one night . . . ouch!"

"Sorry," said the kid, putting on the pistol's safety and shoving it in behind his belt.

"Just . . . just pull it off real quick, will you?"

"Uh, yeah, yeah." He started to tug, then stopped and said, "Look, we, uh . . . we didn't hurt your friend too much, really. We aren't gonna kill anybody. My dad, he was over in Vietnam, too. I wouldn't be part of this if I thought we'd kill any vets. I got too much respect for them."

"Mighty patriotic of you. Will you *please* pull it off quick? The pain's killing me." I suppose I was doing some powerful overacting at this point, but this kid didn't strike me as a closet theater critic, so I figured I was safe.

On his knees, the kid pulled himself straight up, the prosthetic came straight off, and as soon as the leg had cleared away, eleven pounds of paranoid feline fury threw itself straight into his face. His hands flew up to grab Quixote and I expected him to fall backward but he didn't, he fell to the side, and I was able to roll half-over and grab the pistol from his pants, release the safety, and fire three shots into the ceiling.

This would've sent most cats heading for the hills, but it only served to irritate Quixote, who pressed his claws against the kid's throat and sank his teeth into the kid's nose.

"Oh god, get it off me!"

"I really wouldn't move too much if I was you. He don't seem to've taken a shining to you, and I ain't had them claws of his trimmed for a *long* time."

"Uh-huh . . ."

"By the way, son?"

"Uh-huh . . . ?"

"Happy Veterans Day."

When the kid didn't say anything, Quixote growled and scratched him a bit.

"Uh . . . h-happy Veterans Day," squeaked the kid.

I felt proud to be a feline-loving American at that moment, I don't mind saying.

Well, you pretty much know the rest. The cops showed up at my house about two minutes later, the guys down at the VA office panicked and gave themselves up—not one of them was older than twenty-two, and they hadn't planned it out as well as they'd thought—and the rest of them were picked up at various spots along the parade route as they tried to solicit donations for their bogus charity.

Quixote rode on the float with me that day, and I even draped one of my medals around his neck to show my appreciation. He sat up at the front of the float, head high, chest out, looking pretty proud of himself.

As for me and Beth—well, I suppose you figured out from your call earlier and from her answering the door that her and me had ourselves that date, and about a hundred others, and we got married a while back and I ain't had a lonely moment since.

The VA decided that maybe keeping all that money in the safe wasn't such a good idea, so now they've arranged it so that the cash is on hand for only three days every month, and there're armed police officers at the office during those three days, and if there's any vet who can't make it to the office during that time, Beth and me are more than happy to go and give them a ride into town.

Those punks split Jimmy's lip and busted his nose, but since he's healed up everyone agrees that it has improved his looks considerably.

As for Quixote and my leg, I took an ice-pick and hammer and made several air holes in the plastic so he can breathe while he's in there, and once a week I strap on the Ken-doll leg (Beth makes me wear my Terminator leg the rest of the time) and take him out for a stroll. He's real comfortable in there. I added a patch of carpeting for him to snuggle up on, and it's quite an odd sensation to feel the inside of your leg purring as you walk around. Sometimes when he gets real happy, that purring gets a bit loud, and the little kids get a real kick out of it.

Quixote's just this week been named the official mascot of our Veterans Day parade; and, yeah, I suppose this makes me Sancho Panza but I don't care. My cat's as good a soldier as ever I served with.

You'll have to excuse me now; I believe my leg needs to visit the litter box. It was real nice of you to stop by.

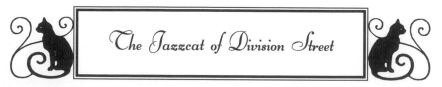

The Jazzcat of Division Street

WAYNE ALLEN SALLEE

MAMACH WANTED TO KICK HIMSELF for steering the conversation toward anything remotely feline. He could have mentioned a different case or collar to Rizzi and Big Ben Christopher, maybe the perp they caught for the A.T.M. stickups after the guy took one victim's money, then spilled his own ID on the curb without knowing it. The ID was a bond card with his girlfriend's address on it. Confessed to a dozen holdups along the North and Clybourn corridor. That would have been a good one to mention. He thought this as his fellow cops waited for him to tell the story from his rookie days.

But, no, Mamach instead brought up the coyote that had been hiding under the cab on Franklin, and Rizzi and his partner had been called to the scene because they had been in traffic court, just across the river. Mamach laughing about Christopher, all 315 pounds of him, rolling on the asphalt, trying to coax the errant animal out into the open. Yep, ol' Mitch Mamach thought this would be a great laugh, what with everybody half snookered on Jim Beam, sitting in Dipple's Printshop, the bar with the alibi built in to the name, where Eastwood dead-ends with Josephine Court. None of the other cops were blinking, not even the *women* cops, for cry-eye. They were all waiting for the cat story. And Rizzi threw it on the table: "Mitch once swore a cat helped him catch a robber back when he was a rookie."

Mamach looked over at the door, wishing some biker would come in and play Van Halen on the jukebox, thus distracting them all. It wasn't going to happen.

"Well. . . ."

"C'mon, Mitch." Dipple the Owner was wiry and muscular with wild red and white eyebrows. "Tell your story and I'll pour some tequila. On the house." Everyone cheered. Good old Dan, nailing the coffin shut. If it was just the guys, he wouldn't care as much, but Felice and Cantu were there, and he was certain that someone was going to bring up Mamach's weight problem back then.

"Fine, fine," he said to everyone, subconsciously pulling at the waistband of his pants. "The way it happened was. . . ."

The way it happened was like this. Mamach had been a few months out of the academy and still being fattened by his mother's cooking—Polish sausage, beef-filled kolàckys, kishka, you name it—when Mayor Daley had started up a new community policing program. Nothing would ever end up as an episode of *Cops* during Mamach's tour, but as beat representative, the then twenty-seven-year-old cop left the station house at Augusta and Wood every day and patrolled northward then westward down Division Street.

The area had just started to gentrify; many students from Columbia and DePaul Universities were finding apartment rentals cheap, but there was still the element of gang crimes and intimidation to be dealt with. Mamach would saunter past the Rainbow Room and the old Luxor Bathhouse, leaving the normal cop greasy spoon hangout of Duk's in favor of Leo's Luncheonette, off Wolcott. He did not mention to those gathered at present that he ate there because of the menu's cheap prices.

Upon his departure one fine spring day three weeks into his tour, he walked past the Bop Shop, a jazz establishment with a holistic rehab center on the upper floors, and a fat tabby streaked from the entrance and kept circling Mamach, as if to tell him something was amiss.

"As if something was amiss?" Remy Petitt, Mamach's new partner, a recent transplant from Baton Rouge, narrowed his eyes. He tilted his head toward Dipple and snickered, "The man don't need no tequila, Dan."

"Just let me get on with it, okay?" Mamach finished off his whiskey out of spite.

"A fat tabby?" Felice, a tall blond out of Narcotics, asked. Like Petitt, she hadn't heard the story, either. "That the best description you can give us? Some cop you are!"

"Sure you're not describing yourself, Mitch?" Rizzi cackled. "Your partner had a bit of a weight problem back during the Reagan administration," he said to Petitt. And now Felice knew, along with Ileana Cantu, if she didn't already. Knowing Petitt, he'd have it written in the bathroom stall before they left for the night.

The tabby wasn't fat in the well-fed way, it simply wasn't one of the scrawny strays one was accustomed of seeing in the area. In fact, Mamach was more aware of this particular cat than others, as he had frequented the Bop Shop several times in the past. The cat had no name, cute or otherwise. Paul Barnes, the bartender, had told him the cat appeared during remodeling once and never left. The music never seemed to bother him, and he often stretched out behind the stage. Patrons came to know the tabby as the jazzcat of Division Street.

"How did it be de cat doan recognize you a cop?" Petitt said, going for his Baton Rouge accent that always turned ladies' heads, bar patrons and mass murderesses alike. "You was still in uniform back then, you."

Mamach explained that the early version of CAPS—Community Activity Policing System—deemed that the individual cops assigned to their beats dress casually, i.e., less than plainclothes, but more dressy than half the hairbags on the detective squad in *any* district station house. So there.

"Now, as I was saying. . . ."

The cat didn't have a cute name, like the fictional ones who solved crimes, or even an atypical name, considering that his surroundings included both an Old Country Polish neighborhood as well as a premiere jazz club. He wasn't named Sherlock 'n Boots or Thelonious Cat. He was just the jazzcat, in lowercase, presumably.

The cat kept circling Mamach in a frenzy, not allowing him to sidestep the feline and move forward. Then the cat leapt at his crotch, though he did not say this to those present at Dipple's that night, and when he did it again, he swiped a paw at the holstered gun snapped on Mamach's belt. (What Mitch did tell his audience was that he heard moaning from the side entrance of the jazz club, which was not entirely true.)

The cat then darted back to the side exit. Mamach, having deduced that the cat was somehow aware of his law enforcement background, and never once thinking that the cat had been perched above the pinball machine on several nights when he had talked cop crap to club owner Kate Smith, drew his weapon and walked to the steel door which faced Hermitage Street. Sprawled on the floor, just inside the doorway, was the daytime bartender, Jimmie Heaslip. He had introduced himself to Mamach months back, saying that a good way to remember his last name was to answer the question "How he get bruise?" He slip, of course.

In this case, he hadn't slipped, rather he had been cold-cocked after taking out some trash. It had been someone in the bar that had followed him to the back door. Heaslip was no worse for wear, having a bump on his head he'd be nursing for a few days. Nothing worth filing workmen's comp for. A quick tally from the register showed about thirty dollars and change missing. Heaslip had just cracked open two rolls of quarters for when the pinball crowd came in. So that was another twenty. The only other person at the bar would be no help, seeing as how he was passed out. And, yes, Mamach had nudged Little Nemo out of Slumberland to be certain the fellow wasn't faking.

Mamach suspected that the cat would be aware of the thief. Looking around, he saw the feline perched atop the ancient Captain Fantastic and the Browndirt Cowboy pinball machine, situated between the bar and the front door, and looking very much like the cat who ate the canary.

Or, at least knew where the canary ran off to.

And so it was, a few minutes later, Mamach and the jazzcat—sheesh, that sounded like the title of an old Cat Stevens album—were walking eastward down Division, closer to the subway, pawn shops, flophouses, and floppier flophouses.

There were also laundromats, such as the one the cat was going ballistic in front of, at the corner of Paulina. One thing Heaslip had mentioned before Mamach left the bar, the cat following a moment later, was that after he had been hit, he had tried swinging the open garbage bag at his assailant. He had only succeeded in spraying condiment packets and droplets of beer on the robber.

The cat started doing his Tasmanian Devil routine as Mamach stood in front of Tina's Ten-Cent Coin-Op, the ground floor of a three-flat with most of the upstairs windows boarded up and empty pint bottles of Wild Irish Rose and Night Train Express along the curb. Mamach shielded his eyes from his own reflection in the window and looked inside.

As he sized up the potential situation, which was easy enough, seeing as how amongst the half-dozen women in various stages of purposefulness or boredom, there was a lone man in the back of the laundromat. Bare-chested, he was watching a washer go through the spin cycle. Mamach later learned that Glines, the perp, had wanted to get the smell of the pickle juice and beer off his shirt, because he was afraid a cop might stop him and ask why he smelled like pickles and Miller High Life, making that giant leap of logic that all crack addicts were capable of.

Meanwhile, as Mamach thought of his next move, he watched through the window as the cat tore through the laundromat and leapt onto Glines's right shoulder, startling everyone inside. The thief yelped in surprise and disdain. Freaked out when he realized it was the cat from the club, Glines tripped on his own feet and tumbled to the floor as Mamach rushed up, gun and badge drawn.

Glines of course denied his culpability in anything, and pulled his empty pants pockets inside out, eager to please in spite of the thin claw marks on his bare shoulder. But then the cat nuzzled against Glines's ankle, rubbing his pants leg up with his cheek, exposing the orange-and-white-striped wrappers of quarters. He had torn one open to remove a quarter for the washing machine.

"He had the bills rolled up in the other sock," Mamach told everybody gathered, non-cop patrons included, as he concluded the tale of the jazzcat of Division Street. The tequila he'd been drinking made him sound a little bit like Jack Webb doing the epilogue to "Dragnet." The cat wasn't mentioned in the papers; in fact, the entire crime rated only a few lines in the *Dziennik Chicagoski,* the neighborhood's Polish paper. In Mamach's rookie days, there was a lot of coverage of a corruption probe into Cook County judges, and a bagman for the Chicago Mob turned state's evidence the very day the Bop Shop was robbed.

The story, far-fetched as it was, had encouraged patrons to stay and order more beers to go with their free tequila shooters, and that made Dipple the Owner happy. He milked the moment.

"Okay, which one of you are gonna top that one?" he said in his gravelly voice and waggled his red and white eyebrows. "I've still got another bottle of tequila here, and I'll pay for any cab ride home, for those without designated drivers!"

Everyone cheered. The cops looked at each other.

"Hey, Rizzi," Mamach grinned lecherously. "Why don't you tell the story about working undercover in drag and how our own boys picked you up. . . ."

Jeepers

ADELE POLOMSKI

LANA GAVE HER COUSIN JULIAN a private smirk before treating Aunt Viola and Jeepers to a winning smile. When the old woman held Jeepers out, Lana held her breath. The huge, fluffy creature the color of smoke hung before Lana and stared at her with glittering eyes.

"Wouldn't you like to hold him, dear?"

Lana didn't think cats were animals that needed to be held, but said nothing. The cat loomed in her face before it sank into her lap, claws hooking into the navy slacks of her airline uniform. "He's adorable," Lana managed in a thin, strangled voice. She was trying not to breathe.

Lana's aunt, eighty if she was a day, was a tiny woman under a pelt of blue hair that she wore curled up in a flip at the ends. Today her aunt was dressed in a stylish pink suit with the collar turned up.

"Should we have called first?" the old woman asked.

"No, I love surprise visits," Lana lied. In truth it hadn't been that much of a surprise. The super had tipped Lana off to the white stretch limo in the parking lot. It cost Lana twenty bucks, but gave her time to swallow a couple of advanced-formula allergy tablets, and time to rearrange her furniture. Aunt Viola and Julian, who sat beside one another on the brown leather sofa, now had a breathtaking view of the terrace and street eight stories below.

"How are you Julian?" Lana asked.

Julian, a scarecrow of a man in a long black coat he refused to relinquish at the door, said nothing. He stared out at the terrace, his unnaturally black eyes bright, the rest of his face as pale as a peeled twig. Equally pale fingers gripped the armrest and a leather cushion. Lana sensed that Julian's discomfort more than equaled her own, and this made her feel better.

Lana was deathly allergic to cat dander, while Julian was only phobic, irrationally afraid of closed spaces, spiders, showers, radiator steam, pigeons. And heights.

The idea to position the sofa overlooking the terrace had been a last-minute flare of genius. When Aunt Viola was out of earshot she would point out to Julian that the terrace door could be opened, and leapt from, should the urge seize him. That would quickly end this contest for Jeepers, and the five million dollars that would accompany the cat.

Lana smiled. "Suppose I show you around?" she said, anxious to get free of the cat who was now clawing the sleeve of her jacket. Worse, she began to feel a tickle at the back of her throat, and a fuzzy feeling in her sinuses.

"One thing first, dear," Aunt Viola said, placing a waxy, liver-spotted hand on Lana's knee. "A little bird told me you were allergic to cats," Aunt Viola said.

"Me?" Lana asked, packing the single syllable with incredulity. "Perhaps when I was younger," she allowed, "but I adore cats. Especially Jeepers."

The cat was rubbing his plump, furry cheeks against Lana's sleeve which had been reduced to shreds. Catnip sewn into the jacket lining of the old uniform represented an earlier inspiration.

Julian made a little gibbering noise, which Aunt Viola ignored. Lana looked at him. A corner of his mouth had begun to twitch.

As if sensing Julian's misery, the cat stretched, got down, and walked toward the panic-stricken man. Lana watched the hopeful look in her cousin's otherwise miserable eyes, and crossed her legs. Immediately, the cat walked toward her, prancing on the tips of its toes.

Jeepers began to sniff the hem of her navy trousers where she'd sewn in more catnip. She bent, rubbed the cat between his ears and looked at Julian who wore a terrorized mask of wonder and disbelief.

"Jeepers will adore it here," Lana said. "His room is all ready." The tickle in her throat had grown worse. She now had to fight the urge to cough. "May I show you?" She directed her question to her aunt, who didn't seem to notice her anxiety. Julian, however, was staring at her.

The allergy specialist Lana had met on one of her international flights hadn't said anything about the new pills wearing off so quickly. But Lana hadn't mentioned she'd be wearing a cat. Long cat hairs carpeted her clothes. She had to get up.

Lana looked down. Jeepers was rolling sensuously in her lap, his pale gray paws stroking the air, his plumed tail swiping back and forth under her chin. Lana thought desperately of the additional allergy tablets in her kitchen.

"I thought Jeepers would be sleeping with you," Aunt Viola said, making no move to get up.

"Oh, of course," Lana said inventing desperately. She allowed herself a small cough. "And I want to show you the changes I've made, to make it safer and more comfortable for my little darling."

"He's not your darling," Julian said in a voice that seemed to have burst out of him.

Aunt Viola ignored Julian, pulled herself up. "You won't mind," she said, "if we look around?"

Julian unfolded, then lifted himself and followed the old woman into the bathroom, his eyes full of longing for the cat.

When they were gone, Lana quickly pushed the cat off her lap. The creature didn't seem to notice the rebuff. It circled her legs like a loopy shark.

Lana hurried into the kitchen, reached into a cat-face cookie jar and shook into her palm two tablets from a plastic prescription bottle. She tossed the pills to the back of her throat and choked them down dry. Then she walked to the bathroom door, where she watched Julian open and inspect the contents of her medicine cabinet: a first-aid kit, a few cosmetics, aspirin.

Aunt Viola, bent over to inspect under the sink, seemed to approve of the deluxe kitty-litter pan, though Jeepers, she pronounced, had his own commode, a large old roasting pan he seemed to favor over anything else.

Aunt Viola walked out of the bathroom, toward the bedrooms. Julian, though trembling, continued his exploration of the linen closet, looking undoubtedly for something to hold up as proof of Lana's inability to act as Jeepers's guardian.

As Lana watched, the bathroom door began to swing closed. Either Aunt Viola or Julian had kicked out the doorstop, and Julian had nudged the door enough to get it going. Lana almost cried out, but caught herself, and grinned when the door snapped shut. Poor Julian, she thought. In his haste to uncover her ailment he had overlooked one of his own: claustrophobia.

Lana found Aunt Viola in her bedroom. Like every other room in the small apartment it was festooned with feline artifacts. Cat vases, ceramic kittens, postcards and photographs of cats in silver frames.

"I want you to appreciate how cat-friendly this apartment is," Lana said.

A moaning sound came from the bathroom. As they walked past Lana could see the glass doorknob rotating, and ignored it. Aunt Viola didn't hear it, and Jeepers seemed too bombed on catnip to care.

In the kitchen, Aunt Viola nodded approvingly at the cat calendar, the cat mugs, more china cats, a cat tea towel slung off the oven door. Lana hardly thought of Julian. Jeepers followed her, purring, rubbing his big cat head against her ankles whenever she stood still.

"Lovely, Jeepers," she said, noticing her voice growing nasal again. She would have to get them out of here, and soon.

"You have a charming apartment, dear," Aunt Viola said when they returned to the living room.

Lana glanced at the bathroom door. The knob had stopped turning. Julian must have realized it was hopeless.

She herself had been stuck in there once. For an hour before the super, who had let himself in to fix a dripping faucet, had let her out.

"I know I don't have a garden, Aunt Viola," Lana said as if apologizing, thinking she would suffer to give Julian a few more minutes of hell, "but the terrace is quite nice. Come see. I do get a lot of birds. Mr. Jeepers could spend hours watching pigeons."

While Aunt Viola checked the lock on the sliding glass door, Lana pulled two videocassettes out of a wall unit. One cassette featured an aquarium with a ballet of live goldfish, the other a well-attended birdbath.

"I've screened them. They're quite acceptable," Lana said to Aunt Viola who had picked up the cat.

A low moan sounded from the bathroom, and Jeepers poured out of the old woman's arms. Lana left Aunt Viola on the couch with the promise of a cup of mint tea and went to the bathroom.

She twisted the knob and Julian tore out, hair wild, eyes blazing. He was speechless with fear. After several deep breaths he rasped, "You knew."

Lana stared blankly at Julian, not admitting she had been after the building super to fix the lock for weeks. The super had said she could wait. Hadn't he just fixed her faucet? What did she want? Everything? After he made the rounds, he'd be back.

"There you are Julian," Aunt Viola said coming up behind them. "As usual, you've missed everything. Lana has been wonderful."

Aunt Viola was smiling at Jeepers who was enjoying the pigeons.

The cat, finally tiring of birds he couldn't get at, sniffed disdainfully at the deluxe scratching post before he tried his claws on the leather sofa. Aunt Viola, who was studying the cat books on Lana's coffee table, didn't seem to notice the tearing sounds, the gathering white stripes. "I never knew you loved cats so much, Lana. I would have brought Mr. Jeepers to you sooner."

Lana excused herself to the kitchen, and downed two more allergy pills, this time washing the tablets down with a glass of water. When she turned she saw Julian staring at her. She waited, but he said nothing.

"Have you got the tea, dear?" Aunt Viola shouted in a voice shrill with happiness. The old woman was clearly enjoying herself.

Lana let Julian carry in the tray. Aunt Viola poured. The third dose of allergy medicine started to kick in, and Lana felt woozy, ebullient. So what if the air was alive with cat fur? Her cat-clawed couch would need a slipcover, but that hardly mattered either. Five million bucks could buy a lot of slipcovers.

"She works!" Julian cried, out of the blue. He sat in a club chair near the door.

"My job?" Lana asked. "Not important. I believe a cat deserves a full-time caregiver. What's the sense of having any animal, but especially a cat, if you don't have the time or ability," and here she looked pointedly at Julian, "to give it the proper attention it deserves?"

Aunt Viola's eyes filled. Julian looked paler than ever.

Jeepers, who had found his second wind, was whirling around the apartment sending up clouds of himself. Cat fur flew into Lana's face, and she laughed. "He's certainly having fun."

Lana got up, set a plate of sugar cookies blanketed with cat fur onto Julian's lap.

"The apartment is lovely, dear," Aunt Viola said taking a final sip of her tea. "But I'm afraid Mr. Jeepers couldn't be happy here."

"But—"

Aunt Viola raised a hand. "I am fully aware that aside from Julian, you are Jeepers's and my only living relative."

Julian stared at the furry cookie.

"Jeepers adores Julian," Aunt Viola went on, "but he is positively enchanted with you."

"We could be wonderful together," Lana agreed. "I know I could make Jeepers happy."

"I believe you could, dear," Aunt Viola agreed. "But not here. Would you be able to live in my house?"

"The mansion?"

Aunt Viola nodded. "And Jeepers loves our Paris home in the spring. And the little villa we own outside of Rome for late summer and early fall. Julian, you may not know, is afraid to fly."

"That's terrible," Lana said, aware that Julian was afraid to drive the cat to the vet. Not that she would bother with trifles like ensuring the animal's health. Not after she had the cat's money.

Jeepers was lying at Lana's feet, belly up, waiting to be scratched. Lana obliged him. One last time.

Aunt Viola smiled. "So?"

"I'd be happy to live with Jeepers," Lana said.

"Shouldn't there be a trial period?" Julian asked between barely parted teeth.

Lana shot him a look. "Hasn't this been the trial period?"

"Well, I suppose an extended visit might be in order," Aunt Viola said reasonably.

The matter was settled. Aunt Viola or Julian, if he wasn't afraid of operating the telephone that day, would call to arrange a visit. Afterward, if the trial period went well, Lana would be awarded custody of Jeepers as his adoptive caretaker and companion, to take effect at the time when Aunt Viola couldn't take care of Jeepers herself. The five million or so in Aunt Viola's estate would be left to Jeepers. After he was gone it would revert to Jeepers's companion.

In her care Lana didn't expect the creature would be around very long. She

couldn't spend the rest of the cat's life on high-powered decongestants and antihistamines.

After Lana closed the door behind Julian, Aunt Viola, and Jeepers, she took
off all her clothes. She shoved everything including her shoes into one plastic
bag, then into a second which she tied up and threw over the terrace, hoping
someone else might have the sense to shove the bag into a trash bin.

Then she took a shower with the bathroom door, the terrace door, and
every window in the apartment wide open. After showering she dressed, vacu-
umed, then showered again.

After she changed her sheets, she lay down on her bed. She had taken a big
risk today. But when she got Jeepers, or more to the point, his money, it would
have all been worth it.

In the following days, Lana sent presents to Jeepers. Gourmet cat food,
toys, treats like Beluga caviar swiped from the airline's first-class food-service
cart. And most recently a certificate Lana had made up herself, stating that she
was trained and licensed to perform cat C.P.R.

Lana checked her answering machine daily, but neither Julian nor Aunt
Viola called. She left the cat paraphernalia lying around. The scratching post,
fuzzy mouse toys, balls of yarn. Except for the videocassettes which went back
to the mansion with Aunt Viola. A reminder of their visit. Lana wanted to keep
herself fresh in Aunt Viola's mind.

After a week with no phone call, Lana began to get anxious. What if Julian
had gotten the old woman to change her mind?

Lana also noticed that the feline bric-a-brac was beginning to get to her, in
almost the manner of Julian's phobias. A dryness in the throat when she caught
sight of a beady-eyed ceramic kitten or the cat pan in the bathroom. She could
feel her throat closing at the sight of the smug pair of Siamese featured on the
calendar for that month. The ugly gray Manx gracing the cover of one of the
cat books made her chest tighten.

She wasn't surprised when she came home one afternoon, and found it immediately difficult to breathe.

On the way into the bathroom to splash her face with cool water, she noticed the red light blinking on the answering machine, but didn't stop to play
the messages. In her haste she barely noticed her foot kicking out the doorstop,
which wasn't pushed in as far as she liked.

The cool water didn't ease the pain in Lana's throat which unaccountably
grew worse. She was reaching for a towel when she noticed that the plastic cat
pan under the sink was missing. It had been replaced with a large mottled-blue
meat roaster. Her heart began to race. They had brought the cat. Left Jeepers
somewhere in the apartment.

Lana's eyes clouded. The pills. The kitchen. She threw out her hands in a

• 362 •

blind panic, and her fingers caught the edge of the door causing it to swing before it closed with an audible snap.

"Julian!" she cried. "I know you're out there. Let me out!"

No one answered and after several minutes Lana's chest hurt as if a great weight lay on it, preventing her from taking a breath. She felt herself slip into a collapse, her body grow weaker as her head filled with a cool grayness.

The police entered the apartment the following day, accompanied by Julian and Aunt Viola. It had been Julian's idea to visit Lana's apartment after his cousin failed to return any of Aunt Viola's phone messages.

Aunt Viola primarily wanted to retrieve the roasting pan Julian had forgotten. She told the police how Julian had paid Lana a surprise visit the previous morning.

The super had let Julian in. Julian played with the cat while the super worked on the bathroom door. Julian had paid the man fifty dollars to fix the lock.

After several hours, Julian, Jeepers, and the super left. Neither Viola nor Julian could explain how Lana died. Julian knew an autopsy wouldn't reveal illegal drug use, something the police always suspected in cases like this. No drugs at all.

He stepped into Lana's bedroom, listening to Aunt Viola.

"I can't imagine why she couldn't get the door open. I didn't have any problem with it." Aunt Viola paused, as if remembering something. "When we found Lana, she looked scared to death. Mental health," Aunt Viola confessed in a lowered voice, "has never been this family's strong suit."

Jeepers lay in the middle of Lana's bed, his plume-like tail slashing the air. Julian clucked and the cat followed him into the living room, where they sat together on the sofa watching the pigeons on Lana's terrace, and waiting for Aunt Viola to finish with the police.

Joey

HUGH B. CAVE

WHEN HER TELEPHONE RANG that Sunday evening, Martha Lawton was seated in her living room, watching *The X-Files*. She liked that sort of thing and, living alone except for her cat, could watch any TV program she wanted to.

Her cat, Joey, had not come home yet. He almost always went out after supper, often staying out most of the night. Martha didn't have to worry about him. The back door of the house was fitted with a small swinging panel through which he could go and come as he pleased. Her nephew, Ned Quinn, had installed it for her.

Suddenly, while Scully was protesting to Mulder that a missing person couldn't possibly have been spirited away by extraterrestrials, Martha half rose from her easy chair, and looked toward her bedroom. Had something made a noise there? But it wasn't repeated, and before she could get up to investigate, the phone rang.

She kept a cordless phone close to her most of the time now, for convenience. Well, not just for convenience. She kept it close so she wouldn't put a strain on her not-too-strong heart by having to hurry through a house that was really too big for her. This evening the cordless lay on a table beside her chair. Lifting it, she said with a little frown, "Yes?"

Ned seldom if ever called at this hour; he checked in earlier. This was probably some salesperson wanting her to sign up for a new long-distance telephone service or an HMO that would send her to doctors she didn't even know.

But it was Ned Quinn, after all. "Aunt Martha, you busy?" he said.

"Uh-uh. I was only watching TV."

"I need to talk to you." It was the voice he used when he was not only Ned Quinn, her beloved nephew, but Ned Quinn, detective. He was forty-three years old, unmarried, and worked for the Brampton Police Department.

"Should I turn the TV off?" she asked him.

"You're watching *The X-Files*, hey?"

"Of course."

"Then just turn the sound off for a minute, Aunt Martha. I won't keep you long."

She touched the mute button on her remote control and said apprehensively, "Okay. I'm listening."

"Aunt Martha, from now on I want you to be sure all your doors and windows are locked when you go out or go to bed," Ned told her in his same Detective Quinn voice, which, she now realized, was a sort of low-key growl. "Sure, Brampton is a small town. I know that. But someone is breaking into houses here now and stealing things. Are you listening?"

"Yes, Ned, I'm listening."

"Most likely it's teenagers looking for money to buy drugs," he went on. "Or for stuff they can sell easily to *get* money for drugs. We don't know yet. All we know is that three houses have been broken into in the past week, and no one should leave doors and windows unlocked any more. Especially elderly ladies who live alone, like you. Okay?"

"I'll be careful," Martha replied without hesitation. "I'm always careful about my doors and windows anyway. You know that, Ned."

"Yes, I know," he said. "But be *extra* careful till we catch whoever is doing this. Will you do that, Aunt Martha? Promise?"

"It's a deal," she said.

"Okay, it's a deal. Sleep well, now. I'll stop by tomorrow morning sometime."

He hung up, and she put the TV sound back on. But the fun had gone out of Mulder and Scully and their extraterrestrials. Teenagers were breaking into houses in Brampton? It was hard to believe. She had been born in this town, had married here, had buried her loving husband, Arthur, here, and intended to be buried beside him in the town's little cemetery when her own time came. Brampton was such a peaceful little place. Why would any of its teenagers want to take drugs, for heaven's sake?

Suddenly she heard a noise from her bedroom again. It couldn't be Joey; he came and went by the swinging cat-panel in the kitchen. This was a noise like that of a bureau drawer being pulled open. Frowning, she pushed herself up from her chair and went to investigate.

She limped as she walked across the living room to the hall. Ever since she had slipped and fallen in the shower a month or so ago, her left hip had given her trouble. If she weren't such a little thing she would probably have to use a crutch, Dr. Crowley had told her. Imagine having to use a crutch when you were only seventy-six years old!

Reaching the hall, she was puzzled to find her bedroom door closed. Had she closed it behind her after tidying up in there a while ago? She didn't remember doing that, but of course she must have. Joey, her cat, wouldn't have closed it, though he was undoubtedly smart enough to do so. As she reached for the knob, her trepidation increased.

Then, as her arthritic fingers closed around the knob and turned it, she again heard the sound of a bureau drawer being slid open. And despite Ned's warning she pushed the door wide and stepped forthrightly over the threshold, prepared to challenge any intruder.

She shouldn't have done that, of course. She never should have walked into that room. But she did. Having been a teacher at Brampton High School for years, she thought she knew how to deal with teenagers.

The young man who stood there at her bureau was not really a teenager, though. When he abruptly stopped rummaging in the drawer he had just opened and swung around to confront her, she guessed he was about twenty or twenty-one. It was hard to tell a young man's age when his eyes were drug-distorted and his mouth thinned in a snarl.

At any rate, he stood about six feet tall and was too heavy for his height, though the extra weight appeared to be all muscle. And he wore gloves. White cotton gloves, so he would leave no fingerprints. Having a nephew who was a detective, this told her right away that her intruder was smart.

Behind him a window was open. Had she left it unlocked? She didn't think so. She wasn't that careless or forgetful. In fact, Ned needn't have called to warn her about keeping her windows and doors locked. Evidently her intruder knew how to open locked windows.

As all these thoughts rushed through her mind, she finally found her voice. "You!" she cried, taking a step forward. "What do you think you're doing?"

What he was doing was standing there by the bureau, wide-legged, staring at her with wide, unblinking eyes, and sort of holding his breath.

Then he lunged.

One of those gloved hands made crunching contact with the side of Martha Lawton's fragile, seventy-six-year-old face. Stumbling backward, Martha made similar crunching contact with the door-frame and sank to the floor, her eyes still open but her vision blurred, her breath coming in feeble gasps.

"Bitch!" the young man said, and thrust his right gloved hand into his pants pocket.

It came out gripping a revolver.

"Stupid bitch!" he said, and pointed the gun at Martha, whose eyes were still open, staring up at him.

"No," Martha whispered. "Don't."

He squeezed the trigger.

A second before the bullet thudded into her body, Martha Lawton was aware of a blurry movement beside her in the bedroom doorway, right there close to her, on the floor. Her last thought was, "No, Joey, don't! Don't come in here! He'll shoot you, too! Run, Joey, run!"

Did that thought actually reach the seal-point Siamese who had suddenly stopped in the doorway and was peering at her as she lay there? *Something* caused the cat to stop. *Something* made Joey look at her, then turn his head and look at the young man with the gun, and then—quick as a flash—leap back into the hall.

The young man had seen the cat. Had actually lifted his gloved gun-hand again as though to pull the trigger a second time. But when Joey so swiftly vanished, all he could do was stand there staring. First at the empty doorway, then down at the gray-haired woman on the floor.

Her face bled where his gloved fist had crashed into it. He looked at his fist and saw blood on the glove, too. Some had even dripped onto the revolver. Turning away from Martha, who now lay unmoving with her eyes closed, the intruder peered at the open bureau drawer, stepped toward it, stopped, and shook his head.

"Damn!" he said, then ran to the open window and disappeared through it.

Martha Lawton lay there, her bosom very slowly rising and falling, until at eight minutes past eight the following morning, Detective Ned Quinn rang his beloved aunt's doorbell. He rang it three times. When no one responded, he took a ring of keys from his pocket and unlocked the door.

"Martha?" he called as he stepped inside.

No one answered.

He called her name again, then shut the door behind him and went looking for her. He found her there on the floor by the door of her bedroom, unconscious but alive, and drove her to Brampton Hospital.

After phoning the police station from the hospital, Ned Quinn returned to the house and looked around, noting the open bedroom window and the open bureau drawer. Joey, his aunt's beloved cat, was nowhere in evidence, he noticed. That was strange. He called the cat's name a few times, but Joey did not respond.

The little guy must have seen it happen, Ned thought. Must have gotten scared and run off.

Three fellow officers arrived presently in a Brampton police car to help with the investigation. While searching the house for clues, they exchanged comments.

"Most likely it was one of our druggies, on the prowl for money."

"Or for jewelry, or something else easy to sell."

"But why did they have to assault the poor old lady, for God's sake? Why shoot her? She couldn't have been a threat to them."

"That's how they are."

"The bullet could tell us something. It's still in her."

"Yeah. Let's hope. This is one piece of trash we have to catch."

The Brampton cops returned to the station. Left alone in the dead woman's house, Ned Quinn sank sadly into her favorite living room chair—the one she had last occupied while watching *The X-Files*—and let the tears flow. Then he returned to the hospital.

Martha did not die, though the bullet had missed her heart by only inches. She would recover, the doctors said. The next day when Ned went to see her again, she was even able to talk to him and describe her assailant. It was no one he knew, he had to admit with a shake of his head.

Then a technician at the hospital, a small, dark man named DeStefano, beckoned Ned to a microscope on a table and invited him to peer into it. What Ned saw on the slide were a number of white, headless snakes. Those, DeStefano informed him, were bits of cotton fiber taken from Martha's battered face.

"How they got into the wound I can't imagine," he said, "unless when the guy slugged her he maybe had a towel wrapped around his fist. These fibers didn't come from the carpet or anything she was wearing."

"Thanks," Ned said. "I'll keep that in mind."

"By the way," said DeStefano, "the slug the medics took out of her was a thirty-eight. Find the gun and maybe you can put its owner where he belongs."

Following the assault, which was a front-page story in the Brampton *Press Journal*, Martha Lawton remained in the hospital while Ned Quinn went every day to her home to look for clues. Beginning with the window through which the killer had entered, he searched every room in the house but found nothing. No fingerprints. Nothing left behind.

On each of his visits Ned also looked for Martha's cat, Joey. His aunt loved the Siamese with a passion, and he was determined to find it. Being a working man who lived alone, he might find caring for a cat until Martha was able to leave the hospital a bit much, he guessed, but if he didn't, little Joey could die of hunger.

Not until the third evening, when he was sitting in Martha's favorite TV chair again, wondering what to do next, did Joey finally turn up. Then the cat made a noise pushing through its panel in the kitchen door—the panel Ned himself had installed—and as Ned rose scowling from his chair, Joey walked into the living room and dropped something white at his feet.

The object was a clean white cotton glove. Ned bent to pick it up and discovered it was damp. The cat stood there looking up at him, as if to say, "Well? Aren't you going to do something about this?"

Ned remembered the white cotton fibers he had peered at through the microscope. "All right, fella," he said. "Where'd you get it?"

Joey responded with a sharp "Mr-r-eow!" and trotted back into the kitchen, with a backward glance as if to make sure Ned followed.

Ned did follow. And when Joey pushed through his little panel, Ned unlocked the door itself and stepped out after him.

The cat waited for him to turn and relock the door, then looked up at him again, this time as if to say, "Okay? Can we go now?"

"Lead on, little buddy," Ned said. "Show me where you got it. But go slow, will you? I can't see in the dark like you."

It *was* dark, and Joey did go slowly, stopping once in a while to make sure Ned was still behind him. Being a brown Siamese with black markings, he himself was nearly invisible, but his eyes glowed helpfully and Ned had no trouble keeping up with him.

Across the yard they went, and around the house to the front, then on down the street—Elm Street, it was called—for a distance of four blocks. In Brampton only the town's main thoroughfare was lighted at night; there were no street lamps elsewhere. Elm Street tonight was dark as a criminal's heart.

Joey stopped after the four blocks, though, and waited for Ned to catch up. Waited, actually, for Ned to bend over and stroke him and say something. What Ned said was, "Is this where you got it, buddy? Somewhere here on Tyler Street?"

"M-r-reow," Joey said, and Ned could have sworn he nodded.

"Okay. Lead on."

They went down Tyler Street to the fourth house. All the houses on Tyler were shabby; this one had been white once but was gray now. The lawn was mostly weeds.

Joey turned up along the side of the house and, with Ned closely following, trotted into the backyard.

There in the backyard a couple of sheets, some shirts, a dress, and a few other items hung from a clothesline. There was no breeze to flap them so they just hung there, most of them visible in the dark because they were white. Near the end of the line, which ran from the house to a pole near a fence some thirty feet distant, hung what looked like a single white glove.

Joey ran across the yard toward it, increasing his speed as he went, and when close enough he leaped high into the air. But not quite high enough.

He tried again while Ned hurried toward him. This time he made it and came down with the glove in his mouth.

As he did so, the back door of the house clattered open, shattering the silence and letting a lane of yellow light stab out across the yard.

Ned stopped in his tracks and turned on one foot. The cat spun about, too. There they were, some ten feet apart, man and cat staring at the doorway's yellow rectangle and the outline of a young man framed in it.

Suddenly the young man snatched at his belt, or at a pocket just below it, and Ned Quinn saw a revolver appear in his hand.

Ned moved even more swiftly, and a gun leaped into his hand too. "Freeze!" he said in his Detective Ned Quinn voice. "Drop it, and keep your hands where I can see them!"

Evidently the youth had seen only the cat. Startled, he spun toward the sound of Ned's voice, and because he hadn't obeyed the command to drop his weapon, Ned fired. You didn't take chances with a creep who would shoot an unarmed, helpless old lady.

There wasn't a better shot on the Brampton police force than Detective Ned Quinn. His bullet went through the youth's wrist and the weapon in the youth's hand went flying.

Stunned, the young man stood there looking down at his wrist for four or five seconds. Then he voiced a wailing scream and sank to his knees, just as a thin, dark-haired woman appeared in the lighted doorway behind him.

Joey, the cat, trotted over to Ned with the glove he had snatched off the clothesline. Ned reached down for it, saw it was a mate to the one the cat had brought home before, and with a nod of satisfaction thrust it into his shirt pocket. Gun in hand, he then walked over to the two in the doorway.

"I'm a police officer," he said. "Is this your son, lady?"

She stared at him in silence for a few seconds, then nodded.

Ned took hold of the boy's arm, just above the shattered wrist. With his other hand he showed the woman the white cotton glove Joey had snatched off the clothesline. "Is this yours, lady?" he asked.

She peered at the glove and shook her head.

"You didn't just wash it?"

"I started the wash," she said. "My son finished and hung it out. I didn't put that in the machine." Frowning, she looked at her son. "What's going on here, Wayne?"

"Never mind," Ned told her. "Do you have a telephone?"

She nodded.

"I'll thank you for the use of it," Ned said.

She led him into the house. He followed with one hand firmly gripping her son's good wrist. Ten minutes later a police car arrived.

There were two others in Wayne's gang. A test of the revolver with which he had tried to shoot Joey proved it was the same weapon he had used on Martha Lawton. Though he had obviously attempted to clean it, there was some of Martha's blood still on it.

Wayne went to jail. So did the others, for earlier crimes. Brampton became a quiet little town again. Martha was released from the hospital.

Ned Quinn continues to visit his beloved aunt every few days, and Joey invariably runs to him when he walks in. Man and cat are now close friends. They understand each other. They talk to each other. Even watch TV together.

Joey, Ned says, has never again come home with anything from a neighbor's clothesline.

Just a Little Catnap

KIMBERLY R. BROWN

BOB SCHERER DRUMMED HIS fingers on the taxi's steering wheel, trying to decide how to pay last month's rent. His landlady's thin, frowning face loomed in his mind, and he feared an eviction notice was coming soon. He often thought it would be easier to rob a bank than to try to earn a living driving a taxi. He just hoped that moving to this new uptown location would net him some higher-priced fares. His ex-wife had always complained that he wasn't enough of a go-getter.

At that moment, Mrs. J. K. Waterman, widow of the restaurant tycoon, stepped onto the sidewalk. Bob recognized her trademark fur coat and matching hat from the society pages of the newspaper he read between fares. At her feet, on a rhinestone-encrusted leash, was the largest, haughtiest looking cat Bob had ever seen. It stepped beside her like a runway model, legs placed just so, head held high. It had the coloring of his aunt's old Siamese, tawny fur with a brown mask and feet, but instead of being whippet-thin, its fur fluffed around it like a dandelion gone to seed. Its aloof face was flat, as if it had run into a wall at high speed.

Bob pulled his taxi beside Mrs. Waterman and, at that moment, the sun moved from behind a cloud and shined on the cat like a spotlight. An epiphany washed over Bob and it seemed as though his prayers had been answered. How much would Mrs. Waterman pay for the cat's safe return, if it should happen to be kidnapped—or in this case, catnapped?

His mind racing, Bob pulled his baseball cap low over his eyes and didn't turn around as Mrs. Waterman opened the back door of the cab. It wouldn't do to have her get a good look at him, in case this brainstorm panned out.

Cat cradled in her arms, Mrs. Waterman got in and said in an aristocratic voice, "Roxie's Grooming Salon, please."

Bob fumbled with the gears of the car and he broke into a sweat, despite the cool fall temperature. It would be so easy just to drive the other way, straight to his small house in the suburbs. But he didn't want to kidnap the woman—no, he didn't want to go down that felonious road. He just wanted to take the cat. Besides, he needed time to work out a foolproof plan. He pulled out into traffic and drove the five blocks to the shop.

In the back seat, Mrs. Waterman cooed to the fluffball. "You're Mama's grand champion, aren't you Lin-Su?" The cat answered in strange, guttural growls which Mrs. Waterman seemed to take as affection, because she redoubled her coos.

Bob risked a glance in the rearview mirror. Mrs. Waterman was rubbing the cat's ears, and the cat looked like she would collapse with ecstasy. As he pulled to the curb, Mrs. Waterman stuffed some bills into Bob's hand. "Will you be good enough to wait? We don't expect to be longer than half an hour."

When the woman and the cat emerged from the salon forty minutes later, Bob started the taxi. He turned the car around and drove the five blocks back to Mrs. Waterman's high-rise. He couldn't believe his luck as Mrs. Waterman said, "If you're available, we must go see Dr. Murray tomorrow morning at ten. Roxie says Lin-Su's allergies are acting up again. Poor baby hates those allergy shots so." Without waiting for an answer, the befurred woman and cat exited the cab.

For the next two weeks, Bob fell into the routine of chauffeuring the show-cat and her mistress between Roxie and Dr. Murray. He began to feel sorry for the pampered animal. Even though she wore a fancy collar and was no doubt served delicacies on fine china, Bob figured so much clipping and dusting and washing must cause its constant allergies. But he was certainly enjoying the extra money the trips provided.

Finally, the time was right. The next morning, Mrs. Waterman would be waiting for the cab to take her to the vet. Bob would snatch the cat, and his money problems would be over.

That evening, he stood in the pet aisle of the super-discount store, staring at the selection of cat toys, litterboxes, little collars of all description, more cat food than he had thought existed, and bags of cat-box filler. He didn't anticipate having his visitor for long—just long enough for Mrs. Waterman to pay ten grand to get it back. Ten thousand seemed like a reasonable amount. After all, the cat was a champion of some sort. It wasn't as much as you'd ask for a person, but then he didn't expect the cat to be as much trouble as a person. He grinned to himself. Why hadn't he thought of this before?

Whistling under his breath, he threw a five-pound bag of bargain-brand cat food into his cart. He stared at the litterboxes, but balked at the price they wanted for a simple plastic box and clay filler. The cat could use a cardboard box with some torn-up newspapers. It wouldn't hurt that coddled beast to rough it a little.

The next morning, Bob parked the taxi in the alley near Mrs. Waterman's high-rise and thought about his plan. Keep it simple, that was his motto. He hadn't followed that motto with a robbery scheme twenty years before, and as a result had spent a good portion of his youth in prison. But this was different. Who would care that some inbred feline had been kidnapped, except Mrs. Waterman? So chances were pretty good she wouldn't even bother to call the police. And if she did, how much effort would they really put into it?

He sprinted from the car to the block past Mrs. Waterman's, pleased that he had kept himself in fairly good shape. He placed a ski mask on his head, rolled up to the top to look like a normal cap. Finally, Mrs. Waterman emerged from the building, the leashed cat at her feet, and looked at her watch impatiently.

It was now or never! Bob pulled the cap down over his face, sprinted forward, and in one smooth movement reached down to snatch the fur-ball. He ran with the wriggling animal held tightly against his chest. Mrs. Waterman's shrieks echoed in his ears as he rounded the corner and ran to the car. He threw open the door, threw the cat in, and drove away. It was that simple.

As soon as she hit the car seat, Lin-Su disappeared under the passenger's side and yowled, an unearthly screech that sent chills down Bob's spine. The cat continued to wail as Bob made his getaway up one street and down the other, to throw off anyone who might have decided to chase him. Finally, he left the city and drove the short distance to his tiny house, confident that no one had followed.

Bob parked the cab and groped under the seat until he felt fur, only to be rewarded with a sharp bite on his hand.

"Ow! You little monster!" Fingers sinking knuckle-deep in fur, Bob grabbed Lin-Su by the collar and pulled her from under the seat. Holding the squirming cat tightly by the scruff of the neck, he unlocked his front door.

With a hiss and a scratch deep enough to rip Bob's only jacket, the cat leaped from his arms. Instead of hiding under a piece of furniture, Lin-Su stopped in the middle of the room, tail held at an arrogant angle, and sniffed her new surroundings. Then, as if to say she wasn't pleased with her new standard of living, the cat opened her mouth and sounds the like of which Bob had never heard before came out.

"Hey, stop that!" Bob said. He threw his torn jacket at the cat. "The neighbors'll think I'm killing a baby in here!" Lin-Su dodged the jacket gracefully and, belly low to the floor, ran under a chair, making unearthly sounds all the while.

Bob pulled down his cracked, yellowed window shades, put food and water in two margarine bowls, and filled a cardboard box with newspaper strips. He would wait until tomorrow to try to make contact with Mrs. Waterman. Let her stew for a while—it would increase her willingness to pay.

Bob spent the night holed up in his bedroom watching his small black-and-white television. He tried to ignore the eerie howls and hisses coming from the living room, but his night was filled with strange dreams of monstrous, yowling felines.

The next morning, Bob moved stealthily down the hallway from his bedroom. He pushed the living room door open and his jaw dropped in wonder at the sight. A sharp, eye-watering odor met his nose. The carpet in front of the hallway door and the front door had been ripped to shreds. A mess of cat food and newspaper strips was strewn over the floor and on the couch. Bob's wary eyes followed the path of newspaper strips over the back of the couch and up the curtains, where a piece of newspaper dangled from the top like a flag.

A big wet spot darkened his threadbare carpet where the water dish had been overturned. Bob saw another wet spot in front of his favorite chair, not as large but much more odorous. Dander floated on the sunbeam coming through the cracks in the window shade and he sneezed fiercely.

In the midst of the mess sat Lin-Su, calmly washing her face with one brown-tipped paw, fluffy tail curled about her brown legs. She leaned back on one haunch, lifted her leg gracefully above her head, and began to wash her nether parts. As she leaned backward, her collar thrust forward, and the sunbeam caught something glittery at her throat. Bob stared at the collar, trying to catch the sparkle again. The paste stones in that collar couldn't be glittering like that! He started forward, but Lin-Su darted under the couch, mewing in alarm.

Studiously ignoring Lin-Su, Bob began to straighten the room. He swept up the cat food and newspaper, then dried the wet spots with an old towel, and poured ammonia on the smelly spot. Just as he finished, someone pounded at his door, making his heart leap into his throat. He twitched the curtain aside and saw the grim face of his landlady.

He opened the door a couple of inches and peeked through the crack. "Mrs. Botnik. What a surprise!"

Mrs. Botnik pursed her lips and crossed her bony arms. "I'm here to collect the rent, Mr. Scherer. This month's as well as last month's."

Bob thought quickly. "I have a new job. I'm expecting a big paycheck next week. I'll have your money then." As he started to shut the door, he felt a softness against his lower leg. Lin-Su meowed loudly, and began to purr as she wrapped herself in and out of his legs.

"You have a cat!" Mrs. Botnik shrieked, and her fingers flew to her mouth. She pulled at the screen, but Bob held it firmly shut.

"I can explain," he said. He pushed Lin-Su away with his foot, but she was immediately on the other side, purring and twining. "I'm just cat-sitting. For my cousin."

To Bob's amazement, Mrs. Botnik's angular face softened into a wreath of smiles. "Such a beautiful kitty!" she exclaimed. She knelt down and made soft clucking sounds, while Lin-Su sniffed her hand through the screen. Lin-Su's tail shook with pleasure. Finally, Mrs. Botnik stood with a loud pop of bony knee joints. "Very well, Mr. Scherer. Please call me next week, when you have the money."

Having been suitably adored, Lin-Su marched away. She sank into a ball on the floor and closed her eyes. Bob tiptoed toward her and touched her soft head. He imitated Mrs. Botnik's worshipful noises and scratched her ears as he had seen Mrs. Waterman do. He was rewarded with a loud purr.

Then, gently rubbing her head with one hand, Bob removed the collar with the other. He held it under the table lamp and examined the stones one by one. There were gaudy red ones and green ones the color of lime gelatin. Most of the clear ones were cloudy and plastic-looking. But the three big stones at the top of the collar! Those glittered and sparkled, catching the light in their many facets. Bob's heart pounded. These were not paste! He held them closer to the light. The settings that held those three stones weren't the same cheap metal that held the rhinestones in, but they were stronger, with more points.

He sat back on the sofa, his mind racing. Lin-Su leaped onto his lap, her purr deepening as he absently stroked her. Why would there be three real diamonds in a cat's collar? Sure, she was a special cat—a grand champion and all that. But real diamonds? He thought about the ten thousand he had been planning to demand for Lin-Su's return. Surely, these stones were worth much more! He gently put the fur-ball on the floor and pocketed the collar.

She went to the empty margarine bowl and mewed piteously. The haughty flat face looked sad now. Did she miss Mrs. Waterman? She probably just missed the gourmet food. He stood and stretched, slowly so as not to startle her. "I guess I could go get you something a little better," he told the cat. "And a proper litterbox." He patted his pocket. "After all, you may get me a fortune."

That night, Bob and Lin-Su curled up on his bed, in front of the television. He rubbed her back, his mind a million miles away from the idiotic television program.

Lin-Su slept all night curled against Bob's side, while he lay awake, his mind ticking over the facts. He thought about show-cats and allergies and rhinestone collars that contained real diamonds. By morning, he had reached a decision. It was time to call Mrs. Waterman.

With Lin-Su at his heels, Bob headed down the short hallway, toward his living room door. The cat stopped suddenly, arched her back, and growled deep in her throat. Bob held his breath, then he heard it too. Someone was in his living room! He tiptoed back to his bedroom for his old baseball bat, then he crept to the living room and pushed open the door.

A tall man and a woman with frizzy red hair stood in the middle of the room. The man held a pistol, which he pointed at Bob.

In spite of his disadvantage, Bob smiled. His grip tightened on the bat. "You must be Dr. Murray and Roxie." He enjoyed the look of surprise on the pair's faces.

Murray jabbed the gun in Bob's direction. "You must know what we're here for, then."

Bob nodded. "I guess Mrs. Waterman told you Lin-Su had been, uh, borrowed."

"You're an idiot," Roxie said. "She knew right away it was you, when you didn't show up in your cab. She called Dr. Murray right away."

Bob frowned. He was the one with the revelations and he didn't want to lose the floor. "It didn't take me long to figure that you two must be passing gemstones between you. And, if you were going to all the trouble to do it with a cat's collar, they must be some hot stones." He tried to keep his voice light and conversational. "I figure you must have two collars. Roxie would get a haul from somewhere, put them in Lin-Su's collar, then tell Mrs. Waterman that her baby's allergies were acting up. Of course Mrs. Waterman would run to the doc right away, where you'd exchange collars till next time."

Roxie twined her long red hair around a finger nervously. "Murray, get the stones and let's go."

The vet's eyes narrowed. "I don't know, Rox. He knows a lot. Maybe we should make sure he can't tell."

Bob's mouth went dry. He'd expected them just to get their jewels and go— he hadn't expected a vet and a cat groomer to be killers. The idea seemed to surprise Roxie, too, because she gaped at Murray.

At that moment, Lin-Su strolled into the room. As she saw Dr. Murray, her back arched and her fur stood on end, almost doubling her size. Then, before they could blink, she launched herself into the air and landed on Murray's arm, hissing and scratching furiously. He dropped the gun and it skittered across the room. Roxie and Bob both dived for it, but Bob felt no compunction about whacking her in the shin with his baseball bat.

"Ow!" she hollered, grabbing her leg, and Bob came up with the gun. Murray had thrown Lin-Su off, but he put his hand to his face, covering deep scratches.

"I guess she remembers you, Doc. Maybe she didn't like all those unnecessary allergy shots you two set her up to get." Panting slightly, Bob backpedaled to the table, holding the gun steadily on the pair. He picked up the phone. "I'm gonna call the cops, so you two behave."

"Wait a minute!" Roxie exclaimed. "You're a catnapper, remember? If you turn us in, you'll be arrested, too."

Bob thought for a minute, then dialed '9.' "I was just babysitting Lin-Su for a while. I never asked Mrs. Waterman for anything." He dialed '1.' "Besides, she'll be so grateful for getting her cat back safe, and for finding out her vet and groomer didn't have poor little Lin-Su's best interests in mind, I doubt she'll press charges. Who knows," he said, as he dialed another '1,' "she may even hire me as her chauffeur."

He spoke to the operator, hung up the phone, and looked at Lin-Su, who sat in the doorway, washing her face. "After I return Lin-Su to Mrs. Waterman, I think I'll pay a visit to the animal shelter. They might have a kitten that needs a home."

Lin-Su, giving Murray and Roxie a wide berth, leaped onto the telephone table beside Bob and sank into a furry mound, tucking her paws under her chest. Her eyes closed into satisfied slits.

Kit for Cat

JULIE KISTLER

JOSIE BARELY HAD TIME to thump once on the massive wooden door before it swung open with a creak. Yeesh. She half-expected someone to say, *You rang?*

But, no. Max O'Connor, the not-so-famous mystery writer, was too darn good-looking for that. Scowling, grumpy, rumpled, and still good-looking.

"What?" he demanded. "What do you want?"

Ignoring his tone, Josie edged around him, eager to take a gander at the interior of the small house. She'd been curious about it for weeks, from over on her side of the property line. There were all kinds of stories about the mysterious Mr. O'Connor, churning out books from his garret, er, carriage house. He rarely ventured out, or so the stories went, existing on a diet of delivery pizza, always fighting his muse for a few pages more.

He moved resolutely into her path, cutting her off before she got any further. "If you're collecting for something, I'm not giving."

"No, no. I'm Josie Kenyon. I live next door. In the Pope-Fontaine mansion." Quickly, she amended, "That is, the Pope-Fontaine Cat Sanctuary."

"Oh, so you got your zoning variance. Even with all the petitions."

"And the lawsuits. Yadda, yadda, yadda." Josie threw up her hands. "The people around here have been so unsupportive. You'd think sharing their fancy neighborhood with a few little cats was going to kill them."

"Uh huh." The mystery writer regarded her with a cynical eye. "And this concerns me because . . . ?"

"Because you're the only person in this lousy town who hasn't signed a petition or testified at a hearing or picketed in front of my house."

There was a pause. "So you've decided I'm an ally?"

"Close enough." Josie cut to the chase. "Look, you must be aware that I've been busy setting up the cat sanctuary that Louella Pope-Fontaine specified in her will. And it hasn't been easy. But, hey, I'm open for business, and I've collected a total of five wonderful cats so far. Only now somebody has stolen three of my cats," she said angrily, "and replaced them with impostors."

"*Cat* impostors?"

"I know it sounds bizarre," she allowed. "But no weirder than your books. I've read them. Murders behind locked doors and on snowshoes and evil twins separated at birth—"

He winced. "Yeah, I never should've done the evil twin thing. Bad idea."

Impatient, Josie got back on track. "The important thing is that you obviously have a fertile mind for oddball plots. So you're exactly the right person to help me solve this catnapping thing."

"If your cats have really been stolen, don't you think the police—?"

"The police? You've got to be kidding," she interrupted. "For starters, my cats haven't just been stolen, they've been *exchanged*. They'll never believe that, because it doesn't make sense even to me. And then there's the fact that the chief of police just happens to be married to a lady named Myrtle Kipp, who is not exactly a fan of the sanctuary."

"Yeah, I think I've heard of her. Hefty lady, owns about forty cats?"

"That's the one." She sighed. "Myrtle thinks all cats should be allowed to run free, unfettered. I spay and neuter, you see, and I keep them indoors. So I'm the enemy. Her dear husband just laughed in my face when I complained about the picketers."

"Okay, so the cops are out. I still don't see what I—"

"But I need help!"

"Yeah, well, it's clear you need help," he muttered, "but somehow I doubt I'm the right kind."

So he didn't believe her? He thought she was a nutcase? "Come on, I'll show you."

Without giving him a chance to object, she dragged him by the hand, back through his front door, down the curving driveway, around through her own gate and onto Pope-Fontaine ground.

"This way," she ordered, leading him inside a glassed-in wing on the back of the house. "They're lounging by the pool. See the little black-and-white one on the chaise?"

He nodded, but he was gazing down at his toe. Or maybe at the orange tabby, the faux marmalade, who was playing with his shoelace.

"The one on the chaise is supposed to be Minnie." She walked over and scooped up the cat. "See, the tag says Minnie. Only this isn't Minnie."

"Right."

"Look at her," she commanded, showing him one flank and then the other, as the cat emitted a small squawk and tried to flee. "I named her Minnie because the black spots on her side looked like mouse ears. But, look—this one's spots are more like a snowman. Clearly, I would've named her Frosty."

"I'm sure you would," Max said in a tactful tone that she didn't appreciate one bit.

She set down the cat, pointing to others who lay around the pool. "They didn't touch Penelope, the Persian, or Demon, the all black one. But Marmalade, the one on your shoe, is a boy. I looked. Only the real Marmalade is a girl. Plus Binky is now a torbie when she should be a tabby!"

Kindly he said, "You seem upset. Why don't you sit around the pool with your kitties, kick back, take a load off?"

"But that's not productive," she protested. "Shouldn't I do something to try to solve this? You know, think up theories of the crime or something?"

"Yeah, sure, okay." But he was backing away. "Start with motive. Figure out who had a reason to trade cats with you. And then I'd look at means, which in this case would be a supply of cats to switch with—"

"Oooh, I didn't think of that. Good point."

"Last is opportunity. Motive, means, opportunity. You work on that and get back to me."

And he was out of there before she had a chance to grab him. Darn it.

He knew it was her before he even picked up the phone. Hiding a smile, Max said, "Yeah?"

"They're back," she told him, not bothering with preliminaries. "Minnie, Marmalade, and Binky. Safe and sound, and the impostors are gone. Only now something else has happened."

Max sat up straighter. "What?"

"Demon. He's gone, without a replacement." There was a catch in her voice. "They must've taken him when they traded back the other three. And I think I found the place where the kidnapper got in. Come over here so I can show you." And then she hung up.

So what choice did he have?

When he got there, Josie Kenyon was standing in the immense sunken living room. Only instead of fancy furniture, there were toys and ramps and carpet tubes all around, as if it were a kitty-cat playground.

"This," Josie said triumphantly, cuddling a black-and-white cat with the telltale marking of a famous cartoon mouse, "is the real Minnie."

Max noted the spot pattern. "Looks like Minnie all right."

"Exactly." Josie led him further into the mansion, past the kitchen and into a walk-in pantry with a narrow, open window at the back. "I saw it as soon as I came in for cat food this morning. The screen's gone, and the window was pushed open from outside. I figure that's how they got in."

Josie didn't wait for him to agree, just carefully closed and locked the pantry door, and then marched down the hall to a nicely appointed office. "Okay, so I did what you said. I thought about theories and all that." She pulled a sheet of paper out of the printer behind her desk. "Here it is. I typed up a list of suspects."

"But if the cats are back, what do you need suspects for?"

"To find Demon, of course," she said quickly.

"Are you sure he's not hiding somewhere in the house?" He looked around. "It's a big house."

"I looked everywhere. He's gone."

"Maybe he ran away, all on his own, unconnected to the others." Max gave her a long look. "Doesn't it seem odd that someone would go to the trouble to do a switcheroo with three of them, and then just grab the last one?"

"The whole thing is odd!"

Well, he had to give her that. She sat back in a huge wing chair, looking like Jonah inside the whale, all small and vulnerable, and Max knew he might as well give in. "Go ahead," he said reluctantly. "Tell me about your suspects."

"There are four. Number one," she announced, "is Myrtle Kipp. We already talked about her. And then I've also got Ophelia Pope. She's Louella P-F's great-niece or something, and she would've inherited everything if not for the sanctuary."

Max pulled out a small pad and started to take notes. "Myrtle the cat lady and Ophelia the heiress. Next?"

"Reverend Gary Roy Ronkus." Josie shuddered. "Have you met him? Scary. And his Stepford-wife, Kathy Lee, is even scarier. He runs the Little Chapel of Eternal Damnation, and he keeps preaching that cats are evil spawn of Satan. He gave quite a speech to the city council to try to keep me out of business."

"Sounds like a contender." Max looked up. "Who else?"

"Dr. Steve Vedekov."

"The guy at the humane society? No way."

"But he came out loud and clear against the sanctuary," Josie argued. "I don't know whether he was afraid of the competition or what, but he was very unkind."

"Probably just thought you were a flake." Max regarded her dryly. "Take him off the list. Steve's a good guy. Used to date my sister."

"Because he dated your sister you want me to absolve him? I don't think so!"

"Listen," he tried, in a gentler tone, "my sister volunteers at that shelter, and she says Vedekov is one of the best. I just don't think he'd go in for this kind of cat-switching rigmarole."

Josie crossed her arms over her chest. "I'm not taking him off the list."

"It's not him."

"It could be."

It was an impasse. Max broke first. "Okay, so what motives have you got for these people?"

She shrugged. "It's the same motive for everyone. The only thing I can think of is that somebody wants to make me look crazy. Somebody who wants the Pope-Fontaine Cat Sanctuary shut down before it ever really gets started."

"I don't know if I buy that. Especially since the cats have been switched back."

But she stopped him. "Can you come up with anything better?"

None that he cared to share.

Josie continued, "I also thought about the other things. You know, means and opportunity? Dr. Vedekov has a big pool of cats to find substitutes. And so does Myrtle."

Max shook his head. "But Myrtle Kipp is three hundred pounds if she's an ounce. If your thief came through that small window, then—"

"My thief isn't Myrtle." She made a dark line through the top name on her list. "Okay, so we're down to three."

"What about opportunity?"

"Well, Reverend Ronkus's Little Chapel isn't far, and neither is the humane society." She frowned. "I don't know about Ophelia, though. She had to fly in from out of town when she tried to get Louella's will overturned."

Max shrugged. "Let's find out." He pointed to the computer. "Do you have a modem on that thing?"

It was quick work to dial in, pull up a handy website, and do a quick search. Max tried not to show off too much. But he had an address and phone number for Ophelia Pope in about three seconds. After that, a quick call found Ophelia safe at home. In Las Vegas.

"No way she got here, switched your cats, and made it back to Vegas. . . ." He glanced at the clock on the wall. "By nine A.M. Scratch Ophelia."

"No Myrtle, no Ophelia." Josie chewed her lip thoughtfully. "That only leaves Doctor Vedekov—"

"Who I still don't think it is."

"Or the Reverend Ronkus. Wait a second. . . ." Josie leaned forward suddenly, almost tipping out of her huge chair. "The only cat stolen outright is Demon. Reverend Gary Roy thinks all cats are demons. Do you think—?"

But she never got to finish the sentence. A terrible din—a kind of howl and then a short, nasty shriek—erupted from outside. Josie and Max were both up and out of there before the caterwauling had even stopped echoing against the house.

"Oh, my God," Josie whispered, stopping dead in her tracks. "It's Reverend Gary Roy Ronkus."

Max was ahead of her. Way at the back of the Pope-Fontaine estate, just inside the fence, the black-clad reverend lay face up, with a very ugly look on his face. The knife protruding from his chest was even uglier. And there were scratches on the man's face. Cat? Or human?

Max felt for a pulse, but he already knew what he'd find. "Better call the police, Josie. This is one ex-reverend."

"I never thought—"

"Yeah. Me neither." Who could've predicted that a wacky little cat-swap would turn into murder?

Josie scrambled back to the house, returning with a cell phone pressed to her ear. He could see her talking energetically into the phone, obviously trying to get out the whole story to a less-than-appreciative audience.

Just as she signed off, Max thought he heard a small, indistinct cry or moan, coming from a stand of trees not far off. He lifted his head. "Did you hear that?"

Josie edged around behind him, using him to block her view of the dead man. "Wh-what was it?"

"I don't know. But I'm going to find out."

As Max cut across the lawn in search of the odd little whimper, she hurried to keep up. "You're not leaving me alone with *him*."

The cries became louder as they neared a big oak. Max slowed, holding Josie safely behind him, but he soon saw there was no need. The woman propped against the far side of the tree trunk was so subdued she was practically catatonic.

"It's Kathy Lee Ronkus," Josie whispered. "With Demon."

Clutching the all-black cat to her chest, Kathy Lee petted it gently, weeping with every stroke. Her hands were stained red, and Demon's fur looked matted where she'd touched him.

Josie slipped out from behind Max, kneeling next to the distraught woman. "Everything's all right now," she said in a soothing tone, carefully lifting Demon away and into her own arms. "Do you want to tell us what happened?"

Through her tears, Mrs. Ronkus mumbled, "I had to make him stop. He brought the Cleansing Sword of Divine Right to, you know, kill the kitty. And then he was going to burn it at the stake, like you're supposed to do with demons. He said—he said we couldn't suffer the demon to live, but I knew it wasn't right." Her eyes met Josie's. "I couldn't let him kill the kitty. Could I?"

They hadn't even noticed the arrival of Police Chief Kipp, who came barreling in with his weapon drawn. "Is this the perp?" he bellowed.

Josie nodded. "Apparently her husband was going to make an example of my cat, I guess because his name was Demon. But his wife got in the middle of it."

"A real couple of fruitcakes, huh? But what was that you told the dispatcher about somebody switching your other cats and sticking fake ones in their places?" the chief persisted. "Okay, so the reverend went off the deep end and tried to steal one. But why replace the other ones?"

Josie shrugged. "Who knows? The reverend and his bride both took a long leap off a short pier, if you ask me. Nothing those two did is going to make sense."

Chief Kipp glanced over at Max. "What do you think?"

Quietly, Max returned, "What she said."

As Kipp and his men busied themselves handcuffing poor, deranged Kathy Lee Ronkus, Josie shepherded Max and Demon back into the house. "I have to wash him off," she murmured. "Pronto."

In some sort of large mudroom, Max helped her hold the wriggling cat as she tried to wipe him down. Over Demon's wet body, he gazed at her, wondering how to broach this. "Josie," he said finally, "there's something I have to tell you."

"Did you really think I wouldn't figure it out?" Josie stood back from the sink, giving him a superior smile. "Okay, so Demon and his totally coincidental adventure with the reverend confused things. But let's see—motive, means, opportunity. Who had the best opportunity? How about the guy who lives next door? Means—your sister works at an animal shelter, right?"

"But when—?"

She kept right on going, her smile growing wider. "But what about motive, Max, that sticky wicket from the beginning? Who had a motive? Who stood to gain if my cats were switched? You did, Max, because you knew I would trot right over and ask for your help."

"Now, just a second. I—"

Josie shook her head. "Sheesh. I've had guys go to extremes to try to meet me before, but only a mystery writer would think up this one."

Lady Windermere's Flan
(with apologies to Oscar Wilde)

ELIZABETH FOXWELL

I CAST AN EYE DOWN A COLUMN debating the return to Greece, after some eighty years, of Lord Elgin's spoils from the Parthenon. "Rather belated now," I muttered crossly and hurled the newspaper into the whatnot, rattling the objects it held. I drummed my fingers on the arm of my Bath chair, bored and unaccustomedly restless. My valet entered the room, a distant cousin to distress sliding across his imperturbable features. "What is it?" I snapped.

"Sir," began Slade. "That creature—"

I frowned. My pique was not improved by endless accounts of What That Cat Had Done Now. Roma was a souvenir of our last encounter* with the Hon. Maud Greystone, playwright and distraction. Maud had turned her luminous eyes on me, and somehow I—and Slade—were transformed into unlikely—and unwilling—Cat Caretakers.

"That creature," continued Slade, automatically retrieving and folding the newspaper, "has interfered with the buttermilk again and left a trail of paw-prints across Mrs. Dunn's newly scrubbed floor. I barely had time, sir, to remove the skillet from her hand."

"You are to be congratulated, Slade."

"It would hardly do to upset Miss Greystone, sir."

I glanced at the whatnot again. It was an elegant piece of furniture, certainly, but I fancied the framed drawing of the woman on its polished surface was the more entrancing.

The bell rang and Slade went out. He returned behind a woman with dramatic cheekbones and thick dark hair upswept gracefully off her swanlike neck. I sat up sharply in my chair, straightening my smoking jacket.

"Good afternoon, Lady Windermere."

Since her debut, Lady Marguerite Windermere had taken the season by

---

*A Roman of No Importance

storm with her irresistible combination of exotic Latin beauty and sizable American income. To everyone's surprise, she had not chosen any of the eligible young bachelors strewn in her path—including the Mexican diplomat Javier García Montez and my equally intoxicated godson, Algernon Moncrieff—but Lord Windermere, a longtime bachelor and collector in the arts some twenty years her senior.

"Señor Bunbury." She flung herself on the carpet in a cascade of crimson, clasping her hands imploringly. "Help me."

I gazed down at the lovely vision on the floor. "Surely a chair would be more comfortable, Lady Windermere?"

The ever-helpful Slade provided a respectful arm to assist Lady Windermere to her feet and a more traditional seat. But she still perched on the very edge of the chair, her liquid eyes wide with appeal.

"Algy said you solved problems of a nature most delicate, señor," she said in her uneven English.

"On occasion," I said cautiously, and mentally consigned the indiscreet Algy to the farthest regions of Hell.

"He said—you are clever. Yes?"

I instantly restored Algy to the land of the living.

"I need a clever man, señor, to rescue me from my folly," she continued with a charming anxious smile. "Thinking with the heart rather than the head."

My thoughts moved irresistibly to Maud Greystone, and I wrenched them back with difficulty. "An understandable weakness, Lady Windermere."

"*Exactamente*, señor. Weakness it is. And it now may cost me everything I have." She sighed. "I notice Lord Windermere returning home later and later at night. I felt there must be another woman."

"Impossible, madam."

She inclined her head, acknowledging the compliment. "You are kind, señor. But I wait outside his office, you understand? And I see a woman leave, late in the evening."

"Are you certain? It was dark. Perhaps the visitor was a man?"

She smiled sadly. "Silver combs in the hair shine even in lamplight, señor."

"I am sorry, Lady Windermere."

"I blame myself, Señor Bunbury," she countered with an ardent candor. "This colder climate of yours has not dampened my hot temper. It has been most hard on Lord Windermere. He is older than I and content to putter about among his pottery and paintings. I am not. But I honor and love my husband."

She sighed again. "This woman fired all the passion of my Latin temperament. Señor Montez came to call and desired my special flan. You know it, señor?"

"It is a type of custard, as I recall."

"Sí. A specialty of my mother's homeland. Javier says no one prepares it as I do. He was most insistent. Flattering." She flushed. "Perhaps if I had not been out of temper with my husband I would not have been so foolish. I made the flan and arranged it prettily on a bright blue plate. Javier admired Lord Windermere's collection, then took the flan away with him. After he had left I discovered my wedding ring was missing. It slipped off while I was cooking."

"Into the flan."

She nodded and dabbed at her eyes with a handkerchief. "I must retrieve it, or I am lost. If Javier finds it, he will think the ring a token of my affection." Her fingers twisted together. "My husband is a good man, but he could not countenance his former rival with my wedding ring. I would well and truly lose his affection to this other woman."

"Do I understand you properly?" I asked. "You wish me to retrieve . . . a *dessert?*"

Slade looked like he had been slapped.

"Sí," she said eagerly.

Silence greeted her words. She faltered, the dark eyes dimming. Every gallant impulse in my body leapt at her distress but my more rational mind resisted. "I have never encountered an—er, edible—problem, Lady Windermere. Surely the 'evidence' has been digested."

"I came to you immediately. Señor Montez is attending a diplomatic affair. He told me he would eat the flan at dinner."

"Could you not go to his house and retrieve it on your own?"

She grimaced. "Juanita—his sister and hostess—has no great love for me. Her duenna would take great pains to inform my husband of my visit." Her scowl deepened. "The lazy Señora Gaston's devotion extends to food, Juanita, and *el gato—solamente*. If not for his sister's reputation, Javier would pack the enormous señora back to her Spanish homeland. Fur and idleness irritate him."

Slade's eyes gleamed, and despite Señor Montez's dislike of cats, Slade's expectation of foisting Roma on the duenna was easily divined. "Could this Señora Gaston sample the flan before Señor Montez?"

The pleading eyes held mine and all my objections—a man in a Bath chair is scarcely an ideal burglar—melted like snow.

"I will look into the matter," I promised.

Slade sat across from me in the carriage. The cage on the floor rumbled ominously with low, feline growls.

"How did you manage it?" I asked Slade, regarding the vocal object.

"A saucer of cream and a pair of gauntlets are invaluable kit." He hesitated. "If you'll pardon my saying so, sir . . . it does not seem like much of a case."

"Doesn't it?" The horses pulled up. Señor Montez's residence lay in Grosvenor Square, its lacy trellises shining white and elegant even in the dodgy sunshine. "I fancy it has one or two features of interest."

"Such as, sir?"

"Why was Señor Montez so insistent about Lady Windermere preparing the flan?"

"What the lady said: His partiality to her cuisine."

I snorted. "A diplomat, with his own hand-picked cook from Mexico? Just follow my lead, Slade."

He stepped out of the carriage, removed the Bath chair, and settled me into it. "I always do, sir."

Another carriage came to a snorting, stamping halt behind us and I heard Slade's sharp intake of breath. "Followed," he hissed, and I heard him wrench open the carpetbag at the back of my chair—the keeper of the revolver.

"What is your business, sir?" I said coldly as the carriage's occupant bore down on us—it does not do to show a fearful countenance to ruffians—then I recognized him. "Lord Windermere!"

The gray-haired husband of Marguerite Windermere was not a bulky man, but his looming over me with clenched fists seemed to pose a clear threat. "My wife called upon you, Bunbury. I want to know why."

"I would suggest asking Lady Windermere."

His square jaw set. "I am asking you."

"Unfortunate weather we are having, don't you think? I am sure a storm is brewing."

"You refuse to answer." His fingers bit nastily into my arm. "I will not have it, sir. If you believe your disability excuses you—"

I looked at the intrusive hand on my arm as if it were an insect, then back at him steadily. Slade cocked the hammer of the revolver, which resounded on the quiet street like a thunderclap. Roma hissed in the cage, and Windermere released my arm.

"This is not over, Bunbury."

I withdrew my case from my coat. "Here is my card. But I believe you already know where I reside."

Windermere stormed away.

"Well played, sir." Slade thrust the pistol back in the carpetbag and lifted the cage, dodging the swipe of an annoyed paw. "Are you injured?"

"No, I am quite all right, thank you."

He looked at Lord Windermere climbing into his carriage. "Interesting, sir."

"Yes, Slade. I thought so too."

He wheeled me to the front door, and I tossed a card onto the butler's polished tray. After a short interval, we were admitted to the drawing room. Juanita Montez glanced up from her needlework, a pretty if somewhat sulky young woman in elaborately embroidered white silk, her heavy black hair twisted with flashy bits of ribbon. Seated near her was a figure swathed in black—Señora Gaston, the duenna, I assumed—her gloved hands folded firmly in her large lap.

On the tea table lay the promised flan—er, land—golden brown and quivering in a crudely shaped and chipped red bowl decorated with birds. On one side of the custard appeared a rather revealing bulge. I looked away hurriedly.

"Señor Bunbury? We are acquainted?"

"Er, I am acquainted with your brother," I said rapidly. "And I wished to make your acquaintance, Miss Montez."

She smiled, some of the sulkiness receding. The mounds of black began to vibrate, like a rumbling volcano. I quickly said, "I am glad to see you are properly chaperoned. So many young misses entering society do not have the benefit of wise counsel."

The volcano subsided, and I saw Slade slide closer to the tea table. Miss Montez pricked her thumb with her needle and bent over the embroidery hoop, the ribbons in her hair swaying. I remembered Lady Windermere's glimpse of the mysterious woman and her iridescent hair ornaments leaving her husband's office. Was Miss Montez the late-night visitor of Lord Windermere? Was that the reason he had confronted me—to discover if his wife had confided in me about his mistress?

"I have brought a gift for Señora Gaston." I frowned at the flan. Something about it nagged at me. It continued to squat in its homely bowl, unilluminating.

Slade bent over the cage and released Roma. The duenna recoiled, throwing out a stiff arm. *"Madre de dios!* Er . . . Señor is generous but—"

A fat black cat sauntered in, and both felines arched their backs, hissing. Señora Gaston sneezed, and I remembered what else Lady Windermere had said. I reached over suddenly and ripped the mantilla off "her" head, and the very bearded Señor Montez sat there, sneezing violently. The cats launched into the flan, each other, and me, sending me hurtling backward in the chair. The red bowl teetered, and Slade and Señor Montez dived as one for the flan. In the tangle of spitting cats, torrents of angry Spanish and even angrier English, rivulets of liquid sugar, and Slade's flailing legs came a clear and unexpected voice. A familiar slim form appeared near my spluttering head.

"And I believed an invalid led such a dull existence," drawled the Hon. Maud Greystone.

"I'm not certain I understand all of this," said Maud presently.

Slade righted my chair and brushed ineffectually at his sticky coat. Señor

Montez, still absurdly attired in the duenna's clothing, peered out between the drapes, then turned. "I am sure the resourceful Señor Bunbury can explain all, Miss Greystone," said he with a charming smile (for Maud) and a saucy curtsey (for me). My valet received a bow. "I apologize, señor, for such rough handling."

Slade murmured something in smooth Spanish, and Montez's eyebrows shot up, impressed.

Miss Montez had retired in hysterics in the care of the real Señora Gaston. The black cat had been equally routed from the drawing room in a final tangle of fur, and Roma had taken up smug residence on Maud's knee.

"What are you doing here?" I asked her.

"Research. I'm thinking of setting a play in Mexico. Now do explain, Bunbury."

I managed a modest shrug. "Lady Windermere wished a compromising flan returned to her in a discreet fashion. What she didn't realize was that Señor Montez had designs of his own for the flan." I turned to him. "Lady Windermere said she arranged the flan very prettily on a blue plate. This bowl is far from blue and pretty nor is it a plate. I recalled an article I read about the Elgin marbles, and that Windermere also is a collector. It occurred to me that perhaps the object was not the flan, but a piece of pottery."

"An Aztec treasure stolen from my country," said Montez. "I offered to purchase it from Windermere at a fair price but he refused. I think he has not forgiven me for courting Marguerite. But matters of state must master *el corazon*, yes?" He peered out between the drapes again. "His carriage is still there, curse it."

"You switched the flan to the bowl before you left Lord Windermere's house."

He nodded. "When he accosted you, I feared he had discovered the theft of the bowl. I had barely enough time to disguise myself before you arrived at the door." He pulled a rueful face. "But you divined my unfortunate reaction to *los gatos*."

"Fascinating," interrupted Maud, "but I don't see how a custard can be compromising."

Before Montez could move, Slade handed the bowl and a knife to me. I cut into the telltale bulge in the flan and held up a ring, its gold and amethysts, even tacky with custard, shining in the light.

"Well, well," murmured Maud. Montez clapped his hands.

"*Excelente*, Señor Bunbury. You are—how do you say?—capital fellow."

"*Muchas gracias*, señor."

He gazed wistfully, even hungrily, at the piece of pottery in my hands. "The next play, I think, is yours."

I looked at the birds on the side of the bowl, graceful in their long-ago flight, and thought of treasures in many forms. "I should not like it, Mr. Montez, if the crown jewels were removed by someone who claimed Her Majesty's Government was an inadequate caretaker."

Maud's eyes shone, and I had to force myself to look from their radiance back at Montez. He was smiling. "You are a wise man, señor."

"Occasionally, sir." I gave him the bowl. "Now . . . I assume you must transport this piece to your embassy?"

"A rather difficult task, señor, with the persistent Lord Windermere on my doorstep."

"But you have an affinity for disguise, Mr. Montez. Please listen to what I propose . . ."

Slade pushed my Bath chair down the walk, accompanied by a querulous monologue from its heavily muffled occupant and several prods from an insistent stick. From the expression on Slade's features, I fancied I would hear later about the stick.

Slade heaved the chair's occupant into my carriage, secured the Bath chair, and climbed in. I watched the activities from behind the drapes. I had refused the loan of Señora Gaston's clothing—a gentleman must retain some dignity—and was clad in Señor Montez's garish yellow dressing gown. But because I possess some considerable inches over the Mexican diplomat, an embarrassing quantity of bare leg was exposed to Maud's interested eye.

My carriage rolled away. But Windermere's carriage, curtains drawn, sat stubbornly in front of the house.

"Hell and damnation," I muttered. "I have a ring to return to an anxious lady."

"Dear Bunbury. Always riding to the rescue of a damsel in distress." Maud arranged the disgustingly pliant Roma over her shoulder. "But it does seem we have some time to fill." She placed a hand on my knee which suddenly seemed warm. *Very* warm. "I propose," she murmured throatily, "to take advantage of your remarkably fortuitous state of undress."

The old restlessness welled up in me again, and I realized it must be laid at her door. My fingertips brushed, then lingered against her imperious cheek. "My dear . . ."

"Yes?"

My hand dropped. She was not for one such as I. "I am a confirmed and crippled bachelor."

"And I am a playwright, not a brood mare." She grabbed her bag and stalked out the door.

"Maud—!"

Maud stormed across the street, cat bobbing and smirking on her shoulder. The curtains were pulled back on the windows of Lord Windermere's carriage, and the horses finally whipped up. As it rolled past, I caught a flash of ruffles and silver hair ornaments—and underneath them, the unmistakable sight of gray hair and a distinctive square jaw.

And as my head reeled with the knowledge of the late-night visitor's identity, I realized Lady Windermere faced a far greater problem than a mislaid diamond or a wayward custard.

Land Rush

JODY LYNN NYE

GIL COULDN'T KEEP SHADOW out of anything. The four-year-old ex-tomcat considered a closed door or any other blocked egress to be a personal challenge and an affront to his feline sensibilities. Although what Great-aunt Erma was speaking about, sitting there at the front of the room in her ancient rocker, could affect Gil's entire future, he had only half of his attention on her. The other half was fixed on the black cat.

Just as he feared, Shadow nudged open the lid of the old coal box next to the marble fireplace and climbed inside. The lid dropped shut with a bang. Aunt Erma turned a gimlet eye toward the noise and cleared her throat irritably. Embarrassed, Gil got up to retrieve Shadow. Thank God coal bins were just for show these days. All he needed was a cat daubing sooty footprints all over the spotless mansion.

"Gilbert Todhunter, are you listening?" Great-aunt Erma asked, turning her wheelchair toward him. She was a deceptively frail-looking old lady with wispy white curls arranged around her narrow head.

"Sorry, Auntie," Gil said, sitting down. He tried to hold the restless cat still. An almost impossible task, with his cousin Charlotte's white English bulldog, Augustus, right behind them, giving him the eye. Charlotte herself was watching Gil. In a room full of cousins, Charlotte was the only one he really worried about. Gil believed the old saw that people and their pets were a lot alike. Certainly he was tall and rangy, with black hair like his cat's. Charlotte was short, pale, and stocky, with bowed legs like her dog, and the tenacity to match. At home in Philadelphia, Charlotte had her own consulting firm. She was an efficiency expert. Gil thought it was probably because she loved telling other people what to do. She had brought Augustus in hopes he could sniff out Great-great-grandpa Todhunter's scent before anyone else.

"I'm old," Erma was saying, "and I've got all that I need for what time I believe I have left. So, what I mean to do is to choose my successor to the Todhunter fortune, while I'm still alive. I have seen too many family fortunes cut up into small pieces and ruined by squabbling heirs. I hate that. I want the estate to pass down the generations intact. I have no children of my own, so I have invited you, my great-nephews and nieces to participate in a little contest. The United States government did it once, and now I'm doing it. I'm starting a little land rush, right here in my very own home.

"You could say my grandfather all but invented land speculation. He waited for homesteading settlers to return here from the land rushes, and made them good offers for their stakeholding deeds. Everybody was happy. They got cold, hard cash, and he got land, which looked worthless at the time." She smiled, and her blue eyes glinted sharply. "At the time, Grandpa knew better. His deals made him very rich. I've lived very well on the interest alone. Most of the deeds have never even been exercised, so I left them exactly where Grandpa did. They're still good, and worth a tidy little fortune. Winner takes all: land, house, and money."

"Where are the deeds?" Charlotte asked, setting her heavy jaw in a way that made her look like Augustus. The twenty or so other cousins leaned forward, avidly.

"Patience, Charlotte," Erma snapped, her stentorian voice belying her ninety years. She looked around at them all. "You'll hear the rules, and not one person will leave this room until you do. You may have one companion to assist you, human or otherwise." The glints lit briefly on Shadow and Augustus. "The deeds are in a small brass correspondence box hidden somewhere in this house. The contest will be over at nightfall, or when someone finds the box. And it begins . . . now!" With that, the old woman lifted a starter pistol from under the shawl on her lap, and fired it in the air.

At the explosive sound, Shadow rose straight up five feet in the air, tail hairs spread out like a bottlebrush, and shot out of the room. Gil scrambled up after him. The nephews and nieces scattered, leaving Great-aunt Erma sitting alone in her wheelchair, chuckling to herself.

Gil cornered Shadow hiding behind a painted fireplace screen in the study next door, where his cousins Brad and Amy were already searching. The house was sprawling, with more than thirty-five rooms, dating back to the last quarter of the nineteenth century. It had been built at the height of the westward expansion, intended to impress the neighbors, and indulge the old man's sense of fun. There were secret doors in plenty, some of which led to priest's holes, others to elaborate underground tunnels, and a few nowhere at all. When Gil bent to pick him up, Shadow pawed at the back wall of the fireplace. Gil saw a thin line. Shadow had found a door that Gil, who had been in the house hundreds of times since he was a child, had never seen before.

"Good kitty!" Gil said. They were off to a great start.

He dropped to his hands and knees and began to feel his way around the brickwork for a catch. He hoped he would be the one to find the deeds. He urgently needed to find a new place to live. His beloved loft in St. Louis had been condemned and was being torn down to make way for a mini-mall, and as an impecunious freelance commercial artist, he couldn't afford both a new apartment and a studio. He needed this inheritance.

The whole rear of the fireplace shifted and swung noisily to the left, revealing a dark passageway. The cat sniffed at the musty air that rushed out.

"Gangway!" cried Charlotte. Growling fiercely, Augustus muscled his way into the hearth, scaring Shadow halfway up the chimney. Gil stood up, banging his head on the mantel. While stars danced in his eyes, Charlotte barged past him through the newly opened door.

"Hey, wait!" Gil shouted, but it was too late. He could hear their voices echoing off the tunnel walls like a couple of questing hounds. There was no point in following them. If there was anything down there, they'd get to it first. Better try another prospect.

The echoingly huge kitchen and pantry were overrun with Todhunter cousins who were turning out every cupboard and shelf onto the stone floor. Two of the younger girls had gotten into a flour fight, and the choking cloud of white filled the room. Shadow sniffed briefly around, checking under the sink, but kept on going out and down the hallway. Gil ran after him. He was counting on the black cat's instinct for finding the best hiding place, the one the old man had chosen.

Shadow ran up to the green baize door that divided the former servants' quarters from the main part of the house, and pawed at it. Gil hurried to open it for him, and the cat scooted through, making for the library. Yes, the library! That would be a good place to try. The thousands of books could easily conceal a small brass box, whether between two of them, or concealed in a cutout cavity. It would appeal to Great-great-grandpa's sense of humor.

Cousin Scott eyed him suspiciously as the cat and man ran by. He was turning over every picture in the long gallery, looking for a niche or a wall safe. Gil could have saved his younger cousin the trouble. The safe was under the floor of the master bedroom, and it had been empty for years. Cousin Yarra had just tried it, and was stomping around the second floor of the house looking for more hollow places under the floorboards.

Gil flung open the door to the library, and he and Shadow dashed in, only to be confronted by Augustus. The dog marched toward them, a menacing expression on his pushed-in face. Gil backed up until he felt the wall behind him.

Charlotte was already there, pulling book after book off the shelves, then tossing them into a heap on the floor. The Todhunter library consisted of thousands of volumes. Gil was pretty sure they'd been bought by the yard, as many nouveau riche people of the nineteenth century had done, and never read. Charlotte had only covered two shelves so far. Gil counted more than thirty to go.

"Let me help," he offered.

"No!" she said, fiercely. "Augustus, guard!" The dog shouldered forward like a street tough.

The last step was too much of an invasion of Shadow's personal space. The cat turned sideways, arched his back, fluffed out his short fur, and showed all his fangs.

"*Eeerooooo,*" Shadow growled warningly deep in his throat. It was his preliminary war cry. He took a pace forward.

"*Mmmruuu-uh?*" Augustus mumbled, looking alarmed. He took a pace back.

"Don't let *a cat* bully you!" Charlotte yelled at the dog, pulling down one book after another. "Guard!" At her command, Augustus waddled forward and planted himself in front of Gil, showing all his teeth. Gil started to move around him, but the bulldog matched him step for step, growling.

"This isn't fair, Charlotte," Gil protested.

"All's fair in love and money," Charlotte said, tossing aside a priceless sixteenth-century book on herbs. "And this is money. Aunt Erma didn't say *how* our companions could help us hunt."

"Shadow, do something," Gil said. The cat sauntered away, and Gil's heart sank. Shadow was giving up. Just as Gil was about to cry uncle and cede the turf to Charlotte, Shadow walked up to the shelf next to where she was rooting, inspected it, turned his back insouciantly, and emitted a jet of urine.

"Ugh!" Charlotte exclaimed, jumping away and batting at her trouser leg. "That's disgusting. Stop him!" Shadow moved on to the next spot that interested him, the floor-length curtains framing the window between two of the bookshelves, and sprayed them, too.

"He's just marking his territory," Gil said. He sidled a pace, hoping to elude Augustus. The dog's attention was no longer on him. He was watching Shadow. Abandoning his guard post, the bulldog strode over to the first shelf and lifted a leg, marking the spot over Shadow's. He followed the cat, covering up each new blast of scent with his own. The room started to reek of dueling animals, but, as Charlotte rightly pointed out, this was war. Gil threw himself at the nearest bookshelf and started to pull out fat nineteenth-century novels. He had to shift this way and that to avoid the warring dog and cat as he moved on through philosophy, geography, and the sciences.

In less time than he would have thought possible, Gil had shaken out almost all the books on his side. Only one shelf divided him from Charlotte. She kept a grim watch on him out of the corner of her eye as she pulled down the last books on Civil War history. The two of them lunged at the same time for the books on gardening. Charlotte got there first.

"Mine, Gil," she said, turning her back on the books to confront her cousin. "I'll let you visit the old homestead once in a while." With his superior height, Gil reached over her head for a volume on growing sweet peas on the topmost shelf. Charlotte elbowed him in the stomach. Gil doubled over, sliding to his knees, in time to see Shadow trot out of the room. He took it as an omen, and stumbled up to follow his cat. Augustus watched him retreat with a smug look.

Shadow hadn't gone far. He was waiting for Gil at the end of the corridor. As soon as the man caught up, the cat trotted through the gallery and into the smoking room.

The cozy, wood-and-leather-paneled chamber was built as a place for the men of the house to lounge around with post-prandial cigars and brandy. A lot of the Todhunter cousins were there, lounging in the big leather chairs under the two-story stained-glass windows or the hunting prints on the walls, or sprawling out on the gallery, drinking up Aunt Erma's liquor cabinet, and eating goodies from the kitchen. Some of them still had flour in their hair. Others were smudged with soot from the chimneys.

"You still at it?" Cousin Scott asked him, around a Corona Corona cigar. "I think the whole thing is a fake. Auntie's gone senile."

"I don't know," Gil said, casually. He watched Shadow slink around the walls, nuzzling a chair leg here, a panel corner there. He must have liked the scent of the rolling library steps, because he ground first one cheek, then the other against them. "It's a good story. I sure could use the money."

"Huh!" said Cousin Yarra, through a mouthful of cheese. "You'd be better off asking the government to re-open the land rushes."

Gil got tired of waiting for Shadow to give him a clue, and picked him up. Shadow squalled, and kicked loose to run. He heard the derisive laughter from the other cousins as he followed his pet back down the long hallway. Shadow reached the middle of the grand ballroom, and began to prowl nervously back and forth.

"Is it in here?" Gil asked, looking around. The big room had already been thoroughly searched, to judge by the disarray of the little gold chairs that were usually against the wall. The curtains were all askew. The only other thing in the room was the big silver and Austrian rock-crystal chandelier hanging from the ornamented plaster ceiling, and anyone could see nothing was hidden in it. Maybe the other cousins were right. There was no fortune. He was sunk. Bye-bye loft.

"You tricked me, Gilbert Todhunter!" Charlotte cried, charging into the room with Augustus on her heels. "You knew there was nothing in the library. I've wasted all that time, and it's almost sundown! Sic 'em, Augustus!"

The dog charged at the cat. The two animals circled, growling at one another, while their owners shouted.

"C'mon, Shadow," Gil urged. "I'll hold down Augustus so you can beat him up."

"You will not!" Charlotte sputtered. "Augustus! Charge!"

Setting his jaw, the bulldog sprang to obey his mistress's order. Shadow had evidently had enough of Augustus. As the dog thundered forward, Shadow sprang up into Gil's arms, climbed onto his head, and leaped into the swinging chandelier.

"Now look what your stupid dog did!"

"Good boy, Augustus," Charlotte said, gloating. "C'mon, let's search while they're stuck."

Torn between curiosity and concern, Gil stared up, wondering what to do. The chandelier was priceless, but Shadow was his cat. Shadow wiggled higher until he was standing at the junction of the arms beside the chain. The whole thing swayed alarmingly.

"Come on down, kitty," Gil said, holding his arms up. Shadow settled himself, his whiskers twitching. "Come on, we'll go get something to eat."

Shadow paid no attention. Instead, he pawed at part of the fancy ceiling. The white plaster curlicue moved aside, revealing a black gap, which Shadow jumped up into. A secret passage! Gil almost broke his neck beating Charlotte to one of the gilt chairs that stood along the walls. He climbed up and pulled himself into the ceiling. The little attic was dim, but beside the boss holding the chandelier he could see a small tarnished box. Gil brushed off a wealth of cobwebs and clutched it, hardly believing it was real. It had probably been hidden in this very spot when the house had been wired for electricity in 1890. Gil looked down through the hole in the ceiling. The chair seemed to be very far away. He looked at Shadow in dismay. That was what the cat had been trying to tell him in the drawing room. He'd wanted him to bring the ladder!

"There's no way down!" he shouted.

"Throw down the box," Charlotte said, stretching up her arms. "I'll hold it while you carry Shadow." Gil saw the glint in her eye. She'd be gone in a minute, probably even move the chair out of reach. He couldn't trust her.

"Nothing doing," he said, eyeing the distance to the floor. Could he jump it without breaking his neck? While he was trying to decide what to do, Shadow shot away and fled along the ceiling beams. "Come back here!"

Clasping the precious box to his chest, Gil tiptoed over the trusses, afraid he would step between them and fall through the ceiling. Charlotte and Augustus, whom he could hear muttering along below, would win by default. "Darn it, cat, where are you?"

Gil heard Shadow's joyous cry from a dark corner of the attic. Gil was covered with cobwebs when he caught up with him. Shadow prowled up and back at the top of his discovery. The cat had led him to another hidden staircase! Thanking the shades of Great-great-grandpa and his architect, Gil descended, box under one arm and cat under the other, and emerged in the drawing room, to the astonishment of his half-drunk cousins.

Triumphantly, Gil and Shadow led a procession into the drawing room to see Aunt Erma.

"Congratulations, Gilbert," Aunt Erma said over the protests. "Now, don't all of you grumble. He won, fair and square. I'm not intending to cut everyone else off completely. The rest of you will get ten thousand dollars apiece, but the rest of the pie is Gilbert's. He earned it."

"Hmph," snorted Charlotte. Augustus looked crestfallen. He had disappointed his mistress.

Shadow rubbed against Aunt Erma's chair, then marched up to the hanging curtains, turned his back on them, and marked them. Gil groaned, as the others snickered.

"It's all right," Aunt Erma said, eyes glinting. "He's just staking his claim. It's an old family tradition."

Letters to the Editor

SHIRLEY ROUSSEAU MURPHY

DILLIE LAKE KEPT A BAD-TEMPERED tomcat to kill the mice that *would* burrow into the Beauty Beautique from the back fields behind Main Street, a cat ugly as sin, scarred and lumpy and the color of dirty scrub rags, their relationship as sour, too, as cat food left in the summer sun; but Oscar was a good mouser and, since the divorce, was Dillie's only companion. Except, of course, for John Findley who owned the *Greeley Gazette* next door. The two establishments shared the ancient building; and what else Dillie shared with John had, in her opinion, nothing to do with John's wife, Lucille, being her best friend.

What was she supposed to do, stop eating lunch with Lucille just because she was seeing John on the sly? Lucille had enough problems. Why upset her? The truth was, she was doing Lucille a favor because if John went home in a better mood, that was Lucille's good fortune.

Besides, he needed someone to talk to, he sure couldn't reason with Lucille about their son Ferdy. If Ferdy'd been *her* child, Dillie would have put him up for adoption. Why they tolerated the boy's smart mouth and stealing ways was beyond her. All Lucille did was fawn over Ferdy like the child was God himself.

Dillie had no idea why her old cat had taken up with the nasty eight-year-old—Oscar followed Ferdy like a dog. Well they were two of a kind, she guessed. Both born to trouble. Why John and Lucille didn't see that it was their own son writing those anonymous letters to the editor that kept arriving at the *Gazette* office, was beyond her.

Oh, it was Ferdy, all right. You'd think John would recognize his son's careful block printing, except nearly everyone under the age of forty printed anymore. You could tell right away if someone was up in his years, by their nice handwriting. Well if John was to publish those letters in the *Gazette* he'd find himself beat up in the back alley some dark night.

Not that Greeley was full of criminal types, but this was rural Georgia, famous for its old sour-mash stills hidden back in the steep ravines, and now the same families turned to growing maryjane in an effort at simple survival.

Well the letter writer wasn't interested in pot-growers; he snooped on the town's dirtier secrets. Every new letter that arrived Lucille would bring over to read to Dillie while they ate their sack lunches in the back room between the nail-gloss table and the tanning bed while Dillie's hired beautician, Shelley Grome, gave a perm or a color process out front. Half their customers copied Shelley's own hair color of the month; they all left dreaming they looked beautiful like Shelley, blonde or redhead or sultry brunette, their hair done just like hers, and that was good for business. Well if Ferdy was there in the corner at noon, chewing on his own sandwich while Lucille read the latest letter, the sly look on the boy's face was too much to miss. But Lucille did miss it, hadn't a clue. What Dillie couldn't figure was, how Ferdy learned those juicy secrets.

She never doubted the letters were true, she had her own sources, whispered in the chair over a haircut or over the shampooing sink. The letter-writer knew all about pharmacist Sid Beuser and Mrs. Holleran, when Mr. Holleran was away in Chattanooga on his selling trips; he knew that twelve-year-old June Bartow often spent the night with Budgie James, the bachelor mail-carrier on Route Three. The nameless writer even knew about Greeley's county judge having an affair with her bailiff. These were not things a boy would learn easily, these were nighttime doings. Greeley, in the daytime, was as dull as chickens pecking in the front yard. Night was the time for hanky-panky, a shadow slipping into the wrong house, a car without lights slithering around a corner. The boy had to be sneaking out at night after Lucille put him to bed, looking in people's windows, mailing his nasty little letters right to his mama's desk at the newspaper and likely taking the stamps right from her desk, too.

And how long would it be before Ferdy came snooping on his own pa, poking around the newspaper office late at night, and see her and John together? Well, that would tear it. And poor John, slaving ten-hour days at the paper and coming home to that impossible boy, knowing that Ferdy, being his only child, would inherit the *Gazette*. John loved the old-fashioned paper, it was all he knew, it had been in his family for three generations. Every Tuesday Dillie could hear, through the wall, the clacking of the old flatbed press that John's pappy had bought back in 1948. The press wouldn't run by itself, you had to hand-feed the paper onto the big roller, and it was a lethal thing; if you were to get yourself caught between the roller and the type bed you'd come out flat as a waffle.

She was just vacuuming up the shop for the night after a late shampoo and set—it was already dark out—when Oscar came slinking in through the open front door mewling for his supper, and Ferdy scuffed in behind him sliding his eyes toward the drawer where she kept her Snickers bars. She could see lights spilling across the sidewalk from next door, and guessed Lucille was still there—when John was alone, only the back lights burned in the press room.

"Where'd you get the sweater, Ferdy? It new?"

"Lyle Farnsworth at school. He give it to me."

"He give it to you?" She looked hard at Ferdy while Oscar crunched away on his cat kibble, scattering little hard biscuits across the black and white linoleum.

"Traded a jar of frogs. He wanted 'em for a experiment."

"I'll just bet he did," she said. But her eyes widened as Oscar glanced up at Ferdy with a smirk on his dirty white face.

Still, maybe she imagined that smile. "Your mother told me she found that expensive gold fountain pen, Ferdy, the one with Lawyer Madden's monogram on it that he advertised for in the paper. Found it in your dresser drawer."

"So? It was laying on the street outside the Red Barn." Ferdy's pale green eyes looked back at her blandly. "How would I know what them letters stood for?"

"That's the pen the Georgia Bar Association give him. When your mother give it back, she told him she found it in the courthouse beside the Coke machine when she went in to pay her taxes. What did you do, Ferdy, slip into his office at noon when he and his secretary were out? Doesn't he lock his door? What else did you take?"

Oscar stopped eating, watching her again, his ears laid flat in a such a nasty scowl that she took a step back—and the boy looked angry, too. She was so interested in their behavior that when Ferdy and the cat left the shop, slipping away into the night, she locked up quickly and followed them.

Walking softly along the dark side of Main Street, she trailed them into the residential section where the shadows of the big old pines struck across the lawns, and at the Baptist church rectory Oscar, his dirty fur brightened by the street lamp, leaped to the bedroom windowsill, peering in.

The cat remained for nearly an hour observing whatever was going on inside the faintly lit bedroom. Now and then he would lean down and Ferdy would slip close, their faces nearly touching. If they'd been two little boys, she'd say they were whispering; then Ferdy found a foothold in the laurel bushes and climbed up to peer in beside Oscar. And when, the next noon, Lucille had received another anonymous letter, it told, plain as day, who had spent Thursday night in bed with their pastor, Johnie Heuger, and Dillie felt cold all over.

"I can't believe such as these letters." Lucille unwrapped the second half of her sandwich. "Who would write such things?"

Dillie rose, fetched a screwdriver from her tool drawer and pretended to fix the loose table leg, hiding her hot, flustered face—knowing it would be only a matter of time until the letter Lucille held would be about her and John. She tried to eat the rest of her lunch, but could only pick at her sandwich. She threw her cheesecake in the trash.

But Friday night after Lucille had gone home to have an early supper and watch her programs with Ferdy, Dillie closed up and slipped along the dark alley as usual and through the back door of the *Gazette* where John was making up the paper.

He left the back desk lighted as if he were working, and they snuggled down on the old leather couch that was wedged in among the work tables and the press. It was an hour later when she rose and pulled on her dress, that she looked up at the high windows above the alley and saw Oscar looking in, his white, whiskered face pressed against the glass. She imagined Ferdy, in the shadows, climbing up on the dumpster to peer in beside him but, hurrying out the back door, she didn't see boy or cat.

Turning back inside, she imagined the letter soon to be in Lucille's shaking hands, and wished she'd had the good sense to offer Oscar a nice dose of rat poison.

But what about the boy?

She didn't sleep well, tossed and fidgeted, her head filled with ways to stop the two. And of course it was too late: the next morning when she opened the shop, a sheet of white paper lay folded under her door.

Why would Ferdy bring the letter here? She snatched it up expecting to see the same block printing as the others, same awkward green-ink printing, accusing her and John.

But this letter was written in black, in a handsome cursive script: John's handwriting. She knew that hand.

She sat down in her customer chair, spinning it around slowly, her hands shaking. It was a love letter, from John to Shelley Grome. She read it again, how much John loved Shelley and how he meant to make some changes so they would be together.

The boy couldn't have written this, he sure didn't know how to write cursive. Examining it closer, she found several little black spots scattered across the white paper, like from a dirty copy machine.

Spitting on her finger, she drew it across the paper. The ink didn't smear, as a pen would. Maybe the boy had found the letter, made a copy right there in the *Gazette* office, had put the original back for John to pass on to Shelley, but saved the copy for a special occasion.

Last night, he'd found the occasion when he saw her and John naked on the couch.

Knowing Ferdy, he wouldn't want to squeal on his own pa and blow up his home life, but he sure would want to get back at her, Dillie, for messing with his dad. And he'd known just how to do that. For an eight-year-old, the boy was shrewd as any backhills bootlegger.

Sick with jealousy and fear, she put a note on the glass door to cancel her appointments, locked up the shop and went home, stayed inside the house all day and didn't answer the phone. And after that terrible morning, the blows came one on top the other. She found John's powder-blue polo shirt stuffed down in a drawer of Shelley's station when she was looking for a pair of clippers and it had Shelley's raspberry lipstick on the collar.

She thought of John's hands on Shelley's body, and knew it was time, now, to worry Lucille. To see Lucille fly into action. Serve John right for two-timing her. Serve Ferdy right for snooping. And at noon when Lucille brought her lunch over, Dillie showed her John's blue shirt with the raspberry lipstick. She held back the letter. The shirt alone made Lucille plenty angry; that very afternoon Lucille, snooping through John's dresser drawers, found Shelley's gold angel pendant hidden under his shorts, and brought it over crying. "It's a love token—the way I gave him my locket before we were married." She was so hurt that Dillie thought Lucille might take care of Shelley herself. Then she, Dillie, would have only Ferdy to deal with, the hateful little beast. Ferdy, and of course Oscar.

She wondered if she could lure Ferdy into some foolish and dangerous act. What if Oscar got trapped on the quarry cliff and Ferdy had to climb down to save him, and they both fell? Or what if Oscar got caught in the old printing press while it was running and the boy dove after him and they got sucked in between the flatbed and the big roller? That would crunch bones, all right. That could happen Tuesday evening, when John left Lucille to tend the press while he ran across the street for a quick sandwich. Lots of times the boy and cat were there. All she had to do was lure Lucille away on some errand, tell Lucille she'd feed the press as she did sometimes when Lucille wanted to get out of the shop.

She sat down in her swivel chair. Dropped her head in her hands. What was happening to her, to have such dreadful thoughts? She was not a murdering sort of person. There were other ways to handle these matters. She'd be a fool to resort to such terrible crimes—not because she loved Lucille. And certainly she didn't love Ferdy. But because she would never get away with such a thing. But before she had time to argue the matter, fate struck, and it struck hard.

Unlocking the beauty shop the next morning and stepping through to the window to open the blinds, she tripped over something large and heavy, and there at her feet lay Shelley.

She jerked the blinds open.

Shelley's uniform blouse was soaked with blood. Dillie's old-fashioned thinning shears with the bone handles stuck out as if driven through her heart. Her blue eyes wide open, the pale oval of her face framed by her newly done, honey-gold curls. The sight of Shelley's blood pooling across the black and white linoleum froze Dillie; she couldn't move, couldn't cry out.

She didn't sleep that night. Long after the sheriff came and the body was taken away, she lay in her bed thinking about how she had wanted to kill Shelley, kill Oscar, and little Ferdy, and she lay tossing and frightened. And the next day, she wanted to be dead her own self, because when the sheriff took her finger-prints, he got a funny look on his face though he tried to hide it; then late in the afternoon she heard sirens wailing down Main Street and police cars skidding to a stop in front of the *Gazette* office, and when she hurried over Lucille was already there, screaming and weeping.

John lay humped over the old press—she thought for a minute he'd been sucked in, the way she'd imagined doing to Ferdy—but the press wasn't running. John lay slumped over the bed of type, which was filling with blood, much blood running out of his neck where a screwdriver protruded, its green plastic handle matching the set in her tool drawer.

Three days later she was arrested. Her prints matched those on both weapons. Two days after that, the grand jury met and she was arraigned for Shelley's murder though she kept telling them she'd done nothing.

It was not until after Dillie Lake was tried and convicted for Shelley Grome's murder—there being no other fingerprints but Dillie's on the thinning shears—and was arraigned for John Findley's murder and sent away to Metro Women's Prison in Atlanta to await the second trial, that Lucille took over the *Greeley Gazette*. She bought out the beauty parlor, too, and hired a nice young man from Altanta to run it. It was at this time that Ferdy began to wash regularly and answer his mother politely. His grades improved, and he stopped stealing. Even Dillie Lake's old cat, Oscar, who moved into the newspaper office, began washing himself. He looked white again and didn't snarl anymore, but instead went around looking as frightened as Ferdy often looked. More than one neighbor said the boy seemed afraid, that the shock of his father's death must have done something terrible to Ferdy.

Ferdy's scared of me? Lucille thought, amused. Her own son, afraid of her? That, for Lucille, was liberating. Ferdy's sudden respect and obedience were fine and liberating—as if he were afraid of meeting the same fate as that little blonde hairdresser. The same fate as his own father. Oh, Ferdy's fear did make her smile.

Of course she didn't mention Ferdy's fear to Dillie when she visited her down in Metro Women's Prison, didn't mention to Dillie how fearful old Oscar had become. In prison, Dillie must have enough problems. Why upset her?

Lin Jee

MARY A. TURZILLO

THE MORNING AFTER OUR WEDDING night, Lin Jee woke us yowling over a sock she had killed.

Almost immediately after, Eric, Tom's best man, appeared in the door. "Somebody's broken in!"

Lin Jee hadn't killed a sock in a long time. She used to kill mice and (sadly) the occasional blue jay. Like the old farmhouse, she was part of the "dowry" my granny had left me in her will. As a kitten, Lin Jee had once gone after a rat bigger than she was. I suspect she'd have killed it, if Granny hadn't snatched her up.

But Granny had passed away ten years ago, Lin Jee's fur had turned cinnamon-dark with age, and the old Siamese curled like a fur croissant in a nest near the furnace and hunted nothing, not even socks.

And I had just married the most wonderful architect in Burton, Ohio.

That same architect, Tom, was standing in his boxer shorts in the middle of our bedroom holding a gray sock. When Eric appeared, Tom tossed the sock to me, and it landed, soggy and cold, in the middle of my chest.

Eric's eyes were wild. "That cat woke me up. God, what a voice."

My little brother, Bobcat, who had apparently slept in his clothes, appeared in the doorway behind Eric. "What's up, Sis?" I looked for signs of drug abuse, although Bobcat had been in a twelve-step program for two years now, since a spectacular car crash on his nineteenth birthday.

Lin Jee ambled over to the bed, scrambled up, and presented her creamy belly for petting.

Tom pulled on his jeans, his only change of clothes since he'd flown in from the base in Hawaii for the wedding, the rest of his gear being at his folks' house until he moved in. I grabbed a long T-shirt, and we all rushed downstairs.

"The back door was standing open," Eric said. "I thought it was just Bobcat, sneaking a cigarette. Then saw all the gifts gone."

I rushed into the parlor, still clutching Lin Jee, who purred her satisfaction at having played watch-cat.

Martha, my oldest friend, and matron of honor, floundered out of the front downstairs bedroom. Great with child, she probably was the only person who didn't have a hangover. Her husband, Chucky, was a cool guy, but he had a weakness for beer. He followed her out and headed for the john.

Eric ran to the back bedroom, where he had slept alone.

It was all too true. My mother had polished up Granny's sterling and put it gleaming into its velvet-lined case. But the case was no longer displayed on the coffee table in the living room. Nor were the food processor, the silver candlesticks, the linens, the crystal vase, the expensive bathroom scale, the big-screen TV my parents had given us.

And the envelopes in which money gifts were enclosed were gone. But then I remembered Tom had hidden the checks and cash in the blue willow vase in the china cabinet.

I ran to the china cabinet, only to discover the vase gone.

Eric came back from the bedroom. "My Rolex is gone! How could I have slept through that? What the hell did you guys put in the punch?"

Bobcat stumbled to the door and looked at it. "There's some scrape marks around the latch. They must have broken in."

"I think that's from where I forced the lock last summer. I locked myself out, and I didn't want to call Mom or Dad to drive all the way over from Champion."

"You're insured, aren't you?" Chucky asked, reappearing and zipping his pants. "Has anyone called the cops?"

"I'll do it," said Eric. "You guys catalog what's missing."

Shaking, I went into the bedroom where Martha and Chucky had been sleeping, to my bill-paying desk. As I was rummaging for paper and pen, Martha took my arm. "This worries me, Mary. Chucky is just pretending to be hungover. He didn't drink anymore than I did."

I looked at her, amazed. "You're saying—?"

"He's been worried about bills."

"But he just got a great new job at the bank, and—"

"Listen to me, girlfriend. The insurance doesn't kick in for six months. And the baby—"

"Is due in a month. But he wouldn't—?"

She hunched her shoulders and looked at me wide-eyed. "He asked if you had insurance."

Sure, we had insurance. But it didn't cover antiques, like the silver.

From the front bedroom, I could see out into the yard. The brilliant sun made the grass sparkle with dew, the lilac tree was blazing purple, and the tulips were just beyond their peak. My little brother, Bobcat, was running up the driveway as if fiends were after him. A moment later, he burst into the bedroom. "My van is gone!"

The police arrived ten minutes later. Sergeant Belkor was saying, "You're saying the thief took a beat-up, nine-year-old Econoline van, and left Eric's BMW, an almost-new Geo owned by Mr. and Mrs. Charles, here, the Sable ready for the newlyweds' honeymoon? And did they jump-start it, or did you leave the key in the ignition?"

"I don't understand why they took it," moaned Bobcat. "But I know how. I left my keys in my jacket, hanging in the hall."

Sergeant Belkor shook his head. "So the burglar needed a van to get away with the loot, and your keys happened to be handy. Bad luck, son."

Bobcat banged his head with his hands. "And I don't have any insurance except liability. How'll I get to Burger King for my Monday shift?"

Sergeant Belkor's partner, Venuti, took a call on their radio, said something to Belkor, and left the house. "And the cat. You say the cat woke you up. How did the burglar get a chance to get all that stuff out of the house if the cat was playing watch-cat?"

"She's probably senile," muttered Eric.

Bobcat picked Lin Jee up and petted her. "Don't say that. She's a genius cat. That's what my grandmother said, and my grandmother was a very smart woman."

Of course Granny also claimed Lin Jee could speak English, but her Siamese cat accent was so bad nobody could understand her.

Sergeant Belkor smiled tolerantly.

"I think I can explain," I said. "She's got a little arthritis, so it probably took her a little longer to climb up the stairs to the bedroom."

Tom said, "Tell them about the sock."

I laughed nervously. "When we stopped letting her outside to hunt, she took to bringing us socks, pretending they were prey. She hasn't done that in two years, but for some reason, this morning—"

Sergeant Belkor stroked Lin Jee between her chocolate velvet ears. The Siamese narrowed her eyes and turned up the volume on her purr. "I'm a cat man myself. Could I see this sock? Might mean something."

Just then Sergeant Venuti returned. "Well, the van mystery is solved. It's parked behind that tall hedge on the road. Key in the ignition. Engine's still warm."

Bobcat jumped up, but Venuti restrained him. "Not so fast. We found this in the bed of the van." He held out a shard of china: the roof of a bright blue pagoda, fading into exquisite white.

Bobcat turned pale. "That's a piece of my granny's vase. She left it to my sister."

"Mmm," said Sergeant Belkor. "You want to tell us what happened to the rest of that vase?"

Bobcat looked down at his bare feet and said, "Sir, I have no idea."

Belkor looked at me and Tom. "Are you going to press charges, even if this turns out to be an inside job?"

I swallowed hard. Lin Jee, tense in my arms, had stopped purring.

Tom came downstairs. "The sock is gone. I looked all over the bedroom for it."

Chucky made a *pshaw*ing noise. "Cat hid it again."

I didn't think so. Lin Jee had been lazing in my arms since Tom had tossed the sock at me.

"I will press charges," I said, "if my husband agrees. But first I want you to hold everybody in this room, while your partner brings out their shoes. And their socks, too, if he can find them. Especially any gray socks."

"Why?" asked Chucky.

"I would recognize the sock. I think it belongs to the thief."

Lin Jee started purring again.

Sergeant Belkor tried to hide his smile, but I could see he was planning to go along with me.

Ten minutes later, Venuti had assembled four pairs of men's shoes and two pairs of women's on the marble-topped table in our parlor.

"And whose are these?" he said, holding up a pair of ladies' lavender dyed silk pumps.

Martha said, "They're mine. And that pair of white athletic socks and the Nikes are mine, too. I can't tell if those are my pantyhose. They might be Mary's."

"Those are my pumps," I said. "The white ones. And the off-white pantyhose. Uh, I assume you didn't go into the closet and haul out *all* my shoes."

"We assume you didn't burglarize your own house for the insurance. But we did look through your bureau. You gave permission. You favor pastels and bright colors, right?"

"Right. And Tom hasn't moved in yet. He only has the shoes he wore to the wedding, plus a pair of rubber thongs."

Next, they turned to Eric's shoes. A pair of black socks were folded neatly inside the left shoe. I felt them. Dry.

Then, Charlie's. He too wore black socks, and though the toes were worn through, they didn't look like the sock Tom had thrown at me.

Bobcat's boots contained no socks at all.

"You came to my wedding with no socks on?"

"Aw, Sis, nobody can tell if you're wearing boots."

"Boots? To my wedding?" How had I not noticed?

Belkor turned to me. "I'm afraid this doesn't look too good. I have to wonder if your brother has hidden the sock you think the cat brought to you as evidence, plus its mate."

"I didn't!" Bobcat wailed, startling Lin Jee, who jumped out of my arms and ran to hide. "Somebody stole my van and used it to transport all the gifts, and—"

"And who was that someone?" asked Belkor. "Listen, I think your sister might be willing not to press charges, even though I made her promise to do so, if you'll just tell us where you secreted the loot."

"And what you planned to do with it," said Eric.

Bobcat looked stricken. It was one of the darkest moments of my life. "Honey," I said, "if you need money, I mean for anything besides drugs, you know we'd loan it to you."

"Heck," said Tom, "we'd *give* it to you."

Bobcat straightened and got a hard look. "This just tops it. Not only do I have to work this lousy job to pay off my debts from that car accident, but now my own sister turns against me."

The conversation was interrupted by a terrifying Siamese yowl. Lin Jee stood in the middle of the hall door, her blue eyes blazing, a gray sock at her feet.

"That's the sock," I picked it up. It was damp. "The sock Lin Jee brought us was gray. Lin Jee, tell me where you got that sock."

The next few moments were a blur. Lin Jee leapt on Eric. Eric slammed her against the wall, toppling a lamp. Bobcat gathered her up and held her defiantly against himself. "Don't hurt my sister's cat!"

Eric looked at me, breathing hard. A slash of red oozed across his cheek. "She attacked me for no reason."

Lin Jee's tail fluffed to twice its size, and she emitted a terrifying growl, far too big for such a tiny, cute cat.

I went over and examined her. Her eyes were blue, sharp with intelligence, and ablaze with hate. She flinched a bit when I touched her right front leg, but she didn't cry out again.

"Put her down, Bobcat. See if she can walk."

Bobcat put Lin Jee on the floor and she limped toward the back bedroom. The room where Eric had stayed.

Eric lunged for her, but Bobcat twisted his arm and the two struggled until Belkor separated them.

We followed Lin Jee.

The other damp gray sock was behind the radiator.

Sergeant Belkor looked tired. "This is yours, I gather."

Eric said, "No. I don't wear gray. The kid probably hid it there."

Belkor shrugged. "Well, we could get a search warrant for your apartment.

And I think I have reasonable cause to detain you. Please read this and tell me if you understand it."

Eric glanced at the Miranda rights card and snarled, "I know your boss, you know. And the mayor."

Tom said, "Eric, I don't understand. It looks like you wore these socks out so as to not wake us up. Then you must have gone out in your stocking feet and gotten the socks wet from dew. Finally, you drove the goods somewhere and stowed them. Otherwise, why did you attack Mary's cat?"

"I didn't! It attacked me!"

Tom and I exchanged sad glances.

"My oldest friend," said Tom. "I guess business school and that fancy job changed you."

"I didn't finish business school. I flunked out. And the job evaporated in early February. I hope you enjoy the food processor. If you ever find it." He angrily wiped his cheek and scowled at the blood on his hand.

"You could tell us where it is," said Tom gently.

"You could go take a flying leap," said Eric.

Lin Jee lay panting on the floor near the radiator. I picked her up, and she was purring through her pain.

Tom said, "You'll pay for the vet bills, too, of course."

"I haven't admitted anything," Eric said.

Sergeant Belkor let me look in Eric's wallet, where I found a receipt for a storage unit only a mile away. The vase, of course, was broken, and we couldn't prove the money in his wallet was ours. He must have planned to do this. How sad.

Lin Jee's leg was broken, and she looked comical limping around with a white bandage around it. Eventually, she gnawed the bandage off, and went back to her post near the furnace. Tom and I bring her upstairs to bed with us every night, a furry warm bundle with sharp blue eyes. Her velvet brown tail twitches in her sleep, as she dreams, no doubt, of hunting mice, birds, and evil socks.

And she tells us off frequently about being so stupid as to trust Eric. I can almost understand her now. Granny was right. She's really much smarter than the average burglar.

Living the Lie

MARC BILGREY

WILL YOU MISS ME, DAVE?" said Sally, as she looked out the passenger side window of the light blue Packard.

Dave held the steering wheel tightly and kept his eyes on the road. For a minute he forgot his name. Since he'd only had it for six months, it was an easy mistake to make. He kept telling himself it was Dave, like *Davy Crockett*, the hottest program on television.

"Sure I'll miss you," said Dave, staring at a police car in the rearview mirror. His heart began beating faster. He watched the patrol car drive up behind him, then silently turn onto a side street and disappear. Dave let out a deep breath, glanced at Sally sitting next to him, then at a passing sign that read Train Station, ¼ Mile.

"It'll be the first time we've been separated," she said.

"Oh, come on, it'll only be for a week. You make it sound like you're going on a trip around the world."

"That's what going back home feels like to me. And now with Mom being sick . . ." her voice trailed off.

"She'll probably outlive us all." The train station came into view. Dave glanced at the imposing, dirty, stone building, then slowed the car down as he navigated between taxis.

"You won't forget to feed Scooter, will you?"

"How many times do we have to go over this? I'll stop by your place every night and feed the cat, don't worry."

"Okay," said Sally, as they pulled up in front of a cab which was dislodging a group of tourists.

Dave got out, opened the trunk, pulled out Sally's suitcase and placed it on the sidewalk. Sally put her arms around Dave and kissed him.

"I'm gonna miss you so much," she said.

Dave looked into her sparkling green eyes and said, "Just don't be talking to any of those Midwest guys."

"Oh," she said, playfully slapping him on the arm, "you're impossible."

Dave kissed her cheek and said, "Me and Scooter'll be counting the days."

She smiled, picked up her suitcase, turned around and walked into the station.

On the drive back, Dave turned on the radio. The Platters sang, "You've Got That Magic Touch." Dave thought about Sally. It occurred to him that he really would miss her. He was already starting to feel lonely. The feeling surprised him. He'd vowed to himself when they'd met that he wouldn't get too involved. She was there to pass the time with, to have some fun with, interchangeable with a hundred other women. Though he had tried to maintain his emotional distance, he had realized early on that it was a losing battle.

A police car with flashing lights appeared behind him. Dave felt his throat go dry as he gripped the steering wheel so hard his knuckles turned white. The police car passed him and then zoomed down the highway. Dave swallowed and relaxed his hold on the wheel.

If it hadn't been for Sally, he'd probably have left a month or two earlier. He knew he was pressing his luck. They hadn't called him Doc for no reason. He'd been the brains, the logical one who thought things out. There was no place for emotion, he'd told them. And yet, here he was, ignoring his own advice.

Dave slowed the car down as he passed a movie theater. There was a new Bob Hope picture playing. It looked good, but, he decided, he just wasn't in the mood. He considered going back to his apartment. What was the point of that? Just to sit and stare at the four walls or watch his new television set? Besides, at this hour, all that was on was *Howdy Doody* or *The Lone Ranger*. He pulled up to a bar and found a parking space.

Inside the bar it was dark and reeked of stale cigarette smoke. He found an empty stool and sat down. An old man at the far end of the bar nursed a drink. The bartender asked Dave what he wanted. He ordered a beer and then chewed on a couple of pretzels from a bowl next to him. The jukebox was playing Doris Day singing "Que Será Será."

The bartender brought his drink, collected on it and then went to the other side of the counter. Dave took a sip of beer and looked at his reflection in the mirror behind the bar. He had dark circles under his eyes. And no matter how many times he saw his mustache and beard he couldn't get used to them. He'd stopped shaving the day after he'd begun his new life. And even so, there'd been a few close calls.

In Boston, a year earlier, a man in a hotel lobby had called him by his old name. They'd gone to high school together. "You must be mistaking me for someone else," said Dave. He left Boston that night. It was probably just an innocent, accidental meeting, but why take chances?

One time, when he was living in Chicago, a newspaper ran an article on the case and printed his picture. He was out of town before the afternoon edition.

That's why it was so odd to stay where he was. He'd taken to moving even when there were no incidents. He took another sip of his drink and watched the bartender ring up a sale on the cash register. His thoughts drifted back to *that* day a year and a half earlier. The armored car, the bundles of neatly wrapped new hundred dollar bills. "See you guys back at the warehouse," he'd said. Then he'd gotten into his car and driven away. He wondered how long it had taken them to realize that he wasn't coming back. A day? A week?

"This seat taken?" said a voice.

Dave snapped out of his daze and looked to his left as a burly man in a rumpled suit and tie sat down next to him. Dave shrugged.

"Bartender," said the man, "I'll have a glass of your best whiskey." Then the man turned to Dave and said, "When I say life insurance, what comes into your mind?"

Dave got up, placed a quarter on the bar and headed toward the door.

"Hey," said the man, "you don't have to be downright rude."

Dave walked out of the bar and back to his car. A minute later he was driving through the streets. He stopped at a red light and forgot where he was. He was used to it. After a while, every place started looking the same. The greasy spoons, the gas stations, the drive-ins.

He hadn't realized that it would be like this. When he'd taken the money he'd thought that he'd be able to retire and just lie by a pool somewhere, surrounded by palm trees and nubile young women in bathing suits, but it hadn't worked out that way. A few days after he'd left, he'd gone to Florida, rented a house, bought a sports car, a boat, new clothes. A couple of weeks later, he noticed that one of the local cops seemed to always be driving around his house. That was when he realized that he'd never be able to sit in a chaise longue with a cold drink in his hand and watch the world go by. Oh, the money was safe. He'd buried it in a secret place, that wasn't a problem, not for Doc. Nor was coming up with fake I.D. and a new life history. That wasn't a problem, either. What *was* a problem was always having to look over his shoulder.

Even Sally had noticed it. He'd told her that he was neurotic. Phobic was more like it. A fear of cops or feds, or anybody in a uniform, or in a suit and tie, that looked a little too serious.

But what he was really worried about was the old gang. After what he'd done, he knew they'd never stop looking for him. When he hadn't returned to the warehouse that night, it was no longer about just the money. He'd even thought about giving the money back, but he knew it wouldn't solve anything. They'd still hunt him down. At least with it, he had a fighting chance.

Dave stopped the car in front of a boarded-up nightclub and walked across the street to a small park. He sat down on a bench under a shady tree. A couple of teenagers in leather jackets went by. A woman wheeling a baby carriage strolled past, followed by a young couple holding hands.

Dave thought about Sally again. He'd met her six months earlier at the diner where she worked. He thought she looked beautiful in her white waitress uniform. He started going back to the restaurant just to see her. Eventually he asked her out. She'd believed his story about being a financial consultant. At first Dave thought it was just a fling, a casual liaison in a strange town. Then, as the months went by, he actually wondered if he should tell her the truth. Finally, he decided that the best thing for both of them was to live the lie.

But he couldn't deny he had feelings for her that went beyond the physical. "Doc don't feel, he just thinks," was what one of the guys used to say. And for the most part it was true.

"Bang bang!" yelled a child.

Dave turned and saw two little boys wearing coonskin caps, and pointing toy muskets at each other. He got up and walked back to the car.

A few minutes later, he pulled into the parking lot of a supermarket and got out. Now what the hell was it that Scooter eats? he thought, as he walked into the store.

He found the cat food section and stared at the different brands. They all had colorful labels and cute names. Then he remembered that Sally had mentioned that she had stocked up on cat food before she'd left. What was he doing here? He shrugged. Maybe Scooter would want some kind of special treat. If Sally were Scooter's mother, then he was an uncle, and wasn't that what uncles were for, to spoil kids?

Scooter was a shaded golden Persian that Sally had gotten as a kitten seven years earlier. She'd seen an ad in the newspaper about him. Scooter was the runt of a litter of purebred show cats. Scooter had been real sick and there was some question about whether or not he'd live. Sally had taken him in and nursed him back to health.

Dave would often watch the cat and study his behavior. Dave noticed a lot of things about Scooter. Like how right before it rained, Scooter would start jumping around and scratch the walls and stand up on his hind legs. Then, as soon as it did rain, he'd calm right down. Sometimes Dave would watch how Scooter would sneak up on a spider and then pounce on it and hold the insect under his paw.

And Scooter was always happy to see him. Whenever he'd visit, Scooter would run over and rub up against his leg. Until he'd met Scooter, he hadn't really liked cats, but Scooter was different. Scooter was a real friend. And he wasn't that way with everyone. If Sally had someone over to fix the sink or a squeaky door, Scooter would run and hide.

Dave picked up a few cans, went up to the cash register and paid for them. Then he got back into his car and drove out of the parking lot.

On the way to Sally's house, he stopped the car by the bay, got out and watched the sailboats go by. He wondered if the people on them were happy. He took off his jacket and glanced at the sun. Even though it was going down, it was still as warm as it had been earlier in the day. Dave adjusted the gun in the small of his back. On hot days it felt heavier than usual. He looked at the water in the bay and thought about tossing the weapon into it. It was something that had occurred to him many times before. He gave up the idea as he saw a police launch cruise past him. Then he turned around and got back into his car.

A few minutes later, he pulled up to Sally's house. She lived in a residential neighborhood on a quiet, tree-lined street. Dave walked up the path to the house, put the key into the lock, and opened the door.

"Hey, Scooter, Dave's here!" he said, stepping inside and closing the door. No response. "I've got treats for you," he said, shaking the bag of groceries. Still nothing. Dave looked around the living room and saw Scooter under one of the chairs. Scooter tensed up. Dave stood silently. He listened, but didn't hear anything. Then he placed the bag on the floor and pulled out his gun.

As soon as he did he heard a floorboard creak in another room. His heart began pounding. He turned and noticed that one of the windows was open. He took a breath, then tiptoed to the sofa and crouched behind it. He said in a loud voice, "So, how you been Scooter? Good kitty, I've got some food for you."

Just then, a shadow appeared on the wall. It came from the direction of the bedroom. Dave kept talking. "Good boy. I know you like tuna."

A man wearing a dark coat and hat and holding a gun peered out from behind a wall. Then he stepped into the living room. Dave squeezed the trigger of his gun. There was a flash of light and a loud cracking sound as the man moaned, grabbed his stomach and fell to the floor.

Immediately another man with a gun appeared. Dave shot him twice in the chest. He dropped to the carpet and stopped moving. Seconds went by. No one else walked out. Dave looked in the bedroom and then the kitchen, but they were empty. He went back into the living room and stared at the two men. One he recognized. He was the cousin of one of the guys in the gang.

Scooter came over and rubbed up against Dave's leg. Dave let out a breath and said, "You saved my life, boy, you know that?"

Scooter mewed.

"C'mon, Scooter, we have to get out of here."

He grabbed Scooter, got Sally's cat carrier out of the closet and put Scooter inside. Holding the carrier, Dave cautiously walked outside and back to his car. He stuck Scooter's carrier on the seat next to him and turned on the car's ignition.

Five minutes later, Dave was on the highway heading north. How had they found him? he wondered. He must have done something careless. He'd stayed too long in one place, he'd been spotted by someone, he'd—Sally. Sally. She had just coincidentally gone to visit her poor sick mother in Cleveland. Sally. He'd trusted her. Somehow they'd found him and had bought Sally off, or scared her, and she'd cooperated. Could she have known about what they'd intended to do? Maybe they'd told her that they were federal agents, something like that. Anyway, she'd gone along and . . . Dave noticed Scooter looking out of the window of the cat carrier.

Scooter's eyes were big, like he was scared, but he wasn't mewing. Dave glanced back at the road, then at Scooter again as he saw him pushing his paws through the slats in the carrier. It was as if Scooter was in his own little prison, thought Dave, a travelling prison. Dave pressed down on the gas pedal. He wondered where the road would take him and what the next town would be like. Then he realized that it didn't matter. Even though it all seemed like wide open country, everywhere he looked there were locks and guards and iron bars.

The Magician's Palace

EDWARD D. HOCH

IT ALL BEGAN ON THE MORNING Dante the cat went missing, seeming to disappear as completely as he did during the various magic performances in which he was a sometimes unwilling partner. Jenny Stowe had come in to help clean the place at 8.00 A.M., just as she did most mornings when she wasn't working as an extra on one of the television films shooting around town. Being part of the crew that cleaned the Magician's Palace wasn't exactly her idea of Hollywood glamour, but at least it brought in a needed paycheck each week while she was waiting to break into the movies.

Jenny had been waiting for thirteen years to be discovered, and occasionally now, in her mid-thirties, she wondered if her time was past, if she'd spend the rest of her life cleaning places like the Magician's Palace while she worked occasional jobs as a film extra. At first the work as an extra had been worth a letter home, alerting the family that she was in the opening scene of this new blockbuster film. Sometimes she even had a line or two of dialogue in a movie, though in the last year or so her work had mainly been confined to crowd scenes in TV films. She'd stopped writing home some time back.

But she wasn't thinking about that right now. She was thinking about Dante the cat and where he might be hiding in the vast labyrinth of rooms that made up the Magician's Palace. Not yet as elaborate as the Magic Castle about a mile away, the Palace was strictly a supper club with magic performances scheduled throughout the evening on the main stage and in two small additional rooms catering to close-up performers. Dante, a fittingly black cat of indeterminate age, usually perched on the counter by the hostess's station, greeting all comers with a benign indifference. Occasionally he performed in one of the magic acts when there was need of a black feline for a proper occult atmosphere.

Jenny had taken to feeding the cat when she came in to clean each morning, getting out the bag of cat food or unwrapping some special treats she'd brought from home. Dante always appeared within minutes of her arrival, purring softly and rubbing against her leg in the only brief show of affection he ever allowed himself. But this morning there was no purring, no rubbing, no Dante!

"Where's the cat?" Jenny asked Alf Frazier after she'd been searching for ten minutes. Alf was the manager of the Magician's Palace, an old-timer who'd made a living doing card tricks in Vegas lounges until he welshed on a gambling debt and got his fingers broken.

"How the hell should I know?" Frazier groused. "Maybe he got ate up by a dog. Serve him right."

"Alf!" She knew most of Frazier's attitude was an act, but she was in no mood for it this morning. "Come on, help me look."

"Can't, babe." Everyone under fifty was a babe to Alf. "I'm waiting for a phone call."

Jenny sighed and went off to continue her search. She'd already covered all the main floor rooms including the kitchen, where Dante was forbidden to prowl, so she headed for the basement stairs. The other members of the cleaning crew were already at work, their vacuums snoring, as she flipped on the basement light and went down among the discarded props and forgotten relics of a dozen past shows. There were concealed trap-doors in the first-floor stages, for use when needed, and she knew Dante sometimes prowled this area down below. Perhaps he dreamed of an unlucky mouse dropping through a trap some night.

"Dante! Here, Dante!" she called, alert to any movement in the shadows.

Then suddenly he came bounding toward her on his padded paws. "Dante—bad cat! Where have you been, you bad cat? You're all dirty." She ran her hand across its fur and looked at her moist, sticky fingers. It almost looked like half-dried blood on the fur, but Dante showed no sign of a wound. "Where have you been?" she asked the cat. "Show me where you've been."

Jenny was not surprised when the black cat turned and ran toward the cushioned area beneath one of the trap-doors. As she followed the cat, she flipped on another light switch for this area of the basement and saw the sprawled figure of a man. She gasped and took a step back, seeing the handle of the knife protruding from his side. She had never been a screamer and she didn't scream now. Instead, she calmly walked up the stairs and told Alf Frazier, "There's a dead man in your basement. He's wearing a silk cape, so I suppose he's one of your magicians."

The dead man went by the name of Carlo the Great, and even Alf wasn't too certain of his real name. "He was booked by the owner. I met him once in Vegas but I never knew him as anything but Carlo the Great."

That wasn't good enough for the detective sergeant in charge of the case. He was a bulky, balding man with a black mustache and tiny eyes. Sgt. Amos Paige. Jenny knew him well. Five years ago he'd threatened to arrest her for prostitution when she refused to cooperate on a narcotics sting operation. She'd never been a prostitute but she'd gone with a cable television producer once in hopes of landing a part in a film. She was disgusted with herself and never did it again. That was why she particularly disliked Sgt. Amos Paige and his insinuating glances in her direction.

"You find the body?" he asked.

"I found the body. I'm on the cleaning crew here. I was looking for Dante the cat."

"You're Jenny Stowe," he said, dredging up her name from the depths of his memory. "We had some dealings once before."

"I remember."

He said no more to her just then, turning his attention instead to Alf Frazier. "So Carlo the Great performed last night?"

Alf nodded, chewing nervously on his cigar. "He produced flowers from his wand, rabbits from his cape. Nothing unusual but the crowd liked his patter. He went on after the late dinner when the customers are feeling fat and rested."

"Did he use a knife in his act?"

Alf thought about that. "I don't— Wait a minute! Yes, he used a long sharp knife to slice through a grapefruit for one trick. Kept it concealed in his cape till he needed it."

"And the trap-door?"

"He didn't use that at all. In fact, that particular one wasn't even—"

Dante had been sitting on Jenny's lap, quietly purring during the inquisition. Now he suddenly leapt to the floor, running to greet a tall blonde woman who had just entered. "Alf, what are all the police cars doing out front?"

"There's been a killing," Sergeant Paige told her before Alf could open his mouth. "Who are you, Miss?"

"Monica Hayes. I'm one of the owners. What do you mean, there's been a killing?"

"A performer who went by the name of Carlo the Great was stabbed to death overnight. One of your cleaning people found the body." Paige was looking her over as he answered. Monica was worth the look.

"Is that true, Alf?" she asked.

"That's what they're saying. He's dead, all right. They need his real name."

"It was Carlos Costa, I believe. At least that's the name on his contract."

"Had he ever played the Magician's Palace before?" Paige asked.

"Not here. We have a place up in Santa Barbara that I booked him into a couple of times. What was it, a robbery?"

"We don't know yet. He was found in the basement, under one of the stage trap-doors."

"I always worry about those traps." She turned to her manager. "Alf, could it have been an accident?"

Frazier rubbed his fingers. "Maybe. He might have fallen through the trap after he finished his act and the audience left. He still had his knife from the grapefruit trick and when he landed, it could have gone into his side."

"How does the trap-door open?" the detective asked. They had finished their work in the basement and were bringing up the body in a black plastic bag. Jenny Stowe averted her eyes.

"There's a lever in the basement that controls it. We installed this particular trap a few years back for a magician who had an illusion in which he seemed to walk through a brick wall. A large rug was unrolled on stage and a solid brick wall was set in place over it. Members of the audience were invited to examine the wall and make sure it was solid. Then the magician drew a curtain while the audience members stood at both ends of the wall to make certain he didn't walk around it. We had someone in the basement to throw the lever and open the trap-door. The magician couldn't go through it but the rug sagged into the hole just enough to allow him to squeeze beneath the wall. When the curtain was opened, he appeared to have walked through the bricks."

"The lever is in the basement," Sergeant Paige repeated. "There's no lever on stage to activate the trap-door?"

"No."

"That would seem to rule out an accident. Even if someone in the basement accidentally pushed the lever, they would have seen Carlo fall and gone to his aid. If the trap-door was deliberately released while he was standing on it, that indicates a premeditated crime." He made a few notes. "Was he having trouble with any of your employees?"

"Not that I know of," Alf replied.

"What about that bartender of yours?" Monica Hayes asked. "When I first booked Carlo the Great, you told me there might be trouble with someone who'd known him in Vegas."

"Yeah. Brian Korol said he had a fight with him once."

"Was this Korol working last night?"

"Sure. He should be coming in pretty soon now, if you want to talk with him."

Sergeant Paige asked to use the phone and was directed to Alf's little office beside the bar. When he'd finished, he asked Jenny to join him in the office. "I remember you," he said. "Jenny Stowe. You weren't so cooperative the last time."

"You wanted me to help frame someone for a crime. I don't do that."

"Still in the movies, Jenny?"

"I get a part now and then. Extra work, mostly."

"Behaving yourself? Staying off the street?"

That only fueled her growing resentment. "Listen, Sergeant, I was never a prostitute and you know it! When I called your bluff, you dropped those charges."

"What do you know about Carlo the Great?"

"Nothing. I never met the man. We come in the morning to clean the place up. He only works at night."

Paige walked over to the wall to study a large planning calendar where Alf had written in the names of the performers in the various rooms. He had CARLOS penciled in for one of the smaller rooms while someone named MAGICO was scheduled for the big room. "Isn't that trap-door under the main stage?"

"I guess so, yes."

"So Carlo the Great wasn't even performing there! What in hell was he doing on the big stage?"

"Don't ask me, Sergeant. I was home watching TV."

"Yeah, I'll bet!" He walked to the office door. "Mr. Frazier, please come in here."

Alf came in, looking worried. "My bartender, Brian, is here now."

"I'll see him in a minute. Look, according to this schedule Carlo the Great was in a small room. How did he happen to be on the big stage when he fell through the trap-door?"

Alf shrugged. "Sometimes after we close, they like to practice in the main room, just to see what it's like. I was in here, going over the receipts. He might have gone anywhere without my knowing it."

"Maybe he never fell through the trap-door at all. Maybe someone stabbed him in the basement and left his body under it just to mislead us."

Jenny knew the bartender, so she strolled out to say hello. "Hi, Brian. Did you hear what happened?"

"Mrs. Hayes was just telling me." Brian Korol was a light-skinned Jamaican who'd come west to work in Las Vegas. Jenny liked him and they often chatted about show business matters after she finished her work for the day.

"Sergeant Paige wants to question you. He heard you had a fight with Carlo once in Vegas."

"That was years ago. He used to think he was a tough guy before he turned to magic."

"How'd you get along this time?"

Korol chuckled. "I don't think he even remembered me."

Paige was coming out of the office, heading their way. Jenny decided it was time to make herself scarce. "See you later," she told the bartender.

It had not been a morning for getting much work done, but it wasn't every morning she discovered a body. Since the police were finished downstairs, she decided to take another look at the basement before heading home. Dante was back purring at her feet, so she scooped the cat up and carried him with her.

The police photographers and the fingerprints people had left every light in the basement burning and, with all this illumination, it didn't seem a frightening place at all. Jenny went immediately to the spot where she'd found the body and started hunting for the lever that would release the trap-door. She found it quickly enough, a knife switch just above a railing. By pulling down on it, she completed the circuit and the doors of the trap fell open, then sprang closed again.

Dante hopped up on the railing and swiped at the switch with his paw. Jenny watched him do it a second time and an idea began to form in her mind.

Ten minutes later she went back upstairs, carrying the black cat in her arms. She found Monica Hayes and told the blonde owner, "I think I know how Carlo the Great died."

Monica eyed her a bit uncertainly. "Look, Jenny," she said at last, "anything you think you know is better kept to yourself. The police don't need a lot of amateur theories and I sure don't want to hear them. You only help with the cleaning here, remember."

Jenny remembered. No one wanted to hear her theories. She stroked Dante's fur and the cat gave a low purr. As she turned to go, she saw Sergeant Paige standing with the bartender and Alf. "If you'll come down to the basement with me, I think I can show you how Carlo died," she told them.

Paige just looked at her for a moment and then gave a laugh. "This your big scene, Jenny? You going to confess, or you going to pull a killer out of the woodwork?"

"Just come down with me and you'll see."

"I'll go," Alf said, and Brian Korol tagged along too. When Paige followed along, Monica Hayes decided she needed to know what was going on.

Once she had them down there, she led the way to the cushioned area beneath the trap-door where Carlo's body had been found. "All right." She stood by the switch for the trap-door. "Now imagine that Carlo the Great is upstairs, after closing, running through his act on the big stage. He's wearing his cape, so the knife he used in his grapefruit trick is hidden in the lining. By chance he's standing on the trap-door, though he doesn't intend to use it in the trick. Meanwhile, most everyone else has gone home. Downstairs here, Dante is on the prowl for mice."

Jenny released the cat and he jumped onto the railing beneath the knife switch. Sergeant Paige took a step forward but Jenny held him back. "Just watch," she whispered.

Dante sniffed around and then boosted himself onto his hind legs. He could barely reach the switch but managed to get his front paws on it. He pulled it down and the circuit was completed. The trap-door above their heads fell open as the bolt was pulled, then sprang back to the closed position. Monica Hayes gasped.

"You see," Jenny told them, feeling like a teacher lecturing her pupils, "Carlo the Great fell through the trap when Dante pulled that switch. I was down here with him earlier and saw him do it, and realized exactly how it happened. Carlo fell on his knife and bled to death. Nobody killed him, unless it was Dante here."

Sergeant Paige was a bit reluctant to accept Jenny's solution, or to admit that anything she came up with might be important to his investigation. But after the scene in the basement, his men packed up their equipment and departed. "I'll want to talk to your employees," he told Alf Frazier, "especially those on duty last night. If I can't find anyone with a motive for killing Carlo, maybe we'll consider this cat business." He glanced distastefully in Jenny's direction. "I suppose stranger things have happened."

Jenny Stowe finished up her work and went into Alf's little office. Monica Hayes had finally departed and Korol was busy behind the bar getting ready for opening time. "It's been a busy day," she told Alf.

"That it has been," he agreed. "I hope the publicity doesn't hurt business."

"It'll probably help. The idea of having dinner at a murder scene will intrigue people."

"I hope so. Monica will blame me if business falls off."

"Alf?"

"Yeah?"

"Why'd you kill him?"

"What—?" He started to protest but then his face relaxed into a grin. "I should have known I couldn't fool you, babe. But you just showed Paige how the cat did it."

"That was an act. I'm an actress, remember. Not a very successful one, but an actress still. I put a little of Dante's catnip on that switch and he went for it, pulled it right down. I tried it earlier to make sure he'd do it, then invited Sergeant Paige down for the big show. I certainly didn't owe him anything else!"

"Catnip! I'll be damned."

"You said you never knew him by any name other than Carlo the Great, but on this schedule here you've written in *Carlos*. You knew he was Carlos Costa. You knew him in Vegas and you knew his real name. Brian Korol told me he used to think he was a tough guy before he turned to magic. Is that when you knew him, Alf?"

He was rubbing his fingers again, as he often did. "Yeah. He's the fella who broke these fingers when I had a little trouble over that bad debt. It was bad enough I couldn't do close-up magic anymore, but then the bastard started doing magic himself! That was more than I could stomach. As long as he was in Vegas and I was in LA, I could put it out of my mind. But when he had the nerve to get booked into the Magician's Palace, that was too much. I acted friendly and last night after we closed, I told him he could run through his act on the big stage. I even showed him the best place to stand, right over the trap-door. I pulled the switch in the basement and, when he fell through, I was on him. I grabbed the knife from his cape and put him away." There was nothing more to be said.

Dante came through the office door at that moment carrying a dead mouse. He dropped it on the floor at Alf's feet. "See?" Jenny told him. "I always knew he was a killer."

Man's Best Friend

NANCY JANE MOORE

I WOULD NEVER HAVE GOTTEN INVOLVED, except for the cat.
Yeah, I know, I've never been much of one for cats. Real men don't do
cats, that's my motto. But, hell, the poor little bugger was sitting out there in the
rain, scratching at the sliding door—you know my apartment's got that patio
door, opens onto a little grassy area in back—yowling pitifully and looking wet
and bedraggled.

Since Laura left I've developed a little more compassion for those in pain.
So what the hay, I let him in, toweled him dry as best I could. Found a can of
tuna in the cabinet. Boy, did that make him happy. He scarfed it right down,
then sat down to lick himself the rest of the way dry.

Nice-looking cat, once he'd cleaned himself up. Big green eyes, grayish
stripes—I think you call it a tabby. Not too big, and kind of lean, like he went
out and got his exercise going after mice or something. He leapt right up into
my lap, made himself at home, and started to purr.

Well, hell, that suckered me right in. I'd been sitting there, planning to take
him to the pound. Feeling a little guilty about it—I always figured taking them
to the pound was just the civilized version of putting them in a bag and throwing them in the creek. But once he started purring, I got to thinking that maybe
having a cat wouldn't be so bad.

So your wife walks out, you get kind of maudlin, okay? Laura had told me
I was boring, and I'd started to think maybe I was. I liked it, getting affection
from someone. Even a cat. I scratched his ears and he purred some more, and I
felt kind of good for the first time in a month or so.

Anyway, I hear pets help you live longer.

Eventually it occurred to me that cats got to eat regular, and they can't just
run out to Mickey D's when they get a mind to. And I didn't have another can
of tuna. Plus he was going to need a bathroom sooner or later, and I did know
you can't just send cats outside twice a day to do their business, like you do
dogs.

So even though the rain was still coming down, I went out. This big guy
was walking just ahead of me in the hall—must have come from the elevators.
Really big guy. Beefy. Looked like he might have played linebacker. He let the
front door slam back in my face.

His black Firebird was parked next to my old Toyota in the tenant parking area. I'd noticed the car a few weeks earlier—hard to miss the silver racing stripes and mag wheels. He'd probably just moved in. I fumbled with my keys while he screeched his tires.

The Giant was full of customers after eleven. I found the pet-food aisle, and about freaked out. You wouldn't believe how many different kinds of food they got, just for cats. And cat litter—my God, they must have had twenty brands of that, in all sizes.

Fortunately, this woman was loading her cart right next to me. Really loading it, I mean—cans and cans of stuff. Turned out she had three cats. And she wasn't some old lady. Kind of a babe, actually.

But she took pity on me. "Keep it simple, for now," she said. She selected a box of dried food, told me which litter to get, reminded me that I needed some kind of container for the litter, that sort of thing.

"And take him to the vet," she said. "Stray cats can have all kinds of diseases."

I could see this pet-keeping might get expensive. I wondered if vets cost as much as doctors.

When I got home I did the usual struggle with the door you do when your hands are full of stuff, finally got it open—and the cat goes rushing out between my legs and up the hall. Kind of surprised me. I guess I was expecting him to be sitting curled up where I'd left him, just waiting for me to come back so he could sit in my lap again.

I put the stuff down, and went looking for him. And there he was, up the hall about three apartments, scratching at this door and mewing like his heart was going to break.

So I picked him up, said, "Hey, boy, what's the deal here?" I tried to think who lived in that apartment. You know, life in the big city, you don't really know your neighbors.

After a minute, it came to me. A woman lived there. In her early thirties, maybe. No beauty queen, but not a dog either. Nice enough. Hadn't lived there long. One evening I'd come in the front door while she was struggling with too many bags, and helped her carry them in. And the cat—my new cat—had come running out the door when she'd unlocked it.

Well, what the hell, I could give her all the stuff I'd just bought. I should have thought about asking around to see if anyone had lost a cat. So I knocked on the door. No answer. Knocked louder. Still no answer.

It was after midnight by now, and a weeknight. And it bothered me. Stupid, really, because I didn't know enough about her to know her habits. I mean she seemed quiet enough when we met in the halls, but maybe she liked to party all night. Or was staying with a boyfriend.

But it bothered me. I guess it was the cat. I just didn't think she'd go off and leave him out in the rain. So I knocked again. Still no answer.

Well, hell, her apartment would have sliding doors out to the same garden area as mine—that's how the building was designed. So I took the cat back into my apartment—he protested loudly all the way—and slipped out my patio door. Counted over apartments to figure out which one was hers. It seemed to have a light on inside.

Her sliding door was open just a few inches. I banged on it, yelled, "Hey, lady, I found your cat!" No answer. So I tried sliding the door. It didn't move. Must have been jammed open just enough to let the cat in and out, without letting anyone else in.

So I reached my fingers in, and pushed the curtain aside so I could peek in. And saw a leg, lying at a funny angle on the floor.

That's all I saw. It's all I had to see. I went rushing back to my place and called 911.

Well, pretty soon we got cop cars and an ambulance, and even a damn fire truck. Lights flashing everywhere, and all the neighbors outside. The resident manager was standing around, looking a little green. The cops had gotten him to open the door, and he saw her lying there. Blood everywhere.

After a while they carried her out all zipped in a body bag. And then the cops started asking me questions.

Well, I'd expected that, you know. I mean, I called 'em. But after a few minutes the questions moved from "About what time did you find the cat?" to "How long ago did your wife leave?" and it finally hit me: they considered me a suspect.

Hell, no wonder nobody wants to get involved. I do my neighborly duty and the next thing you know, I'm going down to the station with a couple of detectives.

Well, they did ask nicely. They didn't arrest me or anything, just said, "Would you mind coming back to the precinct with us?" What was I going to do, say no?

The station they took me to in Wheaton looked like it was built in the Seventies—all brick and glass. Some architect probably told them to make it look friendly, not like all those forbidding police stations of the past. Let me tell you, it didn't make me feel any less scared.

First they fingerprinted me—"Just want to check your prints against others on the scene, to eliminate them." Then they asked, would I mind giving them a sample of my blood. Well, of course I minded. At that point, I thought long and hard about calling my lawyer, only I didn't want to call him in the middle of the night. Anyway he's a divorce lawyer, not a criminal one. So I let them take the sample. I told them, "Hey, I didn't do anything but find the body. I got nothing to hide."

They stuck me in this interview room, and just left me there for a while. It got kind of eerie, sitting there. I kept thinking I should get up and leave. But maybe they'd locked the door. I didn't want to know that, so I just sat there.

After what seemed like a couple of hours, two detectives came in, and started asking me questions. And you could tell from the questions they really thought I'd done it. The guy was doing this nice-guy routine—"Hey, buddy, I know what's it's like. Your wife leaves, other women shoot you down. You got reason to get angry."

But the woman cop, she jumped all over me. "You hate women, don't you? Your wife said you frightened her, that's why she left, isn't it?"

And I found myself thinking, *My God, did they already call up Laura?* I mean, the scenes between us got kind of ugly there at the end, you know. No telling what she'd say about me.

Then the cop went on about the other women in the building, how they felt scared of me. First I'd heard of it. I had visions of the cops waking up all these women up and down the halls, asking them about the murderer in apartment 107.

They kept it up for about an hour or so, and then disappeared for a long time. The room really started to get to me. Nothing to read. No television or anything. Nothing to do but sit there and think. And I didn't have anything to think about, except how scared I felt.

I swore to myself I'd just demand to call my lawyer when they came back. I didn't want to—I figured only guilty people needed lawyers and anyway I'd already paid all my money to lawyers during the divorce—but I began to think I'd never get out of there without help. I remembered some sociology professor I had back in college saying, "It's not whether you're guilty; it's whether you look guilty."

They didn't come back in until about seven o'clock in the morning. And when they did, the male detective started in on the nice-guy stuff again. Brought me some coffee—kind of old—and a donut from the vending machine. The woman cop just sat there, kind of sullen, watching him get all palsy-walsy with me. And I thought, *Well, he's not so bad a guy. I'm not going to need a lawyer here. Truth will out.*

And just as I got comfortable—the caffeine and sugar giving me a pleasant buzz—the woman started in again. She just jumped all over me, mentioning the Web sites I'd bookmarked—hell, I mean, my wife left me, okay. I'm not dating anybody. So I checked out some kinky Web sites. Cheaper than buying *Hustler*.

I kept looking at the male cop, and he'd give me one of those shrugs, like "Sorry, buddy, nothing I can do." And I didn't think it would ever stop, until finally just one thought remained in my head: confess. Just tell them what they want to hear, and they'll leave you alone.

I almost did. You know, we got the death penalty in Maryland these days. Guy kills a woman like that—a sex crime—everybody's going to want to give him one of those lethal injections.

I knew that, and yet I still came that close to confessing. Scary, really, what psychological tricks can do to you. Make you wonder whether you actually did something.

I'm not sure what I would have done if another officer hadn't stuck his head in, pulled both cops out of there. They left me sitting there about ten minutes, long enough to pull myself back together, and realize I'd better demand a lawyer before I confessed to every unsolved murder in twenty states.

And then the male cop came back in, and said, "You can go home now. We've got everything we need." Didn't explain a thing. But he did ask a uniformed guy to drive me home. While I was waiting for him, I heard someone mention something about the lab tests coming back. I guess my blood didn't match.

Thank God for modern science.

I saw the woman detective sitting at her desk, just drinking some coffee. She gave me a look as I left. Didn't seem apologetic, just disappointed.

I got back home at maybe ten in the morning, thinking mostly about crawling into bed. I could hear the elevator doors open when I was unlocking my apartment door, but I didn't pay any attention. Frankly, I was leaning up against the door frame, trying not to fall asleep before I got inside. The cat came out, rubbed against my ankles, and then growled. Before I knew it, he ran up the hall, climbed up the leg of this huge guy standing there, and started scratching his face. I swear he was trying for the eyes.

I said, "Oh, shit." It was the new neighbor, the one I'd seen the night before. The big one. He looked even bigger in the morning light. He swatted at the cat, cursing.

Well, I rushed up there, got an opening, grabbed the cat by the scruff of the neck, and pulled him off. Probably took off some skin. The guy reached toward the cat, like he wanted to strangle him, which I admit didn't seem like an unreasonable reaction, but I held the cat out of range, and said something dumb like, "Bad cat." The cat hissed at me, wriggled around, scratched at my wrist, which made me drop him. He raced off down the hall to God knows where.

I told the guy, "Man, I'm really sorry about this. Look, let me get something for those cuts." I figured, better be conciliatory with this guy, because both he and I knew he could take me apart with one hand.

Funny thing was, he didn't seem particularly angry. Or not at me, anyway. He rubbed a scratch, looked at his fingers, saw blood, and said, "Damn cat." And then, "Yeah, I guess I'd better clean up."

So he followed me. I grabbed a couple of towels and the antibiotic cream out of the bathroom. He wiped the blood off, threw a towel on the floor, then started putting the ointment on the cuts he could find.

I said again, "Man, I'm really sorry. I don't know what got into him." After all, I was thinking, if this guy doesn't beat the crap out of me, for sure he's going to sue me.

He didn't seem to be listening. He said, "You got any beer?" I pulled a Rolling Rock out of the fridge—I keep it around for my friends who don't know what good beer is. He popped the top and chugged about half of it. And then he said, "That bastard cat never did like me."

I got it, then. He didn't think the cat belonged to me. Which meant he knew who the cat belonged to. Which meant. . . .

Freaked me out, I tell you. But I kept my cool. "Just can't tell with cats," I said.

He swigged the rest of the beer, crumpled the can, threw it at the trash. It missed. "Yeah," he said. "Cats and women. You just can't tell." And walked out.

I waited a minute or so, then called the cops. Again.

They acted pretty skeptical at first. "The cat recognized him?" the male cop kept saying. But they finally agreed to come look at the stuff the guy had touched.

The blood on the towel matched some they'd found in her apartment. Not to mention the nice fingerprints he'd left on beer can. The cops were sitting in his place waiting for him when he came home.

Turned out he'd killed several other women the same way. He'd move into some big, anonymous apartment complex like mine, get friendly with some woman living there—preferably someone new to town, somebody who didn't have many local friends. After running into her a few times in the hall, acting friendly, he'd ask her out. And by that point, he wouldn't seem like a stranger.

He was always careful not to be seen with the women. A couple of months after the murder, he'd just move on to a new place. And start the pattern all over again.

Gives me the creeps, just thinking about a guy like that.

The *Washington Post* did a feature piece on me, all about how sometimes neighbors do get involved in this ugly modern world. Kind of nice, actually. Ran a picture of me with Fred curled up in my lap. That's what I decided to call the cat. Fred. Just seemed right, you know.

Actually, Fred should really get the credit. I wouldn't have found her except for him. And I wouldn't have seen the guy if Fred hadn't attacked him, much less invited him into my place to clean up. They say cats aren't too smart, but Fred knows his enemies. And his friends.

No, I think I'll pass on another beer. Got to get home and feed Fred. I've got a date later. Didn't I tell you? The reporter who did the story. She doesn't think I'm boring.

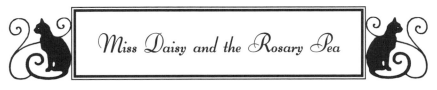

Miss Daisy and the Rosary Pea

SIDNEY WILLIAMS

MISS DAISY KITTYCAT SAT on the kitchen windowsill watching a squirrel in the oak outside. The squirrel was oblivious to Miss Daisy, a gray-and-white tabby-striped queen by birth and attitude. If she had been in the backyard he would have perched on a power line and barked at her. He tended to get disturbed anytime she left the house. Just thinking of that agitated her, and her tail made an instinctive thump, knocking over the salt and pepper shakers.

They were Fitz and Floyd, one shaped like an accountant and the other like his pencil. They mattered a great deal to Ms. Christine; she shouted her annoying "Ahn, ahn, ahn!" every time the tail problem occurred. Miss Daisy was wondering if she could upright them again when she heard the back door open. Mr. Sid was cooking outside, which meant he'd be making several trips. Sliding along the counter, she perched on the bar beside the door, waiting.

A few moments later Mr. Sid came back inside, probably looking for matches. Before the storm door could swing closed, Miss Daisy slithered out and went scurrying across the patio. As soon as she stepped into the grass, the squirrel took notice and bolted, heading straight up the oak trunk. Miss Daisy didn't try to follow. She knew he'd be too fast. She moved along the ground, watching as he hurried out a branch.

She was hoping he'd make a misstep when he tried to make the transfer from the oak to an encroaching pine, but he maintained his balance like an acrobat and kept moving. Miss Daisy stayed with him on the ground, ignoring his protest. It sounded oddly like Ms. Christine's cry when she was angry, but Miss Daisy didn't find it as affecting. She didn't care if the squirrel was mad.

As he left the pine and hopped onto one of the power lines that crisscrossed the backyard, Miss Daisy made her way up the tall wooden fence that stretched across the back of the property. She wouldn't be able to reach the squirrel even from the top, but she'd at least be able to keep track of him. He'd been taunting her for ages and he was going to pay.

He started to bark even louder as Miss Daisy topped the fence. He was pointing at Mrs. Edson on the ground. She was the heavyset lady who chased Miss Daisy with a broom if she came near her garden, although lately it had been worth the risk because the birds were holding conventions there.

Now the lady was stretched out amid jagged wet-looking leaves of bearded black irises. Carefully, Miss Daisy lowered herself over the edge of the fence for a drop to the grass. Quietly she padded over to Mrs. Edson's side and nuzzled the old lady's cheek. No air was coming from her nostrils, at least not the way it did from Mr. Sid's when he slept. Gently Miss Daisy tickled the woman's cheek with her whiskers. There was no stirring.

Miss Daisy was wondering if she should go for help when she saw Lou Elle, the dog from next door, heading around the edge of the fence. Ever nosy, Lou Elle was coming to see what was going on. Miss Daisy made a quick leap into a bush and watched Lou Elle dawdle around Mrs. Edson's feet where a teacup and saucer had fallen.

"Rrrrwwrrrrrr," Miss Daisy warned as Lou Elle started sniffing at the cup. She wasn't fond of Lou Elle. She had a tendency to slobber, but she wasn't as bad as the Labrador that lived two doors down. Miss Daisy didn't want to see her get a dose of the stuff that had obviously dropped Mrs. Edson.

"What's wrong?" Lou Elle asked.

"Someone's poisoned her tea," Miss Daisy said.

"Could've been a heart attack," Lou Elle protested.

"I don't think she keeled over from a bum ticker while sipping tea and admiring her irises," Miss Daisy said.

"You think her husband did it?"

"He's been dead for years," Miss Daisy responded. "Sniff around and see if you recognize anyone else's scent."

Lou Elle pressed her nose to the ground, moving aside grass blades and inching along. It seemed a tedious process, but it was one area she had superior skills.

"Well?" Miss Daisy asked.

"A couple of people have been by," Lou Elle said. Suddenly the wind shifted and her head tilted back. "Mr. Sid's cooking out."

"I know that," Miss Daisy said. "What about the visitors?"

"Mr. Harseman. The new neighbor. He's been by here." She sniffed the ground again and contemplated the smell. "And Mrs. Grendly."

Both were silver-haired people from the same street, not young people like Miss Daisy perceived Ms. Christine and Mr. Sid to be. She didn't have a good concept of age, but she knew they moved slowly like her cousin Charley had on the times she'd met him. He had belonged to Ms. Christine's sister and had visited on holidays until this year.

"What do you think?" Lou Elle asked.

"I don't know why Ms. Christine and Mr. Sid do half of the things they do," Miss Daisy said. "Let alone what older humans might be up to, but maybe if we snoop around a little we can find something that my folks will understand."

"Can we get into her house?" Lou Elle asked.

Lou Elle was able to push open the sliding glass door with her nose. Miss Daisy went in first, her tail high but slightly crooked at the end in caution.

The living room was cool, a room kept much neater than Mr. Sid's office. No books or papers were piled on the floor. A couple of teacups were left on the coffee table, however. Miss Daisy hopped up and walked over to sniff the tea.

"Do you catch the smell of the same humans here?"

"It's the same," Lou Elle said.

"So they all had tea together, then Mrs. Edson walked out to her garden, drank her tea, and died. Everything is kept neat as a high-class litterbox so she wouldn't have let the cups sit for very long."

"So Mr. Harseman and Mrs. Grendly put something in her tea," Lou Elle concluded.

"Maybe just one of them did it," Miss Daisy suggested. "I wonder why."

She strolled on along the coffee table and stopped at the end, looking across at a bookcase. It displayed gardening books and items on humane pest control. It was decorated with several flower pots featuring bright blooms. On a top shelf were gleaming statues and photographs of Mrs. Edson with the black irises, like outside. Blue ribbons were pinned to the edge of the shelf and to the picture frames as well.

"What's that about?" Lou Elle asked.

"She has blue ribbons like Ms. Christine's old cat, Marie, used to win at cat shows."

"Cat shows?"

"The humans take cats to big halls and display them and the best cat gets a ribbon. They do it with dogs, too, but I'd never give a dog a ribbon."

"So Mrs. Edson went to shows with her flowers."

"And the flowers won ribbons."

"Maybe Mrs. Grendly and Mr. Harseman poisoned her because they didn't win," Lou Elle suggested. "My folks would be upset if I was in a show and I didn't get a ribbon."

"They wouldn't be upset. They'd understand," Miss Daisy said, looking over at Lou Elle's tousled brown fur. Leaves and burrs were tangled into her bangs and Miss Daisy didn't want to know about the dried stuff on her tail.

"Both of them garden, dig in the ground and plant things," Lou Elle said. "I've seen them. The first time, when they got out their shovels, I thought they must be looking for bones or something."

"You would," Miss Daisy observed, hopping from the table with her tail straight in the air now. She was about to head for the door when she noticed the small round object just under the end of the couch. She took a quick step over and touched it gently with her nose. It rolled slightly, a hard blackberry or pea.

"I'll have to get Ms. Christine to look it up," Miss Daisy said. "I just have to be careful with it. I wouldn't want to swallow it."

"You think it's what went into Mrs. Edson's tea?"

"There's a good chance of it," Miss Daisy said. "I'm going to take it back to our house."

"What's next after that?" Lou Elle asked.

"We'll need to visit Mr. Harseman and Mrs. Grendly and see if they have anything to say. Now don't talk to me after I pick up the berry," Miss Daisy said.

She carefully took the berry into her mouth and started a slow walk toward the back door.

"Should I wait here?"

With a huff, Miss Daisy spat out the berry. "No, go wait for me at the edge of the fence. I'll be right back."

She picked up the berry again and trotted away before Lou Elle could say anything else. She found Mr. Sid at the grill flipping over one of the big slices of cow he fixed periodically.

"Daisy," he called when he saw her. "Come on back in the house. I was getting worried about you."

Before Daisy could get out of his range, he hoisted her into his arms, closing on her ribs so quickly he almost caused her to swallow the berry. She started to squirm once he stepped through the back door, so he put her down on the living room carpet. She hopped immediately onto the coffee table in front of Ms. Christine and spat again.

"What'd you bring me, girl?" Ms. Christine asked. "Guess we'd better see if it's anything that would bother you."

She walked over to the bookcases at the den's edge and pulled out a big green picture book.

"Oh goodness," Ms. Christine said. "This is poison. Good thing you didn't bite into it girl."

Miss Daisy looked up at her and cocked her head, offering her best inquisitive look. Since she couldn't read she was dependent on Ms. Christine's explanation.

"It has a long scientific name, *ab-ru-us pre-ca-torius*, but it's best known as a rosary pea. Sometimes they're used to make rosaries."

Not sure what a rosary was, Miss Daisy made a soft sound in her throat. Ms. Christine called it murpleing. It usually got her ears scratched.

"Well, we won't let this get back in your mouth," Ms. Christine said, depositing the pea in a pencil holder. Thankfully she wasn't throwing it away.

As Ms. Christine went back to her reading, Miss Daisy sat by the back door until Mr. Sid made another trip outside, then she slipped past.

The squirrel was sitting on the back fence. "Does anybody know there's a dead lady in the garden back here?" he barked.

"Duly noted," Miss Daisy said. She trotted past Mr. Sid and went over the fence to find Lou Elle.

"Let's get down to Mr. Harseman's before dinner," Miss Daisy suggested, and they were off at a mild trot. Miss Daisy moved with her usual grace. Lou Elle lumbered along with her tongue dangling. It seemed so undignified, but Miss Daisy had never been able to convince her not to do it in public.

When they reached Mr. Harseman's cottage at the end of the street, they didn't head immediately for a door or window. Miss Daisy made a check of his yard first, trying to determine if his plants included one that would produce the rosary pea. He had a lot of plants, but none of them matched.

"Does that mean he's in the clear?"

"He doesn't have to grow his own to be a poisoner," Miss Daisy said.

They headed up to the house. Since there was no easy entrance, Miss Daisy hopped onto a ledge outside the bedroom window, trying to peek through the curtain. Mr. Harseman was inside, sitting at a desk under a large framed diploma, one of several. Tilting her head for a better look, Miss Daisy determined he was writing something on a yellow legal pad next to a stack of magazines with plants on the covers. After a few moments he tore the sheet off and folded it, putting it inside an envelope which he licked and sealed.

"If we could get that top sheet of paper, Ms. Christine might be able to see what he's written. Can you do anything with this window, Lou Elle?"

Mrs. Grendly lived in an older house. Built of white wood it stood off the ground on red brick pilings. Miss Daisy and Lou Elle strolled under the edge of the porch and made their way through the powdery dirt. Once under the living room, they stopped, listening for the creak of Mrs. Grendly's footfalls. After a while they could hear her muffled voice, and there seemed to be an urgency to her words.

"I wish I knew what she was saying," Lou Elle said.

"So do I," Miss Daisy agreed. "But we'd better have a look around Mrs. Grendley's garden."

"What about the greenhouse?" Lou Elle asked.

"There's a greenhouse?"

"Over here."

Lou Elle trotted from under the edge of the house and led Miss Daisy across the backyard.

"What's in there?"

"Irises," Miss Daisy said. "Just like Mrs. Edson grew. And look over there."

"What?"

"*Abrus precatorius*," Miss Daisy said. "The plant that produces the rosary pea."

"What should we do?"

"Time for another consult with Ms. Christine," Miss Daisy said.

She picked up the yellow paper from the place she'd hidden it after Lou Elle had pulled it from the house and went over the wall again.

"What have you got there, girl?" Ms. Christine asked.

"Just a piece of legal paper," Mr. Sid said. They'd finished dinner and were settled on the couch. He tossed the paper on the coffee table.

Miss Daisy hopped onto the table beside it and began to meow. The more they ignored the page, the more shrill her voice became.

"She wants us to look at it," Ms. Christine said.

Gently she unfolded the paper.

"Writing, pressed through from another sheet."

She took a pencil and began to brush it across the page.

"What's it say?"

"Someone is frightened. 'I may be in great danger,' it says."

"Who's in great danger?"

She brushed the pencil further down the page. "Mr. Harseman."

"Why?"

"Something about a discovery he's made. Can't read what he's saying here, can you?"

"Looks like something about irises but I can't make out what it is."

"Maybe we should go check on him. I'll get my coat."

Miss Daisy followed Mr. Sid and Ms. Christine around the fence and along the lane that led down to Mr. Harseman's. They were approaching the front door when they heard the gunshot.

"Oh God," Mr. Sid muttered. Then he kicked open the front door and they rushed inside.

Mrs. Grendly was there, a small silver pistol clutched in one hand. Mr. Harseman sat on the sofa, blood streaked across the side of his face where a bullet had drawn a thin line of scarlett.

"What's going on here?" Mr. Sid demanded.

"She's trying to kill me," Mr. Harseman protested.

"Mrs. Grendly," Miss Christine accused. "How could you?"

"He was going to tell everything," Mrs. Grendly said. "We had to try and kill him."

"Who's we?"

"She and Mrs. Edson," Mr. Harseman replied. "They tried to serve me poisoned tea. I was suspicious because they'd asked me over. I swapped cups and then Mrs. Edson went out into the garden and keeled over."

"Tea made from dried rosary peas," Ms. Christine said. "That's where Daisy got that awful berry."

"What was this about?" Mr. Sid asked.

"He knew. He was a botanist with twenty degrees. He knew all about Mrs. Edson's iris problem. She was the queen of the garden club. She'd won so many ribbons. It was all she had since her husband died, and he would have taken it all away."

"How?" Ms. Christine asked.

"*Macronoctua onusta*," Mr. Harseman muttered.

"What?" Mr. Sid asked.

"Jagged, wet-looking leaves, a chewed leaf fan. Clear signs of the iris borer."

"What?" Mr. Sid asked.

"Bugs," Ms. Christine said. "This is about bugs?"

"She did everything right," Mrs. Grendly said. "There was no reason for an infestation, but they wouldn't have let her plants near the show for fear of an epidemic."

"She was too complacent," Harseman said. "She failed to observe proper precautions."

"She would have been drummed out of the Iris Society. It was her whole life since her husband died. She was trying to fight them, using a method of squeezing the stalks to try and stop the borer without chemicals. Then he came, and they asked him to join the society."

They must've uprooted some of the untouched plants and moved them to her greenhouse, Miss Daisy thought, right beside the *abrus precatorius*. As for the bugs, that explained why the birds had been so plentiful.

"Why didn't you call the police?" Mr. Sid asked. "A lady's dead over there."

"I was afraid they would blame me for the death. I am a botanist, and not originally from your country," Harseman said. "Now we're all going to die."

Miss Daisy had other plans. She lifted her paw and spread the razor blades of her nails, extending them like fish hooks. As Mrs. Grendly continued to point the gun, Miss Daisy made a swipe at her leg. The pain showed on the old woman's face as her nylons yielded. She wavered, let the gun tilt downward and when she did Mr. Sid and Mr. Harseman rushed her.

"Why did Mrs. Grendly agree to help in the plot?" Mr. Sid wondered later when everyone was home again.

"I think she lived vicariously through Mrs. Edson's triumphs, and garden club politics can be vicious," Ms. Christine observed. "You never know what people will do."

"You think Miss Daisy knew what was going on? She brought all those things in for you to look at."

"I don't think so," Ms. Christine said. "She's concerned with other matters. Look at her up in that window. She just wants the squirrel."

Miss Daisy's tail twitched and the Fitz and Floyd shakers went rolling.

"No, no," Ms. Christine shouted. "Ahn, ahn, ahn!"

Mrs. Milligan's Cat

GARY LOVISI

STEAMING TEACUPS AND GENTLE old ladies full of neighborhood gossip—not a one of whom was under seventy years of age—were the usual at Cynthia Milligan's house. My name is Delilah, dahling, and I am Mrs. Milligan's prized longhaired Persian. A cat, for those of you not acquainted with the species. In fact, not just any cat, but one of the most graceful and glorious of all felines ever. And one of the most modest, dahling.

I sat watching my mistress and her guests with my usual bored feline detachment and disinterest. After all, it was just another day in Milliganland. Nothing unusual. Nothing unusual ever happened here.

Mrs. Milligan, my esteemed mistress, fairly congenial as humans go, was prattling on as usual, dear old soul. This time she elaborated profusely and, I noticed, with much nervousness to her ladyfriends on how young Roderick Thorpe, the neighborhood rogue—a tom if there ever was one—was seen coming out of Mrs. Beverly LeGrange's residence in the very wee hours of the morning. Beverly LeGrange, being the very young and attractive—in a human sort of way, dahling—wife of rich old Stuart LeGrange—-of the LeGrange Orchards, LeGrange Winery, LeGrange Mercedes. . . . Well, you get the idea. . . .

"Now, Maye," my mistress chortled to her best friend, the dowager Maye Blumenthal, "and that's not all I saw! I'm scared to say this, but I have just got to tell someone . . . I saw young Roderick running from the house—carrying his trousers—*not wearing them!*"

There was muffled laughter, accompanied by feigned sounds of shock. It was all so terrible, so tawdry . . . they were each dying to hear more!

"Really! Why, Cynthia Milligan! How do you know that?" Edith Jones cried out, a bit too indignant for her own good.

My mistress just harrumphed and in that very confident voice of hers simply said, "Saw him! That's how!"

"Saw him? Really?" Maye rasped, Maye rasped, curious now, smelling some new sensational gossip brewing in the small town they inhabited.

"Sure as you, Debra, Edith, and I are here right now playing cards and having tea," my mistress added boldly. She always did love the dramatic.

I heard a collective sigh from the assembled biddies.

"Oh, my!" Debra Wilson replied when she was able to respond. "Bad! Bad! Very bad, indeed!"

My mistress and her three human companions all nodded their elderly heads and wagged their crooked old fingers furtively. More gossip. They said they hated it, but I knew differently.

I yawned. Then meowed loudly. Just to let the biddies know *"Hello, ladies, I'm still alive and . . . still hungry!"*

"Oh, Cynthia, that darn cat of yours just cannot be hungry again!" Edith Jones said between sips of her tea. The recalcitrant old crone, why I'd not eaten in hours! I thought of performing a hop-on-the-lap, spill-the-tea routine, dahling, but just then something caught my immediate and undivided attention. That being my dear mistress Cynthia Milligan, as she suddenly and quite conclusively keeled over dead.

Well, dahling, you can imagine the instantaneous chaos and shock. The ladies dropped their teacups, cards, cookies, and haughty expressions and tried to help my mistress as best they could. Her best friend, Maye, dialed 911. They waited. They tried to make her comfortable, but I knew that she was already gone.

I was aghast! I had a true soft spot in my heart for dear old Cynthia Milligan. She fed me well and often, kept a dry roof over my head, and let me have the run of the house and the yard. All things considered, dahling, a feline could ask for little better.

Now I realized the good life I had enjoyed for so long was all going to end.

✻ ✻ ✻

It did not take long.

Alberta, Cynthia's older sister, comes to the old, dark house now each day. She does not feed me. She merely rifles through her sister's things. Always finding a few choice items to appropriate as her own by right of inheritance—an inheritance I find repugnant since Alberta hated her sister with a passion. I can only watch sadly, meowing for food that never comes. Doomed to watch my dearly-departed mistress's choice personal possessions—the sacred mementos of a lifetime—become the property of one who scarce appreciates them or the memories they house within them, one whose avariciousness is only exceeded by her own cold-blooded selfishness.

The last straw for me occurred when Alberta, using the old ruse of finally giving me something to eat, locked me out of the house and would not let me back inside. I now found myself without mistress, shelter, or food, and there was scant prospect of any of these coming my way soon. What would I do now?

LeGrange Mansion was just down the road, a destination as good as any, and by the way I had curiosity regarding that place and the people who lived there. So, keeping an eye out for marauding mutts, I trotted on over to the big house with a two-fold plan brewing in my furry little feline mind. Food and revenge. But food first, dahling. Then revenge against the human who had caused the death of my mistress, thus also precipitating the plunge in my status and comfort level in this world. You see, we felines, contrary to popular belief, are nothing if not practical creatures.

LeGrange Mansion was large, lonely, and dark. My padded feet made no noise as I scampered over the wall and onto the dewy lawn, through a partially opened front window to enter the huge house. There were dogs on the grounds and this caused me immediate concern, big cat-eating brutes, I was sure, but I could see they were securely locked away. I was safe from them for the present so I concentrated on the more immediate matter of finding food.

It was the shouting that drew my attention. Harsh human words. A man and woman arguing in another room of the house. The man saying "I knew it! I come home and find you with *him!* How could you, Beverly?"

Then a hard thump followed by a man's painful yell, then by a woman's sharp, high-pitched scream. I looked in the room and saw the two lovers: Roderick Thorpe and Beverly LeGrange. At their feet lay a very dead Stuart LeGrange, Beverly's rich husband. He was obviously no longer an inconvenience to the two lovers now.

"You didn't have to hit him so hard, Rod!" Beverly protested. She appeared on the verge of panic. "I think he's dead!"

"Well, wasn't that the plan, to lure him here and kill him, then hide the body? It's done now and I'm glad. Now you can be mine!" Thorpe insisted, pulling her toward him roughly. She did not resist, but fell into his arms laughing, offering passionate kisses, even as the warm corpse of her husband bore silent witness to their lust.

I snorted, thinking, *And humans have the gall to say that felines are selfish and cold!*

Thorpe said between mouthfuls of Beverly, "The scare you put into that Milligan woman worked well, telling her if she ever opened her mouth and spoke about what she had seen or heard, she'd keel over and die."

Beverly laughed, "Just a little mind game. I'm very good at them, Rod."

Thorpe smiled, kissing her all the harder.

I flicked my whiskers in disdain.

"So what did you tell her that got the old crone so whacked out that her heart stopped?" Thorpe whispered as they continued their ravishing embrace.

"Oh, Rod," she crooned, like a feline in heat now. "It was so funny. I threatened all kinds of harm to her property, even to her person. Nothing scared her. She was adamant about reporting us to the police. The only way she finally listened to me was when I threatened her *cat.* Imagine that! I told her I'd poison her cat with antifreeze and then skin the little monster and make a purse out of the fur!"

Thorpe just laughed. He thought Beverly was so funny.

I shuddered: *All right! Now you're going to pay! Justice will be done in the human world and my mistress will be avenged!*

However, I knew that could prove difficult. The murderers had taken the man's body out of the house and buried it in a secluded location on the grounds of the huge estate. The killers had done a masterful job of concealing the grave. I watched from my perch in a nearby tree, knowing it would not be easy for me—a mere feline in a human world—to bring the police to where they would find the secret grave and solve this dastardly crime.

Next day I found the shallow grave and began digging. It was hard work, unseemly for a delicate house cat such as myself, but necessary if I was ever to unearth this mess. My claws had just about reached the body when Beverly LeGrange saw me and ran to chase me away.

"It's that damn cat!" she said to Thorpe. "If I didn't know better, I'd say it was trying to dig up Stuart's grave!"

Thorpe did not like that at all. "I'll take care of her, honey," and he drew a gun from his jacket and took a few poor shots at me in rage.

Beverly quickly put her hand on the gun saying, "No, Rod, that will draw attention. I have a better idea."

I watched and waited, wondering what new horrors they had in mind.

Rod said, "You want to unleash the dogs?"

I dug my claws deeper into the wood of the tree I was perched upon.

"Oh, Rod, lover, that's a good idea, but I have an even better one," Beverly cooed. "Just wait here."

Beverly LeGrange returned soon with a bowl of shimmering fluid, gently calling out, "Here kitty, nice kitty. Come here and have a drink of this nice bowl of delicious antifreeze. It tastes so good and will kill you *sooooo* dead."

Thorpe laughed and gave her a kiss.

What kind of monsters were these humans?

I put the thought of the tempting dish out of my mind. I knew it was poison, my mistress had raised me to be wary of such tricks when she let me out of the house to run at night.

I ignored the antifreeze and concentrated on the problem at hand. Namely, how was I going to get the police to discover the hidden grave of Stuart LeGrange?

My chance came the next day when two plainclothes detectives called at LeGrange Mansion. Shots had been reported.

Of course, there was no way I could get close to the detectives; Beverly and Rod would see to that. And even if I did, there was no way I could make them understand what I was trying to tell them. After all, humans are not adept enough to communicate with felines yet.

"Funny thing about that cat following us," one detective said. He was a large bull-necked fellow in a too-tight suit. He watched me carefully as I played catch-me-if-you-can with young Roderick Thorpe who seemed to protest too much at my presence. "It's almost as if that cat knows something, or is trying to tell me something."

"That cat's a damn pain in the ass, detective," Beverly said smoothly, steering him away from my direction. But this cop was a smart one and would not be steered. Beverly, angry now, added, "I should have had it taken care of a long time ago."

I saw the detective's eyebrows rise precipitously in interest.

The other detective looked at Beverly and said carefully, "Then it's not your cat, Ms. LeGrange?"

Beverly stumbled for a mere second, regained her composure and replied, "Heavens no, detective. I would never own a cat. That's just some stray that wandered onto the grounds the night that Stuart was due home. Been wandering around ever since, just a general nuisance. I have half a mind to sic the dogs on it."

Roderick Thorpe suddenly grew concerned, saw the two detectives beginning to walk onto the grounds, and asked, "Ah, detective? Where are you going?"

"This is such a nice estate here, I thought Wendell and I would look around a bit. You don't mind, do you?" he said, carefully.

Thorpe couldn't reply but he grew nervous as he saw the two cops were now investigating the grounds around the house. That would not do. Not at all. Why, it looked as if they were actually following that damn cat!

"Did I ever tell you my ex-wife had a cat, Wendell?" the cop named Joe Walker said to his partner as they walked further into the grounds, followed by a very nervous pair of murderers.

"All the time, Joe. . . ."

"Excuse me, detectives? Just where do you think you are going?" Beverly LeGrange said with a perceptible twinge of panic in her soft voice.

"Yes, detectives, what gives?" Thorpe added now, rather a bit too insistently.

The larger of the two detectives, a big, brawny fellow by the name of Wendell Paige said, "Just looking, Ms. LeGrange. That's not a problem for either of you, is it? Because if it is . . . Me an' my partner, just looking, is all."

"But, ah, it's cold out here. Why not come back in the house, Detective Paige? Detective Walker?" Beverly offered, trying to cut them off, but they walked on, outflanking her, following the cat walking ahead of them.

"We're just looking. Taking a walk. Lovely day for a walk, isn't it, Ms. LeGrange?" Walker replied.

Now Thorpe was nervous.

He heard Beverly growl under her breath as she walked away, "That damn cat! I'll fix her!"

The dogs were set loose a minute later by Beverly. Big, howling brutes with large teeth, big mouths, and voracious appetites for all things, especially felines. Let me tell you something, dahling, I was not at all amused by this turn of events, but it did give me an idea.

I knew the dogs would be after me soon, they'd scented my spoor and would immediately give chase. I was determined to use that instinct in them, use it to lead the dogs to Stuart LeGrange's hidden grave, even at considerable danger to my own physical well-being. I flew across the well-manicured lawn, down past a thicket of trees and into a secluded meadow behind the house. The dogs were right behind me. There were six of them and they operated as a pack. They had my scent committed to memory and locked onto the sights of their marauding jaws.

When I reached the gravesite I began digging and clawing furiously into the earth. I had a little time. I had to free Stuart LeGrange's spoor from where it was embedded in the ground of the grave, get it exposed to the air where the dogs could smell it. I knew it would be close, that my margin of error was slim, if nonexistent. So I dug and clawed deeper and deeper into the soft soil of the murdered man's grave.

Then the dogs were upon me. They practically flew into the clearing, raging brutes, all fiery eyes and slavering jaws just waiting to take some canine-size bites out of my furry little hide. I hissed and jumped back, trying my best to defend my turf as I did all I could to mix up the spoor of Stuart LeGrange that so permeated the soil with my own. It worked!

First one, then another of the huge dogs began to growl and cry, whine and claw the ground, pushing their great ugly snouts into the dirt and then lifting their great ugly heads and crying loudly to the heavens. By the time Beverly and Roderick arrived, I could see that the two detectives, who each held his service revolver in his hand, accompanied them meaningfully.

The dogs were positively frantic now. They had found the spoor of their dead master, Stuart LeGrange, and were busy ripping into the loose soil of his unmarked grave.

Detective Walker took in the scene immediately and said to his partner, "Wendell, I think we may have solved that Stuart LeGrange missing-person case."

"Yeah, Joe, but I think we just got ourselves another case, a murder case," Paige replied.

Then he took out his cuffs, ordering Beverly and Roderick, "Now you two wanna come over here? Slowly."

The dogs continued to dig. It wasn't long before they brought up what appeared to be a spotted sheet, torn and full of dry blood, and not soon afterward, a man's arm was visible in the dark dirt. The dogs whined madly; they had discovered their master.

Wendell Paige said, "Well, Joe, if that don't beat all. That cat's got real moxie. I think I'll take it home to Martha, she'd like a smart cat like that."

From my vantage point on the hood of the detective's car, I finished my meal of Tasty Tuna, then looked at Beverly and Roderick where they sat glaring at me, cuffed in the back seat of the police car. I gently lifted my tail in the air, giving them a full view of my exposed nether parts, insulting in the extreme. I thought of my dear mistress and rubbed my whiskers in satisfaction.

That will teach you to make trouble for Mrs. Milligan's cat, dahlings!

Feline revenge is sweet!

Rest gently, dear Cynthia.

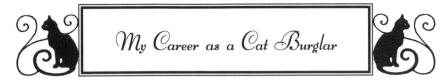

My Career as a Cat Burglar

RON GOULART

I SHOULDN'T HAVE TRIED TO KICK the cat, because I think that turned him even further against me and really prompted him to start contemplating revenge. But the desire to see that smug, fat orange creature go sailing across the cozy parlor of my former wife's cottage got the better of me.

When Margery started laughing at me and telling me that my plagiarism charges were so much hooey, Bosco hopped off his candy-striped loveseat near the deep fireplace and waddled over close to where I was standing, wide-legged and, I hoped, formidable on a throw rug. Smirking up at me, the cat started producing an ominous growling noise deep inside his fuzzy orange being.

"You arrogant jerk," I told Bosco, attempting to boot him into the feebly burning kindling.

But the cat, despite his bulk, was nimble. He deftly dodged me, and my foot continued on up like a jumping jack's. That caused me to lose my balance and sit down, exceptionally hard, on my tailbone.

Margery laughed again, louder. "You're as graceful as ever, Alex," she observed from the bentwood rocker that held her bulk. She'd gained at least fifty pounds since our divorce had become final two years ago. Closer to sixty pounds.

I sat up, glaring at Bosco. "If it wasn't for me, schmuck," I told him gruffly, "you'd still be a nonentity."

The cat smirked again, strutted near the fireplace and, delicately, began nibbling at the cat food in the large bowl that had *Bosco the Cat Detective* painted on its side. After a few mouthfuls, he arranged himself comfortably on the hooked rug closest to the fire and commenced purring with exaggerated contentment.

"You've got it wrong again, dear heart," mentioned my erstwhile wife as she watched me rise, not too gracefully I admit, to my feet. She kept her pudgy hands folded in her lap, and I noticed that she was wearing what looked to be a very expensive diamond bracelet around her fat right wrist. More evidence of her success.

I hadn't seen her in person in nearly two years. In that time she'd ceased to be Margery McGibney Hilligan and had reverted to her earlier identity of just plain Margery McGibney. She'd also sold a mystery novel titled *Bosco's Greatest Case* to Mystery House Press.

The damned thing was on every best-seller list in the country for twenty-seven weeks in hard cover, got optioned by the movies for a rumored $1,700,000, inspired a line of Bosco the Cat Detective toys, as well as T-shirts, hit the best-seller lists again in paperback.

The second mystery in the series, *Bosco's Murder Cruise*, was due out in two weeks and, again according to industry rumors, had earned my onetime spouse an advance of $3,300,000.

You saw her face on the covers of *People, Newsweek, Mammon,* and *Cat Fancier* and a multitude of other mindless magazines. The fact that she'd put on about fifty pounds since hit by success didn't discourage the editorial half-wits who dominate the magazine field from displaying her pudgy portraits on their periodicals.

The thing that bothered me the most about all this was the fact that I'd written those two books. I wasn't a published author and had been, until getting unexpectedly downsized out of a job six weeks earlier, working as a trade journal editor.

Margery had been, until stealing the Bosco mystery novels, a moderately successful writer with seven cozy midlist detective novels to her credit. While we'd been married, working in my spare time at night, I'd written the two books. When I had them both finished, I decided to ask her opinion.

She gave me that opinion on a gray autumn afternoon, sitting on the sofa she kept in the large office she'd had built for herself in our house in Southport. Both of my manuscripts rested on her lap, which was much less wide in those days. "I know you love that old rundown IBM Selectric of yours, dear heart," she began, tapping the books. "But you really have to learn to type on a computer."

"I know how to do that," I'd countered. "I do that every day at work. But when I'm doing something creative, I'd rather use my old—"

"Creative?" Laughing, Margery shook her head. "Really, darling, you'd better stick to *Hardware Spotlight*." She gave me a sympathetic look. "This stuff is . . . how can I be truthful without hurting your poor pathetic little ego? It's tripe, garbage, absolute drivel."

"But mysteries with cats in them are selling like crazy."

Bosco was sprawled out on one of my wife's many metal filing cabinets. When I used the word *cat*, he sat up, licked his forepaw, and then snarled in my direction. Basically he was her cat. She'd rescued him from an animal shelter a year earlier, a serious mistake I'd always thought.

Margery smiled one of those patronizing smiles of hers at me. "True, dear, but those books are written by *professional* writers," she explained. "By professionals, I might add, who *like* cats. I can't, for the life of me, understand why you attempted to use Bosco in these efforts of yours. You two have never gotten along."

"Because he's a cat. And he reminds me of a sort of feline Nero Wolfe," I told her. "A perfect companion for my spinster detective."

Margery stood up, placing the manuscripts on the sofa. "And I don't see why you went ahead and wrote not one but *two* complete manuscripts."

"I got inspired. And also I figured a series would be easier to sell if I had two complete books to show around."

"You trust my judgment, don't you, Alex?"

"Well, sure, that's why I didn't want to do anything until you had a—"

"I could show these to Orlando," she said doubtfully. "But that would only embarrass me and upset him."

Orlando Villanova was her self-styled hotshot literary agent in Manhattan.

"Never mind." Sighing, I shook my head and started toward the sofa to gather up the manuscripts.

"I'll file these away, dear. You lose everything." Margery picked them both up, crossed to one of her many filing cabinets, and bent to toss them in a bottom drawer. "They'll no doubt give us a laugh or two when we look at them again in years to come." Margery had an obsession about filing stuff. She even kept a fat manila folder full of the rejection slips she'd collected back in college when she was trying to sell magazine short stories.

Up on top of a nearby cabinet Bosco lolled over on his back and purred fondly in her direction.

Well, about three months after that Margery filed for divorce. Something about incompatibility, although I had a suspicion she'd been having a fling with Orlando Villanova. I didn't contest the divorce, though, just let her go ahead. By that time her drill sergeant approach toward me had me feeling like some poor rookie who'd been dragooned into service in a second-rate Central American army.

Then, just a few weeks before my visit to her cottage, I'd finally gotten around to reading the first Bosco novel. I figured, when I'd first heard about the book, that Margery had only swiped my idea of using her cat as the sidekick of an amateur sleuth. My title for the book had been *Miss Farquhar on the Case* and it never occurred to me that Margery's book was mine under a new name. Because of my feelings for my erstwhile wife I'd never even picked up the book and skimmed through it at a bookstore. But when I came across *Bosco's Greatest Case* at a library book sale, I decided to spend two dollars on it.

When I finally read the damn book I saw right off that it was basically my book. She'd done a very modest rewrite, deadening some of my best dialogue, messing up some of the descriptions, and inserting some inept similes and metaphors. And she'd changed the name of my spinster detective—the one who was accompanied on her investigations by the surly orange cat based on our own Bosco—from Emily Farquhar to Esme Fotheringill.

Initially I wasn't sure I wanted to do anything about it. Let Margery enjoy her unearned fame and fortune. I was doing pretty well as an editor, plus I had little desire to get tangled up in some protracted legal hassle with her.

Then I got downsized out of my job. That started me thinking that I ought to get Margery to share her enormous profits with me. For refraining from bringing a plagiarism suit against her, I'd settle for a percentage. It wouldn't even have to be fifty percent. Forty percent would be fine. Sure, forty percent of four or five million would sure as hell take care of all my financial worries for the rest of my life.

We'd sold our Southport house after the divorce, with Margery managing to get most of the take from that. I was living in a small place in Westport and Margery had settled into a so-called cottage in nearby Brimstone, Connecticut. Orlando Villanova had refused to give me her address when I phoned him, but I used the Net to track her down.

The cottage was down in a little sort of gully off a winding lane. It was a huge two-story thing, all brown shingles and quaintly shuttered windows. When I'd parked my aging car up on the road that afternoon, I got the feeling somebody was watching me from the sprawling Victorian just across the road.

A curtain at the front window fluttered, but I never actually saw anyone over there.

"You're looking awful, dear heart," Margery had said after letting me in and leading me into her excessively quaint parlor.

I refrained from countering that she was looking immense. At that point I was still trying to be diplomatic.

As I started to sit on the loveseat, she warned, "No, don't sit there, Alex. That's Bosco's chair."

"He's still around, huh?"

"The darling is only seven years old," she reminded me. "And in excellent health."

A growling started behind a wide potted plant and then the cat emerged. He, too, was fatter and seemed to be more vividly orange. He eyed me disdainfully for a moment before he hopped up on the loveseat, sprawled out, and went immediately into a snoring sleep.

"It's about Bosco that I'm here, Marge," I began, deciding to avoid the other quaint chairs in the parlor and remain on my feet.

"You always hated him."

"True," I admitted. "That's why I used him in my two mystery novels. Instead of a lovable cat detective, I wanted one with a nasty edge."

"*You* used him?" Her look of surprise and puzzlement was fairly convincing.

"C'mon, hon," I said, moving nearer to her. "You know damn well that I wrote those books. And, listen, I'm not asking for *all* the dough you've been dishonestly earning. Nope, I'll settle for—"

"Whatever are you ranting about, dear heart?" She settled into a fat armchair and frowned up at me as she gave me a searching look. "I'd heard they'd tossed you out on your fanny from *Hardware Spotlight*, but I didn't realize that getting canned had affected your mind."

"I wrote two mystery novels about a spinster detective and an arrogant cat named Bosco," I reminded her. "You read them and told me they were lousy. Are you claiming you don't remember that?"

My onetime spouse shook her head. "But I don't, Alex." Pity for my sad mental state sounded in her voice. "I can understand how a man of your years, frightened that he'll never find another job, could fantasize that he had some part in *my* success. It's awfully sad to see you in this condition, Alex, but we're legally parted and I really can't humor you in this sad delusion of yours."

"Sad, my ass," I told her. "I wrote the books that you're making millions off of."

Her pitying smile segued into a sneer. "Prove it, jerk," she challenged.

I took another step in her direction. "If I get you into court and under oath, Margery," I said, "you'll have to tell the truth."

"I just told you the truth," she said, standing up slowly and looking directly at me. "Now if you'd kept copies of your alleged manuscripts or had any sort of written proof at all, things might be different."

That was when she laughed at me and Bosco confronted me and I tried to kick him.

I left shortly after that.

But as I climbed back to my car, I figured out what I'd have to do.

Two nights later I was back at Margery's cottage. This time it was after dark and I was certain she wouldn't be at home.

The moment I'd seen the notice in the *Westport News* that Margery McGibney, bestselling author of the Bosco mystery novels, was going to be giving a talk at the Brimstone Public Library at 8 P.M. on Thursday, I knew it was time to put my plan into action. To make sure her house was going to be empty, I'd called the library before leaving my place to inquire if my favorite mystery writer hadn't canceled and was definitely going to appear. They assured me that

Margery McGibney was indeed expected and that, as a devoted fan, I'd be delighted to know that I'd be able to get her autograph.

As I'd noted on my previous visit, Margery didn't have a burglar-alarm system. The lock on her front door was fairly easy to pick.

Bosco was home, though, and he hissed at me when I went sneaking into the two-story cottage at a few minutes after eight.

"Shoo," I advised him as he emerged from the shadowy parlor, a dark lump snarling at me, "or this time I'll punt you through a window."

The cat, after making a disgruntled noise, withdrew.

Nodding, I started exploring the ground floor of the house. Finding no trace of Margery's office on that level, I climbed the dark staircase that led upstairs.

She had converted a huge, whitewalled second-floor room with a slanting skylight into her office. There was quite a bit of moonlight coming in, so I didn't have to use the pocket flashlight I'd brought.

Knowing that Margery had a compulsion to file everything, I was near certain that she'd still have my original copies of the Bosco novels stored away around here someplace.

I recognized some of the old filing cabinets, but noticed that she'd added several more new ones. Standing on the white carpet in the moonlit office, I studied the array of a dozen or so of them.

"That's the one," I decided after a moment.

It looked like the one in which Margery had stowed the manuscripts. She'd obviously taken them out again to steal them, but I was betting her fastidious nature would prompt her to file them back in their original place afterward. With those in my possession—they included title pages with my name on them and had been written on my typewriter—I'd be in a much better position to negotiate with Margery and her literary agent.

The manuscripts weren't in the first cabinet I picked. Although I did come across that folder of rejection slips.

After checking my watch—it was already 8:20—I selected a second cabinet to search.

I didn't hit the manuscripts, but came across something even better. In a lemon-yellow folder labeled *Bosco/Initial Correspondence* I located copies of two letters that would prove my case.

The first was Margery's to her agent—whom she was addressing as Orly Love at that point. She said to him, among other things, "I'm glad you agree that Dumbo's books are saleable. I always thought so but didn't want him to find out that he was a better mystery writer than I am. Now that he's out of the picture, I see no reason why these can't become Margery McGibney books. I'll make some changes, as you suggested. But since I have the only copies, there's nothing much he can do if these do sell and prove to be hits. He's too stupid *and* too cowardly ever to try suing us."

"Bingo," I exclaimed, in a careful whisper, after I'd read through her letter.

Villanova's reply established that he was a party to the plagiarism and went along with Margery's idea to steal the books and pass them off as her own.

Extracting the two letters from the yellow folder, I folded them carefully and tucked them into the right-hand outer pocket of my sport coat.

This would be enough.

And now I was going to ask for ninety percent of the take.

After returning the folder to exactly the place where it'd been, and sliding the metallic door shut, I made my exit from Margery's office.

I was stepping on the second step from the top of the dark stairway when my foot connected with something that hadn't been there before.

I tripped, cried out in surprise, and went rolling and tumbling down the hardwood steps.

The thing that had tripped me went rolling and bumping down ahead of me. I was nearly certain it was that big cat food dish of Bosco's.

I hit the last step hard, whacking my head a good one. I somersaulted over onto the floor and cracked my head again hard.

Then I passed out.

There was noise, voices talking, and light when I woke up. I'd been lifted off the floor and propped against the paneled wall.

A uniformed cop was crouched in front of me. "Suppose you explain what you're up to, buddy?"

"How'd you . . ." My voice didn't sound much like mine. Swallowing, I tried again. "How'd you get here?"

"Neighbors called in to report a possible burglary," he answered. "Turns out they were right."

"Hey, I'm not a burglar," I assured him.

"Oh, so?"

"I'm the one who was robbed," I explained, starting to reach into my outer pocket.

"Easy now," warned the policeman.

I kept my hand hovering in the vicinity of the pocket. "I've got something in there that'll explain everything, officer."

"I'll fetch it out for you." He thrust his big freckled hand into the coat pocket, felt around. "Yeah, this does explain a hell of a lot."

What he fished out wasn't the two letters but that diamond bracelet I'd seen Margery wearing on my last visit.

"If you'd please stand up now, sir," he ordered.

I've thought about this quite a lot since. I can see how Bosco could've dragged his dish up to where it would trip me. But I still don't understand how he got those letters out of my pocket and substituted the bracelet.

Nothing Newsworthy

JEAN RABE

NADA! GRAN'MA NADA!"

She ignored the willowy man who'd just burst in the front door, bringing with him an uninvited flurry of snow and a gust of frigid winter wind. He stomped his feet on the rug, dropped his briefcase on the floor, and furiously brushed at his coat. "Gran'ma Nada!"

"And you're certain nothing else was taken, ma'am?"

The old woman shook her head, freeing several strands of steel-gray hair from her stumpy braid. "No, Sergeant. Nothing else. I'm certain."

"Gran'ma Nada!"

She sighed and shivered, wrapping her shawl tighter about her shoulders. "In here, Rupert! We're in the library!"

"Always in the library," came Rupert's muffled reply. "Musty old place."

"No jewelry?" The policeman continued.

She shook her head again.

"Money?"

Another shake. "I have a large coin collection, Sergeant. Quite valuable and on display in my study. They left that alone."

"Nothing else?"

"Nothing else."

"Gran'ma Nada!" Rupert tromped into the library, tugged off his gloves, and thrust them in his pocket. He smiled tightly when he spotted her. "Are you all right, Gran?"

"Yes, Rupert. I told your secretary I was fine. Sergeant, this is my great-grandson. . . ."

"Gran, I saw the police cars out front, and I . . ."

". . . was worried something had happened to me?" *Or to your inheritance?* she whispered half under her breath.

"Gran'ma Nada, I. . . ."

"Hush, Rupert. I'm not finished with Sergeant Decker." She returned her attention to the policeman, who was busily scratching notes on a small pad.

Rupert huffed and glanced about, his features drawn together so as to make his rosy face look even more pinched than usual. There were three policemen in the library—the one at Nada's side, who was obviously in charge, and two others dusting shelves for fingerprints. Each gave Rupert a perfunctory nod.

"What was taken, Gran? God . . . the paintings?"

She continued to chatter to the sergeant in her tinny, old-woman voice. One of the other officers glanced at Rupert and said, "Newspapers," then went back to work.

"Newspapers," Rupert repeated. He let out a deep breath as if in relief. "From the library."

The library was the largest room in the ancient house, until thirty years ago serving as both a living room and a dining parlor. Then Nada had the intervening wall knocked out and shelves upon shelves upon shelves installed, forcing even guests to eat in the kitchen. A fireplace took up part of the far wall, nestled between overloaded shelves and merrily burning birch logs on this cold February day. Two striped cats, as orange as the flames, were curled up in front of the hearth. A plump Siamese, conveniently named Cat, was sleeping on Nada's rocking chair a few feet away, its tail dangling down like an inverted question mark. A fourth cat, coal black save for the white front paw which gave him the name Boot, was slinking back and forth between the policeman, all the while keeping a protective eye on Nada. The fifth, an Angora as fluffy and white as the snow outside, was perched on a high shelf where she could regally survey the entire room.

"Cats and shelves," Rupert softly growled. "Shelves upon shelves upon shelves."

Covered by stacks upon stacks of newspapers.

Oh, there were some books in the mix, Rupert noted, a half-dozen early Ed McBains and the latest Tony Hillerman. There were two first printings of Edgar Rice Burroughs's *Tarzan and the City of Gold*, one of them supposedly personally autographed to Nada—Rupert had never bothered looking to confirm his great-grandmother's boast. There was a well-worn Southwestern chili cookbook, a thick pictorial tribute to the Texas cowboy, and a rumpled copy of a Lillian Jackson Braun paperback. The books were difficult to spot amid all the newspapers.

"Just newspapers?" Rupert asked. "Nothing else was taken?"

The sergeant raised an eyebrow to the old woman.

"Nothing," Nada repeated to them both. She looked so small standing between the men. Stoop-shouldered from age and from leaning on a three-pronged cane, she barely came up to their chests. Her sadness made her seem smaller still. "Nothing but some of my greatest treasures. Months of my life. Stolen."

"Sergeant Decker!" A fourth policeman came into the library. Boot slipped toward him and rubbed against his pants leg. "Checked all the windows 'n' doors, sir. No obvious signs of forced entry, but the locks are old. Some barely catch." He lowered his voice. "A halfway decent thief coulda picked his way in without leavin' a clue. You need better locks, ma'am. Deadbolts all the way aroun'. A security system'd be a good idea, too. Looks like you've got plenty of valuable things you should be protectin'."

"Original paintings," Rupert volunteered. "A pen-and-ink Picasso—which thank the Lord they didn't spot. A Diego Rivera. A Max Beckmann. Coins. Jewelry and pocket watches and. . . ."

Your precious inheritance, Nada mouthed.

". . . Some unique military memorabilia from her first husband. Depression glass. Cut-crystal vases. No, wait, the vases were taken in a burglary last year."

Sergeant Decker raised an eyebrow again.

"I didn't report that one," Nada explained.

"Her gardener," Rupert cut in.

"He was poor. Had medical bills from his wife. Trimmed the hedges really nice before he left."

"Stole her entire collection of vases and vanished. Year before that, or maybe it was two, a burglar broke in and took two sets of silver and all of her Rosewood bowls."

"That one I reported," she said smugly.

"Gran, at least only newspapers were taken this time. But next time. . . ."

"My newspapers," she said wistfully. "Months of my life. Gone."

Sergeant Decker glanced down. Boot was rubbing against his ankles. "Were they valuable? The newspapers?"

Decker scratched some more notes when Nada answered, "Yes, very valuable."

The old woman shuffled away from the pair and toward the east shelves, pausing in front of the fire a moment to warm herself and acknowledge the orange cats. Newspapers, all folded neatly, stretched from the floor to the ceiling. Only one shelf was bare, and that was by the door. Nada explained that was for the newspapers yet to come.

"Months of newspapers. Taken yesterday, maybe three months ago."

"So you're uncertain of the time?" Decker took more notes.

"Sometime in the fall or early winter, Sergeant. I didn't notice them missing until early this morning when I wanted to read again about Woodrow Wilson's term winding down. Wilson had a cat, you know. So did McKinley. Abraham Lincoln had the first cat in the White House. But I'm not so old as to have papers about those men." She leaned heavily on the cane, drawing her free hand up to the shelf at shoulder-level. Her age-spotted fingers tugged free a newspaper. "It was December of 1920. The *Detroit Free Press* was what I was looking for. Good paper. Good article on Wilson. When I couldn't find it, I poked around and noticed half of December of that year was missing. Five weeks out of 1932 are gone, too. And four or five each out of 1941 and 1944. Months all together."

"If only you didn't have so many newspapers," Rupert hushed.

Sergeant Decker scribbled furiously, recording the string of missing weeks and the names of the newspapers.

Nada shuffled along the shelves and tugged free another paper, then another and another. She continued her work until she had more than a dozen tucked under her arm and was struggling with the burden. Then she went to the north row of shelves, her eyes scanning the newspapers there and the dates scrawled in marker on the wood beneath the stacks. "This one." She pulled free one more. "Sergeant, the town librarian comes out here once in a while to look at my collection. She borrows a few papers from time to time to put on micro-film. Ones of special interest to the town."

"Gran, perhaps the librarian didn't return some of your newspapers," Rupert suggested. "You've called these policemen out here for...."

She shook her head. Nada shuffled to the rocking chair and tapped her foot. Cat slowly raised his head, then reluctantly uncurled himself and plopped to the floor. She took his place, commenting on the propitiousness of having Cat around—he kept your seat toasty warm. The Siamese curled at her feet, narrowing its blue eyes to take in Nada's great-grandson.

Rupert returned the gesture. "If you had a dog, Gran, a big one, he would've barked at the thief, maybe chased him away."

"I like cats." She reached a hand down and scratched Cat's ears. Boot sauntered over for his share of attention.

"You were saying the newspapers were valuable," Decker prompted.

Nada adjusted the papers on her lap and pointed to the one on top. "I really like the *Detroit Free Press.*"

April 20, 1912. The headline read: BLAME OF TITANIC TRAGEDY IS FALLING ON J. B. ISMAY. A secondary head proclaimed: TITANIC'S LIVING ARE ALL TEN-DERLY CARED FOR IN NEW YORK CITY. "This one's worth about three hundred dollars," she said. "Would be worth more if I stored them properly, hanging them from bamboo poles and keeping them in plastic in a moisture-proof room. Too hard to read them that way, though. The fire plays havoc with the papers, too, drying them out, yellowing them. It's this Wisconsin weather, really, that's to blame."

She dropped the paper on the floor and pointed to the next. The *Cleveland*

News, August 6, 1945. The headline read: U.S. ATOMIC BOMB RIPS JAPAN, GREAT-
EST WEAPON IN HISTORY. "Sixty to seventy dollars," she pronounced.

The next was another edition of the *Detroit Free Press*, May 24, 1941: WAR-
SHIP BISMARCK IS FIGHTING FOR LIFE AGAINST OVERWHELMING ODDS, NAZIS
ADMIT. "Probably seventy, more to a World War II buff. All of these are valuable," she added, stabbing a now ink-stained finger at her stack. "None worth
less than ten or twenty dollars."

The *New York Times*, October 2, 1921: YANKS WIN 1921 PENNANT. Pictures
of Babe Ruth and Frank Frisch stared up from the brittle page.

The *Los Angeles Times*, May 18, 1935: LAWRENCE OF ARABIA NEAR DEATH.
Another, from April 24, 1936: HOUDINI WIDOW PLANS SÉANCE.

There were other headlines: CHURCHILL RESIGNS; VICTORY PARADE FOR
IKE; PATTON TO BE BURIED IN LUXEMBOURG.

"This is one of my favorites, though not so old." It was an edition of the
Chicago Sun-Times, Thursday, July 17, 1980. Ronald and Nancy Reagan smiled
from the left-hand side of the front page. The banner read: IT'S REAGAN AND
FORD, FORMER PRESIDENT AGREES TO VP DEAL. "Bad journalism," she observed. "Picked it up when I was visiting a friend in the suburbs. The paper
jumped the gun and printed that former president Ford would run with Reagan.
Ford was thinking about it, that was common knowledge. But he declined. The
papers were pulled from the newsstands, but not before some of them were
snapped up. Like Dewey wins." She wrinkled her nose and made a *tsk-tsk*ing
sound. "Reagan."

"Didn't care for him?" Decker asked.

"A good enough president," she said evenly. "But he had a dog. So did
Ford. I like cats better." The orange cats at the hearth meowed in unison.

"So it had to be someone who knew the newspapers were valuable," Decker
mused. "Someone who knew you kept so many, and someone who knew to
come here late at night when you and your housekeeper were sleeping."

Nada pursed her lips. "A lot of folks in town know I have these newspapers. The local paper did an article about me and my collection early last year."

"What about your housekeeper?" Rupert cut in.

"Celia? Goodness, no! She's a godsend. Wouldn't think of taking anything
from me. Besides, she's not one to read the paper. Gets her news from the
radio."

"Not one to steal . . . that's what you said about the gardener before your
vases disappeared."

Nada ran her finger along the Reagan and Ford story. "By Jerome R.
Watson and Patrick Oster, *Sun-Times* correspondents," she whispered. "Dateline
Detroit. The *Detroit Free Press* wouldn't've run this story."

"Want me to put those back for you?" Rupert volunteered.

Nada shook her head. "I think I'll read these today. And I'll put them back later. You'd only get them out of order."

"Ma'am?" One of the other officers stepped close, the one who told her she needed better locks. "I was just wonderin' why you keep all these newspapers."

She chuckled softly. "These newspapers are my life. I have . . ." She frowned. "Until this theft I had at least one issue for every day I've lived. They mark the years for me. I so love the news."

"Three hundred and sixty-five times. . . ." one of the policemen whispered.

"Times ninety-five," Rupert softly added. "Nearly thirty-five thousand papers. Most of them in here."

"That's a lot of newspapers," Decker said. "Why the fascination?"

"She used to write for a paper in San Antonio," Rupert explained, "before she married her second husband and moved to Wisconsin."

"So long ago," she said. "I had just turned twenty when I got the job. That was sixty-five years ago."

"Seventy-five," Rupert corrected.

"I covered the social engagements, the only woman reporter on the staff. Church teas, marriage announcements, frilly things. The editor called me Nothing Newsworthy."

"What?" This from another policeman. All four were gathered around, listening intently. Rupert had backed away to stand at a narrow window between the shelves. The snow was falling harder, and he scowled to see it collecting on his car.

"Nada," she told the policemen. "My name in Spanish means 'nothing.' And since I covered all the frilly bits, the things the other reporters laughed about and didn't consider news, the editor called me Nothing Newsworthy." She laughed again. "Oh, but sometimes I got the good stories. A church caught fire when I was there covering a social. Then there was the murder of a young woman. I had an appointment with her to learn the details of her wedding." She sucked in her lower lip. "I discovered the body. Turned out it was her husband-to-be. My first front-page story. Let's see, there was a deacon who had embezzled from the parsonage. That was news, too. I was Something Newsworthy then—at least every once in a while. And it was warmer in San Antonio." She held her palms out toward the fire. "I suppose this theft will make tomorrow's *Journal-Sentinel*? If they consider it newsworthy."

"The reporters have access to our reports." Sergeant Decker motioned to his men. "And I am sure they'll consider this very newsworthy, Nada. We'll be checking with antique shops and pawn stores in the area, see if anyone is trying to sell your papers. That's our best option right now. Unless the fingerprints turn up something. In any event, I'll call back tomorrow." He stopped in the doorway. "And see about better locks, ma'am. Please. Maybe a security system."

She nodded and smiled, intending to take care of it a little later today.

Boot followed the men to the front door, then returned to join the orange pair on the hearth.

"Gran. . . ."

She pushed herself to her feet, leaning hard on the cane as she joined Rupert at the window.

"I'm not worried about my inheritance, Gran. I'm worried about you. All alone here."

"I'm fine. I just want the sergeant to find my missing papers. I particularly want the one with the special on Wilson."

"They'll do their best."

"And I'll get better locks. I promise."

"I'd feel better if you didn't stay here."

She made a *tsk-tsk*ing noise. "I want nothing to do with that nursing home, Rupert. You can keep your fancy brochures. Nursing homes are places to die. I'm old, and I'll die soon enough. But I'll die here."

"You'd be plenty warm at Fox Manor, Gran. Three meals a day. There would be lots of people and. . . ."

". . . And no place to keep all of my newspapers." She placed her free hand on his back. "And they wouldn't let me keep my precious cats, either."

"Your cats." He made a huffing sound and reached for his gloves.

"They mean even more to me than the papers."

"I'll stop in to see you at lunch tomorrow."

"Thank you, Rupert."

"And I'll tell Celia to bring in more firewood."

"Thank you, Rupert."

She stayed at the window, watching her great-grandson make his way to his car, clearing the window in front of the driver's seat. She watched him swerve down her twisting driveway and out of sight. Then she returned to her chair and picked up the copy of the *Chicago Sun-Times* again, almost reverently turning it over to stare at the back page: RANGERS HAVE FEAST ON SOX PITCHING.

She drew her shawl tight about her as the fire started to die, read the article twice, and drifted off to sleep, Cat curled between her feet.

Boot was at the window. Celia hadn't yet gone out for firewood. The cat knew the housekeeper's continually slowing routine. She wouldn't be going out until almost dinnertime. An hour away. He meowed softly and looked to the Angora, a silent signal passing between them. Boot meowed again and got the attention of the orange cats, who rose and stretched and padded to the north wall, the 1950s *Cleveland Press* section. Together, the four tugged free paper after paper, careful not to take them all from the same stack, where their absence would be easily noted. Then they pulled them to the hearth, under Cat's approving gaze, and nudged them into the fire. Another few weeks' worth followed, along with the Lillian Braun book—just enough to keep Nada warm until Celia brought in more wood.

One Tiny Slip

JUDITH L. POST

MARJORIE SIMMS POINTED AT the black cat rubbing against the sheriff's legs. "I told Silas not to get a black cat. I told him they were bad luck."

Blacky turned toward her and hissed.

"Your point?" Val Levine asked. He was tall and thin with sandy-colored hair and a graying beard. He'd converted from being a Methodist when he'd met and married a Jewish woman. It had caused a minor explosion in his small town of Grabill.

"Bad enough that you had to marry an outsider," Val's father had complained. "But hell, everyone around here's either Protestant or Amish. We've never had a Jewish family among us before."

Their worries didn't sway Val. From a small boy on, he'd never wavered from doing what he thought was right, whether anyone else agreed with him or not. Now he squatted to pet the sleek cat.

Marjorie glanced at her brother's body, crumpled at the base of the spiral staircase. Silas lay, face down, long arms and legs sprawled, on the marble tile of the foyer, exactly as she'd found him when she'd come to visit this morning. "We always share brunch together on Sundays, and that awful creature was constantly winding around his legs and feet. It's obvious, isn't it? The stupid thing made him trip. It killed him."

Val shrugged. He'd known the Simms family his entire life. None of them were afraid of speaking their minds. Unfortunately, they more often than not spoke before they *used* their minds. "Could be you're jumping to conclusions," he said. "Silas fell, that's for sure, but who's to say the cat tripped him?"

"I tell you, I know," Marjorie insisted. "Just look at those yellow eyes. He's evil, a devil's cat."

"That would make your brother a warlock, wouldn't it?"

Marjorie glared. "Go ahead. Make jokes, but I came to visit Silas every Sunday. That cat never liked me, hissed every time I walked through the door. If I tried to pet him, he ran away. Silas laughed about it, too, but I knew. That cat wanted Silas all to himself. Even that wasn't enough. Now he's killed him."

"And what would the motive be?" Val asked. "Without Silas, the cat's without a home."

"Homeless beasts go to the pound, don't they? He'll be put to sleep if no one adopts him."

"Actually, I was thinking of taking him home," Val said. "Our youngest started college this fall, and the house is sort of empty."

"I thought you loved your wife," Marjorie said. "Do you really want to risk this beast?"

"Paula survived three kids. I think she can handle this guy." Val picked Blacky up and carried him to his car.

"You're being careful, aren't you?" Marjorie asked when Paula stopped to deliver a chicken and rice casserole. "That cat killed Silas. I wouldn't want anything to happen to you."

"We're doing fine." Paula glanced around the untidy bungalow. Silas's funeral had been big. It must have taken a lot of planning. Paula wondered what Marjorie would do now that her brother was dead. Would she stay here, or move back to the family's mansion? How long had she been away? Twenty, thirty years? Paula admired her for choosing to live modestly. Not that she had to. She'd been left a great deal of money. "Blacky's the best cat we've ever had."

"I didn't know you liked cats."

"Love them," Paula said, "but Zack's allergic to them. Since he's in college, Blacky's welcome."

Marjorie scowled. "My brother loved that monster, too. Now he's in a coffin."

"I'm sorry about Silas's death. I know he's all you had."

Paula's sympathy caused Marjorie's face to pucker. Was she going to cry? "Spinsters, townsfolk called us. And I guess that's true. Once you're past fifty and you've never married, there's no hope, right?"

"Did you *want* to marry?" As far as Paula knew, the Simmses had always been loners. That's what Val had told her. After serving on several committees with Marjorie, she couldn't imagine she'd ever had a love interest, even a boyfriend when she was young.

To her surprise, Marjorie's eyes misted. "Perry Bishop's a widow now. Perry asked for my hand after we graduated from high school, but Papa refused him. Said he was beneath us." The Simmses had been the wealthiest family in Grabill at the time, but times had changed. Running the local bank didn't automatically elevate them to the town's highest status anymore. Of course, they were still *one* of the wealthiest families, but businessmen and investors had joined their ranks in recent years.

"Does Perry live around here?" Paula asked. She'd never heard Val mention him, and he had frequent dealings with the Bishop family.

"Oh, no, he moved to the West Coast and married, but we always stayed in touch. He's thinking of retiring back here. Wouldn't that be nice?"

If Perry was like the rest of the Bishops, he wouldn't be a boon to the community. Val spent an inordinate amount of time detaining Perry's brothers and sisters, even their offspring, until they sobered up or someone came to fetch them. *Small communities were like that.* But even in Grabill, people's patience was growing thin with the Bishop family. Perry must be different or Marjorie wouldn't be enamored of him.

Every time Blacky got out of the house, Paula found him at the old Simms mansion, clawing at the front door, meowing to get inside.

"Pretty soon Marjorie's moving back," Paula warned, "and then you won't be welcome. I wouldn't be surprised if she hired someone to shoot you if you came on her property."

Blacky's yellow eyes narrowed, and he seemed to understand, so Paula was vexed when he disappeared five days later.

"That cat won't give up," she told Val. "He acts like he's happy here, but the minute I'm not watching, he slips out of the house and runs back to the Simms home."

Val's sandy eyebrows furrowed and he frowned. "If Marjorie finds him, he won't have any of his nine lives left."

The next time Blacky escaped, Paula couldn't find him. "He wasn't at the Simms place," she told Val on his lunch break. "I've looked everywhere. Maybe he's hurt and he's hiding. Maybe he needs us."

"I can't put out an APB on a cat," Val said.

"I want you to find him." Paula pulled herself to her full five feet.

Even at six-two, Val was intimidated. "I'll do what I can," he promised.

Val was cruising down Main Street, on his way back to the office, when he noticed Blacky on the garage roof of the Simms place. He slowed his cruiser. He could empathize with the cat. A large reason the Jewish religion appealed to Val was its emphasis on morals and traditions. Blacky believed the mansion was his home, that he belonged there. Val parked the car and got out.

When Blacky saw him, he jumped to the ground and sauntered down the driveway.

"Here, kitty. Good cat." Val approached cautiously.

Blacky let him get close, only inches away, then ran to the garage. Val followed. That's when he noticed the strange Mustang parked inside. "What the——?" He took note of the license plate—from California. Marjorie had said that Perry Bishop was from the West Coast, hadn't she?

Blacky didn't give him any more time. He leapt to the garage roof, crossed the slate shingles to the mansion, and climbed to a second-floor window. It was open.

Marjorie's home on Walnut Street had a "For Sale" sign in the front yard, but she hadn't moved out of it yet. Had she let Perry Bishop use the mansion while it was empty? Why hadn't she said something to Val about it? Or had Perry decided to "visit" the mansion alone and "borrow" a few things before Marjorie moved in?

He was ready to return to his cruiser and call for backup when two silhouettes moved past the kitchen window and Blacky disappeared inside the house.

Val pulled himself onto the porch roof, inched onto the house, and worked his way to the open window. "Blacky!" he whispered. The cat's black head popped into sight. "Here, kitty." He reached out a hand, but the cat pounced just out of reach. Val made a small move forward. The cat took a small step back.

So close. . . .

When Val tried to grab him, the cat dodged once more. Val did the inconceivable. He followed a cat in hot pursuit and climbed through the second-floor window.

Voices floated upstairs, muted by distance.

"Why take a chance?" a man's voice said. "Why not wait till the will's read and everything's final?"

"I've waited long enough." Val recognized Marjorie's voice.

"Then meet me in the next town. No one will know us there."

"What difference does it make?" Marjorie demanded. "Silas is dead. So is Father. I can do as I please."

"What if your brother put some clause in the will? What if you lose everything if you marry me?"

"Then we'll live in sin."

There was a low laugh. "Silas and your father must be rolling in their graves."

"You were right about Silas," Marjorie said. "After all this time, nothing had changed. He had a fit when he found out we'd stayed in contact all these years."

"So I take it he wasn't happy when he learned I was moving back?" Perry asked.

"He'd always been too full of self-importance," Marjorie said. "Told me I was still a fool, that a little love talk and I'd been duped again. Said I was unfit to be a Simms."

"See. We should wait. He might have gone straight to the family lawyer."

"He didn't have time." Marjorie's laugh was high-pitched, too loud. "You were right again when you told me that Silas would try to cut me out of everything, even my share of the money, just because I was going to see you."

"Money marries money," Perry said. "That's the way of the world."

"I'm tired of the world. And I'm tired of my family telling me what to do. I'm too old to be under Silas's thumb."

"It was a stupid way to set up a will," Perry said.

"Stupid! It was Father's opinion of me. He never trusted me after I wanted to run away with you. So for my entire life, Silas had to approve of my expenditures each year. Every time he gave me a cent, he thought he was the picture of generosity. I lived in a bungalow while he lived here, and do you know why? That's all I could afford. Then Silas learned that you might come back. He threatened to cut me off without a penny if I saw you again. Can you imagine? I'm over fifty. I told him I didn't care. I was sick of living under the Simms curse, being alone and unhappy because of our family's 'place in society.' "

Perry hesitated. "And his response?"

"He threatened to call the lawyer."

"And you're sure he didn't?"

Marjorie's voice was bleak. "I remembered your story about a trip wire. It was perfect. And better yet, I blamed his fall on his stupid cat! I never liked the thing. Two for the price of one, that's what I wanted."

Blacky's entire body quivered, and he began to pace.

"It would have been perfect justice if the cat had been put to sleep. That way, Silas would have lost the one thing he truly loved, just like he wanted me to lose you."

Blacky shot out of the upstairs bedroom and thudded onto the landing.

"What was that?" Perry grabbed Marjorie's arm, and they headed up the steps.

The lights were low, and Blacky blended into the shadows. He crouched, poising to pounce at Marjorie, when Perry's foot struck him. The cat jumped and yowled. Perry recoiled, falling backward. His body bounced down the open, winding stairway. His head smacked loudly on the marble steps and his body bumped against the oak rails. He rolled to the first-floor foyer, lying in exactly the same place that Silas had occupied only a short while before.

Val rushed to him and searched for a pulse.

"Dead," he proclaimed.

"That cat!" Marjorie lunged, but Val stepped between them.

"Perry tripped on him," Val said. "I saw it. And I heard everything. *This* was an accident, unlike Silas's death."

"It was just talk, and you shouldn't have been here. Doesn't that make whatever you heard inadmissible in court?" A typical Simms no-nonsense retort. Marjorie turned her back on Perry's body, making an effort to collect herself. Emotional excess was short-lived at best.

"You really loved him," Val said.

"That's none of your business."

"Perhaps you've been punished enough."

"I want the cat."

"He avenged Silas's death. Leave it at that."

The cat and Marjorie exchanged stares until Marjorie turned away.

"Sell your house, get your money, and leave town," Val said.

Marjorie raised an eyebrow. "Do you really think people will believe you? You're a misfit. My family's above suspicion."

"Leave, or I won't vouch for what Blacky will do," Val said.

The cat crouched and a long, low growl rumbled in his chest.

Marjorie's face paled. "It's a witch's cat, I tell you. Evil." Then she glanced at Perry's body. "There's nothing here for me anymore anyway."

After that, Blacky sat on the front stoop with Paula when she read the paper, but at night, he curled up on Val's lap. And once a year, on the day of Silas's death, he visits his grave. Val and Paula expected it. They even admired him for it. After all, they did love tradition.

Paw-trait of a Murderer

JOHN HELFERS

THE MAN'S BODY WAS STILL SITTING cross-legged on a woven *tatami* mat in the middle of the room. His chin was resting on his chest, and his eyes were closed. A long writing quill rested in his open right hand, a writing stone was held loosely in his left. On the floor before him lay a pristine scroll of rice paper.

From what Kitsune could see, it looked like the man was sleeping. Only when he walked around the still form did he see the dark stain on the man's ki-mono, the crimson liquid dripping down to pool with the ink from the spilled ink pot beside him. There were strange markings near the puddle of ink that caught Kitsune's attention, but before he could examine them further, a voice commanded his full attention.

"Kitsune! Do not touch anything!"

The boy straightened and turned back to the doorway, where the vaguely middle-aged man who had spoken to him was speaking with the captain of the house guards. Kitsune edged closer and picked up the conversation in mid-sentence.

"—Of course you realize the delicacy of the situation, Ashiga-san. With the generals of Clan Yoshitsune assembled, I don't know how long we can keep the death of the *daimyo* quiet. If they find out, they will immediately begin arguing as to who should take over the province. If this is not solved quickly and the rights of power legally handed down, it could lead to civil war, and we cannot afford that, not with enemies on all sides," the captain of the guards said.

"It is not the enemies outside your province I would be concerned with, but the enemies within," the older man replied. "What of Yoshitsune's son? Surely a suitable governor can rule the province until he is of a proper age."

"That's just it, there are too many generals who would see the *daimyo*'s death as a means to gain control. Once installed as governor, the boy could have an 'accident' and the acting governor could take over," the house captain said, frowning. "Some wouldn't even be that sly about it, they would just use their troops to take over the castle."

"That would be inconvenient," the older man said. "Spread the word that the *daimyo* is ill and will be resting for the next twenty-four hours with no visi-tors of any kind, on my orders. Post only guards you trust around the boy twenty-four hours a day, and let no one see him unless you have cleared the visit personally. I will see what I can do. Please leave me to examine the scene here. My associate outside will make sure we are not disturbed."

"Should the boy be here?" the captain asked. "It might disturb him to be in the presence of. . . ." he motioned toward the body.

"I have every confidence in my retainer's ability to conduct himself in the proper manner. Besides," the man said with a small grin, "he's probably seen things that would disturb *you*. Go now."

The captain of the guards bowed deeply, turned, and strode out of the room. As he slid the paper and wood door aside, Kitsune saw the familiar form of Maseda, his mentor's samurai bodyguard, standing just to the left of the door. He smiled, then quickly turned back to the older man.

"If you are done spying on conversations that do not concern you, then perhaps you would care to tell me what you have observed here so far," the man said.

Kitsune gulped and stepped forward, taking a close look at the body. Now that he was able to study it, the dead man's face wore an expression of calm, not fear, pain, or anger as he had expected. "There is a peaceful look about him, and the quill in his hand is not crushed or broken. Therefore he must have died instantly. Only a samurai or a ninja would know how to kill so cleanly."

The older man nodded. "Very good. What else?"

Kitsune thought for a moment. "The fact that he was relaxed when attacked indicates he was taken by surprise." He looked up at the roof, which was composed of wooden panels that could be opened to let the sun in. "I would examine the roof for signs of someone letting himself in that way, perhaps climbing down on a rope, stabbing Yoshitsune-san, then climbing back up."

"Perhaps," the older man's expression was unreadable, as usual. "More?"

Kitsune walked around the body, pausing when he got to the pool of ink. He bent down to study it and the strange marks he saw earlier, then looked up at his mentor. "Yoshitsune was not alone, Asano." He pointed to the black paw prints that were tracked across the otherwise spotless white floor. "His cat was with him, and escaped either when the assassin fled or when the serving girl discovered the body," Kitsune said.

Asano nodded curtly. "So, based on what you have observed, how would you begin your investigation?"

Kitsune thought for a few minutes before answering. "I would probably question the serving girl to see if she saw anything, then take statements from everyone on the grounds to see where they were at the time of the attack. I would compare the statements to see who was alone or closest to the *daimyo*'s room, and try to find a weakness in those individuals' alibis, thereby hopefully eliciting a confession."

Asano nodded again, more thoughtfully this time. "A sound plan, but aren't you forgetting one thing?"

Kitsune frowned, retracing his plan in his head. "I don't believe so."

"Actually, there are two things. First, the fact that Yoshitsune died cleanly may not only indicate that he was taken by surprise, but that he knew his attacker. One of the generals may have thought that now, with all of the commanding officers attending the council, would be the perfect time to remove his obstacle to taking power, and perhaps even throw suspicion on one of the others. What you will be doing this afternoon is finding out which of Yoshitsune's military leaders was alone at the time of his death."

"How can you be sure it was one of them?" Kitsune asked.

"Because of the skill you ascribed to the killing blow," Asano replied. "As you said, only a samurai or a ninja would know how to strike so cleanly. Besides, if I know the generals, they would trust no one else to take care of this matter."

"And what will you be doing?" Kitsune asked.

Asano smiled. "I will be interviewing the witness."

"What witness?" Kitsune asked.

"Why, the cat, of course," Asano replied.

Later that afternoon, Kitsune trotted back into the castle, searching for Asano. He went to the room where the body was and saw Maseda guarding the door, as still as a statue.

Kitsune went up to him. "Has Asano returned here today?"

Maseda shook his head, pointed down the corridor, and held up three fingers.

Kitsune bowed, turned, and started down the hall. Three rooms down, Maseda had told him. At the third sliding panel, he tapped gently on the wooden frame.

"Enter." Asano's voice came from within. Kitsune pushed the panel open and stepped inside.

Compared to the neatness of the other rooms, with their soft white paper walls, polished wooden beams, and swept floors, this area was a mess. Several pots of paint were scattered around the floor. Dozens of sheets of valuable rice paper were hung on every wall at varying heights, none more than a foot off the ground. These were smeared with paint in dizzying combinations, from multi-colored bursts of red, blue, and green to delicate patterns that resembled flowers or ornate gardens. Multicolored paw prints were everywhere, tracked around the room until it was impossible to tell where one set ended and another began.

In the middle of it all sat Asano, stroking a black Persian which was resting on his lap. When Kitsune entered, the man and the cat both looked up at him at the exact same time. Kitsune shivered involuntarily as he approached, bowed, and sat down.

"What news?" Asano said, his own slitted black eyes remarkably cat-like in the gloom.

"There were three generals who were alone at the time Yoshitsune was killed. General Konami, who was walking in the garden; General Ryuga, who was writing a letter in his quarters; and General Tokushu, who was riding his stallion," Kitsune said.

"Interesting. Did Ryuga say whom the letter was for?"

"He claimed he was writing to his wife," Kitsune said.

Asano nodded. "Did Tokushu have the stable boy get his horse, or did he have it out already?"

"The stable boy said that Tokushu had taken his horse out that morning, and returned it just a few minutes before I came to see him. In fact, he was rubbing it down as we talked."

"Did the horse look winded?" Asano asked.

"Yes, he was sweaty and lathered, as if he had been ridden hard," Kitsune replied.

"Hm. Any one of them could have easily killed the *daimyo*. While you were out, I was having a most illuminating conversation with Ningpo," Asano said. When he didn't say anything more, Kitsune's eyes dropped to the cat, who stared back at him unruffled.

"And?" Kitsune asked.

"She knows who the murderer is," Asano said.

"Great, then all we have to do is assemble everyone who was on the castle grounds, and have her point him or her out. Surely her negative reaction will be enough for a trial," Kitsune said.

"No, Kitsune, you do not understand. I know she witnessed what happened in Yoshitsune's room; however, she does not realize what she has seen. If we were to attempt your test, then Ningpo might just seize on the aura of someone that cats naturally find repellent, and could condemn an innocent man to death. No, there is a way to uncover the killer, and the cat is the key," Asano said.

"But if the cat can't tell you who did it, why don't you just contact the spirits and ask them who killed the *daimyo*? Surely they saw it happen," Kitsune said.

Asano shook his head. "Pah, their assistance is not required for this minor matter. If one goes to the spirits too much, they begin to believe that one relies on them too often, which can lead to all sorts of trouble. Better to exercise the mind and solve this using more earthly methods."

"But how are we to accomplish that?" Kitsune asked.

"That is my business," Asano said. "But I will need plenty of clean rice paper and pots of paint in every color you can find. By tomorrow morning we shall have our murderer."

The next morning dawned clear and bright. Kitsune rose to watch the sunrise and meditate, then went to Asano's room. He'd spent the previous evening hanging the sheets of rice paper and leaving the pots of paint on the floor of the cat's playroom as instructed.

Maseda was standing outside Asano's quarters, as usual. He opened the door for Kitsune, and motioned him inside. Asano was sitting in the lotus position, his eyes closed.

"Asano?" Kitsune asked, bowing.

Asano's eyes opened and the old-not-old man regarded him. "It is time. Have the captain of the guards, Ikama, I believe his name is, summon the three generals and bring them to the room we were in last night."

Kitsune bowed and ran to find Captain Ikama. He located him in the main courtyard and gave him Asano's message, then ran back to find Asano sitting in the middle of the cat-tracked floor in the paint room. The cat, Ningpo, her paws streaked with several colors of paint, was still resting on his lap, smiling her peculiar smile. Maseda, looking as inconspicuous as ever, stood quietly in a corner of the room. Kitsune bowed again and waited beside the door. He noticed that only one sheet of rice paper now hung on the wall, to the left of the entrance.

A few minutes later, Kitsune heard the sounds of men walking and talking amongst themselves as they came down the hallway. Captain Ikama entered, bowed to Asano, and walked over to him, where the two men had a whispered conversation. He then moved to stand on the other side of the door. Then the three generals came in all dressed in kimonos with *katana*s by their sides. Each of their kimonos were decorated on the front, back, and sleeves with patterns representing their regiments. General Konami, commander of the Crane regiment, was tall and thin, with a long nose much like his unit's namesake. His kimono was covered with the image of a crane spreading its wings to fly. General Ryugu, commander of the Tiger regiment, was short but thickly muscled, with his hair cropped close to his head. A long scar wound its way down one cheek. His orange and black robe was decorated with dozens of sitting tigers. General Tokushu, commander of the Lotus regiment, was a handsome man in his immaculately pressed silk kimono covered in lotus blossoms, and perfect topknot. Of the three men, he seemed the most annoyed at being summoned here.

"Gentlemen, once again I humbly thank you for agreeing to meet here on such short notice," Captain Ikama began. "It is my sad duty to inform you that our *daimyo*, Lord Iretsu Yoshitsune, died yesterday." The captain paused to let the news sink in. "He was murdered, killed by a single *katana* thrust to the heart."

The generals murmured among themselves. Then General Ryugu stepped forward, bowing slightly. "But what does this have to do with us?" he asked, the other two nodding in agreement.

"For that answer, I will turn to the physician of the Royal Court of His Most Revered Emperor Yamata, Master Asano Ashiga." Captain Ikama bowed to Asano, who had not moved, but still sat in the center of the room, his nimble fingers stroking the cat in his lap.

"Honored gentlemen, the captain of the guard has asked me, a humble physician, to investigate this most sorrowful matter. This I have done, and I have come to the conclusion that one of you three had both motive and opportunity to commit this terrible crime," Asano said. The three generals looked warily at each other.

"What the murderer did not count on was the fact that there was a witness to this horrible deed," Asano continued. "That witness is sitting on my lap as I speak."

All eyes, with the exception of Maseda's, went to the black Persian cat lounging on Asano's lap.

General Konami was the first to break the silence. "This is ridiculous. How is a cat supposed to tell who may have killed Lord Yoshitsune?"

"Regardless, this cat most assuredly has told me who killed Lord Yoshitsune. The proof is hanging on the wall there," Asano said, motioning.

The three generals, Asano, Kitsune, and the captain of the guard turned toward the wall where the lone sheet of rice paper hung. On it was what looked like rough brush strokes in the shape of a man dressed in a kimono and carrying a *katana*. The robe in the painting was covered with paw prints that decorated the sleeves and front.

"What the murderer didn't know is that Yoshitsune's cat, Ningpo, is one of the rare breed of painting cats. When left here with paper and paint, she produced this rather accurate picture of the murderer."

Kitsune saw the eyes of the generals widen as they studied the painting. Asano continued as if he hadn't noticed. "As you can see by the design on the kimono, it is obvious which one is the murderer."

For an instant, no one moved. Then the steel hiss of a *katana* being drawn split the silence. Kitsune looked back in time to see one of the generals leaping toward Asano, his blade raised above his head to split the sitting man in two with one stroke. Just as he was about to bring the sword down, Maseda was suddenly standing behind Asano, his own *katana* intersecting the other man's and sending it spinning off into a corner of the room. Just as quickly, Maseda's blade was at the man's throat, followed by the swords of the other two generals and Captain Ikama.

"General Tokushu, I hereby arrest you on the charge of murder of our Lord Yoshitsune," the captain said. "Generals Konami, Ryugu, please escort the general to a holding cell and place him under constant guard until his trial."

The two generals escorted the suddenly pale Tokushu out of the room. The once proud general could be heard muttering as he left, "Demon cat . . . how could it have known?"

Once the general was gone, Captain Ikama turned to Asano. "How did the cat know indeed?"

"Well, the cat was indeed part of the solution, but not the entire solution. When I saw that Ningpo was a painting cat, I realized how I could trap the murderer," Asano said. "To be fair, Ningpo is possessed of uncommon skill. I simply left her in here with several sheets of rice paper and plenty of paint, and she supplied me with several paintings. It was then a simple matter of selecting the one that most closely resembled a samurai, and making a few artistic additions to strengthen the image. In particular, I added the paw prints, knowing that would be the final touch that would unmask the villain."

"But how did the paw prints make the difference?" Kitsune asked.

"That was the crucial element for all three men," Asano replied. "Once I found out which regiment the three generals belonged to, I selected the paw print of the cat for the kimono marking because each of the men could identify with it.

"I believe I see what you mean," Captain Ikama said. "Tokushu would see the prints as the marking of the lotus, Konami would interpret them as a crane unfurling its wings to fly—"

"—And Ryugu would see a tiger sitting on its haunches, each one the symbol of their regiment. The killer would think the cat had marked him as guilty—" Kitsune said.

"—And betray himself, although I thought the criminal would try to flee rather than kill the only witness," Asano said.

"You mean Tokushu was trying to kill the cat?" the captain asked.

"Well, both of us actually," Asano said. "That was why I was holding Ningpo on my lap: to present a more tempting target."

"Amazing," Captain Ikama said. "But what of the castle and province? Who will run it now?"

"I think the best way to handle the question of which general will be governor until Yoshitsune's son comes of age would be to make none of the generals governor. Rather, I will draw up formal papers that will make you, Captain Ikama, governor of this province until the boy is of ruling age. I trust this will be suitable?" Asano asked with a smile.

Captain Ikama could only nod dumbly at this most heavenly turn of events. And Ningpo, still sitting on Asano's lap, smiled her inscrutable smile, looking for all the world as if the events of that day had unfolded just as she had wished.

Powder Puff

GAIL TORGERSON

JAMES HID A GRIMACE AS PUFFY'S claws dug into his thigh. Twenty pounds of long-haired gray tabby slow-blinked at him and chortled. At least it sounded that way to James. Puffy hated him.

"He adores you, James. I am pleased," Aunt Lavinia said in that slightly breathless voice she affected. James had heard his great-aunt speak to the servants in a strong, clear voice on occasion. For now though, she played the invalid: a white-haired, frail spinster almost swallowed up by the masses of feather pillows on her huge four-poster, both bed and occupant carefully arranged against any suggestion of dishabille. As if anyone would have the slightest improper thought about the old lady.

At least not the kind of improper thoughts Aunt Lavinia guarded against. James smiled. Would dear old Auntie consider her murder an impropriety? He absent-mindedly brushed the cat, then winced as Puffy responded with another dig. Loose silver hairs swirled through the air.

"Yes, very pleased," Aunt Lavinia continued. "He loves to be close to people. You know I'm talking about you, don't you, Puffy dear?" At the sound of his name, Puffy looked over and made a *mruupp* noise. "I hand-fed him as a kitten, he was so tiny and weak when the gardener found him. A darling little powder-puff of a kitten. I daresay he thinks he is a person, the way he responds when I talk to him. We often chat together, just the two of us." Aunt Lavinia laughed gently as she gazed at the light-gray-striped lump of fur. James forced a chuckle in response. Puffy purred. "He's such a hedonist, isn't he? He loves sitting in laps and being brushed and petted. He's quite particular—all his life when I have had visitors, Puffy would go around to them all, carefully selecting the one he wanted to sit with."

Aunt Lavinia sighed and lay back. "I am so frail now that I tire too quickly to brush him properly. Isn't that dreadful of me? I feel I am neglecting my great big boy. That's why it pleases me so to have you visit and give him the attention he deserves."

"I've always loved cats, Aunt Lavinia. I hope someday to live where I can enjoy the daily companionship of a cat as you do." James mimicked Aunt Lavinia's outmoded speech with ease, after so many months of practice. He smiled tightly, trying not to squirm as the big cat kneaded his thighs with renewed vigor. Puffy meowed, his yellow eyes glinting with malevolent humor. "Of course, no other cat could compare to Puffy."

"That's very true, James. He has the sixth sense, you know. Oh, all cats do, of course, but Puffy has it stronger than other cats. It makes him more intelligent. He doesn't take to many people—he knows when people don't like him, you see. What's the matter, Puffy dear? There's a good boy. He's always preferred the company of men, particularly strong men. Men with drive and ambition."

James tried to look strong, driven, and ambitious.

"I've often felt that Puffy and my dear Poppa—your great-grandfather, James—would have gotten along very well together. Both enjoying their comforts, yet both gentlemen and quite mindful of their responsibilities. You'll think me a silly woman if I say Puffy looks after me in his own fashion, quite as Poppa used to do. Oftentimes when I had company, Puffy refused them all, and *that* told me something about my guests, I can tell you. Sometimes I believe Puffy knows just what people are thinking."

"I imagine he finds most people quite boring, then," James said with a laugh. Puffy laid his paw on James's arm. A cold lump formed in James's gut. He tried to will it away with reason. Cats can't read minds, and even if Puffy could read his mind, he couldn't tell anyone. James laughed harder. Puffy hissed.

"Oh, dear."

"My fault, Aunt Lavinia. I jiggled him. There, there, Puffy. I'll be still." James relaxed as the look of concern faded from his great-aunt's wrinkled face. He felt close, very close, to his goal. He mustn't throw away the cumulative benefit of months of holding the great hairy beast. All the trousers ruined with threads pulled up, the yards of sticky tape to pick up cat hair, innumerable scratches. Most of all, the painfully good behavior, just in case his aunt had him investigated. He hoped she had, after all the sacrifices he made. He smiled reassuringly at the old lady as he stroked the cat with the brush. Puffy relaxed, but his enormous tail switched and beat at James.

"You must be quite weary of hearing me go on and on about Puffy. How is your work, dear? And that young lady you mentioned dining with last week?" Aunt Lavinia settled down to the task of extracting the details of James's life since his last visit. James gave her the all-too-easily-censored version, experience telling him what the old lady wanted to hear most: how his job was going, his prospects with the company, his social life. Aunt Lavinia smiled encouragingly, evidently pleased. She should be pleased, James thought, after all his effort in altering his life to suit her. He'd really let loose, once he could call his life his own again. First he'd dump the pitiful job, or maybe he'd dump his dull and conservative girlfriend first. In the meantime, he recited his activities carefully, answering Aunt Lavinia's prying questions without annoyance. It was all part of the price. James smiled at the thought of the payoff.

"I know you think me a busybody, James, but truly I have your best interests at heart. Dear James, I've grown quite fond of you. I admit I have been concerned about your behavior." James felt a cold hand clenching his guts. "Your past behavior, that is, was less than desirable, but I find you have matured and steadied. My father probably would have quoted some maxim about sowing wild oats, or boys will be boys." James felt his whole body relax. So, the good behavior was paying off. The old lady did have him checked out.

Aunt Lavinia lowered her eyes and blushed—a practiced blush, James felt sure. "I heard tales, suitably cleaned up, of course, about his wilder days. And my brother needed to get some of the wildness out of his system. You remind me of him." She smiled sadly. Her younger brother was her favorite—James counted on that, and the family resemblance, when he came to see her.

"Thank you, Aunt Lavinia. Although I was just a boy when he died, I remember Grandpa fondly." In fact, James barely remembered the old geezer. Mostly he remembered the smell, and all the adults jumping to do the old guy's bidding.

Aunt Lavinia smiled. "Yes, you have matured, James. And you are one of my closest blood relations. These things matter, my boy. I've had my lawyer in— there's another gentleman Puffy adores. Now, don't be jealous, James. Puffy favors you. Poor Mr. Pinchon's wife is so allergic, she simply can't bear cats. Though he always speaks kindly to Puffy, Mr. Pinchon can't hold or even touch Puffy because of his wife's difficulties. Imagine being saddled with such a creature."

"How sad." James had seen the lawyer leaving as he drove in, but Aunt Lavinia made the shyster dance attendance on her regularly, so James had learned not to get excited by the man's presence. Or by Aunt Lavinia's talk of not being long for this world.

Today, the two events seemed weighted with meaning. Perhaps it was Aunt Lavinia's coquettish behavior—the old lady loved a secret, loved the power it gave her.

"I noticed the gentleman leaving, though we only waved in passing. I trust everything is well?" Careful, not too heavy on the prompting.

"Oh, as well as can be expected. I have outlived so many of my contemporaries," she said. "That is why Puffy has been such a joy to me." James stifled a sigh as Aunt Lavinia returned to her favorite topic. It wouldn't do for her to see how anxious he was to hear about Pinchon's visit.

"I have had Puffy for nearly ten years. He looks as fit as a kitten, doesn't he? He's in the prime of his life. I expect him to outlive me, indeed I depend on it. But I've been so worried about my precious, wondering what will become of him when I am gone. I couldn't bear to leave him with someone who doesn't love him and care for him as I do. Someone whom he loves, as well."

James felt his heart beat faster—he reminded himself that Aunt Lavinia had made similar hints several times before, but nothing had come of it. Yet. "Puffy would miss you terribly, Aunt Lavinia. No one could ever truly take your place in his heart. Fortunately, you're going to be with us for a long time to come." As long as it took for James to complete his arrangements. It wouldn't do to knock the old lady off the day after she changed her will, if she ever got around to it. He needed his alibi, too.

The cat he could deal with at his leisure—maybe an accident in a busy street. Puffy turned his head to glare at James. James smiled back. Sometimes he hoped the cat knew exactly what he was thinking.

"Thank you, dear James, but I fear it may not be so. I want to be sure my darling is taken care of. That is why I had Mr. Pinchon in today. I had him draw up a new will, and I signed it today. Oh, don't fret, James. I'm old, dying will be a blessing, a release. I've decided you shall have custody of my dear Puffy after I die. You needn't worry about not being able to care for Puffy as he is accustomed. He does like his comforts. You shall also be quite comfortable with my new will." Aunt Lavinia smiled, still savoring her power.

James tried to control his excitement enough to say something, anything, he thought the old lady wanted to hear, but Aunt Lavinia brushed aside his words.

"There are a few other bequests, of course, but I am a wealthy woman and can afford to be generous without depriving my boy of anything. You will be very pleased, James, but that is all I am saying for now. Yes, you do remind me of my brother, so intense, always wanting to know everything. A lady likes to have her secrets, James, my dear. Indulge me—I have so little time left."

James made the appropriate noises of denial and gratitude. His great-aunt waved them aside, but she looked pleased. "Aunt Lavinia, you are far too generous. You are so very good to me. But I have tired you. You should rest. Shall I call your maid?" He could barely tolerate another minute in the room—he wanted to get out and celebrate.

"I have all of eternity to rest, dear boy, but your solicitude is comforting. Perhaps I shall close my eyes briefly."

Despite his eagerness, James endured Puffy's claws for nearly half an hour to be sure Aunt Lavinia slept soundly before he left. As always, Puffy anticipated his action and kicked off with such force that James grunted from the pain. He'd have fresh, bloody welts from the monster. James silently cursed at the mat of cat hair on his pants and the pulled-up threads. He'd toss all his clothes out, and buy everything new, once Aunt Lavinia made good on her promise to die—and he'd make sure she did. He met Puffy's malevolent gaze from the bed. Your days are numbered, too, James thought. He smiled as he shut the door behind him, thinking of all the accidents that could happen.

James spared a brief nod to the maid as he passed her in the hallway, his mind still on accidents and other unnatural ways to die. He had been patient while he stalked Aunt Lavinia's money, but now he found his patience almost too weak to stand up against his eagerness to inherit. He'd have to force himself to wait a little while, to allay suspicions, then he could complete the arrangements. He knew just the man. James would be surrounded by witnesses far away at the time of the tragic robbery.

James allowed himself a small chuckle as he started briskly down the wide stairs to the front door. His mind barely had time to register the gray mass that darted between his legs. His laughter turned to a scream as he pitched forward.

"*Ahnnnhhg.*" James tried to complain when Puffy jumped on the bed and lay next to him. He feebly pushed at Puffy with his plaster-encased left arm. The big gray cat closed his eyes as he dug his claws into James's thigh. James moaned, a weak, gargling sound.

"Oh, look. James is trying to pet Puffy," Aunt Lavinia said, nothing breathless and frail about her voice now. James had watched helplessly from his hospital bed as his great-aunt took on a new life, getting stronger with each visit, with new clothes and now a new hairstyle. His weak hands refused to clench into fists of rage. "I knew bringing him home would be the best thing. You heard him, Mr. Pinchon, how he tried to say Puffy's name? There is a bond between them—Puffy was the first of us to reach James, after his terrible fall. I can still see him sitting watch over James. I just know James will recover more quickly here, surrounded by affection, than in that cold, impersonal hospital."

"I'm sure you're right, Miss Lavinia. Such a tragic accident, and then to be paralyzed by a stroke. How fortunate your nephew is young and strong. I'm sure he'll make a complete recovery, though you must remember the doctors said it could take years. I arranged for the best nurses, just as you instructed."

James tried to speak again, tried to shake his head. A nurse moved forward to wipe his mouth. She frowned at the sight of the cat but said nothing as she stepped discreetly back. James moaned with frustration—in the hospital they hadn't allowed Aunt Lavinia to bring the damned cat.

"There, there, James, my boy. You rest and work on getting well. Your Aunt Lavinia will take care of everything. I admit I was ready to go, my life's work complete, but I won't leave you, my dear, while you need me. Puffy will be right here with you, too, keeping you company. He'll watch over you as he has always watched over me. He just adores you, James. I know he wants to help you get better."

Puffy meowed at Aunt Lavinia. "There, you see? You and Puffy have a nice nap, dear. You need your rest to get better." Aunt Lavinia kissed her fingertips and touched James's brow. Her loving stroke down Puffy's side released a cloud of gray hairs. James tried to speak, but Aunt Lavinia just smiled and waved as she allowed her lawyer to escort her out of the sickroom.

James whimpered. Puffy purred and dug deeper. Turning his head to look at James, the gray tabby cat slowly blinked both eyes and chortled.

Pretty Kitty

JOYCE HOLLAND

DON'T EVEN THINK ABOUT IT, puss," I said to the little ball of black fur poised to jump into my lap. "I keep telling you, I am not a cat person!" I opened the newspaper and shook it threateningly.

"Ah shut up, Lew!" Maggie said, slapping our plates and two glasses of milk on the table. "I pay for the stupid cat food! And I'm sick of living hand to mouth. We can't even afford a six-pack of beer for crying out loud!"

I stared at my plate. The cat's food looked better. "I'm not very hungry, but this looks great," I lied, hoping to stop an onslaught of endless nagging. Maggie was still on the ragged edge of pretty, but the years were taking their toll. Or the meanness. Nothing made her happy lately. Probably had a new boyfriend. Funny thing was, I didn't really care anymore. Kinda wished one would take her off my hands. I'd give the poor sucker a medal if he could last a year.

The telephone rang and Maggie sprang to her feet.

The feisty feline took advantage of the distraction to jump up on the table. I reached to put her down, but the little devil humped her spine and back-stepped around the salt and pepper shakers.

"At least drink your milk," Maggie hollered at me, as she dashed to answer the phone in the hall.

I turned and watched Maggie go, wondering who could be calling. The fuzzball seized the opportunity, took two quick steps, and stuck her nose in my glass. She sniffed experimentally and shook her head.

The hell with this, I decided. It's her cat; let her share with it if she wants. I set the kitty back on the floor, changed my milk for Maggie's, then drank the whole thing. Anything to keep the peace. A beer *would* have been nice.

Maggie came back and started to eat, watching me with an oddly intense stare. "Wrong number," she said. She picked up her milk and took a long swig, then suddenly grasped her throat and slid off her chair to the floor. "You switched the glasses!" Maggie cried through clenched lips.

Speechless, I watched her death throes.

The kitten jumped into my lap, curled up, and began to purr.

"Maybe I could become a cat person," I said, gently stroking her glossy fur. "Pretty kitty."

The Queen's Jewels

JAYGE CARR

LIZAVETTA, THE CHARTREUX QUEEN, was out for her first breath of fresh air in this newest city of her triumphal tour. Her nose wrinkled in disgust, though she tried to hide it as beneath her dignity. Fresh? This city smelled *terrible*, with rot and old unmentionable bodily by-products as its choicest ingredients.

Beside Lizavetta, her Faithful Companion was chattering excitedly, gaze darting about, feet keeping to a slow pace that matched her queen's shorter legs.

So this is America.

It smelled. Bad.

A hoarse wolf whistle attacked the two. Lizavetta ignored it, but her companion blushed. The two teens, who had been playing with a basketball on the concrete courtyard, ran to the chain-link fence and half climbed it, clinging.

"Woo-woo!"

"Will ya looka that!"

"Ohhh, baby, wanna play?"

Lizavetta had had practice ignoring importunities. But her Faithful Companion was less hardened. She didn't look at the two, but her pace faltered. Lizavetta glanced over in reproach, but already FC had regained her stride. Cheeks glowing, she kept going.

But Lizavetta's attention had been caught by something else. Not far from those two louts—yes? No? Yes!

Unmistakable: two of her own kind. Not royal, not noble, not even servants of a proper court. But two of hers, nonetheless. Young, very young, not nearly as mature as the two men-children clinging to the fence and hollering.

Lizavetta allowed her gaze to catch the older of the two, all patches, but alert and poised for all his mismatched outerwear. Young Patches lowered his head, just briefly, before again favoring her with a cocky grin, then a yawn that showed sharp little teeth.

Lizavetta acknowledged his instinctive obeisance with a grave nod in return.

The smaller of the two was most formal in black, but very young. He wriggled all friendliness, and Lizavetta gave him a nod also. Possible potential there. Good courtiers were made from less.

Though their stroll took the usual time and was at the usual pace— Lizavetta was a stickler for routine, it had long been bred into her—her Faithful Companion did stop and consult for a little with the proudly uniformed guard at the door before they went on in.

Lizavetta paid little attention. There were all the sights and sounds and smells of this new city to absorb.

"Can't say I didn't warn you, m'lady," the guard was saying. "This neighborhood isn't what it used to be. The slums are too close."

"Perhaps you can arrange an escort?" FC murmured softly. There was a crinkle that Lizavetta had heard many times, but a queen never concerned herself with mundane money matters.

"You bet I can," the guard said enthusiastically. He nodded at Lizavetta with a respectful smile. "Wouldn't want anything to happen to visiting royalty, now would we?"

FC thanked him politely in her accented English. Lizavetta concentrated on this city she must accustom herself to.

The guard was right. Back at the courtyard, the two who had whistled at the queen and her companion were deciding how to take advantage the next time they spotted the two out alone. Stripped of obscenities, street slang, and bad English, it went something like this.

Juan, the older one, said, "Wouldn't you drool for a piece of that action?" He was proud of the several children he had sired with his various girls.

Oboya shrugged. He never repeated a conquest, so he couldn't be sure if he was a father or not. "Like a piece of what her hineyness was wearing better."

"Wearing?" Juan popped the basketball through the hoop with ease. Oboya caught it coming down and made a jump to put it through again. Had he been six foot plus instead of not quite six feet, he might have made it into professional basketball. As it was, he was a poor wannabe.

"Wearing," Oboya repeated. "Didn't you see that thingie around her neck? Jewels all over it."

"Fake." Juan began dribbling, so the two went back and forth across the cracked concrete, first one with the ball, then the other.

"Naw. Read't in the paper. All about her hineyness and all. Coming here. The jewels are real."

"Naw!" Juan, who couldn't read, stopped and stared at the slightly taller Oboya. "Y'sure?"

Oboya only grinned.

Slowly, still practicing desultorily with the ball, the two discussed ways to share the wealth. They paid no attention to the two youngsters still playing quietly in one corner of the yard.

They agreed on a snatch, not just a mugging. Somebody would pay plenty to get her hineyness back, and the jewels around her neck would be gravy, too.

Next day, Juan and Oboya were back on the court, dribbling their ball and trying to look innocent. Luckily, because the policemen in the car carefully paralleling Lizavetta and her companion gave them both a long, beady-eyed inspection.

Lizavetta was aware again, not just of the two mouthy men-children, but of the two youngsters of her own kind, who were peering at her from a narrow alley, shy but radiating good intent. She wondered what they were eating, if there was anything she could do. But she had already realized that this rich city in this rich country had many denizens who wanted badly. There was little she could do for so many. But again she awarded the two younglings a regal nod. Again, they smiled back, all friendliness.

Juan and Oboya took four days to come up with a Plan. The routine of the outings helped. Same time, every day, the two emerged from the posh old hotel and headed down the street, in the same direction. They walked the same distance, then came back.

Juan and Oboya walked the same trip several times, until they had the exact spot for their snatch.

For Lizavetta and FC, it was the usual, routine walk. They were on their way back up the slight slope toward the hotel when, just in front of them, a boy on inline skates came shooting out of a side street and zoomed toward them.

"Look out!" screamed Faithful Companion. Lizavetta, as always, was silent, but she stiffened at the sight of the boy racing toward them.

"I can't stop!" the boy yelled, waving his hands frantically.

FC grabbed Lizavetta and stepped back, but was stopped by a high fence that bordered the sidewalk. Quivering, FC flattened herself and her charge as close to the fence as she could.

But the boy seemed to be veering toward them as he came.

The police had stopped and left their car, but they couldn't run as fast as the boy was skating. As he flew by, he reached out—and was carrying Lizavetta away before the police came running up, seconds too late.

"Don't shoot, you might hit her!" Faithful Companion screamed. The two policemen, shouting, pell-melled behind the boy on the skates, but he was still heading downhill, juggling his burden while trying to pull off her collar.

Just then a motorcycle *varoomed* in the upcoming alleyway. The plot was plain. The boy on the motorcycle would carry Lizavetta off. His friend on skates would speed in another direction and hide. By the time the policemen ran back to their car, reversed its direction, and gave chase, Lizavetta and both her captors would be long gone. Radioing ahead might catch one or both of them, but in all these city hidey-holes, they well could disappear before pursuit could be arranged.

"Stop them!" FC was screaming. "*Stop them!*"

Lizavetta was struggling, but the boy held on to her desperately. Once he could hand her over to his confederate on the motorcycle—

Only a weight slammed into the boy on the skates, hard enough to make him lose his balance and fall heavily. Lizavetta, half choked by his attempts to remove her collar, exploded out of his arms and kept running.

The boy on the motorcycle hesitated when his friend went down. In that heartbeat, he lifted his foot off the accelerator, and the motorcycle paused. And something from the collision site attacked the side of his leg, pushing and causing arrows of sharp pain.

"What the—*owwwwww!*" Oboya looked down, saw nothing—except that his leg was bleeding, dark lines running down below the shorts he was wearing.

A warning bullet hissed over his head. The police were coming closer, both with guns drawn. Juan was down, sprawled on the pavement . . . empty-handed.

Oboya sighed and raised his hands. They might be able to argue that he had had nothing to do with it. If Juan kept his head and claimed it was only an impulse. If.

"Where is she?" No avenging angel looked more threatening than Lizavetta's FC.

"Where who?" Oboya had decided on stupidity and ignorance.

"Where's my queen!"

"Queen?" He looked around. Then remembered her hineyness. "What I know 'bout some queen?"

"You two are in trouble," the closest policeman announced, panting. "Answer the lady!"

"Hey!" Juan stuck his hands up higher, looked down. "You shot me f'r nuthin'!"

"I shot over your head in warning." The second policeman skidded to a halt, stared at the two young males, one lying on his side, clutching a clearly broken leg, crying in pain and rage, one standing by his downed motorcycle, his leg bleeding.

"Those are cat scratches," FC said in accusation. "I've seen them enough to know."

"Cat scratches?" Juan looked down. "Lady, if that pussy of yours attacked me, it's your fault."

"I've seen those two together almost every day." FC faced the two policemen. "But there must have been a third, and he has Lizavetta."

"Lady." The older policeman scratched at the balding area revealed by his cap. "I'm afraid your prize cat took off when this scum—" he nodded to Oboya "—dropped her. Don't think there was another one, just these two."

"Oh! We must find her! This city is dangerous!"

Lizavetta had run in total panic. Grabbed, half strangled, then dropped, she had landed on her feet in cat reflex and kept going. Hands had stretched out toward her, people had screamed or coaxed, but she dodged and, despite her short legs, kept up good speed.

But panic wears off. Lizavetta found herself in a narrow cul-de-sac. No humans were near. The trouble was—she began to retrace her path, but she knew she had dodged and circled and crossed her own trail in her avoidance of those grabbing or yelling at her.

It might take a while—

She froze. The scent was clear, and unmistakable. The ancient enemy. Close.

Dog!

He slid out of a back doorway, big and threatening. He knew she was there, had smelled her just as she smelled him. Hunting dog, bred to kill. His mouth opened, showing a row of fangs.

Lizavetta made herself as big as she could. Tried to challenge, but nothing came out. Nothing ever could—she was mute.

Over a wooden fence, she could hear sounds of humans, possible rescuers. But she couldn't call them. It was just her and . . . Dog.

Dog seemed to sense that she couldn't call for help. He came closer, step by step. Ears cocked, teeth bared. Menace incarnate.

Lizavetta raised what she knew was a futile paw, claws bared.

Dog almost seemed to chuckle as he continued his slow death-march toward her.

Then everything happened at once. One scream of challenge flew over the fence toward Dog, paws and fangs raking skin.

Another scream of challenge raced down the alley, and raked Dog on the other side.

Then both defenders about-faced, to stand between Lizavetta and her Doom.

It was the two youngsters whom she had seen each day. The patchy cat and the sleek little black one. Both were howling at the tops of their lungs. Both were showing fangs. Both were ready to take on the canine enemy—who stopped, partly from the sudden pain, partly from seeing three cats where he'd thought there was only one.

And away, voices. "You looking for a cat? There's a real cat fight back there!"

"Cats? Just listen, there they are."

And coming, through a gate, between two houses, down the alley—people.

The dog howled in frustration and ran.

Lizavetta's two defenders didn't.

But the policeman who had come running through a gate took charge. "Stay back." He spoke quickly into the cell phone. "Don't make her run again. That's the one."

As the policeman organized the people, who were squabbling about who had found the cat—and deserved the reward—the two young cats in front of Lizavetta relaxed a little as no one came closer. Until another policeman pushed through the crowd—with Faithful Companion.

FC knelt. "Lizavetta."

With her usual regal dignity, Lizavetta paced toward FC, her new courtiers flanking her.

"Hello," said FC, holding out her hand for the half-grown cats to sniff.

One of the policemen said, "Don't," but she ignored him. Both of the younger cats sniffed her hand, then stepped back, as though acknowledging that she had failed them once, but she'd learned better and could take back her responsibility.

"Those two may have saved your cat's life," one policeman informed her. "There was a dog here, big bruiser, looked like he wanted your cat for lunch."

"I can reward you policemen—"

"Can't take it," the older cop stated bluntly.

"Surely you have a fund for widows and orphans, or to help those injured in the line of duty." FC gave them her best smile. "And I can arrange at least something for those who helped in the search." For the first time she realized that her hands were empty except for Lizavetta. "My purse."

"Uh-oh," said one of the policemen.

"Long gone, if you dropped it back there," the other agreed.

FC shrugged. She wasn't foolish enough to bring anything but a little mad money on a walk. "But what about these two cats? How can I reward them?"

"Street cats. Won't come with you."

But they were sitting, watching.

"Perhaps—" She reached into a pocket, got the treat she always rewarded Lizavetta with after the walk. Clumsily she broke it in half and extended the pieces to the two cats.

Gravely they accepted the offering.

"Come, kitty, kitty," she said as soon as they'd eaten.

The two cats followed, occasionally stropping her legs, as she walked back with Lizavetta.

But they stopped well outside the canopied doorway where Faithful Companion talked with the doorman, and in only a couple of minutes, an aproned man wearing a hairnet came running up carrying a chunk of fresh, raw salmon.

She divided it between the two young cats and they ate eagerly, then, before she could stop them, ran off.

"Do you think they'll come back later?" she asked the doorman.

He grinned. "Probably. Especially if they smell the fish again."

She smiled back. "Then they will. Even after we're gone, I'll arrange something."

Lizavetta was content. She was back with her people. And the younglings who had saved her were being rewarded.

Though she did wish they could see FC preparing her for the new show. She was sure she'd win yet again.

The man in the basement apartment wasn't old, but he liked his little luxuries, like the fine music that was playing on his state-of-the-art audio system. He was in a Mozart mood, and was humming along with it when the cat door flapped open and two of his favorite pupils came prancing in.

"Well, Ollie. Well, Artie. What do you have for us today?" he asked.

Ollie, a.k.a. Oliver T., black and sleek, dropped a woman's purse at the man's feet and waited expectantly.

The man was quick with the usual dried reward.

Patchy Artie, a.k.a. the Artful D., was having a bit of trouble with his offering: it kept tangling in his feet.

"Artie, my boy, what have you here?" The man took the mangled whatever and looked at it—and pursed his lips in a silent whistle. Those jewels looked real.

"Artie—" He went to the fridge, got the chopped chicken livers, and quickly warmed some in the microwave. He split the plateful in two, putting them down in front of the two young cats, who dove in gleefully, just as though they hadn't split a chunk of salmon a couple of hours ago.

"Good boys," the man was saying. "Good boys!"

Artie looked up, grinning all over his patchwork face, then dived back to business.

Life is good. And the important thing is food!

Rescuing the queen and foiling the two men had been fun, and delicious. Perhaps they could do it again tomorrow.

Author's Note

The Chartreux breed of cat, highly prized but rare, is mute. Some can purr softly, but no howls or meows. At most a little chirp is reported.

Rachel and the Bookstore Cat

JON L. BREEN

ONE EVENING IN VERMILION'S Bookshop, Rachel Hennings was eating pizza with Stu Wellman, book columnist of the Los Angeles *News-Canvass*, and trying desperately to change the subject. In recent months, Stu had become more and more worried about the safety of the L.A. streets and was spending an inordinate amount of time and energy trying to convince Rachel to move her business to a safer neighborhood. Tonight he was in full cry, crime statistics at his fingertips, police sirens unwittingly abetting him with dramatic background noise. Rachel, of course, knew she could never move Vermilion's, the home of so many literary traditions and authorial ghosts. Besides, she felt safe there.

To get him off this tiresome hobbyhorse, Rachel mentioned offhandedly that she was thinking of getting an animal for the store, a sort of combination companion and mascot.

"Get a dog," said Stu instantly. "The bigger and louder barking and more vicious-looking the better."

"I don't need a watchdog. And I certainly don't want an animal that will scare off business. I was thinking of one of those Vietnamese potbelly pigs. They're intelligent. They like people. They wag their tails like dogs."

"I thought they were out of fashion now," Stu grumbled.

Rachel waved a hand at the ranges of shelves. "So are most of these authors. That's why I love them. But maybe a bookstore animal shouldn't be quite that energetic. Maybe an iguana would be better."

"An iguana? You're kidding."

"No, really, they're very placid and pleasant animals. They just sit there munching their lettuce leaves and waiting for you to stroke them."

"Maybe so, but they look like prehistoric monsters. Some people would find them at least as scary as a pit bull."

Rachel thought about that. "What then? I think a mynah bird would be too messy . . ."

"Why such exotic ideas? If you have to have an animal, why not get a cat? Aren't bookstore cats sort of traditional?"

Rachel smiled and shook her head. "No, not a cat. Anything but a cat."

"You don't like cats?"

"Sure, I do, but I made a vow some time ago I would never have a bookstore cat. Didn't I ever tell you about that?"

She knew she hadn't. Before Stu could reply with the latest commercial burglary rate, she hurried into her story.

Rachel had been in Washington, D.C., on a combination vacation and business trip. A former Vermilion's customer who had taken a job as speechwriter in the current administration wanted to sell off some of his modern first editions, which included most of the works of Saul Bellow, Norman Mailer, and John Updike. It was a collection valuable enough to justify a flying visit to appraise the books and make an offer. While in Washington, she stayed in Georgetown with a couple of friends in the rare-book trade. Gus and Emma Ordway operated Ordway's Bookshop, located on D Street, an easy walk from the Capitol and the Congressional office buildings. They could boast any number of legislators, political staff members, and lobbyists among their customers.

Gus was a tall, lean, bearded man of about fifty, an occasionally published poet who dressed with the drab casualness of a fifties beatnik. Emma, who had been a classmate of Rachel's at Arizona State, was not quite thirty, lacked any literary talent or aspiration, and invariably dressed like a *Vogue* model. Despite their odd-couple appearance and the difference in their ages, the Ordways had in common a love of books and literature, and their marriage seemed a singularly happy one. They had become a fixture at art gallery openings and bookish events in the Washington area, he dressed in garb that suggested proud homelessness, she in gowns fit for an inaugural ball. They had a sense of humor about it: at one Malice Domestic mystery convention in Bethesda, he had shown up in white tie and tails with a Lord Peter Wimsey monocle, she in torn jeans and an

Elmore Leonard T-shirt. Once they got their laugh, though, the reversal was never repeated.

For all their seemingly idyllic relationship, Emma and Gus had one strong point of disagreement: cats. Gus loved them. Emma hated them. She wasn't allergic, but she was uncharmed by their standoffish personalities and felt loose cat hair put a crimp in her fashion statement. It was a measure of her love for Gus that she managed to tolerate the fat feline named Oswald who was allowed the run of Ordway's. Emma vowed that once the elderly Oswald went to his reward no other cat would browse among their stacks. It was only fair to give Oswald a special dispensation, she realized, since his tenure at Ordway's antedated hers, she having joined the staff only a few months before she married the boss.

Then, too, Oswald was beloved of the Ordways' customers, and Emma, who had a better business head than Gus, knew the cat had sometimes attracted lucrative commerce. That helped her maintain her tolerance, but she still referred to Oswald as the Capitol Rotundo in reference to his girth. Gus, of course, claimed the cat's corpulence was exaggerated, being an illusion created by his lush gray and white coat.

One compromise Emma demanded and Gus agreed to: Oswald never set foot in the couple's Georgetown home. He spent his nights in the store. One morning during her visit, Rachel inquired over breakfast whether that wasn't somewhat risky.

Gus shook his head. "Not a bit. There's plenty of room for him to roam around in, nothing fragile for him to knock over, and his toilet habits are immaculate. We've got the best commercial security system available, so he's safe from catnappers."

"Who'd want him?" Emma said. She glanced at her watch. "Have to open on time today. Congressman Petrie's coming by to pick up that Dortwiler book."

"Amos Cosgrove called yesterday and asked me about that."

"He's too late. The congressman's first in line."

"That'll really frost Cosgrove. Those guys hate each other."

"Rival collectors?" Rachel asked.

"Well, that, too, but they have other reasons. Amos used to be CIA and Petrie is on the House Intelligence Committee. They had a heated exchange in a hearing once over some blown operation or other and ever since they've been don't-invite-'ems. I can't imagine their altercation could have hurt either of them too much. Petrie's still a rising star in the party, and Amos seems to have nothing but time and money on his hands, but those guys would do anything to best each other or embarrass each other or inconvenience each other. In a more civilized time, they might have settled their differences on the duelling ground."

After a thoughtful pause, Gus asked Emma, "What are we charging the congressman for the Dortwiler book?"

"Fifteen hundred."

"A steal. Ask for bids and I'll bet Amos would pay two thousand or more. Set them against each other and there's no telling how high we could run up the price." Gus leered greedily.

"Gus, you know we don't do business that way. We really don't, Rachel, he's just being silly. Besides, Cosgrove talks a good game, but the congressman's a steady customer."

Her buying activities concluded, Rachel was now playing full-time tourist. She intended to continue her walking tour of the capital: yesterday, the White House; today, the Library of Congress; tomorrow, the Smithsonian. Emma would give her a ride as far as Ordway's and she would continue on foot from there.

As Emma aggressively navigated the Washington streets, Rachel said, "I'm ashamed to ask, but who is this Dortwiler? You're getting fifteen hundred for one of his first editions and I've never heard of him."

"Join the club. I'd never heard of him either until Jim Petrie asked us to search for his books. Gus claimed he had, but I think he was snowing me. Gus has to give the illusion he knows everything. Once he spent all evening ridiculing me for not knowing the contribution to American politics of Senator Claghorn, and it turned out he was a character on some radio show." Cutting in front of a limo with diplomatic plates, Emma went on, "Let's see now. Rudolph Dortwiler was a political theorist who held a minor post in the Lincoln and Andrew Johnson administrations. His books apparently had some influence on later politicians, but they were issued in very small editions, and today they're scarce, to say the least. This one's called *Lectures on the Essentials of Political Economy*, published in 1872, and the contents look even more boring than the title. But the book's a hot item to these two guys. Amos Cosgrove wants it for his Lincoln collection."

"A completist, is he?"

"You could say that. He's got things with a lot remoter Lincoln associations than this Dortwiler book. Not that he ever buys anything from us. He just comes in a couple times a week to talk big to Gus about what a great collection he has. He and Gus are old friends."

"How do they happen to know each other?"

"I'm not sure," Emma said, adding with an amused smirk, "I think Gus may have been a spook in an earlier life. I don't much like Cosgrove, but we have one thing to bring us together."

"What's that?"

"He hates cats, too. I can't say I like Congressman Petrie much either, but at least he's done several thousand dollars worth of business with us over the last few years. We've helped him build his Dortwiler collection, and this is the one item he lacks."

Emma pulled her BMW to a screeching stop behind the shop. She unlocked the back door into the stockroom, setting off a loud alarm. Opening a panel inside, just next to the door, she entered a code to disarm the security system.

"If I don't do that in thirty seconds, the D.C. police *and* the security firm are here on the run."

Rachel nodded. "So you've told me every morning." The Ordways really loved this security system.

"Absolutely foolproof," Emma said. "With this in place, you can relax. And you have to have some extra protection in Washington. Or any big city nowadays. I guess you have the same thing in L.A., huh?"

Rachel shook her head. "No, I never felt the need. Of course, I live above the store, so . . ."

"Rachel, that's all the more reason," Emma said, opening the door from the stockroom into the store proper. "You should look into—"

As Emma opened the door, she broke off, and furrowed her brow. Unlike the other mornings Rachel had come to the store with Emma, Oswald did not appear at once with a meowed greeting. Emma had ignored him those other times, but Rachel had kneeled down to stroke him and inquire about his night's rest. This time, Oswald was nowhere to be seen.

Emma walked a few steps into the store, sniffing the air. Rachel sniffed, too, but her nose didn't detect anything but the pleasant mustiness of old books. Emma obviously smelled something else. She flicked a light switch and marched purposefully to the front of the store. Rachel followed her, and by the time they reached the counter, the unpleasant stench was obvious to her, too.

"I'll kill that cat!" Emma shrieked. "I'll kill him!"

"What happened?" Rachel asked, then saw the source of the odor: a soggy-looking old book sitting on the counter in a puddle of liquid.

"He peed all over the Dortwiler. It's ruined."

At that instant, Rachel heard a noise behind her, and she watched the bulky form of Oswald scoot across the floor from under a table of cookbooks to the shadows of the military history shelves. The usually placid cat was certainly agitated, whether out of guilt or for some other reason.

"Well, you should hide, you . . . you . . ." Emma was quivering with rage, too angry to think of an appropriate insult.

There was an almost apologetic tapping on the front door of the shop. Emma walked to the door, turned the OPEN sign outward, and let in the first customer of the morning, while Rachel helpfully switched on the rest of the lights.

The customer was a tall, elegantly dressed man in his forties with the vapid good looks of a Ken doll. Had to be a politician. Rachel wasn't surprised to learn he was Congressman Jim Petrie, Democrat of Illinois.

"I—I don't know how to say this," Emma said, almost tearfully. "The book's ruined. It was sitting here on the counter and I guess Oswald . . ."

"Do you know how long I looked for that book?" Petrie exploded. Rachel was surprised his face was capable of that much animation.

"I know, I know," Emma said. "We'll just have to find another one, I guess. I'm devastated."

"*You're* devastated?" the congressman snapped back.

"If you want it for the text, it will probably dry out reasonably well, and of course we would adjust the price . . ."

"Forget it! I don't want it for the text." Petrie threw her a withering look, as if the idea of wanting a book for its contents was alien or even obscene. "Don't you understand collectors at all?"

Before the flustered Emma could say any more, the door swung open and a second customer entered the store. He was a short and stubby man with an amiable smile offset by the coldest eyes Rachel had ever seen. He looked at Petrie somewhat sardonically. Assessing the animosity level in Petrie's return look, Rachel figured this must be Amos Cosgrove.

"Something wrong, congressman?" he said. "Oh, Emma, I won't be needing that Dortwiler book after all. Picked up another copy over in Arlington. A real nice find. Even though they doubled the price on me."

"You found one?" Petrie said, his curiosity overcoming all other emotions for an instant. "For how much?"

Cosgrove shook his head in mock dismay. "You won't believe this. The Salvation Army store now sells hardcovers for two bucks instead of one. But in this case, I decided I'd pay it."

The congressman stormed out of the store, and Rachel wondered how long it would take him to reestablish his bland political face.

Emma introduced Cosgrove to Rachel, then said sarcastically, "That was a big help, Amos. You know we weren't going to sell you that book. Jim Petrie's mad enough already, and now he'll think we're offering you books we found for him."

"No, he won't," Cosgrove said unconcernedly.

"Did you really find a copy of the Dortwiler at a Salvation Army store?" Rachel asked.

"No, I was just having a little fun with my pal the congressman." He added, as if in explanation, "Jim and I go back a long way."

"Well, now *I* can offer you a copy for two dollars," Emma said. "That's about what it's worth after the Capitol Rotundo got through with it." She gestured at the counter.

Amos Cosgrove seemed to find it all very funny, but his laughter seemed forced to Rachel.

"No, thanks," he said. "Fine condition only."

Amos Cosgrove browsed through a few shelves in desultory fashion while quizzing Rachel about her own business, but within a few minutes he was out the door.

"Emma," Rachel said, "is there anything I can do to help out?"

Emma shook her head. "No, thanks, there's nothing. The damage is done. We're out a two-thousand-dollar sale."

"If the book's that rare, you'd think one of them would buy it, even if it's, ah, slightly damaged."

"I don't think so," Emma said. "Not after that little scene this morning. Neither would give the other the satisfaction of knowing he bought a book soaked in cat piss."

"Well, if there's nothing else I can do, I'll just go about my sight-seeing and see you tonight. I don't know how long I'll be, so I'll get a cab back to Georgetown. I may look at some other bookshops while I'm at it. Do you have a local directory of them?"

That evening Rachel returned from her capital explorations to witness an embarrassingly loud domestic argument between the Ordways.

"If it weren't for that damned cat of yours—"

"Who says it was Oswald? You didn't see him do it."

"I left the store secure last night, and it was secure when I opened up this morning. Who else was in the store to deposit cat piss on that book, Gus?"

"Oh, yeah, and who says it was cat piss? Did you get a lab analysis of it?"

"I don't think the mice or the cockroaches hold that much, do you?"

Rachel said, "I wonder if I could offer something. I don't want to take sides or anything, but I've been thinking."

Both of them looked at her, their natural courtesy to a guest warring with exasperation.

Gus said, "I should apologize, Rachel, for subjecting you to this—this discussion."

"Don't worry about that. I think I know what might have happened. Emma, didn't this morning seem a little too neat and convenient to you?"

"What do you mean?" Emma said, a note of impatience in her voice.

"Amos Cosgrove just happens to drop in to witness the congressman's dismay. Doesn't that seem like too much of a coincidence?"

"I don't know. They're both in the shop quite a bit."

"At the same time?"

"No, but—"

"Amos almost always comes in in the afternoon," Gus said thoughtfully. "It's very unusual for him to turn up in the morning, and I think if he saw Petrie there, he'd turn around and walk the other way."

Emma nodded grudgingly. "Okay, you're right. So what?"

Rachel went on, "I understand Oswald had no history of dirty tricks in the store at night. Am I right about that?"

"Absolutely," Gus replied.

"Up to last night," Emma said.

"Doesn't it seem a little too good—or, I guess, bad—to be true that when he finally turned incontinent he just happened to jump up on the counter and pee on the most valuable item in the store?"

"Couldn't happen!" Gus agreed.

"It could and it did," Emma said. "It's just the kind of thing I'd expect from him. He was just waiting for his chance."

"You're irrational!" Gus snapped. "You have a blind spot about cats."

"Can I say one more thing?" Rachel said. "This whole thing has all the earmarks of a setup. Cosgrove hates Petrie. Enough so he will destroy something Petrie wants. But Cosgrove wanted that book himself, didn't he? I mean he's a serious collector, right? He didn't just want that Dortwiler book because Petrie wanted it too?"

"No, he's a real collector all right," Gus said. They both looked at Emma, who nodded in irritable stipulation.

"So I figured Cosgrove might have been the one to destroy the book, framing Oswald. But he wouldn't do that as long as there was some possibility of getting the book for himself. Unless—" She broke off and looked at her hosts expectantly.

"Unless he found another copy," Gus said.

"And he did!" Rachel pronounced.

"Rachel," Emma said, "that story about getting a Dortwiler at the Salvation Army store was just something he made up to torment Petrie. He admitted it himself."

"Right. He didn't get a copy at the Salvation Army store, but that doesn't mean he didn't get a copy somewhere else. This afternoon I put off my visit to the Library of Congress and checked out a few of the city's rare-book dealers. I enquired about the Dortwiler book to see if any of them had sold one recently. If I hadn't found one, I was going to try some of my other contacts in the trade to see if one could have been sold by mail order or at auction in the past few days. But I didn't have to go that far. There was a copy of Dortwiler's *Lectures on the Essentials of Political Economy* sold in Washington, D.C., yesterday, and by a little mild subterfuge I was able to get the dealer to confirm Cosgrove was the buyer. He has his copy. He doesn't need yours, so he decided to make sure Petrie doesn't get it either."

"A dog in the manager," Gus said, flashing a look at his wife that said, *They don't blame that on cats.*

"He got into the store somehow. How he did it with your security system is the one thing I can't figure out. If he stole the book or mutilated it in some way, you'd know someone had broken into the store. But if he poured urine all over it, he would implicate Oswald, and there would be no reason to look for a burglar. You told me, Emma, he hates cats as much as you do, so the idea of putting the blame for his crime on Oswald would appeal to him. It may or may not have been cat urine. I like to think it was from his own personal supply."

"Can you prove this?" Gus asked.

"Of course not," Rachel said with a laugh. "But you have to admit it fits the circumstances. It explains Cosgrove just happening to turn up in the store the morning after he got a copy of the book in question. It explains that Oswald's inexplicable behavior never happened."

"Gus and Emma finally agreed my theory must have been the true one," Rachel told Stu, as she reached for the next to last slice of pizza. "They confronted Amos Cosgrove with it, and he immediately confessed, laughing all the time. He thought it was a great practical joke, though Emma and Gus never did see the humor of it even after he paid them for their loss on the sale to Petrie. Oswald was vindicated and still roams the shelves at Ordway's, and they all lived reasonably happily ever after. But since going through all that, somehow the idea of a bookstore cat has never appealed to me."

Stu said, "Great story, but there's a loose end."

"Oh, is there?"

"Of course there is. How did he get in the store past that vaunted security system? You saw Emma disarm it before you went in that morning. She was sure she'd secured the store the night before. She would have had a code presumably only Gus would have known." After a moment's pause, Stu said, "Don't tell me Gus was in on it with Cosgrove."

Rachel shook her head. "No chance."

"I suppose the fact Cosgrove used to be with the CIA suggests he could have known something about security systems, but still—"

Rachel said placidly, "Gus and Emma cleared that up. As I fretted on about how Cosgrove could have gotten in, I saw them looking at each other, not mad any more but like people sharing a secret. Gus gave this embarrassed smirk and said to Emma, 'You want to tell her or shall I?' "

"Tell you what?"

"Cosgrove sold them the security system."

Rags the Mighty

WILL MURRAY

PRIVATE INVESTIGATOR BILL BRUNT was patiently listening to the woman's story when a familiar red Jeep Cherokee pulled up to the curb outside his office window.

"If my husband is seeing that tramp, I want to know," the woman was saying crisply. "Don't spare my feelings."

"Just a minute," Brunt said. Turning in his swivel chair, he slapped the cube refrigerator beside the office PC. It promptly stopped emitting an inappropriate snoring sound.

The woman went on: "When can you start?"

"Once I get rid of a pest," Brunt growled.

"Pest?"

The outer door opened and closed, and a moment later a drop-dead gorgeous woman with classic Italian features and bouncy copper hair barged in.

"Where is he?" she demanded in a smoky voice.

Bill Brunt assumed an innocent expression. "Who?"

"My cat."

"You mean *my* cat," Brunt corrected, "and I haven't seen him in days."

"He wasn't sprawled in your tiger-lily patch, so I figured—"

"Be my guest. Look around. No cat here," said Brunt.

While the redhead scanned the office with deep brown eyes, Brunt leaned back in his chair and addressed his client.

"You'll have to excuse my friend. She's kinda oblivious."

"I'm Gina," the redhead said absently. Her eyes fell on Brunt's client. They narrowed. "You have this recurring dream of a hunky man in a white tropical suit—"

The woman started half out of her chair. "What?"

"Stop right there!" Brunt said, lifting a hammy hand.

"—I see him wearing a matching white eye patch."

"What *is* this? I never said anything—"

"Don't listen to her," Brunt said excitedly. "She's a nut. She thinks she's psychic."

"I *am* psychic, you dunce!" Gina flared. Addressing the woman, she continued, "The man in white has been haunting your dreams for years. He's not real, you know. But if you look, you'll find him in the library. Try the magazine section."

The woman gave a bleat of terror. "I never told anyone about those dreams. Not even my husband!" She backed out of the room like it was on fire. There was no stopping her.

Face red, Brunt closed the door after her and turned.

"You," he growled, "just chased two thousand dollars' worth of business out of my office."

"Where are you hiding poor Rags?" demanded Gina.

"You're supposed to be psychic," said Brunt, blocking the refrigerator and inviting her to look elsewhere with a broad sweep of his hand. "*You* find him."

Gina eyed him mischievously. She pretended to scour the office with her narrowing eyes. A slow, knowing smile came over her classic features. "You're right," she said. "Guess he ran away again. It's hot. What have you got to drink?"

"Nothing. Refrigerator's conked out."

The refrigerator selected that moment to give out a long, unmechanical snore. Brunt pretended to cough into his hand. Gina reached past him and yanked open the door.

Inside, curled in a ball of gray and white fur, was a remarkable cat. Apparently some kind of Siamese–Persian–Maine Coon mix, his wide gray face, framed by muttonchop cheek tufts, was splashed with a lopsided milk mustache, making him resemble an old English gentleman of Charles Dickens's time.

"Rags!" Gina cried.

Rags opened his pale golden eyes and wagged his bushy tail vigorously. Otherwise, he declined to stir from cool comfort.

Reaching in, Gina lifted him out. Rags came supinely, all thirty pounds of him. His disordered fur explained his name.

"I," Gina announced, "am reclaiming my cat."

"He's *my* cat," Brunt insisted.

"He was my cat before he was your cat."

"That's never been proved. What do you need him for?"

"A séance. I need protection from lower entities."

"You are *not* dragging Rags into any fool séance."

"I'll bring him back. I promise."

"You never do. . . ."

Brunt barred the door with his huge frame. Gina stood there holding Rags limp and apparently pleased with being fussed over, if his desultory tail action was any indicator.

Gina turned contrite. "It's a lost child problem. I really, really need Rags. His name's Billy. Wasn't that your name when you were small?"

Brunt's shoulders caved. Relenting, he growled, "Have him back by midnight. And don't forget his milk."

"Deal." Gina slung Rags over her shoulder like a baby in need of a burping. "Thanks. *Ciao.*"

Brunt watched Gina Sconderella leave, mentally damning the day he had gotten involved with the woman. A hard-headed private detective who believed in a concrete world, Bill Brunt had no use for self-proclaimed psychics and their tricks.

Brunt was watching an Amazing Randi special when his door-bell rang that evening. The home-security system showed the butch face of Rags peer blandly into the closed-circuit camera.

Bill hit the buzzer. "Drop the furball and be on your way."

"Let us in," Gina pleaded. "Pretty please. I have a business proposition for you," she added in a wheedling tone.

"Every time I listen to one of your schemes, I regret it."

"Not this time. Your cut will be a cool two grand."

Brunt hesitated. Two grand was two grand. Reluctantly, he let her in.

"Remember the missing boy?" asked Gina, handing over a seemingly lifeless Rags. "Crat told me where he is."

"Who the hell is Crat?" said Brunt, dropping Rags to the floor, where he proceeded to roll and roll as if intoxicated with his own roly-polyness.

"Crat is a spirit I contacted through the Ouija board."

Brunt rolled his eyes. "Crat, no less. . . ."

"He's given me solid information before."

Eyeing Rags, Brunt demanded: "Did you slip him catnip?"

"I always reward Rags for protecting me from bad spirits. Now listen, this is important: A three-year-old boy disappeared two days ago. No trace. His mother is a client. She offered me six grand if I find Billy alive before the police do."

Brunt looked interested. If was difficult to tell whether it was money or sympathy that moved him.

"I'm sensing he's alive," Gina went on, "but scared. Which Crat confirmed. I asked where, and it spelled out Gulf West."

"Gulf West?"

"Technically, Gulp West. Spirits can't spell very well. I'm sure it means the Gulf gas station out on the West highway. All we have to do is find him."

"Why do you need me?"

Gina wavered. Her red mouth formed a girlish pout. "Because it's dark, and I'm scared," she admitted.

"You think you're conversing with evil spirits, but you're afraid of the *dark?*"

"Where do you think they hang out? Two grand to back me up."

"Make it three and I'm in," countered Brunt.

Gina beamed. "Great. Grab Rags and let's go."

Brunt shook his square head. "We don't need him."

"You don't know that," Gina said, scooping up Rags in mid-roll. He went without complaint, marshmallow paws adangle.

Rags was snoring boisterously in the back seat of Bill Brunt's bronze Taurus sedan when the illuminated Gulf sign came into view. He pulled off into a weed-choked rest area. He and Gina got out.

"The family stopped to use the rest room at the Gulf station driving back from vacation," Gina was saying as she tested her flashlight. "When they got home, they realized little Billy was missing."

Brunt looked around. "Where are the cops?"

"They combed the area, found nothing, then declared it a kidnapping. Hah! It's a kidnapping like you're a Scorpio."

"Is that an insult?"

"You are *such* a Taurus. Come on, let's see what Crat says."

Gina slipped a wooden Ouija board from a leather valise and set it on the vehicle's hood. Handing Brunt her flash, she pulled Rags out of the back seat in snuffling mid-snore.

As Brunt watched with various dubious expressions crawling over his square face, Gina set Rags before the board and placed a tripodal planchette on it. Rags pushed at it with dim interest.

"Okay, Rags, do your brave duty." She placed one huge white paw on the planchette. To Brunt's astonishment, the cat obediently left it there.

Making a furtive sign of the cross, Gina called out, "Crat, are you with us?"

Brunt watched with skeptical blue eyes. The planchette started moving, Rags's fat paw riding along. The cat shifted with each change of direction. The pointer stopped at the word *yes.*

"Where is Billy, Crat? Please tell us."

The planchette circled the board with eerie smoothness. Gina called out the letter *W*.

"Rags, are you doing that?" Brunt demanded of the cat.

Rags regarded him over his gray shoulder with a stricken, almost helpless expression. The planchette reversed direction, this time coming to rest on *E*. Then it shifted to *L*.

"Keep going," Gina prompted. But the pointer remained on *L*.

"What have you been teaching that cat?" Brunt roared.

"Nothing. Rags gives Crat the energy he needs to move the planchette. I'd do it but my subconscious gets in the way. Rags doesn't have a noticeable subconscious."

"You have absolutely ruined that poor cat!"

Gina fingered her dimpled chin. " 'WEL.' What can *that* mean?"

Brunt said, "You said spirits can't spell, right? Maybe it means *well*. As in well water?"

Gina addressed the board. "Crat, is Billy in a well?"

With Rags's paw still riding it, the planchette moved to *yes*.

"Got a wire coathanger for opening locked cars?" Gina asked.

Brunt popped the trunk. "Of course. I'm a licensed P.I."

Gina took the hanger, bent it into an *L*, and pointed it in the direction of the weeds.

"What *now?*" Brunt growled.

"I'm dowsing, so hush."

Brunt leaned against the car and shared a perplexed glance with Rags, who had released the planchette. It seemed to creep along of its own power, then stopped dead.

"You and I," he whispered, "are going to have a whisker-to-whisker talk."

The wire began twitching and shifting. Gina started into the woods. Playing the light before him, Brunt followed. Rags trotted after them, as eager as a fluffy puppy.

The trio followed a thin path through weeds, but the twitching rod led them off it after a hundred yards. "You lead," Gina directed.

Brunt got in front. The flash ray swirled around, chasing shadows and making them crawl and squirm like furtive fleeing things.

"Slow down!" Gina hissed. "I'm getting water."

Brunt turned. The rod in Gina's hand was switching back and forth as if alive. "You're doing that," he accused.

"I am not! Go left."

Grumbling, Brunt obeyed. And promptly tripped over his own feet.

Gina snapped, "You big oaf!"

"Found it!" Brunt said. His voice echoed oddly.

"What? Let me see." Snatching the flash from Brunt's hand, Gina dropped to one knee, and began pulling up weeds.

It was a cistern. Edged in broken shale, it was half obscured by weeds. Gina poured light into the well. A flash reflection of oily water gleamed. And down below was a huddled shape.

"I think that's him. . . ." Gina whispered excitedly.

"Billy!" Brunt yelled. At the sudden bellow, Gina and Rags both jumped half out of their skins.

"Hello. . . ." The voice was weak, childish.

"That's him," Gina hissed. "He's alive!" She called down: "Help is here, Billy."

Brunt found his feet. "I'll get fire rescue."

Gina got in his way, face defiant. "Not on your life! That poor boy's been down there two whole days. We're getting him out—*now.*"

Brunt squared his chin. "You're only thinking of the reward."

"Don't you dare ruin my chance to be on *Oprah.* You keep a rope in your trunk. Go fetch it."

"I don't think it's long enough."

Gina gave him an impatient shove. "Go and find out, you uncaring lout."

Brunt came back lugging a coil of white nylon rope. As he began paying it out, he warned, "He may not have the strength to hold on."

It turned out not to matter. The rope was short by two feet. It hung over the boy's head, jerking in useless animation.

Brunt called down: "Can you stand up, Billy?"

"I *am* standing up."

"Damn," said Gina. "He's only three."

At that point, Rags ambled up and peered into the well. He gave a tremendous yawn.

"Too bad Rags isn't smart enough to climb down and get him," Gina murmured.

"Maybe he is," said Brunt. He reclaimed the rope, made a loop, and tied it under Rags's thick armpits. "Rags, you happy ape, this is your golden opportunity to be a hero."

"Are you crazy?" Gina said.

"No more than you," Brunt muttered, dropping to his stomach.

Gina shrugged. "Hang on, Billy. We're sending down a friend."

Rags went into the hole reluctantly. His paw pads kept slipping and scraping on the rim. He was understandably not much interested in a nighttime descent into a dark hole.

Gina sneaked a hand under his chin and scratched vigorously. Rags shut his eyes. That was distraction enough. Down he went.

"It's okay, Ragsdale," said Gina, as she guided Brunt with her light. Both were on their stomachs now.

"That's as far as the rope goes," said Brunt at last.

Gina yelled down: "Can you reach Rags's feet, Billy?"

"I think so. . . ."

"Okay, grab one foot in each hand. Hold on and don't let go."

"I got him!" Billy called up.

Rags seconded that with a low, weird growl.

"Pull!" Gina hissed.

Brunt brought the line in hand over hand, just fast enough, he hoped, not to jerk the exhausted boy loose.

He hoped wrong. Venting a terrific snarl, Rags went into convulsions. Billy let go. He fell a short distance. Water splashed sullenly. A puff of gray fur flew up like a stray spark.

"You pulled too fast," Gina scolded.

"If I pulled too slow," Brunt returned, "the kid wouldn't have the strength to hold on. Never mind Rags's patience. He's the strongest cat I ever saw, but he's no Hercules."

"There's *got* to be a way." Gina snapped her fingers. From her purse, she pulled out a pepper shaker.

Brunt had pulled Rags out. He kept stretch-shaking his rear legs by turns. He was not happy.

This changed as soon as Gina sprinkled him with the contents of the shaker, rubbing greenish flakes about his lopsided mustache.

"Pure organically-grown catnip," she said proudly. "Now hurry while he's too whacky to care."

Rechecking the knot, Brunt lowered Rags once more. This time he went happily. His dangling legs came to rest just short of Billy's clutching hands. Billy stretched, took hold of Rags's feet, saying "Okay." Brunt hauled rope in smooth, even pulls.

When Rags reemerged, front legs splayed outward, his ears were folded so flat they had virtually disappeared. Glowing a demonic green in the moonlight, his eyes were scrunched and mean over bristling whiskers. His growling promised impending violence.

Billy came into the light, small fists white and clutching gray and white back legs stretched to the tendon-breaking point. Gina rushed in, gathering him up. That left Brunt to deal with Rags.

Setting him on his feet, Brunt slipped the coil out from his chest and gave Rags a congratulatory pat. Rags returned the favor by uncorking a blinding one-pawed swipe that left a trio of pale track marks on his right temple, which promptly turned red.

Brunt recoiled. "*Ouch!* Damn!"

"Don't you hurt my cat!" Gina flared.

"He took a swipe at me!" Brunt retorted, holding his face.

"Can you blame him? Look what you put him through."

Brunt sputtered. "*Me?* You—I—"

Gina shielded the boy. "Not in front of little Billy."

Brunt swallowed his rage. "This," he said evenly, "is the last time I fall for one of your idiotic get-rich-quick schemes."

"Fine. When the media shows up, let me handle the talking, okay? I don't want you to embarrass us."

Brunt had composed himself by the time the police and paramedics had arrived. A lone print reporter pulled up.

"I'm Gina Sconderella," Gina was saying. "Here's my card. I'm a psychic. I saved that little boy. His mother hired me."

The reporter addressed Brunt. "Is that true, Brunt?"

"Actually, the cat saved the boy."

"Rags only helped," Gina inserted. "But I'm the one who—"

"She claimed a spirit named Crat told her where to find him," Brunt continued, bland of face and tone. "But that was the cat, too. She's nuts. Thinks she's going to be rich and famous."

"Don't listen to that dumb side of beef," said Gina tartly. "He's only my bodyguard."

"What's your role in this?" the reporter asked Brunt.

"It's my cat, and my idea to lower the cat into the well."

"Which you wouldn't have thought of without my psychic powers!" Gina shrieked. She wore an expression of such feline fury that Rags slunk under the ambulance where the boy was being examined.

"I don't believe in psychics," Brunt told everyone. "Never have; never will."

With that, he gathered up Rags and drove off. A torrent of incoherent Italian invective followed him.

The next day, Brunt was squirting Cool Whip into Rags's open mouth when his would-be client of the day before called.

"That woman, Gina? The psychic? How can I reach her?"

"Why would you even want to?" wondered Brunt.

"I took her advice. I looked for the man with the white eye patch in the library. I found him in an old magazine."

"Say again?"

"He was a model in an old shirt ad I must have seen when I was a girl, and completely forgotten." She laughed self-consciously. "My subconscious just dredged him up in my dreams. I want to hire her."

Brunt frowned. "Coincidence, and that woman is no more psychic than my cat. Don't you read the papers?"

Brunt hung up and reread the front page headline of the morning *Globe*:

HERO CAT SAVES BOY FROM WELL
Local 'Psychic' Discredited

"The last laugh," Brunt told Rags, "is always the best laugh."

Rasputin's Hoard

JOE MURPHY

RASPUTIN LOOKED DOWN AT THE squirming little black and white bundles and licked between the spread toes of his forepaw in annoyance. Kittens indeed, what had Alexandra been thinking? Their eyes had been open for quite a while now; already they rolled and tumbled about, piling in the corners of the cardboard box as they tried to pull themselves over the sides. Soon nothing would hold them back and they'd be all over the house . . . his house.

Crouched next to him on the closet shelf was a long-haired female as white as he was black. Alexandra stared back at him, her blue eyes insolently refusing to blink. After a long moment she sniffed.

Rasputin knew that look. She didn't want him around right now. As if all this were *his* fault. Fine. He looked away, jumped off the shelf, and started for his water bowl in the feeding room.

Voices! Loud ones, and angry too. Rasputin ducked into a crouch and crept through a room cluttered with big, cozy chairs, and piled papers. The room smelled of age, and Catherine, their human, a comfortable layer of strange perfumes and tantalizing foods.

But Catherine didn't smell comfortable now; Rasputin knew fear when he found it. She stood at the door with another human who came around sometimes. Rasputin crawled beneath a table to watch.

"But I don't want to leave. This is my home." Catherine covered her face with her hands, shoulders quivering as she cried. She looked up at the taller man. "Once it was your home too, Nicholis."

"Mama, look at the place." Nicholis brushed back his bristly dark hair; he smelled of tuna and beer. "Papers all over the place, trash, broken chairs. And those damn cats, hair everywhere. You can't take care of yourself anymore. I've found you a place at Shady Courts."

"It's not trash, but memories." Catherine drew herself up. "Papa left it to me and it was all we had."

"But we can make a fortune if we sell now. Do you have any idea how much a four-bedroom house goes for this close to downtown?"

"It doesn't matter." Catherine turned away and folded her arms.

"You're forcing me into it, then." Nicholis shrugged. "You never read the will did you? Papa left the house to me, not you."

"That's a lie."

"Look for yourself." The man's voice took a self-righteous turn. "You'll see."

"I have it here. Let me find my glasses. I'll show you." Catherine lifted her hands and began rummaging among the cluttered cabinets and papers.

"I'll bet your glasses are still on the bedside table." Nicholis laughed. "You were always leaving them there when I was home."

"Well, it's not your home now." Catherine fled to the bedroom.

"We'll see about that." Nicholis moved, with what Rasputin considered admirable stealth, across the room to the old rolltop desk. He squatted down, opened a drawer, and took out some yellowed paper. From a coat pocket he produced some different sheets and put them back in the drawer. Rasputin didn't like the sound of his laugh.

He *did* like the sound the yellowed sheets made when the man crumpled them up into a ball and tossed it at the overfilled trash can. The Game! He and Catherine would play in front of the fireplace. She'd crumple a ball and toss it into one of the dark corners. Rasputin would give chase and bring it back. When they tired, Catherine would end the night dozing in her favorite chair with Rasputin on her lap.

Rasputin dashed after the paper. He caught it in midair and landed with his claws dug in.

"Hey!" Nicholis bent toward him.

He decided he didn't like Nicholis, never had, and never would. Most certainly Rasputin wouldn't play this good of a game with someone he didn't like. Biting down on the paper, he leapt away between the tables and lamps, threading the path to the far corner behind some old boxes to his hoard.

He kept all his paper balls here. He had lots. Soon though Alexandra's kittens would come nosing around. They would want some just because they were kittens; it wasn't fair. Rasputin peeked out. Good, Nicholis hadn't followed.

"I may not always be able to find my glasses." Catherine marched into the room and over to the desk. "But I can always find Papa's important papers." She opened the drawer and took out a sheaf of papers. "See here it is, right on top."

"And right down there," Nicholis pointed over Catherine's shoulder, "is the house."

"No. . . ." Catherine's shoulders slumped and she started to cry. "I can't believe it. I can't believe he would do that to me. I hardly looked at the deed. He was such a good man I never doubted his trust or his love . . . until now." The woman fell back in a nearby chair.

"I'll be over tomorrow to help you move, Mama." Nicholis patted her shoulder. "We should have you out by the end of the week."

That night the kittens learned how to escape their box. Rasputin didn't have a moment's peace from then on. They scampered in the halls, climbed in the corners, and even played in his food dish. He was beside himself. Alexandra was no help, she even thought it was funny, pouncing on them and batting at their tails.

Catherine didn't seem to care either. She sat in her chair, staring at the empty fireplace. When Rasputin jumped into her lap she stroked him once and broke into tears. He nuzzled her hand but then the kittens found them. For a moment Catherine stopped crying. She put Rasputin down on the rug.

"Little one," she cradled a kitten almost as black as Rasputin, "I'll never get to see you grow up." A black and white one with blue eyes pounced on his tail; Rasputin decided he'd had enough. He hid out with his hoard until Karla came to visit.

Like Catherine, Karla was an old woman. They sat in the big chairs by the fireplace while Catherine told her about Nicholis. The room smelled of hot tea and cinnamon. Kittens tottered in and out from under the chairs and, instead of petting Rasputin, Karla held Alexandra on her lap while they watched the kittens play.

"Papa said he could always talk to you." Catherine lifted her teacup in trembling fingers. "You were his favorite sister. Why would he do such a thing to me?"

"This doesn't sound right." Karla nodded. "It broke his heart when Nicholis went to jail. He blamed himself. Said he never spent enough time with the boy, too many extra shifts at the foundry."

"But there it was in black and white." Catherine's teacup clinked loudly against her saucer. "With my own eyes I saw it."

"Your eyes aren't what they used to be, you know." Karla smiled and gently put Alexandra on the rug. The kittens piled onto her immediately. "Come, show me the will."

Catherine rose and went to the desk, almost tripping when a kitten dashed between her feet. "Careful, little one." She took out some papers and brought them back to Karla.

"It's here all right." Karla shook her head. "I . . . I don't know what to say."

Catherine buried her face in her hands and began to cry. "All my memories, all my things. What will I do with them? Who will I talk to? I don't know anyone in Shady Courts."

"That place." Karla's voice sharpened. The kittens stopped their play and looked up at her. "I've seen it. I wouldn't send my worst enemy there. You should move in with me."

"That wouldn't be right." Catherine shook her head. "I couldn't take advantage of you."

"For the cats' sake." Karla rose and went over to Catherine. "And the kittens'." She put a hand on Catherine's shoulder. "Shady Courts doesn't allow pets you know."

"Let me think about it," Catherine said. "I have to do something, I guess. You're a good friend to me, Karla."

"And one who will put you to bed." Karla helped Catherine up. "You're tired, dear, and you've had a bad day. Come, I will help you get ready, and I'll ask Dimitri to help tomorrow with the packing."

"Ahh, Dimitri." Catherine started for the bedroom. "If only Nicholis could have been more like your son."

Rasputin couldn't sleep in his rightful spot. Alexandra climbed onto the bed and her brood managed to climb up after her. Instead, he followed Karla out into the hall and back to the big chairs.

"That ungrateful boy." Karla looked down at him. "I should give him such a slap." She picked up the will and stared at it. "Bah, some lawyer's trick or something. My brother would never hurt Catherine so." She started to crumple the papers, then stopped. "Something is wrong here, but I just can't put my finger on it."

Rasputin's ears pricked up. The crumpling sound—would Karla play with him? At least the kittens were asleep now. But the paper ball—Karla hadn't finished it. He could help. He raced for his hoard. The ball he'd stolen from that nasty old Nicholis was right where it should be. He strutted out, as proud of himself as if it were his first mouse.

"Rasputin? What have you got there?" Karla asked. He dropped it at her feet, then batted it across the carpet. The old woman picked it up. She started to toss it, but then halted, her head cocked to the side. "Where did you find this, kitty?"

Karla smoothed out the paper. She picked up the one on the desk and stared from one to the other. "This paper is all yellow while this one is quite new, actually." She began to laugh. "Rasputin, let me open a fresh carton of milk. I think you deserve it. And tomorrow I'm going hunting for a rat."

Rasputin lashed his tail and glared at the black and white kitten. Its wide blue eyes gazed back and it lifted a paw. Enough was enough; Rasputin hissed but the little beast arched its back, fluffed its tail, and danced sideways, challenging him.

"Now, Rasputin." Catherine picked him up and settled him in her lap. "Be a good father to the little ones. They'll need all the help they can get to grow up proper."

"And sometimes even that isn't enough," Karla said from her place by the window. "Ah, here he comes."

"You behave." Catherine stroked him one last time and placed him on the floor. The black kitten with a white star on its chest ran over to him. Rasputin glared at it, then turned to Alexandra. She stared back, lifted a paw, and licked it.

The two old women moved to the door. They stood there, arms folded, an angry scent coming off them in waves like the big heater in the bathroom.

With the first knock Karla opened the door. Nicholis leaned against the frame with his hands in his pockets. He nodded to Karla and stepped inside. A white kitten that seemed a younger version of Alexandra ran over to sniff his shoes.

"Looks like you found someone else to help you pack. I guess you don't need me after all," Nicholis said.

"No." Catherine glared up at him. "I don't need your help. I need a son who'll be good to me and kind. One that doesn't try to cheat me out of my own house."

"Now, Mama, I haven't tried to cheat you, only look out for you." Nicholis spread his hands and smiled.

"I'm sorry for you, Catherine." Karla shook her head. "But you're right, dear, it's a shame. The boy is such a liar."

"Aunt Karla, keep your nose out of this. It's none of your business."

"Don't talk to your elders that way." Catherine lifted a hand and shook her finger beneath Nicholis's nose.

"Hey, this is my house now, not yours." Nicholis's voice grew louder. The kitten down at his shoe looked up in surprise. "And I'll say anything I damn well want to."

"You will not," a voice from the hallway thundered. Karla had brought this man over that morning. Rasputin liked the stranger; they'd made friends in the feeding room. The man was big, much taller and heavier than Nicholis, yet he crossed the room with a sinuous grace that would have made any cat proud.

"Well, uh, Dimitri." Nicholis stepped back and tugged at his shirt collar. "Haven't seen you in a long time. Didn't even know you were back in the country."

"The Army gave me an extra week of leave." Dimitri strode closer until his nose almost touched the other man's.

"As a reward. My boy just made Special Forces," Karla added. "He tells me now he can kill with his bare hands. I'm so proud of him."

"So am I." Catherine took Dimitri's arm. She looked up at the big man. "Papa would bust his shirt buttons."

"Now see here." Nicholis reached into his coat and pulled out some papers. "I'm legally entitled to this house. The will stated. . . ."

"Which will?" Catherine asked. She went to an end table and held up some papers in each hand. "The real one? Or the one you made up?"

"I can explain. . . ." Nicholis started.

"I will not hear it." Catherine shook her head. "Get out of my house this instant. And for both our sakes, please, never come back."

"Fools!" Nicholis shouted. He whirled, clenching his fists, and started for the door. The white kitten by his foot jumped back in surprise. But it jumped the wrong way, toward the door. Rasputin couldn't tell if Nicholis had seen it, but the little one was about to be stepped on.

Someone had once stepped on Rasputin's tail and it really hurt. He didn't like the kitten, but even so. Alexandra rose into a crouch; she'd seen what was about to happen too. But Nicholis radiated a mean smell, thick with fear. Rasputin didn't want his mate, or their kittens, anywhere near the man.

Rasputin sprang forward, dodging between Nicholis's feet.

"Hey, watch out!" Nicholis shouted. Rasputin crashed into the man's leg, rolled, and sprang at the kitten. His jaws closed on the kitten's scruff. It squealed in surprise, but Rasputin pulled the little one to safety beneath the end table.

Nicholis tried to catch himself, but tumbled down to land on his backside. Dimitri hauled Nicholis up by the scruff too. "I never liked you when we were growing up. You were always too mean to the cats."

"Let go of me, you big ape," Nicholis growled.

"Get out." Dimitri shoved him toward the door.

"Yes, get out, worthless child," Catherine said loudly.

"You're making the house smell bad," Karla said and chuckled.

Nicholis slammed the door shut behind him. The kitten looked up at Rasputin then popped him on the nose. Rasputin started to hiss but changed his mind. He popped the kitten back. Alexandra came over and pushed the little one down on its back with her paw. She held it there and began to clean the Nicholis scent off. She stopped for a moment and gazed at Rasputin. Her tail curled and swept the floor in satisfaction.

Rasputin settled down beside her to watch the kitten be cleaned. He would help with them from now on, he decided. Little ones needed lots of help to grow up properly. They would be big, proud cats like he and Alexandra, cats that moved like Dimitri moved. But how could he help? What could he do?

"Well, that settles that," Karla said. "Let's go have some lunch, everyone. Then my son and I will help get this place cleaned up." She crumpled a paper in her hands; Rasputin's head lifted. He waited for her to throw it but she never did. Still, it didn't matter. He had lots more and the best way to help the kittens would be to play with them, teach them a good game.

He dashed toward the nearest kitten, delighted when it sprang after him. Another gave chase and Rasputin led the way toward his hoard.

Rat

TREY R. BARKER

For Ed Bryant

AFTER CAXTON DIED, OWNERSHIP of his cat fell to me.
I'm not a cat person.

But Caxton was a friend and if he wanted his cat with me, I would do that for him. Besides, the cat and I get along pretty well. Caxton called him Rat because the cat loved to haunt Denver's sewers and he always brought back a gift.

Sunday afternoon, while most of Denver watched the Broncos, I sat in Civic Center Park with my beat-up guitar, playing quietly, and thinking about Caxton.

"Hey, Johnny," Nettie said. "Where's Rat?"

"Sewer, I guess."

Nettie was a bag lady; old and withered, gray, half-crazed in a pleasant sort of way. She was one of Caxton's three friends; Rat and I were the other two. "I miss him." She wiped her eyes with a scavenged purple scarf.

I hugged her. "Me too."

After a long embrace, she waggled her bushy eyebrows at me. "If I were fifty years younger—"

"I couldn't keep up."

She laughed. "Play Caxton's song."

"No," I said firmly.

Surprise slipped across her gentle face.

It wasn't much of a song. A few chords, a simple melody, some lines about life on the streets. Not bitter lines because Caxton wasn't that kind of guy. He lived week to week in a flop down the hall from me, but he was happy. As happy as he could be, anyway. He and Nettie and me and a hundred other nomads I knew had adjusted. This was life, make the best of it. Which wasn't to say we didn't try to climb into the next socio-economic strata, we did. That's why I played guitar for spare change in Civic Center Park. I wasn't a C.E.O., but I'd bet most C.E.O.'s couldn't play guitar, either.

"I never heard his song," Nettie said. "Didn't Rat sing it with him?"

"Caterwauled, more like it."

She asked a few more times, but I wouldn't play it for her. It was something I had given to a lonely friend and because he had never shared it, I would never share it.

My lonely friend had been killed and because he was poor, no one cared.

I was too angry to play his song.

Rat brought me dinner.

I live in a dump called Hotel Tunisia. It's across the street from Civic Center Park. When I look out my window, I can see life thrumming and bobbing along Colfax Avenue.

Headed for the communal shower, I opened my door and saw Rat. He was an old yellow cat, one ear bent, the other nonexistent. He had a slight limp and a few patches of fur were long since gone. The damage was from chasing sewer rats.

Rat's smile said, "Wanna share dinner?"

It was one of the nicer things anyone had asked me recently, but dead rat isn't on my personal menu. At least not without barbecue sauce and baked beans.

"Find a little treasure?" I asked. "Why not a winning Lotto ticket or a wallet with no ID and a handful of twenties?"

Rat seemed to laugh at me. *This* is the treasure, you human dork.

After my shower, I played a few tunes for Rat. Knowing he now belonged to me—which meant he would check in with me if and when he felt like it—darkened my mood considerably. Caxton had been dead for nearly a week and I hadn't cried. Even at the quickie service and cheap burial in a pauper's grave, I hadn't cried. I wanted to cry but mostly I was angry. I had never lost a friend and realizing I'd never see Caxton's smile or hear his laugh again infuriated me.

The cops made it worse. To them, Caxton was poor white trash. They couldn't be bothered with a lonely old man who got Social Security and sold his blood to Bonfils Blood Center.

But that night, with Rat and my guitar, I cried. I cried for a man who had few friends and no family; a man who had a simple cross above his grave because no one could pony up the money for a real marker. When Nettie banged on the door an hour later, I was still crying.

"They're going to rent his room, Johnny," she shrieked. "The manager told me when I was coming up. He's got a renter tomorrow. He's going to throw Caxton's stuff out."

Caxton paid two weeks at a time. I had told the manager—a South Pacific islander with a perpetual grin—I would clean his room. I hadn't done it yet because I couldn't bring myself to go inside.

Nettie smiled tiredly. "Won't take long, he didn't have much."

"True." I picked up some boxes I had scrounged for the task and grabbed Caxton's extra key. Nettie and Rat followed me.

It was six doors down from mine, between a Korean veteran who had never really come home and a woman we charitably thought of as an "entertainer." Room 217. It was small and cramped, only one window—screen broken—and decorated in Caxton's personal style . . . Late American Found in the Street.

Caxton's death became real when I went in. Seeing the empty apartment where he and I had sung together—Caxton loved Perry Como—and had drunk free soda from a nearby pizza place made it real. Caxton was gone, knifed and left in the hallway to bleed to death.

"Wow," Nettie whispered. "This is weird."

I nodded as Rat ran into the room, searched out every corner and cranny, and sniffed the three sticks of furniture. When he understood Caxton wasn't there, he sat on the windowsill where he and Caxton had passed warm Colorado nights and meowed mournfully.

With Rat's song in the air, we packed Caxton's life. Everything into a box and in fifteen minutes we were nearly done. My heart crowded my throat. "That was depressingly easy."

"Still have his records," Nettie said, taking one from the sleeve and throwing it on Caxton's portable player. Perry Como wafted from the speaker.

Rat listened to the music and I hoped—uselessly—he would sing. He only sang with Caxton when Caxton sang the song I had given him.

"What are you two doin'?" The entertainer stood in the doorway, wrapped in a tattered red robe.

Rat hissed, claws bared.

"Take it easy, Rat. Just gettin' his stuff, Brenna."

"You keep that psycho cat away from me and turn that noise down. Or off. I got to work in a few minutes." She smoothed her robe. "A home office."

Behind her, a man snorted. "That what you call it?" He laughed. "I like the music, picks this dump up a little."

"Colonel Edgar," I said. "How are you?"

"Any day I'm not six feet under is a good day." His smile faltered. "I can't believe I said that."

Brenna pursed her lips. "That's what happens in a war. All those bombs exploding bruised your brain." Her nose turned up as she looked over Caxton's empty apartment. "Personally, I don't care he's gone, he was crazy."

"Be nice," Nettie said.

Brenna sneered and left.

"Don't mind her, she hated Caxton," Edgar said. "Said his cat peed on her welcome mat."

Nettie snickered.

"Did you see anything that night, Colonel?" I asked.

"Something suspicious? If you're playing detective, keep your eyes on Brenna. She slapped him a couple of times. Threatened to stab Rat."

"She didn't," Nettie said, shocked.

"Did too. Let's see . . . he died Tuesday. I spend Tuesdays at Capitol Hill Books. Got back about nine. I didn't see anything but I heard Caxton singing."

"Mr. Como," Nettie said.

"No, that song he does with Rat. They should have been on *Jay Leno*." Edgar took a deep breath. "I enjoyed that old coot."

"Why would somebody mug him?" Nettie asked us both.

"God knows all he had was that cat and those records," Edgar said.

"And that pocket watch," I said. "The silver one with the gold chain. Got it at Wedgle's pawn shop, said it was like his father's."

"Never worked, though," Edgar said.

Nettie laughed. "Even a broken clock is right twice a day."

Edgar chuckled as Rat left the apartment. Determinedly, he went across the hall, squatted over the threadbare carpet in front of a door, and peed.

"I'll be swaggled," Edgar said. "Brenna was right, just had the wrong door."

Rat looked at me, nodded in confirmation, and hopped through the hallway window to the fire escape. It was time for another sewer hunt.

"Well," Edgar said, "I guess that's good night, then."

When he disappeared, a heavyset man came up the stairs and headed toward us. When he heard Perry Como, he grimaced. "Music?" he asked, stopping at his door. "You'd think I'd get some peace and quiet now."

"Evening, Mr. Geryk," I said quietly.

"The cat still around? I'm allergic. Turn that music down, a man's got to sleep." He opened his door and noticed the wet spot on his carpet. "How many times have I called the super?" He glanced at the ceiling. "He swears it doesn't leak."

Nettie and I remained silent and Mr. Geryk disappeared inside his apartment. The click of his four locks was louder than the Perry Como.

Minutes later, Caxton's entire life was packed. Nettie and I sat in my apartment and cried.

Through the phalanx of open windows, I heard the ten o'clock news. Channel five. A great sports guy but a creepy investigative reporter.

"I told the manager we'd let him know when we were done," Nettie said.

"Sure." On the wall near the door was an intercom. All the rooms had speakers, but few of them worked. I pressed the button and listened as the night manager's voice came back to me around static and what sounded like a mouthful of late night snack. "We're done in Caxton's room."

"Okey dokey," he said.

I hesitated. "Did you hear anything the night Caxton was killed?"

The manager chomped, then swallowed. "You work for the cops?"

"No," I said defensively. "I'm just wondering."

"Didn't see anything, didn't hear anything."

In the hallway, Rat meowed and scratched at my door. Nettie let him in. "He's got a gift," she said.

The intercom spat more of the manager's words. "Took two complaints, though."

"For what?" I asked.

"You better see this," Nettie said.

"Singing," the manager said. "With that mangy cat. That stupid song. I could hear it all the way down here."

"Who complained?"

"Johnny," Nettie said firmly.

Surprised at the anxiety in her voice, I looked at Rat's gift.

"Hey," the manager said. "You still there?"

I clicked off the intercom and stared.

The gold chain from Caxton's pocket watch.

"Oh, man," Nettie said.

Rat meowed and licked his paw.

"Where'd you get this, Rat?" I asked.

He didn't respond.

"Oh man, oh man," Nettie said. "He took his pocket watch, didn't he? The mugger, I mean. Where else could he have gotten it?"

It hadn't been on Caxton's body or in his apartment.

"Oh man." Nettie's voice wasn't so solid. She was nervous and my shaking hands weren't helping.

I stared at her, at Rat, at the chain. Where else? One place sprang to mind and I didn't want to think about that. If the mugger was close enough that Rat could wander in his open window and snag part of the loot, then he was close enough for me to do something stupid.

"Why'd he only bring back part of it?" Nettie asked.

I shrugged. "Why does Rat do anything? He's about as smart as a cat can be, but he's about ninety percent goofy, too. Where'd you get it, Rat?"

Rat's eyes flashed and I half expected him to tell me or write it down. Instead, he jumped out the window to the fire escape and turned expectantly to me.

"Oh jeez. I can't believe—"

"Shhh," I hissed.

At the window, I leaned out and watched Rat jump gracefully from fire escape to fire escape. After a handful of jumps worthy of an Olympic gymnast, Rat disappeared inside an open window.

"Was it somebody in this building?" Nettie sat on my bed, rubbing her forehead. "That's bad, Johnny, bad bad bad."

"Don't worry, Nettie."

"Worry? Caxton is dead and his *cat* is hunting the murderer."

I shook my head. "Rat is being a cat. They wander, they find things. He probably found the chain in the hallway or outside."

"Yeah, yeah," she said hopefully. "That's it, what else could it be?" She sighed deeply, a breath of relief.

Rat turned up his nose at mindless rubber balls and fake mice, but he wasn't Einstein. Yet a part of me thought he might just be trying to tell me something, and that part took over. If there was the slightest chance I could find Caxton's killer, I was going to take it.

"Stay here."

Nettie's jaw set. "I was his friend, too."

She was right. "Fine, let's go."

There were eight apartments on each side of the hallway between me and the end of the corridor. Whatever it was we were looking for, we didn't see it as we passed apartment 208 or 210.

But near 212, we heard it.

"What is it?" Nettie asked.

I tried to clear my ears of everything I heard leaking through the thin walls: nightly news, reruns, blaring radios, an old voice calling "Bingo!" a younger voice moaning a lost poker hand. Further away, a somber clarinet played jazz enthusiastically but badly.

And beneath those sounds, something I'd heard only a few times.

I turned to Nettie. "Get the cops."

"What? Why?"

"Because I said so."

Her eyes wide and scared, she disappeared down the hallway.

I took a few more steps. Between apartments 212 and 214, I was certain. And scared.

Friendship is a strange thing. It can be as casual as unsticking the stuck window of the lady next door, or as intense as giving someone a song. It's full of shadings and shadows and hidden doorways. And in those passages, while Caxton and I sang and played checkers and drank free soda, our friendship became something deeper and more profound.

He had become my best friend.

I stopped at apartment 216.

Inside, Rat sang, scratching the melody of Caxton's song as well as he could. Actually, it was better than the last time I'd heard him. This time it was almost tolerable.

The strange thing was: Rat only sang for Caxton, not for Colonel Edgar or Brenna or the South Pacific islander or Nettie or even me.

The carpet in front of door 216 was still wet.

"He had been telling me," I mumbled.

Rat sang louder.

"Shut up, you stupid cat," Geryk bellowed. "Get out of here."

Before I could think about it, I grabbed the doorknob and shoved.

Four locks, all locked.

"Who's that?" Geryk shouted.

My element of surprise was gone and now I got to think about what I was doing. I turned to leave as Geryk opened the door. I froze. Geryk's mouth opened but he said nothing. Somewhere on my face or in my eyes he saw it and understood that I knew.

He dragged me in and slammed the door. "You think you know?" he asked, his voice competing with Rat's singing and the pounding fear in my ears. "There's nothing to know."

Still singing, Rat dashed into the bedroom.

"Stay out of there!"

A second later, Rat darted out with Caxton's silver watch in his mouth. In a blur, he was on the fire escape and gone.

"You killed Caxton," I said, taking a sad little swing at Geryk.

With a shrill laugh, Geryk smacked me with his meaty hand. The apartment went fuzzy and I tumbled to the floor.

"Why?" I blubbered.

Instead of answering me, Geryk kicked me. His foot connected two or three times and then I heard Rat.

Singing.

Then shrieking.

Geryk howled. I looked up and Rat hung from Geryk's shoulder.

In the hallway, Nettie banged on the door. "The cops are coming, Johnny. Leave my Johnny alone. Come on out here and I'll teach you something!"

I dove for Geryk's legs while he danced with Rat. Rat's claws sank deeper into Geryk's neck. I wrapped Geryk in a pretty good tackle—like my high school coach had taught me—just as he ripped Rat free. Still howling, and now falling on top of me, Geryk threw Rat across the room. I heard a thud, a short, pained squeak, and then nothing except Geryk's and my heavy breathing.

By the time the cops arrived, I had Geryk tied down in his tattered recliner with sheets from his bed. "What's this?" the young policeman asked.

"He killed my friend."

"Why did he argue with me?" Geryk asked no one. "Why didn't he just shut that cat up? I complained twice. I shouldn't have to listen to that."

The policeman frowned. "What's he talking about?"

I pointed to the fire escape where Rat sat, Caxton's pocket watch in his mouth. "Caxton's cat. He sings."

"Sings, huh?"

"You should hear him, he's great."

"Uh-huh. What's the story on that watch? He late for an appointment?"

"It was Caxton's. The cat found it in Geryk's room."

"The cat found it?"

I nodded.

"And I had to go to the academy to learn police work."

After Nettie and I answered some questions, we sat on my windowsill with Rat. I fancied I saw a smile on his furry face when I got my guitar. I played a few blues tunes, then played Caxton's song. Nettie and I sang it and, eventually Rat joined us. Scratchy, squeaky, ear-piercing, but not so bad. Maybe we could get an agent and go on *Jay Leno*.

I'm not a cat person, but this one will be okay, I think.

Revealing Russian Blue, or The Flaming Switcheroo

KURTIS ROTH

THOUGH THEY BOTH WORE BLACK, Basil thought the Poundstone sisters contrasted one another quite glaringly; the Queen of Hearts and the Queen of Spades personified. Portia, the elder, dressed in cascading lace ruffles and a wide-brimmed, puffy-plumed hat, smiled broadly as she greeted her fellow mourners. Penny, the younger, wore a much simpler blouse, skirt, and flats, with no hat or cap of any kind. Judging by the shadows around her eyes, which she had not bothered to cover, she was far more aggrieved than her sister by the loss of their patriarch, Mr. Preston P. Poundstone, Esquire.

And yet her grief did not prevent her from becoming entranced by The Manchester-Surrey Funeral Home's resident feline, a slim Russian blue named Teller, who was even then rubbing up against her leg.

"What a lovely cat," she said to Basil. "What do you call him?"

"Teller," he said. "After the magician. As in 'Penn and Teller.' Penn is very chatty, but Teller—the human one—never says a word. And since our feline friend here cannot speak...."

"It's a delightful name," she said. "But why a magician?"

"Well," said Basil, "he does magic tricks."

"Come now, you can't be serious."

"No, honestly. Watch." He produced a deck of cards from his pocket, spread them in an arc on the floor, and said, "Teller—pick please." Teller studied them and, after some deliberation, tapped one with his right paw. "This one?" said Basil. Teller blinked once, for *yes*. Basil drew it from the deck. Without looking at it, he showed it to Penny. "Remember the card," he said, "but do not tell me what it is." He placed it back in the deck, shuffled, then held the lot up, and said, "And now, your card will rise of its own accord!"

A single card rose slowly from the deck. The Four of Diamonds.

"Is this your card?"

Teller blinked once. Penny said, "Why, yes. Yes it is!"

"See?" said Basil.

"Oh, that's wonderful!"

"Better still, he has his *favorite* tricks. Teller . . . come on, lad. What's your favorite?"

Teller cocked his head to the left, sprang in a half circle so he faced away from them, then sprang to face them again.

"Ah," said Basil. "The Flaming Switcheroo."

"The Flaming Switcheroo?"

"Yes. It's really quite marvelous. Watch."

They repeated the card-picking process, except this time Basil did not wait for the card to levitate. Instead, he plucked one out and said, "Is this it?"

Teller blinked twice, for *no*. Penny's already faint smile grew fainter.

"What?" said Basil, looking at the card, feigning astonishment. "Seven of Clubs wasn't it?"

"No," said Penny. "I'm afraid not."

"Drat it all! That does it. I've had it with this deck!" He drew a butane lighter from his pocket and ignited the offending card. It went up in flames, smoke billowed, a light dusting of ashes settled on his cuff links—and yet, he still held a card.

Now it was the Queen of Spades.

Penny gasped in delight. "Oh! Yes! That's the one!"

Basil smiled and patted Teller. "The Flaming Switcheroo," he said.

It was at this point—just at that moment when he might have begun to savor Miss Penny's lightened spirits—that someone or something behind him hissed, "Basil!"

He turned to find his employer, Mr. Grimson, the funeral director, standing off in a corner, partially obscured from view by a large hanging fern. Basil excused himself to Penny and ran off to see what was the matter.

"Sir?"

Mr. Grimson's face was redder than usual. "Basil, you idiot, where is he?"

"Where is who?"

"The deceased. Mr. Poundstone."

Basil wasn't sure he understood the question, so he posed one of his own. "Isn't he reposing on the catafalque in Visitation Room Number One?"

"No," said Mr. Grimson, "that is precisely what he is *not* doing. Of all the things you might have forgotten, how could you possibly forget this?"

"But, sir," said Basil, "I didn't forget. I put him in place last night before I left."

Mr. Grimson took him by the arm. "Come see for yourself."

Sure enough, the body was not there. No body. No casket. Just a bare catafalque.

Basil was at a loss.

"I swear this place is falling apart," said Mr. Grimson. "The fridge in the lounge is dodgy. The church truck is nearly shot. This morning I found we're an urn short in the display case. And now it seems I have defective employees as well. What next?"

"Sir, I—"

"I'll tell you what next. I will go distract the mourners while you find that casket. And you had better find it quickly. They're supposed to be taking their seats already!"

As Mr. Grimson strode away, Basil thought to himself, *Well, this is a very confusing little building. Perhaps I simply put the casket in the wrong visitation room.* And when he went to check Visitation Room Number Two, lo, there was the Poundstone casket. Delighted, he loaded it onto the church truck, wheeled it over to Visitation Room Number One, shoved it into place, and swung it open.

Only to find it completely devoid of Mr. Preston P. Poundstone, Esquire.

"Or else."

Those were Mr. Grimson's words. Small words, large meaning. Find the body Or Else.

Basil was off to do just that when Penny walked up, Teller padding alongside.

"Basil," she said, "what's going on? I get the feeling something horrible has happened, but Mr. Grimley—"

"Grimson."

"—Mr. Grimson won't tell me a word. He just smiles and nods and scurries away."

"Well. . . ." said Basil.

"Well?" said Penny.

Well, there really was no way around it, and he could certainly use her help looking, so he went ahead and told her. She was surprisingly cool and collected about it.

"All right," she said, "where do we begin?"

"I'm not sure," said Basil. "Normally we let the body rest overnight in the Slumber Room, placing it in the casket only on the day of the funeral. But your sister wanted to begin so early, and I already had to work late, and I didn't want to have to come in at the crack of dawn, so I put him out last night. At least, I thought I did."

"Well, you must be mistaken. He has to be in the Slumber Room."

"Quite," said Basil.

But Mr. Poundstone was not there. Neither was he in the Preparation Room or the Reposing Room or any of the hallways in between. They even peeked into the Family Rooms and the Minister's Rooms—places a corpse never should have been. And at least that much was in order, because he was nowhere to be found in any of them.

Finally, Basil said, "I hope you won't think me crass, but I must ask: was your father by any chance the new messiah?"

"What? Why on earth would you ask such a thing?"

"Because I'm wondering if he was spirited away by some divine force."

"I doubt it," she said, absently stroking Teller. "He was a good man, but hardly angelic."

"Well then. I'm afraid that leaves us with only one possibility."

"That being?"

"Your father's body must have been stolen."

Penny blanched visibly at the notion. "But . . . who would steal a corpse? And why?"

"I don't know. Perhaps someone is harvesting organs? If so, I'm afraid they'll be disappointed. The man was dead for days, not to mention embalmed." Only after he had spoken did he realize how callous he must have sounded. He apologized profusely.

"That's all right," said Penny. "Sensitivity is a luxury I can't afford just now. Let us keep thinking." So they did.

"Could your father have been a cultist?" he asked. "Maybe his masters wanted his parts for some arcane ritual."

"Not bloody likely. That's how he would have said it, too. 'Not bloody likely.' "

"Or maybe some evil magician was working on a worry-free, saw-the-man-in-half trick?"

Penny laughed a bit at that. Teller, either startled by her mirth or reminded of some important business elsewhere, perked up, glared at the two of them, and bolted out of the room like a shot.

Accustomed to this sort of behavior, Basil ignored it and said, "I read somewhere that ninety-five percent of all murders are committed by someone close to the victim. A family member, a friend. . . ."

"But we're not talking about a murder," said Penny. "My father died of a massive heart attack. What we've got is a stolen corpse."

"On the contrary," said Basil, "what we *don't* have is the stolen corpse. Neither do we have any statistics on what sorts of individuals are prone to corpse theft. What we do have is a gathering of the victim's family and friends. Let us go search their faces. Maybe we'll find a motive there. Maybe our thief has returned to the scene of the crime."

In an effort to stall panic, Mr. Grimson had gradually filed the mourners into Visitation Room Number One. Some wondered aloud at why the casket was closed, but none seemed overly concerned. They were much more worried over who was wearing what, who was sleeping with whom, and how much a funeral of this sort might cost. The phrase "Goodness, the flowers alone must have been a fortune" was uttered with some frequency.

Basil and Penny observed from a dim corner up front, partially obscured by a red velour curtain.

"What about that one there?" whispered Basil. "The scruffy fellow in the back. He's got the look of a man with something on his mind."

"Of course he's got something on his mind," said Penny. "That's my Uncle Patrick. Father's brother. They were very close."

"Can you imagine him committing this crime?"

She thought about it. "Is it really a crime, what's happened?"

"I would think so. The body is family property in a sense, isn't it? Stolen property, at this stage. And then there's the matter of the break-in."

"The break-in?"

"Well, one doesn't enter a secured building without picking a lock or two. I'm pretty sure I locked up. I always do. And even if I didn't, our burglar would still have committed unlawful entry."

"Unlawful entry," she parroted. "Watch a lot of cop shows, do you?"

"A bit."

"In any case, no, Patrick couldn't be our man. He's in the back because he can't stand the thought of looking at his dead brother. He hasn't the mettle for body snatching."

"Well, who else then?"

They sifted through possibilities—uncles, aunts, cousins, gardeners, and laundrymen—until Basil was left with only one suggestion. Penny's older sister, Portia.

"Not a chance," laughed Penny. "She wanted this too much, this gala funeral event. She's the one who insisted on the mountainous flower arrangements, the catering by Spago, and Armani suits for the pallbearers. She's the one who cast herself as queen for a day."

Basil winced, sorry he'd brought it up. "Your father wanted something simpler, I take it."

"A bit."

They sat there in cold silence for a few moments, until Basil noticed a strange gray cat padding across the room toward them. It wasn't Teller. It couldn't be. Teller was a Russian blue. His fur would have been a kind of charcoal-silver tinged with azure, and this cat was patchy gray. But it was the same size as Teller, and had the same purposeful, frisky-yet-dignified gait.

When it stopped at Basil's feet, all doubt melted away. It was indeed Teller.

"What on earth happened to you?" he said, bending over to brush him off.

"Are those ashes?" said Penny.

Ashes. He was covered in the stuff. "Yes, I believe so," said Basil. "I'm terribly sorry, he's usually much more fastidious about. . . ."

He trailed off as Teller reared up and began to use Basil's leg as a scratching post. Devoid of claws, all he managed to do was smudge his pants leg with ash.

"What is he doing?" said Penny.

"I'm not sure. This is what he does when he wants his dinner, or a magic trick, but—"

Teller cocked his head to the left, sprang in a half circle, then sprang to face them again.

"The Flaming Switcheroo?" he said. "For Pete's sake, Teller, not now! Can't you see—"

The cat repeated the gesture, and again. Flaming Switcheroo. Flaming Switcheroo.

Mourners were beginning to notice the commotion.

"All right," said Basil. "Enough. I'll do it! Just stop, please." To Penny, he said, "I'm dreadfully sorry. I know how awful this must look."

Before she could respond, Mr. Grimson charged up to them. "Just what have you got going on here, Basil? Where is he? Have you found him yet?"

"Where is who?" said another voice, one as yet unheard by Basil, but which he knew must belong to Portia Poundstone, whose angry mask appeared just above and beyond Mr. Grimson's right shoulder. "Why haven't the services begun? There's something wrong, isn't there?"

"Please," said Basil, "let's take this out of the public eye, shall we?" He herded them into the hallway and drew a deck of cards from his pocket.

"What is he doing with those?" said Portia. "No one is going to play poker on my time, with my money. If I don't get some answers right this minute—"

Her prattle was cut off by Teller, who let rip with a bloodcurdling hiss—one which might have been very much at home in a film starring Boris Karloff or Vincent Price. Or both. By the end of it, everyone was quiet.

Basil said, "If you'll bear with my partner and me for a moment longer, I believe everything will be made clear." Not that he had the least idea *how* things would be made clear, but Teller obviously knew something important and was eager to communicate it.

When no one protested, Basil spread the deck in an arc on the floor. The cat studied them and, after some deliberation, tapped one with his right paw. "This one?" said Basil. Teller blinked once. Basil drew it from the deck and, without looking at it, showed it to the others. "Remember the card," he said, "but do not tell me what it is." Then he replaced it, shuffled, drew another card seemingly at random, and said, "Is this the one?"

They all looked at it, looked at each other, shook their heads. Teller blinked twice.

Basil glared at the card. "Jack of Diamonds, wasn't it?"

"No," said Portia.

"Not even close," said Mr. Grimson.

"Drat it all!" said Basil. "That does it. I've had it with this deck!" He drew the lighter from his pocket and lit the offending card. It went up in flames, ashes settled on his cuff links—and now he held the Two of Clubs.

"There!" said Mr. Grimson. "That's the one!"

"I say," said Portia, "that's quite a delightful trick. But . . . I don't see what it has to do with our father's funeral."

Neither did Basil. He was hoping some secret would be revealed in the card Teller picked. But the Two of Clubs? Where was the significance in that?

"I'm sorry everyone," he said, brushing the ashes off his cuff. "I suppose I'd better just—"

Wait a moment.

Ashes.

How could he have been so stupid?

He knelt next to Teller. "Ashes. The crematory. Is that it?"

There were smears of ash above Teller's eyes, which looked for all the world like human eyebrows. He raised one in an unmistakably sardonic fashion.

"Right," said Basil. "It's off to the crematory then. Follow me."

At first glance, the room seemed normal. Set halfway up the far wall was a rectangular steel door. That was the oven; the crematory proper. It was closed and latched. Nothing unusual about it. But that was the view from the hallway, where one's line of sight was obstructed by a handcart in the center of the room. Basil stepped around it to allow the others in, and when he did he saw what he would have missed before.

Ashes. Scattered, tiny heaps of ashes. And an empty coffee can, a large one, lying on its side.

Teller trotted into the middle of things, biffing ashes this way and that. He looked up at Basil expectantly.

"I believe he's saying these are Mr. Poundstone's ashes."

"But how?" said Mr. Grimson. "You'd remember if you cremated the man, wouldn't you?"

"Yes, I would," said Basil. "But I didn't. What's more, I believe I know who did." Here he turned to Penny. "Is there something you'd like to tell us?"

She said nothing for a moment, just looked at them, looked from face to face until her gaze landed on Teller. Or perhaps it landed somewhere beyond him.

"Daddy didn't want a funeral," she said. "He didn't want to be buried."

"Oh, how could you!" cried Portia.

"How could *you?*" said Penny. "You knew he didn't want a fuss. You knew he wanted to be cremated, but you've never cared what anyone else wants. Well . . . all I can say is, at least one of us truly loved our father. I gave him exactly what he wanted. If that's a crime, I'll gladly pay the price."

"I hope you'll pay for the missing urn as well," said Mr. Grimson.

Everyone but Penny seemed confused by this. Basil said, "Excuse me?"

"The one that's missing from the display," said Mr. Grimson. "Clearly, she didn't use the coffee can she'd brought for the purpose of transferring his ashes. She stole the missing urn."

"The coffee can," said Penny. "It seemed like such a good idea at first. And then it seemed so undignified. Yes, of course I'll pay for the urn."

"And everything else," said Mr. Grimson. "The Manchester-Surrey Funeral Home demands to be remunerated for services rendered."

"Speaking of which," said Basil, "I believe it's time to get the show on the road. Ladies?"

Mr. Grimson showed them the door. Basil sat down next to Teller, paying no heed to the charred and scattered remains of Mr. Preston P. Poundstone, Esquire.

"I was wrong about you," he told the cat. "You're actually a very talkative little fellow. I should have named you Penn."

Teller paid him no mind. He just licked through the ashes on one paw, revealing Russian blue.

Roscoe's Little Secret

KRIS NERI

LARRY WOULD DO ANYTHING for his old Aunt Grace.

Anything, that is, that would hasten her death.

Jobs came and went for Larry, money slipped through his fingers, but the one constant in his life was making himself into Aunt Grace's favorite nephew. A career, practically.

It was work, make no mistake. Catering to her every whim, stabbing the other relatives in the back to keep them off the inside track, bringing her the morsels of gossip she craved. It hardly left him any time for gambling, the only other interest in Larry's life.

To anticipate her moods—and stay on her good side—Larry studied Grace until he knew everything about her. By the time he had the subject down pat, there wasn't a thing about her that he didn't hate.

He hated the way she scrounged for dirt on everyone just to prove her moral superiority. The way she dangled her will before him to keep him on the straight and narrow. He even hated her cat, Roscoe. God, how he hated that cat! Especially annoying was the way Roscoe always seemed to smirk at him, like he had a secret he refused to share.

But mostly, Larry hated that Aunt Grace refused to die.

He'd been content to wait at first. She was old; he figured she couldn't last forever. But the ponies hadn't been running well for him lately, and the bookies wouldn't wait for their money.

He couldn't ask Grace to help. She'd been so furious when she covered his last gambling debt, she swore she'd cut him out of her will if it ever happened again. He just hoped she didn't hear about this debt. But why was he worried? Thanks to Larry's scheming and Grace's sour disposition, she wasn't on speaking terms with any of the other relatives. Who else could she leave her money to?

Larry decided Grace was going to cover this debt, after all—even if she had to do it from the grave.

But he hadn't counted on Grace being so lucky. Larry had already tried to kill her twice, but Roscoe always got in the way. The first time, Larry spiked Grace's food with arsenic. Only Roscoe nibbled it first and promptly threw up, the way cats do. Grace figured the food had gone bad and tossed it out.

The second attempt should have worked better. Larry drained the brake fluid from her car. Only Roscoe had gone along for the ride, and Grace never drove faster than twenty when the mangy feline was in the car. At that speed, the car simply cruised to a stop on its own.

Roscoe, it was always Roscoe! But his final plan was so foolproof, even Roscoe couldn't mess it up. Larry had noticed that the carpet seam had come open on a riser near the top of the stairs. By pulling the carpet out, he could make a snare that wouldn't be visible in the dark. Grace always came down during the night for a snack, and never put the lights on, the cheap old bat. Even she couldn't survive a fall like the one Larry planned for her.

Larry practiced setting his trap when Aunt Grace went to town alone that morning. Sure, Roscoe watched him the whole time and even caught his claws in the carpet once or twice, but now it was Larry who smirked. Even if the cat could have understood what Larry planned, who was Roscoe going to tell?

Larry planned to set the trap tomorrow night. He was staying over tonight, and it wouldn't do for Grace to die when he was in the house. Even though he'd make it look like an accident, the cops might find his presence suspicious. But tomorrow was perfect. He'd go home, then sneak back and set the trap after Grace went to bed. By the time she fell, he'd be back at his place with someone who, for a small part of his inheritance, would swear he'd been there all night. Foolproof.

Larry drifted into sleep that night a contented man. He was just one day away from riches. But he was rudely awakened a couple of hours later by a loud thud from the stairs. He rushed to the landing and threw on the lights.

Aunt Grace had fallen down the stairs, and judging by the angle of her neck, she wasn't going to be spreading any more nasty rumors. Then he noticed the carpet was pulled up as he planned it to be tomorrow night.

But he knew it was patted down when he went to sleep. He'd made sure of that. Who could have done it?

Larry stalled as long as he could before creeping down the stairs past Grace's body to call the police. On the telephone table was a copy of Grace's will, dated just that morning. He couldn't resist reading it.

"Because my nephew, Larry, who spends my money as if it were his own, has once again proved his irresponsibility by accumulating a large gambling debt, I relieve him of future temptations by leaving him the sum of one dollar."

A *dollar*?

But wait a minute. Who else could she have left her money to? He read on to learn the name of her beneficiary.

Larry gasped and looked to the top of the stairs.

Roscoe smirked.

Sam Spayed and the
Case of the Purloined Pussycat

SHIKHAR DIXIT

MEOW."

"Pardon me?" Sam asked, letting his eyes wander down his prospective client's lush, white coat of fur. The shadows of the windblown alley seemed not to touch her at all.

"That was the last thing he said to me. It's been a week since I've seen him. Oh, Mr. Spayed, I'm so worried about him. What if he's been nabbed by Animal Control, or run over?" A mewl of fear accompanied Isabella's moist eyes. *Ah, those lovely emerald eyes,* thought Sam. *Why do all the cute ones come to me?*

"Pookie was just running out to the Fifty-seventh Street dumpster to score some chicken bones or maybe a half-eaten burger. Mr. Spayed, please tell me you can find my Pookie. I can't live without him!"

Sam thought it over, and as much as it troubled him to think so, he knew the probable truth was that Pookie was dead. It was a harsh, biped world out there, and the city had definitely gone to the dogs in recent years. Still, he couldn't say no to those startling, sad eyes, that perky little nose flanked by the finest pale whiskers he had ever seen. Sam started to shudder from the inexpressible excitement.

"Hey there, guy," Isabella whispered, her grief replaced by solicitous warmth. "Don't get your balls in a knot."

"I'm afraid *that's* not even possible, Ms. Isabella."

"Oh," she sighed with something like embarrassment . . . or was that disappointment?

How come I didn't get clients like these before the fix came in? Sam shook the question away. Something else bothered him now. What was this fine feline doing with litter-box trash named Pookie anyway? And why the hint of seduction from someone supposedly grief-stricken? There was something going on here, and beyond the immediate situation, for Sam had noticed that many of the neighborhood cats seemed to have slunk from sight or vanished altogether. "Okay, Ms. Isabella—"

"Just call me Isabella," she purred.

Sam tried to ignore the phantom itch residing in his groin. "Isabella, I'll take the case. My fee is two pieces of uptown refuse per day, plus expenses. And I particularly love calamari."

Isabella pulled something from the shadows behind her. Sam masked his astonished delight as well as he could. An untouched slab of salmon lay at his nose. "I'll be seein' ya, kitty," she whispered beguilingly and disappeared into the darkness.

"Yowza," Sam sighed.

After devouring the fish, Sam headed off downtown. He trotted into the back of Hsung Tai House, darted under a table, and found Chan curled up on a dirty rubber mat.

"Sam!" he cried. "So good of you to drop by. To what do I owe this pleasure?"

Before he could speak, a pair of feet appeared above him, a hand reached down and stroked him behind the ears, and a steaming bowl of wonton soup was set down between the two cats. "Boy, you've really got it made here, Chan," Sam said. "Listen, you hear of a guy named Pookie hanging around in Chinatown?"

"New case?"

Sam nodded. "Missing felines."

"Yeah, I knew him. Really low-class. Mangy. Picked fights with every tom in the alley, even started stuff with some dogs. Who's looking for a fleabag like him?"

"The most incredible girl, a real kitten."

Chan chuckled. "You can't let it go, can you? What's it been, two years now? You can't feel anything, you just *think* you can. Sam, take my advice, shuffle up to a nice middle-class door, find a short biped in a little pink dress—they love adopting—and live the good life. Let all this go. I mean, what do you get out of this, a few fish bones, a torn ear? Leave it alone."

"Leave what alone?" This was suspicious. Chan was his friend; he had never suggested before that Sam return to the slavery that lost him his tomhood in the first place. "Chan, what's going on?"

Seeming to have lost his appetite, Chan backed away from the bowl of soup and curled back up. "Pookie is dead. And if he's not, he might as well be. I don't know what's going on, but I'll tell you this. There's been talk. This fleabag Pookie, he's not just some piece of roadkill. He was picked up."

"What, A.C.?"

"No, Animal Control don't go around in black vans with no windows. No, Sam, something big is going down, and I ain't settin' foot in the street until I'm sure it's over."

Next, Sam darted over to Bleecker Street. He leapt onto a wall, jumped over to the fire escape, and two flights up, slipped easily through a gap in a seventh-floor window. Chanelle, gorgeous and Siamese as ever, licked Tender Vittles juice off her clawless paws. Chanelle still had her sexuality, and the pheromones slapped him in the face like an aromatic bag of bricks. Something about her was off though, and Sam had known for a while that she was ill. The shortcoming only made her seem more kindred to him. "How are matters in the wild kingdom, Sam darling?"

"Disappearances, I hear."

"Yes, I've heard tell of something similar. Just the other day a darling Persian from two floors down told me an entire pack, the Critters, you know—"

"Yeah, street gang. They've got that initiation where they dart across Broadway during rush hour. If they live, they're in. It's no wonder enrollment is down."

"Yes, well, Sam darling, there won't be any more enrollment I'm afraid. The entire group of them has vanished!"

Sam shuddered. What could make the meanest gaggle on the mean streets vanish without a trace? "Did you hear anything else?"

"Yes, darling, and if I tell you, you must promise to find yourself a decent master."

"You know I can't do that, Chanelle."

"Oh, darling," she pleaded, and immediately nuzzled up against him, "please don't pursue this!"

Her body had grown so slim, Sam wanted to nuzzle her back; he *was* touched by her warmth and honest concern. He loved Chanelle in the only way he could, in that Ernest Hemingway's *The Sun Also Rises* way, but at the same time it made him eager to be away from her. "Cats are disappearing here, Chanelle. I can't stand by and let this continue."

She shrugged him off, stalked angrily away. "You're a fool, Sam." She swished her tail, stabbed the air with it. "You can't see the obvious when it's before you. Stay here, stay with me. My master is kind, considerate; he is a lover of animals. He'll take you in if he sees I love you. You can be safe here as nowhere else."

Sam turned and stared out the window. "I can't," he whispered, choking down his emotions before they could overflow.

She was quiet for a bit. Sam didn't turn, afraid he would be swayed by her pain. He felt sure she would be weeping now. Instead she said icily, "They all vanished from dumpsters. Fifty-seventh Street. That's the big one. No cat with half a brain will go anywhere near it now."

"Thanks." Sam leapt through the window without looking back. Maybe when this was all over, when he'd found the source of this mystery, he would return to her . . . and settle down. In the meantime, he needed to keep working, to get the image of her tortured beauty out of his head.

He returned to his alley, his "office." A blot of white awaited him in the shadows. "Anything, Sam? Did you find out anything about my Pookie?"

Before her lay an open plastic bag, and the aroma of squid activated his salivary glands. He peeked his head into the white sack and found the food was still hot! "How'd you do this?"

"I'm a regular at La Française Cuisine. Enjoy."

"Tell me something, Isabella? You're a high-class dame, no question. You're amazingly well-groomed, built like a brick doghouse, and apparently quite wealthy."

"I'm just well-connected. Sounds like you're asking me on a date. What's your point?"

"What are you doing with a guy like Pookie? He doesn't strike me as your type."

Her eyes grew into lusty slits as she pushed past him, plush fur massaging his flank. "Well, kitty, what can I say? I like rough trade."

Sam's underside began to tingle again. The frustration caused him to dive toward the only ecstasy he was likely to find. He wolfed down most of the calamari in three ravenous chomps. "Something's been nabbing cats left and right from local dumpsters. Fifty-seventh Street seems to be one of them. I'll find out more after I eat. In the meantime, I'd just stay off the street."

"Okay, Sam. Just don't 'disappear' yourself."

"One more thing. Tomorrow I want caviar."

"Will do, Detective. You just be sure to 'detect' my honey soon." With that she left.

More troubled than ever, and more wary still, Sam decided to visit the apparent scene of the crime. The Fifty-seventh Street dumpster was a big, snot-green job. Sam leapt onto its lip and slipped inside. Scents of tuna and bad milk commingled with another scent, the musky reek of corruption. There was so much food in the dumpster that Sam felt a stab of sorrow at the waste. Nobody dared grab *these* easy pickings? There would be no mad rush of gutterpuss teeming over this ten-course meal until the catnappings stopped.

A shadow fell over him as he looked up to see the stark silhouette of a biped reaching down to grab him. *Damn!* The hands were quick and rough and, Sam noticed as they retracted him from the riffraff "restaurant," covered in thick, gray gloves. *This is bad,* he thought, *very, very bad.*

The figure that raised him up before its face wore eyeglasses. There were myriad scratch wounds on his face. Sam swiped madly at the catnapper with a mean right, but the biped knew well enough to hold him at arm's length. It carried Sam further into the alley, toward the open doors of a van. It tossed him hard against the back wall. A bolt of pain rushed through Sam's skull as it impacted the gray steel, then, just before the dark closed over him, he saw the figure climbing into the back, something pointy in its hand dripping a single spheroid of liquid.

His skull was a fast-moving truck grille, pounding through his entire body. His eyes ached as he tried to pry them open. Before his face vertical stripes interrupted the view of neatly stacked boxes. Shaking his head, concentrating on interpreting what he was seeing, Sam realized the vertical repetition was bars, the neatly stacked boxes were cages. All this was inside the van, the very same one Sam had been tossed into too rapidly to notice these oddities before. Other bewildered-looking cats sat or paced miserably back and forth in their own cells.
"Well, she got you too, aye?"
Sam turned to find a mangy brown beast glaring at him through the side bars of his carrier. "Yer just anotha sucker like us all. What'd she promise ya, a life of passionate mating, litter-free dry-humps on the beach?"
He wasn't sure how, but all of a sudden he was certain this was Pookie. "You're talking about Isabella, aren't you?"
"Or Gwendolyn, or Lacey, or Madame Louisa—whateva name she feels like usin'."
So Chan was right. This was bigger than roadkill. "All right. Tell me the story."
"Don't know all of it. I do know this: She belongs to it, to the biped. She lures us in, and you don't stay here more 'n a month. I seen a few cats leave this place. They all leave in trash bags."
"They die?"
"Yeah—" he coughed and a thick wad of bloody fur erupted from his mouth. "Some kinda 'speriment," Pookie rasped. "It comes in and gives us all needles, one at a time, then it goes out and gets more. She lures 'em to the dumpster, maybe all different dumpsters, and it picks 'em up and brings 'em here."
"Have *any* cats left here alive?"
Pookie's glassy stare delivered the whole, bleak truth.
Damn. I should have listened to Chan.

He wasn't sure how much later, maybe a day, maybe a week, *she* finally arrived, clutched in the biped's hands. Her white, fleecy fur looked disheveled, her eyes were closed.
"There's the temptress," Sam whispered to Pookie.
Pookie stirred in his cage as Sam began to realize something was wrong.

Isabella wasn't stirring in the biped's arms, and it was taking her directly to a cage. "Who?"

"Her."

Pookie moaned. "Aww no, not *that* bitch!"

"She's a dog?" Sam gasped.

"'S an expression," Pookie spat sarcastically.

Sam watched stunned as the biped dumped Isabella in the cage to Sam's right. "What is going on here?"

Isabella lay still, eyes shut tight.

"Meow." The sound came from outside.

As the biped moved to open the back doors of the van, Sam asked Pookie, "So this kitty's not the one who lured you here?"

"No! That's Fluffy. She's just a mark."

"A what?"

A kitty scurried in and the biped slammed the doors behind it.

"She had a real nice colla, really uptown with diamonds studs. I boosted it last week. Why, she been houndin' ya about it? Yeah, yer a gumshoe, right? So she hired you...."

But Sam had already stopped paying attention. "Sorry darling, but I tried to warn you," Chanelle said.

"You? You've been luring these poor cats here?"

"It's for a good cause."

"That's the broad," Pookie spat. "She done a numba on all of us."

"What good cause," Sam continued, ignoring Pookie's comments, "am I going to die over?"

The biped mumbled some gibberish, stroked Chanelle on the back of her head, and, opening a door, hopped out of the van. As the door's slam echoed through the interior, Chanelle began to cry. "Oh, Sam, darling, I never meant any of this to happen to you. But my master is special. He is a veterinarian, and he seemed so close to finding the cure."

"Cure?"

"Feline leukemia. He hasn't the time for a hospital to approve his research. I thought he could do it, but he can't. I'm dying."

Suddenly Sam understood why Chanelle's coat had started to thin, why her eyes had grown steadily yellow over the weeks. Chanelle was dying, and in an effort to save her, the biped was doing research on strays. "It's wrong, Chanelle. How many cats have already died in the hope you'll live? How many more will?"

"I know, I know," she wept. "It's over." Sniffling, she planted her paws two levels beneath him. Sam could hear the cages shudder, hear other kitties scratch vengefully at her as she climbed. In a few minutes, her paw pushed at the slide lock until it popped over. Then she vanished. Sam heard her thump hard against the ground.

When he leapt out of the cage and landed, he could see she was almost gone. Her body shuddered from some spasm, then went still. "Sam," she whispered, "Sam ... I ... love ... you ..." and died.

"Hey, buddy, can ya maybe get us out of here?"

Sam looked up at Pookie. Then he leapt into action, opening all the cages, receiving plentiful thanks all around. As he slid back the bolt on Isabella's cage, she was just beginning to stir. "Awaken, my client, for I've found your, um hmmm, boyfriend." Sam pointed his nose over at the only other occupied cage. Isabella's eyes went wide.

"Come on, Sammy, let me out," Pookie begged.

"One condition. Tell her where she can find her collar."

"All right, all right, just get me outta here before that biped arrives and flips out."

After Sam freed Pookie, he could hear that last escapee and Isabella bicker incessantly.

"Would you two maybe mind shutting up so the rest of us can listen for the biped?"

They went immediately silent. And all the prisoners waited for the doors to open.

"You sure you won't change your mind, kitty?"

"Your offer's tempting, Isabella, but I don't think so." Sam sniffled. The effects of the injection the biped had given him, perhaps. The escape had been nothing dramatic. The biped had returned, opened the door of the van, and two dozen cats had swarmed over it toward freedom. As Sam had followed Pookie toward whatever hiding place he had for the collar, he'd seen the police cruiser turn on its lights at the end of the alley. He didn't know what the biped official wanted the catnapper for, he was just pleased to see it get arrested.

After that, Pookie returned the stolen collar to Isabella and she'd rushed away clutching it in her jaws.

When she returned to Sam's alley, the collar was snug around her neck. "They weren't even real diamonds. It just had sentimental value to me. My original master gave it to me before I was passed on to his daughter."

"Well, Pookie wasn't the smartest alley cat anyway. I mean, what did he think he was going to do with it, hock it? To who?"

She looked even lovelier with the collar on, and more seductive. "Life isn't between the hind legs, it's in the heart, you know," Isabella purred.

"Maybe, but I could go crazy spending my days around a dame like you and not being able to do anything about it. Besides, you really think your mistress'd want a mangy thing like me around?"

Isabella nuzzled up against him, set his belly and other regions on phantom fire. "I'll be seein' you around." As she slunk off into the darkness, she added lustily, "Kitty. . . ."

That was the last time Sam saw her . . . until the next time.

Scanning for Dollars

LISA LEPOVETSKY

COUNTY SHERIFF TRAVIS WILKENS rubbed his hands together to warm them. He peered expectantly down the long line of traffic stopped along State Route 37, the only road out of Willowsburg. Finally, he spotted the familiar yellow and white sedan creeping up the berm. He swore softly.

"Oh no, here they come again," he moaned, "right on schedule."

Deputy Jerry Parson turned. "What's the matter?" he asked. "Who's coming?"

Travis's breath created little ghosts in the crisp early-evening air. "Millie Hoven and her cat, Patches. I always hope they won't show up, but they do anyway."

"Millie Hoven. Wasn't she at that warehouse fire on Saturday?" Jerry asked.

"And the semi accident the Wednesday before that," Travis answered gloomily, "and the fight over at Charlie's Tavern last Friday night. Picks up our calls on her scanner and hurries right over. She always says she wants to see if she can help, but I think she's just lonely. Since her husband, George, passed on last summer, she's got nobody to keep her company, except Patches. In fact, I hear she's in danger of losing her house—old Crawford Harrison down at First Federal wants to foreclose. Kind of sad, actually."

Jerry said, "Well, Mr. Harrison has more to worry about right now than Mrs. Hoven's house, if this roadblock doesn't catch these crooks. About three hundred thousand things more."

Travis nodded. "Well, I try to be as sympathetic as the next guy, but Millie's got to stop this; she can't keep getting in the way. Unfortunately, I have to set her straight tonight. No more Mr. Nice Guy."

He straightened his tie and headed toward Millie's car. Over his shoulder he called, "You take care of the roadblock, Jerry. I won't be long."

As Travis approached the old car, he wished that cold fish Crawford Harrison could be here to suffer, too. Travis had certainly felt no particular sympathy for Crawford when the call had come in about the bank robbery just before closing time. But procedure was procedure. So far, the roadblock had turned up nothing, and his men were cold and hungry. And now he had to give poor Millie—and Patches—a hard time.

Millie reached across the front seat and rolled down the passenger window. Her wisps of short hair seemed a little grayer in the light from the line of cars behind her, and Patches was in his regular place, snug in her lap. The old calico blinked its pale green eyes at him and stretched, then sauntered across the vinyl seat to rub his muzzle against the window frame, looking for some attention. Travis ruffled his soft orange fur and felt a tug of pity. Millie had taught him freshman English in high school; he'd had tea and scones on her back porch, for heaven's sake. She'd been a terrific teacher—always said that Patches and her students were the children she and George never had.

And now here she was, all alone and trying to make ends meet, when she should be enjoying her retirement. Travis hated the sorry way Crawford Harrison was treating his mortgage customers, not giving them any slack on their payments, no matter what the circumstances. He bent and leaned into the open window.

"Evening, Mrs. Hoven," he said.

"Oh, Travis, isn't it awful about the robbery?" Millie's eyes looked excited and frightened behind her thick glasses. She clucked her tongue and shook her head. Her thin fingers reached out to ruffle the fur along Patches's back, and the old cat arched his spine in satisfied response. A loud purr began deep in the cat's chest as it leaned back against her hand.

"Yes ma'am," Travis said, "it is awful, but you'll have to go back home now."

"But I think Patches and I can help," she said with a smile.

"You always say that, Mrs. Hoven."

"But I really think we have something for you this time."

"Did you witness the robbery?" Travis asked wearily.

"Well, no, I didn't actually see the robbery happen," she answered slowly. Her fingers stopped moving for a moment, and Patches meowed softly to get her attention. She smiled and stroked his head.

"Did you see any of the perpetrators?" Travis asked.

"Um, well, no." Millie's smile faded.

"Then there's nothing you can do here, Mrs. Hoven. Please go on home and let us do our jobs. It's getting late."

Someone called Travis's name, and he glanced up. "Be right there!" he called back.

"But sheriff, I don't think you understand," Mrs. Hoven began, a frown creasing her brow.

"Please, Mrs. Hoven," Travis said, exasperation heavy in his voice. "I don't want to be rude, but you'll have to leave. This time things could get dangerous. I know you always want to help, but the fact is, you and Patches are only in the way here."

Patches mewed indignantly, as though he'd understood what Travis had said, and moved back from the window.

"But—" Mrs. Hoven tried again.

"No more arguments. Turn the car around and go home, Mrs. Hoven. Patches looks chilly. I'm sure you would both be more comfortable in your own home. If I need you, I'll be sure to call."

Travis stepped away from the window to eliminate further conversation and motioned firmly for her to leave. Millie seemed to consider for a moment what she should do, then Patches stepped into her lap again, put his head down, and closed his eyes. As if that was some kind of signal, the old lady raised her window, made a neat three-point turn and drove back the way she'd come. Travis muttered a prayer of thanks and headed to the front of the line where Jerry Parson waited impatiently.

Millie Hoven drove slowly along the wet roads, one hand on the steering wheel and one stroking Patches's soft fur. She needed time to decide what she was going to do.

"Well, Patches," she murmured, "things didn't go at all the way I expected them to back at the roadblock. Young Travis Wilkens was so abrupt with us, did you notice? It wasn't like him at all—he's always been such a nice boy."

Patches purred in agreement.

"Well, I suppose the stress of police work affects people that way sometimes. But he never even gave me a chance to tell him about what I found."

She'd been putting on her coat to go to the supermarket when the call came across her scanner about the bank robbery at First Federal. Actually, she'd turned if off as she'd gotten her purse, but when Patches had leaped onto the counter, pacing impatiently for her to pick him up, he'd stepped on the switch.

"Good thing you turned the scanner on again," she said, snuggling her fingers deep into the fur at the base of the cat's neck, just the way he liked it. "Otherwise, I'd never have heard the announcement about the roadblock." Patches purred louder.

When the all-points bulletin had come across the police band, any thoughts of plastic wrap and mayonnaise had flown right out of Millie's head.

She'd never seen a roadblock before. So she'd tucked Patches under her arm and hurried out to the car. She'd headed down Main Street, right past the First Federal building, her heart racing with anticipation.

She'd nearly missed seeing the cloth sack, because its gray color almost blended into the sidewalk. But Patches had suddenly yowled and leaped to his feet in the car, causing Millie to swerve over to the curb to see what was wrong. And in the glare from her headlights, she saw the bag just beneath the big blue mail receptacle outside the First Federal Bank. Realizing what it was, she'd lifted it and carefully placed it beside her on the floor of the car.

She'd been amazed by how much a sack of money weighed. As soon as she'd seen the First Federal logo on the bag, she'd known it must be part of the robbers' booty. They'd obviously dropped it in their hurry to get away. Millie hadn't seen anybody on the street to inform about her find, and then she realized that all the policemen would be at the roadblock. So she'd continued on her way, planning to hand the money over.

But that Travis Wilkens hadn't even given her a chance to tell him about it. He'd refused to listen to anything she had to say. And now she was in possession of a large sack stuffed with money, and nobody knew she had it.

"You know I've always been an honest woman, Patches," she said softly as she continued stroking the cat's head. "I realize this money isn't mine. I should return it to the bank, I really should."

But she kept remembering how difficult it had been to keep up the payments on the second mortgage once George's arthritis got bad and he lost the repair business. He'd finally gone into the bank last spring to plead with that awful Crawford Harrison to give them a little more time. But Harrison had refused to listen. And less than two months later, George was gone. And she and Patches were left trying to make ends meet, in danger of losing their home.

"You know, Patches, those robbers aren't going to tell anyone they stole more money when they're caught," she mused as she pulled into the driveway. "*If* they're caught."

She opened the door and Patches jumped into her arms. She sighed. "Well, maybe I'll go down to the bank tomorrow morning and hand it over."

Patches stopped purring and gazed hard into her eyes. He meowed once. "Then again," she continued, "maybe not."

Scratch Ticket

CHRISTINA BRILEY

JEANNE OPENED THE BEDROOM DOOR and looked down at the two felines pacing the landing.

"Mrreow-ow?" asked Butterscotch expectantly, and headed down the stairs with her usually graceful glide. The effect was always marred somewhat by her little "oof" as she hit the bottom step, as if someone had poked her in the stomach, but she never seemed to mind. Butterscotch looked back, waiting for Jeanne to follow.

"Move, twit!" Jeanne spoke affectionately to the tomcat who remained on the landing. He crouched down on the top step, leaving his back end sticking up in the air, and began very deliberately clawing at the carpet. "Come on, Fireball. If I step over you, you'll decide to move, and trip me, and that'll be the end of us both."

Jeanne shoved him gently with her foot, but he went on leaving his mark on the rug. She kicked a little harder, but it was like kicking a massive padded wall. "Ooh, you may have been a little fireball as a kitten, but you're some lump now!"

Fireball stopped his clawing and looked up at her casually, as if to say, "Did you say something? I'm ready for breakfast now." He started leisurely down the steps, but began picking up speed as he neared the bottom, for his stomach's demands now overruled his natural feline dignity.

Jeanne padded down the stairs after him, and around the corner, through the dining room, and into the kitchen. She looked at the cats' dishes and sighed. "For Pete's sake, guys, do you always have to drown your prey?" She bent down and pulled the little wire egg dipper out of the cats' water dish.

"It figures. You like little metal things that skitter across the linoleum nicely, don't you? You're always sneaking up on the counters to steal key rings and bobby pins. I should have put these things away, but it didn't occur to me that you'd be stealing them, too."

Jeanne picked up the water dish, washed away the little rust stains the dipper had left, and filled it with fresh water. As she reached to turn off the faucet, she watched the water splash in the cups stacked in the sink, each with the residue from a different color of egg dye. Tomorrow was Easter, and her three kids had insisted on dyeing Easter eggs with her, even though this was a "Dad" weekend, and there would be no egg hunt here tomorrow morning.

"So, you two want to hunt Easter eggs tomorrow?" The cats looked disdainfully at the water dish she'd just placed before them, and then up at their mistress in annoyance. "No, what you want is some food. Sorry." Jeanne took out a can of their favorite brand of food and divided it evenly between two plates, which she then put down on the floor. For several minutes thereafter the room was silent, except for the moist chewing noise of the cats gobbling down their food.

She watched wordlessly for a few moments before heading upstairs to get dressed. As she turned to go, Jeanne glanced back sadly over her shoulder at the two of them and spoke. "You'd better enjoy the good food while you can. We're headed for some very lean times around here."

While getting dressed, Jeanne mulled over her list of things to do. She'd have to hit the grocery store, and the post office, and then get back here to work as quickly as possible, even if it was Saturday. With her ex having been laid off, and then finding a new job at half the pay, every sewing job she could finish meant that much more to offset the huge drop in child support. Even so, no matter how hard she tried, Jeanne could never make up the difference, and losing the house was becoming a very real possibility.

Jeanne looked down as Butterscotch wandered into the bedroom, licking her chops. She rubbed against Jeanne's legs and uttered her usual "Mee-rrrow?" which easily translated into "Pet me, *pleeease?*"

Jeanne reached to pet the cat's long, orange fur, and muttered in frustration. "What am I going to do? Sewing is great 'cause I can work around the kids, but it just doesn't pay well enough."

She straightened up again and sighed. "I think I'll splurge and stop at Little Peach for another lottery ticket. The jackpot's way up there at the moment. I could sure use it!"

The young man at the convenience store recognized Jeanne when she came in, for once or twice a week she would invest the few dollars she felt that she could spare in a megabucks ticket, and maybe a scratch ticket as well.

"Hi there, Jeanne!" he greeted her. "The usual?" he asked, glancing at the ticket dispenser.

"Yes, please." She always played the same number. It was the day of each child's birthday, the day of her own, and the day they had picked each of the cats out at the local shelter. "And a one-dollar scratch ticket. I don't care which one."

"It'd be nice to win this one, eh? It's up to almost twenty million!" The clerk smiled, and leaned over conspiratorially. "You gonna be sitting in front of the TV for the drawing tonight, waiting with bated breath?"

"Actually, no." Jeanne laughed, in spite of all her worries. "The kids are with their dad, and a friend invited me out for dinner. Her treat, of course, or I couldn't afford it. I never pass up a free meal these days."

"I sure know what you mean!" he called after her, as she hurried out the door to get home to work.

When she got home, Jeanne threw her keys on the counter, and took a minute to scratch the instant-win ticket, before heading into her workroom.

"All right!" she announced happily. "Twenty bucks won't save the farm, but it sure don't hurt none, neither." She grabbed a big paper clip from the junk drawer in the kitchen, clipped the winning ticket to the megabucks ticket, and tucked them under the salt and pepper shakers on the dining room table. With the tickets there in plain sight, she'd be sure to remember to check the megabucks numbers in tomorrow's paper, before running up the street to cash in that twenty-dollar ticket.

By the time Jeanne's friend, Diane, stopped in to pick Jeanne up for dinner, the lottery tickets had been forgotten, and Jeanne, and her poor tired back, were all too happy to get away from uneven hems and stubborn zippers. The evening was a pleasant diversion from her troubles, and Jeanne was in high spirits at the evening's end when she waved good-bye to Diane, and walked toward her own back door.

"Oh. . . ." Jeanne froze, her key halfway to the lock. The glass pane closest to the lock had been broken, and the door stood ajar. She raced to Diane's car, for her friend had waited to make sure Jeanne got into the house okay, and climbed back into the passenger's seat.

"Let's get out of here!" Jeanne cried out shakily.

"What in the world . . . ?" Diane protested.

"Just drive; it doesn't matter where. And give me your cell phone." Jeanne dialed 911 to report the break-in. By the time she hung up, there was no need to explain to Diane what had happened, as Diane had been listening intently to Jeanne's end of the phone conversation.

"Thank God I waited for you!" Diane said. "Should we go back? Would the police be there yet?"

"Let's just drive around a bit," Jeanne answered. "It'll give the cops a chance to make sure it's safe, and give me a chance to let my heart stop pounding." Gradually, fear for her own safety turned to concern about her home, and her workshop, and then to anger at having her home violated. "I'm okay now, let's go back and see what they found. Damn, I sure hope they didn't trash the place."

The women arrived back at Jeanne's house to find the police leading a man out in handcuffs. As he passed under the porch light, Jeanne drew in her breath. "You! Why would you break into my house? Cripes! I've told you enough times how broke I am. Or did you think that was an act?"

The clerk from Little Peach looked at her disgustedly. "No, I believed you. But you sure ain't broke now. You musta had that winning lottery ticket with you all the time."

"You broke into my house for a twenty-dollar scratch ticket?" Jeanne stared at him disbelievingly.

"What twenty-dollar ticket? Try twenty million." He looked at her in surprise. "Don't you know? Your numbers won!"

Jeanne gasped, and her heart leaped happily at the news. Her joy was short-lived, though, as she realized that the man could not possibly have missed the ticket sitting out in the open, yet he seemed to think it wasn't in the house. She brushed past the clerk and his escorts and ran into the house.

She hardly saw the kitchen drawers lying on the floor, their contents spilled everywhere, nor the downed mail rack that had hung on the wall, nor all the other signs of a desperate and thorough search, as she rushed into the dining room. Linens and silverware covered the floor where the sideboard drawers had been pulled out and dumped, but the dining-room table lay bare of everything except one salt shaker that had rolled over on its side, and tiny grains of salt and pepper scattered across the tablecloth.

Jeanne stopped where she was, and simply sank to the floor. There she sat dazed and fighting tears, as she struggled to comprehend what she had gained and lost, all in a few minutes. Slowly one question began to work its way through her confusion.

"How *did* I lose it?" she asked aloud. "If he doesn't have it, and I don't have it, where is it?"

"Excuse me, ma'am. Are you all right?" The police officer who had just walked into the room looked down at her with concern.

Startled, Jeanne looked up. Suddenly, suspicion began to gnaw at her. Had the cops found it? She tried to act naturally, as if no such thought had occurred to her. "Uh, yeah. Fine. Just a little shell-shocked."

"He did make a mess, didn't he?" The officer answered ruefully, surveying the wreckage. "Your insurance should cover anything he broke, and maybe pay for some help to clean up."

Jeanne wondered why he didn't mention the lottery ticket. Surely he had heard the suspect talking about it. Maybe he thought it wasn't his business. Or maybe. . . .

It was all too much. "Thank you, Officer, for your concern. You should be right about the insurance." She spoke quietly, but inside a voice was screaming at him, *What about the lottery ticket!?* Struggling to keep calm, she spoke aloud again. "Do you need to do anything else here tonight? You caught the man in the act, and he didn't take anything. And I'm really very, very tired. I don't think I can face all of this anymore tonight." Jeanne abruptly remembered the cats. "My cats! Has anyone seen my cats?"

"No, ma'am. We checked the whole house for accomplices, but we weren't looking for cats," the officer answered. "They could be hiding in one of the places we ruled out as too small for a man to hide. Let me check with the other men, in case they saw them and didn't mention it, and then I'll help you look."

No one else had seen the cats either, but it didn't take Jeanne long to find them curled up under the dresser, a bit edgy from all the commotion, but unharmed. She found their presence comforting, and after showing the police out, and saying good-night to Diane, who had been hanging around to see if she could help, she made it a point to dig the cats' food dishes out from under the chaos on the kitchen floor. Jeanne wanted to make sure they had dry food and fresh water for the night.

She would deal with cleaning up the disaster and repairing the broken window in the morning. Tonight, all she could think about was laying her head on a nice soft pillow, and trying to stop all the thoughts that were spinning around inside it.

Ignoring the jumble of clothes that now littered her bedroom floor, she crawled thankfully into her bed. Despite her usual habit of closing her bedroom door to prevent unwanted attacks on her toes during the night, she welcomed the cats' company just now, and made no effort to evict them.

Jeanne slept fitfully, but arose in the morning anxious to get to work at putting the house back to normal.

"Well, life goes on!" she spoke with ironic amusement, as Butterscotch and Fireball paced the landing, just as they did every morning. "I don't suppose you two have seen that lottery ticket?"

Butterscotch merely trotted down the stairs, quietly. Quietly, that is, except for the little "oof" at the end. Fireball nonchalantly decided to do his rug thing.

"Damn it, Fireball! I don't know whether to laugh or to cry!" she exclaimed, as the cat blocked her, as always. This time her patience failed her, and she carefully stepped over him, just as he decided it was time to move. She managed to catch herself, and human and cat charged down the stairs together.

By the time Jeanne had picked her way through the rubble on the dining-room floor to the kitchen, the cats were anxiously awaiting her by their dishes. Fireball sat with his front feet up on the edge of the empty, dry food bowl and looked like nothing so much as a large, furry, orange and white pear.

"How dignified you are, sir!" Jeanne spoke to him, laughing. She knew if she couldn't laugh at something, she would surely cry. The burglary, the broken window, the mess, and the incredible frustration of knowing she had held the ticket that would have meant the end of all her money problems, but could not prove it, even should the ticket surface in someone else's hands, all seemed too much to bear.

"Oh, you guys!" she announced, as she glanced at the water dish. "Not again!" She reached to pick up the dish. This time it was a paper clip that sparkled up through the water.

Jeanne stopped in midreach. Slowly, a smile spread across her lips. Tears began to roll down her face, as the smile grew into a grin, and then turned to laughter. There, in the bottom of the water dish, lay the two lottery tickets, still clipped together, and, to Jeanne's utter relief, still legible.

Shiny

JOE MURPHY

THIS IS BETTER THAN A SHREW, or even a vole nest—especially since I've already eaten. Stones, pebbles that scatter the sun in bright flecks over the cabin's mossy walls. Shiny stones on a string, but what's curious is the scent that clings to them. It's so faint, I can't remember where I've smelt it before.

My Branigan is calling. Normally I don't come, but my Branigan always has something good to eat tucked in her pockets. Today I'll bring her a treat too, because the Daddy won't let her play in this old cabin with the tumbled-in roof. Not safe, the Daddy scolds, and stay out of the woods, girl, too dangerous.

"Turtlefur, what you got there?" My Branigan squats down by the big pine where the squirrels live, drawing her naked legs up into her dress. She pats her lap, and it is a bit chilly, so I hop onto her and drop the string of shiny stones. She picks them up and her eyes gleam almost as bright as the stones. "Turtlefur, they're beautiful!"

She's proud of me! I rub up against her, sniffing the big pockets of her dress, nosing into the one with treats. She even lets me help myself.

But then she scoops me up, all the way until we touch noses, and she says in the same serious voice that she used when I brought her a vole to eat in bed, "Where did you get these?"

Why doesn't she follow the scent? I look toward the old cabin, all but one wall hidden by a stand of scrub spruce, gnarled and tangly. I love my Branigan but she's thick as a tree sometimes, the way most people are. Still, she's young, just a kitten of her kind with long wiggly braids that are fun to catch. I have great hopes for her but this time she doesn't get it.

"Well," she says, standing up. "We'll have to show Daddy." So it's off to the trailer where our den is. The sun slants through the trees, late afternoon and Daddy should be home; he does something in a place called Nenana High School. I followed him once just to see, but it was awful noisy so I came back.

The Daddy gets big eyes when Branigan drops the stones into his paw. "Where'd you get these, sweetheart?"

"Turtlefur found them. In the woods."

"What'd I tell you about going into those woods?" The Daddy's voice starts to growl.

"You said not to go past the big tree, and I didn't," my Branigan says; at least she's learned how to purr.

"We've had some thefts up at school." The Daddy dangles the stones and they're so inviting I climb onto his lap to bat them around. "This looks like the bracelet Mrs. Carmical was missing."

"Mrs. Carmical is an ugly old hag." The Randy stomps into the house and tosses his things on a chair. The Randy is my Branigan's older brother. He does something at the school too, but the Daddy says it's sure not work. The Randy is okay though; good for bits under the table whenever we have salmon.

"We've been through this already, son. She may be an old hag, but she's your homeroom hag and you've got to get along with her."

"I try, Dad. Me and Larry Gibbons bust our buns and she's always on our case."

"Larry's got his own problems." The Daddy shakes his head. "But I've seen your work. You can do better."

"Where'd you get those?" the Randy asks, staring at the stones.

"Turtlefur found them in the woods," my Branigan says.

"Oh yeah, I'll bet."

"He did, he really did."

"You're making that up, microbrain." The Randy sweeps his dark hair out of his eyes. "I know you are."

"You two stop your fussing," the Daddy says. "It's time to get supper on."

Supper is good; I get lots of chicken bits from my Branigan 'cause she's proud of me, and quite a few from the Randy who seems uncharacteristically without appetite.

Later that night, after a good nap on my Branigan's bed to make sure she sleeps well, I jump up on the Daddy's big chair to stare him into letting me out.

"Ready for your nightly hunt?" The Daddy strokes me right to the base of my tail, the way I like it. "Good idea." He picks up my string of shiny stones and drops them on the table. "Think I'll just step outside too."

There's plenty of moonlight. A night breeze teases my fur, making my muscles twitch with anticipation. The scent of a new vole family drifts from under the trailer, but the Daddy is stomping around after me. Those big feet will scare them all away. He liked the stones; if I take him back to the old cabin maybe he'll get interested in the other stuff. I can get some hunting done then.

Wish the Daddy would learn how to walk quietly. His feet crash through the brush. Just when I turn to stare him into silence there's an even bigger crash and he disappears, drops right through the ground! Where'd he go? What for? I must know. Trouble now, he's found one of the mine shafts the hard way. The blood smell drifts up with the scent of old earth and rotting wood. He's lying on some boards and the quiet now is a bad thing.

Can't get down to him but maybe my Branigan will know what to do. Faster than fast I'm back at the house. She hates it when I jump off her dresser and land on her tummy but that's what I do.

"Turtlefur, go away." My Branigan rolls over and pulls the pillow onto her head.

"Here, kitty, kitty, kitty." The Randy sounds sad but not sleepy. He's sitting on his bed in the next room, dangling his feet, long black hair hiding his eyes. "Turtlefur," he whispers as he picks me up. "I think I'm in trouble."

That kind of night, I think. There's a smell to him that I hadn't noticed over dinner. Whatever it is was on the stones too. The Randy's bigger than my Branigan, and at least he's awake. Now if I can just get him out.

"I'm hungry." He picks me up, carries me to the kitchen, and puts me on the table. "Sssshhh! Don't wake Dad."

Shiny stones on the table, flashing colors when he opens the fridge. I bat them over to the salt shaker.

"Hey, cut it out!"

Got the string of stones in my mouth. Off the table, over to the open window, perched on the sill I turn and look back at him.

"Turtlefur! Drop those!"

I'm out the window. The Randy thumps through the trailer and comes outside. Soon as I'm sure he sees me, we're off. At least he thought to bring a light. Sometimes that boy is smarter than his daddy. It's not far now; staying just ahead of the Randy is delightfully easy.

"Turtlefur?" the Randy calls out.

"Randy?" The Daddy's voice is weak. The blood scent not as strong now.

"Dad?" The Randy drops to his knees, shining the light into the shaft.

"I'm hurt, son. I need help."

"Yeah, Dad. Hold on!" The Randy jumps up and runs for the house.

Sunrise and it's so noisy out here that I'm hiding in the brush. The Randy is back and my Branigan too. Plus, a big truck they call the Fairbanks Rescue Unit and a bunch of people. Some smell like neighbors, some not. They have to use some special ropes to get Daddy out. He's on a stretcher now, and the kids are on either side.

"I'm sorry, Dad. It's all my fault." My Branigan begins to cry. "If I hadn't given you the bracelet, you'd have never come out here."

"No, it's my fault." The Randy lowers his head.

"You took that stuff, son?"

"Me and Larry Gibbons. The rest of the things are in the old cabin."

So that was the scent! The Larry Gibbons always smells that way; his father runs a dog team . . . yuck.

"I'm sorry, Dad."

"We'll work it out, son." The Daddy smiles up at him, and touches his arm. "It'll be all right."

"Turtlefur?" My Branigan's face seems rather pale in the bright lights from the truck. "Has anyone seen Turtlefur?"

She won't have treats, 'cause her pajamas don't have pockets. But her voice quavers, and the way she hugs herself, poor thing, she's scared. I come out of the brush and rub up against her leg. She scoops me up and it feels good to be held next to her warm body.

"Here's the real hero." The Randy reaches out to stroke me. "You won't believe how I found you, Dad."

All this fuss over some shiny stones. Well there's another shaft just past the cabin. It caved in when the snow melted and I found some real shiny rock, with bright streaks that catch the sunlight and glitter gold. Maybe I should bring one home?

Six-Toed Ollie

MICHAEL A. BLACK

I NOTICED SIX-TOED OLLIE SLEEPING on the roof of my rear porch when I came back from my run that spring morning. The roof was easily accessible for a cat, since the banisters of the elevated back steps made it only about a four-foot jump. I stepped onto the porch and called his name softly, holding my hand up by the gutter and rubbing my thumb and index finger together. Six-Toed Ollie raised his flat, triangular head, squinted at me sleepily, and then gave an acknowledging mew.

The cat belonged to my neighbor, an elderly lady named Mrs. McCarthy. I figured that she must have been somewhere in her eighties, with iron-gray hair and large, gold-rimmed glasses. But she was a tough old bird. Every spring I'd seen her kneeling in front of her house planting flowers, and she'd put me to shame working on a garden in the backyard. She was always pleasant and said hello to me when I'd come trotting up the block from my morning run. I lived two houses away on the same side of the street. It was on one of those mornings about two years ago that I'd seen her sitting on her porch holding this big tan and white tomcat. She motioned to me as I went past.

"Mr. Parker, come see my new boyfriend," she'd said.

I walked up the sidewalk and smiled.

"I'm going to name him Ollie," Mrs. McCarthy said. The cat looked dreamily at me, then closed his eyes. "And look at this." She held up one of his paws and pressed it gently between her thumb and index finger. A flange of six claws fanned out momentarily. "He's got six toes on each foot. That must mean he's special."

Hence the nickname I assigned to him: Six-Toed Ollie.

Mrs. McCarthy was always very careful about not letting Ollie run loose in the neighborhood. She was very proud of her bird feeder in the backyard, too, and didn't want him "marauding." So the only time I saw him out was when she had him on a leash. That's why I was surprised to see him on my roof.

I called to him again, and this time he got up, stretched by raising his rear end high in the air, and sauntered over to the edge of the roof. He rubbed his face against my upraised fingers then deftly jumped the four feet down to the two-by-four banister. Marveling at his display of agility, I picked him up with two hands and walked over to Mrs. McCarthy's front door. He must have weighed a good fifteen pounds. A rust-covered blue Chevy Cavalier was parked by the curb. I'd seen the car there before and knew it belonged to her nephew, Paulie, who came over infrequently to cut the grass and do other minor chores. He pulled open the front door after I'd rung the bell, staring at me through the metallic netting of the screen door.

"Is Mrs. McCarthy home?" I asked, trying to be ingratiating.

"She's sleeping," he said. "I'm her nephew. Why?" He was about medium height but grotesquely fat. His little dark eyes seemed to be two dots of obsidian stuck in a slab of pastry dough.

"Her cat was sleeping on my porch," I said.

"Oh, sorry." He opened the screen door and grabbed Six-Toed Ollie by the scruff of the neck like he was snatching a gallon of milk. Ears flattening out, Ollie hissed and took a couple of swipes at fat Paulie's pants leg. He held the cat down by his side and pulled the screen door closed.

"Hey, you're not supposed to hold a cat like that," I said without thinking. He glared at me momentarily, then let Ollie drop to the floor. The cat scurried off inside the house, still hissing. "Mrs. McCarthy's usually very careful about her cat. Is she feeling all right?"

"She's fine," he said slowly. Then asked, "You the cop that lives over there?" He canted his head to the right.

I nodded.

"I'll tell her you brought it back. Thanks." He closed the door.

I didn't dwell on the incident too much as I showered, ate, and got ready for duty. I worked an afternoon shift assignment and got off at midnight every night. I did notice the blue Chevy parked in front of the house again the next morning when I got up to run. I spent more time than usual walking around my yard cooling off, hoping I'd see Mrs. McCarthy out planting her petunias. But I didn't.

When I was getting ready to go to work I got a call from my lady friend, Cathy.

"Can you do me a favor?" she asked.

"Name it," I said.

"I got a call from the Animal Welfare League. They have a cockapoo that I've been waiting for. I need you to go by and put a hold on it for me." She'd been waiting for about a year to get a suitable dog for her young son. "This dog sounds like a dream."

I told her that I'd head right over, since it was on the way to the station anyway. Thirty minutes later I was pulling up in front of the brick building with the mural depicting various types of adoring dogs, cats, and other animals. After explaining why I was there, and putting a cash hold on the dog, the girl behind the desk asked if I'd like to see the pooch.

"Sure," I said, and she began leading me back toward the rows of dog cages. That was when I heard a familiar plaintive whine. Turning, I saw the big, angular tan and white face staring at me from behind a steel mesh door. Our eyes locked momentarily, and the cat opened his mouth and cried again. I stopped and went over to him.

"Are you interested in a cat, too?" the girl asked.

At that moment twin paws, each containing six awesome-looking claws, curled around the box-like steel bars.

"I think that's my neighbor's cat," I said. "Six-Toed Ollie." With the mention of his name, he emitted another mournful sound. "He's got six toes on each foot."

"Oh, wow, he sure does," the girl said, walking over. "Give me the information." She wrote down the cage number.

The record showed that the cat had been brought in as a stray late the previous afternoon. Since it was obviously well cared for, the usual procedure was to hold it in case of inquiries. I didn't know Mrs. McCarthy's phone number, but explained that I would let her know of Ollie's whereabouts the next morning.

"She's an older lady," I said. "Why don't you take my number just in case."

She did.

The next day the blue Chevy was again parked in front. I changed into my sweats and running shoes, but walked over and rang Mrs. McCarthy's bell before I started the run. I could hear the sound of a hammer pounding inside. I leaned on the doorbell several more times. The pounding stopped and presently the fat nephew came to the door and opened it just enough to frame his big head in the space.

"Yeah?" he said. He squinted at me through the screen door.

"Is Mrs. McCarthy home?"

"No. I took her to the doctor," he said. "Why?"

"I just wanted to let her know that her cat's at the animal shelter," I said. "Did he get loose again?"

"Oh, yeah. He did. I been looking for him, too. What place is he at?"

I told him the address and phone number.

"Okay, thanks a lot," he said, grinning. "I'll give 'em a jingle and we'll get him this afternoon."

"Give my regards to your aunt."

He said he would and pushed the door closed.

Later that evening my partner and I were in the middle of a boring shopping-center surveillance when my cell phone rang. I answered it.

"Mr. Parker, this is Jeannie from the Animal Welfare League," the voice on the other end said. "Were you able to get a hold of your neighbor about the cat with six toes?"

"Yeah," I said. "I talked to her nephew. He was supposed to be contacting you."

"Well, nobody's called, and my supervisor doesn't seem to think we can place a full-grown cat his size."

I glanced at my watch.

"What time do you close?" I asked.

"Seven o'clock, but we have somebody on duty till midnight."

"How about if I drop by around eleven-thirty?" I said. "I'll pick the cat up and deliver him back home."

"That would be super," Jeannie said.

I picked up small bags of kitty litter and cat food at the shelter, and figured I could find a suitable plastic box to allow Six-Toed Ollie to spend the night at my place. After all, it was after midnight by the time I got home. Then in the morning I could talk to Mrs. McCarthy.

But when I pulled down the alley I noticed that the lights were still on in the back rooms of her house. I stopped by my garage and was waiting for the overhead door to finish going up, when I saw Paulie's blue Cavalier swing out from the space adjacent to Mrs. McCarthy's old decrepit garage. He kept going in the opposite direction from which I'd come. I backed in my garage and hit the button on the remote to close the door. Unfortunately I also opened my car door out of habit, forgetting about my rider, and Six-Toed Ollie shot off my lap like greased lightning. My hand immediately shot up and hit the button again, freezing the descent of the door, then, swearing, I lumbered out of the car in time to see the big tomcat run into the alley and turn right. Pulling out my small mini-mag flashlight I went after him, thinking what an idiot I was for not holding on to him better. The beam lit up the alley and I saw Ollie stop and pause in the light, his eyes gleaming like two beacons. I strode purposefully, but not too fast toward the crouching feline. Six-Toed Ollie stayed in the circumference of the light watching my progress with an almost patient expression, until I was a few feet from him. Then he burst forward with alacrity toward Mrs. McCarthy's backyard.

I quickened my pace, thinking that if he paused on her porch, I could probably grab him there. The flashlight traced the trotting tan and white body, which now leaped up the old wooden steps, stopping and sitting by the back door. He cried once and lifted his front legs up almost to the door catch, letting all twelve claws dance over the jamb. Slowly, I reached down and secured him in two hands, picked him up, and held him to my chest. Since I was there, and the lights were on, I figured that I might as well try to rouse Mrs. McCarthy. I was a little bit disturbed by the events of the past few days, and wanted to be sure that she was all right and knew what had gone on with Ollie. After pounding several times, I listened for sounds inside the house. No voices, no movement, no television. . . .

I licked my lips and pulled open the screen door. The back door was locked. Letting the screen door slip closed, I went to the windows at the back of the house and peered inside. It was the kitchen. Stacks of pots and pans littered the floor, and dishes were everywhere. The cabinets stood open, and I could see what appeared to be large holes in the walls. That uneasy feeling continued to grow, and the cop in me took over. I went around to the back section of the house where a triangular wooden structure covered the entrance leading down to her basement. The storm doors weren't locked, and I pulled them up and shone the flashlight down inside. Past a maze of cobwebs, an old padlock dangled unlocked from a hasp on a door at the bottom of half a dozen cement steps. Carrying my squirming burden, I went down the steps, brushing the wispy tendrils away. I removed the lock from the hasp, and pushed on the cellar door. It opened with a creaking sound. I stood debating what to do for a few more minutes, then Six-Toed Ollie made the decision for me. He managed to wriggle out of my grasp and ran into the dark interior. Heaving a sigh, I followed his progress with the flashlight beam, then stepped inside, closing the door behind me. What the hell, I thought. Cops are sort of kissing cousins to burglars anyway.

The basement smelled musty and stacks of cardboard boxes were everywhere. I heard the pit-a-pat of the cat's feet bounding up a slanted wooden staircase ahead of me. Cautiously, I followed, trying my best to be as quiet as a mouse. The stairs went up to an open trap door that led to a pantry. Afraid I would knock something over, I swung the flashlight around and caught sight of the hanging cord of a light bulb. I pulled it and switched off the flashlight. Six-Toed Ollie sat on the table watching me, the ovals of his greenish eyes split by perpendicular slashes of black pupils. I held out my fingers again and clucked softly, hoping this would allow me to grab him again. But no such luck.

Now inside the main part of the house and desperate, I called out, identifying myself. It felt stupid at this point, but since my intentions had been honorable, I figured I would be able to explain my presence.

"Mrs. McCarthy!" I called out again. "It's Tom Parker, your neighbor. I've got your cat."

No response.

I'd searched enough buildings to know the feel of an empty house. I tried one more verbal announcement, as Ollie darted off the table and into a small room next to the kitchen. In one impressive bound he leaped up and landed with a resounding clunk on top of a large deep freeze. The small room appeared to be another pantry of sorts, and I switched the flashlight back on. Instead of doing another fancy leap, the big tomcat watched my approach and delivered a haltingly uneven howl. Then his big claws extended and retracted in rhythmic fashion on the metallic surface. By this time I'd gotten a whiff of something that I knew from experience wasn't spoiled meat. I went to the lid of the deep freeze and Ollie nimbly jumped up on top of an adjacent refrigerator.

Slowly I raised the lid, already knowing what I'd find. The two plastic garbage bags had been rather hastily duct-taped together, but a fringe of iron-gray hair protruded from a tear near the seam.

Suddenly I heard Six-Toed Ollie begin with a hiss that transformed into a feral growl. His ears flattened and he shot off the top of the refrigerator like a white and tan cannonball. That's about when I caught the hint of movement behind me, and whirled in time to see fat Paulie coming at me holding an upraised shovel like a harpoon. The cat passed between us in a flash, and twenty-four sickle-shaped claws dug into the substantial gut bouncing over the dark blue work pants. Paulie screamed, smacking Ollie away while trying to aim the shovel at my head as he swung. The curved metal edge sank into the top of the freezer with a sharp thump. He grunted and tried to lift it for a second swing, but the fingers of my left hand were already curling around the shaft. And a second later my right fist collided with his nose. The shovel came away in my grasp, and Paulie seemed to sit down rather hard on his corpulent backside. A stream of red flooded from his nostrils, and the beady black eyes stared up at me in defeat and exasperation.

From a few feet way, big Ollie arched his back and delivered an accompanying hiss, his tail flaring as big as a raccoon's.

"It was all because of that damn cat," Paulie said, the sobs wracking his voice. "After all the things I always done for her, she was gonna leave her money to that damn cat." He swung his hand in an effete gesture toward the feline, but received only a defiant slap from the Six-Toed Ollie.

I pulled out my gun with my right hand, dropped the shovel behind me, and grabbed my cell phone with my left. I thought about saying, "Tell it to the judge." But sometimes the silence plays better.

Paulie kept right on squealing during his interview with the investigating detectives. For my part, all I had to do was twist things a tad by saying that I heard what I took to be screams from inside the house and went to investigate. Could I be faulted if it turned out to be the cat? After all, a cat's scream can sound awfully human sometimes. . . .

But, like I said, Paulie spilled his guts almost immediately anyway, telling how he had strangled poor old Mrs. McCarthy in a fit of rage after finding out that she intended to leave a substantial portion of her estate to provide for the care of her beloved kitty. Believing that the old lady had secreted a stash of money somewhere in the house, Paulie had been systematically dismantling the interior searching for it. When the odor from the deep freeze started to become a bit noticeable, he'd decided to bury her in a nearby wooded area. Having been a fan of the old *Columbo* TV show, Paulie figured that it would be smart to dig the grave first, then go back and reconnoiter, before returning to pick up the body. That's when he saw me chasing the cat in the kitchen.

Naturally, after the story broke, all kinds of other family members, who'd never even given poor old Mrs. McCarthy the time of day when she was alive, came out of the woodwork trying to vie for a piece of the pie.

And as for Six-Toed Ollie. . . .

I watched him this cold winter's day as he adjusted his back to get more of it against the heating vent in my living room. Then, as if sensing that I was looking at him, he raised his big, triangular head and bleated a cry that sounded more like a baby sheep than a sixteen-pound tomcat. But as Cathy pointed out, he turned out to be the perfect pet for a guy who works afternoons like I do. He sleeps most of the day, eats when he feels like it, and tolerates my presence the rest of the time. But then again, how many many other guys can say that they have a roommate with nine lives, six toes, and a tail, who just happened to have saved their life?

Slightly Guilty

MORRIS HERSHMAN

CARL WEST HATED GETTING INTO this cheap all-wool suit with that tight vest and two-button jacket that never fit right because the padded shoulders dragged down to his arms. It made him feel like he was still working for some two-bit twerp instead of being his own boss.

Bunny, watching him, smiled impishly. "I won't go out with you later tonight if you put on cheap clothes like that."

Carl didn't have to tell her that he was only doing it because he never wanted the boys to think he was high-hatting them by going to the distillery when he was dressed like a million.

Instead he buttoned his fly disdainfully and told her what she needed to know. "You ain't going with me later on."

Bunny's face didn't exactly crumple, but her cherry-red lipstick seemed to shiver a little. "I thought we'd both get dressed for that ritzy place you want to go to."

"I'm going out now on business and then I'll come back and go out alone to the Yard Boys Dinner." The Yard Boys was an organization of New York City hot-shots who raised money to sponsor cultural events in the city "for a happier 1926," as somebody always said at a speech, naming the current year. Carl got a kick out of pledging ten thousand to help pay for a performing visit by the Russian ballet, for instance.

Bunny said softly, "Gee, just think how great we'd look, with me in my French crepe and—"

"You gotta work," he said briskly. "Remember?"

"Mr. Grady said I can take a couple of nights off if I want." Bunny was a dancer at Revels on the Roof, popping out of a giant cardboard cake while people swilled illegal liquor in the town's best known speakeasy. Sometimes, though, she felt as if this was the night for her to be discovered as an artiste, another Marilyn Miller or Ann Pennington.

"Don't bother taking time off," Carl snapped.

"You mean you really don't want me at that big dinner?"

"Now you got it." A high-pitched meow near his feet was enough to annoy him, like it always did. "And I wish to hell you'd get rid of that cat before I do."

He had told her a few times that he'd needed to sleep close to a lot of god-dam cats in his days of being flat broke, and he hated seeing even one cat in this high-class Fifth Avenue apartment.

"I'll keep Ziggy out of your way," she promised for the hundredth time and believed it. The red tabby had been named for Mr. Florenz Ziegfeld, who produced the stylish yearly editions of the Follies. Bunny had never been near the great man, but she liked calling the cat by Ziegfeld's nickname. It made her feel like a show business insider.

She was snuffling as she picked up the growling red cat and moved slowly into the hall and then to her own room. Ziggy padded back just as Carl was irritably climbing into a cheap black cowhide jacket. He aimed a kick at the beast and missed by a mile.

He liked his city car pretty well, a Rollin two-seater that could get thirty miles to the gallon on a good day. He kept a Pierce Arrow Runabout at his other home in Saratoga Springs where he lived in racing season. A different girl decorated that place, a girl demure and stylish, a girl who talked good English, the right sort of a girl for a guy who was nearly rich.

He drove out to Castle Hill Road in the Bronx. Eventually he pulled up at a garage he knew was as cold as an icebox on the inside. He paid a dime to have a boy drive it in. A three-block walk brought him to a two-story gray brick building where workers had made his current easy living possible. It was a distillery licensed to produce medicinal whiskey only. A mint of money had

bought the place and fetched the needed permits to produce and sell the stuff—
not for medicinal purposes, really. Profits came in so soon that he'd been happily repaying loans in no time.

"Maybe trouble will come tonight," the assistant told Carl solemnly in stiff
book-learned English a few minutes after he walked in. The assistant, Sergei
Ivanovich, claimed he had been a Grand Duke in Russia before the Communist
revolution. His bony face reminded Carl of the President of the United States,
Silent Calvin Coolidge himself. "There is talk of a jacking very soon."

"So Ned Reese thinks he'll hijack even a drop of my booze! Well, put two
boys on the truck to ride shotgun with tonight's shipment along with the usual
four. We'll fix Reese."

"Where will I get two men?"

"Take one rifle yourself and offer fifty bucks for—" he looked around at
the shabbily dressed workers busily packing whiskey bottles in large cartoons
"—the closest one."

That worker turned slowly. He was thin, and only the frames of his glasses
were thick. Carl knew him.

"You're Four Eyes Fred Fitch! I'm pretty sure my girlfriend introduced you
to me a while ago."

"Bunny Hatton, yes. She said you'd be an important guy, but I thought she
was dreaming again like she usually does."

"That time she wasn't dreaming. Stick around and you'll have more money
than you'd expect. Fifty bucks extra goes to you for tonight's ride."

"If you remember me at all, you know I don't carry nothing heavy and I
don't hurt nobody."

"You better carry a rifle and ride tonight if you want to be here tomorrow—got that?"

Four Eyes was quiet.

Carl was already putting on the cheap wool cap he wore for these visits in
winter. Gesturing Sergei Ivanovich to follow, he strode to the door and turned
to talk quietly.

"That Four Eyes will never put an eight-ball in the side pocket. He's a flop-
peroo, a guy who'll be broke forever." Carl didn't add that he wanted nobody
working for him who had known him even casually during hard times. "After he
does the extra job tonight, fire him."

He took off that cheap cap and jacket at the first traffic stop and put on his
plaid lined coat. His mind was roaming, which happened to be unusual for him.
It was hard to keep wondering, for instance, how soon the state government
would get done building that bridge from Fort Lee in Jersey over to Fort
Washington in uptown Manhattan, a sure time-saver for everybody when it got

done. Now that he thought about motion, he made a mental note to put down a bet on Bubbling Over for the Kentucky Derby when the time came.

He was humming *I found a million dollar baby in a something-or-other*, not remembering the words five-and-ten cent store, when he reached Fifth Avenue again. In front of the garage he used, he called for an attendant to park his car. In respect for the young man's snappy uniform, Carl paid out a quarter this time.

Before going upstairs to his apartment he tore up the crossword puzzle magazine that Bunny had left in the car. Bunny enjoyed that new fad because she was sure it improved her vocabulary. Leave it to Bunny to waste her time and think she was improving herself.

He had taken off the cheap clothes and jammed them into his hall closet only a few minutes after he got back to his apartment. Deciding that his skin was rough, he spent a few minutes with his fancy new vibro-shave electric razor, keeping one foot on the new saddle-seat toilet top all the time. He had put on a stiff white shirt and bow tie with his knife-crease tuxedo pants and was trying to decide which blackskin shoes to wear for the charity dinner tonight when he heard the front door.

Ready to bawl out Bunny for coming home early as if she could change his mind about not taking her to the dinner, Carl charged into the hall. There must have been steam coming out of his ears.

The door had opened on—he didn't believe it!—Four Eyes Fred Fitch. Four Eyes was walking in slowly, practically tiptoeing as he closed the door behind him and turned.

He was facing Carl West.

Carl knew from experience just how to deal with people who didn't have as much money as he did: surprise them. Smile when they expected scowls, for instance, or use the fists before they could guess what they had done wrong. The trick was to keep poor simps off-balance.

"Come in here," he said roughly, knowing that Four Eyes was expecting to be pitched out.

Carl gestured the intruder into his living room and walked in behind him. Four Eyes gaped at the mirrored walls that reflected both of them along with the hard angular furniture. In particular Four Eyes stared at the loudspeaker radio console, showing admiration for the item rather than for the man whose shrewdness made it possible to own such a treasure.

"Give me the key," Carl said, trying not to show he was annoyed by the misplaced awe as well as by the intrusion. "You got in with it, and I want it. Then I'll have all the locks changed."

The key was handed over, a warm metallic chunk without lettering on the stubby part. Carl made sure that the metal would let somebody into his apartment.

"Where'd you get it?" he snapped, striding back to his living room.

"Made it," Four Eyes said with furtive pride. Even the reflected light in his thick glasses glowed with his pride. "I can put a blank into any door and punch out the pattern without ever leaving the outside hall."

"I don't believe it."

Four Eyes took out a cloth handkerchief from a coat pocket. Half a dozen small instruments gleamed when it was opened. Carl had never seen the likes of them. If he'd had those pieces and had known that trick only a few years ago, he wouldn't have needed to sell logs that had been washed ashore from the Hudson River as firewood. On the other hand, Four Eyes had probably known the key trick for years, but was now shaking in his shoes at being alone in Carl's presence. While Four Eyes was running to get out of the road, in other words, Carl was riding over him.

"I suppose you figured to sneak in if I wasn't home and to take some of my stuff," Carl said with lofty understanding. "You must have been so set up at using those tools that you convinced yourself I wouldn't be here and I guess you were sure you could lie your way out of trouble if you got caught. Okay, go ahead and lie. Let me hear how an idiot punk does it."

"I guess I wasn't thinking clear." Four Eyes swallowed. "I knew I wouldn't be working for you after I told that Russian guy I won't carry a rifle to get a shipment of booze where you want it to go. Before I left town to get away from your boys, I figured I might as well—you know."

"Uh-huh. Steal, you mean—hey, what the hell—"

Carl had been incomplete control up to that point, showing his classiness, proving how much smarter he was, as well as being better off. No human being could have made him lose control, and no human did. It was a cat which made the difference.

Ziggy, the red tabby who caused Bunny to giggle occasionally and say she belonged to him, had originally jumped to the base of the window from here. On this, a favorite perch, he would usually gaze out at the blurry sky and the tall buildings. Every so often, usually in spring or summer, he had a chance to scare off a pigeon who paused on the outer ledge. He would make some clicking noise which the bird certainly couldn't hear, but it was enough to send the youngest of birds back into the air. Bunny, giggling again, would say, as if she believed it, that darling Ziggy gave those little birds their flying lessons.

As soon as he sensed the rising tenseness in the room, Ziggy did what every cat is programmed to do in the case of quarrels among humans: he ran for the exit. He didn't stop, even though his person's person was standing close to the door. Ziggy put on as much speed as Bubbling Over would hopefully put on in the Derby, getting away from that nasty human.

Carl turned the air purple with profanity. To have seen some animal whose species reminded him so much of his own hard times in the past was bad enough. For that beast to have nearly defiled his soup-and-fish—Ziggy had come as close as a whisker—was nothing less than the outside of enough.

Carl was instantly proved wrong in his assumption that nothing could be worse. When a red rim of anger cleared from in front of his eyes and he focused on Four Eyes again, he saw a glint of amusement behind the man's thick glasses. Four Eyes was clearly amused by Carl's discomfort and anger. Disgusted, Carl made up his mind to be sure that any sign of pleasure was wiped off the features of this bozo who did donkey work, wiped off forever.

He kept his voice calm. "Four Eyes, I guess you want me to forget what happened here and even forget that you refused to do your whole job for me, maybe even give you another chance to work for me and I'll swear you never again get asked to ride shotgun with booze or anything else. Isn't that what you want?"

Four Eyes turned serious again. "What would you expect from me in exchange?"

"Catch that cat," Carl said, smiling more widely, "and kill it."

Four Eyes put up a hand in front of his face. "I wouldn't use violence against any creature, and that means I wouldn't wring a cat's neck."

"Who said anything about wringing the damn animal's neck?" Carl was good at making believe he was being perfectly reasonable. "What you do after you catch him is you take him into Bunny's room—there—open the window and throw him out."

"I couldn't do anything like that, either."

Carl swiftly reached back of the standing azure pillow of the nearest soft chair and brought out a gleaming Colt. He pointed it toward the ceiling, but made sure that chandelier lights reflected from its oily surface. Four Eyes couldn't miss the sight.

"Turn down that simple request, Four Eyes, and I might soon be telling my friends the cops that I shot a burglar with a police record. I'd be awfully sorry if I killed him."

"You'd do all that over a cat?"

It wasn't a cat for its own sake, but Carl wouldn't justify himself. He simply glowered.

Four Eyes nodded unwillingly and started down the hallway after that red tabby. When he walked back into Carl's view, the cat was complaining loudly in Four Eyes's clumsy grip.

He said doggedly, "I don't want nobody seeing this," and closed the door of Bunny's room behind himself. The window was opened. The feline squeals came to a stop suddenly. The window was shut.

Slowly the door opened a little way. Four Eyes had to squeeze himself out of there.

"Open it all the way and don't never let me see you again."

Even as Four Eyes hurried to the outside door, in response to Carl's crude gesture, he murmured, "I knew you'd double-cross me."

A draft of wind from the opening hall door opened the door to Bunny's room. Carl, glancing inside, saw the damned cat eating hurriedly from its dish. No doubt it had quieted down when Four Eyes put him there; Carl had originally insisted that the animal's food dish be kept in Bunny's room, and the pan in her bathroom.

The next seconds were a nightmare for cat and man. Ziggy sped away from tension, taking the only possible space to freedom by scooting out between Carl's legs. Carl, seeing his tuxedo actually desecrated with cat hair, making his hand shake in fury, fired down at the cat with what had to be less than perfect aim. . . .

Bunny hurried into the apartment by the back way, the front key having got jumbled up in her ring. Maybe she was too excited to pick it out. There was a good reason for that. After her night's work in the chorus at Revels on the Roof, a British producer had asked if she'd like to work for him. He must be an important producer, about that much she felt sure.

Thank heavens that Carl had insisted she go to work instead of being taken to some society dinner. He'd sacrificed himself for her career. She should think of that as one favor he had done for her. He wasn't always easy to live with. Now that she could help herself in her career, she realized he was sometimes rough on her, very rough on her.

Another girl, a girl who wasn't so forgiving, might've been glad to get out of this arrangement, to be the one who broke it off. Another girl would almost be looking forward to saying those necessary goodbyes.

She stopped to coo at Ziggy on the kitchen windowsill, looking a little— she thought—guilty for some reason. Making her face serious as was fitting for this occasion, Bunny walked to the front of the apartment.

She didn't scream at what she saw there.

Stalker Goes A-Viking

JORDAN STOEN

STALKER SAT IN THE LONGBOAT'S curved bow, eyes, whiskers, and ears pointed toward land, wide tail plume trailing behind. He ignored the soft mist that rose from the river as much as fell from the clouds. Droplets gathered on his long, thick outer coat, turning dark gray hair to black and his lighter markings charcoal.

Aft, at the steering oar, Gunnar Olafson smiled through his wind-tangled blond beard. His ship's cat enjoyed Jorvik—York, the Saxons called it. While only average size for his sturdy Norse breed, Stalker's size and muscle nearly doubled that of cats native to this softer land. He fared well during their visits here.

As he guided the boat past the ancient Roman wall to the beach below the thatched warehouses, Gunnar hoped to do as well. Once again he reviewed his Orkney holding's winter needs. The harvest had been meager. He sent a prayer to Niord that his profit from the summer's raiding would see them past the Hunger Moon.

The ship scraped onto shore beside a row of similar vessels. The sail had already been furled; now ten men shipped oars, then stretched while Gunnar assigned watches. Stalker balanced on the gunwale, casting impatient glances at Gunnar. Gunnar wished the rest of his crew were as courteous, but Vikings weren't known for observing formalities.

"Yah, we go ashore now," Gunnar said. He vaulted to the sand. The cat followed with a soft *thud*, then the rest of the party hit the beach.

They strolled between tents and fires belonging to other voyagers, stretching their legs, adjusting to land again. Stalker strutted foremost, upright tail fluffed wider than Gunnar's wrist, broad head held high above his thick fur ruff. The cat's stately progress looked more regal than that of the emperor Gunnar once served in Constantinople.

They proceeded first to Coppergate, a narrow, timbered street lined by workshops and merchants' stalls. The crew scattered, but Stalker accompanied Gunnar, surveying everything as calmly as a jarl inspecting his subjects.

Grains to feed people and animals until spring took more of Gunnar's silver than he liked. Then they visited the crowded warehouse of Edmund, a chunky Saxon merchant. Here Gunnar found his other needs: ax heads and hoes, a plow blade, knives and spoons, an iron pot. He bargained shrewdly, determined to get full value for his furs, walrus-hide ropes, and what silver he could spare.

As the men talked, a small girl with wispy reddish hair and huge blue eyes crept from between large sacks of furs. The child stared at Stalker, then stood and toddled toward the cat. Gunnar watched closely. Stalker shared his breed's tolerant disposition, but wasn't used to children.

Edmund smiled at the girl. "Asti won't hurt him. She loves animals."

Asti offered Stalker the crumbling oatcake clutched in one dimpled hand. Stalker sniffed, then looked to Gunnar. His wide-set, slanted eyes clearly asked, "Does she think I'd eat *this*?"

Gunnar held back laughter, not wanting to hurt the child's feelings. "It's good of you to share, but Stalker prefers meat or fish."

Edmund said, "I'm afraid we've none of that today. My wife is in childbed, with all our household's women running to and fro. Asti and I are on our own this afternoon."

He opened a wooden box on his cluttered table and took out a leather bag. "See what I have to reward my wife's efforts." Edmund opened the bag and spilled its glittering contents into his palm.

Gunnar's eyes widened as Edmund suspended a necklace between both hands. Beautifully wrought silver links joined to an oval pendant. At its center gleamed a large sapphire, with four smaller ones set around the edges. Excellent workmanship, highest quality stones—and their deep blue matched Inga's eyes. Gunnar pictured the stones on his nearest neighbor's middle daughter, and how those eyes would sparkle over such a treasure.

Stalker jumped onto the table and watched the pendant sway gently between Edmund's hands. The cat raised one broad paw toward the swinging bauble, and Edmund snatched it out of reach with a chuckle.

"You like this, hey?" said Edmund. "Well, it's spoken for. I got two fistfuls of these stones from an Arab trader a few years back. Some became earrings for Thora when she gave me Asti two years ago. However, I have something else you might appreciate."

He took another small leather bag from the box. It held a charming silver brooch of the same fine workmanship, set with three more blue stones. None so large as those in the necklace, they were gorgeous all the same.

"Feel how heavy it is: the best silver." Edmund handed Gunnar the brooch.

Gunnar turned it over, enjoying its smooth feel, admiring the craftwork. He gave it back reluctantly. "It's a rare treasure, nearly as beautiful as the woman I'd give it to. But I need to keep what little silver you've left me for emergencies."

Hearing truth in his voice, Edmund slipped the brooch and necklace back into their bags. "Perhaps next year." They then arranged to exchange goods the following day.

Outside Edmund's door, Stalker gave a questioning meow.

"Yah, today's business is finished," Gunnar told him. "I want a bath and a taste of wine. Enjoy yourself as you like."

Stalker looked slowly from side to side, then strolled with lordly dignity toward the pier where fishing boats landed. Gunnar laughed aloud. Many city cats congregated there toward day's end. If past experience was any guide, Stalker would have some fine fights, a good dinner, and make a grand impression on Jorvik's female cats.

Gunnar sat long in a wineshop where an excellent skald recited sagas for customers. He returned to his ship late, and found Stalker there before him. He also found several town cats, all intent on boarding the vessel. From the looks of them Stalker had already demonstrated they stood no chance, but they continued to slink around the boat, voicing occasional *rowls*. Stalker paced the gunwales, rumbling threats back at them.

Gunnar rolled up on deck in his sealskin bag, proof against the light drizzle, well padded with eider ducks' down. But the prowling cats prevented sleep. Twice he rose and chased cats away, tossing water on them from a hide bucket. They returned before he could slip back into his sealskin. Just as he started drifting off in spite of the feline disturbances, Stalker gave a loud scream. He launched himself at a foolhardy black-and-white who had leaped onto the ship at one side while Stalker patrolled the other. Muttering curses, Gunnar took to the beach. He knew enough of cats to realize when it was pointless to interfere in their business.

The following morning's sun shone through wispy clouds. Cats still prowled near the ship. Gunnar couldn't guess what it meant, but warned Kark to keep them off. Stalker watched Kark while most of the crew collected trade goods to complete Gunnar's transactions. Then, satisfied that the ship's guardian could handle his job, the cat escorted Gunnar into town.

After the grain merchant's donkey cart started for the ship, Gunnar and Stalker returned to Edmund's warehouse. Three of Gunnar's men had delivered the trade items. Edmund inspected them. It only remained for Gunnar to hand over his silver.

"A good bargain." Edmund set aside his scales and held out his right hand.

"A good bargain," Gunnar repeated, slapping Edmund's palm. His crewmen carried away his purchases.

Stalker had disappeared. Now a soft giggle came from behind a barrel. Gunnar and Edmund exchanged glances, then peered over the barrel.

Young Asti sat in a nest of blankets. Stalker covered her legs like a plump fur robe. The girl held something to Stalker's mouth, and laughed as he nibbled.

"So, she has her way, as usual." Edmund smiled fondly. "My brother brought a fine fat goose to celebrate last night, and Asti insisted on saving some for your cat. You don't mind?"

"Certainly not." Gunnar wondered what Edmund celebrated, then remembered yesterday's conversation. "All went well with your wife?"

Edmund's smile broadened into a proud grin. "A fine healthy son, my first heir."

"How did Thora like the necklace?"

Edmund shook his head. "I was so excited when the thrall came with the news, I ran home without it. I even forgot Asti! Thank the holy Madonna, the slave had enough wit to lock the door and bring the child."

He moved to the box as he spoke and brought out the necklace. It sparkled in sunlight from the open door.

Gunnar watched without envy. Someday he would buy a lovely trinket that he could offer for Inga. Surely she would favor a man who gave gifts almost as lovely as herself.

"Pretty!" Little Asti stood gazing up, delight on her round face.

Her father nodded. "Perhaps when you're older Mother will let you wear it."

Shouts sounded in the street just then. Something thumped the wall. Gunnar and Edmund hurried to the door. Two men fought three of the city guards, yelling and throwing wild punches. The guards quickly subdued the men and marched them off to settle the matter away from the watching crowd.

As the street cleared, Gunnar took his leave. A fair wind was rising; he hoped his grain was loaded. Stalker trotted ahead and reached the ship long before his master.

Cats still prowled the beach, twice as many as earlier. Kark reported difficulties tripping over them while loading the grain, but thought none had boarded. Gunnar frowned in puzzlement, but soon forgot the riddle of the cats as he made ready to sail.

He was about to give the order to shove off when a spear rapped the ship's prow. Looking over the side, he saw a dozen city guards in chain mail and round helmets.

"Where is Gunnar Olafson?" one demanded.

"That's me."

"You must come with us, in the king's name. A freeman has accused you of thievery."

Gunnar stared at them, dumbfounded. After a moment he found his voice, but not his wits. "Thievery? What freeman?"

"Edmund the Ironmonger."

Why would Edmund say such a thing? Gunnar had been accused of many crimes in his days a-viking, but never something he hadn't done. And never by a friend.

Stalker leaped to the prow and hissed at the guard. The man stepped back, startled, as well he might. With ears back and fur on end, the husky cat looked ferocious.

"Stalker, down!"

The cat relaxed somewhat, but his tail switched dangerously.

Gunnar's men grumbled behind him. They would be foolish to fight the guards. Even if they escaped, the king's warships would make short work of Gunnar's ship, perhaps even sink it. This must be a mistake he could set right.

When Gunnar jumped to the sand, Stalker landed beside him. The guard captain ordered Gunnar's men off the ship also, while most of the guards boarded to search it. "And you," he finished, pointing at Gunnar's crew, "get rid of these cursed cats!"

Two guards escorted Gunnar back to Edmund's warehouse. There the stocky trader glared at Gunnar.

"Thora's necklace!" he growled. The venom in his voice startled Gunnar. "You stole it while I was distracted by that street brawl."

"I swear by Odin's eye, I never touched it! I went with you to the door, then left. I wasn't near it."

"Don't bother lying." The merchant's tone rang colder than the iron he sold. "I heard the yearning in your voice yesterday. You spoke of a beautiful woman, a suitable gift. After you left, the necklace was gone, and no one here but me. The necklace left with you."

Despite Gunnar's protests, the guards searched him thoroughly. When they found no stolen treasure, they threw him against a wall to await news from those searching the ship.

Gunnar stood proudly, refusing to hang his head. Was the merchant plotting against him? Did he want Gunnar bound to him, to work off this debt? Perhaps he planned to demand wergild payment for Gunnar's freedom.

But Gunnar had nothing to pay with except his ship or his land. The land was his security, a place to start a family. The ship meant income to build his holding into a profitable farm.

He ground his teeth. Edmund would regret this treachery.

Stalker leaped atop a barrel and butted his head against his master's arm. *"Mrowr?"* The tone meant "Can we leave?"

"Not yet." Gunnar sighed. "They think I stole that shiny ornament you liked. We can't leave until it's found."

Stalker gave him such a thoughtful look, Gunnar almost believed he understood. The cat leaped to the table. He sniffed the wooden box where the merchant stored his jewels, then examined the table's surface. Next, Stalker jumped to the floor and padded off between the barrels and sacks.

Gunnar turned to the guards who stood in the doorway between himself and freedom. Edmund stood with them and glared at Gunnar. The Viking glared back.

"No!" a shrill voice cried. "Mine!"

Stalker's battle growl sounded. He backed from between two barrels, something shiny stretching from his mouth. As he emerged, more shining links appeared, then the sapphire pendant, followed by the rest of the chain. Which was clutched at its other end in a chubby fist.

"Bad cat!" Asti yelled. "*My* pretty!"

Edmund gaped. Then, as his eyes met Gunnar's again, the trader flushed a deep, dull red.

Gunnar let loose a bellow of relieved laughter. The guards, looking from cat to child, from Edmund to Gunnar, laughed too.

Edmund closed his eyes. "Holy Mother of God." He swooped on his child while Gunnar bent to pry the necklace from Stalker's jaws.

"Your property, I believe." Gunnar handed the necklace to Edmund.

The merchant flushed even redder, but to his credit met Gunnar's gaze squarely.

"I am in your debt. Can I ever compensate you for this unfortunate incident?"

"Let me sail before I lose the wind. And next year, give me a good price on a gift for a farmer's lady."

"I can do better than that." Edmund put down his daughter. Opening the box, he removed the brooch in its leather pouch. "Take this."

Gunnar backed away. "That's too much for a simple misunderstanding."

"But not for unfairly staining a man's honor. And as reward for recovering something of much greater value."

Gunnar shrugged. "I did nothing. Stalker found it."

Everyone looked at the cat, who stood near the door, obviously impatient to leave.

"Come to think of it, how did the cat find it?" Edmund asked.

Gunnar studied Asti, his mind working rapidly. He knelt, taking her tiny hands in his own rough palms. After examining them, he straightened. "May I?" He reached for the necklace.

Edmund, staring at Stalker, passed Gunnar the pendant.

Gunnar inspected the chain. "Goose grease!"

"What do you mean?" a guard asked.

"Asti has goose grease on her hands, and some caught here in the links."

He pointed. "She must have touched the table when she took the necklace, and Stalker smelled goose. He remembered the lunch she fed him, and went looking for more. With the necklace smelling of goose grease as well, he thought to get another bite. He took it to chew on."

Edmund nodded, but kept a speculative eye on Stalker. The guards clapped Gunnar on the back, then went to end their comrades' search of the ship. Gunnar made to follow them, but Edmund stopped him.

"Your cat solved the crime; the reward is his. But since a cat has no use for jewelry, you take care of it for him." Edmund spoke firmly, but his eyes held a pleading look. Now Gunnar understood. The trader's shame at accusing a friend of his daughter's deed could be relieved only by this generous payment.

Gunnar nodded. The pouch changed hands, then Gunnar held out his right palm. Edmund slapped it smartly, smiling for the first time since the guards delivered Gunnar to him.

Approaching his ship, Gunnar saw men busily restowing goods displaced during the search. Two, however, worked to repel cats that jumped onto the ship faster than the men could throw them overboard. Stalker dashed down the beach with a wild battle cry and went to work dispersing the feline horde.

Once finally under way, Gunnar handed the steering oar to Kark and looked for Stalker. On the way back from Edmund's warehouse he had bought a fine fresh cod. Now Stalker would have his reward. After all, the cat had saved his master's freedom, ship, and land, and earned the brooch that might win Inga—although Gunnar must learn first how Inga felt about Stalker. If she didn't admire the cat, she would never see the lovely breastpin; he'd find a woman with more discerning taste.

Stalker didn't appear when called, and wasn't in any of his usual spots. The Viking began to worry that his cat had been left behind in the rush to embark. Had Stalker chased an enemy up the beach, and not returned in time?

Gunnar searched through cargo under the aft half deck. He was on the point of ordering the ship to turn back when an unfamiliar noise came to him over the ship's creaking. It sounded like a cat's cry, but too high and soft for Stalker. Did they have a stowaway after all?

He wormed his way between water barrels, crawled over boxes of dried herring. Finally he reached the long wrapped bundle of extra sail. Behind it lounged a large mound of long gray fur, unmistakably Stalker. Enough light came from the open center cargo well to show the delicate red-gold feline nestled against his side. The smaller cat stared at Gunnar with round blue eyes, then closed them and stretched her neck as Stalker licked her cheek.

Gunnar chortled. "So. You vanquished your foes, won a treasure, and carried off this beautiful lady. Perhaps you should be chief instead of me." He reached into his tunic and drew out the cod. "And as you brought me a gift for my lady, here's a gift for yours."

The man watched the two cats share the fish. Stalker showed uncharacteristic restraint while his dainty companion sniffed and nibbled. Then Gunnar crept away to leave them in privacy. He grinned. Wait until his crew heard why they had been besieged by cats.

Swirls of Midnight

JUDITH POST

LAWRENCE TRIPPED OVER A CLOD of dirt and swung his flashlight back and forth, up and down. The Pearsons' mausoleum glowed bone-white in the moonlight. Jessica's fresh grave was four tombstones to the left of it, her humble granite headstone overpowered by its high dome and marble columns.

She wouldn't like being in someone else's shadow, Lawrence thought. She'd never liked being second best.

When he reached the pile of dirt that covered her coffin, he swung his flashlight up its length. Yellow eyes reflected his beam. Nothing would bring Lawrence into a cemetery at night except for the love of his cat, Midnight. Black as ink, impossible to find in pools of darkness, Midnight was the best cat Lawrence had ever had. The best *anything* he'd ever had, in fact.

"Let's get out of here." He reached for the cat. "It's time to go home."

Midnight moved away, turned to the gravestone, arching his back. A breeze whistled past them, and Lawrence swallowed hard. His skin went clammy, his breathing shallow. He had no idea how the cat had found Jessica's grave. All he wanted was to leave this dreary place and return home. "Midnight, please...."

A sharp hiss was the cat's good-bye to Jessica. Then Lawrence understood. Midnight had wanted to make sure that she was gone, that it was final.

"From now on, it's just you and me," Lawrence said.

Satisfied, Midnight allowed himself to be picked up and held close.

It had never been a question of who was master once Midnight came to Lawrence's door and scratched for comfort. He'd been a tiny kitten, barely weaned. Lawrence had been immediately touched when the cat curled on his lap and suckled his arm while falling asleep.

"Removed from his mother too soon," the vet had proclaimed. "He still needs to suckle to feel secure. He'll outgrow it."

But Midnight never had. Whenever he needed comfort, love, he suckled Lawrence's arm. To sleep, he curled against Lawrence's chest on the big king-sized mattress that had once bedded Lawrence and Jessica before Jessica met Mark.

Lawrence did his best to understand. Women deserved romance. And Mark was full of flowery language. Women deserved beauty. And Mark was Grecian with curly dark hair and soulful brown eyes. Women deserved love, and Mark espoused his devotion each day and every night. How could Lawrence, staid and devoted, ever compete with someone like that? It hurt, but didn't surprise him. He'd never really expected Jessica to stay.

Midnight, on the other hand, roamed the apartment, meowing pitifully. No treats, no cuddles could alleviate the cat's suffering. "Things change," Lawrence proclaimed.

The cat turned his head and snubbed him.

Lawrence scooped tuna into the cat's dish. "I did everything I could." Midnight refused to eat.

He poured a saucer of milk. "What more did you want? When you were a stray, I took you in. I let her live here, rent free, while she went to college. Same thing. I even asked her to marry me." Midnight ignored him.

He piled shredded cheese in a bowl. "I treated her every bit as well as I treat you." The cat turned his head and listened. "It's not like we ditched her. She was the one who dumped us." Midnight went to the tuna and began to eat.

A few weeks later, Lawrence bumped into Mark at the corner bar.

"You probably hate me," Mark said. He was drinking at least one beer too many.

"I don't hate you." Lawrence spread sales brochures on the bar in front of him. He wanted to buy new furniture for the apartment. Since Jessica had left, he had a lot more spare cash.

"She wants me to be more like you," Mark said, taking a long draw from his glass. "Hold a steady job, make more money."

"She said my job was boring, that I wasn't rich enough to be exciting. She said I wasn't ugly or handsome enough to be remarkable."

Mark blinked. "She told me looks aren't all that important when you really get to know a person. She told me that talk is cheap."

Lawrence pointed to the photo of a seven-foot-long velvet sofa. "What do you think? Midnight would love stretching out on that."

"She used you, man. Free rent all through college. Then she talked you into co-signing for that little convertible she loves so much and stuck you with the payments."

Lawrence shrugged. "I thought she was worth it. I counted myself lucky every day she was mine."

"She ditched you the minute she graduated and got a job."

"A good job, too. I was happy for her," Lawrence said.

"Even when you found out she'd been sleeping with me while she was living with you?"

"Pretty girls need a diversion. I was her security until she got on her feet, could make her own way."

Mark banged his glass on the bar, sloshing his beer. "All she talks about is you and that black cat. I'm ready to boot her out, send her back."

"Oh, don't do that. I didn't satisfy her the way you do."

Mark tried to push himself to his feet. "You, my friend, know the true meaning of the word 'love.' Me, I'm selfish. I wanted her, needed her, to make myself happy. Now I can't stand her, God help me."

Lawrence paid both of their tabs and walked Mark to a cab. "You're used to getting what you want. I'm not. You wanted Jessica, and she wanted you."

Jessica came to the apartment a few days after the furniture was delivered. "It's breathtaking," she said, walking around to inspect the wine-colored velvet couch, the tapestry chair, and Oriental rug. She sat on the sofa and sighed. When Midnight jumped beside her, she gave him a sharp smack on the head and pushed him down. "Pets aren't allowed on the furniture."

"He's always slept on the sofa during the day," Lawrence protested.

"That piece of junk? What did it matter? But now that everything's new, he'll leave hairs on it. It'll be ruined."

Midnight paced to the plush Oriental rug and kneaded his claws in and out, in and out.

"Stop that!" Jessica rolled a magazine and struck him.

Midnight ran to hide behind Lawrence's legs.

"Mark said he met you at the bar," Jessica said. "That's where he spends most of his time. You could probably tell that we're not doing very well."

"It's early. Every relationship has start-up bumps."

"Ours didn't."

"That's because I'm so boring."

Jessica stood and crossed the room, put her arms around Lawrence, and sobbed softly against his shoulder. "I'm so unhappy. I'm almost desperate."

Lawrence's body sagged. He gave a deep sigh. "Try to hang on," he finally pleaded. "You love Mark."

Her gaze roamed the apartment, the new sponge-painted walls, gold-rimmed mirrors, and stained-glass lamps. "I'll try." But her tone wasn't encouraging. As she crossed the room to get her jacket, she absently kicked Midnight out of her way.

When Lawrence opened the door to collect his mail, the cat bolted from the apartment. It was the first time he'd stepped outside since the night he appeared on Lawrence's doorstep. It took an exhaustive search to find him. When Lawrence finally located him, Midnight was high in a tree branch that overhung the street.

"What do you think you're doing?" Lawrence yelled. He was furious. "You've worried me half to death! If anything happened to you—"

His words were cut off by a car's engine roaring their way. Jessica was flying toward him, several suitcases on the seat beside her. Her long, wavy hair blew in golden waves behind her. The convertible's top was down, as usual.

When she darted toward the curb, Midnight pounced, leaping from the tree branch into the front seat of her car. Her arms flew in front of her face and the car veered into a parked van. As it bounced back into the street, Midnight leapt onto the sidewalk. Brakes squealed and a Lincoln caught the front of the convertible, spinning it. A pick-up truck hit it square-on, and it rolled. By the time it stopped moving, the convertible was upside down, and Jessica was dead.

Lawrence glanced at Jessica's headstone before turning to leave the graveyard. Ironic, he thought. The angel perched on top of it had long, narrow eyes almost exactly like Midnight's. He stroked the cat as he carried him home. Midnight burrowed his face against Lawrence's arm and began to suckle.

"It was self-defense," he told the cat. "We loved her, but she didn't love us. You knew I wasn't strong enough to survive her again. You did it to save me."

It was the first time he'd said it, even thought it. Midnight curled close against his chest and began to purr. Lawrence finally realized that the cat *did* have a sense of honor and loyalty, unlike Jessica. Lawrence had found them both and given them a home. Midnight would never forget it. Or lose it. Ever.

Tea and 'Biscuit

JON L. BREEN

DO HAVE A CUP OF TEA, and I'll tell you a story.

My nephew Jerry Brogan sometimes accuses me of trying to escape reality. That is, of course, absurd. No one my age would think such a thing possible. Reality will always come after you, whether in the form of the unavoidable processes of aging or the more dramatic form of finding a dead body on the grounds of your own home, as I did some years ago when jockey Hector Gates was murdered there. I solved that one, with some help from Jerry, and yet when he has become involved in other puzzles of a criminal nature, he has never called on me, despite my deep knowledge of detection from a lifetime of reading about it. Am I trying to evade reality or is Jerry trying to shield me from it?

I should introduce myself before I go on. My name is Olivia Barchester, widow these many years of the late Colonel Glyndon Barchester, who campaigned Vengeful and other fine thoroughbreds on California tracks. I myself raced Vicar's Roses, among others, after my husband's death.

Odd to say I raced them. I never saw any of my own horses in person, since I never went to the track after the Colonel died, but they ran in my colors. So if a trainer or a jockey's agent can say, "I hooked the favorite at the head of the stretch and beat him a nose at the wire," I suppose I can say I raced Vicar's Roses.

While I won't admit to evading reality, I do take the prerogative of one who is fairly advanced in years and comfortably off (say old and rich if you must) and control my environment to the greatest extent possible. I don't consider myself a recluse, but I see little need to leave my home and my books. After my husband's death, I decided to follow racing to the extent possible on television. More recently, I decided not to watch live races on television. That decision came after Go for Wand's tragic death in the Belmont stretch the day of the 1990 Breeder's Cup. Now I videotape the races on my VCR and watch them at my leisure the evening of the day they are run, relying on Jerry to let me know if anything tragic occurred that I can shield myself from seeing. Self-indulgent, I'll admit, but I can enjoy a race so much more when I know all the runners and their jockeys will reach home safely.

Now I must introduce you to my black cat Seabiscuit, a handsome fellow from a rather distinguished litter who has been my companion for the past fifteen years. All of Seabiscuit's siblings were named for notable one-word race-horses—Stymie, Citation, Equipoise, Swaps, Nashua, Regret. They were born on the backstretch to a stable pet from the barn of an English trainer who insisted, contrary to American superstition, black cats were *good* luck.

There are many cats in racetrack stable areas, though most of them are strays, semi-wild. They are seldom pets for racehorses. Goats are more often cast in that role, for their calming effect on the highstrung thoroughbred.

Thus it is hardly surprising that, while most of Seabiscuit's litter found homes with persons connected to racing, only one followed in his mother's footsteps as a stable mascot. That brings me, you'll be relieved, to the subject of my story.

On a coolish fall evening, toward the end of the annual Surfside Meadows meeting where my nephew Jerry works as track announcer, I was visited by an old acquaintance, trainer Walter Cribbage. I brought him into my library, where Seabiscuit was lying by the fire and I had been engrossed in a vintage Agatha Christie novel from my extensive collection. I offered Walter a choice of beverage. I was sipping tea, but he opted for a straight bourbon, an indication of his troubled state of mind.

Walter is of my generation, thus nearing eighty, but he still has a trim figure and an erect, almost military carriage, and he still is up early mornings seeing to his string of horses. On this particular evening, we began by exchanging good-natured banter in the old way, but it seemed a bit forced on his part. He was clearly worried about something, and I was relieved when he got to the point of his visit.

"Olivia, Exterminator died this morning."

Remembering the post-World War I gelding, I said, "I should think he died years ago."

"Not the horse. The cat. He lived in my stable all these years. He came from the same litter as Seabiscuit. Remember?"

"Oh, of course. I am sorry to hear it. Still, fifteen is a good age for a cat, and one cannot hope—"

"That litter is notably long-lived, Olivia. Citation and Stymie are both still around. And he didn't die of old age, Olivia. He was murdered. Poisoned."

"Oh, dear. But why? Some superstitious backstretch worker, I suppose."

"He survived fifteen years without superstition getting the better of him. I think I know why he was killed. I have a horse in my barn named Band Wagon."

"Walter, as I think you know very well, that was one of the last horses I bred. Odd to say I bred him—I wasn't there in the shed after all—but I did plan the mating of his parents, Red Band and Hay Ride."

"I thought you'd be concerned about his welfare."

"Most certainly. You're doing very well with him, I understand. Jerry tells me he may be favored for the Surfside Handicap. But I'm sorry he doesn't belong to my friends the Burnsides any more."

Walter made a face. "As one who has to deal with the current owners, Mr. and Mrs. Preston Fremont and son, I sometimes share your sorrow. Still, if the Burnsides still had him, I wouldn't have got the chance to train him, would I? I got him just over a year ago. He was a bad actor and had never run up to his potential. Since I've had him, he's gotten better and better, and I don't take a smidgen of the credit. He fell in love with Exterminator. As long as that black cat was around the barn, he was as calm and as kind as can be. He started training well and racing better. That black cat made him a stakes horse. Now he's gone into a tailspin, not eating well, acting up. In the state he's in now, I don't think he'd win a ten-thousand-dollar claimer, let alone the Surfside Handicap."

Very sad, of course, for my last good horse to fall on bad days, but how could I help? After considerable hemming and hawing, Walter finally got to the point.

"Olivia, I have a big favor to ask of you. I want to borrow Seabiscuit."

"Borrow Seabiscuit? You must be joking."

Hearing his name twice in quick succession, Seabiscuit woke from his slumber and strolled over to sit by my chair, happily oblivious to the significance of our conversation.

"He and Exterminator are virtually identical," Walter continued. "Maybe having him around the barn would bring Band Wagon back into form."

I shook my head. "Walter, I'd like to help you, but I can't believe you'd ask me that. To begin with, cats, even much younger ones than Seabiscuit, don't always adjust well to new surroundings. He has grown accustomed to this house and these grounds, a quiet and predictable environment." I reached down to scratch Seabiscuit's ear, and he appreciatively rubbed his head against my palm. "Put him in the middle of the furor of the backstretch at his age, and who knows how he would react? Second, cats as much as horses have very distinct personalities. There is no reason to think Seabiscuit could establish that same special bond with Band Wagon simply because he and Exterminator are closely related. And finally, Walter, you are asking Seabiscuit to fill in where his brother has already been poisoned. You think I would consider putting him in that situation?"

Walter looked crestfallen. "You're quite right, of course. I never should have asked. But I don't know what else to do."

It was at that moment that Jerry phoned to assure me that the day's racing at Surfside, as well as ESPN's coverage of a midwestern stake, had passed without a hitch and was safe for me to watch. Not sharing my nephew's tendency to keep a mystery to himself, I invited him to join Walter and me for a discussion of the problem. He seemed to treat it as a command appearance, though of course it was nothing of the kind. He turned up at my door within minutes.

When he had settled his considerable bulk into an easy chair and accepted a cup of tea and a scone, Jerry listened closely to Walter's story and said rather archly, "It reminds me of the curious incident of Barnbuster's goat."

Walter seemed to brighten slightly. "Barnbuster had no goat."

"That was the curious incident."

"Really," I said, "while nothing delights me more than Sherlockian allusions, I haven't any idea what you two are talking about."

"Don't you remember a horse called Barnbuster a few years ago? He only lived up to his name when his pet goat Mary Poppins wasn't around. The owner-trainer was down on his luck and forced to sell the horse. He got a good price based on the horse's record, but he cleverly withheld Mary P. Barnbuster proved unmanageable for his new owner, and the original owner was able to buy him back for considerably less than he'd been paid for him. Reunited with his nanny, Barnbuster resumed his winning ways."

Walter chuckled at what was obviously a familiar story, then turned grim again. "Doesn't apply to my situation."

"Not exactly, no, but I wouldn't rule out the former owners. Could they be looking for a way to get Band Wagon back cheap? Or maybe seeking revenge against the new owners?"

I was scandalized. "Jerry, what a suggestion! You've known Matthew and Helen Burnside all your life."

"A lot of people probably knew Jack the Ripper all *his* life, too."

"Do be serious! He's just talking this way to irritate me, Walter."

"All right, all right. I don't really suspect the Burnsides, okay?"

"Besides, they've been living on Maui for over a year," I had to add.

"Then let's see what else we can figure out," Jerry said, truly applying himself to the problem for the first time. "How do you know Exterminator was poisoned?"

"The vet recognized the symptoms," Walter said, "and it wasn't the first time someone had tried to kill him. A week or two before, I discovered someone had put a rubber band around the poor cat's stomach. It was eating into his flesh, and there was nothing he could have done about it. It surely would have killed him eventually, and very painfully. I got it off him, and saved his life."

"What a terrible thing to do to an innocent animal," I said, more thankful than ever I had declined to loan Seabiscuit. He cooperated reluctantly as I protectively gathered him into my lap.

"Any new stable employees?" Jerry asked.

"They've all worked for me for years."

"Any of them unusually superstitious?"

"Perhaps, but not about black cats."

Annoyingly, Jerry resumed his anecdotal posture. "It's not always just black cats. I once knew a hotwalker who was heavily into numerology. To him, *any* cat was bad luck in a barn. You take a horse's four legs and add them to a cat's nine lives, and what do you have? Thirteen."

Walter seemed as impatient with Jerry's digression as I was. "Everybody who works for me loved the cat," he insisted.

"Do the owners of Band Wagon visit the backstretch often?"

Walter nodded. "What a bunch. If I didn't like their horse so much, I'd dump them in a minute. Old Preston Fremont is a mean bastard with a short temper and no real regard for horses. He'd run them into the ground if I'd let him. He's smart enough not to even try to do that to Band Wagon, though, and he certainly wouldn't have harmed the cat no matter how angry he was. He loves the money Band Wagon makes him too much.

"Then there's Millicent Fremont, his wife. Kids herself she can dress like a woman half her age, and every time she comes to the stable she seems to resent those filthy things you have to have around a barn—you know, dirt, dung, people. Imagines herself a horse-lover, though. Makes a big deal of feeding her horses carrots. I wonder how'd she'd react if one of them bit her polished nails!

"And the son is the prize of the lot. Young Delbert. Twenty-five and never did an honest day's work. Doesn't know one end of the horse from another but always has big plans for the stable. A terrible snob with all his other sterling qualities. It was his bright idea Band Wagon should prove his worth by racing in Europe next spring. Even had his old man half convinced it was a good plan. I told them it was impossible, and Preston understood, but the kid practically threw a tantrum."

"What relationship did the three owners have to the late Exterminator?" Jerry asked.

"Relationship with the cat? None at all, really. Preston understood why we had to keep him around, but I don't remember he ever came near him. Millicent would make a big fuss over him until he got pawprints over one of her thousand-dollar dresses one morning. Since then, she's kept her distance. Delbert's gone on record as hating all domestic animals, and I guess that includes horses as well as cats, though moneymakers like Band Wagon he manages to take some interest in."

"Are any of *them* superstitious?"

"Just the opposite, if anything. You have to understand, Jerry, the role of Exterminator in that barn was not a matter of superstition. It was just the relationship he had with Band Wagon. They were pals. Mr. and Mrs. Fremont accepted that, but the son always figured it *was* superstition, and the idea drove him nuts."

"How frequently do you see the owners, Walter?"

"More than I want to. I sometimes think they're there every day, but it probably just seems that way."

Jerry nodded. "I think I know who killed the cat," he said, with the offhand casualness appropriate to a brilliant amateur. I'm sure he puts that on for my benefit. "Not that it will do you much good. Killing a domestic animal isn't nearly as serious a criminal offense as it ought to be, and knowing who did it won't help your problem with Band Wagon . . ."

Jerry shook his head solemnly and stared into the fire, letting his dramatic pause lengthen intolerably.

I cleared my throat. "Jerry, if you'll permit me, whodunits form a large part of my recreation. I still might like to know who the killer was."

"So would I," Walter said.

"Sure," Jerry said obligingly. "It has to be the son."

Walter wagged his head. "How on earth did you figure that out?"

"Go back a minute, Walter. You didn't say racing Band Wagon in Europe would be just a bad idea because he didn't like to run on grass or something. You said it would be impossible. Why impossible?"

Before Walter could answer, I belatedly caught on to Jerry's line of reasoning. "The quarantine! A domestic cat would probably have to be quarantined for months before he would be permitted in a European country. It wouldn't be possible for Band Wagon to travel with his pal. And without Exterminator's companionship, Band Wagon would have been useless on the track. So the idea really was impossible from your point of view, Walter."

Jerry nodded. "But young Delbert thought Exterminator's role was just superstitious nonsense. He thought if he killed the cat, and if Band Wagon then carried on his winning ways as before, his scenario of campaigning the horse over European tracks could be realized."

"I ought to have known!" Walter Cribbage exclaimed. "The last time Delbert visited the stable area he had a scratch on his face."

"Probably he got that on his first attempt, when he put the rubber band on Exterminator," Jerry said. He reached down to stroke Seabiscuit, who had fled my lap when the thrill of detection made me too animated.

So among the four of us we seemed to have solved the whodunit. But what good did that do Walter Cribbage, you ask, in his effort to restore Band Wagon to form? Jerry was able to offer him a small ray of hope. One of Regret's offspring, thus a nephew of Exterminator, was a backstretch resident at Santa Anita and might conceivably be available as a new companion for Band Wagon. If bloodlines meant anything at all, Jerry argued, why not give him a try?

I remained dubious about the probable success of a surrogate, but when I heard the cat's name, I felt it was a good omen. It was Vengeful, after my late husband's best runner.

Band Wagon did win the Surfside Handicap, but Delbert Fremont wasn't around to see it. Died of an infected cat scratch, poor lad.

Well, I wouldn't have told you the story if it didn't have a happy ending.

Tombs

JOHN R. PLATT

THE CHURCH WAS QUIET AND DARK. It felt like home.
The gray-haired man placed his bags on the floor, then slowly closed the door behind him, cutting off the light from the street lamps outside. Now, just a few candles cast their weak shadows on the frescoed walls.

He picked up his bags—one of them hissing slightly—and walked further inside.

Thick white votives sat on either side of the confessional. He put his bags down once again, and stepped in through the open door.

He lowered himself to the hard wooden seat, rubbed his tired eyes and raised his head.

"Forgive me, Father, for I have sinned. It has been three days since my last confession."

A sigh came from behind the small opening in the wall. "What did you do this time, Max?"

Max began.

It started yesterday . . . in Geneva of all places. A city of peace.

I had been sent to take care of a woman, a scientist on vacation—no one special, really. Just another cog in another government's wheel. But take care of her and you leave her people several months behind in developing a new computer chip, or something like that.

They don't always tell me these things.

I saw her sitting there, alone, looking out at the snow-capped mountains, and I realized, for the first time in fifteen years, that I just couldn't do it.

I know you know what I mean here, Father. Don't make me say it.

My plane had barely landed back in the States before I heard that the Old Man had requested to see me. I expected to be reprimanded—hell, I knew I'd be lucky if that was all I got. Instead, the Old Man simply said he needed me to make a delivery.

A delivery. I was on my way out, perplexed, when he called my name.

"Max."

I turned back toward him. The morning sun was just rising in the window behind the Old Man, turning his skin translucent, his long white hair into a glowing halo. I had to squint just to look straight at him.

He reached down into a drawer, pulled something out, and placed it on the edge of the desk. "You'll be needing this."

I hesitated, my mind finally beginning to question what was going on. "Why do you need me to make a simple delivery? Wouldn't a courier do just as well?"

The Old Man glared at me. "Just do it, Max."

I took the package and left.

Noon in the city brought out the businessmen in droves. Hundreds of people rushed past me, their marching feet a heartbeat faster than any city deserved. Stuck in the middle of it all, I sat alone, one of the few patrons of an outdoor cafe. I sipped my drink slowly, put my feet up on the chair beside me, and waited.

I spotted my contact easily. She moved with an easy grace, but underneath it all was a coiled feeling of self-control. Her clothes were tight, but not too tight—enough to distract a male opponent, but not enough to restrict movement. Her blonde hair was cut short, stylish. And then there was the edge in her eyes. . . .

I realized that this was no ordinary agent, and I knew then that this was no simple delivery operation. I began to wonder what I had gotten myself into.

The waiter pointed her toward my table. Now I could see her more clearly. Leather skirt, high heels, and a low-cut silk blouse that revealed none-too-subtle cleavage. She didn't appear to be armed, but her very appearance could be a weapon on its own.

She flashed me a bright and undoubtedly fake smile as she reached my table. "Mr. Allen?" she asked, and I nodded.

She sat down, uninvited, and said, still smiling, "I believe you have something for me."

I placed the package on the table between us.

She let it sit there for a moment, touched my knee as if we were old friends—acting for the crowd—then picked the package up and placed it in her purse. Standing, she kissed me quickly on the cheek, and then she was gone, disappearing back into the crowd, her ass bouncing teasingly from side to side in her leather skirt.

Damn effective weapon.

I stayed behind, sat in the heat, and mused.

"What was in the box?" I questioned.

The Old Man still sat behind the giant desk, but this time moonlight shining through the window made him appear hard and cold. No one knew if the Old Man ever left the room. Some newer recruits who had never met him doubted he really existed, laughed at the legend. Unfortunately, I knew better, had known now for quite some time. Knowing sometimes kept me up at night.

"That's not something you need to know," he said.

I crossed my arms, tried my best to look serious. "I disagree."

He sighed and turned his chair around toward the window. "You used to be one of the best, Max. You're slipping."

"What was in the box," I repeated. This time it wasn't a question.

There was a pause before the answer finally came from behind the high back of the leather chair. "A muzzle."

"For a dog or for a person?"

He turned slowly and met my stare, his own shadowy eyes looking tired, bored. "Don't patronize me, Max. You, of all people, know exactly what I mean."

And I did. He was talking about the barrel of a gun. Putting a new "muzzle" on a pistol would make any bullet fired through it untraceable. All ballistics records from registered firearms would be useless. Such a gun would effectively be invisible.

"Why?" I asked him, knowing the answer full well.

"Why else?" came the reply.

I left the building feeling restless, confused about the plans the Old Man had in store for me. I didn't know what to do or who to turn to. So I did the easy thing. I went grocery shopping. Even killers need to eat.

It was after midnight when I finally got home. The Siamese kitten sat just inside the doorway, silently standing guard over the apartment. I greeted her with a smile, kicked the door shut with my foot. The kitten, slipping clumsily on the tile floor, followed me in to the kitchen.

The apartment was dark, and I dumped the bags of groceries onto the table pretty much by feel. I rubbed the small of my back with one hand as I reached for the light switch with the other, and wondered to myself just when I had gotten so old.

The light flared briefly, burning itself into my eyes, then popped softly and burned out. I cursed and reached down to pick up the kitten, who had almost faded into the darkness. "These things never happen in the daytime, do they?" I asked. She purred in reply.

I walked out into the living room and felt around for the light switch. My fingertips touched it just as the package landed at my feet.

The light came on and I turned to see the blonde from that afternoon sitting casually on my sofa. A pistol, level with her breasts, was trained at my head. I didn't need to see the shine on the gun barrel to tell me that the box at my feet was empty.

"So," I said to her. "It's already come to this."

She shrugged. "What did you expect, Max, a reward? You shouldn't have let that woman in Geneva live."

I scratched underneath the kitten's chin. "That 'enemy of the American people?'" I asked sarcastically.

The blonde snorted and shook her head. "You used to be one of the best, Max. We all looked up to you. What happened?"

I stared at her. "I was never anything less than the best. I'm just tired of killing people in the name of politics.

"We used to believe in the greater good," I said to her. "But maybe you're too young to remember that."

I looked away from her, touched my lips to the soft, dark fur on top of the kitten's head. "You know, this kitten's mother died after giving birth. She was the only one of her litter to survive. She'll grow up to be strong."

I glanced back up. The blonde looked unimpressed.

"She's Siamese, you know," I continued. "Great warriors. They were bred to guard temples and tombs from desecration. Now *there* was a culture that understood death, worshipped it, didn't ignore it like today."

The blonde laughed and tossed her hair. Any other time the movement would have been seductive. Now it just made her look cold. "Big old killer kitty sure did a good job of keeping me out, now didn't it?" she asked.

"Not their job," I said. "They only attack what they perceive as a threat."

Her smile faded. "You don't see me as a threat?" she asked, pointing the gun at me.

"Quite the opposite," I said. "Anyone stupid enough to use a gun is a threat. *Moses.*"

On command, the kitten's sire leapt out of the shadows and landed on the blonde's gun hand, digging in deep before jumping at her face. She screamed, and the gun clattered to the floor. She tried to protect her eyes as the massive Siamese tore into her hair and forehead.

I picked up the gun and whispered a command for the cat to stop. He disappeared instantly back into the darkness. The blonde stared at me, shaking a little, eyes scanning the room, probably not all that sure about what had just happened. A small trickle of blood ran down from her hairline and mixed with the heavy makeup on her cheek.

I smiled at her. "Now you're not a threat."

She was up then, a blade in her hand. I sidestepped the knife. It snagged in my coat—something that never would have happened as little as a year ago—but even so, I was still the faster of the two of us; two hard fingers up under her rib cage and she lay coughing at my feet. I picked her up gently and placed her back on the sofa.

I knelt down beside her. "You make a living dealing death," I said, "but you don't understand it, do you?" She only coughed in reply.

"Look at yourself," I continued. "In nature, death is just a part of life. But you've corrupted that. Not just what you do for a living—your skirt represents an animal slaughtered just for its skin. Your perfume and makeup are based on boiled-down animal fats. The hairspray alone is a nightmare. You kill, but you don't care about the repercussions."

I felt like an old man, an old man lecturing her on environmental nonsense that wasn't really what I was talking about at all. I realized then how alone in this life the job had left me, and how much I wanted somebody to share what little I had left. "You can get out of this before it's too late," I said, my voice barely a whisper. "You don't have to live like this forever." I looked into her eyes for a sign of approval.

She threw a punch at me instead. I dodged it easily, but still felt the pain of the impact inside me.

I stood up and cocked the pistol. "Take off your clothes," I said. When she responded by looking confused, I screamed, *"Take them off!"* She hesitated, then kicked off her heels. The leather came next, then the silk, then the stockings, and more silk underneath. She stood that way for a moment, then, uncertain, walked toward me, thinking sex was all I wanted in exchange for her life.

I shook my head and pointed toward the bathroom. "You're going to wash—until every ounce of death is off you. Then we'll talk."

She looked at me like I was crazy. Maybe I was.

I yelled orders to her through the fogged glass door of the shower, making sure she got everything unnatural off her body—no more hairspray, eyeliner, nail polish, or perfume. From the other side she watched as I cut the leather skirt into thin strips with her titanium knife—easier said than done. The kitten sat on the radiator, purring.

After twenty minutes, I told her to stop. The glass door slid back and she stood there, dripping, seeming much smaller without her high heels and with her hair flattened to her head and shoulders. Her skin was raw in places from the scrubbing, and her cuticles were bleeding from where she'd tried to remove the nail polish. White plastic-surgery scars stood out faintly on her skin against the reddening from the hot water.

I hopped off the sink to stand in front of her. "How do you feel now?"

She stared down at the floor. "Naked," she said.

I put my hand under her chin and gently lifted her head. I looked deep into her eyes. "Then you never really knew how to live."

My hand slipped down to her neck. Two pops and she was gone.

I gathered together the few things I needed and got the cats into their traveling case. The closed bathroom door stood behind me. No feline warriors would be staying behind to guard this tomb. "I'm sorry it had to happen this way, kid," I said. "See you soon."

I walked out and locked the door behind me.

Max stepped out of the wooden box and into the cool air of the empty church, then bent down to pick up the two small cases. Moses hissed as his hands closed around the handles.

Oh God, he thought, *not here.*

He could feel it now, the adrenaline in the air, the metallic smell of a well-oiled automatic pistol. Bending down into a crouch, he looked out between the pews. Nothing moved, but he knew someone was out there. Where were they?

A scraping sound came from the confessional behind him. "Father," Max whispered, looking back over his shoulder, "get back inside."

The priest stepped out into the candlelight. "Why, my son? Whatever is the matter?" His smile was jovial, but his eyes were hard. He raised the pistol toward Max and fired.

And missed.

Max grabbed the priest's gun hand at the wrist, twisting, while angling in closer. His other hand went in quick. Up, under the breastbone. Into the heart.

End of sermon.

He lowered the body back into the confessional and slid the door shut, then slammed his fist into the wood. "Hail fucking Mary," he said between clenched teeth, then grabbed his cats and marched out.

Now he knew the world had truly changed. The killing no longer served any greater good. Now it was just a question of survival.

Under the Circumstances

MAT COWARD

TRAGICALLY," I SAID, BEGINNING the first conversation I'd ever had with my husband's former lover, "I have to inform you that Robert died yesterday. The funeral's on Tuesday. You're not invited, obviously."

I hadn't expected her to cry quite so much. I suppose I'd never before pictured Jan as someone who really loved Robert—merely as a nuisance, a marriage-threatener, a life-spoiler.

Her prolonged sobs turned to endless bawling, with never an intelligible word in between, and I began to worry about my phone bill. I was tempted to ask her to ring me back; if she really wanted to spend the evening long-distance weeping, let her pay for it herself.

After what seemed like a week, Jan's howling degenerated into gurgling sniffs and chokes, and eventually she managed some real English words.

"What—what happened? Was it an accident?"

"It was his heart."

"But he was only thirty-nine!"

So? What did she want, an appeal to the High Court? "Hearts ran in his family," I explained.

"Oh," she said, with more sniffs and coughs. "I didn't know that."

"There's no reason why you should," I replied, with what I felt, under the circumstances, was a forgivable level of smugness.

She said nothing for a while, though I knew she was still there from the continuing Mucous Symphony which echoed down the transalantic line like Muzak.

"Will you please accept my most sincere condolences, Mrs Mead," she said at last.

"I will," I agreed, graciously.

"And could you tell me please, what is the address of the chapel of rest?"

Now why the hell did she want to know that? Was she checking up on me? "Why do you ask?"

I heard her frown. After a lifetime of Sunday night phone calls to my mother, I knew what a frown sounded like.

"Well, I need to know where to have the flowers delivered."

"Oh, I see. No, no flowers please. Robert wouldn't have wanted flowers." I certainly didn't want flowers. "A donation to your neighbourhood cats' home, made in his name, would be more appropriate. Robert was very fond of cats."

Jan started crying again. "This is so incredibly awful!" she gasped.

"Yes it is, isn't it? Anyway, must run—things to do, you know." I hung up.

Bit of an abrupt farewell, I admit, but there was a new American sitcom starting on channel 4 and I didn't want to miss the beginning. Besides, I'd just heard Robert's car pull into the drive, and for obvious reasons this was a conversation I would rather he didn't overhear.

Jan Lucas had been a spectre haunting my life since the day Robert Mead and I were married.

Robert started his working life as a junior clerk in local government, but he was always more interested in trade union activity than in form-filling. A bright, friendly, attractive young man, he rose rapidly through the ranks, and by the time he was twenty-five was a full-time organiser. In 1986 he was the British delegate to some international union jamboree in Boston, Massachusetts. He met Jan there, in a singles bar, and they had the sort of holiday fling which young people have: you know, all sex, torch songs, and ethnic food.

The day after he returned to Britain, I started work in his office as a temporary typist. I was never terribly keen on unions—to be frank, and while not wishing to sound snobbish, I simply wasn't from that sort of background—but I was keen on Robert, right from the start. Keen and determined.

The first I heard of Jan was when Robert's best man—his cousin Larry— was reading out the telegrams at the reception.

"... 'don't do anything I wouldn't do STOP Not that there is anything I wouldn't do STOP,' and that's with lots of love from Aunty Mary. Now, next one is from America, and it says ... ah. ..."

Larry stopped reading. He blushed and glanced over at Robert. So did I, just in time to see an expression of weary resignation crease my husband's face, before he hid it behind a champagne flute.

The best man flustered for a while, unaccustomed as he was to public dissembling, but eventually replaced the offending telegram with yet another unamusing double entendre from Robert's plentiful supply of proletarian relatives.

I had the full story from Robert as we lay in our first marital bed. Not a great start to a honeymoon.

"We broke up by mutual consent, Debbie, I swear to you."

"Her telegram doesn't sound very mutual," I said. I'd made poor Larry show me the American wire.

"No, well. I thought it was mutual. God, I'm sorry about all this." He put an experimental arm around my shoulders, and I rewarded his apology with a slight thaw. "At least there's one good thing," he said.

"Really?"

"Think about it, love—we're in London, Jan's in America. There's a big, cold, comforting ocean between us."

Jan sold up and moved to London two months later.

She was never dangerous. She didn't stalk us, or hang around the house like a wronged Victorian woman. There was never the slightest hint of a physical threat.

I never met her, never even spoke to her. When she rang, I would say nothing, and pass the phone to Robert in silence. Taking it from me, he would sigh like a brave martyr, and send me apologies with his eyes.

She rang at least once a month, usually more. "Is Rob there, please?" Endlessly. Whenever she lost a job, or couldn't understand how to fill in a form, or how to find a plumber in the Yellow Pages. Or the time when she was convinced she'd contracted "cancer of the teeth" and the only way she could be cured of this belief was by talking to my husband for four hours solid. When he eventually got off the phone, Robert was so desperate for a pee that he was walking cross-legged.

Robert insisted that talking to her on the phone was the best way of keeping her at a safe distance. So we established rules: he was never to ring her; they were never to meet in the flesh. That was how we lived, the three of us.

"Jan no longer sees our relationship as a romantic one, I'm sure of that," Robert assured me, five years after our wedding, during a short holiday on Guernsey.

"Are you?"

"I don't blame you for being sceptical, Debbie, but yes, I'm sure. She's got over that. Now I'm just a friend. Her only friend, perhaps. That's progress of a sort, isn't it? My hope is that eventually she'll find someone else, for real, and we'll be free of her."

His excessive optimism was not one of the qualities which attracted me to Robert.

We never had children. We could have, but I chose not to. If we had children, I knew, the day would come when I would have to explain the "Jan situation" to them, and I wanted to spare myself that humiliation.

One humiliation I never worried about was sexual infidelity. Robert was an exceptionally ethical man—pathologically so, in my view; we'd have been able to afford a much bigger house if only his damned principles had been a little more flexible. He'd no more have an adulterous affair than he would kick a cat.

Jan's hold over my husband was far more powerful than sex. It was his own conviction that, if he "abandoned" her, she would kill herself.

"That old trick," I sneered, the first time he admitted that this was what he feared.

"Just because it's old doesn't mean it's not fatal," he said. "Come on Debbie, you know I can't risk it. We'd both feel terrible if she did do herself in."

I made no reply to that, since I could not find one which was both honest and socially acceptable.

My name isn't Debbie by the way. It's Deborah. I gave up so much to marry Robert, you can't imagine.

I suffered Jan's haunting for ten years, unable to act for fear of losing Robert altogether, until one day a solution presented itself.

"Poor thing," said Robert, putting down the phone after a forty-five minute Jan Session. "You know her mum's got Alzheimer's? Well, she has. And now her dad's gone and died." He paused for me to make sympathetic noises. I carried on reading the paper. "Well anyway," he continued, "this will interest you. Jan's flying back to Boston tomorrow. To nurse her mum."

"For good?"

He shrugged. "For as long as it takes, she says."

My momentary feeling of liberation soon died. Jan's mother wouldn't live forever, and then. . . .

And that was when it came to me. She'd only come back if there was someone here for her to come back to.

I gave her a couple of days to get settled in, found her Boston phone number in Robert's personal organiser, and called to give her the bad news about my husband's premature death.

Perhaps maritally infected by Robert's foolish optimism, I didn't expect to hear from Jan again. She'd have no reason to contact me, now that Robert was dead, would she?

"Debbie? It's Jan. Look, I'm real sorry to trouble you during your grieving process, but—"

"What the hell do you want? Robert's dead, and you and I surely have nothing to say to each other." It was Saturday afternoon; Robert, thank God, was at the football game.

"Look, I know, I'm really sorry—but it's about the cats. You know, Rob's cats."

She'd lost me. Robert did indeed have two cats, and would happily have filled the house with mangy strays, if I'd allowed him to. He never could pass a Cat Protection League collecting tin without emptying his pockets into it. But what Aneurin and Hardie (two stupid names for two ugly animals) could possibly have to do with Jan, I couldn't imagine.

She talked on through my baffled silence. "I guess it's all a bit more complicated now that I'm back in the States, but—well, you know, I'm sure we both want to respect Rob's last will and testament. Rob said you wouldn't mind. What with you not being a cat person, and all."

To give me time to think, I had to pretend I knew what she was talking about. I had to tell her it wasn't convenient to talk now, and promise to phone her back—God, the irony of that stuck in my throat!

We'd both made wills about two years earlier, but I'd never read his. Why should I bother? It wasn't as if he had anything to leave—except his damn cats, apparently. I didn't imagine Jan was lying or mistaken: now I came to think of it, Robert might well leave the cats to her, presumably because he didn't trust me not to have them put down the day after his funeral.

What was I to do? Jan wouldn't let this drop, that was obvious. I knew from half-listening to Robert talk about her, that she was as soppy over cats as he was. I couldn't tell her the cats had died; losing a husband and two pets within a fortnight, that might arouse her suspicions. I could send the cats to her in America, and try to convince Robert that they'd both happened to get lost simultaneously, but that would cost money—expenditure which Robert would be sure to notice. On his measly salary, we were always short; I'd given up telling him that if he was such a great union man he ought to be able to negotiate a decent pay deal for himself.

And I certainly couldn't tell Robert the truth, even if I was willing to give up my dreams of a Jan-free life. With his moral mania? He'd never speak to me again. Might even leave me.

No; there was only one way out of this mess that I could think of. A way that I felt was entirely justified, under the circumstances.

"Must be something in the air," I told him when he got home. "First your Jan's father—"

"She's not my Jan, Debbie."

"—and now my mother. She rang from New York while you were out. She's had a heart scare, and she wants me to fly over."

"That's wonderful!" said Robert. "I mean, that she wants to see you again, after all these years."

None of my family had attended my wedding to that common little Bolshevik, and I hadn't seen my widowed mother since she'd moved to America, seven years earlier.

"I've managed to book a flight for tomorrow. Look, Robert, I know this sounds awful, but—whatever you do, don't phone. You know what Mummy's like. If there's a chance of patching things up with her before she dies, I don't want to spoil it. You do understand, don't you, darling?"

It was a large, secluded house in a wealthy suburb of Boston. She answered the door herself.

"We meet at last," I said. "I'm Deborah Mead."

Jan couldn't have been more welcoming. So pleased was she to see me—"The two women who loved Rob the most, united in remembrance"—that she didn't even ask me what I was doing there.

Killing her was delightfully simple. She insisted on showing me around the house, and when we reached the top of a long, steep staircase, I shoved her with all my might. From the angle of her neck, it was obvious that I'd achieved my "primary purpose of visit."

I'd already established that there was no-one else in the house but her mother, whose dementia was so advanced, that, as Jan had told me, "There's no point introducing you. She doesn't know who she is, let alone who I am." A quick search of Jan's room convinced me that even if her death wasn't treated as an accident, there was nothing amongst her effects likely to connect her life with mine and my husband's. I slipped her address book into my overnight bag, just to be sure.

I flew straight back to London (I'd tell Robert that Mummy had changed her mind, and refused to see me), exhausted almost to the point of death, but happier than I'd been in years.

The moment I saw Robert's face, I knew something had gone terribly wrong.

"Jan's lawyer phoned me from Boston," he announced without preamble. "Jan's been found dead."

"Bloody hell," I said, genuinely shocked: I hadn't expected news to travel so fast. "But—why did her lawyer ring you?"

He shook his head, sadly. "Apart from anything else, because it turns out, amazingly, that I am the sole beneficiary of Jan's will."

"Amazing," I agreed, thinking nothing's gone wrong, after all! In fact, everything's gone better than I could ever have dreamed!

I realised that I hadn't asked him how she died, and that I probably should. "Was it," I said, lowering my voice tactfully, "suicide?"

Robert sighed his martyr's sigh, and I felt the ice return to my spine. "Before we talk about that, I'm afraid I have to make a confession."

"A confession?" I said. "I don't understand."

"Debbie, I've never lied to you. You know how I feel about dishonesty, in any form."

"It's one of the things I love most about you," I lied.

He held up a hand to stop me talking. "I've never lied to you ... except about one thing. I've never told you this before, because I knew it would make you angry, but—well, the fact is, Debbie, I am the owner of fifty cats."

He made a small, ingratiating chuckling sound. I said nothing; frightening connections were forming in my mind.

"You know what I'm like about cats," he continued. "I hate to see them suffering, but it wouldn't be fair on you to fill the house with them. So, a couple of years ago, I bought a row of derelict lock-ups over by the river. Had them converted into a feline sanctuary and re-homing centre. Rounded up some volunteers through the union to run the place. Anyway, that's where I spend half my time these days."

"And half our money," I said, light dawning at last, far too late. Robert flinched. "Why are you telling me this now?"

"Ah," said Robert. "You see, that was the other reason Jan's lawyer phoned. Apparently, the day before she died she'd been to him for some advice. Told him that a friend of hers had died suddenly, leaving her responsible for a cat home. In London. Wanted to know about animal import regulations, that sort of thing. He was rather surprised when I answered the phone, instead of you."

"Robert. . . ." I said, but he hadn't finished.

"I needed to talk to you about all this, as you can imagine, so—despite your instructions, and I apologise for this too—I rang your mother in New York." Robert started crying, very quietly. "She was rather abusive, as always, but she did stop swearing long enough to assure me that her health was as robust as ever."

I was crying too, now. Robert put his arms around me and held me. He didn't say "It's all right," because of course that would have been a lie.

"I've already spoken to the union's top lawyer, Debbie, an excellent man. He's on his way over now. He'll accompany us."

I pulled free of his embrace. "Accompany us where?"

"To the police station, of course! I mean, come on, Debbie—I don't see what else we can do, do you? Under the circumstances."

And under the circumstances, all I could think of to say was, "It's not Debbie, for God's sake! It's Deborah!"

Watch-Cat

ARDATH MAYHAR

I WAS AT THE WINDOW, AS USUAL, taking note of the street below. At two-thirty on an afternoon as dingy as yesterday's litterbox, of course, nothing was happening. I tend to become bored and irritable before the People come home from work.

Lying on the window seat, my silver-gray tail twitching to startle the gold-fish in the bowl on the small table at my feet, I pictured the pleasing effect I must make against my blue velvet cushion. As a Persian, I have an appreciation for aesthetic detail.

Unfortunately, no one was at home to appreciate *me*. At last I rose and stretched, washed thoroughly, and stalked into the kitchen, where I stared ac-cusingly at my empty food dish. This business of one meal a day until I lose weight had me out of sorts . . . grouchy, in fact.

As I grumbled about that, I heard steps in the service hall beyond the kitchen door. That was *not right*. Nobody went there except to take the garbage bags to the chute. Only when the janitor did his yearly cleanup was there any-one out there except my own family and others whose back doors opened onto this corridor.

This bore investigation! I jumped onto the counter (strictly against Melinda's rules, of course) and scrambled onto the top of the cabinet that ran around the corner of the kitchen to the edge of the door. There was a vent above the door frame, and once I flattened myself enough I could get an eye into position to see a part of the hall.

A blurry shape, carrying something, passed my position and stopped at Miss Patterson's kitchen door. It fumbled for a moment, the door opened, and it went inside.

Definitely *not right!* By the time it came out again, I was regretting my years of overeating and underexercising. My stomach felt as if it were being squashed, but I hung in there. The figure was dressed in gray, and the hall was dim, but I could see that it carried a toolbox that seemed heavy. When it passed out of view I leaped down (I have to admit I landed with an ungraceful plop), and went to my special cushion for a good wash.

☆　☆　☆

Melinda came home at a bit after five, and Paul was not long after her. So engrossed was I with the puzzle I had found that I didn't hear them come in, and Melinda's voice made me jump.

"Pammie, what are you doing?" she asked, picking me up and cuddling me. "You always meet me at the door. Are you sick, huh?" She felt my nose and looked anxiously into my eyes.

I winked solemnly, wishing for the thousandth time that human beings had the wit to understand Cat. Before I could try sign language, Paul arrived, followed by Miss Patterson from next door, now twitching and sniffling even more than usual.

"Linda, Miss Patterson says her apartment has been robbed. Call Officer Burt right now!" he told her.

Melinda almost dropped me, but I managed to get down gracefully. By the time the police arrived, they had Miss Patterson settled down a bit, though she began to sob when Burt came in to question her.

"They took my grandmother's gold necklace! And my V.C.R. and TV. I think my pearl ring is still there, but it's cultured pearl and they must have known it isn't worth much."

I listened for a bit, but the things people value don't mean much to me. Instead, I wandered around inspecting strange sets of feet.

"Did Henry see anyone unusual?" Paul asked the officer, who shook his head.

"Said nobody signed in all afternoon. Not even a delivery came."

I sniffed. As if the apartment house had only one door! I had escaped from the back door once, gone down the garbage chute, and found myself in a fascinating complex of basements and alleys. Anyone who could open the service doors could come and go without Henry having a clue.

I mewed softly. Nobody seemed to hear. I meowed loudly and set my claws into Paul's trouser leg, but he shook me off absently and kept talking to the Law.

There was another man with the officer, a quiet fellow in a gray suit and black shoes. When he spoke at last, he said, "This is the fifth burglary in this block of apartments in the past six months. Have you seen anyone outside who looked at all suspicious?"

"Everybody," said Paul, and Melinda nodded. I agreed. The neighborhood had gone downhill in the past few years.

I reached for the gray pants leg and pulled it gently with my claws. The man looked down, and I lashed my plumy tail and headed for the kitchen. He followed, but when he got there he didn't take my hints at all.

He decided I was hungry, and Melinda put some dry food in my dish (yecch!), which I ate, just to be polite.

When the men left, nobody was at all the wiser, and Miss Patterson twitched back to her apartment, where we heard her propping furniture against the front door. Not, you notice, against the back door. People sometimes have very limited vision, I find.

My long period of deep thought had not been wasted. I decided I must watch everything carefully and figure out some way to see into the alley alongside the apartment building. That was where the service hall came out, at a grimy door in the brick wall. I had investigated that, too, during my brief period of freedom. Anyone who could open it had the free run of every dwelling on this side of the building, as he could obviously open their back doors.

There were three windows across the front of our family room. I tried every one of them, straining my neck severely as I attempted to find a way to see more than the barest glimpse of the alley's entrance. And then I realized that the dress shop across the wide street had a plate-glass window. If I lay in our farthest window and watched the reflections in the shop glass, I could see if anyone entered the alley.

Not that I thought our thief would actually return, but I felt it was better to be cautious than careless. Melinda wondered aloud why I changed my favorite lounging window, but I kept my own counsel.

Two more burglaries happened nearby, though not in our actual building, over the next week. The thief was becoming bolder. That was when I redoubled my watch, spending most of each day with my gaze fixed on the dress shop. I lost weight, for I was so concentrated upon my task that I actually forgot to eat when Melinda began keeping my bowl full again.

There was talk of taking me to the vet, but I paid little attention. When I was a kitten, the family used to watch a TV program about Sherlock Holmes. I found him almost cat-like in his dignity and intelligence, and his methods seemed really effective. Using mental abilities seemed an excellent way to cope with our burglar.

I reached really svelte proportions in a month and a half. Yet so caught up was I in the thrill of this unusual chase that I ate absently, with one ear tuned to that back hallway.

Of course, when he came it was while I was eating, rather than when I watched. The world is strange that way. Indeed, the only tomcat I ever found remotely attractive had suffered an operation that rendered any interest we might have in each other academic, at best. Nothing ever goes as one wishes or plans, I have decided.

I was nibbling a bit of that dry food, wishing it were tuna fish, when something scritched at the door. I looked up, alert and ready for anything. The door opened to let in a skinny man wearing coveralls and carrying a toolbox.

He might fool those who didn't know the staff, but I knew everyone. This was not the janitor, who never came in that way, particularly when the family were not at home.

He glanced down, said, "Hello, pussycat," and moved past me into the family room, which combined office, sitting, and dining space. He went straight to Paul's rolltop desk and opened it.

I thought quickly. Then I acted. I jumped up onto the desk beside him, acting fascinated by his hands as he unlocked the little doors at the back. Managing to knock the stamp pad onto the floor, I leaped down again and set all four paws on the inked part.

As the man rummaged through the desk, then went into the bedroom and made searching sounds there, I put my pawprints on every item in the pile he had left on the desktop.

When he returned, carrying Melinda's little jewel box, I met him with a loud purr and put pawprints all over the back of his pants and even on the leg above his sock. I also put prints on the floor and, as I followed him back to the hall, beside my dish.

He was about to close the door when I had a flash of brilliance. I shot out of the door into the hallway, so quickly he didn't really see me. Then I crouched in the shadows beside the garbage bags and watched as he moved to the stair door and out of sight.

I sighed and curled up for a nap. It was still early. Paul and Melinda wouldn't be home for hours yet, and I had no way to get back into the apartment. I slept hard for it had been a long time since I rested completely. My job was almost done, and the knowledge allowed me to relax at last.

I woke to frantic calls. "Pammie! Pammie! Where are you?" came the cry from Melinda.

I rose, stretched every limb, groomed my fur a bit, and went to the door. "Mee-yowww!" I shrieked.

Paul's voice asked, "Where is that coming from?"

Then I yowled again, and two sets of footsteps rushed to the service door. When it opened, I jumped into the first pair of arms I could find.

"The *back* door," said Paul, looking down the hallway.

"Of course!" Melinda replied. "Why didn't we think of that? We have to call. . . ." Then she realized what my being there meant, and they both rushed back inside.

The gray man came back to investigate the burglary. I gave him time to talk with Paul and Melinda, then I rubbed against his ankles until he looked down. I went over to the desk and jumped up. He followed me and stared at my artistic arrangement of blue pawprints.

"I suspect," he said very slowly, "that our burglar may well have blue ink on him. All over what he took, too. And possibly . . . identifiable prints, as well. I do believe Princess Pamela marked him well and truly."

"Oh, it's clear she followed him out—why I will never know—but she is only a cat, after all, though a highly intelligent one," Melinda said.

I flexed my paw, giving her a touch of the claw. But not even when they apprehended the man in coveralls, not even when they recovered all of my family's possessions, plus Miss Patterson's and a dozen other people's, did they truly believe that I, alone and unaided, stopped the rash of thefts.

Whether Paul and Melinda know my role or not, I find it amusing to be the only cat ever "fingerprinted" by the Markham City Police, for my prints were used to convict the burglar, as well as to identify our own possessions.

However, noblesse oblige. My family are, after all, only human. And I am Princess Pamela of Dirhan, noble heir to an ancient bloodline. One cannot expect mere people to comprehend or to appreciate my abilities.

The Web Designer's Assistant

ROBIN REED

I SNEEZED VIOLENTLY AND THE CAT jumped up and ran away. Served him right. I had been trying to accommodate him, letting him turn around on my chest until he decided to lie down, all the while blocking my view of the TV. I really was trying to be nice to the furry monster, but I didn't understand how cat people let their cats take over their lives. I was sitting there in order to watch TV, not to be a cat-warmer.

"And if it turns out I'm allergic," I told him, "all bets are off. It's the pound for you, buddy." The cat had jumped up on the card table across the room and was staring at me. I glared back at him. My statement didn't seem to bother him at all. He just looked at me, golden eyes in gray fur, and wrapped his fuzzy tail around his feet.

I had to be crazy to take in this creature. I wasn't a pet person. My mother had never allowed animals in the house. I brought a hamster home from school once, and Mom shrieked so loud the neighbors called the police.

So I had no background whatsoever in taking care of animals, and thought I never would have a pet until Mr. Gray Fur showed up. I told him that he couldn't stay. I told him that I couldn't take him in. I told him I didn't have any food for him. I was standing on my front porch, holding two bags of groceries, and talking to a cat. I've always thought pet owners were crazy for talking to their animals, and I was doing it two minutes after meeting the beast.

Nothing I told him fazed him one bit. He sat, like a lord in his castle, as if this was where he belonged, on the windowsill next to my front door.

"Shoo," I said. "Go away." He gazed at me, seemingly trying to decide if I was worthy as a potential owner. He was quite a good-looking animal. He didn't look like he'd been stray for long, either. Not too thin, or torn up like an alley cat can get.

Still, I was a little afraid of him. You can't grow up in my mother's house and feel completely safe around animals. They destroy the furniture. They bring in fleas. They might even attack you in the middle of the night. I actually asked Mom for a pet once, when I was about eight. I heard all the above reasons and more for not ever having an animal in the house.

He certainly didn't seem afraid of me. He opened his mouth and let out a little tiny "meow." I sighed. It couldn't hurt to take care of him for one night, could it? I managed to open the door while juggling the grocery bags, and held it open a little longer. It was up to him if he wanted to come in.

He strolled in like a star inspecting his dressing room. I went into the kitchen and put away the groceries, all the time worrying that the cat was destroying my furniture, or worse. I heard a "meow" and turned to find him standing at the kitchen door.

This was the tricky part. Even I, who had never had a pet, knew what he wanted, but I didn't think I had anything. Nothing I had brought home from the grocery store would appeal to a cat. It looked like I would have to go back to the store. And leave the cat in my house all that time to do whatever horrible things cats do when you're gone? My mom's voice in my head told me that wouldn't be a good idea.

I scrounged in the cupboards and came up with three cans of tomato soup, a week's supply of Ramen noodles, and, yes! a can of tuna. I was saved from going back to the grocery store.

The cat ate the tuna like he hadn't had anything for some time. I still didn't think he'd been stray for long, but he certainly hadn't eaten much in that time. I also put down a bowl of water.

Was I really thinking of keeping him? Against all my mother's anti-animal propaganda? Or was the eight-year-old who wanted a pet finally getting her wish? I hadn't really thought of getting one in my adult years, I guess mainly because I moved around a lot. I had lived in four cities in the last six years. But buying my house meant I was going to be here for a while. Maybe I should keep the cat. Maybe I was nuts.

While I was thinking all this, the cat finished the tuna and looked up, licking his lips. I approached him and touched him for the first time, rubbing his head and running my hand down his back. He didn't object at all, and in fact pushed his head into my hand, asking for more. His fur felt wonderful.

"I suppose I should look for your owner," I said to him, "but if I can't find him, or her, I guess you're here." An amazing rumbling purr came out of him that I could have heard across the room. That was it. I hoped I would never find his owner.

It was a couple of hours later that the cat tried to impose himself on my TV viewing. He had done an inspection tour of the house, and I had followed him around, hoping to avert any damage to the furniture. Then I realized, what the hell, all my furniture came from thrift shops. So I sat down to watch TV and, three or four sitcoms later, there he was trying to curl up on me and blocking my view. I tried to work with him, I really did, but I found myself craning my neck to see the TV. I could have booted him off completely, but I didn't. Maybe I was already becoming a cat-owned person. Anyway, the sneeze ended our attempt to get along.

It was time for the news, so I turned to the TV again. I just have to hear all the awful things that happen each day. It makes me feel better that none of them happened to me.

The first story was about a murder, of course. A pretty unusual one, though. Early that morning a rich lady had been found, shot dead, in her home, one of the big mansions near the lake. She had been found by the maid, who also found the front door wide open. The TV station was reporting only the latest development in the story, assuming that viewers had seen earlier reports. This was the first news I had seen all day, however, and it was all new to me. The latest part of the story was that the woman's husband had collapsed while being interviewed by the police and had been taken to the hospital. "Poor man," the well-coiffed female anchor said. "I'd be upset too." Then they went to the weather report.

When the news was over, I looked at the cat, still on the card table, curled up and ignoring me, and announced, "Bedtime for kitties. And me too." Only at that moment did my brain come up with a useful bit of information. I groaned. Mr. Gray Fur had eaten and drunk in my house. Sooner or later he would need to do something else.

I put my shoes back on and went back to the grocery store after all. Luckily it was open twenty-four hours. And they did have litter pans and litter.

I've heard cat people say that their cats act as alarm clocks. I found out what they meant when a cold nose thrust into my face at about six A.M., almost an hour before my clock-radio was set to go off. Groggily I rolled over and tried to go back to sleep, but there it was again. I sat up. The cat aimed those bright yellow eyes at me and said, "Mrrow!" in a demanding tone.

I staggered into the kitchen. I gave him some of the cat food I had bought at the store, in one of my own cereal bowls. I staggered back to bed and did not fall asleep. So I got up.

With an extra hour to kill I decided to catch some morning news. I sat and watched the anchors, impossibly bright and neatly dressed and made-up for that hour of the morning, tell me all the terrible things that had happened during the night. I munched some cereal as I watched.

"We have an interview with Mrs. Grodnick that was taped in her home for our series on prominent women in the area," said the male anchor, and I chewed on my Cheerios without registering that I'd heard the name before. "Since her unfortunate death yesterday morning, we have decided to show you that interview to show you what a lively, likable person she was."

"Yes, it's terrible," the female anchor piped in. "She was such a dynamic person. Let's show the tape."

Now I knew who they were talking about. The dead lady in the big house. The tape they played showed a handsome older woman sitting in her house in front of a computer. She had a nice set-up too. A P.C. that was a lot newer than mine, and about three times as expensive. She had a big monitor, a scanner, and a color printer. She was sitting in front of the computer because she designed the Web page for the charity she worked with.

"Call me Ann," she told the interviewer, and something about her just made me like her. She had a warm smile and crinkly eyes that seemed kind. In the interview she said that she was very surprised that at her age she had taken to computer work so well. "I work with the Polish Society for Disadvantaged Youth," she said. "We decided we should have a Web page, but none of us knew how to make one. I volunteered, and took some courses at the university. I bought this computer, and now I design the Web page." She and the interviewer chattered for a while.

I heard a "meow" and looked around for the cat. He wasn't in the room. I heard it again. I looked back at the TV. Mrs. Grodnick smiled fondly off-screen and reached out. "This is Tyler," she said, bringing a cat on screen. I sat up and almost spilled my Cheerios.

Mrs. Grodnick smiled and petted the cat. "He's my assistant. He helps me with all my computer work. He sits right by me and gives me advice." It was the cat. It was *the* cat. It was *my* cat. My stray, adopted, golden-eyed, gray-furred visitor.

Then the TV station cut to a reporter standing in front of Mrs. Grodnick's house. It was a huge place surrounded by a tall fence. If that's where the cat came from, he was sure coming down in the world living at my house.

I scrambled for the phone. I didn't know what number to call, so I looked up the police non-emergency number. The police operator answered.

"I'd like to talk to someone who's working on the murder case, um, Mrs. Grodnick?" I said, hoping I didn't sound like a flake.

"Do you want to speak to a detective?" she asked.

"Uh, yes. Please."

"What's his name?"

"I don't know. Can't you find out? This is really important." I didn't know if it was really important, but I thought she'd be more likely to put me through if I said it was.

"Hold please."

I held for long enough that I was thinking I should give up and get ready for work. Then the phone clicked and man's voice came on. "Espinoza."

"Hi. My name is Laurie Cole. Are you a detective?"

"Yes, ma'am."

"Are you working on the Mrs. Grodnick case?"

"Yes. Do you have some information?"

"Well, I think I have her cat."

"Her cat?"

"A stray cat showed up at my house last night, and I think it's the same one that I saw with Mrs. Grodnick on TV."

"It could be any cat, ma'am, they often look alike." I heard another voice ask Detective Espinoza a question. "Can you hold a minute?" he asked me, and without waiting for an answer he put the phone down. He must have put it down on the desk, though, and not hit the hold button, because I could still hear him talking to the other man.

"We searched the house. Nothing."

The other voice rumbled but I couldn't make out the words. Espinoza responded, "Of course it was the husband, whether he was out of town or not. I just don't have any motive without the papers."

Another question.

"When she came to me, she said she had proof that her husband was into something bad. She said she copied the papers from the safe and put them in a safe place."

A rumble.

"The safe was cleared out. He must have destroyed everything. If we don't find her copies we don't have a case." The other voice said no word that seemed to end the conversation.

Detective Espinoza picked up the phone. "Hello?"

"I was calling about the cat. I don't know what to do with him."

"Keep it, take it to a pound, I don't care. Or did you think it was going to testify in court?" Then he hung up.

I tried not to get mad. The man was trying to catch a murderer and didn't want to deal with my cat problem. Fine. He didn't have to hang up on me.

At work I typed on my keyboard, thinking about Tyler and Mrs. Grodnick, and her husband. The rat. Collapsed because he was so distraught over his wife's death. Right. Found a way to get out of interrogation and into a nice comfy hospital, more likely.

I raced home and found Tyler sleeping curled up in my TV-watching chair. That was all right. I had no intention of watching TV just then. I went to my computer and turned it on.

I got on-line and chose a search engine. What was the name of the charity? Polish Society for something. I entered "Polish Society" and hit the search button. The computer churned for a while and came up with 1,456 matches.

I got Polish organizations, Polish jokes, and sites that were *in* Polish. I hadn't gone too far down when I saw "Polish Society for Disadvantaged Youth." I hit it.

The site was pretty bland, telling about the wonderful work done by the society. But then there was a link at the bottom that said, "This Web page was designed by Ann Grodnick. To see her home page, click here." I did.

The home page was simple to a fault. There was a picture of Mrs. Grodnick, some information about who she was and what she did, and further down a picture of Tyler, with a caption that said, "My beloved cat, Tyler."

There were no links of any kind to any other part of the site. The home page appeared to be the whole shebang. I passed my cursor over each of the pictures. It did not turn into a little pointing hand, so neither picture was a link.

I thought for a minute. Just then, Tyler surprised the hell out of me by jumping up into my lap. I thought for a second I was being attacked by a dust mop. I guess he just wanted to be with me, just like with his former mistress.

On a Web page, you have to program a link if you want different parts of the site to be connected. But you don't have to link everything. I looked at the little bar near the top of the Web browser that shows the address of the site I was currently looking at. This page had a long complicated address because Mrs. Grodnick had just used the free Web space provided by her Internet service provider.

I clicked in the address bar and moved my cursor to the end of the address. I typed a slash. If there was anything more in her site, I could find it by typing the name of the new directory after that slash. What name would she have given it?

I was scratching the cat's ears, and suddenly I knew. I typed "Tyler."

A new page formed on my screen and when I saw what was there I fired up my printer.

The people in the police station were not at all happy to see me, especially since I was carrying Tyler. A couple of big uniformed cops blocked my way. "I need to see Detective Espinoza," I told them.

"You can't bring that animal in here," one of them stated flatly.

"Then the detective won't be able to solve the Grodnick case. Oh well." They looked at each other, then indicated that I should follow them.

Espinoza was a balding man with a sharp nose. He looked at me like I was nothing but an intrusion. I thought he would change his expression soon.

"This is Mrs. Grodnick's cat, Tyler." I told him. "I brought him just because I thought you should see who cracked the case for you. And this," I juggled the cat in my arms and brought up the manila envelope full of what I had printed out at home, "is the evidence from her husband's safe, which she scanned and loaded onto her Web page."

Tyler meowed and I put him on the detective's desk, petting him and keeping him in one place. Espinoza took the envelope from me and pulled some of the pages out. He looked at them, then looked at me. I was right about his expression. He smiled and asked me to have a seat.

I had a lot of explaining to do, but in the end, everything I told the police checked out. The evidence from the Web page detailed everything illegal that Mr. Grodnick had done. Through the names in the papers they found all his associates in crime, including, eventually, the hit man who had killed his wife.

The newspapers got hold of the story but got a lot of it wrong, so I wrote up this story for posterity. If anyone wants to know what really happened in the famous Grodnick case, heralded in the papers with headlines like CAT SOLVES MURDER CASE and KITTY DETECTIVE, all they have to do is look at my home Web page. Tyler likes to help me when I'm working on my computer.

Ann, I hope you approve of Tyler's new human.

What a Cat Has to Do

WILLIAM F. NOLAN

KNOW THERE ARE A LOT OF OTHER cats in this book and a lot of them solve murders and are really smart. A lot smarter than I am, because I'm just an ordinary, run-of-the-mill house cat with what I guess is an average feline brain.

I'm a girl, and my name is SnoBall, and I live in Southern California, in the San Fernando Valley, so I've never seen what I was named after. Snow, that is. You just don't get snow in this part of California—but I've seen it on TV. Looks clean and nice. Something it might be nice to skitter around in, but it's a really hot summer outside, so I don't know if I'll ever get to see it.

Pamela owns me now. She found me at the pound. Pamela had looked at a lot of cats, but when I rolled over in my cage and showed her my tummy, she decided she'd take *me* home, which made me pretty happy. My tummy is white. In fact, I'm mostly white all over, and I've got very long fur. Pamela says my eyes are "ice blue" and that my ears are "champagne-colored." I don't know what that means, but it must be good because she's always warm and loving when she says it. My tail is very white, big, and bushy. Pamela's always telling me that she could use my tail for a feather duster, but I think she's kidding me.

Pamela talks to me all the time just like I was a person. I learned the meaning of human words from another lady I lived with for about a year. Her name was Edna and she didn't treat me very well. When I lived with Edna I was hungry all the time. She said cat food cost too much, so I didn't get to eat as much as I needed. And she didn't scratch me behind the ears like Pamela does. Finally, Edna said that I was "too much of a bother" and she took me to the pound.

That's where Pamela found me. She saved my life. They were going to kill me the next day. They call it putting you to sleep, but what they really do is kill you. I was real sorry for the other cats and dogs there because they didn't have Pamela to rescue them.

Anyhow, here I am, living with Pamela and another cat-friend named Betty. She's white with big black spots all over her face. Like a mask. She shares Pamela's pillow at night, but I'd rather sleep on a folded towel on top of the dresser.

Betty gets kind of cranky sometimes, but we get along okay. We bump noses every morning just to let each other know we're still friends. And Pamela has a rope we like to chase together over the rug. But mostly we just go our own cat ways. (I used to chase lizards in the yard, but Pamela got real upset about it so I stopped. I guess she likes lizards a lot.)

There's a point to all this. I mean, you have to know who we are—me and Pamela and Betty—so you can *empathize* with us when I tell you what happened. It means you can really understand what happened just like you were there. That's a good word that Pamela always uses: empathize.

The problem we had was Mr. Murch.

He met Pamela when she took us (me and Betty) to the vet for our shots. Mr. Murch (who is long and bony) was in the waiting room with a male dog he called Flopsie. (Stupid name, if you ask me, but the dog *did* have floppy ears, so maybe that's why he was named that.) Flopsie had broken his front leg and he needed to get it fixed.

I listened to what Mr. Murch told Pamela.

"I notice that your black-and-white talks a lot," he said, nodding toward Betty in her carry-cage.

"Yes, she does. Betty is very vocal," said Pamela.

"I must tell you," said Mr. Murch, shaking his head, "that your Betty is *not* a happy animal."

"Really?" Pamela frowned. "She certainly *seems* happy."

"No. She's very disturbed."

"About what?"

"Well, I can't say at the moment. She needs to be brought to my office for evaluation."

"I don't understand."

He handed her his card. "I am a trained animal empath. I read animals: pick up their thoughts and emotions, study their reactions, treat their psychological neuroses." He clucked this tongue. "Betty needs therapy. She's severely troubled."

So Pamela was talked into taking my friend to this Murch guy for a "reading." At the end of the first office visit, Murch said that Betty needed more "counseling," that she was mentally ill, and that only *he*, Mr. Murch, could guide her back to mental health.

I knew this guy was phony from the moment I saw him, but Pamela loves me and Betty a lot. She's always trying to do the best thing for us, so she kept taking Betty back for more readings. Murch was making a lot of money off of Pamela, telling her all this phony-baloney junk about Betty.

Finally, last weekend, things got bad. *Really* bad. Murch told Pamela that Betty needed to be "put to sleep"—that she could never be cured and would soon go totally out of her mind.

"A crazed cat is dangerous," he warned. "She could attack you with devastating results."

Pamela did some crying, but reluctantly agreed to have Betty put to sleep "for her own good." Murch would take care of it for a hefty fee, and it would happen in a week.

That's when I knew I had to do something about the situation. I began to talk and mutter a lot (the way Betty does), knowing that Pamela would take me to see Mr. Murch.

Which she did.

"Oh, we have a real problem here," Murch declared. "SnoBall is suffering from an obvious case of *dementia praecox*. Really quite serious."

Pamela was worried. Could he help straighten me out? Yes, indeed. He was sure he could.

"Just leave her with me over the weekend. I'll put her through my most intensive, advanced therapeutic program."

So that's how I came to be alone with Mr. Murch in his office on the top floor of the Prescott Building in Santa Monica on the hottest day of the year.

While Pamela was there, Murch held me in his arms and tenderly stroked my neck. I kept muttering until she left, then I shut up and glared at Murch.

He leaned down and opened the door of a metal cage in one corner of the office. "In here, you furry little bitch," he snapped. The mellow voice he used with Pamela was now hard and mean.

That's when I clawed his left cheek and jumped to the floor. He said "Ouch!" and staggered back toward the window, which—since this building was a registered historical landmark—was unscreened and open.

Mr. Murch was shocked and off-balance. I took a flying leap at him, thumping into his body and burying my claws in his chest. He tipped backward—and fell right out of the window.

Seven floors down.

To the concrete sidewalk on the street.

Splat!

When Pamela got me back home I told Betty what happened and suggested that she quit muttering to herself. If she just shut up, then Pamela would figure she was mentally okay again. Betty agreed that this was the sensible thing to do.

So Betty quit muttering.

That solved everything. Mr. Murch was very dead (the newspapers said he had likely committed suicide) and we were all back home together in our own happy family.

That's my story.

I know this makes me a self-confessed murderer, but I don't feel any guilt about it. Murch was ready to kill Betty—and probably me, too, once he got a lot more money from Pamela.

I had to do what a cat has to do.

And I bet you don't blame me.

I bet you *empathize.*

Don't you?

Where the Cat Came In

MAT COWARD

WAS LOCKED IN. JUST ME, THE CAT and twenty thousand pounds in cash.

I took a deep breath, and did what I always do when I'm in a hole. I panicked. I find it helps to get it out of the way right off—clears the mind, leaves one better able to cope with the long hard slog of extrication.

So I took my head in both hands and beat it against various available surfaces—walls, doors, floor—as if attempting to gain entry to an unusually coy coconut, while the cat, taking its cue from me, ran up and down the walls and across the ceiling with its ears stretched back along its body like those fins you see on old American cars.

Coconut panic; aerodynamic panic. Each to his own. Yeah, we can do you vanilla, but you'll have to call back.

I'm what the Crime Prevention people term a "creeper"—a burglar who creeps into your house on a hot afternoon when you leave the back door open for the breeze while you're upstairs making love to your sister-in-law—and I was just having a little look around the snooker room when I heard a sound that pretty much froze my blood.

There are a number of sounds that'll do that, obviously, to a man in my line of business. Shotguns tumescing, sirens approaching, hairy baritones asking "What the hell do you think you're doing with my wife's panties?" right in my ear when I'd thought I was all alone. But this particular noise was more blood-freezing than any of those. It was the faint, but preternaturally penetrating *bleep-whurr-clunk* of a top-of-the-range, state-of-the-art security system being activated by a departing householder.

I was locked in. Me, the cat, the cash.

A creeper isn't a cat burglar, isn't a safecracker, doesn't really carry much in the way of specialised equipment, doesn't possess any particular skills. The ability to move about very quietly is an advantage, and of course one does require guts. That's not boasting, it's just true: I make my living strolling into people's houses in broad daylight and stealing their valuables from literally under their noses. Well, OK, not *literally* under their noses, but literally behind their backs, as often as not.

I once had a VCR out of a bloke's living-room while the bloke himself was snoring on the sofa with a beer can in his hand. The beer can could have dropped from his grip at any moment and he would have woken up, but the VCR was brand new, an expensive make, and I had to have it.

I had it, got clean away, and whenever the guy finally did wake up, he must have thought the bad fairies had been. This was about two o'clock in the afternoon, and that kind of thing takes guts. I even ejected the video he'd been watching and left it on the arm of the sofa for him, because it was rented and he'd have got into all sorts of form-filling hassle if I'd taken it away. Besides, he'd fallen asleep halfway through the film, and he'd want to know how it ended. I thought, like, maybe he could take it round to his neighbour's place and finish watching it on her machine and it would turn out she was a pretty widow and years later they'd place an ad in the local paper publicly thanking the burglar who brought love to two lonely people.…

My point being, creeping takes guts. But it doesn't take any fancy equipment or magical tricks of the trade. No breaking-in, so no breaking-in tools. And thus no breaking-out tools.

The house I was in was a big one. I like stealing from big houses, not only because they are demographically more likely to have something in them worth robbing (I'm a cash and jewellery man myself, given the choice; aren't we all, given the choice?), but also because, when stealing from the rich, I can fool myself that I'm not a common creeper at all, but some sort of brothel-soled Robin Hood.

(Point worth remarking: just because you know you're fooling yourself, doesn't mean you're not fooling yourself.)

I don't do much scouting out. What's the point? It would only increase my chances of being seen and described. Instead, I get up in the mornings, put on a decent suit and a prosperous tie (because your average creeper is a fourteen-year-old boy with his arse hanging out of his trousers), prepare my excuse, and head out to where the rich folk roost. (I never go anywhere, do anything, without having my excuse prepared and practised. Something I learned at school. Probably the only thing I learned at school.)

And in I go. Upstairs, downstairs, it doesn't matter; places like that have something worth nicking in just about every room. I once found a very nice gold ring sitting in a soapdish in a downstairs loo.

On this particular day, in this particular house, I started in the basement. Rich people, for some weird reason, love to own facilities that they never use. A swimming pool with no water in it, a squash court with no scuff marks, a sunbed still in its plastic wrap, that sort of thing. Maybe when I'm rich I'll understand this better. Maybe when I'm rich I'll buy a Jacuzzi and forget to plumb it in.

Anyway, snooker rooms are favourites in this category. Almost every rich house has a snooker room, and it's always in the basement, and it's very rarely used except as a place to dump stuff. And, interestingly, to keep valuables. It's like the fat wallets reckon that since they never go down there, the burglars won't bother either. (Does this puzzle you? Because it puzzles me. You never meet a rich person with a brain, right? So how did they get to be rich in the first place?)

As I crept down the stairs to the converted basement, I could hear noises of habitation coming from somewhere above, and I kept half an ear open to that while I scanned the snooker room. Didn't have to scan very thoroughly, as it turned out, because right there on the virgin baize table itself, more or less the first thing I noticed as I entered the room, was a large, bulgy canvas bag.

Some times you just *know*, and I'm telling you—if that bag had contained anything other than used tenners, I'd have eaten it: zip, luggage tags and all.

I opened the bag and looked inside. My stomach remained empty of canvas even as my heart filled up with joy: twenty thousand pounds was my guess. Could have been more, I was always a conservative guesser.

A month's wages, probably, for the guy who owned the house. A day's wages, if he was even more crooked than most rich people. For me, the biggest single haul of my entire creeping career. By a country mile.

I had the dosh bag in my left hand, and was preparing to decamp, when I heard hurried footsteps clatter down the main stairs, from the upstairs to the hall; heard the front door open and close; and finally heard the aforementioned *bleep-whurr-clunk*. Which was, if you'll forgive the heavily laboured irony, where we came in, right? I was locked in. The creeper, the feline, the readies.

I didn't really do that panic bit that I mentioned earlier. I mean, I did it, but only internally. Externally, what I did was stand very still, stiller than you have ever stood in your life, and listen. I detected no furthers sounds of humanity, which was pretty cold comfort under the circumstances.

There was no point searching for an open window. All the doors and windows had been locked automatically at the moment of *bleep-whurr-clunk*. That's the whole idea of the system: saves you having to troll round your big house checking every little entry point every time you go out. Great breakthrough for obsessive-neurotics, and fat wallets in a rush.

Once the doors and windows have been locked using the electronic "key," they cannot be opened, from inside or out, except with that same key.

In other words, the only way I was going to get out of this house was to wait until the owner got back, and talk my way out. Well, I still had my excuse ready. I just had to hope the owner hadn't left on a Caribbean cruise. Meanwhile, I needed to use the loo (what I lack in glamour, I make up for in candour, right?).

I located it, went in, enjoyed the amenities, and when I reemerged found myself looking at a tall, blonde woman in her late thirties, who I was quite sure hadn't been there a couple of minutes earlier. At least she'd waited until I'd emptied my bladder before confronting me, which showed good breeding, I thought. She was rather attractive in a stern sort of way, and one thing I knew about her from the start: she was a better creeper than I was, since she'd heard me and I hadn't heard her.

"OK, who the hell are you, and what the bloody hell do you think you're doing in this house?" Heaven knows what made me say such a thing. I should have played my excuse and left. But her sudden appearance had caught me on the hop; well, zipping my fly, in point of fact.

She made the obvious reply: "I live here, this is my house! Who are *you*, more to the point?" Her accent was American, and matched her big white teeth.

Something about the way she said it—something about the way she looked at me, calm and considering, not scared or angry—made my say: "You're not the lady of the house, lady. I happen to know that lady very well, and she doesn't look a bit like you."

She sighed theatrically, and said, "Oh, why pretend? I guess I know who you are, and I guess you can guess who I am. Right?"

This whole thing was getting a little wacky for my taste, so I said nothing.

"And I guess," she continued guessing, "that you have as much right as I have to be here." I said nothing again, so she spelled it out for me. "I'm Simon's *mistress*, OK? Christina." We shook hands. "And you'd be Pete, right?" I nodded. "Justine's *toy-boy*. Well, my, what a family, huh?"

I felt *toy-boy* lacked the dignity of *mistress*, but I didn't get huffy. Instead I got down to the main business. "So, Christina, do you have a key to get us out of here?"

She sighed again. Theatrically, again. "Look, Pete, I'm going to level with you. This is going to sound crazy, but you have to trust me."

"OK," I said.

"I think Simon wants to kill me," she said.

"OK," I said. "What makes you think that?"

"Long story," she said, "but basically, I don't have the key, we're trapped in here, and I think he's going to burn the place down. Isn't that horrible?"

"It is," I agreed. "Why would he do that?"

Yet another sigh. "I did a foolish thing. I threatened to tell his wife about us. I realise now that he never intended to leave her—because of the money, you know."

"Sure," I said. "So what about the phone? We could ring for help."

Christina shook her head. "Not working. That's where he said he was going, just now, to report the fault. And he doesn't allow mobile phones in the house, because he says they give you cancer."

"So where's the wife now?" I said. "I mean, of course, *Justine*, my beloved."

"Shopping," said Christina.

"Great. Then maybe she'll get home before—"

"Abroad," said Christina.

"Shopping abroad? Oh, right. Pity." Should Pete have known about that, I wondered. And then I wondered a bit more, and finally I said: "One thing I don't understand."

"Yes?"

"The cat."

"Cat?" said Christina.

I pointed at the cat.

"Oh, yeah," she said. "That's old Mouser. Yeah."

"So what's she doing sitting in the hall inside a carrying basket?"

"Long story," said Christina. "Basically, she has an appointment with the veterinarian. She's supposed to be there right now, poor little kitty."

"And instead Simon's going to burn her to death? Just to get rid of a troublesome mistress?"

"I guess it all adds to the authenticity. Besides, Mouser's not Simon's cat. It's Justine's cat, and he hates it. Kind of like transference, you know?"

"So what do we do now?" I said, genuinely curious.

"OK," she said. "I'm thinking, there has to be a spare key here somewhere, right? If we can find it before Simon does whatever he's planning to do . . . I think that's our only chance."

"What are we waiting for?" I said. "I'll take upstairs, you do the living-room."

As soon as I entered the main bedroom, I started screaming. I screamed like a girl in a horror film, and within seconds I could hear Christina's valiant steps running up the stairs to save me.

The minute she poked her head around the door behind which I was hiding, I hit her as hard as I could with a ski stick (still in its plastic wrapper, naturally). Even so, she managed to squeeze off four incredibly loud shots from her big handgun before succumbing.

"That's a good idea," I told her, as she lay on the floor. She wasn't dead, but she certainly looked tired. "Shoot the windows out, why didn't I think of that?"

My scream had been a ruse, planned mere seconds in advance, but it came out more authentic than I'd anticipated, because I'd never before seen a garrotted corpse. Not until the moment I burst into that bedroom and saw the lady of the house lying on her bed, corporeal proof that you can't take it with you when you go. She looked horrible.

I'd been expecting something of the sort, because by then I knew for certain that Christina was neither the wife nor the mistress. Nor yet the cleaning lady. She was, though, hired help of a kind.

While I was searching Christina for the key, I worked out the rest of the story. Or at least, a version that made sense to me.

(See, I can come up with some pretty good stories myself, like that thing with the VCR, how I stole that VCR from under that sleeping man's nose. Not really true. I did steal the video, yes, but the man wasn't asleep, he was dead, had been for days according to my nose, and I could've made all the noise I liked. Or, to look at it another way, if he *had* woken up, a burglary charge would've been the least of my worries.)

Obviously, Christina was a freelance killer, hired by this delightful Simon character. That's what the twenty grand was for. He lets her in, they murder the unfaithful wife, then Simon drives off, leaving the coast clear for Pete, the toy boy, to arrive for his rendezvous with Justine.

Presumably, Christina would have taken care of him, then fired the place, making it all look like a tragic accident. When I showed up, she must have thought I was Pete, taking my cue a bit early. She didn't have time to wonder how I got in—she was too busy making sure I didn't find the body in the bedroom.

Which meant she had to have a key to let herself out. So where was it? Believe me, I searched every fair inch of her recumbent loveliness before giving up.

Then it hit me. Why hadn't she shown me the gun right off? Why the "let's look for the key" ruse? Because the gun was somewhere else, and she had to go and fetch it. And that's where the key would be.

Sure enough, in the dining room, at the other end of the house from the snooker room steps, I found the tools of Christina's trade, neatly assembled in an expensive leather evening bag. Lipstick, paracetamol, spare ammo, spare key.

That was when I heard the cop sirens. I told you those gunshots had been loud.

* * *

I had a decision to make and it had to be made quickly. The cat was in his cat basket in the hall, and the cash was in its cash bag down in the snooker room, and it was pretty clear I couldn't hope to collect both of them and still pass Go before the cops, or the toy boy, or both, arrived. Hard choice, huh? Not really.

I skittered down the hall, scooped up the cat, keyed the security system, and disappeared through the back door, without so much as a sad look back in the direction of the money.

After all, I owed that cat my life. If Christina hadn't lied about knowing "Mouser," I might not have figured out who she was, and she'd have killed me at her convenience. Besides, me and Leo (*Mouser, indeed!*), we've been partners a long time.

I mentioned excuses earlier. Well, here's mine, and it's a damn good one, which has got me out of trouble on more than one occasion:

I get caught creeping round someone's basement, and the householder, reasonably enough, wants to know what I'm up to; I act all embarrassed, and say, "I'm so sorry, but you see I was walking Leo to the vet and somehow he escaped from his basket and ran in here, and I just wanted to get him back before he disgraced himself on your lovely carpet."

So you see, my hard choice wasn't hard at all. Twenty thousand quid may be a lot of money, but a good excuse is worth its weight in diamonds.

(There, now: I bet you'd been wondering where the cat came into it, hadn't you?)

ℐcknowledgments